THE Y(

M000315802

Book One

THE GOLDEN SPAN

Christopher Laing

Copyright © 2012 By Christopher Laing
Signal Flag Publishing and Promotions, LLC
Madison, Wisconsin
Cover art courtesy of tonyschwartzphoto.com

www.theyoungoaks.com

1

**For Wifey,
My Valkyrie**

My Deepest Thanks to:
Ben and Emily
Claudia and Tony
Tom
Mark and Kate
Dwight
for my oldest and truest friend Jerry, who must otherwise remain
anonymous.

Dan McGregor *drove north along the river in the van, the shovel and pick rattling in the back every time he hit a bump in the road. The river spanned the space out the window, huge and dark, taking up the right half of his world, the left half being the towering limestone bluffs that dropped down to the road. Gravid clouds bulged down overhead as if they had been filmed with a fisheye lens, and lightning glimmered now and then in their great depths, silent with distance. Dan drove with his elbow out the van's window, the fresh wind gusting in the cab. There were a few scattered lights in the dark to his right, barges making their slow way, and boaters returning to river towns. Up in the hollows and on the bluffs, down in the sloughs, Dan knew, were occasional shacks with hardpacked dirt for yards, surrounded and hidden by deep woods, and some of them still had no electricity, the homes of river rats and hermits, hippies, dopegrowers, and other small time lawbreakers, people who lived at right angles to society.*

It was a lonely road. Splattered possums, raccoons, and the occasional flattened rattler were the only evidence of other traffic. The green light of the van's dashboard hollowed his eyes and reflected sharp highlights on his cheekbones, fading down to greasy stubble. There was a scar through his eyebrow, a scar on his lip, scars on his arms. Although he still wore an earring, the spiky, dyed-black hair he had once worn was long gone, cut and regrown to its natural brown. He was a young man and might have been handsome in better times. When he occasionally looked in the rearview mirror, his wide right eye stared back at him, but he was unaware of his appearance. Part of his mind took care of the driving, but his eyes stared at nothing.

He would have been drunk if it weren't for the acid he had taken, or might have gotten too close to the edge on the acid if he hadn't drunk so much, a familiar balance for him. He reached down into the cooler on the floor of the passenger side of the van and fished out another beer, steering with his left hand and watching the road. He opened the can with a practiced pop and drank deeply from it, watching the road around its rim, the cold beer easing the queasiness that the acid gave him. He wondered if he should pull over and vomit, but the idea of it made his stomach clench.

He was sure he would feel better when it was over. He would do this and then he could rest. He would get a hotel room, or go back to the Hephaestus Forge. He would shave and take a bath and eat a good meal, and he would sleep for a long time. He fought other images that came to him, visions welling up unbidden and unwelcome. There was the man in the alley, lying bloody where he had slid down concrete steps, blood gaining volume under his body until it flowed into the gutter. This Dan saw again and again. He saw his own hands, and thought of the things he had done which he could never change.

Dan tried to replace all this with pleasant images, with thoughts of Kate, of the beach with the booming waves, the sound of the lighthouse in the night when they made love. He tried to concentrate on these things, but soon his mind would wander and spiral slowly down. He popped the Ramones cassette out of the console and fished around for a moment before finding the copy of Smetana's Moldau and popping it in.

Imposed on the river's geography was an overlay of memory; he had fished with his grandfather off this island, his grandfather had explained the habits of eagles as they watched them from that bluff; there they had had a picnic with his grandmother, Mae. He was torn: he felt that he no longer belonged. He felt that he was truly home.

For the thousandth time, he thought of screaming at his grandfather in the kitchen. "What did you *ever live through?"*

Dan came to where the road up to the bluff came down to the river road and took a left onto it, his rear tires spinning briefly in the gravel of the smaller road before taking hold. Some of the roads in the hollows here were steep and had unpredictable turns, and part of Dan's mind told him that he was driving too fast. He pressed on the accelerator.

Through gaps in the trees, he could see flashes of lightning reflected in the water of the river now far below him. The trees roared around in the growing wind, their branches swaying in the cone of his headlights.

When he came to the cemetery, he turned left again onto a fireroad that went steeply up the hill across from the cemetery's decrepit gates, and drove up the road far enough to hide his van in the trees. He killed the engine and put on the parking brake and sat for a moment in the windy darkness, trying to get used to the darkness, drinking a beer. He took several cans out of the cooler and put them in his backpack.

He got out, taking the backpack, and went to the side of the van gathering the tools. He bundled them over his shoulder and walked down the fireroad, and came out of the trees, walking across the road to stand in front of the gates of the cemetery. All the landscape seemed in motion with the wind, undulating, the long grass growing by the cemetery's fence bent with its force.

Dan walked through the gap of the leaning gates, and headed through the grass among the huge oaks and neglected tombstones. There were a few mossy crypts just inside the fence on the high part of the grounds, put there long ago when people of importance were buried here, their names inscribed and now forgotten. Dan shifted the tools on his shoulder and walked down the slope to the far end of the acreage, past tilted obelisks and broken tombstones, the details of their engravings softened by the rains of years, down the slope to where the graves were more recent and less proud, near where the vinegrown fence was close to the edge of the bluffs. To the paupers' graves.

Dan came to the one he knew and put down his pack and all the other things he had brought. Reaching into the pack, he took out a beer and popped it open. For a long time, he stood before the cheap flat concrete marker almost obscured by long grass.

WILLIAM J. MCGREGOR

That was all is said.

Dan stared at the marker, taking in a deep breath and slowly releasing it through pursed lips. He ran his tongue over his lips and drank from the beer, still looking at the cheap marker. He walked a few feet and set the beer can on top of a stout fencepost and looked out past the edge of the bluff, to the space of sky and river in the growing darkness beyond. Then he turned back and picked up the shovel next to the grave and began his task.

Willy McGregor had come out to the river only because he had finally become cynical even about his cynicism. Perhaps, he thought, when one becomes cynical about cynicism, the only thing left was hope.

The letters from his friend Emilio Benitez had been *full* of hope, of optimism, two things of which Willy was in short supply. Emilio's letters, written with a sharp literacy which might have embarrassed native speakers of the English language, had made Willy scoff at first. He imagined that his friend had gotten soft after coming home from the Great War. The hope and optimism were so relentless, though, that Willy began to wonder if the place and the state of mind which Emilio described were possible. Emilio seemed to have found some kind of peace, of a sense of home, and Willy became curious as to whether such a thing was possible. Perhaps something awaited him, some meaning, some purpose.

It wasn't the quest for such simple things which put him on his path, but a search of glory, perhaps; at least for credibility. He had enlisted in the Army and gone to the war in France; being large for a sixteen-year-old, he didn't get a second glance when he wrote down the date of his birth as being two years earlier than it was. It would later be difficult to summon up the feelings of that long ago kid (they were so alien now), but he would remember as a fact that he had been enflamed by some kind of romantic zealotry that posed as patriotism, as boys in search of adventure are prone to do. His father was familiar with such facades, and had somewhat wearily tried to talk Willy into another course of action, namely going to college to study engineering and eventually building lighthouses like himself. McGregor and Son. His father had emigrated from Scotland during his own years of restlessness, but had come to hope that he and Willy might work together; Willy was a bright boy, his father had said, and could make something of himself if he'd just settle down.

There it was, though, that indelible human trait, that inability to absorb the hard-earned wisdom of another. Willy had been a hothead at that age, and his contrariness had warped his father's suggestions into something verging on isolationism and even cowardice, and he said as much. His father was patient, possibly recognizing himself in the boy and wondering if such unfortunate belligerent obstinacy weren't a McGregor family trait, and stolidly stood his ground, saying that Willy could think about it until he was eighteen. Willy was a step ahead of his father, though, and graduated high school early, then promptly jumped ship and lied his way into the military. He thought years later: if he'd have listened to his father, he would have missed the war altogether.

It would seem to Willy that his memory of the war became blurry and impressionistic with unusual speed. Emilio would remember day to day events with a clarity that baffled Willy, who would remember sensations. At all times, even on the front, Willy kept a notebook, writing down impressions and poems, a lifelong habit. It struck him strange, years later, to read what he had written in the hundreds of pages. Sometimes he had no recollection of the events at all, and it was as if he'd opened a dusty door to a forgotten landscape hidden for years.

He'd gone into the Army, in contradiction to his family's long naval heritage. That much he would remember. Enlistment, falsification of his papers, his physical; these were things he would not long remember, and not at all after ten years. Boot camp and training, there would be glimpses of that. The timeless, grinding voyage across the ocean on a coal-fired steamer would be a bright memory, mostly due to the stink of vomit of the soldiers unused to the sea, and of him being on deck in the crisp wind and fresh spray, there to escape the smell. Willy would remember standing on deck, comfortable in the roll of the boat, thinking that he should have gone into the Navy after all. He would hardly remember landing; he had misplaced something, searching angrily while other soldiers disembarked. There would be impressions of a long journey to the front. Willy had boxed. There was boxing. He had always been good. He had met Emilio there, and would always have a clear picture of his friend smiling up at him with a bloody lip and swollen eye, the lid already turning purple.

Then there was the thing itself, the war, the combat. Another human failing, the tendency to forget what one wants to remember, and to remember what one wants to forget.

Willy was a private, the lowest of the low. Most of the time he had little idea of where he was, only of the objective, only what he was pointed toward. There were rat-warrens of trenches, often with retaining walls of latticed branches, studded with occasional muddy bunkers. There was cold mud, freezing mud. If he'd experienced hot mud, he had no recollection of it. He would remember bedding down in woods, the trees there shattered and ripped, falling asleep on thick grass and lumpy ground, thinking it was the best thing he had ever known.

What he would wish to forget and what he would try to forget usually involved senses other than vision. There was the din, yes, the din. That was a thing he would remember, wish to forget, and try to find a word to describe it. Chattering, shuddering, booming, sounds so loud that his hearing went blank white and fizzed back to the screech and howl of men screaming and the patter of gunfire. And after all the cowering in a stinking trench, staring at the retaining wall or his hands around his rifle, when a whistle had sounded and he had clambered up a flimsy ladder and run howling with his rifle into the roar, seeing the silent spark of machine guns in the grey and brown and black and green, seen fresh red on either side of him, he had jumped down into the next trench and killed and killed, first through training and then through inspiration.

Willy had stood in the trench, covered in fresh red, howling over the bodies of boys like him at his feet. It was *that* he would like most not to remember. And it came with medals.

Like millions of young men over thousands of years, he had sought experience and found more than he wanted. Perhaps it was hard to find the right measure; there was either too little or too much.

Willy's parents, at home on their island in the ocean, had died in the influenza epidemic. Back stateside, blank from the war, Willy had sat in the attorney's office, staring at a painting on the wall as the man had explained to him the circumstances and their aftermath. Willy felt indifferent about the sum of money he had been left. After making a brief effort at doing what his father might have wanted him to do, he gave up the study of engineering, then switched to literature and poetry, something of which the old man would never have approved.

In all the time of going through the motions of a life, he felt as if he were observing his own society as dispassionately as a science experiment. He sat in his classes, trying to be a proper student, but the droning of scarless classmates who had never seen the brains or blood or intestines of friends did little to capture his interest. His mind wandered so obviously that a concerned professor pulled him aside and asked him about it.

"No, I'm fine," Willy said, neither knowing nor caring if he were lying as the words came out of his mouth.

Willy began a friendship with another young veteran named Glen Farnsworth. They had noticed each other on campus. Willy saw in Farnsworth's eyes a look he suspected Farnsworth saw in his. The first time they struck up a conversation and shaken hands, Willy couldn't help but observe that the other young man was missing a finger. The healing wounds on the right side of Farnsworth's face and neck were a contradiction to his aristocratic looks, and to Willy, that made him likable and trustworthy.

They went to a speakeasy together and were disgusted by the furtiveness of it, not to mention the prices. Although they rarely talked about their experiences in combat, they rehashed stories again and again about their days of furlough, in Paris and the smaller towns in the French countryside, of the food and the women and the great bouts of uninhibited drinking.

"I'm going back," Farnsworth said one night. The brown smudges under his eyes made him look years older, and Willy thought that a change would do him good.

"So go," Willy said.

"I don't belong here anymore," Farnsworth said. "*You* don't belong here anymore. Let's just say fuck all this and go to France."

Willy realized he had no objections, no reason to stay.

"Sure," he said.

He didn't even bother to withdraw from school. He simply left.

Farnsworth never showed up for their rendezvous at the steamer. Willy waited for over two hours, well after the steamer had left, the smell of the port and the stack gas, the deep bellow of the departing ship's steam whistle making him anxious and angry. Soon the ship was out of sight. Fucking Farnsworth, Willy thought.

He was loyal, though. Following one referral after another, he called a telephone number at what he knew to be a ritzy exchange. He had not been raised impoverished, but was surprised to have his call answered by someone who was obviously a servant.

Farnsworth, the young woman informed him, had hanged himself in the family dining room.

Willy had no feeling about the news, other than wondering what would cause the young man to do the obvious in such a spiteful manner. He snorted and shook his head, holding the receiver of the phone to his ear but turning from the mouthpiece.

"Sir?" the servant said after a few moments.

"Yeah, I'm here," Willy said.

"Is there anything else I can do?"

"Sure," Willy said. "Give it to me straight. Was Farnsworth an asshole?"

"I'm sure I don't know what you mean."

"Yeah, you do. Just us chickens. Was he?"

"No," the young woman said, a hitch in her voice. "No he wasn't. He was a good boy."

Willy booked passage on the next steamer for France. Before he left, he posted a letter to the last person he knew of who had survived the war and who had been, for however long, his friend. He never expected the letter to reach Emilio Benitez, and wrote sheet after sheet of thin paper as if he were going to stuff a letter in a bottle. In the end, he sent it to Emilio's last known address. The letter was so thick that it resembled a flattened lozenge. He posted it with little hope of a response, just a message into the void.

Willy's father might have recognized his symptoms: wanderlust, itchy feet, something McGregors over the generations had endured, rarely understanding it until they had outgrown it. His father might have explained that it was this that had made them go to sea when others had stayed behind, it was this that had driven his father to a new land.

Staying in Paris for some time, Willy casually befriended other young Americans and their acquaintances. He followed a string of relationships with women less inhibited than those he had known Stateside. There had been Marie-France, a petite French girl with short dark hair and a heart-shaped face, Inez, a Spanish flamenco dancer ten years older than Willy, and Gunta, a tall, pale German girl, rather moody and neurotic. All had their charming attributes; all left him knowing it would be a lie to say he truly loved them.

Moving from one overlapping social circle to another, he spent time in Provence, falling in love with it immediately. The hills and the vineyards, the quality of the light settling onto the green and golden land; it was hypnotic. One morning he sat outside a tiny café, trying to puzzle his way through a French newspaper as he drank a cup of coffee and ate a croissant. He absently put his hand out onto the small table, as if to hold the hand of a woman who was not there. Realizing what he had done, he recoiled slightly, puzzled. Sitting alone at the café, he had been unobserved; conversations continued around him, a dog barked in the distance. It was the strangest sensation, as if he had had a memory of a future habit, had been reaching out to hold the hand of a woman he did not yet know.

Willy moved on the next day.

Marseilles was an interesting place, vibrant and noisy. As an industrial port, he found it familiar, and with his money running low, he began to look for work. By pure chance, he ran into someone from his division who remembered Willy for the prowess in boxing and for his handiness in combat, something Willy refused to discuss. Dick Ryan was in France to placate his surly wife, he said, but had left her behind in the hotel room while he went out for a drink. Without hesitation, Ryan offered Willy a job with his bootlegging operation on the east coast, saying that someone as smart and tough as Willy would fit right in. Willy woke up the next morning a bit hung over, but charged with a sense of possibility and purpose. After the morning at the café in Provence, the time he was spending in France had begun to seem empty and pointless. He contemplated the prospect for a couple of minutes, admitted to himself that bootlegging was easily the best of his few options. Willy found that he was excited to return to the States.

First stop, though, was at the Ste. Pierre et Miquelon Islands- a French possession just south of Newfoundland- where Ryan had warehouses for his product. He was in the process of spreading his operation to the Virgin Islands and other ports throughout the Greater Antilles, he explained, and needed good men to work for him. His procedure was always the same, and always effective: he loaded the hold of a clipper ship with the crates of the finest booze, then rendezvoused in international waters with known contacts to the mainland, who brought out cash in speedboats for the transaction. Business was so lucrative that bootleggers almost always had better boats than the Coast Guard- although pirates, at times, gave them a literal run for their money- and things proceeded as a matter of routine. Ryan and his men trained Willy to run booze to ports in New England, many of which were already familiar from his childhood and his father's profession. Willy caught on quickly and loved the work, wondering what his father would have said about it.

Bootlegging took cunning and nerve, and had the added advantage of flouting a stupid law. It was profitable, and even somewhat glamorous. Although Willy never would have admitted the importance of the last aspect, but bootleggers were folk heroes, their exploits reported glowingly in the press. Legal opposition was scant; what with the "remunerated complicity" of local authority and the outright ineptitude of agencies like the Coast Guard, which was under current scrutiny for both firing on an Ivy League crew team and accidentally shooting up a lighthouse on one of the Great Lakes, wounding the lighthouse keeper. There was a reported two percent chance of actually getting caught by the law. Far more dangerous were the turf wars, and worse, the piracy that evolved as more people wanted to make a profit while they could. Willy understood the ethic behind turf wars- there was a certain etiquette involved in bootlegging- but pirates he considered to be parasites, preying on entrepreneurs who made a living by fulfilling a public need.

Throughout the 1920s, Willy's responsibilities grew with Ryan's operation. He worked in the Virgin Islands and the Carolinas, most of it going without a hitch, although there were occasional run-ins with pirates and once, oddly, with the KKK. Willy often responded in such situations with violence; his desire for adventure was diminishing, though, and when he resorted to these skills, it often left him feeling depressed for days.

It was during these times that his correspondence with Emilio Benitez increased. Willy's message-in-a-bottle letter to Emilio had found him, and Willy was astonished to discover a reply in the post office box he kept and checked infrequently. Emilio had found a place in the middle of the country, on the River, in the North. He described it lovingly, Willy was touched to read, going on about his adopted home. It sounded peaceful, and Emilio surprisingly pacifistic, as though he had found a place for his gentler sentiments to take root. Emilio began a habit of inviting Willy to come for a visit. "Go to New Orleans," Emilio wrote. "Find the river. You can't miss it; it's big. Find it and come north."

As the business began to get more crowded and violent, Willy began to think about making a change. It was Dick Ryan's suggestion that Willy, with his own boat, bypass New Orleans and go up the river, far enough north that he was unencumbered by the bootlegging bailiwicks of the South, but not quite far enough that he was too close to territories where booze was brought in from Canada, northern industrial cities like Cleveland, Detroit, and Greysport. This was not a tip, Ryan told Willy, that he had bestowed on anyone else. Willy was thankful for the man's kindness. When another of Ryan's men was shot by pirates, Willy's mind was made up.

Having long since saved the money to be independent, Willy bought a new cabin cruiser in New Orleans, one with a large storage capacity, a powerful engine, a few bunks and a small galley, and broke it in with a cruise to Atchafalaya Bay, and then to Pascagoula and Pensacola. He pushed the engine to its limits, got to know the boat's idiosyncrasies, and soon felt ready to move up the river. He contacted a member of Ryan's organization, made a pickup in the Caribbean, and was soon headed upriver with a laden hold, solo for the first time.

It was strange to be away from the sea, but there was something compelling about the powerful river, something epic. As he headed north from the gulf and the river rolled out bronze and pungent before him in the hazy dawn, filigreed with islands and sloughs and backwaters, shacks sheltered by trees hung with spanish moss on the low and marshy shore, with river traffic from canoes to barges, Willy felt light- perhaps even cheerful- with wonder.

Although most of the point of this first trip was for the exploration and the adventure, finding new towns and customers, Willy had one destination in the northern river town of MacDougal, built on a crescent-shaped island accessible by boat and bridge, where Emilio had settled and become a carpenter. In their correspondence over the years since the war, Willy had found out more about Emilio than he had when they had seen each other almost daily. Emilio was a fellow boxer, and a talented one, and the Army in its wisdom had taken this small, ferocious warrior- with a sharp mind for science, to boot- and turned him into a cook, apparently not seeing him as fit to fight alongside decent white boys. Emilio bore this insult with a characteristic weary irony. His parents had come to the States after the government had leveraged the revolt of that part of Colombia which would become Panama in order to obtain construction rights to, and control of, the Panama Canal, his parents feeling that, as long as they were going to be under the thumb of the United States, they would at least like to be able to vote. Willy had seen Emilio take stupid, senseless, and demeaning orders with a deadpan face, a pause of some seconds, and a sigh, acts which were not quite insubordinate, but nonetheless humorous to the fellow underlings. He could change gears into a mode which was a subtle parody of obsequiousness, an insult so fine that it was usually lost upon the victimized superior officer. It was for this that Willy had liked him. Like Willy, Emilio also read constantly, and his literate nature was finally something that Willy trusted enough to break through his habitual barrier of self-protection to actually show Emilio some of his poetry, that aspect which he had kept very secret. Emilio had seen him constantly jotting notes in a rather furtive manner, and had begun to pester Willy about his actions out of boredom and curiosity. It could easily have become the kind of friendship that faded away, but the diligence of their correspondence kept it alive, and had Willy cruising up the river to MacDougal Island.

After the war, Emilio had pursued a woman to MacDougal, but discovered upon his arrival that she had moved on, leaving no forwarding address. Out of money and ideas, Emilio found work as a carpenter and soon had built enough of a reputation that he could be his own boss. When Willy had finally taken Emilio up on his invitations and written about his plan to do business up the river, Emilio's response had been enthusiastic. From the vantage point of his adopted home, Emilio could tell Willy that there was a great demand for good liquor in that region, the thirsty populace having been relegated to home brew and the often dangerous products of secluded stills. There was a clamoring market for top quality products, Emilio insisted, and he had the connections along the river and in his own town to make distribution simple and Willy's transition to a new market seamless, all without stepping on anyone's toes or getting shot at.

The topography changed as Willy cruised north, the land bunching into hills and the river itself seeming to contract into something still huge, yet smaller than a moving plain of water. There were stops along the way suggested by Emilio, medium-sized river towns, where he sold cases of booze, spent a night in a hotel or at a cathouse, then refueled and continued north. He soon noticed that the people he spoke to no longer talked with southern accents, and he knew he was nearing his destination.

In the North, the river was perhaps more beautiful, strung with random wooded islands and shoals, lined with bluffs thick with oak and maple or faced with sloping fields like alpine glens. Around every bend in the river was some new vista, and fascination and curiosity drew Willy on. Bald eagles soared serenely on thermals, their burning focus on the water for prey, and the sight of them made Willy forget everything else in wonder and a joy that made him laugh aloud. Some places were too beautiful to bypass, though, and in quiet sloughs and backwaters, away from the river's traffic on still waters thick with Canada geese, mallards, herons, and cranes, Willy would drop anchor. He would get out his rod and reel and fish, then cook up his catch in the galley (using garlic in the French way, which he had brought from the mouth of the river) and eat in the cockpit under a wild sunset, the sky and clouds titanic, life perfect and free as he smoked a cigar and drank scotch from a mug, sometimes writing his impressions in a notebook, perhaps in prose form or in a poem, squinting out over the water in search of the right words. If such a night were fair, he would sleep in the cockpit under army blankets, feeling tiny but enveloped under the sprawl of stars.

Emilio had given him directions to his home, and Willy began to spot landmarks, finally finding the place on a late summer morning when the river was heavy with golden haze. Emilio had a fine cabin on a south side of MacDougal Island, on a crescent-shaped cove protected from the southward flow of the river. It was off a little road that lead to the town, peaceful and surrounded by pine trees, set sturdily on the bank above flood level and looking down on the dock which Emilio had put in himself.

On the south end of the island, Emilio's cabin was a testament to his skill as a carpenter and woodworker, for which he was now known throughout several counties. His work for others was exacting and beyond reproach, but it was clear to Willy that the cabin was built with love, that it was Emilio's successful attempt at creating a personal heaven. It had varnished siding and green shutters at the windows, and a broad porch with two rocking chairs that Emilio had made himself, and flagstone steps leading down the short hill to the path that lead to the dock. The front door had a brass knocker and a brass lamp on the wall next to it, and the door itself was meticulously carved with remarkable hunt scenes, carefully and accurately rendered, done late at night in the woodshop farther up the hill under a stand of pines behind the house.

It was a Saturday afternoon when Willy showed up at Emilio's house and tied up at the dock. Emilio came out the front door of the little house, a grin on his face. He trotted down onto the dock and regarded Willy, shaking his head.

"Well," Willy said, "I'm here."

"I know. I can no beeleef it." Emilio said, his accent undiminished. The two men embraced, thumping each other on the back.

"I am very glad you are here," Emilio said. "Welcome to my home."

Emilio showed Willy around and led him to a spare bedroom with a small bed, where Willy laid his duffel bag. They sat on the big front porch of the cabin and got amicably drunk together.

Willy liked Emilio's corner of the world, but he was less than impressed with the town of MacDougal. Its heyday had been in the last half of the previous century, when its Grand Hotel had catered to the captains of riverboats and businessmen involved with shipping and trade, and was actually almost grand at the time, perched on a bluff overlooking the road into the rowdy town. When Willy first saw the hotel, it was a pretty and proper place, with white walls and neat green shutters, and at the foot of the veranda a narrow, clipped lawn and benches looking out over a low stone wall at the edge of the bluff and down on the broad dark river with its docks on the near side, smaller islands dotted across its width, and across to the wooded shore in the hazy distance beyond. In the summer, young men in suits, crisp collars, and derbies strolled on the lawn with young women in the flapper-inspired fashions from the east, or sat on the green-painted benches in the breezy, cooling evenings, watching the color of the sky change and listening to the sound of the piano come through the large open windows of the hotel, a sound which could be heard faintly by those passing on the road below, who perhaps paused to look briefly up at the source of the sound, up over the lush and windshifted trees to the high amber windows of the hotel glowing out from the bluff and shaded from the setting sun. When Willy first saw the hotel, though, he knew at a glance that its day was waning, that it was a shade off perfection, but he did not guess that in the time of his grandson's young adulthood, the hotel would have continued its trend of decay to become a paintless grey and vinegrown ghost building, its few remaining windows glinting in the moonlight in the shadows of the cliffs which press down black in the night over the lightlined streets of the humble little town.

When Willy first came to MacDougal, it was a place of riotous nightlife, unlike the directed, businesslike bustle of the daytime, and it was here that Willy would make his money. When Prohibition had come in, the bars in the town had made an immediate conversion to private clubs featuring a variety of home brews, a move supported by the Sheriff, a lazy and amiable man fond of drink and sure that this current silliness would soon pass. The Sheriff was unworried about federal authorities; they had too few people and too much to do in cities like Greysport, the industrial giant and harbor town, which, in any event, was a few hundred miles to the east. Emilio informed Willy that whatever anxiety the Sheriff suffered was abated by any number of payoffs. Emilio introduced Willy around, and the quality of his booze, unseen in the area for years, created a sensation. MacDougal became Willy's safe haven, his own comfortable and profitable niche in the world of bootlegging. He said to Emilio that he thought of it as a gig that would work for awhile, until he saved up enough money to set out again, perhaps back to Europe. All the time, almost secret even to himself, was the thought that perhaps this was it, perhaps this was his home. He wordlessly hoped but didn't know that it was in MacDougal that he was going to meet the woman who would become his wife.

The music that he'd heard wafting down from the Grand Hotel was what had brought his future wife to Ole's Sportsmen's Club, though indirectly; a classically trained pianist, Mae Palmer had returned to MacDougal after college to stay with her parents, who owned the Grand Hotel, and consider her next move. Her mother loved her eternally- Mae would always be her baby- but her priggish father was distressed that she hadn't found a cultured professional for a husband while in college, and was aghast at what he perceived as her crazy, headstrong, suffragist views. He had never anticipated experiencing such discord with a daughter, but she had become so much the opposite of submissive that the arguments began almost as soon as she came back. Old man Palmer's threats to cut her off financially, he was dismayed to note, appeared to have no effect. The final blow came when Mae announced that she would soon begin to play the piano in the hotel, and her father countered that they had not spent all that good money on her going to college just to have her become an entertainer, that she was from better "stock" than that. It would appear immodest! Mae's mother, always loving and supportive, enthusiastic about the notion of Mae playing in the huge front room of the hotel, had submitted yet again to her husband, to Mae's mixture of love and disgust.

So Mae, with a grim set to her pretty face and the sound belief that further argument would prove pointless, had left the hotel and walked into town, penniless. She immediately got a job at Ole's Sportsmen's Club, doing this by simply walking in- to the craned necks and muttered comments of those at the bar-sitting down at the bar's upright piano, and playing such a dazzling lineup of everything from ragtime to nocturnes that she was able to state her price as the stunned crowd of member-patrons got over their gaping surprise and began to applaud. Ole, who got her cheap anyway, had dollar signs in his eyes. Mae became a fixture.

When Willy first saw her, he and Emilio had come in the backdoor of the bar from the alley to have a drink while Ole's boys unloaded cases of booze from the back of Emilio's carpentry truck, and Willy, surprised to hear Chopin played in such surroundings, looked to the front of the bar where Mae sat in the diffuse light of the dirty front windows, hypnotized by the act of playing the piano. Her copper hair glowed in the light, her skin shone like living pearl, her eyes were half-closed. Anyone would have said she was beautiful

Willy drew up short as if he'd hit the end of a leash. "Holy *shit*," he said. Emilio glanced at his friend, did a doubletake at the look on his face, smiled and said, "Uh oh."

Simply seeing Mae in that unlikely setting had put things in motion. After all his involvement with women, it perplexed him that Mae seemed uninterested. It wasn't that Willy was vain; he simply thought that he looked better in comparison to most of the locals.

He tried to engage her in conversation and was occasionally successful, but she usually seemed simply indifferent.

"Maybe she's a *lesbiana*," Emilio said.

Willy thought about this for a moment. He shook his head. "Nah."

On his trip back down the river to the Gulf, he fantasized about taking Mae with him overseas, showing her Paris and Marseilles. Or, St. Pierre et Miquelon, for that matter. Perhaps she would make life in any of those places complete. Perhaps it was her phantom hand he had gone to hold outside the café in Provence.

Willy had returned with a hold full of liquor and been rebuffed by Mae yet again. This threw him into a funk, and he procrastinated on making another run to the gulf, and thoughts about returning to France had disappeared from his mind altogether. Emilio watched him staring with a furrowed brow out at the sliding water of the river and shook his head. In many conversations, they had talked about the notion of love, Emilio having lived through it and been disappointed but still maintaining hope, while Willy had simply come to believe that it did not exist. Now, though, his confidence in that belief and others had been shaken.

Willy pursued Mae with an obstinacy that Emilio appeared to find embarrassing, but Willy could not be reasoned with. It may have been something akin to love at first sight, but after he had talked to Mae the first few times, he began to love her spirit even more than her beauty, and at that point there was no going back.

Although she worked in a thinly veiled speakeasy and saw herself as living in liberation of her father's snobbishness, Mae was still partially a product of her upbringing, a fact she would have vehemently denied. Its result was that she spurned Willy; his boxer's build and brawling tendencies somehow offended her, and he was not the kind of person (she would later admit) that she could ever see becoming responsible. She supposed she found him attractive- it would be lying not to admit it- and he was well read and philosophical in a way that was jarringly contradictory to his appearance, as if he were a character actor wearing the odd costume of a dockworking hoodlum while discussing Plato between scenes.

For a year Willy pursued her. He brought her flowers, he tried to make her laugh, he took her to dinner-when she consented- at the best places within fifty miles that he could find, and to the area's one movie theater upriver in the large town of Black Marsh. Mae had one of the sharpest and most wide-ranging minds Willy had ever come across, and they talked about everything: Margaret Mead, Havelock Ellis, Prohibition and Suffrage, fascism and communism, Hitler and Mussolini, Lenin and Stalin, Kahlil Gibran and Mohandas Gandhi, Houdini, Mae West, and Mickey Mouse. Mae had a better formal education than Willy, and was at least his intellectual equal; he often found himself scrambling to keep up. On trips back down the river, he took stacks of reading material.

Willy was chivalrous and thoughtful, never pressing too hard, but never withdrawing. Mae hoped and expected that he would give up, realizing his quest was fruitless, and that he would get over his infatuation and find someone else. She was often faintly surprised to see him return after a run downriver; a man of his pride and independence would surely, at some point, feel foolish and gather about himself the tatters of his dignity and walk away. But then there he would be, at Ole's or in the town park or on the street down in front of her second-story apartment, and his eyes would brighten upon seeing her, and he would begin, in his brash and cheerful way, to tell her stories about his trip south or about what he'd been reading, all the while seemingly enjoying a specific blindness to her indifference.

She didn't see him the way Emilio saw him; away from her, he became moody and irate, and his tart observations about everything, including Emilio, reached a level of acerbity previously unknown. In his frustration, Willy became anxious to make runs downriver, and would jump aboard his boat with boxes of supplies and toss the mooring lines on Emilio's dock, saying to him, "See ya when I see ya," and churning full throttle out into the river.

Emilio became accustomed to the fact that Willy would undergo a metamorphosis somewhere downstream; he returned with a hold full of alcohol, doing a beeline to Emilio's dock, and, after perfunctory greetings, pumped Emilio for information about Mae. Had she left town, was she still playing at Ole's, was there anyone else in the picture? Emilio had noticed that she'd told Willy she was considering jobs in the cities to the east, maybe Greysport, but never took them. He wondered if she were just toying with his friend.

It made Emilio sick to see. After Willy would seek her out and casually establish that at least his standing with her had not deteriorated, he would return puzzled and distant. He seemed almost to be reviewing points by counting on his fingers: she's not seeing anyone else, while Willy was good-looking, smart, and flush with cash. He was a rumrunner, a modern Robin Hood! He just didn't get it.

Emilio tried to get Willy's mind off it. A stalwart friend, he tried to talk Willy out of his feelings, only to be stared at with incredulity. He tried to get Willy drunk, but half the time Willy would be too distracted to keep drinking, sitting sullenly on the porch, or the dock, or his boat, glowering out over the water. The other half of the time, he would succeed in getting Willy drunk and Willy would become belligerent, insisting that they go off and find a fight in a town somewhere down the river, the door once again open to his capacity for violence. Emilio would say that his days of fighting were over and leave Willy to it.

After one such event, Willy came back loaded enough to run into Emilio's pier and do damage to both the pier and the bow of his boat. This mishap had the ironic side effect of temporarily lessening Willy's lovesickness; his mopey contrition while doing the repairs necessary to both the dock and the boat kept him quiet and occupied for three days, while Emilio managed to make it last by constantly pointing out Willy's comparative shortcomings as a carpenter, all the while struggling to maintain a stern demeanor and a straight face. "Missed a spot, *pendejo*," he would say, pointing with his chin, and when Willy would respond with a meek and remorseful nod, Emilio would have to turn away, trying to keep from laughing, turning back only when he felt sure he had reasserted his cool gaze.

Emilio would eventually see that he had underestimated Willy's stubbornness and drive; a war hadn't killed him, his outlaw life hadn't killed him; he appeared capable of surviving even a dire and unrequited love.

One day it had begun to rain in MacDougal, a long summer rain, and the water had poured from the bluffs in waterfalls, and down the gullies in torrents. The gutters had run dirty for awhile, then clean, and thunder drummed overhead and the days were dark at noon from the thickness of the clouds. As the river began to rise, some of the people of the town grew worried, while others were fatalistic; these were river people, and they responded in habitual ways to the vagaries of their environment.

Emilio had anticipated this, having grown up in a part of the world where flooding was also customary, and had built his house far enough up the slope that it would only be affected in the most severe circumstances. Willy's boat was tied tightly to the dock in the backwater, its fenders rubbing gently against the dock as the boat bobbed in the slowly rising water. Willy and Emilio sat in the rocking chairs on the porch, drinking coffee and watching the rain fall in shifting veils, rendering the trees of nearer islands ghostly, obscuring the far shore altogether.

Willy, as usual those days, was silent and distracted, his eyes turned outward to the rain but looking at nothing. Emilio alternated between watching the beauty of the rain and the river, sipping his coffee, and doing a crossword puzzle on a clipboard on his knee. Although English was his second language and he would always speak with the accent which Willy often found amusing, his vocabulary was terrific, and only when he was talking too fast, as he often did, would he accidentally confuse words. When he had time to contemplate, he suffered no such lapses, and it gave him deep satisfaction to complete a difficult crossword puzzle in his adopted language.

Emilio contemplated his friend's plight. It was obvious that Willy's affection for Mae was not only sincere, but long-lasting; it was his approach that kept him from winning her heart. Emilio was correct in assessing his own skills at planning and at strategy, however, which told him not only how Willy should approach

Mae, but how Emilio himself should approach Willy. An oblique approach seemed in order for the latter. He tapped his white teeth with his pencil.

"What is-" he asked Willy- "a eight letter word for lovesickness. Begins with a 'y', ends with 'i-n-g'."

Willy didn't answer, staring out at the rain and the water.

"Willy."

No answer.

"Willy!"

"What?" He snapped, annoyed.

"I asked you a question," Emilio said unflappably, pronouncing, as was his habit, two syllables in the word "asked".

"What?" His eyes had lost their look of trance, but still rested on the rain and the water.

"What is a eight letter word for lovesickness. Begins with 'y', ends with 'i-n-g'."

"Oh fuck, don't get me doing that again. I hate crossword puzzles."

"They are good esscerise and you are good at them," Emilio said. "You just don't have no patience."

"Any patience. What was the question again?"

Emilio smiled to himself, his eyes flicking to his friend, and repeated the question. Willy stretched his legs out and laced his fingers behind his head. He squinted. "Yearning," he said presently.

"Hey, good," Emilio said. "See, I tole you. Now, what is a word- nine letters- for extreme sexual frustration in the male. Begins with a 'b' and ends with 'l-l-s.' "

Willy thought for a few moments, then sat up like a shot and slammed his feet to the porch. "Gimme that paper, goddam it!" he said, snatching it out of Emilio's hand before he could stop it. He looked at the puzzle then looked at Emilio with a droll glare. "What's on your mind, buddy?" He couldn't suppress a bit of a smile.

Emilio managed to maintain an air of seriousness. "I think you are being estupid."

"How so?"

"You have tried everything with this woman, right? You have brought her flowers, taken her to dinner, tried to be charming and kind- which must be difficult for *you*- you have been around all the time, all the time, but nothing works, right?"

"Yeah, so?"

"I'm just saying that I thin' you chould try another approach," Emilio said, shrugging. They watched each other.

Willy gave first. "Such as?"

Emilio affected a look of sagacity, folding his hands with his index fingers pointing up, touching his lips. "It is time to espose that which is secret inside you."

"Espouse?"

"Ex. Pose."

"Oh. *Expose*. Like how?"

"Show her your poetry."

"Are you nuts?" Willy started to bluster. "I couldn't-"

Emilio, a superior look on his face, held up his hand, "Ah, ah, ah, ah! No! Listen to me, my friend! Trust me when it comes to matters of the heart!"

18

Willy huffed disgustedly and shook his head.

"It's the one thing you haven't tried," Emilio persisted. "What have you got to lose? What are you afraid of?"

Willy stared at Emilio for a moment. "I'm not *afraid* of *anything*, pal."

Emilio stared back; neither dropped his eyes. "Oh yes you are."

Willy dropped his gaze.

"Why don't you get her to read your poetry?" Emilio asked.

Willy scoffed. "God, no!" He shook his head, laughing.

"Why not?"

"It's not ready."

"When will it be?"

"I don't know, but it isn't now."

"I thin' it is," Emilio said. "I've read bits of it for years, and it was ready *then*."

"It's proof of my questionable judgment that I showed it to you in the first place."

"She is a person of intellect and taste," Emilio persisted. "Show her your heart."

"No," Willy said. "I would show her some work if we were married, or even serious, but as it is, no."

"So you are only brave in certain ways," Emilio said, and Willy gave him a look.

Emilio gazed back and said, "You have to do something to counteract your brutish appearance."

"Not that."

"Then it is a conundrum. You would only share with her if you had her love, but she might only love you if you share with her."

"You're an annoying person," Willy said.

"You are brave in that you are not afraid of physical consequences," Emilio continued. "That's one kind of bravery. You have *medals* for that kind of bravery, of course."

Their eye contact broken, Willy now studied the water.

"But there are other kinds of courage, my frien'," Emilio said. "You coul' be the toughest guy in the worl' and not be able to tell someone you loved them, you could act like you were too tough to show such things, and so, in reality, that toughness is a form of cowardice, a way to avoid doing what you fear the most."

Willy licked his lips and swallowed.

"There could be some pimply little kid in college, weak and small, and he could write about the sadness of the death of his mother when he was fourteen, and that skinny kid could have the courage to take those raw feelings and have them publish' in the college literary journal. And why does that kid do it? Because he has a different kind of courage. He has the courage to say what is true.

"And you have something that makes you different, something that makes you...especial. Even beautiful, to a woman like Mae. She will not be impressed by your considerable brutality, I assure you. You mus' share what is beautiful within you."

Willy capitulated. Willy brought out sheaves of his work, and they talked about it, Willy nervous and reticent at first, but then opening up as he felt more comfortable with Emilio's reactions. Soon he was candidly asking Emilio what he thought about this or that piece, although he had sworn his friend to secrecy. It would become a habit of their friendship, and Emilio wouldn't have to disguise his feelings, thinking Willy's poetry quite good, for the most part. Willy would be deeply flattered one day when his friend committed some of the poems to memory. When Emilio would encourage him to seek a publisher, Willy waved him off, saying, again, that he wasn't ready yet. Willy often thought of his scribbling as an affliction rather than an ambition, although Emilio tried to talk him out of such a notion. On that day, though, Emilio convinced Willy that it was his work that would win Mae over.

Willy gathered up what he thought to be his best work, putting it in a large manila envelope it the selection he had already shown Emilio, addressing it to Mae. He put on a black slicker and hat, holding the manila envelope.

"Mind if I borrow your truck?"

Emilio smiled. "The keys are in it."

"Okay. Okay. I'm gonna..." he held up the envelope and wiggled it.

Emilio nodded.

Willy started down the steps, hesitated, turned around and said, "Thanks, Emilio. You're...probably right."

He went out to the truck and drove up the river road in the rain. When he got to Ole's he found that Mae had the day off and Ole had no idea where she was. Willy sighed and shook his head.

"What's eating *you*?" Ole said. "You look sick."

"It's just...look, give this to Mae, will you?" He handed Ole the envelope.

"Sure," Ole said, putting it next to the old cash register.

"And don't read it."

Ole shrugged.

"I'm serious," Willy said. "It's personal."

"Fine," Ole said.

Willy held his eye for a moment and went back out into the rain.

The next day was Saturday, and threatened to rain yet again, but never did anything more than sprinkle. Willy refused to go into town to see if Mae had gotten his package, but the wait was painful. It felt as if he had eviscerated himself and left his guts behind on the sidewalk to be poked at by strangers. To pass the time and divert his attention, he alternately did calisthenics on the porch and read a book. He walked up into the pines where Emilio was at work in the woodshop and offered to spar with him, but Emilio put him to work instead to give him something to do with his overflow of energy. After a few hours, they went down to the kitchen and cracked a bottle of whiskey, drinking while Emilio prepared some perch for dinner. They avoided the subject of Willy's sacrificial offering of his work, talking about anything else in one of their wide-ranging conversations. As Emilio grew happier with the whiskey, he warmed to the topic of marsh ecology, going on at length while Willy found himself to be half interested and half distracted. Emilio broke out some hard cider to augment the whiskey, and soon they reached a point of hilarity, listening to music on the scratchy radio. Emilio noticed, though, that the smile would occasionally fade from Willy's face, that he would tune out and become distant. Emilio would do something to make him laugh, and they would be off again.

The next day they were a bit bleary, but better after coffee and a good breakfast. Willy started to do sit-ups and push-ups on the front porch, then chins on one of the porch's crossbeams.

"What is it with you and the constan' essercise?" Emilio asked, looking up at Willy from the door. "Is it some kind of nervous tic?"

"Just when you get soft is when things are gonna deteriorate, pal," Willy grunted, chinning himself. "Trust me."

"I'm too hung over for that shit. I'll be up in the shop."

"Don't chop off any fingers," Willy grunted.

In the afternoon, they sat on the porch, Willy with a book and Emilio with another crossword puzzle. The atmosphere felt heavy and the trees drooped. The river slid by unperturbed. Willy read the same paragraph over and over again, and Emilio could see from where he sat that he had not turned the page in quite some time. After awhile, Willy let the book hang between his knees and looked out at the river.

With a nearby detonation of lightning that made them both jump, it began to pour.

"Ja see that?" Willy said. "Lightning just hit across the river."

"Maybe it's a sign."

"You don't believe that any more than I do, but I'm willing to pretend it's one."

He got up and went inside, bringing out a bottle of whiskey and two glasses. "I'm going to have to gird my loins for this."

"It was smart of you to wait until it started raining," Emilio observed.

"It's more miserable this way," Willy said, pouring.

After girding his loins, Willy had put on his rain gear and walked into town in the rain, declining Emilio's offer of his truck. He stomped up the road through the brown puddles, muttering to himself and occasionally producing a flask for a pull. A black Ford tore down the road toward him, splashing puddles and honking its horn, the inhabitants hooting drunkenly. They didn't recognize Willy, in his black slicker and hat, as their favorite rumrunner, but the size of his thick shoulders and his baleful glare caused the driver of the vehicle to swerve enough out of the way that he went off onto the gravel shoulder, tipping the Ford for a few precarious moments on two wheels, eliciting frightened and delighted screams from the riders. Willy swore at them.

The town of MacDougal was in the beginning stages of flood, that much was apparent. The docked boats rode high next to the sinking piers, and where the road met the ends of the cobbled streets, mud and silt accumulated and oozed. The town's frequent hubbub was quieted by the ominous weather, but here and there a cheerless horse, harnessed to a work wagon or simply alone, stood tethered to the hitching posts that lined the streets' raised sidewalks, among a dotting of occasional automobiles.

Willy turned off the river road and stepped over deep puddles and onto the sidewalk, the heels of his workboots thumping as he strode. He muttered to himself a little, going over scenarios in his mind in which the obstinate object of his desire succumbed to his dignity, his wounded princeliness, seeing at last into the depths of his blue eyes, seeing the worth there. He almost didn't dare to think about the consequences of her despising his work, for that, surely, would be that. It was almost a relief to think that it was too late to change anything.

As it was, he clomped up the raised sidewalk, under the awnings of storefronts, out again in the hissing rain, the rain thrumming on his hat and his shoulders. Irrationally, he was headed for Ole's, although it was too early for Mae to be there, but before he could get to the door of the place he spotted her walking toward him down the street, sheltered by a black umbrella and carrying a small bag of groceries, black and lean in her hat and long coat, her spill of red hair, lank in the rain, the only color. He straightened himself up and walked toward her.

She saw him coming and their eyes met, her face remaining blank. She maintained her pace and walked toward him, but stopped under the awning of a clothing store, mannequins standing in the window behind her. He drew himself up and closed the distance between them, his shoulders taking on an almost belligerent roll.

Crossing a sidestreet, Willy held his head up in spite of the rain. He looked at her, expecting to see a look of disgust or annoyance, but instead saw- what- tenderness? Affection? He sped up his pace involuntarily, and his bootheel came in contact with a patch of slick submerged clay. He slipped, his boots soared into the air and he landed with a splash on his back in the running water and the mud. He lay on his back, staring up into the rain, and his hat flopped off ignominiously into the water. He thought that if a horse came by and pissed on him, it might be more humiliating, but not much.

Mae's mouth dropped into a little O, and pity overtook mirth on her face; she set down her groceries under the window of the clothing store and went to help him up. When he blinked away some rain and saw her standing over him, he waved off her proffered hand.

"Are you hurt?" she asked.

He shook his head. "Just thinking," he said.

She bent over him and held a sheaf of red hair back with her pale hand.

"I loved your poetry," she said.

"Yeah?"

She smiled, and it was the best smile he had ever seen. "Yeah," she said.

He rolled over onto his side and got up. He stood up, dripping, muddy, and ashen with embarrassment. "Ah, shit," he said.

Trying to maintain a straight face but giggling intermittently, Mae extended her hand to him. "Here," she said. He stood, and she looked up into his woebegone face and wiped some of the mud off his cheeks with her pale fingers, and looked into his eyes, which were wide and defenseless. She inclined her head slightly, he leaned forward, and they kissed. They kissed for a long time. When they drew apart, her eyes were wide, and she put her hand to her hat. They looked into each other's eyes, their gazes curious and exploring.

The rain poured over them. Mae gestured vaguely over her shoulder in the general direction of her groceries and said, "I was going to...phone you at Emilio's...cook you something. I didn't know...."

They kissed again.

Emilio's mouth dropped open when Ole's Packard pulled up in front of his cabin and Willy and Mae climbed out, waving to Ole before he pulled away. Emilio talked politely to Mae, serving her tea, while Willy washed up and changed clothes. When Willy came out in fresh jeans and work shirt, his blue eyes calm and happy in the first time in ages, Mae courteously continued her conversation with Emilio, but her gaze was locked on Willy. They left rather abruptly at Willy's suggestion, putting on their coats and heading out to the dock, where Willy helped Mae aboard the boat, then loosed the mooring lines and got aboard. He started the engine and pulled the boat out into the swift and swollen current. They were gone for two days, up the river to Omicron Falls, a place famous for young couples, where they stayed in a little hotel overlooking the river in a room with clean trapunto quilts, where they started their lives together in room number eleven.

Their wedding was a thing that Willy had looked forward to with some dread; once she'd agreed to marry him, occasional moments of reality began to sink in. He didn't like crowds unless they were customers, and the idea of meeting Mae's parents was one that filled him with a secret stagefright nausea. At that heady time in their relationship, he was pleased, beside himself really, when Mae told him that their wedding was not for her parents, especially her father, her mother being malleable clay in her father's unyielding hands. She didn't want it to be the kind of typical, formal wedding that was even more common in those days, and the idea of her father paying for some "grotesque affair", culminating with the stuckup bastard "giving her away" was one that evoked loud and bitter laughter on her part. She figured that her parents wouldn't even come. Locked as she was in a battle of stubborn silence with her father and only secretly talking to her mother, she looked upon the occasion, in one sense, as merely another battle in the long war with her father.

"Fuck him," she said, her use of the expression amusing him. "I feel sorry for my mom and I wish she could come, but if there were one thing in her life to make her stand up to that bastard, this should be it." She looked him deeply in the eyes and held her pale, fine hand out to his tan face, slowly stroking a scar there and running her hand into his hair. "I love you, Robin Hood. You're my future. They're my past."

It wasn't that easy, and Willy knew in retrospect that it rarely is, and that he should've been wise enough to see it even at the time. He didn't ask her why she wanted to stay in the town that seemed to hold her down, but was happy that someone as beautiful and talented would want such a mug as himself. He didn't want to fuck anything up with common sense.

Emilio felt that he had succeeded, that it was all his doing, everything coming into place. Not only had he found his friend a love and a home, he'd just met and begun cautiously dating a plump girl of Norwegian extraction, loving her roundness where others did not, and his quiet, poetic nature and limpid eyes kept her watching hopefully out the windows of the diner where she worked. Her name was Solveig, and she was unaware that her name had a place in literature, something Emilio found charming. She had a large older brother who had protested rather strenuously to Solveig dating a "spic"- in spite of the high regard Emilio enjoyed in the community- a protestation which Willy quickly thwarted, in spite of the brother's being a head taller and sixty pounds heavier. For this alone, Emilio would have stood up in Willy's wedding.

Mae, for her part, didn't have many friends in town. Willy chose to see that her complexity made her incomprehensible to the people of MacDougal -many of whom were fans in any circumstance- but others saw her as being somewhat chilly and remote, pointing to the tendencies of her arrogant father and supposing worse about her socially furtive mother. Mae had gotten to know and like Solveig, with limitations related to Solveig's own. Solveig was vivacious and fun, capable of drinking large amounts on their picnics on the river and excursions to the towns up and down its banks, funny when she ruined jokes in her high-pitched voice and laughed harder at herself than anyone else, and she was a terrific cook besides. She made a good counterpart to Mae's thin, smart, sarcastic persona; both of them saw it. All four of them were as thick as thieves. Mae asked Solveig to be her maid of honor.

The day of the wedding came, and Willy found himself surprisingly calm. This was, he supposed, because he was secure in his knowledge that he was marrying the right woman. The preparations had all been taken care of, and the only thing that mattered to him was that, barring unforeseen circumstances, he would be married to the woman he loved by the end of the day.

The dawn came misty and quiet to the river, but slowly blossomed into one of true Indian Summer; by eleven o'clock, the temperature had reached almost eighty degrees, and the area was at the peak of fall colors, the bluffs and islands and far shore glowing red and yellow and orange, the marshgrass and cattails faded tan, the river flowing fast, black and broad through all, flickering in reflection the depth of the blue sky. Willy had pleaded to flee upriver and elope, but finally gave the reins over to Mae's will. The wedding was planned to be held in the town's park by the river and conducted by the Justice of the Peace, a departure from the traditions of the time. Mae was happy with the plan, seeing it as a thumb in her father's eye.

Willy pulled his boat up to the pier by the park where Emilio and Solveig were already setting things up. It seemed as it things were slowing down, becoming more clear. Perhaps Emilio had been right, his optimism, his hope. Willy stood in the boat and watched the preparations, watched strangers and those who had recently been strangers as they prepared for his wedding day. Who had ever shown him such regard?

Emilio had gotten kegs of a local Octoberfest beer from Ole, who, along with the Sheriff and some of his hangers-on, was helping Emilio set up the kegs under a large oak tree. Solveig, assisted by nearly a dozen of her girlfriends, was spreading white linen tablecloths over the park's picnic tables, which had been set in a long line by some of the town's men already in attendance. A large rectangular slab of concrete in the park had been set aside for dancing, its perimeter staked out with Japanese lanterns strung from poles and leading into the oaks. People had already begun to show up. The veterinarian was talking to the physician, and, as they were customers, Willy knew their dynamic; Dr. Homburg, the young vet, looked up to the old, somewhat boozy Dr. Ambrose for his experience and many tales, while Dr. Ambrose was impressed by the younger man's vivacity and amazingly clear and encyclopedic memory of scientific fact, even under the dint of drink. The butcher, the barber, the grocer, and their wives formed a familiar sextet, and Willy knew they were playing their game of making humorous, derisive comments about their neighbors, while making up fabulous stories about those in attendance whom they did not know.Willy liked them, smiled at them, and knew they were enjoyable customers. The bank president was talking to the publisher of the small newspaper and they were pretending that they were great movers and shakers in the world, while the truth of their existence could be guessed at first glance. A knot of bargemen and a similar group of railroadmen were craning their necks over each others' shoulders to see how the tapping of the huge kegs was coming along, and when the first one spouted foam, they all shouldered for position around the beer with a little predictable jostling and mutual derision, the Sheriff spreading his hands and calling for order, and being pretty much ignored.

Emilio spotted Willy tying up his boat, and pointed to it, getting a few of the boys around the keg to take some hand trucks down to the pier and offload the cases of scotch, gin, whiskey, and champagne that Willy had on the deck. They gave each other a thumbs up, and Willy indicated the cases and stood by as they were unloaded, fielding comments about the coming wedding night.

Mae, for her part, was getting ready in the clothing store across the cobbled street from the park. Solveig bustled back and forth between the two, finally seconding the food and cake preparations to her sister, and putting all her attention on Mae and her simple trousseau. It was no exaggeration to say that Mae looked radiant, although a little ornery.

"Are you nervous?" Solveig asked.

"No, I'm not nervous," Mae said, watching through the wavy glass of the store's window as a truck pulled up with the polka band and their equipment. Farther away, by the river, she could see Willy, in jeans and workshirt, leaning against the cabin of the boat, arms crossed, as men unloaded cases from it and talked up to him. She smiled wryly for a moment, then her face settled again into a thin scowl.

As soon as the wedding plans were firm, she had told her mother. The two still talked frequently, and saw each other surreptitiously on occasion, to Mae's mild disgust. She and her father had not spoken in the many months since their argument, Mae being at least as stubborn as he, and she didn't like the idea of having to skulk around to see her mother. She tolerated it, though; her mother was so meek, kind, and sweet that she was easily rolled over by the arrogant windbag that was her father, and it was her mother's almost saintly component of compassion that took away from her any ability to fight back. Her mother saw her father as a man of thwarted ambition, in need of her kindness, love, and coddling more than anything else that she could give, a fact that galled Mae, who thought he needed a swift kick in the ass. Her mother's compassion merely made Mae love her more, in a wistful kind of way, but that sentiment had dissipated in the face of the hotter and more immediate emotion of anger on the day of her wedding. She would remain indifferent to her father's very existence until he summoned the reason and strength to apologize (and for that she could wait forever), but her mother's absence at her wedding- not to mention the fact that she would be walked down the aisle by Ole- had her feeling an anger the direction of which was atypical. As Solveig adjusted her veil, Mae glared out the window, south down the road to the hotel. More people gathered in the park, and the streets were packed with vehicles of every variety from Model Ts to trucks, with even a few horse-drawn carriages were still in evidence. There was, however, no sign of her mother. She looked back over the gathered people to the pier, looking for Willy, but the deck of the boat was empty.

Willy had watched in amazement as people continued to arrive. Due to his trade, he had gotten to know most of the people in the area, but was nonetheless surprised by his and Mae's apparent popularity. He was mostly unaware of the notoriety that he had garnered, that he had become something of a local hero, and was completely unaware that even the Sheriff looked up to him. Seeing all the people, though, smiling, laughing, still bringing dishes of food and jugs and bottles of hard cider and home-made brandy, brought him a bit of a lump to his throat. He had something that he had apparently been missing for a long time: a sense of being home, a sense of being with...his people. Looking over the crowd from the deck of the boat and being greeted by the genuinely warm and happy waves and smiles of the many people he had come to know made an impression on him that he would never forget. He had thought himself a loner, but the simple sense of inclusion was satisfying on an unplumbed level. He would refrain from speaking about it, but on that day, the simple view from the deck of his boat was something that changed him. When Emilio had come down the pier and suggested he start getting ready, Willy, in a contemplative daze, complied.

"Oh, this is gonna be great," Emilio was saying. "Everythin is set up. You would not believe the food, I mean aside from the stuff we already provided for. There is roast venison, roast goose, pheasant, duck, a rabbit stew... it's just a bacchanal, hermano."

"Bacchanal, huh?" Willy grinned.

"Yeah, a *pinche* bacchanal, I kid you not. This is going to be a thin of legend. And the band's here, they're almost set up. It's time for us to get dressed."

"Yeah, okay," Willy said, but first went to the cooler and got out a couple of beers, opening them and handing one to Emilio. "Um," he said, clearing his throat, "I just wanted to say, you know..."

"Thanks?"

"Yeah, thanks. A lot."

"Ah, what the hell. We'll be around a long time, so you'll have a long time to pay me back. Le's change clothes."

They had, waiting in the cabin, a couple of new dark suits, pressed and spotless, and new white shirts with starched collars. Neither of them being the type to wear such clothing, they grumbled to put them on, Willy especially, his thick neck feeling constricted in the tight collar. The more Willy grumbled, the more Emilio laughed. Willy put on his dark tie, and then the suitcoat, shrugging his shoulders around to get it to settle.

"Your tie is crookit," Emilio said, reaching out. "Lemme-"

Willy slapped his hand away. "I can do a tie, goddam it."

"Apparently not! Settle down." Emilio fixed the tie to his satisfaction while Willy rolled his eyes, then they put on the carnations they were to wear, a white one for Willy and a red one for Emilio. When they were finished, they watched out the portholes of the boat as the Sheriff organized an aisle through the crowd.

"Nervous?" Emilio asked.

"Hell, no." Willy said. "Tell you one thing, though. I don't like it that Mae's obstinate prick of a father isn't going to come to this thing. He's a shithead, but Mae's awfully close to her mother, and this's going to make the day less for her. Weddings are pretty much for the women anyway, and if that old bastard hurts Mae's feelings any more than he already has, I might have to go and knock him on his ass."

"Ah, Mae's a tough girl. Don't be surprised if she does it herself."

Mae was having that same idea. She was all ready and in a serene state as Solveig and some of the other girls busied themselves around her, all wanting to be part of the moment. She didn't watch the road that went south to the hotel, she stared at it, seeming to float above the chatter around her.

Solveig knew her mind, and said while making some last minute unnecessary readjustments to Mae's gown, "It's just a shame that your mom isn't showing up for this. I mean, it's her only daughter's wedding and all, and that old ogre has to keep her away from her. I never! But you're right to stick by your guns and, dammit, you've got that big, handsome guy waiting for you."

"It's okay, Solveig," Mae said coolly. "It's all just fine." She looked out the window to where the Sheriff was crossing the street toward the store, then down to the park where the Justice of the Peace had set up a little podium. Farther down, she saw Willy and Emilio approaching the podium from the river. She'd never seen Willy in a suit before, and on some level that subverted all her political theories and her social consciousness, her heart swelled and she smiled, her cheeks coloring. Solveig saw her reaction and laughed adoringly, then followed Mae's gaze out the window and across the park to where their men stood talking to the Justice of the Peace.

"Oh, my, my, my!" Solveig said, and clicked her tongue salaciously, and they both giggled and hugged, girls lost in the moment.

The Sheriff, a tall paunchy man with grey hair and bad posture, came into the shop with his hat in his hand. "Well, now, aren't you a sight! Things're all ready, if you'd care to accompany me. We'd better get Ole to take you down that aisle while he can still walk without weaving."

And so they walked across the street, Mae with a bouquet in her hands, Solveig and the other girls trailing behind. A face in the crowd turned to see them, which instigated some nudging and more turning of faces, until almost the whole assembly had turned to witness the arrival of the bride. A wolf whistle shrilled out, but was silenced by shooshing and what sounded like a slap to the skull.

The Sheriff was in the process of entrusting Mae to Ole, who was, indeed, redfaced and mirthful with beer, when Mae's mother and father pulled up in their car. Mae's eyes went wide, but she kept her mouth from dropping open. The crowd was silent; knowing all the gossip, they knew the shocking importance of the moment, but it was anyone's guess what would happen. Down in front of the podium, Willy started and made to stalk up the aisle, but Emilio stopped him with a forearm across his chest.

"Mommy," Mae said in a soft, small voice, and tears started to her eyes. Her mother looked back with a radiant love the like of which only the kindest mother can summon, and got down from the passenger's seat of the car. She walked across the cobbles and the two embraced.

"Oh, Mommy, Mom," Mae said, sobbing.

"It's just fine, honey," Mrs. Palmer said, holding her daughter gently, delicate tears on her face. "Just fine. My, I knew you'd be beautiful, but this..."

They broke apart, and Mae looked over to where her father sat in the car and irradiated him with a black look.

"Just stay here, dear," her mother said, and walked around to the driver's side of the car. At a merciless look from his wife, Mr. Palmer dropped his eyes and turned off the ignition. He got down out of the car, his wife taking him by the elbow, and they walked over and stood in front of Mae, who noticed that, on the cloth at the elbow of her father's jacket, her mother's knuckles were white. Looking up, over his familiar purple nose and pince-nez glasses, and under the brim of his somber hat, she saw that her father had a good-sized mouse on his cheekbone, and that the eyelid was in the first stages of swelling shut. Mae suppressed a snort of laughter.

"Don't you have something to say to your lovely daughter, dear?" Mrs. Palmer said in her sweet voice, which, shocking to Mae, seemed for the first time to contain a thin sharp bit of meanness.

"Well," Mr. Palmer stammered, meeting neither of their eyes, "I wanted to say that I apologize…" Mrs. Palmer subtly but sharply jerked the cloth at his elbow "…no, no, that I'm *sorry*, very sorry, you see…"

With another jerk of the elbow, Mrs. Palmer said, "Not that, dear."

"Oh, oh!" he said, looking over at his wife's shoulder, "No, I wanted to say that it would mean so much to your mother-" another glance at the shoulder "-and, and to me, of course, if you would allow me to escort you, um, down the aisle. If that would be…permissible."

"Okay by me!" Ole said beerily, moving forward to slap Palmer staggeringly on the back. Mae made a snap decision, and put her anger aside.

"Sure, Dad," she said in a tone bereft of daughterly reverence.

"Sure. You can do that."

Mae shot her mother an inquiring look, and her mother merely smiled lovingly, then leveled a brittle gaze on her husband and said, "I'm going to find a place down in front, and you join me there when you've escorted your beautiful daughter perfectly down the aisle. Dear."

"Certainly," Palmer said.

"Honey," Mrs. Palmer said, looking back at Mae,

"Nothing would have kept me from being here today. Nothing." It seemed to Mae that her mother willed her to feel warmth and encouragement, and then she was off down the aisle. Even though almost no one in the crowd had heard what was said, they all cheered, and Mrs. Palmer was greeted enthusiastically among the girls in the front, where she graced Willy with an affectionate smile. Willy, shaking his head and pressing his lips together in a grin, nodded gratefully back.

When the polka band, assisted with florid grace notes from the accordion, began playing "Here Comes the Bride", Mae started down the aisle with her father in tow, and the crowd burst into spontaneous applause.

It was dizzying and surreal for Willy to exchange vows with Mae, and so focused was he on her eyes, and on the love he finally saw there, that it seemed as if the practiced drone of the Justice of the Peace faded, muffled, into the background. It seemed as if there were a roaring in his ears, and, outside of a clear column of vision that led to Mae's glowing eyes, the world smeared to a bright blur of impressionistic colors. Although, as with most people, time would play tricks with his memory, wiping some areas clean and bending others, this sensation would stay with him for the rest of his life.

The dinner ensued and that, too, was a blur. Among the requests for speeches and the ringing of glasses for the bride and groom to kiss, Willy passed up an opportunity to read Mae a poem he had written for her, suddenly finding himself overwhelmed with terror, which manifested itself as a grumpy form of embarrassment. Emilio took up the slack well, and gave a rather beautiful speech for the new couple, after which everyone applauded, and Solveig looked up at him, beaming.

After the dinner was time for dancing, and as the sky turned lavender overhead and the bluffs became dark, the multicolored lanterns around the dance area glowed gaily, bobbing gently back and forth in the cooling breeze. Mae and Willy split up to talk to the guests and a brief scuffle broke out between some bargemen and railroad men who were interested in kissing the bride, but it was quickly quelled. Willy had a warming conversation with Mrs. Palmer, her husband meek and uxorious by her side with an eye that was beginning to purple, and it took all his will to summon his scant diplomacy and not ask, even in the most polite terms, what had happened between the two of them. At the same time, he was surprised to realize that Mr. Palmer was fairly drunk. When Willy moved on to another set of guest congratulations and Mrs. Palmer was talking chirpily to Solveig and her friends, he paid attention as Mr. Palmer silently moved away and wandered over to one of the picnic tables where the banker and the newspaper editor were drinking glasses of whiskey. Having heard endless stories of his teetotaling hypocrisy from Mae, his eyebrows shot up in humorous surprise when he saw Mr. Palmer, in public, pour himself a very stiff drink and down most of it. Moments later, Mae came up quietly behind Willy and linked her arm in his, and when he indicated with his eyes and a nod of his head what her father was up to, she said,

"Well, I guess the cat's out of the bag."

And they danced and danced. Having talked to all those they could, they danced under the starry sky in the glow of the lanterns, and everything faded but each other. The party became more raucous; an inevitable fight broke out between the railmen and the bargemen. Some time later, the local bad-ass troll, wife-beater, and maker of moonshine Bud Sletto, who was not invited to the proceedings but had an irrational hatred for Willy and his "high-tone booze", showed up roaring drunk and looking for a fight, and was subdued and taken away by a now-comradely self-appointed squad of rail- and bargemen who all had their hands full trying to teach Sletto what it meant to be uninvited. Everyone close laughed uproariously when Mr. Palmer, relieved at last of the secret that he had kept from no one, relieved himself as well of his dinner and a copious amount of whiskey and beer, all with firehose accuracy, on the shoes of the banker and the publisher, wiping his mouth primly after the fact and apologizing like a courtier. Mrs. Palmer also seemed grimly pleased with the turn of events, and behaved like an old hand when she got two burly boys to load the sodden Mr. Palmer into their car and drive him back to the hotel, accompanied by the jeers of men who had for years considered him stuck up, but now thought that me might not be that bad a guy. Palmer waved like a wounded hero from his supine position in the backseat.

People became more distracted and riotous, and Willy and Mae took the opportunity to quietly thank Emilio and Solveig, walking with the two of them down to the pier. Emilio cast off the bow and stern lines, and Willy hoped to make an unobserved getaway. When he started the engine, however, those nearest the shore heard it and realized what was happening, and began to cheer. Soon, the whole gathering was cheering, and Willy and Mae waved as Willy pushed forward the throttle and cruised off into the night.

The party lasted late, and when Emilio came back in the morning to clean up, he found the Sheriff there with some of the bargemen and railmen. The Sheriff supervised as the others cleaned up; hung over and contrite, showing signs of both bruises and laughter, the men cleaned up to avoid the threat of fines and jail that he hung over their heads. When they were done, though, he saw to it that they had sandwiches, and some of the leftover beer.

Willy and Mae cruised north on the river, which gradually grew narrower, although still remaining huge and powerful. Some nights they would anchor in the still water of an island, and some nights they would find a hotel in a town and make love in the cool, clean sheets, taking a break for as fine a dinner as the night's restaurant could provide. Their favorite hotel was their first, the one in Omicron Falls, and they stayed in room number eleven for three days, in no hurry, sleeping and making love when they wanted. In the mornings they would take off again, moving slowly up the misty water in the brisk and golden autumn sunlight. They picnicked on the banks of the river for lunch, and sometimes hiked up the towering bluffs to look down on some new vista. They had plenty of money and no worries. Willy made the awkward metaphor that their future was as broad, golden, and mobile as the river itself, a golden span- a metaphor he immediately attempted to retract in favor of something more poetic- but Mae kindly stilled him with a hand on his forearm and told him that she knew what he meant.

"The Golden Span," she said. "The Golden Span."

In moments of quiet and beauty when Mae was asleep below deck, Willy wrote poems in a notebook and guiltily concealed them if he thought he heard her move. Then he joined her in the bunk, fascinated by her pastel moonlit beauty as she slept. In the end, though, they stayed in MacDougal. Mae's mother had a lengthy bout with pneumonia and Mae could not bring herself to leave, especially after the demonstration of loyalty and love at the wedding, not to mention her inflexible, and apparently correct, opinion that her father was useless in such a situation. Willy knew that Prohibition was going to end, and when Ole offered to sell him the bar for what Willy thought was a ridiculous price- and at a ridiculous time- Willy gave him cash on the barrelhead and renamed it the Eyrie. Ole took the opportunity to move out to the west coast, where his brother had a bar on the beach. The end of Prohibition followed quickly on the heels of these events. Shortly after that, Willy bought the bungalow on Bluff Street, also for cash. Mae showed a flair for ingenious domesticity and began to redecorate the place with gusto, with the help of her mother, who had recovered gamely from the pneumonia. Mae was thrilled to come home one day and find that Willy had bought her a piano for the living room, and on summer nights, Willy would sit in the dark on the screened front porch with a glowing cigar and a scotch as Mae played nocturnes that rolled sweetly out the windows and through the open door, down the cobbled streets and as far as the darkly encroaching trees at the bottom of the bluffs while children played kick the can and neighbors listened, smiling, in the dark.

The Depression didn't hit MacDougal quite as hard as it did some towns, and, having made a wise move in buying the bar before the end of Prohibition, Willy was able to set aside most of the remaining money that he had made running liquor on the river. He showed the heavy oak box he hid in plain sight among other clutter under the basement workbench to Emilio, sliding it out with a grunt and opening it. Emilio whistled. It was full of stacks of gold coins: quarter eagles, half eagles, eagles and double eagles.

"Insurance policy," Willy said as Emilio frowned and nodded. "We'll make enough money, and I can't take this to the bank. Tell me if you need a loan."

"I've got enough," Emilio said as Willy slid the box back in place.

Willy sometimes felt confined by his new daily responsibilities, but was able to escape to do some fishing or hunting with Emilio if things got too tight. Mae didn't mind; she still played piano at the bar when it suited her -she also tended bar to pitch in- and with a house that was paid for and a stable life in uncertain times, she was happy. The fortunes of her parents' hotel seemed to be dwindling, but, she came to realize, her mother seemed to manage to quietly keep things on track, especially after the climactic change in her parents' relationship, which her mother never completely explained. Mrs. Palmer liked Willy, characterizing him as "a wild one, but good", and saying that such a thing would never come to pass in their lives together. About Mae's father, Mrs. Palmer would only say, "I always knew the measure of that man."

Many people were surprised to note that Willy and Mae's marriage was not brought on by biological necessity, both of them seeming too independent to fall quickly into such an institution, if at all. When enough time had passed to prove the suspicious wrong, it seemed even to those skeptics in the town that the marriage was one of equals.

When Mae got pregnant more than a year after the wedding, everyone was pleased. Mae's mother was beside herself, and even her father's chest puffed up, the opportunist beginning, however belatedly, to sense the change in the winds. Emilio thought it was the natural course of things- being in the process of getting ready to marry Solveig- and Solveig kicked into a vicarious overdrive of preparation.

Mae was a bit disgusted by the brute animal nature of everything involved with giving birth, but she smiled quietly to watch Willy immediately embrace the idea, never seeing the moments of white-faced panic he allowed himself when he realized that this was the final nail in the coffin of his freedom. In moments like this, he would sit by himself and watch the river flow away and down into the waters of the world, gone forever, but, admittedly, always replaced by something new. These moments of overthinking the situation were few, and were soon washed away by a massive swell of the pride of fatherhood. He would never have guessed that he could be so happy.

The baby was due in November, and Mae slowly expanded through the mild summer, to Willy's fascination and her own irate disgust. When Emilio and Solveig got married, Willy and Mae reciprocated by being best man and maid of honor, although this wedding was much more typical. Emilio was raised Catholic but had grown into a comfortable agnosticism, and for all his rational argumentation, was unable to gently shake Solveig from her simple religious beliefs, so he mildly accepted the idea of having the wedding in the Catholic church. Willy and Mae, as outsiders, were puzzled by most of the goings-on. They were happy for their friends, though, and organized everything under their purview flawlessly, finally allowing themselves, during the ceremony, to dare each other to laugh with the secret glances of couples. Emilio looked dashing in his formal wear, Solveig was beautiful in the gown bought at her father's expense, and Willy never mentioned the fact that he had to have a terse conversation with Solveig's looming and obtuse older brother about the fact that the brother didn't like the idea of Solveig marrying a "spic". Had any of the townspeople known- most of whom had come to love Emilio for his kindness, intelligence, talent, and humor- the brother would probably have received a much more public, though less frightening and emphatic, dressing down.

The summer was beautiful, and they took as much time off from the bar as they wanted, leaving the running of the place to the second-in-command, Ole's former manager, Alvin "Runty" Schommer and a new employee, Bob Two Bears, whom Willy had hired both for his size and his deadpan sense of humor. As Mae's pregnancy blossomed, they had tranquil days on the river, sometimes fishing, sometimes anchored by a quiet island or the base of a bluff, reading aloud to each other as barges went by or an occasional train roared up the tracks that ran the length of the river. Mae disregarded the advice of the time to treat pregnancy as a frail and aberrant condition, and swam with Willy in calm spots in the river, finding the additional buoyancy a relief.

Fall came on again, and Mae's girth became huge. Like many women, she considered herself disgusting in such a condition, and like many women, the condition made her practically throb with beauty. Willy took her for picnics up on the towering bluffs, looking out over the vastness of the river and into the smoky, bright woods of the autumn land beyond. Mae painted landscapes with watercolors while Willy lay on a blanket and read from books held up in the air over his face. At night, they cooked quietly in the cozy kitchen, or Mae played piano in the amber light of the living room.

November began unusually balmy, and Mae heaved herself around grumbling while Willy hid at the bar. He was concerned, anxious, and solicitous as he could be- more than was common for fathers at the time- but after that point, when he knew he could do no more, he ducked his head between his shoulders and made for the door in a desperate and tactful attempt to avoid Mae's hormone-soaked wrath. Solveig would come over and keep Mae company, along with the other girls of Solveig's group who had become Mae's friends, and Willy and Emilio would slip away.

It was a good year for duck and goose hunting, and at dawn along the river the popping of shotguns could be heard. As often as possible, Willy and Emilio wanted to be among those doing the popping. Willy would drive to Emilio's cabin while it was still dark, and the two men, dressed warmly against the foggy chill, would load the jonboat with their shotguns and thermoses and other gear, start the

Johnson outboard and cruise off into the gloom. After a morning spent like this, they drove into town and went to the bar for a breakfast of steak and eggs and strong Irish coffee.

This posed no problem for Mae, who was glad to be alone or with her mother and Solveig. The men, the latter two assured her, were superfluous in this situation, and best chased out of the house. The men stayed comfortably low key, and things progressed naturally.

When Mae was overdue, however, some consternation began to set in. It was a late Saturday morning and the two couples were in the living room one afternoon, Mae reclined scowlingly on the couch, a nervous silence overall.

"Little shit's never going to come," Mae said, just as her mother came through the door from the kitchen with a tray of tea. Mrs. Palmer gave her daughter a mildly disapproving glance, to which Mae said, "Little shit *isn't*. Turd."

Willy and Emilio were sitting quietly, exchanging hopeful smiles with their spouses and exquisitely covert looks of tedium with each other, when Dr. Ambrose came in, rather blearily, according to Willy's snap analysis. Willy and the doctor had become friends, and knew each other well enough to trade their own look. Ambrose gave Mae the once-over, never escaping the skeptical glare of her lidded eyes, and said that she was fine. Things would take their course.

"Okay, then," Mae said to the doctor, "can't you get them to leave?" She jerked her head at Willy and Emilio. "*They're* not doing any good."

Dr. Ambrose looked off into space for a moment, as if in divine calculation, and said, "Sure! You boys do some duck hunting, and if you bring something back for me, I'll reduce the fee!"

Before anyone could say anything else, Mrs. Palmer said, "That's right. You fellas get out of here. There's not a thing you're going to do but get in the way."

"I don't like you staring at me," Mae added. Even though he was getting kicked out of his own house, Willy thought her pout was cute.

The two men acted unsure, but allowed themselves to be quickly bundled into their jackets and shoved out the door. Once outside, they looked at each other and laughed. Before they knew it, or anyone else had paid attention, they were in the jonboat and headed north to their favorite spot.

Approaching the place, they saw that two other men were already there in a jonboat, camouflaged with reeds; strangers, from the look of them, otherwise they would've recognized and respected the fact that it was generally Willy and Emilio's spot. One wore a large, yellowish cowboy hat of a type rarely seen in the area, and unsuited for duckhunting in any event. Willy gave an irate look at Emilio, who shrugged back philosophically, and they motored quietly by. The two waved at the strangers, who lifted their chins in return, and continued up to another spot a mile beyond. That spot proved to be uneventful, and they went farther up the river. Seeing no waterfowl there, they changed positions again, and Emilio commented on Willy's unusual edginess, telling him not to worry about the delivery, that everything would be fine.

They had secured themselves, and were passing back and forth a bottle of whiskey for amusement and against the cold, at the same time that Mae went into comparatively mild contractions. They had reached a point of mild and quiet hilarity, there in the forlorn mist, when Mae's water broke with an audible pop. She was sitting on the sofa and the rush of fluids, to the surprise of everyone including herself, reached her knees. Some of Mae and Solveig's friends showed up at exactly that moment, and there was great bustling in the house and an attempt to get Dr. Ambrose, who had left on "other business", on the phone.

Emilio indicated to Willy some ducks flying across the clouded horizon, but they were out of range, and neither of the men even moved their shotguns. After the breaking of her water, Mae's contractions became intense and painful. The wind shifted to the north, seemingly squeezed out from underneath the swollen black clouds gathering there, and a dazzlingly cold blast hurled down the river, blowing dead brown leaves off the oak trees of the island and over the heads of Willy and Emilio, who cowered in sudden astonishment in the lee. Snow whipped across the water and the islands at a sharp angle. The windows rattled as Dr. Ambrose tottered into the bungalow, inspected Mae, and said that she was far from delivering the baby, and went home to get some sleep. "Or sleep it off," Mae said.

The temperature dropped sharply. It was not known until afterwards to be a record, one which remained unbroken for decades. Ice began to form quickly in the usual bit of water in the bottom of the boat. "'Nough of this," Willy said, and Emilio nodded, pulling up the small anchor to the bow of the boat. As they watched, ice began to form in the lee of the slough, as if it were rolling out, crackling, from the whitening shore.

Mae's contractions continued, and her mother and Solveig ministered to her efficiently. Willy and Emilio motored downstream toward the town, the outboard stuttering occasionally, ominously, as they passed the spot where the two strangers had had their boat. They sat there, still, dark shapes obscured by the snow, although the silly hat was still visible. Encroached by freezing water, and Willy and Emilio shouted out to them the need to move. The outboard faltered then, though, and Willy toiled to get it started again, and by that time they had been borne down by the water closer to the town. They were glad just to get the boat ashore in the late twilight, and left it where it was as the snow mounted immediately against its side. With their shotguns, they leaned against the north wind and the spattering snow, walking up through the park to the cobbled street and then to the bar.

They pried open the door to the bar and it slammed shut behind them, all the customers looking their way. They stomped their feet and brushed the snow off themselves, and sat down huffing, thumping their shotguns onto the bar. Runty Schommer came down the bar and gave them both a generous whiskey, and said, "Solveig called. Mae's in labor."

Willy started up from his barstool, but Runty said to Emilio, "Told me to tell you to keep him here. Said there's no need to have him lumberin' around, bustin' shit up." He looked at Willy. "That's what she said, boss."

Willy went to the phone and picked up the earpiece and dialed, turning his back so the conversation was shielded from the covert listeners of the bar by his large shoulders. After a moment's conversation, he jerked a bit, and Emilio could see that his eyebrows shot up, and he put the earpiece back in its cradle.

"Guess she's okay," he said, and the fathers present nodded calmingly at Willy without belief, exchanging wry glances amongst themselves.

Solveig hung up the phone at the bungalow and proudly announced, in her piping voice, that she had chased the men off. Mae resented it, but was in the midst of a wrack of contractions, and was unable to say anything, even though (in spite of her duress) she had no idea what Willy would do if he were present.

Emilio hoisted his glass and Willy followed, if somewhat automatically. They put their shotguns in the corner and began to play a distracted game of eightball against two of the regulars, losing the first two games but winning the last three, when Willy finally got irate enough to give the game his full attention. Time passed slowly.

Time ceased to exist for Mae. She was angry at the fairly blase attitudes of her mother and Solveig. Couldn't they see the epic nature of this battle? Dr. Ambrose checked in after awhile, but had been there for perhaps fifteen minutes when he was tracked down on the telephone. Solveig answered and indicated that the call was for the doctor, and he listened, he nodded and grunted several times, muttered something into the phone, and hung up.

"You're not nearly dilated enough yet, Mae," he said, suddenly serious, "I'll be back, but it seems a few boys caught out in this norther just barely got back in, almost trapped by ice. There's some frostbite and hypothermia, so I have to go look after it."

"Will they be all right?" Mrs. Palmer asked.

"They probably will, but there's reason to believe that there are plenty of other men trapped out there, and not much we can do about it until morning. I'll know more after I take care of these boys. Could be nothing. You're doing fine, though, Mae, just fine, and I'll leave you in these ladies' capable hands."

The wind continued to howl from the north outside, thumping into the roof of the bungalow and making its frame groan. At the bar, men stood by the windows with drinks in their hands, watching the unusual developments. Dr. Ambrose was down at the boathouse in the town park where the huge potbellied stove was stoked and surrounded by sodden men in blankets drinking soup and hot chocolate. Ambrose catered to their symptoms and looked at their frostbite, some of which was bad; one man had three fingers that were dead white and tingling painfully, the ears of another were pale and lifeless as wax. Ambrose feared the outcome, but did what he could. No hospital was nearby, and in any event, the roads were becoming impassable and the river too dangerous and icy for boats.

Willy, nervously gnawing a thumbnail, phoned the house for an update, and was told by Mrs. Palmer where Dr. Ambrose was and why. He became irate at this, there being no telephone at the boathouse, and in a moment of abrupt decision that would later cause years of small arguments with Mae, called Dr. Homburg the veterinarian to look in on his wife and render what assistance he could. He knew his wife would object, but also knew that Homburg had been a medic and was much more abreast of recent medical developments than Dr. Ambrose. After this, he bundled up in a heavier winter coat he kept in the back room of the bar and put on a watchcap, getting ready to make his way through the howling snow to the boathouse to assess the situation. Emilio couldn't miss this and got some similar gear from backroom, and they headed out into the night, hunching their shoulders against the cold. When they banged into the boathouse and saw the situation, they were aghast.

"Jesus, Dave," Willy said to a blond young man shuddering in a heavy wool blanket next to the stove. "What the hell happened?"

Dave Russell shook his head and said, "We were up by Cat Island and the weather changed. We just didn't think it was gonna change that much. Almost got trapped in this ice. Had to break our way out with our oars at one point."

"Holy shit," Willy said, exchanging a glance with Emilio. "Is anyone else out there?"

"Well, yeah," Dave said. "Pete Leahy and his brother-in-law, I think, and maybe Larry Cornwall and one of his boys..."

Emilio said, "Yeah, and those two guys up by our spot. That one with the hat."

"Holy shit," Willy said again, staring off and gnawing his thumbnail. "We've got to do something."

"Nothing you *can* do," said one of the blanketed men by the stove. "Too rough out there. Lots of ice. Most of the big boats are out of the water this late in the year anyway."

"Ah, those boys'll be all right," said another. "If they have any sense, they'll get their boats out of the water and use them for shelter. Make a fire and tough it out 'til morning."

"Where's the Sheriff?" Willy asked.

"Think he was dealing with Bud Sletto. He's out of jail again and got rough with the wife."

"That fucking prick," said Willy, disliking even the mention of the troglodytic Sletto. "The Sheriff'll just have to keep him in the lockup."

"When he gets him," someone said. "Sheriff's out looking for him now."

Willy thought about Mae, and he thought about the men out on the river.

"What're you going to do," Dave asked him, "go out in your jonboat? That's crazy."

Willy walked to one of the large windows overlooking the river and stared out into the darkness, the heavy, almost horizontal snowfall illuminated by a spotlight on the roof of the boathouse pointed at the water, which was barely visible in contrast to the snow, but obviously choppy with the fetch from the north, whitecaps visible.

When Willy had come back from the war, he had tried to forget things he had seen and done, to push them down into some deep oubliette of the mind where he would not stumble over them. The images locked down there included the deaths of friends, of brothers, and he wanted those images contained. He had come back with the unspoken notion that to care much about anyone or anything was to wound oneself, and he had, he saw now, wrapped himself in a false and numbed imperviousness. Slowly, though, he had come alive again. It had started with following his friend to this beautiful place, then falling in love with Mae, and then with a place which became his home, with the people of his home. It had happened so gradually that he hadn't even noticed it, but now here he was, alive again.

Emilio was standing beside him, looking rather fatalistic.

37

"We'll put the cabin cruiser in," Willy said.

"The ice-" Emilio said, a light suddenly in his eyes.

"Hipwaders, in case we go through, the prybar and axes-"

"Right."

They went for the door. Doc Ambrose said, "Where're you boys going?"

"We'll be back," Emilio said.

They took Emilio's truck and drove through the snow down to his cabin, where Willy's boat had been winched out of the water on runners for the winter. They put on hipwaders and got the tools they would need to break the ice, and went out and freed the boat. The ice was getting thick, but not thick enough to bear the weight of the boat, and when they pushed it down the runners and out onto the ice, it broke through with a crash. Emilio held the bowline while Willy jumped aboard and started the engine, which coughed a couple of times and began to hum. He thought that it was fortunate that he had put off winterizing the engine; they would have been unable to use the boat.

Emilio grabbed Willy's gloved hand and hopped aboard, and Willy gunned the boat out to open water, the grinding and whining of the ice on the hull- which they had laboriously refinished just last March- making Emilio wince. Out on the black and choppy water they headed north toward the closest group of dense islands and sloughs, both of them squinting though the windshield of the cabin cruiser, as Emilio worked the spotlight and the snow came down, ice building on the boat.

Mae went through another set of contractions, forgetting for a moment her anger at Willy, the dilettante father, for sending over the veterinarian to see to the birth of their child. She liked the man, but didn't like Willy's implication that their child was an animal of some sort. Although she would have bitten Willy's head off if he were there, she was fuming that he wasn't, admittedly because it stripped from her the opportunity to bite his head off. The contractions subsided, and Dr. Homburg reassured her that she was still not dilated enough, and she imagined smashing Willy in the temple with a brick. When she chuckled aloud at this image, her mother asked what was funny, and she said, "Nothing."

"You keep up those good spirits," Homburg said, obviously impressed by the woman's heroism.

Willy and Emilio motored up the river in the dark, and from time to time, Emilio had to get out of the cabin with a broom and clear the windshield of the heavy buildup of snow. It was only through their detailed knowledge of the river that they did not get lost, and when they came to the leeward side of one island the wind abated, and they could see trees in the cone of the spotlight. They steered toward a likely spot, and after some minutes, sure enough, they saw the light of a fire through the heavy snow. They got as close as they could to the shore, the water being too shallow at that point, and the ice too thick, for them to get any closer. In the spotlight, they saw that it was Larry Cornwall and his teenage son Dennis, and that they had been in the process of breaking up their boat for dry firewood while using the bow of the boat as a shelter against the wind. The Cornwalls waved and Willy indicated upstream to where an old oak tree had fallen into the water, which the two could use to get out onto the boat. Willy pulled alongside the barkless old oak, and the two Cornwalls precariously moved out along its trunk, while Emilio leaned over the gunnel with his hands outstretched. Larry Cornwall boosted his boy aboard too hard, so that the boy toppled headfirst into the boat, and Cornwall's momentum precipitated him chestdeep into the drink. Emilio leaned over the boat and Cornwall grabbed his hand, and while the boy frantically clutched at his father's jacket, Emilio pulled him aboard. He took them into the cabin and shut the door tight behind them, giving the man and the boy blankets.

The boy was shuddering, unable to speak, but Larry Cornwall said, "You fuckers are off your rockers being out here, but we sure as shit are glad to see you."

"Why didn't you two idiots have the sense to get in out of this?" Willy barked, craning around from the helm.

"Just happened so fast..." Cornwall said, shrugging.

"We actually almos' got caught ourselves," Emilio said, handing the boy a cup of hot chocolate from his thermos.

They motored around to a few more likely spots in the dark, the snowy limbs of black trees suddenly looming out of the whirling darkness in the spotlight. They were beginning to wonder if it was all in vain when they heard shouting off to their left. The two Hansen brothers, George and his supposedly dimwitted brother Steve, were crouching under a large tree with Barnacle Brad Verhelst (called "Barnacle" not only for his time in the Navy, but for his tendency to be fixed by his ass to a barstool when not hunting). They were close to the shore, but a table of thin ice thrust out from the black bank. There was no boat to be seen, nor did they have a fire. George seemed the most prudently dressed of the three, wearing a heavy jacket, gloves, and a hat with earflaps, while Steve had covered his pearlike body with a couple of sweaters and a duckhunting vest, his long hair a tangle of icicles on his shoulders. Barnacle Brad was clad in his usual bib overalls, a sweatshirt, and a denim jacket, his footlong grey beard (which he trimmed by igniting its end as a malodorous bar stunt) a mat of snow as he stood pretending imperviousness, his arms crossed over his chest. Willy and Emilio smiled at each other; there had to be a story here.

After shouting back and forth the best options for picking up the stranded men, Willy came to the conclusion that the best thing to do was take the bull by the horns and ram through the ice, while Emilio and Larry Cornwall waited on the bow to help the men onto the boat. He backed up into the current, maneuvering against its force, and rammed the boat through the ice, feeling the keel dig into the sandy mud underneath. Emilio and Larry pulled the men on board and got them back into the warmth of the cabin.

"Cock*sucker!*" Barnacle Brad said, beating snow out of his beard and stamping his feet. "What a fucking motherfucker out there! Got any whiskey?"

"Thanks, Willy," George said, then looked at his brother and said quietly, "You idiot."

"You're the idiot," came Steve's retort.

The two brothers were known to have entire arguments in such low tones of voice that Willy had to lean forward and turn his head to hear them. The story gradually came out that the Hansen brothers had freed themselves from advancing ice and were heading in when they heard Brad calling to them from the bank of the slough. Brad had been out all day to avoid his wife, who was so sweet that everyone believed that the only reason he ever wanted to get away from her was because he was so foul. He had gotten drunk enough to misplace his boat, and was still stumbling around in the dark looking for it, barking his shins on deadfall, when the Hansens had come by. Brad was getting bored and lonely at that point, having tripped and sprawled flat, shattering his bottle of whiskey on a rock, and was therefore ready to get picked up. The Hansens had pulled up to get him, looping back upstream against the current and grounding on an icy sandbar, both getting out of the boat at the same time, each trusting to the other to hold onto the bowline. George, the more nimble and fit of the two and therefore first out of the boat by a hair, claimed that it was Steve's responsibility to hold the bowline, whereas Steve said that, as first man out of the boat, the responsibility was clearly his brother's. The two had gotten out of the boat and were laughing at Brad's predicament when Brad had begun laughing harder, pointing downstream to where the boat, eased off the bar by the current, was lazily whirling away from the slough. After the initial astonishment on the part of the Hansen brothers, they'd all had a pretty good chuckle at the irony of that, until the gravity of their situation had settled in upon them. Willy blamed the loss of the boat on the fact that the Hansens grew their own very potent reefer, having inherited a knack for botany from their father, and were known to overindulge in their crop. He was also convinced that Steve was actually very bright, but usually under the influence of his smoke. His mellowness had escaped him at the moment. The arguing and accusation had reached the point where the brothers were muttering audibly at each other, each mildly shoving the other's shoulder- an unprecedented melee for them- when Willy turned around from the helm and barked at them to knock it off.

Willy wanted to search for more men on some of the islands upstream, but Emilio said quietly to him that he didn't like the looks of the Cornwall boy, so they reluctantly turned back to the town. As they moved down the river, they occasionally crunched into massive slabs of ice in the dark. Each impact sounded large enough to sink the boat, and the slabs ground along the hull as they passed. They exchanged looks that were both excited and horrified, and shrugged off the work done on the hull. They finally got to the dock by the boathouse and bulled their way through the ice, tearing at the hull, and tied up to the dock, ushering everyone up and into the boathouse.

Once inside and having seen to the rescued, Willy and Emilio were pounded on the back by the men around the stove, and Dr. Ambrose shook his head ruefully. "Ever think about your wife before you go joyriding around like that?"

"Of course I did," Willy snapped, "What am I going to do? Go home and pull the kid out by the head? She made it pretty clear that she didn't want me around anyway-"

"Well, sure she said that, you dullard-"

Willy waved a hand at him exasperatedly and went out to check on his boat. He saw at once that it was listing, and when he got on board and looked down in the bilges with a flashlight, he saw that a seam had been popped against some ice, and the boat was taking on water.

"Ah, shit!" he said, and went back into the boathouse.

When he told Emilio about this development, Emilio's eyes went wide and he bobbed his head philosophically, and said, "Well, that's the end of that. Don't worry though, we'll fix it. This was more important." They got one of the men to give them a ride up to Willy's, Dr. Ambrose saying that he'd be along shortly. They fishtailed all the way there.

Nothing that happened that night had given Willy any pause, but outside the bungalow on the snowy walk he had to take a few deep breaths before coming into the house. Emilio clapped him on the back, and they went in. It was warm in the living room and smelled of soup and fresh bread, and Dr. Homburg and Solveig were on the couch playing cards. Solveig squealed in delight, jumped up, and hugged Emilio, who embraced her back and kissed her a dozen times on the face. Willy went by the kitchen, where, indeed, a pot of what smelled like tomato bisque simmered on the stove at a low heat. With a bit of trepidity, Willy stuck his head around the corner of the bedroom where his wife lay in a white cotton nightgown, tired and cross-looking, her red hair tied up loosely behind her head. Mrs. Palmer sat beside her in Willy's wingbacked red leather reading chair, reading to Mae from a women's magazine, an effort which Mae appeared to be ignoring. She saw Willy and said, "Oh! Wonderful! Mr. Bigdick! How kind of you to grace us with your presence!"

Willy forced a rather ghastly artificial smile. He opened his mouth to speak, and Mae said, "Where the hell have you been?"

"Just out-"

"Sure, just out with the boys, lounging around the bar. Great! Meanwhile, I'm left here by myself, trying to push this fucking little McGregor-"

"Language, dear," her mother said mildly.

"- out of me, and the kid's got a head the size of a keg! You really should have told me about this, Mom! Jesus!"

"You wanted me to leave," Willy said, spreading his hands.

"Oh, when the fuck was that?"

"Language." Mrs. Palmer slapped the bed with the magazine.

"Yeah, yeah. Okay, Mister Bigdick. *Now* I want you to leave."

Willy opened his mouth to defend himself, but Mrs. Palmer got up and laid the magazine on the bed, inserting herself between the two and ushering Willy down the hall towards the kitchen.

"Mister Bigdick!" Mae shouted down the hall. "Hey, everybody, it's Mister Bigdick, local hero! Hi, Mister Bigdick! Delivery for Mister Bigdick! Come and get your fucking baby!"

"Holy smokes," Willy said, sitting dazedly at the kitchen table. Mrs. Palmer helped him out of his soggy coat and hung it over the back of a chair near the stove, bringing him a bowl of soup and some fresh bread and butter. "I always knew women get irritable but...jeez."

"Oh, Mae's always had some spark. You just have some of that soup."

Emilio came in and sat down, and Mrs. Palmer brought him the same thing. The two men realized how hungry they were and dug in with gusto.

After some more contractions, the baby was born. Dr. Homburg was on hand in case of emergencies, but Mrs. Palmer and Solveig, both farm girls with much experience in life and death, delivered the baby capably. Willy, with the most experience in death, had the least experience in birth, and was gaping in astonishment as the baby's redly slick and puckered head came out of the birth canal. As this happened, it occurred to him that he had seen death that was neither as fascinating nor as disgusting, just sort of banal, like a bullet thumping into the greatcoat of a friend beside him and leaving a neat little hole in both the coat and the heart of its wearer, who had looked at Willy in vaguely disappointed way and died. He also recognized that the more gruesome forms of death he had seen were what prepared him to witness this opposite end of the spectrum of life, and it was a revelatory thing, that coming in and going out were both transitions of blood and pain. Was afterwards just the same as before? Was birth a point where a person became, for a very short time in the eyes of the Universe, an individual, as if someone had splashed their hand in the water of the river, sending droplets in the air, each individual droplet a human life, spinning softly for a span in its own sunlight before dropping again to the surface of the water and becoming, once more, part of the whole? Or was before and after simply darkness, and the time between merely an odd state of matter in animation, any meaning an illusion?

But as his healthy and bawling son was held in a clean white blanket up to his mother's arms- she beautiful, laughing with relief, alight with love- all thoughts of life's meaning as illusion were blown away on a strong wind, warm and bright, and he laughed and cried in a love he had never know before.

Willy had collapsed on the couch in the living room after putting Emilio and Solveig in the spare bedroom, and Mrs. Palmer had seen Dr. Homburg quietly out and Dr. Ambrose quietly in. Ambrose checked on the peacefully sleeping mother and baby and went on his way, having to look after a patient who might still have to have fingers amputated after the freak event of the Norther. He told Mrs. Palmer what Willy and Emilio had done, and after she had seen him to the door, she went to where Willy was stretched on the couch and covered him with a blanket, tenderly smoothing the hair back off his forehead. She spent the night in the chair next to her daughter, reading and napping.

The wind shifted again in the early morning, and again abruptly, until it was warm and from the south. When dawn came, the warm air over the cold land and fresh ice created a dense fog, thick and pale gold in the growing light. The river was calm but swift, and men waited by their jonboats or in the boathouse to head out onto the river once the fog thinned to search for those who might still be stranded. The Hansen brothers- their argument over- were there, and Barnacle Brad, as were Larry Cornwall and Dave Russell. In that golden light, warmed by strong coffee, they looked worried and purposeful.

Willy and Emilio showed up still tired, and congratulations went all around, both for the birth of Willy's son and the rescue of various local idiots. Remarks were made about Willy's sanity, going out on a night like that when he had the best reason in the world to stay home, and Emilio pointed out that it had been safer on the river. Everyone laughed.

The sun got higher as Emilio and Willy prepared the jonboat. Emilio started the motor without a word, and Willy jumped in and they headed up the river, while the other men were still milling around on shore.

The bluffs over the river stood free of the low-lying fog, their faces glowing in the morning light. Emilio, trusting Willy's boathandling skills more than his own, gave the tiller over to his friend and sat in the bow with a boathook to fend off any chunks of ice that Willy had a hard time avoiding. Navigating became easier in the mists as they neared their favorite slough, Willy able to discern where they were by the familiar patterns of the trees, the snow that had crusted them melting now in the growing sunlight and warm breeze, tiny droplets of water and ice sparkling in the light.

It was still gloomy, though, in the dark downstream curvature of the slough. The fog was clammy and Willy slowed the motor to trolling speed, squinting into the gloom with the light in the tree limbs over the fog. It was another world, like the arches of an ethereal cathedral, reaching their untouchable height in the pink and gold clouds fragile in the sky overhead. They came out from a wall of fog into a clear patch some hundred feet across, the surface of the river black and calm in this backwater. There, across the clear space at their favorite spot, sat the two strangers in their boat. The large yellow hat was visible in the shifting sheets of fog. Willy and Emilio looked at each other and arched their eyebrows, and Willy gunned across the clear water. Emilio waved and shouted out, but the men didn't reply.

As they drew near, they could see that the boat of the strangers was two-thirds surrounded by melting ice, the bow free and pointed downstream. The sun came over the treetops and illuminated them; they sat hunched in their seats, forearms across their thighs, as if crouching against the cold. Ice and snow were melting from the yellow hat, drop by drop off the inclined rim, and when they were close enough they could see that the man's eyes, milky and vacant blue, stared at the middle of the boat. His face was peaceful, contemplative. The other man had his eyes squinted shut, as if he were counting to ten to regain his patience, and under his cap his face was rimed with ice.

Willy pulled close enough so that Emilio could grab their bowline, and it took a few smacks with a sledgehammer to free the boat from the remaining ice, which cracked and floated away downstream. They towed the boat through the dissipating golden fog back to the park boatlaunch, where others, including the Sheriff, helped secure the boat and take the dead men, frozen in sitting positions, out onto the gravel of the drive.

Willy decided that he'd had enough, and walked wearily up the cobbled street through the rivulets of meltwater, and went home to the bungalow on Bluff Street. It was warm inside and coffee was on the stove, and his wife was in the cheery sunlit bedroom with the baby in her arms and her mother at her side. She smiled when he came in to the room, and he leaned against the doorjamb and sighed, completely alive. They named the boy Gordon.

Their son Daniel was born a year and a half later. Life was kind and peaceful, with Willy working at the Eyrie and living as much outdoors as he could around the time he spent with his wife and child, and Mae showing a flair for motherhood as she kept little Gordon with her while she gardened and cooked and read. Gordon was the pet of the bar, which had become the *de facto* town hall; he tottered around among the legs of the barstools and played under the pool table, sat by his mother when she came down to play the piano. He was a happy and beloved child, if somewhat imperious, and Mae and Willy, talking quietly in bed late at night, had difficulty imagining what their lives had been like before they were parents. They were so mystified and fascinated by the development of this new person, an amalgam of them both but entirely himself, that as every change occurred they felt as if they hadn't had nearly enough time to absorb the last one.

They were in the midst of a flood when Daniel was born- life on the river rarely being boring when it came to the forces of nature- and Willy was considerably less concerned about the prospect of new fatherhood than he had been the first time. Mae, too, knew what was in store, and was less ornery with Willy than she had been. Willy hated the feeling of helplessness he had when the labor started, knowing that it would last a long time, and walked with little Gordon down by the river toward the wall of sandbags he had help set up and watched the powerful water for interesting flotsam. He had only to hold the boy in his arms and look out at the water for the restlessness to go away. Thoughts of other places in the world still came to him, and memories of things good and very bad, but less often and less intensely. The satisfaction of his sense of home was a perfect anodyne for the loss of his freedom.

Dr. Ambrose was in attendance for this delivery, sober and unhurried, as were Mrs. Palmer and Solveig, who had had a daughter of her own in the intervening period. As the time passed, Willy and Emilio sat on the front porch with their children on their knees. Gigantic thunderclouds moved in from the west, turning the early afternoon to dusk, and with a ripping sound the sky let loose and the rain poured down. They watched, the children delighted, on the screened-in porch, knowing that they were high and dry, everything battened down, while others in the world were in danger. Daniel was born before the rain and the thunder stopped, and Willy's awe was renewed.

It was astonishing how quickly the boys grew. Willy and Mae talked about it, that an individual day might seem like a long time, but a year was over in a puzzling snap of the fingers, time moving slowly and quickly all at once. When Willy was at the Eyrie alone, presiding over the regular customers, time ground on, and he had to force himself not to look at the clock until he could see his wife and boys. Then whatever hours they did have together, on the weekend or a stolen day during the week (stolen from himself, as he had to pay Runty Schommer or Bob Two Bears out of the till to cover the shift), were over so fast that the next day he couldn't remember exactly how they had filled the hours. It didn't matter much, though; he retained from them a sense of golden satisfaction.

It seemed that their lives were blessed, and this sometimes made him fearful. He had seen things he didn't want to remember that had shown him how the world really was, and he pitied anyone who thought that the bubble of happiness in

44

which they lived was the natural order of things. Their house was paid for, as was the business, he had money hidden away, everyone was healthy...and disaster happened all around them. In industrial cities like Greysport, in agricultural areas to the south, people were suffering in numbers and severity that seemed almost epic, as though they belonged to another era, a storied time, not something as mundane as the present.

One summer, he and Mae took the boys to the county fair, the kind common in those days, with crooked games of chance and skill, boxing matches calling for challengers from the audience, freak sideshows, the works. Willy had Gordon on his shoulders and Mae had little Danny in her arms as they watched the boxing for a bit; a large local boy was throwing haymakers at the carnival professional and taking predictable punishment, and Willy emitted disgusted hissing and grunting noises. Mae nudged him with her elbow, and gave him a coolly challenging look, indicating with a humorous tip of her chin that he should get in the ring, and Willy gave a droll look in return that stated that such a thing was beneath him, although part of him wanted to get into the ring and beat the living shit out of the "professional". He bounced Gordon on his strong shoulders and squinted up at him, as Gordon laughed and played with Willy's hair.

Under an old oak they had a picnic lunch of hotdogs and potato salad, and beer for the adults. Danny made an utter mess of himself with ketchup and mustard, somberly, as if he were adorning himself with warpaint, and Willy made a comment about it and began calling him "Chief", a name that was to stick for the rest of his life, solidifying when he was old enough to object to it. Gordon was excited about the highlight of the day, which involved a man, The Amazing Rotelli, who was to perform hair-raising acrobatic stunts on a hotair balloon and to culminate his feats of daring by parachuting to the ground. Gordon was obsessed with the idea, and Willy agreed that he was pretty fascinated himself. The act was announced with fanfare, and the carnival goers craned their necks to the Amazing Rotelli's gaudy balloon as it wafted overhead and Rotelli performed acts which caused the crowd to gasp but which made Willy and Mae look at each other with expressions that were humorous and underwhelmed. Even Gordon stated that it was all "pretty crappy". The finale did not disappoint, though, in that the Amazing Rotelli, swandiving ostentatiously from the basket of the balloon, shot to earth like a brick when his chute failed to open, and smacked down unambiguously in an apple orchard near the fairgrounds. Chief had stopped paying attention before this, but Gordon, Mae, and Willy looked back and forth at each other's faces with round-eyed stupefaction. The crowd was silent for a moment, then a fat woman screamed and fainted as if on cue, and this seemed to signal a general hubbub and a race to the apple orchard. The McGregors, knowing the outcome, took that as an indication that it was time to go home.

At the breakfast table the next day, Willy read in the paper that the Amazing Rotelli had shot down to the apple orchard in a horizontal position, and that, in a vain attempt to arrest his fall, he had held out his hands to grab branches, which skewered his hands like spears. Unimpeded, the Amazing Rotelli had hit the ground with his legs locked straight out beneath him. When he was found, his feet, in their delicate acrobatic shoes, were just below his pelvis, his legs having been thrust up into his chest cavity. When the coroner pulled the legs out to prepare the corpse for burial, it was found that the man was still six inches shorter than he had been in life, a condition which was mysterious, but without apparent remedy.

They clucked their tongues and shook their heads, and Willy continued to read while Mae fed Chief and Gordon played with his cereal. When the timing was just right and Mae was drinking from a glass of milk, Willy said, "That Rotelli. He sure was amazing."

Mae blew milk from her nose in a snort of laughter and Gordon cheered, causing Chief to cheer, as Willy, laughing so hard it was inaudible, feebly slapped the table. Mae wiped her face, laughing in spite of herself, snapped Willy in the arm with a dishtowel, and said, "Good one, McGregor."

They seemed so fortunate that people took notice. Willy was written up in the local paper as a person of interest; mention was made of his being a "war hero" with some sanitized versions of his exploits offered to the reader, as well as what Willy thought was an embarrassingly fulsome account of his adventures on the river as an "entrepreneur". The article finally arrived at his and Mae's ownership of the Eyrie, which offered the "best steak dinners and hamburgers on the River, accompanied by Mae McGregor's talented renderings on the piano". When it came time for the accompanying photograph to be taken, the family posed in front of the bar for the photographer, with Chief in Mae's arms and Gordon in front of Willy, who put his hand on his son's shoulders. The photographer, about the best that the small town could afford, had equipment that predated disposable flashbulbs, having, instead, an ignitable flashstrip that he held in the air and touched off when he took the picture. The McGregors, set off by Gordon, were already giggling about the man's appearance as they posed for the photograph- his resemblance to Larry from the Three Stooges was remarkable- so that he hardly had to ask them to smile for the picture. When he ignited the flashstrip, however, he also ignited the large tuft of improbably ulotrichous hair on that side of his head, burning it all off in an instant. The photograph registered the first flash of the McGregors' astonished mirth at this development; their mouths partially open, their eyes wide in the second before outright laughter. Mae and Willy rushed over to see to the man, concerned but struggling with laughter. The photographer was mortified but unharmed, and the reporter was embarrassed, thinking that his incompetent cohort reflected poorly upon him. Willy, feeling guilty at having laughed at the unfortunate man and half-guessing that one reason the reporter wanted to run the story was to get a free meal, treated them both to steak dinners and all the beer they could drink.

Mae's father was chagrined by this publicity, his hotel in gradual decline and now barely able to afford its own pianist, but her mother was overjoyed. Emilio and Solveig framed the picture from the paper, and, years later, Emilio would laugh at the expressions on his friends' faces.

Between the satisfaction of running his own successful business and being no one's lackey, and the deeper joy and completion of his life with his family, Willy was happier than he could ever have imagined being. If he ever felt the least bit dissatisfied, he knew the cause of it, and so did Mae. When he began to pace and seem distracted, Mae knew it was time for him to go out on the river. By himself, with Emilio, or, more and more, with the boys, she would shoo him out and he would come back in the evening, or a day or two later, a man refreshed, joyful and alive. Mae realized that it was a delayed pleasure for her; Willy never made love so voraciously as when he returned smelling like crisp wind and woodsmoke. It seemed to Willy that he had two worlds at once, one being his small subjective world of love and fatherhood, with a snug home, warm family meals, and bed in cool fresh sheets next to his sweet-smelling wife. The other world, as though it existed outside of a small, safe bubble, one of immense richness and beauty, powerful and complex, with the ancient towering bluffs, millions of years old, resolute and immobile, and the endless river, huge and unstoppable, flowing through eons to the sea, and all the while the sun gliding across the sky, spelling the seasons and the centuries, and at night the magnificent turning of the silent stars, their light older than everything, their grandeur encompassing everything, seeming to hum with a deep unknowable power that was felt in the bones of the planet itself.

When he took the boys out, he taught them what he could about these things, as well as playing pirates or Indians or explorers. When Emilio came along, he added his amateur expertise in the workings of botany and the ecosystem, pouring it out for the boys (he and Solveig's daughter, Marita, was afraid of the water and of boats), finding great satisfaction in the dawning understanding in their eyes.

When Willy and Emilio went out alone, it was a male thing. They loved their wives, but it was necessary sometimes to be away, to smoke cigars and drink beer and scotch, to speak as filthily as they wanted and to engage in the type philosophical arguments that neither of their wives, especially the cheerful Solveig, seemed to have much time for.

A current track that Emilio had been on was the notion of pacifism, with which Willy found it easy to argue. Although he had started out as a boxer and had had a demonstrable talent for violence, Emilio had changed during the war, and now felt that there was nothing worth his committing an act of violence. Willy heard him say this again and again, and challenged him on it.

"So you see a big guy on the street, a big guy, okay?" Willy said, "and the big guy is beating the shit out of the little guy-"

"I'd have to know why the big guy was beating the shit out of the little guy. The little guy might have just cut the throat of the big guy's daughter. Who am I to interfere?"

"Fine. You have knowledge that the little guy just braced the big guy about fucking his wife, and the big guy started to beat him, in a most uncivilized manner, for his temerity."

"Then," Emilio said, "I would stand between the two men, calm them down, and reason with them."

"Okay," Willy said, "suppose it's someone like that Bud Sletto, someone who has no respect for reason or what's right, and he starts beating the shit out of both of you. You're a boxer, for fucksake."

"I am no longer a boxer, I am a humble carpenter with a wife and a child and a business-"

"Bullshit. You'd take care of the situation-"

"If I could not, justice would prevail," Emilio said serenely.

"Justice? Since when could you depend on justice? Christ, your folks had to leave their homeland because it was advantageous for some corporate interests to start a revolution there-"

"Oh, there you go with the corporate interests-"

"Ah, fuck that." Willy exasperatedly swigged from his beer. "Look, you should know better than anyone. The only justice that we can depend on is the justice we provide for ourselves."

"That would be mayhem." Emilio drank calmly.

"Yeah. What do you have in your old country? What have we had in this one?"

Emilio looked at him stonily. "I assure you, there is no comparison."

"What the fuck. No workers in the States have been killed in labor riots? By corporate troops? Ever heard of the Haymarket? The Greysport Massacre? And what would it have gained them to be pacifists?"

Emilio snorted. "That was the best place for them to be pacifists."

"And this would work where you come from," Willy scoffed, casting his line.

"In time," Emilio said.

"Wouldn't work where I come from."

"Thas because you are all barbarians and pooritanical idiots. I come from a country of cultivation," Emilio said soberly. A moment passed. They looked at each other and stared. They drank their beers and narrowed their eyes, staring. Then they laughed. They drank some more. Their children got bored with this kind of thing.

Willy held the unspoken conviction that there were hidden forces of irony at work in the universe, forces as ineluctable as the forces of gravity, but less open to explanation. He thought that such a notion conflicted with his disbelief in an overall plan for the universe, that we rode the wave of an initial ignition so infinitely complex that it was the utmost of our capabilities to understand that we were chaff upon the wave at all. He did not, could not, believe in predestination, but had seen so much ironic death or unearned victory in his life that he was unable to deny his own experience. He had lived through desperate times with the feeling that the nature of his life would keep him alive to endure more misery, and now that his life was happy, he felt that his happiness could not continue on unpunished. The shortcoming he had in all this, and to which he was oblivious, was that his sense of irony was so touchy and hair-trigger that he was like a hunter so intent on stealthily pursuing a rumored tiger in the night that he failed to see a pit right in front of him, clearly marked "Pit".

There could be no more obvious a villain in Willy and Mae's peaceful life than Bud Sletto. The man (who could more properly be called a troll) had been a problem in the community long before Willy had ever come upon the scene. Bud was the "worst of a bad lot" as was often said of his place among his kin, a tribe of southern pig farmers who had come up in search of a place to further their livelihood, witlessly bypassing a state of great reputation for such enterprises and ending up in the next one to the north, in the top tier of states and right across the stretch of river to the west of MacDougal. They had never made much of a go of it, something which was apparently typical of their kin. It was initially understandable to their new neighbors why they would come to the area, but the question as to why they would stay became more and more difficult to explain. An offshoot of a southern clan which was obstreperously Confederate, the Slettos were even disliked by their neighbors in the south, who mostly pitied the pigs they raised for having to suffer such masters. Tending to be large, blubbery, and ill-tempered, they created their own demographic anomaly in the area, pushing the average down toward a baseline characterized by violence, filth, drunkenness, and, according to some, unusual forms of affection for their livestock. It was theorized that they stayed just to make things unpleasant for their neighbors. It would be unnecessary to exaggerate their lesser tendencies; they were already caricatures of themselves, and Sletto was a caricature of *that*. Unsurprisingly, during the life of Willy and Mae's grandson, one scion of the Sletto brood would move to an Eastern industrial state and become a major figure in the American Nazi Party, a pathetic bunch if there ever was one.

Bud Sletto, at the time largest and most bellicose of the clan, first found something to hate in Ole at the beginning of Prohibition, when Ole refused to sell the rotgut homemade potato vodka that was Sletto's pride and joy, Ole fearing that the liquid would render his patrons blind or dead. Sletto, perhaps once a lonely child wounded by the exclusion of others and unaware of the burden placed upon him being born to his parents, was as an adult one capable of developing ill will and harboring a grudge at the drop of a hat. Ole's refusal to sell his booze flicked the one-way piss-off switch on Sletto, who, having indulged at length in his own product, would from time to time show up at Ole's to start trouble. One on one, most men were afraid to take him on, and even as a group were wary; Bud's usual coating of body grease and pigshit made it undesirable to touch him even if he were unconscious on the floor. The Sheriff, ever the well-intentioned but incapable bananaman, handled him mostly with coddling diplomacy and prayed that he would stay on his side of the river, preferably on his own farm, with his own people. Ole had gotten him to leave the bar once or twice by speaking to him calmly and reasonably, leaving Sletto room to save face, while tapping his left palm with a baseball bat which he held in his right. Sletto made a grand and glowering exit, threatening everyone in the room, and went his way into the night. Ole thought that this method was the best; no one could predict what vicious and sneaky mischief Sletto might get up to if sufficiently aggrieved. After he left, the front and back doors were left open to air the place out.

Sletto's animosity towards Ole and his place merely increased when Mae began to work there. He knew and hated Mae's parents already, finding them "snooty", and had seen her around MacDougal and lusted after her, squinting his eyes in a porcine private reverie that only he could imagine, and which might have involved pigs. When she began playing music at Ole's that he overheard and also deemed snooty, and found out that she was the daughter of the Palmers, these factors and her sexual unapproachability combined into a deep, keen hatred.

Willy's appearance on the scene was the final straw, Willy being everything that Sletto was not: adventurous, free, fit, successful without being an ass-kisser, well-liked, and attractive to women. Sletto figured women *would* find him attractive, not in a soft-skinned, pretty kind of way, but in a way that Sletto found a bit cool-eyed and penetrating, like he could look at you stonily across a big crowded room with those blue eyes and know just what you were thinking and warn you without moving that you'd better behave. This made Sletto feel kind of fluttery, so he looked for some fault in the fact that Willy's clean jeans and work shirts smacked of a man who thought he was too good to work a real job and get dirty like a real man, preferring instead to float around above everything like fresh laundry sunning on the line. The growing stories about Willy being a tough guy or some kind of hero during the war and after- stories that kept getting new additions- didn't leave Sletto the solace of impugning Willy's manliness, instead causing his hatred to deepen and darken.

Willy had first taken notice that he was in a feud when he was negotiating the purchase of the place from Ole, sitting at the bar with him on a quiet late afternoon and discussing the assets of the business over a beer. The paperboy came into to deliver the local daily pamphlet and to get a free soda from Ole, a tradition that Willy would keep when the boy grew up to be a cub reporter on the paper, before moving across the state to the city of Greysport. Willy already knew and liked the boy; for a gradeschooler, he was bright, articulate, and cynical, and could tell a joke better than most adults. Willy patted the empty barstool next to him in invitation and the kid hopped up in what seemed a practiced and worldweary manner, putting the paper on the bar and nodding to Ole, who had already gone around to get his customary root beer. Willy suppressed a smile.

"How's biz, Jeff?" Ole asked the boy, setting the stein of rootbeer in front of him.

Jeff shrugged and took a sip. "Bad news sells papers, but nothing much happens around here. It's a good thing I've got my deliveries." The boy's convincing imitation of a middle-aged man made Willy and Ole exchange a glance of amusement.

Willy chatted with the boy about events in Europe while Ole, as a matter of habit, wiped down the clean bar surface with a rag, slowly coming back around to resume business with Willy. Suddenly, the room dimmed as the open doorway was blocked from the light as though a beer truck had pulled into a parking space on the street. Ole looked up and saw that the doorway had been filled by the bulk of Bud Sletto. Ole's face dropped, and Willy looked over to the door, squinting to see details against the glare from outside.

Sletto reached out his massive hand and opened the screen door with a creak, then thumped over to the bar about six feet down from Willy and Jeff. The kid wrinkled his nose. Willy watched expressionlessly.

"Bud," Ole nodded coolly, trying to remember where he had last had the baseball bat.

Sletto slowly scraped a barstool out of his way across the floor and stood leaning on the bar, his huge arms definitionless but powerful, and caked in patches with mud or shit, Willy couldn't tell which. His overalls were stiff with filth and grease, and his grey t-shirt, from which the sleeves seemed to have been violently ripped, was a variety of different shades. "Gimme one a them Pilsners," he said, and tossed a quarter on the bar.

Willy watched as the quarter shivered to a stop and Ole filled a glass and put in front of Sletto. He ignored the smell, but put together the fact that Ole and Mae had told him about the man. Sletto's eyes were as red as if he had salted them, and his hair, face, and bristles of beard were as slick as if they had been wiped down with rancid lard. Willy was as fascinated as he was disgusted, and he realized that he owed Mae and Ole an apology for thinking their descriptions were an exaggeration. Little Jeff turned on his barstool so his back was to Sletto, and pantomimed a gagging, nauseated face to Willy.

Sletto stared straight ahead and downed his beer in a long gulp, then slapped the bar for another. Ole took the glass between two fingers and filled it, setting it down again in front of Sletto, who cleared his throat, a rumble deep in his chest.

"The Prohibition's most up," Sletto muttered.

"Scuse me?" Ole said.

"Prohibition's almost up," Sletto muttered again, but louder, "and you never did buy none a my likker."

"Don't be starting that again, Bud," Ole said, getting more frantic in thinking about where he might've put the baseball bat. Willy seemed frozen, his face inscrutable, watching Sletto.

"You had your goddamn chance," Sletto said, his voice rising. "Coulda helped a fella out. Tough times we're living in, and you coulda helped a fella out, steada buyin some kinda high flight likker from some goddamn outsiders-" he turned halfway toward Willy, and Ole noticed that Willy had begun to smile.

"You all think you're better than anyone else? You an yer damn high flight likker?"

"Don't make me get the Sheriff, Bud," Ole said.

"That faggot! Why, I'll fuck him in the ass until he loves me, that piece a shit. Call him."

Ole didn't move, and Willy sat there smiling, but Jeff got down off the barstool and slowly made for the door, moving as if to make a semi-circle around Sletto, who finally turned to look straight at Willy.

"You all think you're better than me, goddamn it? With all yer high flight likker? You think you're better'n me?"

"Jesus, mister," Jeff piped, snorting with laughter, "my *dog's* better than you." He made a dash for the door.

With surprising speed, though, Sletto snapped out a hand and grabbed the boy by the arm, holding him in a grip that encased the boys upper arm with thumb and fingers overlapping and raising his other hand to strike him. His mouth turned down as if he were about to cry and his eyes bulged and seemed to become a deeper red. He glared down at the boy and the hand he held in the air, the size of a catcher's mitt, curled into a fist.

"Will I be mocked by a boy? Will I be mocked by a *boy*?" he shouted, spitting, actually seeming to gnash his teeth. Before the blow could fall, though, his tunneled vision was torn away from the boy's flinching eyes- the fear there made him feel a twitch in his pants- by a crunching grip on his hand that freed the boy's arm, turned his thumb down and palm out, and popped something in his elbow. He looked down and saw Willy smiling up at him with those keen blue eyes before he

51

wrenched Sletto's arm up behind his back, hard, popping something in his shoulder as well so loudly that Ole could hear it. The boy fled into the shadows of the bar as Willy shoved Sletto towards the door, kicking him keenly in the coccyx. Sletto barked and turned around, and, amazingly, seemed to shake his twisted arm so that everything came back into place. He reached around and felt his ass, and muttered, "Cocksucker done broke m' assbone."

Willy raised his eyebrows and frowned, impressed, as Sletto charged back across the bar like a wild boar. Without even raising his fists, Willy merely stood aside and ducked at the last moment, stuck out a workboot, and sent Sletto stumbling heavily to the floor, knocking aside chairs and a table. As Sletto got up on his hands and knees, Jeff came from the shadows with a pool cue raised over his shoulder, and with a whistling swing brought the butt end down hard across the back of Sletto's head with a sound like a line drive, the cue bouncing back, quivering, almost out of Jeff's hands. Ole stood behind the bar dithering, unable to find the bat, then got on the phone to call the Sheriff.

Sletto slowly got up, feeling the base of his skull and saying, "God damn it," then feeling his ass and saying, "God DAMN it!" He turned around and Jeff brandished the poolcue again, and Willy held up his palm to him and warned the boy off with a look. Sletto shook his head like an animal, as though trying to clear enough anger out of it that he could see straight. For no apparent reason, he snatched up a barstool and flicked it over the bar and into the mirror behind it, smashing the mirror and several bottles and turning on a beertap on the rebound. Ole shied away from the flying glass and talked into the telephone mouthpiece, finally seeing the baseball bat stuck behind the wooden pillar to which the telephone was attached. Sletto charged again, this time anticipating Willy's dodge and reaching out to grab him, but Willy's dodge was a feint, and he bobbed nimbly out of the way, landing a solid right on Sletto's ear in the process.

Out on the street, the Sheriff, who was coming up the sidewalk with two cronies to have a few beers for lunch at Ole's, heard the crash of the broken bottles and chuckled, thinking that Ole had dropped a case and that he and his buddies could rib him about it. Always one to avoid a confrontation, yet interested in keeping his usually effortless job, he faced a conundrum when he walked through the door, his friends behind him, and saw that Ole had not dropped a case at all, but was standing behind the bar amongst a litter of broken glass, telephone earpiece in one hand and baseball bat in the other, looking unbelievingly from the phone to the Sheriff, and that his most hated and feared employment shortcoming, Bud Sletto, was holding his bleeding ear and panting like a boar while glaring at Willy, who stood in a loose and agile fighting stance, smiling a little and moving his fists in small, anticipatory circles. When Sletto saw the Sheriff, another person on his lengthy lifetime hate-list, balking in the door, he picked up another barstool and flung it at him. The Sheriff ducked, and the seat of the barstool hit his friend Tim Butler in the face, breaking his nose and sending him backwards out onto the sidewalk. Willy motioned Ole to toss him the bat, and Ole did, as Jim Butler, too enraged at his broken nose to be fearful of the legendary Sletto, burst in from the street, shoving the Sheriff and his friend Ed Mayfield aside and charging Sletto, who struck him in the chest hard enough with his fist that Butler skidded across the floor and up against the base of the piano hard enough to make the strings inside hum. The Sheriff's sense of job preservation outweighed, for a moment, his fear, and he and Ed Mayfield came forward and grabbed and arm apiece on Sletto. Although Sletto was an unusually large man, they were both surprised by the apparent ease with which Sletto flung them around, knocking over stools and swiping the bar clear of glasses. Willy waited a moment, amused to see the Sheriff earning his money for a change, and, at the right instant, accurately thumped the end of the baseball bat, with considerable pounds-per-square-inch of impact, into Sletto's solar plexus. Sletto's eyes bulged and he made hitching sounds as he tried futilely to catch his breath, and slowly slumped forward to the ground, taking the dazed Sheriff and Ed Mayfield with him. Willy stood over Sletto and put a bootheel on his broken coccyx, leaning his weight on it, causing Sletto to grimace in breathless pain, and told the Sheriff to put the cuffs on him. The Sheriff seemed to come to himself and complied.

"Better get him in a cell before he gets mobile," Willy suggested, and the Sheriff and Ed Mayfield complied, struggling to get the limp Sletto to his feet. Sletto was too dazed to fight, and was relieved to have the pressure off his broken tailbone, dimly fearing more abuse from Willy. As he reeled blearily between the Sheriff and Ed Mayfield, the Sheriff's two part-time deputies and full time hangers on, responding to Ole's call, came through the door.

"Cocksucker done broke m' assbone," Sletto, his breath barely back, repeated wheezily.

"Cad I have a bar rag?" Tim Butler asked Ole, tipping his head back, his face wet with blood.

"Sure can," Ole said, giving him a clean one and, realizing the tapper was still running, put a glass underneath it and filled it, sliding it over to Butler. "You just come in for a free one anytime you have a thirst."

"Thags," Butler said, sipping the beer and squinting suspiciously at Sletto around the bar rag as he was lead out, as though he would suddenly regain his wind and burst free from his handcuffs to begin the real chaos.

Willy and Ole looked at each other.

"Nature of the business," Ole shrugged.

"Oh, I know it," Willy said. "You have to pay for the mirror."

Willy went through the familiar feeling of settling back to normal after the jolt of violence, a sensation that was at once triumphant and shameful, exultant and nauseating. And he continued with his life, thinking that that particular problem was solved and on the lookout for others, little knowing that he had just touched downfall, been in the presence of disaster.

In the years that followed, Willy dealt with pool sharks and card cheats and mountebanks of every variety, but it was one of the things that kept the work interesting. Mae was every bit as shrewd and hardheaded as he was, and considered her dealings with such people to be a fascinating slice of life which she would never have experienced had she followed the path that her parents- mostly her father- had initially laid out for her. She didn't think it was bad for the boys to spend time in the bar and learn about the world, not wanting them to be as shocked by its less desirable aspects as she was at one time, and she knew that their lives were well-balanced with the fresh outdoorsman's world that Willy showed them and the world of books and ideas and music in which they both immersed them. Mae was adamant that they learn to play the piano, and in spite of their squirmy restlessness, as soon as they were old enough she sat them down and began to teach them. No amount of pleading, pouting, or black muttering would get them out of it, and, although Willy never said it, he saw in her in those moments her father's stern and dictatorial nature. Old Palmer might be a prick, he thought, but the attitude got results.

Neither had any worry that the boys' spirits would be broken by too regimented an existence. In almost any weather, if they could be corralled long enough to get their chores and small children's homework done, they virtually ran wild, bolting a lunch on weekends and banging out the door into whatever weather awaited them. In the winter, they came in from the snow breathing hard, red-cheeked and runny-nosed, having stayed out as long as they could and stripping off their sodden layers of clothes before sitting in the warm kitchen to dinner, their parents smiling at each other quietly over the things they said. When early spring rolled around, they were gone in the fog and the late snow to watch the developments of the river as the meltwater flooded it, and they were trusted to treat the water with respect, having had unflinching horror stories of drowned children drummed into their heads. When May arrived and the weather warmed, they climbed the bluffs and haunted the woods, learning forest craft from Willy and Emilio, making forts in the shady green recesses of the trees, putting lunches made by their mother into knapsacks and staying gone all day. In the summer, business slowed for Willy and they all spent more time out on the cabin cruiser or on the simple jonboat, exploring the river and the complex configurations of its islands and backwaters, fascinated by its wildlife. In the fall, when the air smelled like apples and woodsmoke and the river and the sky seemed darker even on bright days, the leaves an impressionist fantasy of color, they roughhoused in leafpiles and banged into the bar demanding hamburgers and rootbeer, to the amusement of the customers, who knew them well. And winter came again, and the first snowball fight, and the first soaking clothes and hot chocolate, and warming recuperation in the living room by the dim orange light of the radio dial.

Being rambunctious boys, they were no strangers to the ministrations of Dr. Ambrose. While being chased by Gordon in the bar after watching an Errol Flynn movie, Chief demonstrated his derring-do by leaping evasively from the floor to a chair to a table, across three barstools- two of which toppled behind him, creating an obstacle for Gordon- and up onto the bar. He ran down the surface of the bar, the daytime customers Steve and George Hansen and Brad Verhelst snatching their drinks out of the way, and looked back laughing at Gordon just getting over the fallen barstools. Chief was so fixed on this sight that he ran right off the end of the bar, landing in such a way that he fractured his left radius and ulna. Willy had gone into the back room for what seemed an instant before coming out to find the customers clustered around Chief, who appeared more chagrined than in pain. After Dr. Ambrose had set the bones and applied a cast, Willy felt that he didn't need to give the boys much of a lecture, and merely reviewed the events of the day, making sure they paid strict attention.

This set up an unfortunate theme in that Mae began to perceive Willy as somewhat negligent, which wasn't true; he was simply more permissive, and added spice to the mix by finding the boys antics entertaining. He had to admit, though, that the worst things seemed to happen when he was in charge and when he turned his back for the merest instant. He had finally sat the boys down to take turns practicing piano one day, gauging the relative peace in the house by the reverberant sounds of their unskilled plunkings, and had gone into the basement to get some tools when, ominously, the sounds of practice stopped. Willy's head snapped up, he cocked an ear, and the sounds of thumping and cursing came from the floorboards overhead. Chief was younger and smaller, but a strong kid, and losing consistently to his older brother didn't do much to keep him out of the fray. This sounded like one such fracas, as the thumping and slamming rolled across the floor over Willy's head toward the front porch.

"Hey, knock it off up there, you guys!" he shouted. "I mean it!" The rumble continued unabated, though, and he ran for the stairs and up into the kitchen, seeing through the living room that the boys had each other in headlocks and were struggling to throw the other to the floorboards of the front porch.

"Knock it off!" Willy bellowed, and Gordon let go, holding his hands up in a surrendering gesture to his father. Chief apparently saw this as a sign of weakness, though, and butted his head into Gordon's stomach, sending him assfirst through the bottom half of the porch's screen door. Willy ran out onto the porch, where he saw Mae pulling into the driveway at the same time that he saw Gordon, hooked by his knees on the lower wood portion of the door, release his tenuous one-finger hold on the door and fall backward through the buckled screen, cracking the back of his head on one of the concrete steps so hard that it bounced.

Mae had stopped the car and put it into park and sat staring at the tableau. Chief was in a crouched, post-ramming position, a look of mingled mirth and mortification on his face, and Gordon's sneakers stuck up through the bottom of the ruptured screen door. "Hi, honey," Willy said to Mae.

From the porch stairs Gordon said, "Ow, my fuckin' head," and began to laugh, at which Chief began to laugh, and Mae said, "Watch your language, dammit!"

She got out of the car and they righted Gordon on the steps, where there was already quite a bit of blood. Gordon felt the back of his skull, grimacing but laughing, and pulled away his hand smeared with blood, saying, "Hoo, boy!"

Chief, seeing his brother in such a state, looked sick and began to cry, saying again and again that he was sorry. Gordon tried to reassure him that it didn't hurt much but sure was funny, starting to look a bit dazed, and Chief worked himself into a state of near inconsolability. Gordon patted his shoulder and got blood on his t-shirt. Mae shook her head and clucked her tongue at Willy, who spread his hands and began to explain how short a time he had been in the basement. Dr. Ambrose was called and put thirteen stitches in the back of Gordon's head and checked his pupils for signs of concussion, advising the parents to keep waking him periodically during the night.

"Serves you right for being the kind of kid you were," Ambrose said to Willy on his way out.

"You didn't *know* me when I was a kid," Willy said.

Ambrose snorted and said, "I didn't have to."

"See you for happy hour," Willy said.

"Yep," Ambrose said with a wave over his shoulder as he retreated into the twilight.

That night, hiding in the basement from Mae's wrath, lifting weights and working out on the heavy bag, Willy wondered how much grey hair he had put on his own father's head. Then he wrote a poem about it.

The boys' injury list lengthened, but they never made the same mistake twice unless it came to fighting with other kids in town, in which case it was the other kids who usually ended up on the injured list. The boys seemed to share Willy's type of luck; they might get in trouble, but they usually got out of it when other boys didn't; they might get injured, but it was the least harmful of injuries on a large spectrum of possibility. Gordon slipped while climbing a precarious bluff and cracked his ribs landing in the crotch of a tree, whereas if he had fallen another foot in either direction, his distance to the ground would've been another thirty-five feet. With his fractured ribs, it took him awhile to climb the rest of the way to the ground, after which he tried to cover up his injury. Willy only got to the truth by tricking Chief into explaining how spectacular the fall was, and Gordon was unable to punch him due to the pain in his side.

Chief could have lost an eye to a rock thrown at him by a neighborhood kid, but saw the rock at the last instant and inclined his head, taking the rock in the upper orbit of his eye socket and sustaining a wound that left him with a scar through his eyebrow for the rest of his life. When the other kid's father brought his son over to the bungalow demanding an explanation and an apology for the subsequent beating that his rock-throwing son had received (most of the blood on the kid's shirt had been Chief's), Willy merely had Chief come out onto the front porch and showed the father the stitches. Chief stared the other boy down while the boy's father finally put two and two together realized who Willy was, and it all ended with a blustery retreat and stammering suggestions of a father and son outing, to which Willy said, "Hey, there's an idea," while the man backed out of the drive, running gracelessly up over the curb and into an empty garbage can, while Chief continued to glower fixedly from under his stitches.

There was the time that Gordon got a screwdriver in the cheek, and the one where Chief learned why you whittle *away* from you, and where Gordon learned that you can't really swing from vines like Tarzan, and where Chief proved that a knotted bedsheet makes a poor parachute, especially when jumping from a second-story roof (which particularly annoyed Willy, the Amazing Rotelli story being one commonly retold among the family and friends), and the time where both boys proved that you shouldn't play chicken on your bicycle against your brother, whom you know to be impossibly stubborn.

Willy, though, knew that boys would be boys, and hoped against hope that the scars the boys attained, along with their mother's smarts, would keep them from getting into the next war, whatever it was and wherever it would take place. He stared back at his own stupidity with blankfaced disgust, seeing his friends' blown out heads and halved chests and legless bodies and disembodied arms and....

He would shake his head and focus on the day. He would go out on the river, alone, or with Emilio, or with the boys. He would write small, sad poems and immediately hide them away. He would look outward. He would lose himself in sex with Mae, who gave no thought to the source of his intensity.

It was when the children succumbed to illness that he felt powerless and afraid. He could tell his strong and cheerful boys how to avoid many pitfalls, and had an indelible faith in them to survive the rest with comparatively minor damage, but he could not teach a boy how to avoid getting sick. A cold was bad enough- seeing his rugged boys temporarily lose their spirit, their constant motion, caused him to withdraw into a mute and motionless horror- but when they were struck by something as frightening as the flu, he retreated completely, hiding behind a newspaper or a book, perhaps seeming gruff and disappointed but all the time terrified. He thought about the men he knew who had died in the war, and knew it to be true that nearly half of them had died of influenza caught in the prime breeding ground of the trenches, tough and deadly men carried away as helpless as babies, buried far from home not killed by the war at all, another useless, pathetic waste. There was a town up the river and in the hills and apple orchards, the town of Mt. Pleasant, which, although stuck with an unoriginal name, suffered the unusual catastrophe of losing two-thirds of its population during the influenza epidemic of 1918, two-thirds of a population of sound and self-sufficient people, surviving people, gone as if their knowledge and strength meant nothing, blown away like dust. However tough and strong his boys were, and however much he could teach them, they were unprepared to take on an enemy like that. He silently squelched the urge to flee to the river, take it all the way down and out to sea and across to France where nightmares like this, this fatherhood, did not exist for him, to get away because he was unable to watch. He marched himself into their bedroom to read them stories of heroes as they lay pale and quiet in their beds. Then they got better, and were back to their noisy selves, and in a few days he forgot that he had ever had such a penetrating sensation of fear.

When he was still aware of his fear, though, when it was right in front of his face and could not be brushed away, he could speak of it to no one. Mae seemed at her best when the boys were sick; some large well of compassion seemed to be suddenly tapped, and she ministered to them with more love than she already showed. She didn't mention Willy's deceptive gruffness, and seemed to accept, even to relish, the fact that these were situations in which she flourished. Her mother was present as much as she was needed, there to give her experienced advice, but Mae was such a natural that they conferred more as equals. If Solveig came over and the three of them all at once were demonstrating their unassailable skill, Willy went and hid in the basement, pretending to putter while drinking scotch, or home made vodka from the Hansen brothers when in a particularly cathartic mood.

He couldn't even talk about it to Emilio, who came closest to guessing Willy's malaise, if not its depth. Emilio now had three daughters, Katita and Gabriela coming after a rest period following Marita's birth.

Emilio was typically philosophical. "We can do only the best that we can do," he said. "Other than that, the fates of our children depend on factors which we cannot affect."

Willy had read in the newspaper regarding polio that "there is no disease about which both the laity and the medical profession feel so apprehensive and helpless". Reading that passage made the hair on his forearms stand on end. He looked out the kitchen window to where Gordon and Chief wrestled in the backyard's summer sunlight, both of them brown-skinned and white-toothed, grinning and panting like wolf cubs, Chief with the scar in his eyebrow faded from pink to white. Willy alternated between reading the article in the paper and watching out the window to his boys, his imagination descending a cruel and uncontrollable spiral, and he finally folded the paper, slapping it disgustedly on the table, and walked out the screen door, letting it bang behind him as the boys did, which always annoyed Mae.

"How's about some fishing, you guys?" he said.

"Yeah!" they both barked delightedly, immediately breaking off from this latest explosion in their ongoing rumble and running out to the driveway to clamber into the back of his pickup.

A week later, Chief came in unusually early from the afternoon, saying that he wasn't feeling well. He said he was tired and had a headache, and, after drinking half a glass of lemonade, vomited copiously into the toilet. Willy came home from the Eyrie to find Mae holding a cold cloth to his head. She explained his symptoms to Willy, who nodded silently throughout, and then she added, "he's also feeling fatigued and...he's got pain in his arms and legs." They exchanged a deadpan and penetrating look.

Willy's flesh crawled, but he felt his eyelids droop. "Did you call Doc Ambrose?" he asked, amazed at the calm sound of his own voice.

"On his way," Mae said, her attention back on Chief, who actually whimpered. Willy felt momentarily dizzy and groped robotically into the kitchen to sit down at the table.

After Ambrose had looked Chief over and run some tests, he sat down in the kitchen with Willy and Mae.

"Well, I want you both not to worry..." Ambrose said, carefully looking them both in their eyes in turn. "He appears to have poliomyelitis."

Mae's hand tightened on Willy's although her face remained impassive and her attention bored into the doctor. Willy felt faint, but forced himself into a wooden rigidity.

"Now," Ambrose said without hesitation, "the thing about polio is that it's feared much more than it deserves. There can be terrible consequences, yes, even death, but that happens only in a small percentage of all cases. Eighty to ninety percent of those afflicted with polio come down with what's known as the minor, or abortive, form of it. Symptoms begin after perhaps five days from the time of exposure and last from twenty-four to seventy-two hours. In most cases, they subside and do not return."

Mae looked at Willy with a small, brave smile, and Willy reflected it automatically, overwhelmed with surreality, a roaring in his ears.

"In the major form of the illness," Doc Ambrose continued, "it can return after the symptoms have subsided, perhaps a week later. Even this is not as frightening as it's made out to be in the press. Of the small percentage of polio victims who contract this form, only a quarter of them have any lifelong symptoms or disability."

"But those symptoms can include paralysis," Mae said, holding her chin up. "They can include having to use an iron lung for the rest of your life. They can include death."

Ambrose looked in her eyes for a moment, kindly. "Yes, Mae. Yes they can." He looked at Willy and said, "And there's no use in looking all murderous, Willy. There's nothing here you can fight." This struck Willy as such an obvious thing to say that it was bizarre, and he almost barked in terrified laughter, turning it instead into more of a snort.

"Now, I've got some medication here for the fever and the muscle aches," Ambrose said, "and I've got a copy of other instructions to follow. Only the three of us are to be near him, and maybe your mother, Mae, in a pinch, and by no means is Gordon to have any contact with Chief. I mean none. The more people are exposed, the more chance of something bad happening, and we don't need that. Remember, though, that most victims of this son of a bitch escape unscathed. We'll just keep an eye on the situation."

They escorted him to the door, Willy still feeling more disjointed from reality in his own home than he ever had anywhere else in his life. Dr. Ambrose murmured reassurances to them and Mae nodded and he mimicked her, his mind wheeling. When Gordon came home just before dinnertime asking where his brother was, they told him. He sat down, suddenly looking very serious and much older than his years. "Jeez," he said. "What can I do?"

"You have to stay away from him," Mae said. "He could still be infectious, and children are most susceptible, so you have to stay away no matter what you do."

Gordon's uncomprehending kids' fear of a disease which made the adults around him afraid worked for awhile, but his loyalty to his brother was stronger. Before he went to bed that night, he was silently capering outside the door to his brother's bedroom behind Mae's back as she applied a cold compress to Chief's head. At first Chief just gazed at him, pale and motionless, but that wasn't enough, so Gordon increased the rudeness of his miming until Chief began to laugh weakly. Mae snapped her head around and told him curtly to go to his room.

Willy didn't fare as well. He sat in the basement among his tools and weights, dangling a glass of whiskey between his knees. He was powerless to help his son, his own son; there was nothing he could do. And his sense of powerlessness made him hide, and the hiding made him disgusted with himself. He'd gladly risked his life for virtual strangers, but now when it came to his own beautiful boy, there was nothing he could do. He also sensed that Chief felt his reaction was one of disgust, and that thought wrenched him. After struggling despairingly with this feeling for some time, he swallowed the rest of his whiskey and forced himself to walk up the basement stairs and into the kitchen, then into the living room, where he retrieved a book from one of the shelves. He willed himself to walk down the hall, almost letting himself believe there was something else he had to do in the basement, but he mastered the notion and stood in the doorway of Chief's bedroom. Mae was talking quietly to Chief, a tender smile on her face as though she were sunning the boy with love, and when she sensed him there, she turned around.

Willy held up the book and tried to speak, but his voice caught in his throat, so he cleared it and tried again.

"*The Time Machine*," Willy said. "I thought I'd read to my boy for awhile."

Mae looked at him with such love, such triumph, that he knew that she had had his number all along, and was merely waiting for him trustingly on the other side while he, not trusting himself, sorted out his thoughts. She got up, kissed him, and left the room.

He sat down in the wingback chair next to the bed and looked at his boy, his heart breaking so with helpless compassion that he mercilessly crushed the impulse to weep, crunched it far down into his chest. "You've probably read this one almost as much as I have, but still...."

Chief nodded, smiling wanly at his father, and snuggled into his customary pose when he was read to in bed. Willy began to read from the book and soon settled into his rhythm. After a half an hour, Chief made a noise in his throat, a clutching sound of discomfort. Willy saw that he was attempting to cover up a wince of pain. "What's the problem, Chief?"

The boy looked embarrassed and said, "I got a leg ache. In both of them."

"Oh! Well! Dr. Ambrose gave us something for just that very thing!" He didn't know why he was sounding cheerful, but got up and went into the kitchen and got the bottle of medication for the boy and a glass of cold water to wash it down. After the boy was settled again and Willy prepared to read, Chief said, "Dad?"

"Yep?"

"Am I gonna be okay?"

Willy looked the boy straight in the eye and said in a scoffing manner, "Sure you are. Huh! You're gonna be fine. Kinda scary, though, isn't it?"

Chief seemed a bit embarrassed, but said, "Yeah. A little."

Willy gently stroked his son's hair and said, "You'll be fine. Just takes awhile."

He started reading aloud again, feeling as though he'd just told a very successful baldfaced lie to his own son.

Sometime later, he felt a hand softly laid on the back of his head and muzzily awoke. He'd been drooling in his sleep on Chief's cowboy-and-Indian bedspread and wiped the drool off his chin with the back of his hand. Mae stood looking at him, her head tilted to one side, her eyes glistening. Chief was peacefully asleep.

"Come on to bed, tough guy," she said. "Our son's fine."

He groggily got to his feet and obeyed. Having broken his initial fear, he spent as much time as he could by Chief's side, going into the Eyrie if he had to or if his wife or Mrs. Palmer insisted. Dr. Ambrose stopped by from time to time and said that all the symptoms- headache, vomiting, pain in limbs- were normal and now, that they would just have to wait and see.

Three days after the symptoms began, they disappeared. Chief got weakly out of bed and wandered out onto the front porch, where Willy had just gone to check for the mail. Willy turned around and almost bumped into the boy, who looked up at him and smiled.

Almost a week had passed and Chief was back running wild in his usual summer manner, having started out slowly and gained momentum. Willy felt as if he had been retrieved from hell. The boys burst into the bar demanding hamburgers and rootbeer, and Willy felt his chest swell. There had been times in those days when Willy had wished to feel the deadness inside himself that he had known after the war, when he was connected to no person or place, but now he saw the ridiculousness of such a notion.

Things seemed to have gotten back to normal when Gordon slammed into the bar one afternoon, terrified and panting.

"What is it?" Willy said.

"We were down- by the boatlaunch- and Chief- he grabbed his head and said it really hurt- said it really hurt and he just fell down- and he says he- says he can't move his *legs*!"

Willy threw his barrag at Runty Schommer and ran out the door, getting into the pickup truck where it sat in front of the bar and turning the ignition as Gordon jumped into the passenger seat.

"The boatlaunch?" Willy said

"Yeah," Gordon gulped. "He didn't want me to tell nobody down there, I think he was embarrassed."

"Didn't want you to tell *anybody*," Willy said automatically, pulling the truck out into the street and punching the accelerator, roaring over the cobbles to the boatlaunch. He could see, on the grass under a tree, half hidden by a picnic table, Chief's little body lying supine in the sunlight. He stopped the pickup and yanked the brake lever, got out and ran across the grass to where Chief lay, Gordon right behind him. Kneeling in the grass, he looked in his son's face; Chief was sweating and pale, his skin clammy. "What happened, son?"

Chief parted his lips stickily, gritting his teeth, and said, "My head just all a sudden hurt real bad and I think I kinda fell down or something and I can't move my legs and they hurt real bad, too. Maybe I should take some a that medicine."

"Okay, son," Willy said, gathering the boy up in his arms, "that's just what we'll do. You're with me now."

Dr. Ambrose came out of the boy's bedroom and closed the door behind him quietly. "He's fine for the time being. You're going to have to watch him very closely, and if his condition worsens we'll take him to County Hospital."

Willy and Mae looked at each other; Willy thought that the look on his wife's face could best be categorized as resolved.

"You are not to panic," Ambrose continued. "As I told you during the first onset, only a small percentage of those afflicted with the major form of this illness are permanently affected. Chief's chances are very good."

And so they began to watch again, and to wait, and they took care of the boy as, this time, the pain was greater in his head and in his limbs, as he weakly vomited the soup they encouraged him to keep down. Willy read to him and they took turns sleeping in the chair by his bed. Gordon descended into a wide-eyed silence. Emilio and Solveig were willing to help in any way, but there was nothing they could do, so they went home slowly and were unusually affectionate to their own daughters, even for them. Mrs. Palmer came to cook for Willy and Mae and was gentle with them, no stranger to heartache, and even the perenially aloof Mr Palmer came by to give the boy a present of some comic books and a toy rocketship. The Sheriff came into the bar to express his condolences and broke into tears, and Willy had to console him with a beer and a few shots of whiskey.

Willy found that it was now easy to do this. He felt that he was washed clean of emotion except for a kind of automatic tenderness to others. Most of it went toward his endangered son, whom he read to and sat next to as if he were storing loving memories for some darker time, and then to Gordon and Mae, who seemed like some kind of heart-swelling transient phenomena, some temporary but profound illusion of happiness. It would all go down to misery again, he knew, and the golden span that had been their lives was not to last; it would fade and be gone, and only the familiar landscape of sadness would remain. It was with that feeling of melancholic sweetness that he reached out his strong brown hand and grasped the Sheriff's forearm, and, looking the weeping man lucidly in the eye, said with undiminished depth, "Thank you," and slid him another shot.

Little Chief fooled them all, though, and shrugged off the illness with what seemed like impatient contempt. After a period of cranky convalescence, he got slowly back to normal, and was gaining his customary speed. Mae expressed her faith in her boys, and Willy walked around in a daze for weeks.

Fall came back to the river after a particularly hot August, during which they went boating and camping, and had picnics in shady groves of oaks with Emilio and Solveig and the girls. The girls took to doting on Chief, who was not yet quite strong enough to run away from it. Marita, Katita, and Gabriela fluttered around him, pretending he was a wounded soldier and they were his nurses, and Gordon, in disgust, took a long, forked stick and went off to the bluffs to look for rattlesnakes. The adults sat on a blanket by the river, under the shade of a huge old oak, drinking whiskey sours and talking quietly, their speech still soft and somewhat wistful after the catastrophe which had so nearly mauled their clan. Willy sat with a drink in his hand, watching the motion of the river, feeling wrung out but somehow cleansed. The desire to go down the river had left him again, and he thought of all that he had, of this unimaginable home, and he felt too lucky for the man he was. He looked at his wife, loving her more than he could ever have thought he would love anyone; after all they had been through her serenity and grace seemed ...fascinating. He kept drifting off into thoughts like this, a vacant smile on his face, and was frequently called back to the conversation by one of those who sat nearby.

Gordon's unmistakable bark of "Holy Moly!" made him jump, thinking that, in spite of all his training and admonitions, his son had finally been bitten by a rattlesnake. He saw, though, that Gordon was merely reacting with disgusted amusement to the discovery that Chief had finally succumbed to the girls' pampering, and was lying with his head in Katita's lap, a bottle of pop in his hand, while Gabriela fanned him with ferns and Marita applied makeup to his face. He'd apparently begun to like it, and had caved completely in his brother's absence, but now was on his feet, redfaced under a lurid makeup job, blusteringly defending himself as his brother, weak with laughter, began obligatorily to start a fight. Before Willy could get over to them to break it up, they were scuffling in the dust, and Chief was doing pretty well for someone who had just been gravely ill. He pulled them apart before they got really angry and sent them opposite directions, the girls' faces changing from expressions of delight to disappointment. He went back and sat down on the blanket next to his wife, and noticed that Emilio, stretched out with his head in his own wife's lap, was gently snoring. Willy shook his head and fixed another drink.

They spent the night in tents after eating around a bonfire and telling ghost stories, and Willy was up first in the morning, making cornmeal pancakes for everyone in his giant skillet.

The leaves began to change, though, and there was a crispness in the morning air, along with the first hints of woodsmoke. Willy would stand out on the porch in the morning, stretching away the early stiffness in his back, and breathe deeply of that scent, smiling just for the joy of that specific sensation. The constant odor of the river changed with the seasons, from crisp to fecund, and later there would be the smell of fallen, fermenting apples chilled by frost and releasing their vapors as they warmed in the sun. He loved *knowing* that, loved anticipating those small changes in small things. The kids were back in school at Bluffside Elementary, and when Emilio had a day free, Willy would get Bob Two Bears or Runty Schommer to take over at the bar and they'd sneak out onto the river to drop in some lines. They talked about the fact that, the older they got, the more sweet the autumns became, and agreed that there had been a time for both of them when they wouldn't have imagined getting so old, or of having traditions that were so enjoyable as fishing together out on the river. They kidded each other about the tiny traces of grey that were appearing in their hair.

"I guess I had a vague idea about getting older," Emilio said, reeling in his line and pronouncing the word "vay-gyoo", which Willy didn't bother to correct, "but it din't involve being here or living the way I do. I thought I'd have a lot of sons." He shook his head and laughed. "Having daughters is somehow...is a beautiful thing. You know? With Solveig and the girls, being the only man, I feel especial. I am surrounded by love."

He cast his line out again, plunking the leader in with accuracy among some yellowing lily pads. "Sometimes it's like being in a fairy tale, like I am the king, surrounded by all my princesses. Not like you. With you, it's like living in a cowboy movie."

Willy laughed short and hard, then got silent.

Emilio looked over, saw that distant expression, and said, "It is a terrible thing to have a child get so sick. How terrible to have one die."

"I don't think I could survive it. You know?"

"After all you've been through."

"That's just the point. I feel like I'm out of ammo."

"You are such a tough guy. I am surprise to hear you talk this way."

"I'm drunk."

"Yeah, me too," Emilio said, laughing. "We wouldn't talk this way if we weren't."

"It's like Mae and Solveig. Jesus."

"Well, confession is good for the soul," Emilio said.

"Don't get all religious on me."

"Give me a little kiss," Emilio said, puckering his lips.

"I'm married. How 'bout a beer."

"I guess it will have to do."

They were quiet for awhile, thinking, sipping their beers. After some time, Emilio said, "You know, before I was born, my mother and father lost three children."

"Yeah, I remember you saying. That's tough. My folks lost one. I don't remember it."

"It makes you wonder why they hang on."

"What else are you going to do," Willy said automatically, but then looked at the river and remembered his brief but shameful thoughts of escape when Chief was so sick.

"I thin' you have to have some kind of faith about the future, or it's all pointless." Emilio said.

"Well, I don't believe most people think that way. I think they mostly keep on living just out of stupid animal habit, no matter how shitty things get. Me, I just don't want any more surprises," Willy said.

Emilio shrugged. "Doesn't matter. Life will provide them anyway."

Willy slowly moved his head and looked at his friend, saying with gelid sincerity, "That's what I'm afraid of."

Emilio thought about this for awhile and said, "The Buddha says, 'the only thing that life guarantees us is misery'." He drank his beer, letting that percolate for a bit.

"The Buddha, huh? I don't think we're reading the same books."

Emilio shrugged.

"Kinda bleak, don't you think?" Willy said.

Emilio's eyes brightened, and he focused on Willy. "No, not really. What he is saying is that there is a certain basic level of life that is indeed misery, and that this is inevitable, but if one has the ability within oneself to react *well* to such misery, and to accept it with grace, then, everything else- everything- is some kind of beautiful gift." He spread his hands and smiled in anticipation.

"Hang on, I got one," Willy said abruptly, and, seizing his rod, began reeling the fish in.

Willy knew that surprises came when one didn't expect them, otherwise they wouldn't be surprises. The next big one came on one of Bob Two Bears's and Runty Schommer's off days, when Willy couldn't indulge his avoidance of work and had to be behind the bar. It wasn't that he minded it; he still loved being his own boss and loved the business, and the healthy sum of money he had put away in those most profitable years would only slip away if he didn't protect it, but the notion of any infringement on his freedom was a chafing one.

The Hansen brothers were at the corner of the bar playing chess, bent over the board and concentrating, and Barnacle Brad Verhelst was blearily trying to watch them, after winning four games of pool, then losing two, to one of the regular bargemen. Willy was ostensibly doing the books and looking over Runty's inventory report, but was mostly watching the chess game. The Hansens stared at the board perturbedly, occasionally sipping from their beers. Barnacle Brad raked his long beard with his nails, squinting and nodding. Willy knew the board and was waiting for the next move, glancing up from time to time to see if there had been any progress. This went on for awhile when George, the older Hansen, said, "Make your move."

Steve, who looked a bit like Benjamin Franklin, set down his pint and sighed. "It's your move, shithead."

Barnacle Brad looked up at Willy and began to guffaw, and Willy laughed with him, drowning out the ensuing muttered argument between the brothers. The Hansens then reset the board, and, with a mutual doleful look, walked out the back door of the bar to smoke some reefer in the alley. Brad gulped his beer down and followed, acknowledging this by pointing his bearded chin once at Willy, signing "one" with his finger. Willy looked back at the books for a moment or two before he felt someone sitting at the bar.

He looked up, and there sat a girl of about seventeen. She was a bit chunky, had a pale, almost watery, complexion with a few dozen faded freckles, and pale pigtails tied with unmatched ribbons of blue and black. She had on worn but clean overalls and was quite busty, and the white t-shirt she wore, Willy realized, had not only been recently bleached, but pressed. She had a pug nose, pale pink lips, slightly buck teeth, and faded blue eyes, and might've been somewhat pretty if she had not already been victimized by a diet that might someday render her porcine. When she realized she had Willy's attention, she nodded meekly to him.

After waiting for her to speak for a moment, Willy said, "What can I do for you, miss?"

"Aren't you Mr. McGregor, sir?" she said almost in a whisper.

Willy noticed a faded, greenish-yellow bruise rimming one of the girl's eye sockets, and a white scar across her chin. On the outside of her left arm was a bruise that looked like it could have come from a thumb, which was confirmed when she moved and Willy glanced four more bruises on the soft white inside of her arm. Her nails were raggedly bitten to the quick, two of them black with small scabs. He leaned his forearms on the bar and said kindly, "Yeah, I'm Willy McGregor."

She nodded and stared at the bar.

Willy waited again and said, "And what's your name?"

"Um, Mollie?"

"What can I do for you, Mollie?"

She moved her pale lips to speak once or twice, then attempted to nibble at a chitinous flake of fingernail. Willy tried to resist the urge to take her hand away from her mouth, but finally, with slow movements, reached out and took her wrist in his hand and gently moved it away from her mouth, trying to look her in the eyes. "What can I do for you, Mollie?"

"I's wonderin if you had any work to do round here?" He could perceive a hint of Southern accent in her voice, not terribly common in the area.

Willy attempted a tone of levity by saying, "Well, there's always work to do around here, but try getting my employees to do it! Ho!"

He saw the sudden, tiny look of hope in her eyes and instantly regretted it.

"Right now, though," he said, "we're not really looking for anyone."

By the look of despair on the girl's face- outright heartbreak, really- he suddenly knew that it had taken all that she could muster to come through the front door of the Eyrie.

He found himself babbling. "It's just that, right now, we have bartenders for most days and all of the weekends, and we have people for the restaurant business, in the kitchen, which is usually Friday and Saturday, those're the big nights, and the kitchen is pretty well taken care of....I just- what is it exactly that you'd like to do?"

She seemed to have lost her voice again and stared at an ashtray on the bar. Willy gently put his hand on hers and moved his face into her field of vision until she could not help but see him. He mugged in a way he hoped was comical, waggling his eyebrows. She seemed to resist for a bit, but then something in her relented. Her reticence dropped and she looked him in the eye, practically glaring.

"Mister," she said, "I'd be your damn dog. I'd sleep under that pool table yonder and guard the place for you at night, and for nothin but food and to sleep there. I'm pretty tough, believe you me. You wouldn't believe the shit I seen. Pardon my language," she said, dropping her eyes again, looking suddenly miserable, as if she'd committed a fatal error by swearing.

Willy looked at her, thinking. He poured a glass of icewater and set it in front of her, but she appeared not to notice. He was afraid that he *would* believe the shit that she had seen, but wouldn't be able to stomach the fact that she had seen it. There was a loud break of pool balls as some of the barge and rail men continued to play.

He was pondering what he could do when Mae walked in. The screen door clacked behind her, and, limned in the sunlight from outside, her hair glowing copper, the tiny new lines in her face blurred away, she looked as beautiful and young as she did all those years before, the first time he had seen her playing Chopin in this very bar. He nearly gasped with relief.

Mae sat down at the bar, a droll look on her face, and said to Willy, "I always knew what you were up to at work."

Willy opened his mouth to respond, but his wife had extended her hand to the girl. "Mae McGregor. And you are?"

The girl blushed and said, "Mollie! Mollie Sletto! I heard you play the piana in here before when my ma was shoppin! I sat out front! A couple a times! You're famous!"

"Well, I wouldn't go that far, really..." Mae said, stalling, looking the girl over keenly, but then her eyes and Willy's locked in the dawning comprehension of the girl's identity.

"Sletto, did you say?" Willy said.

This brought the girl's gushing to a halt. "Oh. Yeah. Sorry." She appeared to struggle with hanging her head, but finally gave in.

"Are you Bud Sletto's daughter?" Mae asked.

Mollie nodded. "He said that you were sweet on him at one time, but that you were too much above everybody else, snooty and all, so he had to break your heart."

Mae looked Mollie in the eye.

"I didn't *believe* it," Mollie cried. "Holy crow! I might be ignorant, but I ain't stupid!"

Mae laughed.

"She's looking for a job," Willy told his wife. They shrugged, and their mutual gaze resolved the issue.

Within an hour, Mae and Mollie had cleared out an upper back room with a view of the alley and a glimpse of the river, and Mae had Mollie scrubbing the floor with wood soap. Mae spelled Willy at the bar while he moved a cot frame into the small room and beat the dust out of the small mattress from the top of the building's fire escape, and set it up under the bare window of the small room. Willy flipped the girl a burger while she sat at the bar, drinking a pop, and Mae went home to get her some fresh bedding and toiletries. Although it was a weeknight, Mae played at the piano, eventually bringing out much of her full repertoire. Mollie sat on the floor, her arms clutched around her knees, her head against the piano where it formed a safe corner by the front window. The regulars sat and listened, and people began to come in from the street, quietly ordering drinks as Mae played, her eyes peacefully closed. She finished with a rendition of Fur Elise, and the patrons, drunk and blissfully melancholic at that point, raised their glasses mistily as Mae stood up finally from her small, hard stool. There was no diminishment of respect for her as she went behind the bar and began to serve the customers, who soon became clamorous again. Willy slipped away for a moment to pick up Mollie from where she slept by the piano, and took her up to the small bare room.

They found her there in the morning, in clean sheets, her thumb in her mouth, the pale autumn light clement on her face. They managed to find things for her to do in the kitchen and around the bar- nothing that couldn't have been handled by the existing staff- but they knew they could do nothing else. Mae was so strongly reminded of her own situation when she first came into this very bar that she felt irreversibly protective, as if this were her chance to pay back Ole for the chance, and the life, that he had given her.

Mollie proved to be unafraid of hard work and desperately eager to please. Willy and Mae conjectured that she *had* been someone's dog- and worse- when she had lived among the Sletto pack, in essence born into a position of servitude until she could make good her escape, which she had just done. They both knew better than to think that Bud Sletto- who, after a stint in jail, had not been in MacDougal for some time but had been heard from in other parts- would let such a deed go unpunished, but, though Mae was a bit worried, Willy was merely watchful. He had known since that long ago brawl that he had not seen the last of Bud Sletto.

Although Mollie was not a worldly girl, she had been taught a healthy distrust for humankind that often came in useful in the bar. When a greasy river conman whom Willy had kept his eye on before tried to shortchange her, she remained pokerfaced and calmly came and told Willy about it. Willy had then discreetly taken the weaselish man out into the alley, pinned him with a larynx-crunching grip against the brick wall so hard and fast that the man's teeth clacked shut and his greasy hat slid forward over his eyes. Willy then patted him down for all the money he had, leaving just enough for him to take a boat somewhere else on the river. He set the man loose and turned him down the alley, but, dissatisfied, kicked him so hard in the ass that the man was lifted from the cobbles and tried to trot away while limping and rubbing his ass. Willy called after him that if he hadn't liked his treatment, he should feel free to bring it up with the Sheriff. He went inside with the largish bankroll in his hand and covertly tapped Mollie on her hip with his knuckles, then handed her the wad. Her eyes lit up, and he winked at her, walking back behind the bar. When she took her next break, she went to her room upstairs, and Willy knew it was to hide the money where no one else could find it.

Mae made an attempt to teach Mollie about makeup and dress, but Mollie didn't seem interested in much more than staying meticulously clean, if simply so. When Mae took her shopping, she frugally duplicated the clothes she was wearing the first day she had shown up at the Eyrie. Mae tried to interest her in a girlish but practical winter coat, but Mollie saved her money and instead took Mae up on a previous offer of a sturdy jacket that Mae had used for years when camping or boating in the fall. Mollie calmly squirrelled away the money they gave her, working hard, and seeming happier by the day. Other than working, she didn't do much but read comic books, listen to the radio, and occupy herself with Gordon and Chief, who seemed to take great amusement in her earthy presence. Willy and Mae both knew that she was too polite to share with them the kind of coarse humor which delighted the boys, and they couldn't help but feel a little disappointed about it. Her greatest joy seemed to be taking at least one long bath a day, soaking and soaking in hot, soapy water while she listened to the radio. She would come down fresh and happy, pink-cheeked from the warmth, and wait on tables cheerfully, joking with the customers, who enjoyed her unpretentious company.

When Halloween approached, Willie began to set up for the annual party at the bar, which he had started as a lark, but which had become such a successful tradition that it had spread until all of downtown MacDougal had become an oasis for adult partying with the Eyrie as it's center. They laid out a spread of food: ham, turkey, roast beef, fresh bread, apple and pumpkin pies. There were hourly drink specials, and, at the end of the night, an award for best costume, which was arbitrarily assigned when the time finally rolled around to give it out.

This year Willy had dressed as a swashbuckling pirate, with a black outfit and a real rapier, and the boys had followed suit in a rather more tattered manner with kerchiefs over their heads, stubble pencilled in by Mae and Mollie with mascara, and cutlasses made by Willie in the basement workshop. Mae herself was a vision as Marie Antoinette with a high, ornate wig (she and Solveig refused to tell how it was done) and elaborate hoop dress. There was ingeniously gory makeup around her neck as if her head had been lopped off and then replaced, enabling her to walk around imperiously once more. When she played the piano by candlelight, the effect was successfully macabre.

She felt surprise and pity when she discovered that Mollie had never been allowed to go trick-or-treating, so with some quick creativity, she turned Mollie into a large Raggedy Ann, with a wig of red yarn and large red circles on her already doll-like face. Mollie was tickled with the results, and went out into the cool dark night with the boys, going from door to door in that familiar scent of woodsmoke and fallen apples, some houses welcoming with doors open and yellow light streaming from the windows, here and there a house made scary by an enthusiastic adult.

Barnacle Brad Verhelst's small house was the best in this category. Dark and creepy anyway, but now with tilted tombstones in the front yard, the only light coming from a dozen jack-o-lanterns on the porch and in the windows, and Barnacle Brad himself in the shadows of the porch in an upright plywood coffin, ghastly with white and black makeup, his long grey beard adding to the effect, waiting silently for the more intrepid kids of the town to come up onto the porch before he burst screaming from the coffin. Most of the kids who had dared his house ran away in terror without even grabbing a handful from the large and tempting bowl of candy on a chair on the front porch, but when the McGregor boys stole up with Mollie in tow and Brad, just over laughing himself breathless about the last group of kids, raised his arms and staggered moaning out of the coffin in his best living-dead manner, Mollie screamed in true terror and the boys loosed warcries, charging forward and slashing at the zombie-like creature with their wooden cutlasses, Gordon scoring a blow on its elbow and Chief one on the side of its knee. When Brad howled and leapt back, Gordon sprang in front of the chair with the bowl of candy on it and held open his paper bag, and Chief poured half of the contents of the bowl into the bag. They ran off into the night, each towing Mollie by a wrist, while Brad yelled after them, laughing in spite of himself. When he shouted that he knew who they were, a fusillade of eggs sailed out of the dark and thumped into the siding of his house.

"Fuckin' McGregors," Barnacle Brad said ruefully, getting back into his coffin.

When all the town's children had wandered home tired, things began to cook at the Eyrie. Mollie had dropped the boys off at home on her way back to the bar, and they had gone cooperatively inside and gotten ready for bed. At the Eyrie, which was now packed with costumed, rowdy customers, Mollie waited tables while Mae played the piano and Willy and Runty Schommer tended bar. Willy had drinks with customers but kept downing black coffee to offset the alcohol until it got to the point where the alcohol was barely keeping the edge off a suspenseful caffeine buzz; he always wanted to keep an eye on the situation. There would be some eventual repercussions for their hiring of Mollie, he knew, although they would not be immediate.

The Sheriff had told them that Bud Sletto was in jail in a county downriver for something yet again- drunk and disorderly, assault, mayhem, multiple chicken rape, something- which explained the absence of immediate retaliation that Willy had expected. "He wouldn't dare," was Mae's only reaction to the situation. Willy kept his eyes peeled nonetheless. When trouble broke out in the bar, as it inevitably would, it usually seemed so easily solved as to be anticlimactic.

A scuffle did break out toward the end of the night, some relative strangers from another town, here for the legendary party, drunkenly quarrelling with the Hansen brothers and Barnacle Brad about something insignificant. The boys were sitting, as usual, at the front corner of the bar by the plate glass window. Steve Hansen was dressed as Benjamin Franklin and looked exactly like him, while his brother was dressed as a passable Abraham Lincoln. Barnacle Brad had arisen from the coffin on his porch and was perfect as some kind of ghoul.

The out-of-towners were all three dressed as clowns, and when they tried to act tough to the drunk and obstreperous Brad, it looked so ridiculous that, as the conflict progressed, the usually quiet Hansen brothers were leaning on each other almost weeping with laughter. It was only then that Brad, with beer froth in his beard giving the appearance that he was foaming at the mouth, shoved one of them, sending the clown backwards through the crowd, slipping in spilled drink and slamming into Mae, who sat at the piano bench playing away. It turned ugly when Mae stood up, righted her towering wig, and yelled at the clown, who actually shoved her. As Willy readied himself behind the bar, Mollie saw what was happening and dove forward but was restrained goodnaturedly by a couple of patrons. To resolve the difficulty, Mae merely reached out deftly, grabbed the clown's scrotum so hard that the muscles on her forearm stood out like halyards, and twisted. The Hansen brothers and Barnacle Brad pummeled the other two clowns, the dead overwhelming the ludicrous living, while Mae sneered down at the crumpled clown on the floor, the red gore on her neck glistening, saying something to him that Willy couldn't hear but didn't have to. The clowns were dragged and beaten from the bar- no regular would allow harm to come to Mae, in spite of the harm she was quite capable of doing by herself- and once on the street they were invited not to return. When Mae came back through the front door dusting her hands, followed by the others, a victorious cheer arose. She clasped her hands, shook them on either side of her head like a boxing champ, and sat down at the piano to play a rousing version of The Beer Barrel Polka. The crowd sang along deafeningly. Willy watched his wife pound at the piano, his heart hot in his chest.

Things wound down, though, and at last the final customer tottered out, Mollie locking the door behind him. They sat at the bar, Willie and Mae having whiskies while Mollie had a ginger ale and Runty Schommer a beer, talking and laughing while Willie counted the cash out of the till. Mollie went upstairs to her bed after Runty left, and Willy and Mae went out the back door on the alley, Willy locking the door and looking both ways down the alley. It was empty and quiet, not even a cat in sight, and so was the street in front of the bar. They walked home arm in arm, the pirate in black and the reanimated corpse of headless royalty, through cones of light cast by the occasional streetlamp, leered at by the dead-eyed jack-o-lanterns on front porches, other pumpkins shattered on the cobbles of the street. In spite of their exhaustion, they made love bruisingly, finally falling asleep not long before dawn. Willy got up a few hours later, long enough to get the boys their breakfast and send them out the door, then coming back into the cool light of the bedroom where his wife slept under the quilt, her hips a pleasing curve, the faint stain of red makeup still evident on her pale neck.

The weather got colder and more blustery, and crisp gusts carried brown, yellow, orange, and red leaves out onto the dark water of the river. Willy and Emilio met before dawn at the boat launch to cruise out into the mist with their shotguns to drop anchor in their favorite sheltered spot and wait for waterfowl. They did it wordlessly, contentedly, each accustomed to his duties. The only new

70

addition to their routine was Emilio's yellow labrador Payaso, just old enough to come along and be of assistance, sitting grinning and excited in the bow of the boat next to Emilio. The first day of the season that they went out, they came back with two Canada geese, walking with them up the street to the bar with their shotguns under their arms and the geese held by the neck in their free hands, Payaso trotting happily along beside them. They cleaned the geese and put them in the big freezer in the basement of the bar to save for Thanksgiving, then sat at the bar and had beer and chili while Payaso jawed on a bone at their feet.

Thanksgiving came under heavy skies and flurries of snow, the clouds gigantic and moving fast out of the north so low and huge that it seemed to Willy as if they rumbled with a power and gravity too deep for human hearing. Most of the trees were bare, and the water was black and crested with whitecaps. Geese huddled on the brown grass in the park by the water, while more flew honking in formation overhead as if hurled southward by the wind and desperately trying to keep up. Snow was beginning to stick on the grass and the north side of trees as Willy and Mae loaded the car to go to Emilio and Solveig's for dinner.

Thanksgiving dinner had become something of an occasion with the McGregor and Benitez families. It wasn't that they were competitive, but somehow loose seedlings of gourmet sentiment had taken root and grown in their little clan, and whether they were going on a picnic or to a more formal dining occasion, each faction did their utmost to please and amaze the others. They traded off places to hold such events, but the mood was always one of hand-rubbing anticipation.

Mae had put considerable effort into this year's contribution, a roast goose with caramelized apples and a garlic, onion, and sage stuffing. Willy hovered and helped in a way not typical of husbands at the time, and when he got too overwrought (and therefore bossy, in the manner of many small business owners), she sent him to the basement to putter or hit the heavy bag until he settled down. She timed everything perfectly, leaving the final roasting of the goose to take place in Solveig's kitchen. Mollie was around for the final preparations, and together they whisked the food out to the trunk of the car, covering it, at Mae's insistence, with a white linen table cloth. They rounded up the rowdy boys and got them into the backseat, where each continued taking pokes at the other so that Mollie sat in the middle.

Willy drove on the river road to the south side of the island where Emilio's cabin overlooked its crescent-shaped cove. Emilio had slowly built onto the house, adding a largish dining room with a stone fireplace and carved wooden mantelpiece, the big table and comfortable chairs all made in his shop on cold winter days. He'd added a spacious bedroom for the girls with windows that looked out up the slope behind the cabin and into the stand of evergreens there. Willy approached down the south road then turned off into the evergreens that surrounded the drive to the cabin, slowly negotiating the gravel. Mae elbowed him and said, "Careful, the goose!"

"I'm *being* careful!" Willy said, driving slowly around a pothole.

Emilio was down by the cove where he had a firepit full of brush cut from the previous fall, with some untenably knotty logs set to the side. He was redcheeked in his sheepskin jacket, Payaso on the ground nearby gnawing on a log while

Emilio threw another bundle of brush on the pile. Emilio waved and Willy tooted the horn, parking the car and getting out while the boys burst out on either side and renewed their hostilities on the way into the cabin. Willy opened the trunk and the wind caught it, thudding it open, and Mae and Mollie reached inside for the goose, and for the mince pie and fresh bread in a wicker basket. They hurried inside, and Willy brought out another basket with bottles of wine and whiskey, struggling a little against the wind to close the trunk. He held the bottles up for Emilio to see, and Emilio gave a thumbs-up.

He walked up the steps and into the house, which smelled so good it nearly made him weak. Emilio and Solveig had contributed by making a goose with a sauce of oranges, shallots, and Madeira, and not only was the kitchen warmly glowing with its polished wood and brass fixtures, it smelled orange and caramel and gold. Solveig had a gingham apron on and was smiling, rosy and damp, pushing back a strand of her blonde hair with her wrist as her girls bustled around her in the heat and confusion of the kitchen. Willy smiled and said hello to the girls, set down the basket and fled outside, slipping a bottle of whiskey out of the basket as he did, taking advantage of the distracting clamor his sons made upon entering the kitchen.

Dr. Ambrose was pulling up in his carefully polished burgundy Studebaker as Willie fairly skipped down the flagstone steps, watchcap pushed forward on his head to his eyebrows. Ambrose's wife, Harriet, sat next to him, and Willy could see that they were arguing. Ambrose parked the car next to Willy's, which had already accumulated a dappling of snow, and when they got out, both he and his wife were smiling.

Harriet Ambrose ducked into the backseat of the Studebaker and brought forth a large, covered serving platter, the kind that would conceal a turkey. By the daggerish looks in their eyes, Willy could see that their argument was not over, and when Ambrose looked over to Willy and Emilio, he gave them an instantly recognizable look of husbandly resignation and disgust. He produced from his side of the backseat a large jug and walked over to where they stood by the firepit, somber in his black overcoat and hat. Emilio knelt to set the brush on fire and Ambrose unstoppered the jug and took a swig, handing it to Willy.

"She insisted on roasting a turkey," Ambrose said. Willy took a swig from the jug and found the contents to be Ambrose's excellent hard cider. He handed it to Emilio, who also drank.

"I told her that both of your wives would be fixing the main dishes," he said, taking the jug back from Emilio, "but she seems to think your wives are young and incompetent and prone to setting kitchens ablaze."

Willy and Emilio laughed. Although the firepit was somewhat sheltered by a contour of the hill, the wind coaxed the fire along and the three men stood passing the jug and watching the flames grow.

Some minutes later they heard the crunch of tires on the gravel, and the Sheriff pulled up in his squad car. He parked downhill, close to the river, coming to a rather abrupt and lurching stop under a pine tree close to the water. He got out of the car and his mournful basset hound Coach flopped out of the front seat and was immediately investigated by Payaso, both of them strenuously wagging their tails.

The Sheriff reached into the backseat and brought forth a case of beer, more expensive than he would usually buy, and as he walked up the hill it was apparent that he had already been at the contents. He looked at the two dogs sniffing each other and said, "You know why dogs lick themselves?"

"Because they can," the other three chorused.

"Yeah. Well. I brought some beer," the Sheriff said a bit dolefully, setting the case down away from the fire. He produced a can opener from one of the leather pouches on his Sam Browne belt and opened a bottle, apparently forgetting the one he had set at his feet. The other three exchanged glances and didn't smile. They proceeded to tell jokes so old that they may well have dated back to the Roman Empire, a notion that Willy mentioned, which caused Dr. Ambrose to digress on a brief lecture about the ancientness of jokes and their place in oral tradition, culminating with the one about the two centurions walking down a street and coming upon a dog in an alley who was licking his own dick and the first centurion says, "I wish I could do that," and the second one says, "You'd better pet him first."

Of course they had all heard the joke before, but the doctor's style was so literate, and the way he slipped the joke in with the history lecture so smooth that Willy howled until he had a coughing fit.

The next to arrive were three of Solveig's single girlfriends, all at loose ends for the holiday and apparently in high spirits about it. They all got out of their car chattering and laughing at once, waved gaily at the men around the fire, and produced from their car an array of desserts that made all the men stare with interest. They had just taken all of this into the cabin when Dr. Homburg, the veterinarian, arrived alone, and Willy saw what was on Solveig's mind by inviting them. Homburg parked his car neatly and got out brandishing two bottles of champagne, and saying, "Hiya, fellas!"

"Better look out, Sheriff," Willy said, "he's here to check you for worms."

"I'd like to suggest neutering while you're at it," Dr. Ambrose said dryly, taking a swig from his jug.

"Gonna need a fire axe to chop off *these* balls," the Sheriff said, holding up his beer. "That'n a shitload a stamina!"

It was always the same, and Willy smiled amid the general laughter, looking around at these familiar, happy faces. They all got serious when another car came down the drive, and Willy saw at once that it was Mae's mother, conspicuously alone in the front seat. Dr. Ambrose gallantly stepped over to the car and opened the door for Mrs. Palmer, doffing his hat soberly.

"Good afternoon, Edith," he said.

"How very courtly of you, Arthur," Mrs. Palmer replied. "Afternoon, gentlemen."

"Afternoon, ma'am," they said in unison.

"Where's the ol' ball and chain?" the Sheriff said, holding up his beer.

"Mr. Palmer will not be attending," Mrs. Palmer said coolly. "He's feeling unwell."

"You mean he's drunk!" the Sheriff shouted, laughing.

"Apparently that didn't keep some of us from coming," Mrs. Palmer replied, to the smiles of the others.

"Who?" the Sheriff said, hunching his shoulders and looking around conspiratorially, as if to catch drunks staggering in from the woods or up from the river. Dr. Ambrose slapped his hand to his forehead and Willy and Emilio laughed, handing off Ambrose's cider jug.

Mrs. Palmer made a beckoning motion to Willy with her head, and when Willy came over to the car, she said, "Can you help me in with this, big fella?"

Willy looked in the backseat of the car. "You roasted a turkey?" he said.

"Well, yes. And I made a couple of pies. Two loaves of fresh bread. Creamed corn. Green beans and mushrooms..."

"God, Edith, you're supposed to be our guest!"

"Oh, I didn't feel right just doing nothing. Besides, it kept me busy in the kitchen rather than contemplating the murder of that old idiot I married. He is drunk back at the hotel with the piano player. Come on now and help me with this."

Willy smiled. "Okey-doke." He had suspected this would happen; he knew that Palmer was scared enough of him on a man-to-man basis, but he was now terrified of his daughter and even more terrified of his once-obedient wife, and the prospect of all that hovering fear being compressed into one place had to prove too much for the poor bastard. Just as well, Willy thought. He could never stand the man anyway.

The blaze grew in the firepit and Emilio threw on larger logs. The boys had come out of the house to cool off and to play with the dogs, playing fetch with Payaso and Coach, Payaso bounding ahead and Coach lumpily trying to catch up on his stubby legs, enthusiastic nonetheless. Solveig ushered her daughters outdoors, and they complained a little at first but then seemed interested in being around the boys. Her girlfriends were next, having proven useless obstacles in the kitchen, and Dr. Homburg was neatly entertaining them all with champagne and jokes by the fire. Noticing this, Ambrose, Emilio, and Willy exchanged looks of surprised amusement, none of them ever having thought of Homburg as a ladies' man. The Sheriff attempted to play fetch with the boys and dogs for a bit, but slowly toppled over in an attempt to pick up a stick and seemed to think the better of getting up, lying on the ground with his chin resting on the palm of his hand and his gut hanging out loosely, drinking a beer that he had produced from his coat pocket. A cauldron of spiced cider was brought out and set by the fire for the children, and a huge pot of coffee and ceramic mugs. The grey sky grew rosy through the pine trees on the west slope, and those present, happy by the fire, began nonetheless to glance inquiringly at the house, where the windows glowed with a gold and elfin light as blue smoke flew south from the stone chimney.

Gordon and Chief came up beside Willy, waited for a pause in his conversation and said, "Jeez, Dad, when are we gonna eat?"

Willy and Emilio exchanged a shrug and the front door of the cabin opened. Mae and Solveig stood there, and Mae said, "Come on! Time to eat!"

There were enthusiastic comments and a few cheers and those around the fire began to move toward the house. Gordon ran over to where the Sheriff lay snoring with his arm folded under his head, Coach curled next to his belly, and kicked the Sheriff in the butt. The Sheriff started and looked around muzzily, not seeming alert enough to Chief, apparently, who kicked him in the butt again.

"I'm up! I'm up! Rarin' to go!" He got up laboriously and dusted himself off, leaning over woozily and slapping at his knees, his dog regarding him mournfully. The boys raced toward the house and barged through the hips of the adults, and inside.

They both came to a dead stop and the adults crowded in behind them, stopping as well.

"Wwwwow!" Gordon said.

"Holy shit!" Chief said.

Willy poked him in the shoulder with a knuckle, but Dr. Homburg said, "You got that right, kid!"

A fire crackled on the stone hearth in the living room, and beeswax candles seemed to be everywhere, in brass wall sconces on the varnished paneling, in candelabra on top of the fireplace's mantelpiece, on every end table and available surface. There was no artificial light. A kids' table was set up on the rug in the living room, small and elegant, and through the arch into the diningroom they could see the adults' table, the sight of which made mouths drop open further.

Three large and ornate antique candelabra lit the large table, and the fireplace had a larger blaze than the one in the living room. The white linen tablecloth was set with sterling and china, all perfect in the golden light.

And that was nothing, just a backdrop. What made them gasp, what made them weak, what made them salivate, was that on every other available surface there was food. The cabin was packed with its scent, the windows steamy with it. One goose sat in front of each of the heads of the table, and two turkeys sat on a buffet to the side, all of them golden brown and gleaming with their own glaze. Everywhere else sat dishes of acorn squash, sweet potatoes, baked potatoes, mashed potatoes with garlic and herbs, potato gratin with sage and pearl onions, corn bread with cranberries and golden raisins, carrots with maple syrup and brown sugar, cranberry sauce, creamed corn, green beans and morel mushrooms. Bowls bulging with oranges, apples, and grapes. Fresh bread, rolls, plates of butter. Relish dishes with pickles, olives, herring in cream sauce. A whole table of desserts; mince pie, pumpkin pie, cherry, apple, rhubarb. Willy's favorite, sour cream and raisin. Something appearing to be an obscenely rich chocolate cake, studded with candied cherries. Tarts of every variety.

And wine everywhere. Burgundy and cabernet. Rhine and liebfraumilch. On a more local level, plum, cherry, rhubarb, and an excellent dandelion kept on ice. Dr. Homburg's champagnes, of which he'd had a case in the trunk, were in silver and brass ice buckets as well. Willy did not fail to notice that on the mantelpiece in the living room there was an array of scotches (many of them presents from him), bourbons, and a cigar humidor. He shook his head, grinning.

Mae and Solveig stood by the arches leading into the dining room, Mollie, Mrs. Palmer and Mrs. Ambrose back in the dining room itself, on either side of the fireplace. All but Mae were clutching their hands in anticipation. Willy looked around. All the people in the doorway stood with their mouths open. Dr. Ambrose,

75

his eyebrows arched in amazement, started to applaud, and they all followed suit. Even the children.

Solveig turned bright red and glanced at Mollie, who had a look of radiant, bashful joy, happy to be included. Mae said, "Well, let's eat, then."

The spell was broken and they all discarded their hats and coats and moved in to the tables, Mae, Mollie, and Solveig showing people where to sit. Emilio put on a 78 of Beethoven's Sixth, and people settled into their places as it started.

Willy and Emilio sat at the heads of the table and carved their respective geese. The turkeys had already been partially carved, and those so inclined helped themselves. Dishes were passed in a general hubbub of activity, after which everyone settled in to eat.

There was a general silence at the adults' table, punctuated only with the clank of tableware and clink of wine glasses. Then someone tasted some of the goose and said, "Oh. Oh, my."

"Holy cow!"

"I never in my life..."

Dr. Ambrose said to his wife, "Honey, this is the best turkey you've ever made."

His wife brushed it off. "This *goose*. How could I know?"

Mollie watched over the kids' table, and even they were quiet except for groans and slurping from milk and cider glasses. Dr. Homburg seemed to be adroitly doling out his looks of sensual reverie to each of the young women, who ohhhed and mmmed and took turns holding out forkfuls of something notably tasty, with a hand cupped underneath, for the young man to try. Mae and Solveig smiled at each other, Mae with an I-told-you-so look and Solveig with one of a younger sister's adoration.

Willy had been quiet, and Mae said to him, "Well, what do you think, tough guy?"

Willy waggled a hand. "Oh, it's okay, I suppose..."

There was an immediate tumult of protest and cries of outrage drowning out Willy saying, trying not to laugh, that he'd had better in France; he sheltered himself under his hands as he was hit by two napkins and a roll and saw that one of Solveig's friends was drawing a bead on him with a spoon catapult loaded with peas. Finally, bursting into a grin at the skeweringly tart look on his wife's face, he cried, "No! No! I'm kidding! I've never had anything like it! Serious!"

There was some indignant muttering at his expense while he said, "Kidding, honey."

At this point, Homburg stood up and said, "I'd like to propose a toast!" He waited until everyone had settled down, then raised his wineglass and said, "I don't know about you folks, but this day has changed for me my idea of what Thanksgiving is about. It can so often be a day of stifling obligation, of enduring the presence of those with whom we did not, would not, choose to be connected. The best company is the company we choose, and this is the best company!"

"Hear, hear!"

"Cheers!"

"Well said!"

Solveig stood up and clapped her hands and said, "Let's all say what we're thankful for!"

There was a general, happy agreement to that idea, and Dr. Ambrose started off with a suprisingly poignant speech in appreciation of his wife and their "long and glowing years" together. Homburg, at the other end of the spectrum, spoke rather gaudily about sensual pleasures of all sorts, saying it so languidly that it was almost to the point of being lewd. The young women watched lambent-eyed, and Willy and Mae exchanged a glance of marvel, as if the young vet were on the verge of taking all three of the women home. The Sheriff, who had recovered somewhat with lots of black coffee but was still drunk, began maundering on about unrequited love, "a love whose name no man can speak" -seriously- and since he had been single as long as anyone could remember and no one knew what he was talking about, this caused some puzzlement. When he seemed on the verge of drunken tears, Willy said, "Oh, dammit, just sit down." One of the young women sitting near him patted his arm compassionately and mentioned that he was supposed to say what he was thankful about, the Sheriff said, "Well, this food is pretty damn good. Thank you, ladies." There were cheers to that, and everyone drank some more.

Solveig said that she was thankful for her loving husband, that she could never have guessed that life could be so "satisfying", giving her husband a private look that made the other girls say "Woooo!" in unison. Solveig was further thankful for her daughters and her beautiful house and for all her friends. From the kids table, Chief said, "I'm thankful for farts," and all the children laughed, except for Mollie, who, in her role as the table's supervisor, slapped Chief on the arm.

"Well I am," Chief said, and leaned sideways and farted. This drove the kids wild, and Willy was forced to quell the disturbance with a dadly "Knock it off!"

Emilio stood and gazed in his wife's eyes, his own glowing with emotion. "Tu eres mi amor, y mi amor, y mi amor," he said. "Tu eres mi corazon, mi vida, y mi alma. Para siempre. Gracias al Universo para ti."

Everyone awwwed at this, although most of them didn't speak a word of Spanish. It was evident that Solveig was affected when she held the knuckle of her forefinger to her mouth and her eyes welled. Before sitting down, Emilio said to Willy, "How about something from the poet?"

Willy gave him a shocked and betrayed look and made a palms-down, easy-does-it gesture, but it was too late.

"Poet!" the Sheriff barked, as if somehow betrayed himself.

"Yes," Dr. Ambrose said, "let's have a poem."

Willy gave a deadpan look to his wife, who smiled and shrugged. He slowly stood up, pinning Emilio with his eyes. Emilio laughed and slapped the table.

"Okay," Willy said. "Poem:

Midst darkling dreams
And twisted ends
We find surcease
Among our friends"

He drank quickly from his glass and sat down.

"How cheerful," Dr. Ambrose remarked.

"Kinda depressing," the Sheriff said. "*Poet.*"

"Come on," Emilio said, "something serious."

Willy sighed and stood back up. "How 'bout this. I wrote it for Mae, it's called The Golden Span:

Here I floated aimlessly
The life behind me left
Past dead was I, abandoned,
Unburied, and bereft

Yet here I found you waiting
On this unenvisioned shore
You held me to your glowing breast
And I wandered never more

A valkyrie, you picked me up
From the meadows of the dead
Your kiss sparked light and breath again
Alive, I raised my head

This gentle land our kingdom
Our boys beside us stand
And through the wheeling of the seasons
We behold our golden span

He glanced around furtively and sat back down, staring at his wine glass. One of the girls from Homburg's entourage sniffled. Most of the rest of them stared at him.

Dr. Ambrose cleared his throat and murmured, "Why, William. I must say."

"Yeah, yeah," Willy said.

"That's kinda sad, too," the Sheriff said, scowling at him with a sort of friendly, drunken belligerence. "What are you thankful for?"

Willy gave him a droll look, but Mrs. Palmer said, "Yes, Willy, what're you thankful for?"

He had to answer his mother-in-law. "What am I thankful for? Jeez. I'm thankful I'm not dead. That's just a flat-out miracle. After that, everything is...a gift. The fact that I wake up next to Mae every morning, that she's beautiful, loving, intelligent, my partner...I...I...those two boys over there, what would I do without them? And all my friends...this beautiful place...." he looked around, his emotions suddenly welling dangerously, "I'm just so fortunate that it's almost...."

"Embarrassing," Homburg offered kindly, watching Willy with warmth and understanding. Willy pointed at him and nodded his head. He sat down and Mae took his hand, glowing, and reached out with her other hand and stroked the hair behind his ear. As they gazed at each other, Mrs. Palmer stood up with her glass and took the opportunity to express her gratitude for the fact that her husband was not here, that he had decided to hide at home with the pansyish piano player who was depressed about something or other- and it was always something- and that the two sadsacks were better left in isolation. She was further thankful for the fact that she'd had a daughter who'd had enough grit to show her how useless her husband was, and what it could be like to be around people who knew how to live with a little joy for a change, present company emphatically included. People around the table were grinning, and as the speech continued, Mae's jaw dropped with amused wonder. No one there had ever seen Mrs. Palmer either so inebriated or so outspoken, and everyone was delighted. She stood with one fist on her hip and her glass in the air, sipping from it occasionally as she talked, a pose that was so unlike her former self of years ago that Dr. Ambrose and his wife hooted and slapped at the table, and Willy laughed out loud. As she sat down, though, and the table applauded. Willy noticed out of the corner of his eye that Mollie had been standing up at the children's table but was in the midst of sitting, cider glass in hand. He looked at her and raised his eyebrows, making an encouraging palm-up gesture, but she dropped her eyes and shook her head. He watched her for a moment, but she wouldn't look at him, so he returned his attention to the table, where Harriet Ambrose was taking her turn.

After dessert, the women in charge ushered the non-essential outside. The boys burst from the door first (their post-feast energy amazing the adults) along with the dogs, and then the girls, and all the rest of the entourage who been around the fire, with the exception of Mrs. Palmer and Harriet Ambrose, who stayed in the warmth of the kitchen, and the Sheriff, who was almost immediately snoring on the couch. Emilio put more wood on the fire outside, which was now a huge bed of coals, and, since the wind had died off, was quite warm. The crispness of the evening air woke them up, though, and soon cigars were passed around to go with hard cider and whiskey, and one of the girls who clung in orbit around Dr. Homburg smoked one with him, rather expertly, to the amusement of her friends. They all talked and told stories while the children played with the dogs, and Willy furrowed his brow and smoked his cigar, trying to recall times in which he had been so content. He had to admit, when he finally gave in to the simplistic nature of happiness, to how easy and obvious it really was, that his times had been many. He wished that he'd said something like that during his toast, which he found to be both inadequate and inarticulate. Perhaps he could get a poem out of it. Perhaps, one day, as Mae and Emilio both said, he would write something he wasn't embarrassed to publish.

He was talking to Emilio about hard cider and cigars when Mrs. Palmer and Mrs. Ambrose came out the door bearing their scrubbed cookwear. They thanked Emilio, who replied with dependable Latin gallantry, helping them to their cars with their burdens. Mrs. Ambrose collected her reluctant husband, who was flirting a bit with one of the young women, and when she took his arm rather firmly and guided him to the car, muttering something in his ear, he replied, "I was not! Don't be ridiculous!" Emilio and Willy smiled.

The Homburg group had decided to go out for more drinks, and Willy told them that the Eyrie would be the only bar open in MacDougal, manned by Bob Two Bears, who didn't think there was too much to be thankful about on this particular holiday. They all piled cheerfully into Homburg's car, promising to get the other one the next day, and were off up the gravel road, hooting out the windows.

Willy and Emilio stood outside by the fire in their customary manner, silent and content, watching the coals and the flames. Before long, the wives and children appeared at the front door, Mollie herding the now-exhausted boys to the car while the girls waved from the porch and Mae and Solveig talked. Willy said goodnight to everyone and got in the car and turned the ignition, and waited the five minutes he anticipated for the wives to keep talking while Emilio nodded his head impatiently and rolled his eyes, making a circular motion with his hand. Willy laughed. It was always this way. Finally he tooted the horn and Mae broke away, still talking her way to the car. She got in and said, "Well!" and Willy drove off down the driveway, his sons apparently asleep in the backseat, cushioning their heads on Mollie's large breasts.

They got home and led the groggy boys into the house and to bed, and Mae got the couch ready for Mollie to sleep on, as she did about half the time these days. Willy got ready for bed and brushed his teeth, then went out to the kitchen for a glass of water. On his way back, he saw that Mollie was still awake, bundled up cozily on the couch and reading a comic book by the light of an end table lamp. She didn't notice him, so he watched her for a while, smiling. She seemed much happier than when he had first seen her across the bar, peaceful and more healthy. Her grammar had begun to improve in idolatrous imitation of Mae, and she had expressed an interest in learning how to play the piano. While he and Mae had first taken her in out of a feeling of obligation, she now seemed necessary around the bar and particularly in their home. The boys adored her, and he himself smiled whenever her solid and somehow apologetic form entered the room.

He cleared his throat without thinking, and she looked over the comic book at him. "Oh, hi," she said.

"Um, do you want anything before I turn in?" Willy asked. "Glass of milk?"

She shifted comfortably on the couch and said, "Nah, I'm okay. I'm still stuffed, in fact. I've never seen anything like that in my life."

Willy wondered if she had celebrated Thanksgiving with her family, but every time he asked her about her former situation, she became gloomy and reticent and he didn't want to ruin her mood. "Well, you can look forward to it next year. It'll be our turn to have it over here."

"Maybe I will have digested by then," she smiled.

Willy walked in and sat by her feet on the couch. "It looked like you were about to give a toast tonight and we didn't see you. You should speak up for yourself."

Mollie shrugged.

"Have something you want to say?" Willy said, patting her knee encouragingly.

Mollie's cheeks colored and her gaze shifted to the bookshelf over the couch. "I just...you know."

"No, what?"

She shrugged and squinched her eyes shut, trying not to smile.

"Come on, Mollie. It's your old pal. You can tell me." He poked her in the stomach.

She cleared her throat. "It's just that...you live one way for a long time and you get to thinking that that's the only way there is to live, and, and anything else you hear about or read about or catch sight of is just...some kind of story. Like a fairy tale."

She stopped for awhile, and Willy said, "Yes?"

Mollie shrugged again and continued. "Then you start living the way you once glimpsed, and you do it long enough, and you don't wake up and it doesn't go away, and you start to trust it, you know? Then you get to thinking that the way you used to live was maybe like a bad dream or a scary story or somethin', and that the farther away you get from it, the less real it becomes, until maybe one day it'll just be gone altogether and you won't even have to try not to think of it no more."

"Any more," Willy said kindly, patting her knee.

"Any more," she said, smiling shyly. "And I got you and Mrs. McGregor to thank for that."

Willy looked her in the eyes while thinking about this, and said, "You have yourself to thank. We couldn't have done anything if you hadn't gotten here first."

"Well, that's what I was gonna say, anyway. At dinner. About you folks."

"Anybody else'd do the same thing," Willy said.

"No they would not," she said emphatically. "I've known all kinds of folks did nothing."

Willy watched her eyes, smiling at her until her sternness went away.

"I just can't ever thank you folks enough," she finally said.

"You don't have to. You just pass it on yourself some day. That's all I'm doing, you know, in my life. Or trying my best to. And I know how you feel. I came here a long time ago just wandering like a ghost. Emilio was my only real friend. I slowly found myself starting to belong somewhere, to have a home, and I'll tell you, I didn't realize how lost I was until I was found. I think maybe we should try to stick together and give the people who need it that same feeling. Okay?"

"Okay," she said.

"Well. I'm going to bed. Might do some duck hunting tomorrow." He slapped his knees and stood up. He was about to go down the hall when Mollie said, "I love you guys."

He looked back and saw that she had tears in her eyes. "Well, we love you, too, Mollie. You can just get used to that, okay?"

"Okay."

He went down the hall and found the bedroom door open, Mae waiting for him in the dark. He got into bed and she put her arm over his chest and said, "You're a good guy, you know that?" She kissed him on the cheek.

"Ah, go to sleep," he said, kissing her back.

Almost a week later, Willy had opened the Eyrie after an early morning of duck hunting alone on the river. The morning had been cold and frosty, with no fresh snow but a brittle rime of frost on the grass as Willy and Emilio crunched across to where they had drawn the jonboat up onto the shore, Payaso running ahead and marking trees and stones, his breath smoking in the chilly brass light, his piss steaming prodigiously as he smiled back at them while lifting his leg and hosing down a target. They headed to their favorite slough through the mists on the water, and, once there, drank coffee from a thermos as they watched and listened to the morning sky. The morning was spent fruitlessly, though, and they ended up heading back empty-handed, but happy they had gone nonetheless.

They had more coffee at the bar, their shotguns put behind the counter, and eventually Emilio went on his way, girded against the chill he would be working in. Willy watched out the front window as his friend drove his truck up the street, people waving to him as he went by.

Mollie had slept in her room upstairs the night before and came down looking pinkly scrubbed and cheerful. With few words, they went about the usual chores of setting up for the lunch crowd, the regular railmen and bargemen and river rats, the small business owners and other locals that made up their dependable business. Willy went into the basement to change a keg while Mollie efficiently set up the restaurant area with place settings and menus.

In the dungeon-like stone basement, with shelves everywhere up to its heavy beams, Willy looked over the inventory of liquor bottles, making notes of what he needed to order from the distributor. It was all above board, and at times he felt a little wistful about his fast-and-loose days running liquor. This never lasted long, though; he was too wise to question the worth of the life he had. His mind wandered and he thought about the .22 rifle he was going to buy for Gordon for Christmas, and the chemistry set for Chief, books for Mollie, and the scotch for Doc Ambrose. Emilio always seemed perfectly content with everything he had and was therefore a problem, and Mae had always been a puzzle, so Willy had fallen into the habit of getting her presents big and small, bombarding her with things, panicking in his last minute shopping until he resorted to a scorched-earth policy of generosity. He didn't know that he was a problem for anyone to shop for because, like Emilio, he truly believed he had everything he needed, and he was also unaware of the fact that the small and sentimental gifts he gave his wife were the ones she cherished the most.

He was writing things down on his list of liquor and tabulating the list of gifts in his head when he heard a crash of glassware from upstairs. He'd thought he'd heard voices, but the old building was so solidly built that it was almost soundproof, and with the front door still locked, anyone upstairs was likely to be a delivery man, someone Mollie could generally take care of. It was unlike Mollie to break anything, though, and he cocked his head, listening. Then he heard what sounded like the scrape and thump of a chair being knocked over, and the muffled sound of Mollie's voice in what seemed to be fear and anger. The hair suddenly prickled on his neck and forearms, and he raced up the basement stairs two at a time.

He came out from behind the bar and found Bud Sletto, bigger than life and smellier than week-old death, with his daughter's right forearm engulfed in the grip of his left hand. She had a bloody lip and a pink welt on one cheekbone, and despite that fact Bud had a grip on her arm that bent it at an awkward angle, close to breaking it, she valiantly aimed a workboot and kicked at his balls. Either she missed or it had no effect, though, because his answer to her temerity was to take a short jab like a mulekick at her face, breaking her nose and making her eyes roll back in her head as she went to one knee, her arm now twisted awkwardly over her head

This all took place in a span brief enough for Willy to grab his shotgun from behind the bar, chamber a round, and move in front of Sletto. His very first impulse was to give him a blast of shot right in the chest; perhaps he'd pushed it down, kept it out of sight, but the hot urge to kill was right there, immediately, as if he'd snapped back in time and found himself in the mud and smoke of a field in France. It was the layer years of different habit, though, that slowed him down, and he thought of Mae and Gordon and Chief and his home. He sighed deeply, suddenly frustrated, and instead of firing, butted the barrel of the gun into Sletto's lips, which jerked Sletto's head back and caused his lips to dribble blood. Sletto smiled, the asymmetrical cluster of dark and stumpy teeth in his mouth dark red with blood.

"Let go of her arm, Sletto, or I will pull this trigger and empty this gun into your fucking eye," Willy said matter-of-factly.

Sletto huffed laughter and let Mollie go. A dark red bubble of blood inflated and popped, a few flecks hitting Willy's shirt, the rest rolling down Sletto's chin. "I guess you ain't got nothin' but birdshot in that gun," Sletto said.

"Let's give it a try and see what happens," Willy said, his face expressionless, the gun aimed right at Sletto's eye.

"That's my girl, there. I aim to take her with me."

Mollie got to her feet and wiped blood away from under her nose, smearing the entire back of her hand. The bridge of her nose was pale and crooked. "I turn eighteen next week, Daddy, and you don't have nothin' to say about what I do any more!"

"What, are you suckin' his cock now, you little hoor? You ain't got but one daddy!"

Mollie gasped in rage and picked up a sharp-cornered ashtray and brought her arm back like a major-league pitcher, but Willy was faster and swung the shotgun away from Sletto and brought the barrel back with a hard thud against his temple. When Sletto involuntarily opened his mouth in pain, Willy jabbed the last four inches of the barrel into it. Sletto gagged, his eyes wide, and Willy pushed his head backwards with the gun.

"Open the front door, will you, please, Mollie?" Willy said. She took a wide berth around her father and unlocked and opened the front door, then stood back. Willy poked the gun into the roof of Sletto's mouth and steered him backwards to the door.

" I don't want to blow your brains out in here," Willy said conversationally, "we'd have to clean it up."

He backed Sletto to the door, Sletto staring crosseyed down the barrel, his hands out as if for balance. The moment he got Sletto to the arch of the open door, the Hansen brothers pulled into the parking space just outside at the curb, right on time for lunch and a couple of beers.

"I don't know if I'd park there, fellas," Willy called around Sletto's bulk. "I was just getting ready to blow a skullful of pigshit all over the street, and that nice Chevy of yours might get some on it."

The Hansen brothers shrugged and dutifully went to move their vehicle, and Willy said, "No, no, I'm just kidding. You guys have to have your parking spot, and our buddy Sletto here was just leaving."

He prodded Sletto with the barrel again, and Sletto gagged and backed out onto the sidewalk, blinking in the sunlight. The Hansen brothers, and a few other locals, watched with a mixture of amusement, fear, and wonder.

Willy said, "Bud Sletto, you don't deserve to be called a human being. If it were up to me, I'd kill you right now, because sooner or later, someone's going to have to, and it's anyone's guess as to what kind of mischief you'll get up to before then. One thing you are not going to do, though, is interfere with this girl's life." He jerked his head at Mollie, who stood by Willy's side, her eyes narrowed in hatred at her father, tears running down her cheeks and dripping, mixed with blood, off her bunched and quivering chin. Her lips were pressed together in a thin line, a tight smile of long-awaited victory.

"So, Bud Sletto," Willy continued, "if I ever catch you on this island again, messing with this sweet girl or anyone else, I'm gonna kill you. I might beat your joints and ribs with a ball peen hammer until you're a dirty sack of jelly. I might feed your living guts to your hogs while you watch, or I might just hang your fat ass from a tree in the woods and leave you there 'til your neck rots through. I'm sure any number of people around here would be glad to help." There were sounds of assent from the witnesses who had gathered.

Willy raised his voice, "I expect to be held to my word! If Bud Sletto shows up on MacDougal Island again, he's not leaving here alive!"

He took the shotgun from Sletto's mouth. "Now get out of here."

Sletto glared at him, trembling, but Willy stared back impassively until Sletto dropped his eyes and turned around, making his way down the sidewalk, people backing away as he approached. Sletto turned once to rest a baleful gaze on his daughter, but continued down the sidewalk.

Willy lowered the shotgun. Everyone watched Sletto. Just as he was about to turn down the alley, a rock flew from the crowd and bounced off the back of his skull with a crack. Sletto yelped, putting a hand to the back of his head and bringing away blood. Willy turned and saw Mollie dusting her palms, smile tight on her bloody face, nodding in satisfaction. Sletto regarded her with a look of dull hatred before turning down the alley. The Hansen brothers hurried and looked down the alley after him. The sound of a cranking starter could be heard, then the backfire and roar of an old engine, and the sound of Sletto's truck reverberated down the alley, faded, and was finally gone.

Willy looked around at the crowd, now feeling a little sheepish. "I guess we ought to call the Sheriff. Come on, Mollie," he said, and went back into the bar. His heart was hammering, and he felt nauseous and brilliantly alive. He forced himself to breathe slowly and deeply, slowly and deeply, and gradually stopped the shaking in his hands.

After he had called the Sheriff's office and found that he was out, he sat Mollie down as if he were a corner man and set her nose, then gave her a bar rag packed with ice to put on it to keep down the swelling, although the swellings under her eyes were already turning color. He told her to go upstairs to her room and lie down, but she refused with a solemn shake of her head that he didn't want to dispute. She sat at the bar while he brought the Hansen brothers a couple of beers and barbecue beef sandwiches, watching him all the time. Runty Schommer came in and the Hansen brothers left off congratulating Willy- and Mollie- and dropped their habitual low tones to tell Runty what had happened, and their growing parts in it. Willy waved off Runty's congratulations and went around the bar to sit next to Mollie.

"You're not working today, if that's what you're thinking," he said, putting his hand on her shoulder.

"I've worked with worse than this," she said, staring in his eyes around the bundle she held to her nose.

"Well, not today, you're not," he said, dropping his eyes. "I'm calling Mae to take you home. If the Sheriff wants to talk to you, he can do it there, while you're on the couch with your feet up."

More regulars came in and the story spread. Soon there was an enthusiastic hubbub; there were already different versions of the facts. Willy called Mae and sat with Mollie until Mae showed up. The mood of the bar was ebullient- Bud Sletto being feared and hated for years- Runty was run ragged, and three men had already said that the day was too great for them to return to work. Willy sat next to Mollie, fussing over her and patting her hand, ignoring the others in the bar, until Mae came in. Mae slumped when she saw Mollie, her face turning pale, then deeply angry. She raised her eyebrows at Willie, and he shrugged and spread his hands. Mae put her arm around Mollie, who rested her head on Mae's shoulder.

"You come home, now, sweetie," Mae said, cradling the girl. Mollie stared at Willy, and Willy smiled at her kindly.

"Go on, now," Willy said to her. Mae led her to the door. Runty and the regulars cheered, but Mollie only turned around once to gaze briefly at Willy before Mae led her out the door.

Fifteen minutes later, the Sheriff came in and sat at the bar. Runty tilted his head at the taps and the Sheriff nodded enthusiastically. Willy came in from the back room, and the Sheriff said, "Hey, there Willy. Could I talk to you?"

"Sure," Willy said. The bar went silent.

"Just thought I'd tell you," the Sheriff said quietly, looking over both shoulders, "that Bud Sletto is out of jail across the river and he's been seen in the area. Better be on your toes."

The bar exploded with laughter and jeers, and Willy thanked the Sheriff dryly and went upstairs until the explanations were handled. The last thing he heard distinctly was the Sheriff shouting, "You'd better watch it or you're gonna get a ticket for driving while ugly!" This was followed by more raucous laughter.

The Sheriff's search for Bud Sletto could only go so far; Sletto lived across the water in the next state. Willy knew that the Sheriff in that county was somewhat more skilled than the local one, his inept friend, but even he could only report back that, quite some time later, that Bud Sletto's shack had burned down and his livestock were gone or dead. Rumor had it that Sletto had had a little get-together attended by some local lowlifes, and when the fire in his stove, which was fashioned from a fifty-five gallon drum, had begun to dim down to coals, Sletto had attempted to replenish it from where he sat in an old wingback chair he had found at the dump, taking a ladle he was using to drink from the zinc bucket of potato liquor which lay, mostly filled, at his side. His plan, unsurprisingly, had backfired, in that when he splashed a ladle of the liquor into the stove, it had ignited and followed the splashline of liquor back to the bucket, which had in turn exploded. The flames, reportedly, had engulfed Sletto's right side, burning his face, arm, and shoulder and removing the hair native to that region, and he was forced to run into the bare earth yard surrounding the shack and dive into the pigpen, breaking through the crude fence and dousing the flames by rolling in snow and chilly pigshit, apparently to the howling laughter of his cohorts. When Sletto, half-scorched, half-hairless, and covered in pigshit, had emerged berserk and steaming from the pen, they had seen what was coming and salvaged what bottles of booze they could and evaporated into the night as the shack was gobbled by flame. Some said that Sletto had recovered his shotgun, and, with one side of his head and body charred and blistered, had strode howling, silhouetted by the flames of his enveloped shack, as he shot the pigs that tried to escape and those that cowered, trying to jump over each other, in the corner of the pen.

The first big snowstorm of the season hit not long after, starting late one evening and piling up silently through the night. Willy watched it, parting the curtains with one hand and gazing down the street, the large snowflakes illuminated as they fell through washes of streetlight and porchlight to make their soundless addition to the growing drifts. He eventually padded back to bed, past the couch where Mollie slept cozily under three mismatched quilts, lit by an amber nightlight he had installed after the small but happy birthday party they had had for her, her pale hand and forearm outstretched over a comic book which lay open on the floor. He checked on the boys where they slept breathing softly, their rooms dark, ghosts of snowflakes floating by their open-curtained windows against a field of deep blue. He went back to his bedroom and got into the warmth under the quilts with Mae, who rolled over in her sleep and put her arm across his chest, resting her forehead against his cheek and moving her smooth, hot thigh across his.

In the morning, Mae got up, as usual, a bit earlier than Willy, rousting the boys out of bed and getting them ready for school. Gordon was usually up quickly, enthusiastic about the day, but Chief had a tendency to drag around until he woke up, which was generally about halfway through breakfast. Now that Mollie had become an addition to the household, her habit was to shuffle into the kitchen blearily, wrapped in a quilt with her hair a bird's nest. Mae had eventually changed Mollie's habit of servility, and had gotten her to accept, with shyly appreciative eyes, a cup of strong dark coffee from Mae. The coffee itself was a habit that Mollie had picked up from Willy, although she adulterated it with sugar and cream to an extent that Willy found comically disgusting. After she had a chance to sit with her hands around the steaming mug, watching the brothers eat their breakfast, Willy eventually came in wearing pajama bottoms and a sweater, hugging Mae and tousling the hair of the three at the table, before pouring himself a mug of black coffee and opening up the morning newspaper.

The boys burst out the door on their way to school after yelling goodbye to the others. Willy went out and shoveled the sidewalk, and when he finished, Mollie came out bundled up for the walk to the bar. Although her nose was healed, her eyes were still swollen and purple, but starting to get greenish at the edges of the bruising as they healed. Mae had asked her hesitantly if she wanted to try to cover the discolorations with makeup, but Mollie had shrugged and said, "Black eyes are black eyes. They usually heal up pretty quick."

The walk to work was brisk after the snowstorm, and Willy pushed his watchcap down over his eyebrows. The streets hadn't been plowed yet, but most of the sidewalks remained uncleared as well, so they walked in the street. Mollie shuffled along, kicking the snow, and lagged behind at one point so she could pelt Willy in the back with a snowball.

"Knock it off!" Willy said over his shoulder and Mollie laughed. People were parked on the main street as best they could, going about their business, and the town's snowplow finally came through. Willy kicked through the deep drift in front of the bar and got out his keys, felt that something was unusual and did a doubletake at the bar's front plateglass window. There was a hole in the window about ten inches wide that went right through the E in Eyrie, painted there just after he had purchased the bar from Ole. The cracks ran throughout the window, which, in any event, would have to be replaced.

"Goddammit," Willy said. He opened the door and Mollie came in behind him, her eyes narrowed in suspicion. Inside, the barstools were up on the bar and chairs upside down on tables, everything neatly swept up from the night before. Out of place were the shards of windowglass scattered on the floor by the piano and across to the bar. Wind came in through the hole in the window, and there were traces of snow on the cover of the piano's keyboard. Willy was looking at this disgustedly when Mollie tapped him on the arm.

He followed her finger to where she pointed at the barrail two-thirds of the way down the bar. Sticking out from under the barrail was what, at first glance, appeared to be a dirty rag. He went closer, bending over with his eyes narrowed, and kicked gently beneath the barrail with his workboot. A large, clear quart bottle rolled out, filled with clear liquid. Stuffed into the neck of the bottle and held in place with a small cork was a rag, the end of which was blackened by flame with a brown border where the flame had gone out. Willy bent down and picked up the bottle by the neck with his gloved fingers and set it on the bar between two upended stools. Holding the bottle in one hand, he pulled out the cork and the rag, setting them on the bar. He sniffed the contents of the bottle and coughed. It contained   the feints from potato vodka, the undrinkable first product of distillation, as strong as it could be made. He looked at Mollie.

She looked tough for a moment, but her chin began to quiver and tears came to her blackened eyes. Willy realized that there was something about his expression that was unintentionally brutal, and Mollie started to cry, saying defensively, "That's...it's my Daddy...that's one of his..."

Willy went and put his arms around her.

"It's okay now," he said, making himself sound lighthearted, "it's okay. Nothing happened. We're okay. You're safe."

The tough girl sobbed into his chest, clinging to his jacket underneath his arms, burrowing her bruised face into him. He put his chin on her head and held her. She cried as if she had never done so before, and he held her and told her she was safe, she was safe, she was safe.

When she settled down to hiccupping gasps, Willy took a barstool down for her to sit on. He called the Sheriff's office, merely as a technicality, and amazingly the Sheriff was in, undoubtedly perturbed to be rousted from his reading of westerns over coffee and pastries.

When he started taking the other stools down, she dully stood up to help him, but he told her to sit, made some coffee, and gave her a cup, with all her necessary defilements. The Sheriff came in shortly thereafter, looking despondent and obviously discomfitted by the cold, and Willy explained what had happened, showing the Sheriff the bottle and other apparatus.

The Sheriff looked at the hole in the window, the glass on the floor, and the bottle, and whispered to Willy, "So, you're saying he thought she still lived here, and he was trying to burn up his own daughter, along with the bar?"

Willy gave him a deadpan look.

"Well, I'll be goddammed," the Sheriff said. "That Bud Sletto always was one no-good piece of shit."

Willy called Mae and asked her to come and take Mollie home, explaining the situation. Mae came through the snow with a .38 in the pocket of her long coat. She looked at the hole in the window angrily, then looked at Mollie, and her expression changed to one of such tenderness and compassion that Mollie burst into tears again. Mae put her arm around the girl's shoulder and took her home. Mollie couldn't see any good reason to stay there, though, and came back in an hour, saying nothing, but going to work with the lunch crowd, smiling and joking as usual.

Christmas had gone for Willy pretty much the way he'd thought it would. It had started out wonderfully the night before; he and Mae had stolen into the living room, lit only by the large, colorful bulbs on the Christmas tree, and deposited presents around the tree's base. Mollie had slept obliviously throughout, and, by the slack expression on her face, he knew that she wasn't faking it, but out to the world. Once the presents were set out, they sat in the darkness of the kitchen together, looking through the arch of the door to the living room at the warm scene, holding hands across the kitchen table and silently drinking old fashioneds.

The very instant the rising sun came up over the trees on the eastern shore and shone across the river, setting aglow in orange light the snowy little town in its protective crescent of western bluffs, the threads of smoke from chimneys turning from pale blue to gold, the boys were up and yelling in the living room. Mollie raised her voice and told the boys not to open any presents yet, but it was obvious that she was too late in one instance because Chief had discovered, and was banging atonally on, his new guitar. This noise stopped and Willy tried with groggy optimism to return to sleep, but then the boys were on either side of the bed, mercilessly yanking on his and Mae's wrists until they got up and out of bed. They shuffled into the kitchen where Mollie smiled at them as she poured them cups of coffee.

They gradually came to in the living room, sitting on the couch and drinking more coffee as the boys and Mollie opened their presents. As with Mollie's small birthday party, it was quietly obvious that this was the first real Christmas she had experienced; she marvelled at the lights, which really weren't all that special, and went on about the coziness of things and being genuinely touched to be given simple gifts just for her. She shyly approached Willy and Mae with her gifts for them: a hardback copy of *The Grapes of Wrath* for Willy and some Beethoven 78s for Mae, including the Sixth and Seventh Symphonies. They both expressed their gratitude effusively, not having to feign it a bit. They exchanged secret looks of marvel over the quality of the gifts; Mollie was obviously learning quietly on a level that neither of them had guessed. For her, they'd gotten a red sweater, a black and grey plaid skirt with threads of red in it which she seemed unlikely to wear (although they retained hope), and a few books. She seemed pleased and deeply touched.

The boys had torn through their gifts in an instant, predictably, and sat among the toys and games fondling their favorites, the .22 rifle for Gordon and the chemistry set for Chief. Willy gave Gordon yet another sober talk on gun safety, where and when and what and why to shoot, and Gordon nodded, gravely intoning that he understood. Chief received a similar talk on the nature of chemistry sets, that, although they could be fun, they were a learning tool, and not to be used for the forces of chaos. Chief nodded with chiefly solemnity, saying in turn that he, too, understood.

For the others, the boys had pooled their resources and bought the following: a malodorous bar of soap on a rope for Willy and a copy of (but not a subscription to) *Field and Stream* magazine, a bottle of cheap perfume and some oven mitts for their mother, and something in what appeared to be a professionally wrapped box for Mollie. When they gave the gifts to their parents, they did it absentmindedly, like an afterthought, but when they were distracted from their own gifts long enough to give Mollie hers, they seemed to remember some strenuously contained excitement. They nudged each other and nodded knowingly, bright with anticipation.

All eyes were on Mollie as she slowly opened the gift. She took off the white ribbon and the red wrapping paper, and, apparently torturing the boys with the drama, carefully removed the top of the box, then dug through the layers of white tissue. She finally gasped, the object revealed, and Mae said, "Well, what is it?"

Mollie blushed, and held up from the box a ruby-red bra with florid lace and a pattern of faux pearls sewn into it. Willy blew coffee out of his nose.

"D cup," Gordon noted, with a connoisseur's air, to his parents. Chief nodded matter-of-factly.

"Try it on," Chief suggested to Mollie, who sat transfixed by the object she held.

Willie coughed spasmodically, wiping his eyes, while Mae patted him distractedly on the back, convulsed with laughter.

"I'll try it on later," Mollie said. "It's very nice."

After some more lolling in the living room, Mae went into the kitchen to make some breakfast. Mollie followed to help and the boys followed her, and after a few moments of silence in which he regarded the mess in the living room, Willy came in search of coffee. After breakfast, when all the kids seemed distracted, Willy gave Mae a lidded-eyed, concupiscent gaze, to which she, as was habit, responded with a bland look and a pursing of her lips. As if not wanting to startle wild animals, they checked out the kids in the living room with imperceptibly slow movements, then crept back down the hall to their bedroom.

Willy quietly locked the door with the key and slid a chair under the doorknob as a precaution; the boys had once seen a movie in which the hero had slid a newspaper under a locked door, then pushed the key out from the other side onto the newspaper, pulled the newspaper with the key on it back from underneath the door, and unlocked it. The boys had done this to Willy and Mae's bedroom on a beautiful autumn weekend day when they had thought the boys would have no reason at all to be home, and Willy had kidded Mae for being overly cautious when she locked the door. The boys had sprung into the room- "Surprise!"- with spectacularly bad timing, ruining a crucial moment for the parents and eliciting talks on both the sanctity of privacy and the nature of sex among adults.

Not to be so surprised twice, Willy made sure the chair was snug under the doorknob, then took off his pajamas. Mae looked at him admiringly; all the working out he did had kept his body muscled like a heavyweight boxer. Her heated look was so sultry that his cock sprang to riveted attention- he imagined an upward-whistling note- and when, backlit by the light of a brightly snowy day diffused through the sheers over the windows, she dropped her nightgown from around her shoulders and exposed her pale skin, full breasts and pink nipples tinged with peach, the copper hair delicate between her soft and glowing thighs, a discrete tuft, he gasped for the thousandth or ten-thousandth time, laying her down on the bed and entering her all the way - but slowly- in one thrust, both of them groaning. He made love to his wife quietly but with a strong rhythm, staring in her eyes, and when her eyes grew distant then clenched shut in orgasm, he put a hand over her mouth to stifle her cries and spurted hard deep within her, their orgasms overlapping. He lay still for awhile on top of her until the breathing slowed and he could roll from between her legs and lie next to her, encircling her with his large arms. She sighed laughter and smiled looking at him, shaking her head.

Miraculously, they were able to shower and get dressed with no interruption from the boys. They set about preparing for the obligatory visit to Mae's parents' hotel, happy in the kitchen together as Mae made a mince pie and Willy roasted a goose under Mae's supervision. Emilio and Solveig stopped by in the early afternoon with the girls in tow, each of them showing off a new doll or article of clothing, and the women talked in the kitchen while Willy and Emilio put on their jackets to smoke cigars and have a spot of whiskey outside while Payaso clowned in the snow. They were talking in the snow on the front walk when they heard the "pop-pop!" of a small rifle from behind the house, and went down the driveway to find out what damage had been done.

Gordon had been showing off his rifle and had apparently found himself unable to resist demonstrating it for the girls, doing so by hanging a can of red primer paint from the picket fence in the back yard and shooting it twice with the.22. He seemed surprised by how much of a mess the primer paint made as it blew out of the back of the can onto the fence and poured from four holes into the snow and was still seeming impressed by the results- Chief was wide-eyed with delight, but the girls looked a little scared- when Willy came around the corner with his cigar clenched in his teeth and bellowed at Gordon to freeze where he was and hand him the gun. He emptied the chamber and put on the safety and put the gun on the back porch, telling Gordon to get a bucket from the garage to put the paint can in and to get some turpentine and a rag and wipe off the fence.

"You've got to try to grow some common sense!" Willy said to Gordon's back as he trudged into the garage.

"*Sorry!*" Gordon said in angry embarrassment, hating to be dressed down in front of the girls, who looked moon-eyed and a little terrified at Willy's vehemence. Chief was chortling in vicarious delight at seeing his brother get yelled at, but a look from Willy made him put on a deadpan face. Willy gave Emilio the same look, but Emilio kept on laughing soundlessly.

Later, while Willy and Mae got ready to go to the Palmer's hotel for dinner- rather morosely, as they were only going out of loyalty to Mae's mother- when they heard a strange sound like a thump from down in the basement. It was an unusual sound, and they froze in the process of getting dressed, sharing a look of suspicion and cocking their heads. The house had become silent. Willy went out of the bedroom and looked in the living room, where he found Mollie, dressed in her new red sweater and plaid skirt, reading on the couch.

"Did you hear that?" Willy asked her.

Before she could answer he left the room and went to the door at the top of the basement stairs, throwing it open.

"I think they're playing with the chemistry set," Mollie said.

A pall of stinging blue smoke rolled out from the open door. Willy coughed and shouted, "Goddammit! What're you guys doing down there?"

There was a flurry of urgent whispering from the basement, then both boys said simultaneously, "Nothing!"

Mollie came in from the living room with her book in her hand, fanning it in front of her face.

Willy felt tired. "I'm afraid to look," he told her.

She patted his arm and went downstairs. He hesitated, not wanting to listen, but morbidly fascinated nonetheless. He heard some more whispering, and Mollie said, "Jesus! But the fire's out?" followed by more whispering. Willy went into the kitchen and opened the backdoor to let in some fresh air, stopping to pour himself another mug of coffee. Pausing at the top of the stairs, he called down, "There'd better not be any damage down there!"

"Everything's under control!" Mollie called cheerfully.

"No damage!" Gordon added, followed by giggling from Chief, who he heard whisper loudly, "That was so neat!" before he closed the basement door.

He returned to the bedroom rubbing one temple with his fingertips.

Mae was finishing her makeup and said, "Everything okay?"

"Oh, yeah," Willy sighed, sitting on the bed and drinking his coffee.

On the way to the hotel at sunset, Mae lectured the boys to mind their Ps and Qs, taking over for Willy, who had obviously done his share for the day. They sat in the backseat on either side of Mollie, who had never been to the hotel before, and were excited because they wanted to take her exploring. Through the halls and basement and attics, outside on the porches and in the front yard leading down to the stone wall by the bluff and the stone walkway along it, through the kitchen and into the woods, when the boys visited their grandparents at the hotel, they could barely be restrained to five polite minutes of awkward conversation before being unleashed to "explore". The obligatory pain over with, the boys would then shoot out of whatever room they were in, usually the high-ceilinged main hall by the huge fireplace, and bolt out into any area where there were no adults.

The only thing to happen that caused Willy a moment's pause on the short drive to the hotel was when Chief asked him, from where he snuggled against Mollie, where someone could buy potassium nitrate.

"Oh, a chemical supply store, I suppose," Willy said. "Why?"

"There wasn't any in the chemistry set."

"Was there supposed to be?"

"No," Chief said. "How 'bout sulphur?"

"Same place, I guess. Why?"

Before Chief could answer, Mae nudged him. They were driving by the bar, and Barnacle Brad was at the front door waving at them. Willy tooted the horn and waved back. When Brad saw the kids in the backseat, he grinned through his heavy beard and gave them the finger, and all three of the kids flipped him off in return in a manner that was not covert enough for Willy to miss. As they turned south on the river road then up the bluff road to the hotel, it occurred to Willy that potassium nitrate, sulphur, and charcoal were the ingredients of gunpowder. He looked into the rearview mirror (which, out of necessity, was aimed at the boys and not out the rear window), where he saw Mollie enjoying the view, while Gordon and Chief, under the guise of snuggling with her, were slowly grinding their cheeks into her large breasts while exchanging evil leers. Now he understood about the bra. He was simultaneously angered and amused; the emotions fought for stasis and he sighed.

"It won't be that bad," Mae said, unconvinced herself, patting his knee as they approached the hotel.

"What won't?" he muttered, but she didn't catch it.

The Sheriff had made it a tradition to patrol the town and the island alone on Christmas night, letting the part-time deputies Tim Butler and Ed Mayfield, who were family men, spend time with family at home. For Marvin Purdue- who, due to something he didn't like about his name or his past or his character, insisted on being called the Sheriff- Christmas was melancholy, but in a sweet way. He slowly cruised the snowy streets in the squadcar, imagining himself the protector of the island, an illusion he could usually maintain until trouble actually arose, an infrequent phenomenon, and one usually over by the time he arrived. When it did, he found that, statistically speaking, there was only a small chance that he could be in any position to do something immediate; it was usually a case of cleaning up the mess, smoothing feathers, and filling out the appropriate paperwork when the dust settled.

He drove along the streets this Christmas, though, peaceful and wistful, a man whom others thought was happily a bachelor, but whom circumstance had decreed would live a life more solitary than he would have preferred, his one secret love kept from him by convention. He drove listening to Christmas music on the radio with the window of the cruiser open, looking at the strings of large, multicolored lightbulbs draped from shrubs and adorning doorways. He looked into the warm windows of the quiet houses, Christmas trees in some front windows, wreaths on others, here a husband smoking his pipe and reading the paper while his wife knitted, their eyes meeting for a moment, a warm connection, a glimpse of their palpable love. In the next house rambunctious children chased each other in the living room in front of the tree, their voices muted but still audible through rimed windows, one of the children wearing an Indian headdress. At another house, a young couple in overcoats, the man carrying a bottle of wine, rang the front doorbell and waited until the door opened, yellow light pouring out with cheerful greetings and the scent of ham. The couple went inside and the door closed behind them, muffling the hearty voices and leaving the Sheriff alone in the dark, the ice crunching under the tires of the squadcar as he rolled past.

He swung by the McGregors' bungalow and found it quiet and dark except for the lights on the shrubbery in front of the porch and a lamp on behind the drawn curtains of the living room. The houses on either side were bright and alive. The Sheriff knew that the McGregors- with Mollie along, of course- were at the in-laws, up on the bluff in the drafty old hotel, having prime rib with Mr. and Mrs. Palmer and the few guests who were present, if any, and the piano player, Frederick Ferrier, who, the Sheriff knew only too well, suffered a loneliness which was a mirror to his own. Willy had said that Mr. Palmer had, before these rare get-togethers, usually been drinking slowly and steadily all day, and that if there was any time during the year that a familial conflagration of emotion were to take place, this would be it, the smoldering resentments in the family bursting finally into flame, the misunderstood and unappreciated artist Ferrier contributing his own flaming behavior to the blaze. Willy seemed to find it an annoying but humorous obligation- his loyalty being to Mae and Mae's to her mother- but it made the Sheriff sad in a way he tried bury in an onslaught of Sheriffly dutifulness. This train of thought made him morose, and he drove down the main street to the boat launch, where he looked out over the river, listening to the news broadcast for Christmas, 1940, and drank from a pint bottle of rye as he sat in the dark. The news was largely about the effects of the Blitz in London, and although it all seemed very far away, the Sheriff began quietly to weep, moved by the plight of the lost and lonely people in the world.

When the news broadcast was over, an orchestral version of "O Come Let Us Adore Him" came on the radio, and the Sheriff, suddenly disgusted with this involuntary slip into the maudlin, wiped his eyes and blew his nose with a red kerchief, took a snort from the bottle, and muttered to himself that he'd better get serious. He got out of the squad and walked through the snow to the boathouse to check the doors and windows, stomping his feet and whistling along with the music that came out of the open door of the squadcar. Silently, it began to snow in huge flakes.

Satisfied that the boathouse had in no way been desecrated, the Sheriff returned to his car and pulled out onto the river road and headed north towards the bridge, the windshield wipers working against the falling snow. He got to the base of the bridge as he had done ten thousand times before, and decided to drive across it, east to the shore which was black in the night, the only thing visible being the falling snow illuminated by his headlights. "Silent Night, Holy Night" played on the radio, and he took out the pint bottle again and had a pull from it as he drove across the long bridge, looking out at the ice and snow on the river and the patches of black, cold water where the ice had not formed over the river's fast-moving surface.

Halfway across the bridge, the headlights of another vehicle grew brighter out of the darkness and falling snow. One of the headlights was dimmer than the other, a fitful amber on the verge of burnout, and as the vehicle approached, the Sheriff saw that it was a battered pickup and heard its blown muffler. As the vehicles passed each other on the bridge, the Sheriff caught an obscure glimpse of the driver, a very large man, mostly a shadow, eyes reflecting in the instant the driver glanced at the Sheriff as he passed. Was there something wrong with the face, a waxy reflectiveness, a missing eyebrow? The glimpse had taken only a second and was obscured by snow and darkness, but a feeling of dread settled into the Sheriff and he slowed the squad as it approached the end of the bridge.

The Sheriff drove to the other end of the bridge to turn around on the opposite shore. He drove off onto the gravel shoulder, but it was deeper with snow than he had anticipated and the tires lost their traction. He tried to extricate himself, putting the car alternately into first and reverse, but the tires whined and spun, crushing and melting the snow to ice. He swore, envisioning himself caught stuck by one of the citizens of MacDougal, some of whom, he knew, regarded him in a less than serious manner. He spun the tires, almost ready to cry with frustration, and got out of the squad to assess the situation, taking a pull from the bottle and putting it back inside his coat. He suddenly remembered Emilio Benitez liberating himself and his truck from such a situation by putting some brush under the rear tires for traction, then rocking himself out. He cast around in the snowy darkness for something to put under the tires, suddenly feeling old and fat and weak and uselessly tall, and he was on the verge of tears again.

At that moment he heard through the flurrying darkness the scrape of a snowplow coming down the road and turned to see the headlights of a large truck. It was painted orange and emblazoned with the name of the county on its door. The driver and the Sheriff knew each other. The Sheriff nodded ruefully at the driver's sarcastic comments as he hooked up the squadcar with chains and pulled it free in moments, and cut short his county employee chitchat, alluding mysteriously to important business afoot on the island. It even made him feel brave and important for a moment.

He crossed the bridge back onto the island and took the river road south into town. Most of the bars were closed, but the Eyrie showed signs of life, as usual. The Sheriff parked in front of the bar and walked in, dusting the snow off his arms and shoulders. A few regulars were there, the Hansen brothers, Barnacle Brad Verhelst (it would be surprising if he weren't), and even some of the wives of those who had them. The mood of the place seemed jovial, even boisterous. Everyone wished him a merry Christmas as he came in. Bob Two Bears was tending bar, and automatically poured him a whiskey when he came in the door. The Sheriff was feeling unusually directed and hesitated for a moment, but then stepped up to the bar, took the glass in his hand and downed half of it.

"See anything unusual tonight, Bob?" he asked.

Bob Two Bears shrugged. "Barnacle Brad gave me a fifty cent tip. That's pretty fucking unusual."

"Nothing else?"

"Nope. Why?"

"Probably nothing. I just..." he shook his head- "Nothing."

"Okay, then," Bob Two Bears said, and went to wait on a customer as the Sheriff finished his drink and turned to leave the bar.

Once outside, he buttoned up his coat, looking up and down the street. It was so quiet, he thought he could hear snowflakes as they settled on the snow already on the ground. The sidewalks were covered with fresh powder. He glanced at his watch; it wasn't that late. When he readjusted his sleeve over his wristwatch, he noticed footprints in the snow beneath the window of the bar. They were quite fresh, and the funny thing was that they didn't come up to the door of the bar. They sort of sidled up, next to the wall, and stopped as though someone paused to look in the window from an angle. As though to spy into the bar. He saw that the heels of the prints were close to the wall, as if the person who made them had put his back to the wall, flattening against it so as to watch unnoticed. The prints were bigger than his own, and that was saying something. The compacting of the snow at that spot made it seem that the person who had been spying in the window had been there for awhile, then the prints reversed direction and went back the way they had come.

With a deflating realization, the Sheriff knew where he had to go next. He hesitated for a moment, looking into the window of the bar and entertaining a brief notion of deputizing a posse- something he had always wanted to do- but he knew the way he was ridiculed already for his cautious handling of the infrequent dangerous aspects of the job, and bolstered himself with a chastising internal speech about how he should for once earn his paycheck as something other than a gladhanding, grinning officiator of public events, punctuating this spate of muttering with another shot from his bottle. Thus girded, he got back into the squad and drove up the street, with the lights out, to the McGregors'.

He rolled slowly to a stop in front of the neighbors' house, got out of the car and quietly closed the door, leaving it slightly ajar. Although the snow silenced his footsteps, he was still a caricature of stealth as he approached the darkened house. He was breathing deeply, his eyes wide, and was starting to get into the role of Lawman, like something out of a western he had read. His senses felt wide open, and he cocked his head, listening for anything. There was a small gust of wind, and up the street flurries of snow swirled under a streetlamp. No one stood on the corner under the lamp.

In the fresh snow on the sidewalk, there was one set of footprints. They went back up the sidewalk and around the fence between the yards, as though coming from the neighbor's driveway. The Sheriff knew Willy's back yard was fenced in. The prints paralleled the short hedge in front of the bungalow and turned a right angle, going up the shadowed driveway. The Sheriff approached the prints and saw that they were the same ones from in front of the bar. He stood there in the darkness, staring at the prints, his mind suddenly blank but his chest clamped with fear. Pride made him shake his head and pull himself together. He breathed deeply. It suddenly occurred to him that, on such an occasion, he would be justified in pulling his gun. He did so, and the heft of it in his hand lifted his spirits.

In a crouch, he sidled shuffling through the snow. He could see no broken windows on this side of the house, or anything amiss with the front porch. Something small sat in the dark shadows on the top stair to the porch, though, and he approached it, squinting, bending over.

Surrounded by a small Christmas wreath, which seemed placed there as if in triumph, sat the body of a large black cat leaning sideways against the riser. Its head was turned backwards, the eyes burst and hanging out of their sockets as if the skull had been crushed by a large fist. Its teeth were bared, and stood out bluely in the shadows. A ribbon around the wreath had been written on crudely with grease pencil, and said "Mollie".

The Sheriff grimaced and straightened up away from the tableau. He backed up a step so he could look around the corner of the house and down the driveway. The huge black shadow that stood there was Bud Sletto, who said, "Evenin', Sheriff," and dropped him with a fist to the temple.

After the dark red flash inside his skull, cold snow on his face brought him to. He realized he was being dragged by the collar of his jacket into the backyard of Willy's house. He struggled to get hold of himself. When he brought hands up protectively in front of his face, Sletto let go of his collar and kicked him twice, very hard, in the solar plexus. When the immediate pain subsided but he was still struggling vainly to breathe, he realized that Sletto was talking to him while cuffing his hands around a fencepost.

"You musta knowed I was in jail there for a bit. Up the river, just like the sayin'. Didn't we laugh about that. Ain't so bad, jail, 'cept for the guards. Didn't much like the way they'd give a fella the ol' finger wave when they was searchin' fer contraband. Without s'much as a by-your-leave. Always thought I'd like to give a little back to 'em. Always said I'd fuck you 'til ya liked it, you old goat, and boy howdy, here we are."

Sletto got down to where the Sheriff knelt in the snow with his arms outstretched to the fence post and roughly yanked off his utility belt, then undid the belt to his pants and his zipper and pulled the Sheriff's pants and undershorts to his knees. The Sheriff, dizzy with horror, looked back over his shoulder to where Sletto stood, one eyebrow missing in a mass of waxy tissue, the hair on that side tufted and patchy, with his pants around his heavy greyish thighs. Even in the dim, snowy light, Sletto's thick, pallid, and uncircumcised cock looked greasy. He pumped it casually with his unclean fist.

"I always figgered you was a little sweet," Sletto grinned, showing his remaining rotten teeth.

The hotel was decorated in an icily cheerful way, with strings of white lights in the shrubs and white imitation candles in all the windows. The large green double doors at the entrance had big wreaths with white ribbons trimmed in silver. Even with their waning income, Mae's mother managed to summon some regal style, and Willy shook his head in admiration. He'd noticed, though, that few cars were parked in the lot and knew that business continued to be poor.

Mr. Palmer had been waiting for them to arrive, though, and opened the door with a flourish. He was all boozy bonhomie, red-nosed and almost reeling with a daylong drunkenness that only habit could conceal. He draped his arm up over Willy's shoulder in a comradely way that he would never do in the increasingly rare times that he was sober, but for years, since Mae and Willy's wedding, he had been at least partially alleviated of the responsibility of feigning his sobriety. His Prohibition Era posturing as a teetotaler had fallen silently by the wayside, and, out of good manners, was never mentioned to his face. Willy still didn't like him much, but, when offered a drink, took him immediately up on it, knowing that the evening was going to be a long one.

Palmer had never met Mollie (although his wife knew her well and liked her) and said to Willy, "Well, is that the nanny?"

This somehow surprised Willy, even with his foreknowledge that the man was a jackass, and he did a doubletake at his father-in-law. "No, that's, uh, that's Mollie." He was still wondering how anyone could perceive him and Mae as being the type of people who would have a nanny for their children, in spite of Palmer's obliviousness, when they reached the sideboard, where Palmer poured them both whiskeys from an ornate decanter on a silver tray into antique glasses. Willy took a good blast of the whiskey, which, he was unsurprised to find, was cheap.

Willy came up to the hotel as infrequently as possible (although he occasionally sent business up the road, which Palmer reportedly treated with sneering condescension), and surveyed the place with some interest as Palmer yammered inconsequentially. One of the few guests was sitting and reading in an old leather wingback chair by the large fireplace in the main hall, obviously a businessman unable to make it home for the holiday and enjoying the warmth of the large fire. Frederick Ferrier, the piano player, sat at the carefully maintained grand piano, painfully thin, overdressed in a crisp tuxedo, his hair meticulously pomaded. He was playing something currently popular, a saccharine tune which he embellished even more with frilly grace notes. Willy looked for his wife so he could give her a glance and a nod to see if she shared his opinion that Ferrier was wearing some kind of makeup- Mae always ready to share a laugh at expense of the man who had crowded her out of a job when she first returned home from college- but she and the kids were being shown the huge Christmas tree, sparkling in white and silver, so he was left in the loyal and husbandly position of drinking and nodding with a half-smile on his face as his father-in-law yapped. When a few words settled in through his haze that indicated that Palmer thought Adolph Hitler was a "dynamic individual", Willy stopped dead still and watched him for a moment, then turned to the decanter and poured a giant whiskey.

The kids were released to explore after bringing in the mince pie and goose, and Willy and Mae and her parents sat by the fire with drinks exchanging small talk. As usual, Mae and her mother could talk on at length, seemingly endlessly, and Willy and Palmer were relegated to itchy silences. Dinner was served mercifully soon, with everyone but Palmer helping Mrs. Palmer and her one kitchen helper bring food out into the large, empty dining room. The single guest in the wingback chair had disappeared.

The dinner itself was less than comfortable and, Willy imagined, just plain strange for the kids. The food was good, the atmosphere gelidly festive, but Palmer had begun to get very drunk and was becoming maudlin. Willy never saw his wife so irate as when she had to deal with her father, and he could see by the sharp look that had settled into her eyes that she was watching him and holding back comments. He furtively glanced at his watch.

When Frederick Ferrier came over to the table and sat down at Palmer's request, Willy knew it wouldn't be long before they left. He never did understand the bond between the two men; perhaps Palmer thought that Ferrier was refined in a way that had nothing to do with his piano playing (Mae herself was a far better musician, and had better taste), that his effeminacy brought some panache to the place. Mae couldn't explain it either, but she knew her mother and Ferrier didn't get along, and that his continued employment at the hotel was a bone of contention between the Palmers. Willy knew that Ferrier shared Palmer's distaste for him and his business, but didn't hold it against Ferrier, seeing the man as sad and lonely and past his prime, clinging to anything that might give him an illusion of dignity. He noticed, upon closer inspection, that Ferrier *was* wearing makeup, a thick orangeish pancake, as though to give the impression that he had just gotten back from Ft. Lauderdale. Some of it had rubbed off on his otherwise pristine collar. With a few flicks of his eyes, Willy communicated this to his wife, whose eyes widened almost imperceptibly, her mouth pursing in a concealed smile. The boys were getting antsy again, Palmer was reeling in his chair, staring crosseyed at Ferrier's wet lips as he spoke. Ferrier was guzzling champagne and it was obvious that he'd been drinking, too, and when he became maudlin and began to speak of life's disappointments, and Palmer knocked over a glass of water, Willy said, slapping his knees, "Welp! Getting late! Guess we should probably hit the road. The boys here've been up since about three this morning! You know how boys are."

"Huh! I know too much about boys already," Ferrier chirped, resting his hand on Palmer's forearm as if to get him to share the joke, and downing a glass of champagne.

Willy smiled as if delighted by this witticism, but started the motions of leaving. He knew he had to be abrupt and begin the process now; Mae would back her way to the car talking to her mother, and, depending on how long it took, he might have to round the boys up as many as three times. It was made worse by the fact that Mollie was obviously smitten with the beauty of the place, throughout dinner pulling her eyes away from the conversation between Mae and her mother to look around with a glowing gaze. She looked adorable in her new sweater and skirt, and Willy thought that, in her entire life, she might never before have been dressed so well or eaten in a place so pretty. It made him feel tender for her.

He managed to get them all out of the door and into the car, though, and, their obligation fulfilled for another year, they headed home. It was snowing rather heavily as they drove down the bluff from the hotel in the dark.

He looked into the rearview mirror and saw that his lecherous sons were at it again, Mollie seemingly oblivious in the middle. He glanced at Mae, who was relaxing already, looking out at the snow, every yard away from her father seeming to reduce her pressure. He looked back at boys again, and, in spite of the day's mischief, he smiled, loving them intensely. They were not bad boys; they did well in school, seemingly interested in everything, and in spite of their unusual rowdiness they were not bullies, always, instead, following what he drilled into them and sticking up for the underdog. They minded Willy and Mae as long as their attention spans and energy levels would allow them to, and most of the things they did made him laugh in secret, just as soon as he was someplace where it was safe to put away his stern face. They were just like he was at their age, and now he understood his father's frustration, even rage, when Willy, sure he knew everything, imperiously told his father what he was going to do with his life. If he could just keep the boys out of whatever trouble was convenient, if he could just teach them how simple happiness really was, he would be able to rest with the idea that he had fulfilled his role as a father. He suddenly missed his own father very much, with his thick Scottish burr- often incomprehensible to Americans- and his martial ways offset by his riotous sense of humor. Willy's life had not been anything like what his father had foreseen for him, but he hoped that, if the old man were still alive, he would see that it had not been a life misspent. He had never had the chance to tell his father how right he had been about things, but the notion that he was doing right by his boys gave him some solace.

He drove by the bar and saw that it was doing fine business for a Christmas; knowing it was a perfect time of year for family acrimony, he liked to give the customers who had provided him with a comfortable living a place to go and hide out when the homefront became too claustrophobic, and the atmosphere was usually so congenial that he always had volunteers to work. He saw that the snow was piling up, though, and hoped that Bob Two Bears would leave off bullshitting with the customers for a minute to duck outside and shovel it off.

As he drove up through the crunching snow on Bluff Street he saw the Sheriff's squadcar in front of the neighbors' house with its lights off and its door ajar. He immediately knew something was wrong, and prickles started in the small of his back and worked up over his shoulders. He stopped the car and backed down the block a bit and parked it, turning out the lights.

Mae looked at him with her eyebrows furrowed and Gordon said, "What's going on?"

"Probably nothing," Willy said, but drew Mae close as if to hug her.

"I don't suppose you have the .38 with you," he whispered in her ear.

She shook her head. "Why?"

"Something's wrong. Just...when I get out of the car, slide over and take the wheel. Lock the doors. If anything happens, go to the bar and I'll find you there."

Mae nodded. Willy looked in the back seat. Mollie looked terrified, but had her arms around the boys protectively. "Whatcha doin', Dad?" Chief said.

"Just keep quiet and look after your mom and Mollie," Willy said. "Lock your doors."

He slid quietly out of the car and Mae took the seat. He closed the door and slowly and leaned on it until it clicked, and Mae locked it from inside. He edged up the street to his driveway, saw the two sets of tracks in the snow going down the drive. Neither of them came out. His scalp prickling, he slipped through the snow. He saw the cat and the wreath, and read the signs in the snow, then, seeing the Sheriff's handgun almost covered with snow beside some tracks, picked it up and checked to see if it was loaded. He followed the dragmarks and the dark spots of blood, holding the handgun exactly as he had first been trained. His heart pounded and he suddenly felt hot and joyful. He knew it was Sletto and wanted to kill him, wanted to shoot him in the face and blow his brains out the back of his head and into the snow, wanted an end to it. He wanted to see Sletto's brains in the snow, steaming.

Willy came to the corner at the end of the house and walked wide of it, expecting Sletto to be there. He trained the gun on the shadows; no one was there. It had stopped snowing and there was a rift in the clouds and moonlight suddenly shone through, turning the white siding pale blue in the light. His senses were wide open and the mild wind seemed to howl in bursts over the collar of his jacket. He went through the gate into the backyard. He saw the Sheriff at the same time that he heard someone trying to start a large engine, a truck engine, a few houses away down the alley. It sounded like the engine wouldn't turn over, and he stared at the Sheriff.

The Sheriff was looking at him from over his shoulder from where he was handcuffed to the picket fence, on his knees and pantsed with his ass in the air. In spite of everything, Willy laughed. "Well, it's Sletto, goddammit!" the Sheriff said. "Get him!"

The engine down the alley fired in ignition and Willy sprinted through the backyard. His gloved hand slipped on a picket as he tried to vault the fence, gashing his wrist. He caught his foot and landed in the alley on his back on the other side of the fence, but never dropped the gun. He got to his feet and saw the taillights of the old truck and aimed the gun at it but the truck went around a corner and was out of sight. He ran down the alley two houses and it occurred to him that Sletto might think to double back and would see his family, and Willy cut up the driveway of a neighbor's house and saw that his car was parked where he'd left it and that everyone was unharmed. He heard the truck's roar dwindle in the distance and ran back to the back yard.

The Sheriff was still in his ignominious position, of course, and when Willy saw that he was mostly unharmed, Willy bent over in silent laughter.

"Let me up, goddammit! The cuff keys are on my belt!" Willy did so, and the Sheriff got up and shamefacedly reassembled himself, finally buckling his utility belt and holding out his hand to Willy for the gun. Willy gave it to him and said, "He's gone for now. What the hell happened?"

Dusting snow off his knees, the Sheriff spat, "That crazy-ass pigfuckin' son of a bitch got the drop on me and was about to *cornhole* me, goddammit! If you hadn't shown up...Don't tell anybody about this, okay? I was checking on your house and...just don't tell anyone, okay? Goddammit!"

"We'll just say that he knocked you out," Willy said. "Add that to his other warrants." Willy settled down and began to get angry. Sletto had been *right here*. "Look, I have to tell the wife that everything's okay. Do me a favor and hide that dead cat under the bushes and come back and get rid of it later, got it?"

"Sure, whatever you want. Just don't tell anyone, okay?"

"Yes! Jesus!" He turned to go to the car, but stopped and turned back to the Sheriff. "Look, I might as well tell you. I can't have this threat to my family. I'm going to kill Bud Sletto."

"I'll *help* you, goddammit, that son of a bitch! You're deputized! Just tell me what you want me to do! What the hell is wrong with a man like that?"

"Just won't take no for an answer, I guess," Willy said, and walked down the driveway.

Willy went out to the car to tell Mae that it was safe to come into the house, doing it in a manner that would reassure her but not alarm the kids. The Sheriff did as Willy told him and hid the mutilated cat under the bushes. Willy cased the yard and the house, looking for broken windows or anything else amiss, and, finding nothing, came back inside. Mae was putting the boys to bed. Mollie stood in the kitchen.

"It was my daddy again, wasn't it," she said.

"Well, yes." Willy said.

She sighed, looking bleak and older than she was. "He won't stop, you know."

"We'll stop him."

Mollie shook her head. "You don't know him like I do. He won't ever let anybody one-up him. People bein' afraid of him is all he's got. It's all he's got to hang onto and he'll hang onto it like a drownin' man."

"We'll stop him."

"He killed a friend of his for cheatin' at cards. I guess nobody knows that, though some have suspected. Friend didn't trust him, though, knew he'd get riled, and slipped away 'fore Daddy could get to him. Daddy acted all friendly, bygones be bygones, and when the man lowered his guard one day, Daddy hit im in the head with a axe and fed him to the hogs. Wasn't nothin' left but a piece of skull and a boot with a foot in it. Daddy made me pick that out of the pen and burn it in a brush pile. Said if I ever told anybody, I'd get the same."

Willy felt part of him slipping back into the wartime blankness where any horror was possible and any goodness an evanescent illusion. He had a sensation of how precarious was the goodness of his own life, that the golden span of his life, the happiness he had with Mae and the boys, could be erased and made not to exist by forces entirely out of his control. He could only fight to protect it. He had nothing to say to Mollie. He merely put his hand on her shoulder.

"I wish I didn't have him in me," she said desolately. "What does that make me? Am I like him? My Mommy was sweet, as far as I can remember, but bein' part him makes me feel dirty inside, like I can never get clean."

Willy put his arms around her. She clung to him desperately.

When he went to bed, he told Mae everything. Her face hardened in the blue light, and she nodded at what he said. "Well, I'm with you all the way. You're my husband. Hard times are when you're at your best."

When Willy got up early in the morning after a sleepless night, Mollie was sitting on the couch in the clothes she had worn the night before, as if she had never gone to bed. In her hands she held what appeared to be letters.

"Whatcha got there?" Willy said, going into the kitchen to make coffee.

"Letters," Mollie replied.

"I see that. Who're they from?"

"My aunt. My mom's sister. She lives in Greysport."

"Greysport, huh? The big city. I didn't know you had any relatives."

"I had an old address for her," Mollie said. "Once I was here, I wrote her and said she could write me back care of the bar. I couldn't do it before. My daddy wouldn'ta let me."

"That's pretty exciting. Maybe you could pay her a visit. You could take the train across the state and get a look at the city. It's right on the Lake there. It's like the sea," Willy said, feeling that he was babbling just to make reassuring sounds.

"Actually, she asked me if I wanted to move there." She looked at him from where she sat on the couch, tentatively, almost fearfully.

"Well, that's...quite an opportunity. Do you want to go?"

She shrugged. "I'd have to think about it. I sure love you guys, and the boys, and I've never been happier, but...maybe I should go. My daddy, he'll be back."

"Oh, I think we'll take care of that problem."

The day after Christmas that year fell on a Thursday, and the midmorning found Willy at the wheel of his pickup truck, crossing the bridge to get to the last known residence of Bud Sletto. His pump shotgun was loaded with double-aught buckshot and sat in the gun rack over the rear window. Emilio sat next to him, looking morose, but had insisted upon coming along. Willy didn't say anything to Emilio about his pacifist's credo; the sad look on his friend's face as they had gotten ready was enough to keep him silent. Emilio's punctiliously maintained shotgun was held with the stock between his knees, an empty chamber, and pointed at the roof of the truck.

The Sheriff sat next to the passenger side door, leaving Emilio rather uncomfortably in the middle. The Sheriff was dressed in civilian clothes, going, as they were, across the river and west into another state, out of his jurisdiction, but had confessed to Willy that he was so petrified at the idea of Bud Sletto out anywhere loose that he knew he would never sleep another good night until the matter was closed. He could take Sletto back and lie on the reports to put him in jail, he didn't care. For the first time in his life one fear had outweighed another, and he was on his way to kill them both. He felt filmically noble at moments, then reverted to being just plain scared. He wore two pistols and had a shotgun, checked by Willy and rechecked by Emilio, between his knees.

They drove up into the bluffs and coulees on the west side of the river, up into a dark valley heavy with old trees, bouldered breakdown from ancient stony escarpments snowcovered and next to the road. Willy had known the road for years and suspected the location of the Sletto farm since having first become aware of the man, and with Mollie's information and the little the Sheriff knew, he was sure when he drove by the Sletto mailbox, rusty and dented as if picked from a trashpile and hung through a bullethole on a nail on a large stick.

Willy drove by slowly then pulled around down the road and came back. There were tire tracks on a trail through the snow up over the rise and into the woods, either a few sets or those of a vehicle that had driven in and back out again, but there were enough of crossed-over tracks and new snow to make it difficult to read, although some of the tracks were fairly fresh. Willy parked the truck and got out for a closer look, and when Emilio followed and assessed the tracks as well, they traded unsure glances.

"What do we have here?" the Sheriff, marching through the snow, said in tones that reverberated among the trees. Emilio gave Willy a sour look and Willy made an emphatic palms-down gesture to the Sheriff to be quiet.

"Oh, sorry," the Sheriff said in a stage whisper, and Emilio rolled his eyes. The Sheriff adjusted his belt with two pistols, slung low under his belly, and seemed to think about the pistols for a moment before vomiting in a forceful spray on the ground, splattering his boots and calves. Willy watched him for a moment, then walked to the truck for his and Emilio's shotguns. He clapped the Sheriff's shoulder on the way, saying, "You stay here and watch the truck. We might need to get out of here fast." The Sheriff nodded, wiping his lips with a handkerchief. Emilio patted him on the shoulder while looking at the snow on the ground.

Willy and Emilio moved up the little road soundlessly, as if they were hunting deer. It wasn't necessary to mention that this particular prey had guns and the home advantage. With this knowledge, they slipped along the edges of the road as silent as smoke. Willy concentrated so hard it was as though he could almost see through the boles of trees. Dark old trees crowded the road, their thick, twisted trunks like pillars, their limbs overlapping above the trail against the pearly overcast. Brambles and other underbrush grew heavy beneath the trees, blocking their field of vision as they followed the curves. Finally the road took one more broad turn uphill and widened out into a large clearing, revealing the top of the hill as a bald, snowy knob, cleared of trees for some acres at the top of the bluff, the fields surrounding it bristling with the stubble of cornstalks sticking out of the snow. At the crest of the knob, atop an outcropping of ancient, stratified stone, stood the burned bones of what had been a large shack. The upright timbers stood black against the snowy sky around the remains of a stone fireplace and chimney, sooty and cracked, standing like the ruins of a dark altar. It began to snow again.

The sheds and outbuildings on the property had been burned as well, and the pig pens were either burned or broken. Here and there in the snow lay the corpses of pigs; one had been shot in the head with a shotgun then been picked at by scavengers and decomposition before freezing, another, close to the remains of the house, had been burned, its eyesockets black, its hide resembling the skin of some ancient barbaric drum. Willy moved through the snow and kicked it softly, and indeed, it thumped like a drumbeat. He looked across the remains of the pen and saw a burned pig's head stuck on one of the uprights of the fence, its flesh seared black, crowpecked, its jaw opened wide, exposing brown teeth.

Scattered around in the snow were rusted cans and empty moonshine bottles, farm implements and old tools. Surrounding the remains of outbuildings were the rusting snowcovered remains of old machinery and a rotten cart, once drawn by horses. Willy followed the tracks of the truck, stopped and stood. In the snow next to the tire-ruts was a yellow stain of snowed-over piss in front of huge bootprints. An empty moonshine bottle lay nearby, as did a huge can which had recently contained beans, its lid ratcheted open but still attached.

"He slept here in his truck, and he's gone," Emilio said, and Willy nodded. Emilio sighed and lowered his gun.

"Let's get the fuck out of here," Emilio said, shuddering. Willy looked around, his eyes narrowed, his lips pursed, and slowly lowered his gun. He listened to the wind for a moment, and to the snowflakes hitting his shoulders. He sighed, long and deep. Then they turned and walked down the way they had come.

They checked up and down the river in places they thought likely to harbor a man like Sletto, clusters of shacks or lone outposts on the floodplain out in the swamps and dead marshgrass and black leafless trees, huts sometimes built on stilts or made of old boats, where riverrats lived, men who did as little as possible to survive, getting money from bounties on pelts or rattlesnake tails, living on possum stew and rattlesnake meat and moonshine, men who drifted up and down the river as suited their temperament, and who were impatient with society. Willy spoke to dozens of these men and came to understand that Sletto was feared, that there was an aura around him of lethal unpredictability, best known among these dispossessed, where an altercation between those on the twilit rim of human affairs could result in the disappearance of one of the parties, to be buried in a wet and shallow grave by a marshy slough, or perhaps gutted to release decomposition gasses then wrapped in wire and weighted with stones and dropped in a deep channel, to rot and be eaten by scavengers while barges thrummed through the muddy sunlit water overhead.

Many of those he spoke to had heard of Willy and some he recognized from occasional appearances in the bar or in town, but even those who seemed favorably disposed to him seemed to have nothing they wanted to say. In some cases it was plain that their mouths were sealed by fear, which Willy understood. Why would these forgotten people have any reason to believe that they were protected? One riverat, a furtive, skulking creature weighing perhaps a hundred and twenty pounds and missing his four top front teeth, a cap pulled down over his bloodshot eyes, drunkenly told Willy that he'd heard Sletto had killed a man in a knife-fight and fed his corpse to his hogs. The man whistled when he spoke, and Willy tried not to obviously withdraw from his stench. As soon as the words were out of the man's mouth, though, the man began to beg Willy to forget what he'd heard, then shifted to a tactic of pretending it was all just a joke and that he'd had Willy going good, then shifted again to hissing at Willy that if he ever repeated what he'd heard he'd regret it. Willy's only reaction to this was to stare at the little man until he dropped his watery eyes and retreated, muttering to himself.

So Sletto had, in effect, disappeared. The Sheriff did what little he could to enlist the aid of local law enforcement, but many of them were aware of Sletto, too, and seemed to be equally powerless, or, in some cases, disinterested. Willy was amazed that the troll-like creature was so wily.

He tried to settle back into his routine, but found it difficult. He, Mae, and Mollie worked New Year's Eve at the bar, and Mae dropped the boys off at Emilio and Solveig's on the pretense that it would be fun for all the kids, but with the understanding that their snug little cabin on the south side of the island was actually more of a safehouse. Willy had a strong feeling that Sletto would show up that night for a cataclysmic showdown which would wreak maximum havoc, and, in spite of his preparations and readiness, was on edge and somber all night, dodging questions from his concerned regulars. Mae and Mollie seemed more at ease, perhaps because they felt that he was in charge of their safety, and Mae played the piano while Mollie laughed and joked with the customers. They kept the bar open almost until dawn, though, as the year changed to 1941, and there were no incidents more unusual than a few broken glasses, a broken barstool, a scuffle between drunken patrons, and Barnacle Brad using a lighter to set fire to the end of his beard, which smelled awful and prompted Willy to tell him to knock it off. As they closed the bar, the last to leave were the Hansen brothers, who were more aware than many others of the situation with Sletto and had deputized themselves to Willy for further backup, going so far as to drink only moderately that evening and to lay off the smoking of weed altogether. Willy thanked them for their loyalty and locked the front door behind them. Only when all the doors were locked and he sat at the bar with his wife and Mollie did he feel a sense of anticlimax, along with a heavy fatigue. They drove home to the bungalow as the sky began to pinken in the east. He woke up briefly when he heard the boys get dropped off by Emilio, then slept until two o'clock

The next few weeks passed uneasily for the adults. The boys went back to school cheerfully and were right back into the routine of homework and play, and the patterns of their lives reestablished themselves, tinged, mostly for Willy, with the ominousness of unfinished business. He felt that there was more that he should do, and twice went back to Sletto's gloomy homestead hoping to finish things himself, but there was no evidence to indicate that he himself was not the last person there. Mae tried to tell him that Sletto had finally realized who he was dealing with and had lit out for good, but Willy didn't feel it to be true, as much as he wanted to.

Mae stopped in for coffee one afternoon in mid-January and was talking to Willy at the bar when Mollie approached them with an air of unusual diffidence. She stood before them, inspecting her nubby fingernails and only glancing at them for a moment.

"What is it, sweetie?" Mae asked, and Mollie, aware that some of the few customers at the bar were listening, nodded at one of the tables. They sat down and drew in their chairs.

"Well," Mollie said, clearing her throat, "I don't know how to say this, seeing as you all are like my family, but I'm just sayin' it anyway. It's time for me to move on." Mae seemed surprised and concerned and leaned closer over the table, laying her hand on Mollie's wrist, but Willy had known it was going to happen ever since he'd seen the letters in her hand.

"You're going to go to Greysport, then?" he asked. She looked at the table and nodded.

"Well, what're you going to do for money?" Mae asked "What about a job and a place to live?"

Mollie leaned back in her chair and withdrew from her front pocket a fat round roll of bills with a rubberband around it. "I've been savin'," she said, "and I don't spend much. My aunt who lives there wants me to stay with her, and she's got a job for me at the bakery where she works." She shrugged. "Guess I'd like to try it."

"Oh, honey, you're sure?" Mae said, her eyebrows drawn together.

"Yeah, I guess so. You all have your hands full around here."

"We'll have our hands more full after you leave!" Willy laughed, trying to lighten things. "I hesitated hiring you, now I don't know what we'll do without you. You're part of the family!"

Mae had tears in her eyes, and seeing this, Mollie teared up, too, taking Mae's hands in hers. "Well, jeez, I'll be back," Mollie said, "I'll be back soon as...well, soon, anyway. Jeez!"

In spite of himself, Willy felt a lump in his throat, which he cleared harshly and said, "Guess I won't have to give you that raise, now. That's a relief."

Mollie laughed. "Raise, huh? I sure as hell deserve one, coverin' for you when you go huntin' all the time with Mr. Benitez." She looked at Mae. "Guess I shouldn't have let that one slip."

"It's nothing I'm unaware of," Mae said, with a cold look at her husband that made the others laugh.

For two weeks, they tried to talk her out of leaving, but with waning conviction. Willy knew that she would be safe far away, especially in a huge city like Greysport. He also knew that, with her gone, his family would be safer, and the recurring images that haunted the sleepless stretches of the night, the horrible things that his imagination showed him happening to his wife and boys, would be gone.

Gordon and Chief were wounded at first by the news of her leaving, but she smoothed it over with them with time and affection and her promises to return. It was unusual for the boys to cry, but they did when they were first told, and Willy watched them, knowing that they were learning an early lesson of loss. They gradually accepted the idea, and began planning a going-away party for Mollie.

Her last day working at the bar was a good one, and the regulars, who had come to love her, tipped her well and gave her little gifts as a send-off, comic books and photographs and even some scented bath soap from the Hansen brothers. At home, the boys had baked a cake under Mae's supervision, and although it was lopsided and unevenly frosted, Mollie was moved. Conspiring with Mae, they had gotten her a locket with their pictures in it, and when Mollie opened it, she gasped and clutched it between her large breasts. She pursed her lips, her eyes shining, and shoved the boys, each in turn, on the shoulder, saying, "You guys! Jeez!"

Mae gave her a copy of *Gone with the Wind* to read on the train. Willy took her aside and gave her a roll of bills, holding up his hand when she tried to voice her appreciation, and a letter in an envelope. When she went to open the envelope, he tried to stop her, but she opened it anyway, giving him a look of sassy defiance.

There was only one sheet of paper inside. Upon it was printed, in Willy's neat block capitals, "DO NOT FORGET. THIS IS WHERE YOUR HOME IS:" then gave the address of their bungalow and their phone number, followed by, "WE LOVE YOU."

Mollie pressed it to her chest, then threw her arms around him.

When they had stalled as long as they could, they got into the car and headed out of town to the bridge, crossing over to the east side of the river to make the drive north to Black Marsh, the large town on the river that was a nexus of rail and river transportation. They were all dressed nicely, the boys wearing clip-on bowties, Mollie wearing her Christmas gifts of the red sweater and grey plaid skirt under her practical warm coat, and even Willy wearing a loud tie over his workshirt. They were quite early, so they drove around for awhile looking at the large town, Mae and Willy pointing out what historical tidbits were visible and telling stories about the town, which had started as a French trading post when the first Europeans had come to the area. This soon wore thin, so they headed for the station. They parked in front and walked in with Mollie, buying her ticket at the window and going to the correct track, the boys carrying her sparse luggage. They were still early, and there was a forty-five minute wait until the train came, so Mae and Willy and Mollie sat on a long wooden bench while the boys explored. They made small talk and looked around the station, watching people and commenting on them as they walked by.

The boys came back after awhile, looking dejected, and Willy knew that it had dawned on them again that Mollie was leaving. They sat next to her on the bench and hugged her, and Chief began to cry, which seemed all the more piteous as he was never one to cry much in the first place. Mollie hugged him to her and said over his head in a whisper, "Why don't you just go. I'll be fine."

Chief began to cry harder, clinging to Mollie, and Mae nodded and took him away from her. Gordon stoically hugged her and Willy stood and put his hand on her head, saying, "You drop a line as soon as you're settled."

"You bet," Mollie said, smiling. Mae, with Chief held to her, bent over and kissed Mollie on the forehead. "Come back anytime you want. You always have a home."

"I know," Mollie said, closing her eyes and nodding.

The family moved away from her, leaving her sitting alone on the long wooden bench, and she waved at them when they went out the door and onto the street.

They drove south along the river, the huge bluffs towering along the left side of the car and the expanse of the river to the right, most of it frozen and covered with snow, ice fishing shanties here and there in the white space, away from the black patches of open water due to the current and downriver from locks and dams. The boys stared disconsolately out the windows, and Willy thought that he should take them ice fishing when they got back, in order to get their minds off Mollie's departure. Thinking along those lines, he said, looking in the rearview mirror, "Hey, fellas. When we get back, why don't we write a big fat letter to Mollie. You could put in some funny pictures and stuff. How about that?"

"Okay," the boys chorused glumly.

"Did you get her aunt's address in Greysport?" Mae asked.

Willy looked at the river for a moment and said, "No. Didn't you?"

"No. I thought you would."

"Shit." He thought for a moment, then raised his voice and said, "Hey, boys, did Mollie give you her new address?"

When they said no, he shook his head. "That was stupid."

"Maybe she left it somewhere at home. Otherwise, we'd better hope she's a good letter-writer."

When they got in the door, Willy and Mae looked around and couldn't find anything with an address written on it. "I can't believe we were so stupid," Willy said.

"She'll write. She might even call when she gets there. I told her to reverse the charges, but she seemed a little hesitant."

"Well, shit," Willy said. The boys were still glum, but he managed to get them to smile with the time-honored pull-my-finger trick, and then ushered them outside to get some fresh air.

Life slowly returned to normal. The boys went to school and did their homework at night. One of them set a small fire in the garage which Mae put out before it could spread, fortunately, and neither brother would say who was responsible, so they were both grounded. Willy and Mae went through some sort of mid-winter, boredom-induced horniness and were at each other constantly, to their mutual amusement. Willy played hooky occasionally with Emilio and went ice fishing in their snugly constructed shanty on the river, and one sunny Saturday, they bundled up their families and had a little party out there, grilling steaks and drinking beer on the snow-covered ice, having a big bonfire (the ice too thick to melt through) and hot chocolate, hot dogs, and marshmallows on sticks for the kids, the boys and girls chasing each other around on the ice. They missed Mollie and were beginning to get irritated by her not writing, but carried on the way they always had, with Mae and Solveig talking and laughing together while Willy and Emilio either smoked cigars together in companionable silence or talked intensely about some point of immediate interest.

The pall of danger which had existed over the winter seemed to diminish, leaving only a durable trace, and Willy shrugged it off and continued business with the bar. He hired a local girl to fill in the position which Mollie had made for herself, and she did fine, although he could tell that she would never become close in their lives. He booked bands for Friday and Saturday nights after the dinner rush, getting blues acts (something he had become increasingly enthusiastic about) and the occasional bluegrass group, which he paid less. On Wednesday nights, he encouraged a gathering of local Scottish and Irish musicians for a Celtic music night, which gained momentum until one night there were fifteen musicians playing everything from Uileann pipes and tin whistles to fiddles, banjoes and drums, and the house was packed and loud while drinkers danced jigs and reels. He danced with his wife, who threw back her head and laughed loudly, lost in her joy, so beautiful it broke his heart.

He took the boys up onto some nearby bluffs for a Willy-style picnic one Saturday, making a large fire and cooking chili in a cast iron pot with the panorama of the riverland spread out below them. The day was sunny and the snow fresh, and he built the fire in the lee of some evergreens, so when the boys came back puffing and red-cheeked from running in the woods, he ladled up bowls of steaming chili and they dug in with gusto. The next day, he and Mae rounded up the boys and drove to Black Marsh to watch a double feature at the movie theater. During the Movietone newsreel, Willy wondered what it would take to push the country over the line and enter the war in Europe. Countries, like people, could engage in conflict for the most ridiculous reasons, and yet hide away from the truth when it was obvious that action was necessary. As much as he still shied away from memories of the last war, he knew that the country would be in this one, and that it was necessary; the chaos was necessary, the misery was necessary, the death was necessary. It was a situation where pacifism was worse than useless. Humans would not change, at least not soon enough to notice. He thought of Emilio saying, "The only thing life guarantees us is misery," and he knew that Emilio was right. How would he talk to the boys about this? Wouldn't he say the same things to them that his own father had said to him, and that Willy had scoffed at? He thought about this throughout the movie, and afterwards had to force on a face of joviality when they went out to dinner.

Business at the Palmer's hotel had gotten threadbare enough that Mr. Palmer finally had to let the pianist, Frederick Ferrier, go. Mae, knowing that Ferrier's employment had caused the decisions in her life that had led her to Willy and the boys and a life she loved, nonetheless harbored a grudge against her father- who had never apologized for his position- and said that she wouldn't play at the hotel until he was dead. Ferrier picked up and left without ado, taking the train to Greysport, pronouncing that he had been sick of this little hicktown for longer than he could remember, and that it would be nice to be ensconced in culture for a change.

They still hadn't heard from Mollie and were all, including the boys, dividing their emotions between annoyance and worry. The boys had compiled a large packet of notes and drawings and were waiting for an address to send it to, getting grumpy over the fact that they had nothing to do with the product of their labor. "She'd better write, and pronto," Gordon said.

"She's probably already got a boyfriend," Chief said wistfully.

"I'm sure she's just settling in," Mae reassured them. "It's a great big city and Mollie's aunt is probably showing her all over. They have museums and movie theaters and all kinds of stores. People from all over the world. There's probably too much for her to do every day. But she'll write, just you wait."

The Sheriff began to seem distracted and despondent for reasons he left unexplained. Willy tried to get it out of him when he came into the bar with his dog Coach and sat hunched over a whiskey, staring into the glass, his face creased and baggy with care, looking not terribly unlike his dog, who lay flopped bonelessly at his feet.

"What is it, your love life?" Willy joked.

The Sheriff huffed a bitter laugh. "Yeah, the ol' *amore*." He looked Willy in the eye for a second and dropped his gaze back to his glass, which he tipped up and finished.

"Career not going the way you'd like it to?" Willy tried again, smiling and filling up the Sheriff's glass.

"Thanks. I just have some things on my mind. I'll work it out."

Willy wiped down the bar, knowing when to leave things alone, and went down the bar to where Runty Schommer and Bob Two Bears, on their day off, sat playing cribbage. He later felt badly about it.

He knew that something had gone terribly wrong when, one morning in early March, he was home in the kitchen drinking coffee and reading the paper when the doorbell rang, and, going through the living room to answer the door, he saw on the curtains over the window the shadows of state troopers' hats. He almost always knew who would be at his door; people usually called ahead, and he rarely had unannounced visitors. The silhouettes of the broadbrimmed hats smacked of officialdom, and he suddenly felt vaguely nauseated. He opened the door, and there stood the Sheriff with two state troopers. Both troopers had their hats on exactly horizontally, had identical thin moustaches, gleamingly polished Sam Browne belts, jodhpurs, kneeboots, and revolvers. One had a clipboard, over which he held a pencil as if ready to start writing. Willy had seen state troopers on the island perhaps a dozen times in all the years since he had first come to it, and he knew that their presence at his door betokened nothing good.

"Hey, Marvin," Willy said, slipping and calling the Sheriff by his downplayed first name.

"Mornin', Willy. These fellas want a word with you."

"Are you William McGregor?" the one with the clipboard said.

"Yeah," Willy said, sensing from the trooper's tone that he wasn't about to be arrested. "Yes, I am. Why don't you come inside. It's cold out there." Willy looked at the Sheriff to try to divine some information, but his friend dropped his eyes an instant after Willy saw how red and teary they were.

He offered coffee all around and had the three seated at the kitchen table, the one with the clipboard cleared his throat and said, "As to our business, Sheriff Purdue here told us you could help us." He opened a manila envelope he had held underneath the clipboard a piece of paper that had a folded, worn quality to it. The trooper placed it on the table and moved it around so Willy could see it.

"Is this your handwriting?"

It was. In his capitals, the letters blurred as if by water, the note said, "DON'T FORGET. THIS IS WHERE YOUR HOME IS:" Their address and phone number were written there, followed by "WE LOVE YOU." It was the note he had given to Mollie the day they had left her at the train station.

"I'm sorry, Willy," the Sheriff said.

"Why do you have this?" Willy asked, feeling sick.

"It's your handwriting?" the Trooper asked.

"Well, yeah, it's..."

"It was in the coat pocket on a body found in the river south of Black Marsh. We believe it to be the body of a Mollie Sletto. We understand that she lived here with you, and that she had been in your employ."

"Yes."

"We're going to need you to come with us up to Black Marsh to the coroner's office to identify the body."

Willy sat looking at the piece of paper. "I have to leave a note for my wife," he said numbly. "She's out shopping."

The drive to Black Marsh was spent in silence. He sat in the Sheriff's cruiser, following the troopers along the river highway. Every once in awhile the Sheriff started to cry, but seemed, with an effort, to stuff it back into himself. Willy retreated into the burnt-out area of his psyche which had seen all horror and to which nothing was new. It roared like flame in there. He knew that the boys didn't have such a place and he wondered how he would explain things to them. He thought about his hard-headed, graceful wife, and knew that, tough as she was, this would be new for her, too.

The county courthouse in Black Marsh was the main headquarters for the Sheriff's Department, also housing the county jail, a branch of the state troopers, and the municipal offices for the county. It was a heavy granite building like a thousand others serving identical purposes, and it smelled like granite when Willy walked into its echoing halls. He followed the troopers down a reverberant stairwell to the coroner's office, where he was first put to the task of identifying personal effects. On two tables in a stark, windowless room were spread things that were familiar to him, but took a moment for him to recognize them, so out of context were they. On one table lay the red sweater Mollie had worn when they had left her at the train station, and the black and grey plaid skirt. There lay the locket the boys had given her, and there lay the large, scarlet bra. The clothing was laid out neatly, but rumpled, muddy and damp.

On the other table were her bags, the clothing within sodden, a bloated copy of *Gone with the Wind* in front of them. Laid out and catalogued were other things a young woman would have in her bags.

A sudden thought occurred to Willy and he said, "Did you find any letters? There should have been a packet of letters from her aunt in Greysport." The two troopers looked at each other and the one without the clipboard left the room.

"There are no panties among the clothes," Willy said.

The trooper looked at Willy for a moment and dropped his eyes to his clipboard. "That's all in our report."

The other trooper came back in with a manila envelope just like the one they had produced in the kitchen at home. He handed it to Willy, who opened it up and looked at the contents. Envelopes were on top, and letters, dried and wrinkled, were underneath. The envelopes were addressed in Mollie's handwriting. To herself. They were the envelopes he'd seen her holding in the living room that morning, but hadn't seen closely enough.

Willy began to read one of the letters, also in Mollie's handwriting.

Dear Mollie, one letter began, *please come to live with me in Greysport. It is a beutiful place and a big city, and there are many men like Willy here who are strong and smart and will pretect you. You can be like Mae here and play the piana. And have fine boys like the too you wrot me about. There arnt no peeple like yor dad here, curse his name. You are who you are like Mae and Willy said and arnt no part of him....*

Willy almost dropped the folder, but clutched it, slapping it shut. "There were no other letters?"

"Just those," the trooper said.

Willy stared at the red sweater and the red bra.

"We need you to identify the deceased, Mr. McGregor," the trooper said.

Willy nodded and followed them to the morgue.

Mollie's feet stuck out from under the white sheet which covered her on the metal morgue cart. Her toes and feet were a bloodless green-tinged yellow, like raw chicken flesh. Her toenails were painted candy-apple red, and Willy knew that Chief had helped her paint them. The coroner, dressed in white scrubs, pulled back the white sheet from Mollie's face. Her hair was wet and seemed to be combed back, as if she had just taken a bath, but her cheeks were not rosy. They were the sallow yellow of her feet, and blotchy black and purple bruises stood out by one eye and on her chin. The sheet had been drawn down far enough to reveal the very top on an incision on her abdomen, between her breasts, and there were dark bruise marks around her neck that were obviously made by very large hands.

Willy forced himself to stand up straight, feeling very old. "That's our Mollie," he said.

The cause of death had been strangulation, not drowning, and she had been raped. She had been weighted and thrown into the river, after the perpetrator had "ventilated" the abdomen to assist in the sinking of the body. Two fishermen had found her just downriver from a bridge, and her body had been fairly well preserved by the cold water. The only lead they had was that a janitor at the train station had seen a scuffle between a young woman matching Mollie's description and a very large, dirty man with long hair and a beard whose face appeared to bear burn scars.

"We'll be looking to question a Bud Sletto," the trooper with the clipboard said.

Willy stared at him for a moment and walked away.

Willy and Mae paid for the funeral when the coroner released Mollie's body. Having no idea about Mollie's religious background or beliefs, if any, they got a Unitarian minister to perform the ceremony. The day was flukishly warm, the kind that can happen in that country and yet be followed by snow, but felt and smelled that day like the coming of spring. It had rained in the morning, the first thunderstorm of the year, but had cleared up and stayed breezy, giving people the sense that they could smell the outdoors again after the sterility of the winter.

"It smells all wormy out," Chief said on the way to the car after the visitation at the funeral home. He was dressed in black, as they all were, and was pale with circles under his eyes. Gordon went to punch him in the arm for saying such a thing, but unclenched his fist and put his arm around his brother's shoulder instead.

"Guess I shouldn't say stuff like that," Chief said.

"Doesn't matter," Gordon said.

Willy watched Mae watching the boys. It seemed like she was struggling with restraining herself from rushing forward and taking her sons in her arms and hugging them and kissing them, as she had been for days since Willy had come home and told them what had happened. The look in her eyes was one of such intense love and great fear that he knew she could barely contain it. Her boys were alive, though; their hearts were broken for the first time in their lives, but they would mend. As he watched her, she turned and looked at him, as if to say, They *will* mend, won't they?

He put his arm around her and walked her to the car, opening the door and holding it for her as she got in. They would heal, he thought; the human heart is mostly made to heal.

Mae had sat down hard when he first told her what had happened, then asked him to repeat the story three times. Although he was diplomatic, leaving out the details from the morgue, he kept nothing from her. Her horror and her pity were so deep, and her love for the lost girl so evident, that he knew there was nothing to do to help his wife, only sit across from her at the kitchen table holding her hands while the truth of it pervaded her.

He didn't lie outright to the boys, but sanitized the information enough that it was nearly a lie. He would tell them everything one day, but now it seemed enough to let them deal with this one truth of life and let them deal with it purely. Gordon had kept saying, "What? What?" over and over again, and Willy had simply kept repeating himself, patiently and kindly. Chief had at first treated it like Willy was playing some kind of twisted joke, then became enraged when he wouldn't stop. He threw a violent tantrum and finally had to be restrained on the couch, Willy with his arms around the boy and Gordon, with some difficulty, holding onto his kicking legs. When he finally settled down, he had stared off into space for awhile and begun to cry. The first night he had come into their bedroom, saying in a very small boy's voice, "Where's Mollie?" They had gently put him back to bed, and Mae sat with him until he cried himself into exhaustion.

They'd had a closed casket for the funeral; Mae had felt sure that Mollie wouldn't like the idea of people staring at her in such a helpless state. They were surprised by the turnout; it seemed that most of the people of the town were there. It was stuffy in the funeral home, and Willy didn't pay attention to the service, registering only that it seemed banal and generalized, as though the minister had on hand a generic service he used for those who died young. Emilio stood beside him and Solveig stood with Mae, the children in front of them, Marita and Katita standing with Gordon and Chief, and little Gabriella in front of them all, fidgeting out of boredom until Marita gave her a look which made her stop.

There was an entourage of cars to the Coeur de la Riviere cemetery, and Willy got there first, followed by a long line of cars which parked outside of the cemetery's gates on the gravel road. The cemetery was up on a medium sized bluff looking east over the river, and where the snow had melted, surprisingly green grass was exposed among the tombstones and black, leafless oaks. It was said that one of the first French traders was buried here, his tombstone long decayed or covered by leaves and grass, and it seemed to Willy like a good place, overlooking the flow of the black river and the breaking ice, the waters moving down as they had ever done to join the waters of the world.

Higher bluffs stood to the north and west of the cemetery, the woods there dark with trees and emitting a slow fog from the bones of snow into the balmy air. People assembled at the gravesite where the white coffin had been placed on a bier covered with emerald green satin. The people, in black, stood among the tombstones as still as the tombstones themselves. Two oblivious children were chasing each other among the legs of the adults but were quickly stopped.

Dr. Ambrose and his wife stood amidst the crowd, next to them were Dr Homburg the veterinarian and two of the young women from the Thanksgiving feast. Regulars from the bar stood in a large, clannish group: the Hansen brothers and their wives, Barnacle Brad and his wife, known for her saintly patience, Patty. Runty Schommer stood with his boys, and Bob Two Bears with his family. Pete Leahy and Larry Cornwall and his son Dennis- whom Willy and Emilio had rescued in the blizzard on the river years ago- stood somberly among the crowd after nodding at Willy when they approached. Back behind the crowd, as though hiding himself among the tombstones, stood the Sheriff, looking as is he had aged fifteen years. He looked at Willy and dropped his eyes, and when the final service began, fought with his emotions and lost, finally sobbing openly, his head bent, as the Unitarian minister droned on.

Willy stood with his arm around Mae, the boys pressed against the front of them as if to keep warm from the fog that issued from the old woods. Gigantic clouds slid by quickly overhead, their shadows moving over the landscape and the people in the cemetery. The white coffin on the bier shone in the moments of sunlight.

Willy thought of Bud Sletto, and it occurred to him that, as devious and capable as he had turned out to be, he could be somewhere in the woods or up on one of the higher bluffs, looking down on the funeral of his daughter, his victim. The thought made his skin crawl, and he stared around into the trees, thinking that, if Sletto were there and could see him, he would know that Willy knew, and that Willy was watching.

The service ended and Willy invited people back to the bar for sandwiches and drinks. They drove slowly down the hill and into the town, the sun out and meltwater running down the cobbled streets as people parked their cars and filed, dark as crows, into the dim bar. Willy noticed that the Sheriff was the last to leave the cemetery, staying behind, standing and looking at the coffin. He showed up half and hour later at the bar, looking calmer and somehow resolved.

It was a somber gathering at the bar, and people watched Willy warily, as if waiting for something explosive and inevitable. He did, indeed, find himself staring off into space with a whiskey in his hand as Emilio and others talked around him. Mae sat at the piano and began to play, working her way into tunes that people could sing along with. Once they got started, people sang with brio, their arms around each other, a loud and increasingly boozy catharsis.

At the peak of this, Willy slipped out the back door and went around to the car, bringing a bottle of whiskey with him. He drove back up to the cemetery, where the gravediggers had finished filling in the grave and were tamping down the loose soil. He gave them the bottle in thanks, and one of them opened it and passed it around. Willy drank deeply from it, as the gravedigger who had opened it said, "This is a terrible thing."

Willy nodded.

"A thing like this can't go unanswered," the gravedigger said.

Willy shook his head. They watched him as if he were about to say something memorable, but they were disappointed.

"Keep the bottle," Willy said finally. "I brought it for you. And come on down and have a sandwich at the bar."

The men thanked him, gathered up their tools, and left the cemetery. The sun had gone behind the bluffs and it was getting cold. Willy stared at the grave. After a time, he said, "We will remember you, and we will see that you have peace."

He stood awhile longer and said, "Also, I wrote you a poem. I thought I'd read it."

He pulled from his pocket the bar napkin upon which he had written his latest poem, one which had seized his mind at the bar one night and which he had had to write down immediately, fearing it would evanesce, telling people who talked at him to shut up while he wrote. He cleared his throat and read:

Cover that cold sacrificial stone
With dust and dirt and grass
And grass again and soil my friend
And then be oaks at last
And when the oaks fall down
And then the new oaks grow at last
Then soil be deep upon the stone
And peace be there at last

And peace be there at last, my friend
And peace be there at last
Lay down with stone
The weary bones
And peace be there at last.

He folded the rumpled napkin and put it back into his pocket. "You rest easy now, honey," he said. He left and went back to the bar. It didn't seem that anyone had noticed his absence.

That night he had an evil dream. Mollie was under the river at night, cold and alone, and the black water rushed overhead. Please, oh please don't leave me here, she wept. Please don't leave me here. Willy forced himself up into wakefulness as if he'd been beneath the water himself. We went into the kitchen and read a book until the mists of the image had left his head. He finally went to bed just before dawn.

It got cold again for a bit, and parts of the river that had been open refroze. There was a wet snowfall, the time for powder behind them, and Emilio and Willy had the notion of getting in one more morning of ice fishing before having to take the shanty off of the ice for the season. They stopped at the bar for some ham and eggs and coffee before heading out on the ice, and as Willy opened the door, he kicked an envelope that had been slipped through the mail slot. Willy's name was written on the envelope in a large and sloppy hand. Willy and Emilio glanced at each other, puzzled, and opened the envelope, sitting at the bar to read the letter within.

Dear Willy,

I have left town. There is a note explaining my actions at the office, but this one is the real truth as I thought I owed it to you being my best friend. Emilio might be with you and tell him to as he is a good man and I know had kept many a secret. It is a given you will tell your lovely Mae who is noble and fine and trustworthy. Please keep this under your hat otherwise though buddy.

My whole life is a lie and because of it Mollie has paid. I didn't have any more business being Sheriff than the Man in the Moon and now look what happened. How did I ever get such a job in the first place? I bragged and I lied that's the long and the short of it. I lied about damn near everything and now I'm caught out.

And you might as well know now that I'm confessing to you that I lied about something else and it is this: I am a man who loves men, a homosexual as they say. I have had an association with Frederick Ferrier at your in-laws hotel. I have loved him. He is elusive and has at turns broken my heart and made me the happiest man in the world. He is a delicate creature and beautiful. When he moved I knew that was it for me.

They are also closing down the MacDougal office of the Sheriff's Department for budget reasons and some "reorganization" bullshit, but that is another thing. Central office in Black Marsh now, so you can do what you want. That is a joke because you always do what you want and are more of a Sheriff than me anyway. Hahahaha.

In some places it is not wrong for a man to love another man. Why is it wrong here? I learned it when I was a boy (and never felt one way or another about girls) and I never thought it was wrong just hushhush until Christmas night and what Bud Sletto almost did and you saved me. I thought if I am like Sletto I am rotten through and through. And with Mollie- that dear girl- and everything else is just more than I could bear.

I am not rotten through and through. I am just an imperfect man who loves who he loves and never should have been a damn Sheriff. I am going to find Frederick and whatever courage I can. Maybe I can hold my head up in Greysport, because I sure can't here.

I am going now. My hand hurts from writing this whole thing. I was thinking of going out to your ice shanty and blowing a hole in my head, but I thought that would be chickenshit. I've been chickenshit enough for one life. Besides, now my hand is too tired! Hah hah!!! How do you write poetry? You should share that more. You act ashamed. Do not be. I am going to try not to be ashamed myself.

Your Friend
Marvin Purdue, formerly THE SHERIFF!!!!

No one in the town seemed to feel any less safe with the Sheriff gone. His absence made it all the more obvious that the one they depended on for their safety, their enforcer, was actually Willy. Someone said this to Willy and he got quite angry, actually flying off the handle. "It's not my responsibility!" he ranted from behind the bar. "It's *all* of our responsibilities to look out for each other! If a big guy is pushing around a little guy in here, or anywhere else for that matter, we should *all* get up off our asses and *do* something about it!"

People nodded their heads and agreed with that, but knew that there was the unfinished Sletto business, and, however much they blustered and talked big, they also knew that Willy would end it.

The rest of March and early April were mostly dreary and rainy, and on days when the boys were home and the bar was slow he read to them in the living room. They enjoyed most stories of heroism, tales of King Arthur, Rob Roy, Robinson Crusoe, and anything about pirates. Their very favorite was a children's version of Beowulf, which Willy read to them again and again. As they became accustomed to their grief over Mollie, some of their boisterousness reappeared, but they were generally more solemn than they had ever been before. Willy worried that they would be changed forever, but Mae reassured him that they were hardy and adaptable and while they would never forget Mollie, they would eventually bounce back.

May came in beautiful and welcome after such a sad winter, and the boys were soon banging in and out of the screen doors, and were back to climbing the bluffs and playing in the woods and down by the river. Willy and Emilio took them out fishing on the river. While fishing one sunny day when the water was vast beneath them, the bluffs on either bank of the river small with distance, and the clouds colossal overhead, Gordon grew quiet and pensive, looking upriver towards Black Marsh. Willy knew he was thinking about Mollie, but said nothing, waiting the boy out.

Gordon finally said, "Dad, what happens when you die?"

Chief's head snapped around, all his attention on his father. Emilio stopped reeling and listened.

Willy cast out his line and said, "Well, there's a lot of conjecture on that subject. People have whole different beliefs about it, religions and whatnot, and often use the difference in their beliefs as one reason to fight each other."

"That's no answer," Gordon said.

"Nope," Willy said. "No, it isn't. You want to know what I personally believe? I personally believe that all evidence points to the fact that, once you're dead, you don't have to suffer anymore. You don't feel anything any more than you did before you were born. From all empirical evidence we can see, the body ceases to function, the forces of decay take over, and the body returns the earth until it is used as nutrients and is involved in the cycle of life once again."

"No heaven or hell?" Chief asked.

"Nope. Those ideas are just to scare people into behaving themselves, like scary stories for little kids about the boogie man or something. Most religions have them to keep simple people in line. We try to do the right thing because we want to leave the world a better place than we found it, and have minds enough to imagine what it would be like if everybody acted that way. We try to do our best and give the best of ourselves because we are rational beings."

Gordon wasn't satisfied. "Yeah, but doesn't anything happen after you're dead?"

Emilio laughed. It was a conversation that he and Willy had had many times over the years.

Willy said, "Well, you'll have to ask your old Uncle Emilio about that one."

Emilio said, "I thin that it is arrogant to believe that we humans can understand all of reality, all of what really happens in the Universe. The more we learn, the more we find out we don't know. I cannot remember the name of the philosopher who said, 'What we know is tiny, what we do not know is immense'. It would be like an ant trying to understand an internal combustion engine. Even though it is beyond the ant's ability to comprehen, it does not mean that the engine cannot exist. The ant could be on top of the engine when it starts and feel the effects of its heat and vibration, all while being unable to understand them. I have no doubt that there is much, much more going on in the Universe than we will ever understand, but part of our job is to keep on trying to understand more of it. For example, at one time we did not even know that bacteria existed, but through the curiosity of many smart people, we now know much more and have more control over what happens to us. Like when you had polio, Chief. Someday it will be a fact that no one will get sick from polio anymore, because smart people have decided to do something more courageous than to say, 'It is God's will.' "

"So we never have to take some stories that somebody made up as any kind of final answer," Willy said.

The boys thought about this for awhile. Finally Chief said, "So, what happened to Mollie? Her spirit or whatever?"

"Well, she's at least at peace," Willy said.

"And who knows what else is possible," Emilio added. "I think it is nothing that anyone has ever imagined."

"It's the Big Mystery," Willy said. "We'll all find out someday, so don't worry about it. The one thing we are sure of is that we are alive and that we have days like this, and that we're going to make them last."

Mollie had taken on a life of her own in Willy's dreams. He had the dream about her being under the black water again, weeping and alone, and it woke him up and left him afraid to go back to sleep. He sat in the kitchen with all the lights on, reading nothing more serious than the funny pages. Mae got up at one point to go to the bathroom, and came blinking and bleary into the light of the kitchen.

"Are you okay?" she asked, putting her arms around him from behind, kissing and smelling his hair.

"Yeah. I just...can't sleep."

"Really?

He wanted to tell her but didn't want to disturb her. "Yeah," he said.

"Okay. Well, come back to bed soon. I miss you."

After an hour he did. He slept for awhile and had a dream that he was in a swamp somewhere off the main flow of the river. It was late fall or early spring because the landscape was brown and tan and black, foggy and wet, and stands of leafless trees stood dim in the mists between sluggish backwaters of the river. He heard the sound of weeping coming from back among the trees and the sound of it made him feel a deep sorrow. He followed the sound and went back among the trees, and there, in a clearing, sat Mollie on a large, mossy, rotting log. Her limbs were covered with mud and her head bent and she was weeping.

"Mollie," he said. "It's okay now. It's okay. I'm here."

"Can you please take me home?" she said softly.

"Yes! I'll take you home! We'll get you washed up and you can sit by the fire."

"Take me home. Take me home!" Mollie cried.

He looked around in the swamp for a way out, but suddenly had a horrible and heavy realization that he had no home, that there was nothing there, that there was only this trackless swamp to the ends of the world. The realization crushed him and he began to panic. He stood frozen in the swamp and Mollie raised her head to look at him, pointing her gaze directly at him, but her eyes were closed and looked as if they had been blackened by charcoal.

"Have I been bad again, Daddy? Don't leave me out here all alone."

He forced himself awake and didn't go to sleep again that night.

After a few warm days, the trees burst forth dense with leaves and there were flowers everywhere. They left the windows open for the first time of the year at night, but for the first time ever, Willy left the doors closed and locked. He grew tired and anxious but was unable to talk about it. One morning he got up and had a light breakfast, waited for Mae to leave on errands, and got his shotgun out of the basement. He cleaned and oiled it, and loaded it with shells. It felt good to put the shells into the gun, good to be doing something. He put on brown pants and a green shirt and a tan hunting vest with more shells in its loops. After finishing another cup off coffee, he took the gun out to his truck and put it on the seat, started the truck and drove through town. He saw people he knew and waved, and was soon out of town and on the bridge to the west side of the river.

He crossed the river and drove again up into the coulees, now leafing out in pale green, the road seeming like a tunnel or grotto as it wound through the hills and bluffs on either side. The dented and rusty mailbox hung on its bullethole on the stick, and Willy passed the drive and parked the truck around a curve in the road.

He got out and checked his shotgun once more, then started out through the burgeoning undergrowth. He walked silently and slowly, blending in to the leaves and trees, shotgun ready. He flicked into the mode of predatory concentration, his senses almost roaring, mindful of the cunning of his target, of the traps he might have set, that he himself was a target as well.

In spite of his concentration, glimpses of possibility showed themselves in his mind. Sletto waiting behind a tree with an ax and watching, Sletto having set a bear trap, Sletto catching him alive. He slipped through the tessellated patterns of growing leaves and sunlight and limbs of brush, and forced himself to visualize Sletto sitting among the ruins of his homestead, disconsolate and drunk, oblivious to Willy's approach until he looked up, squinting in the sunlight, to see Willy standing before him with the shotgun aimed at his face. Willy wouldn't say a word, just fire. Maybe some of his hogs were loose and feral in the woods, ready to make a meal of him.

Willy finally walked into the clearing on top of the hill looking up at the bald knob where the house had stood. Wind moved the new green grass that sprouted in the blackened ruins of the house. He approached and saw the bones of pigs in the new grass and the pig's head still on the stake, but now it was picked and almost clean, the bone yellow and white. The body of the burned pig lay near the house, its scorched hide cured like leather.

There was no evidence that anyone had been there in some time. Willy stood there for awhile looking at the blackened knob, sniffing the sodden ashes on the spring breeze, then turned and went back to the truck.

Two weeks later, the annual carnival came to MacDougal. It was the usual cheap affair that sprouted up in small towns, but was so much more convenient than the county fair and represented such a transformation of the placid town that its citizens were jubilant.

Willy stood in front of the bar with Bob Two Bears on that Friday afternoon, watching down the length of the street to the park by the boathouse where the fair was being set up. The rides and other amusements they could see from their vantage point included a rusty-looking Ferriswheel, a tilt-a-whirl, a cheesy little roller coaster for children, a semitrailer set up as a portable freak show, another one claiming to house the frozen remains of a Neanderthal man in a block of ice. There were also the various other predictable booths with whack-a mole, ring toss, crooked air-rifle games and the lot.

They watched the goings-on for awhile, the increased activity on the streets, strangers here and there, a feeling of more energy in the air than was usual.

"All this activity lends a sort of carnival atmosphere to the town," Bob said emotionlessly.

"You could say that," Willy replied without smiling.

They went back into the bar and a few moments later the boys burst in the front door, assailing Willy for some change to go and see the Neanderthal man and to go on a few rides.

"I guarantee you that there is no Neanderthal man in that trailer," Willy said, never giving in easily to their demands for money. "It's a scam."

"Come on, Dad," Gordon said.

"Please!" Chief chimed in.

Willy stared at them until they squirmed, then said, "Okay." He dug in his pocket as they jumped up and down. "But you guys owe me some work around here."

"Sure!" they both said, and bolted out the door.

They came back later looking flushed, but a little dejected. Willy poured them both rootbeers and set them on the bar. The boys climbed up onto the barstools and returned greetings to some of the regulars.

"So, how was the Neanderthal man?" Willy asked.

The boys were silent for a moment, then Gordon said, "Ah, it was a gyp. It looked like a wax dummy with hair on it and you couldn't even see the face, the ice was so messed up."

"Live and learn," Willy said.

Chief said, "We talked to a dwarf and a really big huge guy with no hair and tattoos all over him, even all over his head."

"No kidding," Willy said, wiping a glass with a bar rag.

"Yeah," Chief said. "He looked like a monster."

"A *troll*," Gordon said.

"Troll, huh? How 'bout that." Willy wiped another glass.

"Yeah," Gordon said. "He said he thought he knew you."

"Who, the dwarf or the tattooed guy?"

"Tattooed guy," they both said.

Willy squinted, trying to remember. "I don't think I know any guys with their heads tattooed," he said finally.

"He said he knew *you*," Gordon shrugged, drinking his rootbeer.

They asked him for more money to go back to the fair, and Willy said, "Save it for tomorrow, you'll be there all day. Right now, you'd both better go home and see if your mom wants help with anything before dinner. Tell her I'll be home pretty soon."

It being a Friday afternoon, the business picked up in the next half hour to the point where Willy didn't have time to think, just kept serving drinks and working smoothly in concert with Bob Two Bears. He was glad when Runty Schommer showed up for his shift and he could duck out the back door, taking his time walking home to dinner in the cooling spring air. Mae had made a roast with potatoes, onions, and carrots for dinner- which he loved- and after the boys bolted out the door and back to the fair he sat out on the front porch with a scotch and a cigar while Mae played the piano, the sound of it floating out the windows and down the darkening street after the boys, soon to be silenced by distance, and overwhelmed by the light and noise of the fair.

Their plan for the next afternoon was to let the boys go down to the fair with money for rides and games, while he and Mae would pull the boat up to the dock at the boat launch and meet the boys there to pick them up, cruise out onto the river long enough to relax and have a late picnic, then come back in time to tie up to the dock and watch the fair's fireworks display with Emilio, Solveig, and the girls.

Willy and Emilio had spent hours over the winter refurbishing the boat for the coming season, and although the boat was no longer new at all, its brass and woodwork shone like new, and the engine had been fussily maintained. Willy and Mae drove to Emilio's, where the boat was tied to his slip, and Willy started the engine while Mae told their friends when to meet them at the public dock. Mae took off the stern and bow lines and skipped neatly onto the boat, joining Willy at the helm as he pushed the throttle forward and moved upstream into the current.

The fresh smell of spring on the river and the sound of the engine and the wind seemed to dilate Willy's veins, the blood flowing strongly. He looked at Mae and she looked back and they smiled at each other. He glanced at his watch and saw how early they were, and gave Mae his heavy-lidded lothario look. She smiled at him and said, "Dirty boy."

He laughed and steered out into the stream, heading for a spot outside of the commercial lanes where he could drop anchor for awhile on the broad water, their boat just one among many. Once the boat was secure, he took his wife below deck, and they did to each other some of the nastier and more excellent things they saved for special occasions. They both climaxed hard, taking advantage of their place on the distance of the river to shout and scream as they came, afterwards laughing weakly in each other's arms. After awhile, they composed themselves, weighed anchor, and headed in to the dock.

Other people had had the same idea and the dock was full, but at the last moment, a man shoved off from the very end of it and they took his place. The boys were nowhere to be seen, but they waited for awhile before getting concerned; the two boys never particularly accurate or punctilious when it came to being anywhere on time. The rides of the carnival were noisy with the screams of the riders and the lights began to stand out in the purple shadows as the sun went behind the towering bluffs. Willy took out his binoculars and scanned the crowd for the boys, but couldn't find them in the chaos. He thought that if they were close enough for him to see them, they would come to the boat.

He finally put down the binoculars and said, "I'm going to go find them."

"Okay," Mae said. "Don't get mad, they're just kids."

"When do I ever get mad?" Willy said, and jumped onto the dock.

Once in the park, he jostled through the crowd, looking for the boys in the most likely places. He had loved such things as a boy himself but was suprised at how, seemingly with every year that went by, he could tolerate crowds less and less. This crowd was getting rambunctious, full of people he had never seen, with families shying away from scuffles here and there between groups of rowdies. He wondered if the boys had somehow gotten their wires crossed, and went up the street to stick his head in the Eyrie.

Business was pretty good, and it took a moment to get Runty's attention. "Did my boys come in here at all?"

"Nope. What'll I say if they do?"

"Tell 'em we're down at the dock on the boat and that they're late," Willy said, and left.

The main street of downtown had turned in to a party, and men walked and jostled each other as they drank from bottles. Willy headed back for the dock and had only walked a few doors towards the river when something more than a scuffle broke out. The time-honored antagonists, bargemen and rail men, had broken into yet another brawl, and at least eight of them had joined this one, with more coming. It was just fists and feet so far, but an empty bottle whistled through the air and smashed into a brick wall somewhere ahead of him. He thought of the boys getting hurt and got angry. One of the combatants, propelled backwards, thudded into him and pushed him into a wall, and Willy grabbed the man by the shirt and swung him sprawling into the street. Two more grappled with each other right in front of him and he was ready to shove them out of the way when a brick flashed over his left shoulder, just missing his head, and thudded into the neck of one of the fighters before him, who fell to the ground with a face contorted in pain.

Willy whirled to see who had thrown the brick at him, and saw, twenty-five feet away, a huge man, big-bellied but heavily muscular, grotesquely covered with tattoos. They lined his thick arms in the form of huge scales, and his bald head was inked so that he seemed to be spouting red and black ram's horns from under his sleeveless t-shirt and up his neck, curling behind his ears and up over his head and around over his cheekbones and coming to points on his eyelids. The man's eyes were filled with a piggish glee, his rotting teeth exposed in a stumpy grin, and Willy knew he was looking at Bud Sletto.

A pulse surged through him. In less than a second, he thought of Sletto with his boys, a man who had raped his own daughter and nearly raped the Sheriff. He thought of his boys screaming in pain and terror as Sletto sodomized them. Where were the boys? The pulse surged through him and he felt like his blood was made of hot helium and his eyes went wide and he felt like an animal and he roared and charged through the crowd after Sletto.

Sletto, seeing Willy's eyes, took a step backwards, his eyes narrowing, and fled up the street. Two women stood in his way and Sletto charged them down as if they were made of cardboard. Willy raced after him, slipped on a bottle and fell to the cobbles, feeling like he was in a running nightmare and wanting Sletto so badly that he would use his teeth to kill him if he had to. He got up, his knee hurting, as Sletto dodged into the hardware store up the street from the bar.

Willy entered the hardware store and found its proprietor, old Larry Eckel, sprawled on the floor by the checkout counter with his bifocals askew and his keyring dangling from his hand, as if he had been just about to lock up when bowled over by Sletto, who was lumbering down the aisle for the back door and had almost made it. Willy picked up a claw hammer from a bushel basket of them on sale and hurled it down the aisle like a tomahawk at Sletto, hitting him right behind the ear with the head of the hammer as though it were a bloody circus act. The impact of the hammer and Sletto's own momentum sent his upper body crashing through the frosted glass of the back door's upper half, but his hips caught on the heavy door without breaking it and he sprawled back into the room, bleeding from behind the ear and from the cuts on his upper body. He tried to get up but fell over in the back row of goods, his boots sticking out into the aisle.

Willy helped Larry Eckel to his feet, sitting him back against the counter and saying, "You okay, Larry?"

Larry fixed his glasses rather primly and said, "Just what in the sam fuck is going on around here, Willy?"

"Call the Sheriff," he said, looking down the aisle and seeing that Sletto's boots were gone from view. The blood surged again, the light hot feeling, and he ran down the aisle and turned into the back row where Sletto, bloody and panting, was standing, swinging a sledgehammer at Willy's head. Willy dodged but the handle of the sledge caught him in the left shoulder and Sletto smeared his shirt with blood and Willy slipped out of the way and grabbed a three pound cross peen hammer and thudded Sletto in the ribs with it with all the strength he could put into such a short blow. Sletto barked in pain and swung the sledge again but his aim was off and he shattered some clay planters instead and Willy hammered him in the cheekbone so hard that Sletto's eye popped from its socket and dangled on his cheek. Sletto howled and lifted the sledge with one hand but Willy was faster and hit him with a full swing to the forehead, leaving a large round dent from the hammer, blood spurting in gouts, and Sletto went to his knees, his one good eye, like a feral boar's, fixed on Willy with bloody hatred. Willy hit him with the hammer in the side of the head and he fell to the ground and Willy was over him hitting him more in the chest and head and shouting unintelligibly (a boy in the trenches) until he could see Sletto's yellow curds in all the blood and knew that he was done. He stood up, struggling for breath, and dropped the hammer on Sletto's chest and staggered out into the main aisle. He saw that his shirt was covered in blood and ripped it off, tossing it down the back row into the large pool of Sletto's blood.

Larry Eckel teetered down the aisle craning his neck to see what he could, and said, "*Ho*-ly *shit*! You kicked his ass *but* good!"

Willy started laughing, laughing harder and harder, but with an effort got control of himself.

"Did you call the Sheriff?"

"The Sheriff is gone," Larry Eckel said. "Office closed. Hafta call up to Black Marsh."

"Yeah. I forgot for a second. Look, could you give me a workshirt? Extra large. Put it on my tab. I have to find my boys."

"Well, if that feller in the back row was that Bud Sletto, I guess you can have the shirt. He was a piece of shit if there ever was one. You got a little somethin' on your chin, there."

"What made you think that was Sletto?" Willy said over his shoulder.

"How many big-ass fellers you made a promise to kill if they came back to the island, tattoos or no?"

Willy washed up in the back bathroom, getting the blood off his face and putting on the new shirt. "Look, Larry. I have to find my boys. I'll clean this up when I get back. Just lock the front door and wait for me, okay? Turn out the lights except for the office."

"Fine," Larry said. "Kicked his ass *but* good, the cocksucker! 'Bout fuckin' time!"

Willy went out the front door and ran down the street to the dock.

Out on the street, the brawl had settled down or moved on, but there were onlookers who seemed to be waiting for him and watched him run by as he went down the street. He moved through the crowds and skirted the carnival, got to the foot of the dock and ran out to the end. The boat was still there, and Mae stood up in the cockpit and looked at him, her face blank.

"Where are the boys!" he shouted.

"Right here," she said. As he got close enough, he could see that they were sitting in the stern of the boat, eating sandwiches. He jumped into the boat and hugged the boys so hard they protested, then hugged his wife.

"What the hell happened?" she asked.

"Look," he said, "cast off the lines."

"What about the fireworks?" Mae asked.

"Just cast off. Please. I'll explain."

"Why are you wearing a new shirt?"

"Please just do as I say," he said. "Please."

She did so and got back onboard as he started the engine, then pushed the throttle and gunned out into the river as the fireworks began in the night sky behind them.

Some time later, they came back. Mae jumped onto the dock and secured the boat. Emilio and Solveig and the girls were there waiting. So were a lot of other people, like Doc Ambrose and Dr. Homburg, the Hansen brothers and Barnacle Brad. So were the two identical state troopers in mountie hats and johdpurs. The one with the clipboard wanted to have a word with Willy.

Willy never mentioned to the other prisoners that, when he was sentenced, most of the town was in the courtroom and had stood in silence as he was lead away. He never mentioned that he killed Bud Sletto to protect his family and the golden span of his quiet personal heaven, or that he had broken the span and dashed it forever in his defense of it. He never mentioned Mollie or the nightmares he had of her helplessly awaiting rescue beneath the cold dark waters of the river. He never mentioned that he had been fatalistic about his defense, or that his lawyer was not up to the task, or that a young prosecuting attorney he'd never known and an old fundamentalist Christian judge- who had agreed with Prohibition, and who had apparently known Willy by reputation, as Willy did him- had seemed to work almost in collusion to put him behind bars, as if for things he had done in the past. He never mentioned that, when the manslaughter sentence came down, he had thought something like this would happen, that he had been too happy and life had been too good.

When asked, in rare conversations on the topic, if he were guilty of his crime, he would say "I'm responsible for a killing, not guilty of a murder," and nothing else. Most of all, he never mentioned that, on some stratum of his being, he missed Mae and the boys so much that it was a physical pain, as if all his cells were pervaded by the same black and growing cancer.

Built in the Twenties, the prison was an attempt at enlightened thought in penology. The linoleum tile floors of the place were a dark, vegetable green with lighter streaks, like the outside of a watermelon, while the walls were the pale, cool green then popular in bureaucratic and other institutional use. Even the bars to the individual cells were this color.

The surfaces of everything were kept clean, and assigned inmates, during daytime hours, were constantly at work with mops, squeegees, rags, brooms, and dustpans. There was no dankness or mold to the odor of the cells, tiers, and hallways; rather there was the scent of cleansers and floorwax, and the cells' underlying smell was of freshly washed and methodically bleached bedding, just like the prisoners' white uniforms, bleached white almost to blueness, always crisply redolent of chlorine.

Any prisoner obstinately adhering to a regimen of poor personal hygiene was eventually given time in "Contemplation", which was known as "Solitary Confinement" in other prisons. The Warden, who believed in rehabilitation rather than punishment, would sigh disappointedly if anyone referred to it as "Solitary".

"We just want the men to contemplate the effects of their actions on others," The Warden would say. "If we are to make the best use of our time here, shouldn't some of that time be spent in learning how to *contemplate* the repercussions of our actions? Building the habit of *contemplation* is how we disable our tendencies toward impulsivity that get so many of us into the kind of scrape that might have us, well, *detained* here for awhile. Besides, the life uncontemplated is the life unlived." The Warden even used this approach on hardened men serving life sentences, men who didn't know quite what to make of him, but decided to mind their Ps and Qs, because they knew they had it better here at the Oakwood Medium Security Facility than at some of the state's harsher, higher security prisons.

The Warden, Dexter Ver Voort, was a chipper young man with a neat moustache and rimless spectacles who wore tweed jackets with elbow patches and snowily bleached oxford shirts, often without a tie. He had a PhD in psychology and a masters in Penology, and he considered the former his true calling, and the latter a grim necessity which qualified him to help as many of these men as he could. His offices, all mahogany and brass, smelled of woodsoap, pipesmoke, and leatherbound books, and he sat in a red-leather, wingbacked swivel chair behind his large desk. Where another warden might have made the place intimidating, his casual demeanor and the way he occasionally hooked an argyle sock-clad ankle on the edge of his desk while he searched the high ceiling for words was so easy going as to be disarming.

Willy was suprised that he liked him immediately, sitting in front of the desk as the Warden reviewed his file. Liking the Warden didn't dispel the overall gloom he felt about being in prison, but he saw that the ordeal was not going to be as bad as he had first imagined, at least not in obvious and ostensible ways. He had seen himself petitioning the Warden to put together a gym for the prisoners to work out in, and maybe even a boxing club, but was stunned to find that the Warden had already beaten him to the punch on both counts, as it were.

"Oh, the men need physical outlets and good healthy competition," the Warden said. "Cleanliness, good manners, good health, and contemplation, that's the ticket. You might think it's a ridiculous idea, but I can foresee a time when the men are allowed conjugal visits, by which I mean-"

"I understand," Willy said.

"Oh, of course," the Warden said, looking in the file. "Says here you have a some years of college, specializing in Literature. Men of letters are rather a rarity here at Oakwood, as they are in most prisons. That bears out my theory that most of these men were raised in circumstances that lacked stability, dependability, civility, *cleanliness*....I see this as one of my tasks: to make the men more civilized." The Warden looked at the file and back at Willy. "That wouldn't have made a difference in your case, would it?"

Willy shook his head.

"You were raised with all those advantages. You are a prisoner of your own conscience."

Willy sat watching the Warden.

The Warden sat watching Willy.

"I don't think your time here should be too difficult," the Warden finally said in a tone of summing up. "We'll look into finding you a job that will make use of your abilities. Some men find that their time goes by almost quickly. I hope this is true in your case. Please send in the next man from the waiting room."

The Warden was as good as his word, and Willy found himself working in the surprisingly well-appointed prison library. The time in prison, indeed, was shaping up to be not nearly as hellish as he had imagined, and it was only after his new life became routine that he realized it was not to be his external environment that would provide him with years of torment. It was that inescapable black cancer of his loneliness, and the slowly growing sense of claustrophobia that seized him if his mind wandered to the woods in sloping coulees like bottlegreen grottos and the epic, embracing sky that changed like the moods of gods over the river, the river, the river. That river that could carry him away down and out into the waters of the world.

He did whatever he could to distract himself. He exercised to exhaustion during his free time in the gym and soon found himself in the best shape of his life, in spite of being in his forties. He read whatever he could in the library, and tried to concentrate on building the library with new acquisitions. He began to play chess and cards (and any other games he could get his hands on or devise) with another of the inmates who worked in the library, an erudite, leathery old black gentleman named Banana Jack Spoerle, who had worn, in less incarcerated times, all matching primary-yellow clothing: necktie, vest, shirt, pants, even his shoes and socks. Willy had never seen him in this attire, of course, but Banana Jack still sported a yellow ascot with his prison-issued clothing, and this somehow gave warmth to his kind face and complemented the gold incisor that gleamed when he smiled.

"Actually," Banana Jack confided to Willy when they had grown closer, "the yellow clothing was merely an affectation which reflected the nickname I had acquired through dint of my reputation."

"How did you get the nickname?" Willy asked, almost smiling.

"It is not only through my charm and silver-tongued grace that I am so successful with the ladies," Banana Jack said with an affected modesty, although glancing significantly at his lap. Willy, staying deadpan, laughed in spite of himself, again nearly smiling.

It was through Banana Jack that Willy began to meet some of the other prisoners, or sometimes they were merely pointed out. One such was Benjamin "Squinty the Yegg" Schulsberg, a short and whippet-thin thief with a nervous stomach and a doleful look who complained relentlessly about his allergies and everything in the prison, although he admitted that his situation could be much worse. He had acquired the nickname Squinty from times where he had set down his glasses and was forced to grope for them, blinking like a mole in the sunlight. "Yegg" was a term falling into disuse for a safecracker, which had been Squinty's profession and had landed him in prison. He had been the type, at one point, who had sanded down his fingertips to increase their sensitivity when he carefully worked the tumblers on safes to finesse them open. His downfall had been switching to the more ostentatious technique of using nitroglycerine, which he made himself, to blow a safe in a bank where he knew there was large stash of bills for a payroll. With two compatriots, he had circumvented the bank's alarms and broken into the building, where he had thoroughly packed the seams to the door of the safe with cotton, which he then carefully soaked with the nitroglycerine, or "soup", administered with a basting syringe. He either used too much soup or had made it too strong, though, for when he lit the long fuse to the soaked cotton and scurried for cover, the nitroglycerine, upon ignition, had worked so successfully that it had not only blown the heavy door off the hinges of the safe, but out through the brick front of the building and into a women's clothing store across the street. The force and blaze of the explosion had also scorched the money in the safe, rendering it useless, and Squinty's comrades had disappeared into the night while Squinty himself, determined to make his efforts pay off, scrabbled through stacks of charred bills looking for one bundle which might still be intact. Temporarily deafened by the blast and covered with soot, he had been found in the midst of this activity by the local sheriff, who had responded to the scene and had placed his beefy hand on Squinty's shoulder before the yegg had heard a thing. Squinty had looked over at the sheriff, smiled and nodded sadly, pointing at the money and spreading his hands. He had reacted to his arrest philosophically, and, in spite of lengthy and intense interrogation, had wearily refused to give up the names of his companions. This loyalty had added time to his sentence, but he never complained about it. When Willy met him, Squinty's time was almost up, although he didn't seem to be as delighted at the prospect of freedom as one might expect.

"You haven't met my wife," Squinty explained. "Oy, that woman will make me pay. Let's not talk about it. Let's have another game of chess. It'll get my mind off my stomach." Willy enjoyed playing chess with Squinty, although he didn't keep up his own end of the conversation, which usually circled around Squinty talking about the benefits of communism and the coming revolution. Willy also liked the fact that, although the little man was quietly devout, wearing a yarmulke on the Sabbath, he never talked about religion, saying only on the matter, "Jews don't proselytize."

Another was Ben Cherry, a handsome young man with very dark skin and aura of sadness, perhaps reproach, who was also possessed of a heroic physique, something that could have been sculpted by Michelangelo. When he worked out or took off his shirt in the course of grounds maintenance or working in the woodshop, those nearby would stop and look. He had an aura of gravitas that neutralized any thoughts of physical confrontation, and if anyone attempted to call him "Buck" as a pun on his name, he would slowly turn his head and then his eyes upon the perpetrator and, if the pithing gaze didn't seem clear enough, he would say, quietly and slowly, "I ain't no *buck*. I ain't no *slave*, neither." If the person were particularly obtuse, Cherry would raise his eyebrows and stare at the man with an expression which was somehow both a plea for intellectual union and a dire threat.

Ozymandias Root was his opposite. A squat, light-skinned black man, he was one of the ugliest humans Willy had ever seen. His head was asymmetrically conical, set down like a weight on his thick, puttylike neck, which seemed to engulf his receding chin. His teeth were a scaly and disorganized jumble of yellow dominoes, and his pointed pink tongue, inhumanly long, lashed out slickly over these teeth during his lurid descriptions of sex acts which went on, intensifying in depravity, until disgust outweighed amusement and those around him finally shut him down. His eyes, of a red-rimmed, unnatural gold color- another asymmetrical feature- were pushed like dark goggles into the surrounding yellowish skin of his face. He looked like a goblin. Willy found him fascinatingly repellent.

Ozymandias fell into the category of those so obtuse- those very few- who were capable of goading Ben Cherry almost to violence. Root was in prison for rape, and not only was he not silent about his crime, he bragged about it and others like it, apparently seeing himself, in some twisted way, as a force for justice and

130

rectification in the world. "Uppity goddam bitch had it comin' and *loved it,* motherfucker. She be screamin' and cryin' and *awwww* that shit, but she be *lovin'* it, man, if I'm lyin', I'm flyin'!" Root's tongue lashed out wetly, as if he were trying to draw an infinity symbol with its tip. "I be gettin' all up *in* there and *hammerin'* that shit, bam bam *bam,* motherfucker, I be doin' some *cunt*punchin', know what I'm sayin'? Gettin' *in* there! Damn!" He leered, popping his golden eyes as his tongue flickered and he mimed holding and humping a large ass.

Ben Cherry would lean against the pale green bars of his cell with his arms across his chest, the prison whites jarring against his complexion, observing Root's gyrations with what appeared to be impassivity tinged faintly, very faintly, with a dark and poisonous contempt. Cherry was so sphynxlike in his silence that Willy, watching from his cell over the top of a book, wasn't sure if he had imagined it or not.

Ozymandias Root's foray into Ben's psychological territory expanded from ridiculing him for a crime he claimed not to have committed - a robbery and double homicide at a corner grocery store in Greysport- to saying what someone like himself would do to Cherry's wife and young daughter while he was "slavin' it in these motherfuckin' slams."

An incredulous silence froze the air at this, and eyes clicked to Ben like nails to a magnet. Ozymandias Root was caught in the midst of his lewd babble when Ben Cherry, quick as a mongoose, silenced him with a black and muscular hand shooting out and pinching Root's larynx. Ben gave Root one of those looks, his eyebrows raised, his dark eyes looking down into Root's gold ones, and there seemed to be the momentary union of souls, Willy thought, like that when a redtail hawk looks almost with curiosity and compassion into the eyes of the rabbit it has just hooked and is about to consume.

Ben released his grip but held Root with his eyes, Root gulping in spasms but mesmerized. Root finally dropped his head in involuntary obeisance, walking to his cell and lying down on his bunk, his face turned toward the wall. Cherry straightened up in a way that was almost regal, and, turning back to his cell, seemed to encompass each witness with his sad gaze.

It was some time after this event that Ben Cherry received the news about his wife and child. He had had a union job as a dock worker in Greysport before his incarceration, his wife working part-time at a dry cleaners. They had saved sedulously for a house near the port and were close to a twenty percent down payment and an affordable mortgage when Ben was arrested unceremoniously. After a brief yet expensive trial defended by a bigoted but opportunistic lawyer, Ben found himself in prison. His wife, with the tatters of their savings, was forced to move to a tiny apartment next to a tannery on the Mesquakee River not far from the port. After six months of stoic residency, their apartment, at four in the morning, was engulfed in a fire which had started in the tannery. His wife and daughter had died screaming in the flames.

Those who saw Ben Cherry upon hearing the news may have superimposed their own expectations on his behavior. He came back from Warden Ver Voort's office in a manner which may have been more slow, sad, and thoughtful than usual, but may not have. Willy watched him while pretending to read. Ben Cherry entered his cell, stretched out on his bunk, and laced his hands behind his head, every bit as he always did.

In spite of all the rantings of Ozymandias Root, not to mention the general clamor of the tier between work hours and lights out, by far the most annoying impediment to Willy's futile attempt at peace was the Pfister and Pfelcher duo. Friedrich Pfister and Hans Pfelcher were originally known as Fred Pfister and Hank Pfelcher before their inbred sense of inferiority found a source of overcompensation in the form of Fritz Kuhn and the German-American Bund. These American Nazis had had a following of some substance in the 1930s, boasting around two hundred thousand members, twenty thousand of whom showed up at one famous meeting in a city on the east coast. The attendees somehow managed to overlook the fact that the stadium in which they met was surrounded by more than one hundred thousand people who were howling for their blood, while the Bund members strutted about the large hall in home-made Nazi uniforms and self-appointed leaders made operatic speeches fulminating about the strengths and virtues of the Nazi party and their spiritual father, Adolph Hitler.

Hank and Fred attended this meeting (saving up money to go to it by robbing gas stations and liquor stores) and came away from the whole thing as Hans and Friedrich. When leaving the stadium, the two farm boys- built like bulls, thicknecked, bulletheaded, closecropped blond- pounded their way through a throng of multiracial protestors in a manner as savage as it was artless, skills they had developed and honed while thumping the dozens of other witless and bored farmboys of their homeland. From this experience, they took away a mistaken belief in their Aryan invincibility.

It was their crime of the beating death of a rabbi's wife that brought them (inevitably, according to some who knew them) to the Oakwood Medium Security Facility, Dexter Ver Voort their host. They had heard that the rabbi had kept a safe full of cash and jewels, and had accosted the old man and his wife in an attempt to obtain it.

When the rabbi, a frail but obdurate man, refused to cooperate, the enterprising young Nazis began to slap around his equally frail wife. The rabbi finally relented, sobbing with rage at the sight of his bloody and semiconscious spouse.

When the rabbi opened the safe, the bulletheaded boys were more than disappointed to discover that the safe held only $74.27, some postage stamps, legal documents, and "some kinda old lookin' candle holder thing", the last of which they proceeded to use to beat the old couple. They yelled at each other and at the old couple, and finally, after some head-to-head muttering in an adjacent room, decided to take what they could get and stick to the original plan, which involved conking both of the oldsters on the head with a rubber mallet and knocking them out, so that they could make safe their getaway.

They seemed ambivalent about the conking itself, and had to resort of One-Potato-Two-Potato, not because either was reluctant to deliver the blow to the prime target, the rabbi, but because both of them *wanted* to, and badly. Friedrich finally won, after some dispute, and conked the rabbi forcefully on the head, who fell to the floor and lay motionless in the fetal position. Hans then followed suit, conking the somehow less desireable target of the wife, who went down hard, but who, as the boys were arguing over their paltry haul, started to move again, groaning, and pushed herself up on her frail, veiny white hands. Friedrich gave Hans a sneer of contempt and held his hand out for the rubber mallet, then conked the poor woman on the head again, sending her down.

"*That's* how you knock somebody out," Friedrich said.

"Well, she...she...fuckin' A. What a bitch," Hans replied.

The young geniuses drove with their booty to a Dog'n'Suds and had a shitload of chilidogs, all with a stolen menorah stuck in their front window, right there on the capacious dashboard of their Packard. It actually did not occur to them that they would get caught for their crime, or that the old woman they had beaten would die of a subdural hematoma, or that her husband would identify them exactly. Part of their problem was in thinking- insofar as they were capable- that everyone hated Jews.

For a while, they were the most obnoxious cellmates on the tier. Nobody did a thing about them. They were loud and they were huge- jugheaded juggernauts- and they used the word "nigger" a lot. In 1941, this didn't get much more than meaningful stares, but one time, during such an obnoxious rant, Willy laid down his book in tired disgust and happened to look across at Ben Cherry, whom he found to be leaning, arms across his chest, against the bars of his cell. Willy found that Cherry was watching him, and, with a very grave face, Willy minutely flicked his fingers from the front his book, as if to say, "So? What?"

Cherry looked at him in a way that Willy thought was almost a smile, then turned around and laid down on his bunk, fingers laced behind his head, while Pfister and Pfelcher called someone a nigger, someone else a mick, someone else a spic, and so forth.

Willy was trying to read some Dickens, and in some depth this time- unlike his drunken perfunctory college years after the war, which he barely remembered- and when Pfister and Pfelcher's ranting became too annoying at one point, Willy, who was sticking to his plan of trying to do his time quietly and get out as soon as possible, was finally unable to contain the increasing heat of his rage and, for the first time, said something loudly on the tier.

"Would you Kraut cocksuckers *shut the fuck up!*" he bellowed, startling everyone in the surrounding cells on the tier. His heart was pounding, sending the leatherbound book on his chest bouncing. There was a moment of silence, in which the young Nazis could be heard whispering incredulously to each other, and Willy went to drive the point home. "Just *shut the fuck up* or I will kick *both* of your *pigfucking asses. Shut up!*"

There was an expectant silence, and someone began to titter. Ozymandias Root started to guffaw, and Banana Jack said, from his cell two down from Willy's, "Well said, young fella." Even Ben Cherry had sat up and had an uncustomarily mild look on his dark face.

"Who said that?" Hans Pfelcher said.

"William J. McGregor, dogdick," Willy said, thinking he might have erred in breaking his silence, but knowing that now was no time for backpedaling.

There was some muttering among the young assholes, and Friedrich said, "What, the fucking library guy?"

"Library guy kick your fuckin' *ass*, white boy," came a latin voice from down the block. "He all a *boxer* and shit. Fuckin' *war* hero and shit."

Willy recognized the voice as that of Ricardo Espinosa, a Puerto Rican thief whom he was quietly tutoring in literacy as a means of distraction. He had no idea where Ricardo had pieced together any elements of his past. Willy slowly slapped his palm to his forehead.

"Motherfucker killed *shitloads* of Nazi cocksuckers like *you* all before," a black man down the line said. "Ain't no *thang* to McGregor. Ain't no thang at all, killing mothefuckin' Nazis like *yo* ignorant asses."

"There weren't any Nazis in the World War, you dumbfuck," someone chimed in.

"Same shit, different bucket," someone else said.

"Who said that?" one of the Nazi boys barked, and Hans said, "We'll be seeing *you* around, McGregor."

Willy slid his hand from his forehead down over his eyes, and someone said, "We'll be seeing *you*, you Kraut asshole."

The climate in the cellblock changed. It was as if the fields of energy had reoriented and somehow aligned themselves around Willy, who wished he'd never opened his mouth, and against Pfister and Pfelcher and their fellow goons. This energy did not seem to form itself necessarily along racial lines (although some died-in-the-wool bigots found Pfister and Pfelcher to be beyond tiresome, but were forced to back the boys out of a sense of racial loyalty), but seemed to coalesce a grim unity among groups and subgroups who would, under normal circumstances, at least dislike each other. Willy could feel it, though, and could not ignore the comments or the approving nods of those in his favor any more than he could ignore the baleful glares of Pfister and Pfelcher and their crew during chow or when passing in the corridors.

Dexter Ver Voort had heard about what had taken place, and, in a meeting in his office, confided to Willy that, if matters stayed at a level of mere talk, there was little he could do.

"Whereas I would hope the men could settle their differences among themselves in a civilized manner," Ver Voort said, "I'm not unrealistic about the odds of their doing so. People rarely act in a civilized and mannerly way in *general* society; it would be ridiculous to expect more of the men in this institution. Here, however, we do have the added advantages of both inculcating the men with the stability of environment and the opportunity to learn good manners and civilized behavior that they, and anyone else, for that matter, might have previously lacked. After we've done the best we can, if the men still refuse to contemplate and then to correct their behavior, we have the option of moving them to another facility, one which will not, unfortunately, offer them the advantages which they enjoy here."

Willy nodded, half-smiling at the younger man, and the Warden added, lighting his pipe, "But don't forget these guys are a couple of halfwit assholes, and they're not above pulling a shank. We just don't have any evidence yet that they *will*, and so are administratively unable to act beforehand. We are still obligated to give them a chance, however small the possibility of success may seem. Allow me to congratulate you, however, on the *eprit de corps* you seem to have fostered on your cellblock."

At this, Willy sighed dejectedly and excused himself from the office as the Warden relit his faltering pipe; he was certain, yet again, that he had made a huge mistake in ever opening his mouth.

Willy felt ambivalent about visitation. The prison was hours away from the river, toward the wooded center of the state, and he told people not to bother to make the long drive, yet waited desperately for them to come, just for the brief surcease from the surprisingly painful cancer of his loneliness. Emilio came at least once a month, often bringing Doc Ambrose and Dr. Homburg, the veterinarian. Steve, George, Runty, Bob Two Bears and Barnacle Brad showed up spottily, and they all seemed nervous about the venue- possibly suffering from the strong suspicion that they might well have ended up in such a place themselves- and Willy suspected they used such an event to barhop their way home on the empty, wooded roads back to the river. Larry and Dennis Cornwall, rescuees of the blizzard on the night of Gordon's birth, brought Jeff, the newskid who was in the bar during Willy's first set-to with Bud Sletto and who was now in college in Greysport and came when he was home for a break. Jeff quite obviously was in awe of Willy, even more so than any of the others, and Willy felt mildly depressed at the thought that he was the object of anyone's hero worship. "If I'm a hero," he said to Emilio on one visiting day, "this society is in big trouble."

The pain and joy of seeing Mae and the boys was so intense that he sometimes vomited beforehand. He had thought of making an order that the boys not be brought at all, that they not be subjected to seeing him in such a position, but he missed them so much that he sometimes had to force upon himself a stony face to seal in the tears that, he knew, awaited just under his eyes. He hoped that no one could see this, but was sure that when he sat across a table over a game of something or other with Banana Jack, those calm, kind eyes across the board from him saw deeper than his granite mask could protect. Nor did he think it was his imagination that, when he snapped out of staring into space after being lost in thought about his family, and his eyes met with those of Ben Cherry where he leaned against the pale green bars of his cell, that there was a crystalline corridor of understanding between the two of them, and they were linked by the eyes, if only for a few moments. He tried to bury his feelings deeper, and put on a brave and jocular face for the boys.

His feelings for Mae were beyond torment and passion. If the weather was fair, visitation was in a large square grassy courtyard set with neatly ordered picnic tables, surrounded by high stone walls and almost pleasant except for the discreetly placed armed guards. She was so beautiful in the sunlight, her skin pale and her hair copper shot with gold and a few strands of grey, that, as he talked to the boys, one of them, perhaps, on his knee, his eyes searched deep into hers, and with them he tried to say, "I'm sorry. I love you. I want you. Forgive me. Please don't leave." And in her eyes, those eyes he knew best of all, he saw her love, and her passion, and her sadness, and there also in those depths lay a tragic and seemingly ineradicable reproach. He tried to ask with a look, "What could I have done?"

135

And he was sure that her look in return, inconcealable tears in the sunlight in her eyes, said, "Nothing. I love you. Forgive me for being angry. I can't help it. Come home, come home, come home."

And a tear, unnoticed by the boys, slid down her cheek, and he swallowed at the piece of gravel that seemed to appear in his throat, and rubbed his eyes as if he were tired.

Willy quietly maintained his scribbling of poems, mostly as a distraction, and recognized that he had never before had so much time in his life to do so. He also wrote letters, and found that two of the best respondents, other than his wife, were Emilio and Doc Ambrose. He did receive letters and postcards from others, but these were usually terse and lacking in the slightest literary merit, let alone decent punctuation.

The letters from Emilio were often about physical descriptions of the river and coulees, and went off on tangents about Emilio's increasing interest in, and knowledge of, the surrounding ecology. Emilio had become quite an astute amateur scientist, and Willy found his writing about ecosystems and medicinal and other uses for plants to be interesting. He was even impressed with Emilio's writing in his adopted language, which, without the added flavor of his accent, made clear what a keen and intelligent mind operated behind his humble facade. Emilio also took the boys fishing and hunting, and as much as this made Willy feel almost claustrophobic- he wanted to pant and rattle the bars of his cell, but held this down deep- he was warmly grateful to Emilio for keeping the boys out there, for continuing to keep them close to beauty and to their freedom.

Doc Ambrose's letters were surprisingly eloquent and touching. Willy thought about them a lot, some more than others. One such letter was on the subject of talent and obligation, and it kept Willy up late at night, a book open on his chest, staring at the ceiling of his cell.

The letter said: "Most of us possess skills, abilities, talents, what have you, that we have in a variation of abundance, and it is our obligation to contribute these abilities to the greater good. Those who would complain about people and the world without trying to better the situation are worse than dead weight, they merely add to dysfunction without contributing to its betterment. Whatever talents we have are those we must endow. I, personally, do this partly because it confers upon me the right to complain. My other talents include knowledge and practice of medicine- this is my most obvious contribution- kindness and patience to my beautiful but vexatious wife (who keeps me in good form to show kindness and patience to those many who are less deserving), and sharing my deep and hard-won wisdom with young idiots like yourself.

"Idiocy notwithstanding, you are not without your own talents. You have proven your valor in life, time and again, even when you seem sure you have earned your rest, your peace. It is your gift and your burden to do what is right even when largely unsupported by those around you. There are those who know the right thing to do and yet are, through some shortcoming, unable to do it, and there are those who are willing to act but haven't the vaguest idea how to proceed. You are able to see what must be done, and to do it without hesitation.

"This leads to another of your talents, and that is leadership. However much you might cringe when faced with the notion, you are a leader, one who can galvanize the unwilling and the unable and the directionless, one who can summon them to action, not through any kind of desire for power, but through the inspiration of your own actions."

During the first reading of this particular letter, this passage made Willy sigh tiredly and close his eyes, but he picked up the letter and continued reading. "You are familiar of the expression 'The only thing necessary for the triumph of evil is that good men do nothing'. It is men like you who can move others to remember that they are, in fact and in deed, good men. They, too, are not without their abilities- abilities which you might lack- but it is this ability of *yours* which brings them to their feet, my boy."

These letters were disquieting to him, especially in the face of the ongoing tension with Pfister and Pfelcher, to whom Willy and Banana Jack referred to, between themselves, as "those two Nazi assholes". Willy could clearly see their watchful animosity, and could also sense that the other prisoners were expecting some kind of confrontation. He saw his own reputation as grossly exaggerated, and, wanting only to serve his time quietly and quickly, he was hoping the two Nazi assholes would make a large mistake and be moved to another facility, or that Warden Ver Voort would make a move himself. He felt, again, perilously close to disaster- he could practically smell it- and seeing the two hulking halfwits glaring at him at any given opportunity was something that filled him with unease. In spite of his skill, he felt certain that he could not take them both alone. Nonetheless, he found himself staring back at them.

Ambrose sent him another letter which was even more annoying than the last one.

"The points I touched upon in my last missive," Ambrose wrote, "are quite obvious positive attributes, and you are not a subtle man. Or are you? There is one aspect of yourself which you are loath to share, and it is your most subtle. Your poetry, my boy, your poetry. Both your undeservedly excellent wife Mae and your stalwart friend- that self-appointed Sancho Panza, Emilio- have shown me some," -and Willy gasped in horrified embarrassment- "although hesitantly, fearing your reaction, and I must admit my surprise at the talent hidden beneath your thuggish exterior. Why have you not shared this? Why do you not publish? It is through Art and through Science that we explore our Universe, and every discovery we make of both the physical and the spiritual worlds is a building block, a contribution to a bridge that spans to an unseeable but better future. If we fail to contribute, we fail, and the bridge will not be built. There are contributions which only you can make, and their individuality makes it obligatory for you to force them into reality, to contribute them, as I have said *ad nauseum*, to the common good. Even if you do not see their utility, others might. One small thing you think- and think unimportant- may be the lynchpin to another's existence.

"Do not make the vile mistake of thinking that a man of action and a man of poetry cannot exist in the same body. Both pursuits take courage, but courage of different kinds. It is, apparently, within your nature not to fear danger (or, at least, to perceive some things as more important than that fear), just as it is in your nature to follow your own compass and to disregard "popular opinion". Have, then, the courage to share what you have in your most private recesses, to share it with the world. It is a different kind of courage altogether that makes one able to expose his intellect and his soul to others, to eviscerate himself that others might divine the truth from the reading of his entrails. There are others who are incapable of facing the risks which you have overrun without hesitation- even, seemingly, with glee- and yet they are able to summon easily the subtle bravery and grace that seem to elude you.

"*Summon the courage that is your birthright.* You are a scion of Scotland, and your ancestry is peopled with poet-warriors. This is an endeavor in which you must summon the courage, summon the courage to stand up!"

On that first reading, Willy resisted the strong urge to ball the letter up and throw it in the toilet, but forced himself, instead, to neatly fold it and set it aside. He read it countless times afterwards. He quietly continued to write poetry, and his poetry sang with loss. He put it away before turning to his cot at night.

And sometimes he awoke in the early hours and asked himself in a whisper, "Am I a coward?"

Halloween came and Willy spent it blackly depressed. It was one of his favorite holidays, and he sat at his desk in the library with a book and notepaper and pen before him, all disregarded as he stared off into space. It was Friday- perhaps the best day for Halloween- and he imagined quite accurately what was going on at home. Mae would be in the bungalow, getting the boys ready for trick-or-treating after they got home from school, where there was a party in the afternoon and the children were allowed to wear their costumes. Runty Schommer, Bob Two Bears and the others would be getting the bar ready for the party and the costume contest, and Barnacle Brad and his wife Patty would be making their house scary in anticipation of the kids. Mae would stay home with the house decorated with pumpkins carved by the boys, and she would play the piano- parts of the Pier Gynt Suite and other timely tunes- with the door open to the front porch as children came up the steps for candy. After this, she would go down to the bar and play piano there, and would hand out awards for different categories of costume. This year the boys would come to the bar after trick-or-treating, and Mae would leave fairly early and take them home and put them to bed, then turn in herself, alone.

This time last year, Mollie had been there for the boys. Willy closed his eyes. After awhile, he had an image of making love to Mae when she had been made up as Marie Antoinette and he had worn the costume of a pirate, and this image filled him with another kind of despair. That night, he stretched out on his bunk and stared at the ceiling, thinking about being out on the October river with its blaze of color reflected in the black water, the boys laughing in the bow of the boat as Mae sat beside him with her hand in his lap.

Willy pecked at the calendar in his cell. Prison had lost any of its original novelty and had become grindingly monotonous; even his disheartenment, loneliness, and claustrophobia had become monotonous. It got cold in the prison yard, and the first flurries swarmed in the grey sky. He could look across the yard to where Pfister and Pfelcher hung out with their usual cronies, and he, for his part, stood and talked desultorily with those who were familiar and loyal to him, most of them longtime allies of Banana Jack. He was prepared to say, if asked, what he intended to do about the Nazi assholes, which was nothing; he just wanted to do his time and mind his own business and go home. Nobody ever asked, though. He was sure, however, that some of them were furtively watching him while he watched the Nazis across the yard. The guards, aware of most of the major tensions in the facility, watched them all watching each other, and Warden Ver Voort could be frequently seen in the windows of his office, smoking his pipe and looking down over the yard. Willy worked out hard, to forget himself and to keep his edge, and tried to not to think about the glacial passage of the days.

Armistice Day came, and he remembered the sense of freedom he had had on that day long ago, the sensation that he had been sprung from hell, and the sensation that had sent him on a howling spree of following his every lust. The war had been a hell of chaos, though, whereas this was a hell of order. He felt that, although he had been very young, he had preferred the hell of chaos. He felt that way now, he supposed, so trapped, and with so much trapped inside him, that he was almost vibrating with it.

Thanksgiving Day approached, and Willy thought back on the one a year before, how perfect it had been, and he told Banana Jack and some of the others about it, his enthusiasm at the memory of it overcoming his usual taciturnity until he was telling them about every detail. Some of the men groaned or whistled at his telling of the event. Due to Ver Voort's progressive policies, the food at the facility wasn't too bad- although the men, of course, constantly complained about it- but Willy's detailed descriptions of the opulence of that day had the men mesmerized.

Willy summed up by saying, "When we're out of this shithole, you guys're going to have to come out to my place for Thanksgiving."

"Although that sounds magnificent," Banana Jack said, "I don't know if I can wait another four to seven years." The other men laughed.

"Hell, Bananaman, I don't think you've got much choice in the matter," Willy replied to more laughter.

Willy insisted that Mae and the boys not come up that Thanksgiving, that they continue the tradition of having the dinner with Emilio and Solveig and the girls, and everyone else they could get to attend. He communicated this in a letter and would not budge on it, finally issuing a plea that the tradition be unbreakably seated by the time he got out, so that he would have something to look forward to.

Thanksgiving Day came, and in the afternoon, the men filed into the cafeteria for "chow", as it was traditionally called, although today it was something special. The cafeteria actually smelled, above the usual scent of bleach and cleansers, of turkey and stuffing, mashed potatoes and pie. There was even more chatter than the usual din, and the line of white-uniformed men shuffled forward across the green floor to the serving line, men craning their necks to see around those in front. Willy stood in line with Banana Jack and Ricardo Espinosa talking now and then as the line moved slowly forward.

"This does appear to be something special," Jack said, "although it might not be quite to the level of your lordly standards, Willy."

"*Que culero*," Willy said to Espinosa, nodding at Banana Jack, and Espinosa laughed.

They got their trays and handed them to the servers on the other side of the cafeteria steam tables. It actually looked good, and Willy was surprised. "It's something of a tradition here," Jack told Willy, "since Ver Voort has been around."

"Could be a lot worse," Willy said.

They sat down at their usual table. Willy saw Ben Cherry sitting alone across the aisle at his usual place. He never invited Ben to sit with them, as he was aware that Banana Jack had on several occasions but had always been turned down. He nodded at Ben nonetheless, and Ben nodded gravely back.

When most of the men were seated and had already begun eating, as was inevitable, there was a squeal from a microphone at the head of the cafeteria where there was a stage, and the men turned to see Warden Ver Voort standing at the microphone, a few guards behind him. Ver Voort tapped again at the microphone, creating some feedback, and the prisoners all watched, some laughing, others grumbling.

"Men," Ver Voort said, "I'll keep this short, but as you all know, it's Thanksgiving, and I'm sure that many of you are thinking about your families and loved ones. That's good, we should be thinking about our loved ones. They are what is important in our lives. And thinking about them, and on their behalf, perhaps we should spend a moment to think about what brought us here, what past behavior of ours it was that is keeping us away from them today. Perhaps we should contemplate-" some of the men groaned at the use of this word- "honestly, without blaming anyone else, how much we are responsible for the fact that we are here today-"

"Boy, *you* sure fucked up royally!" a gruff voice shouted, and the prisoners laughed.

"I sure have, Jenkins," Ver Voort said, addressing the man directly, "but if I keep learning from you, I should be perfect by the time I leave!"

The men laughed again, and Ver Voort continued.

"The point is that being given time to think about things might not be all that bad, and that if we think about things long enough, we might see that there are many aspects of our lives for which we should be grateful, and that we'll treat these aspects as precious and of the greatest importance when we get out. I just wanted to give you something else to chew on during your meal. Remember, most of you aren't bad guys at all but have just made some bad decisions. You don't *have* to make bad decisions, and you can be thankful for that. Happy Thanksgiving, gentlemen."

There was actually a light patter of applause for the warden, which suprised Willy. He began to eat the turkey, which, he thought, could use a little garlic and rosemary. Men continued to file to their seats.

"Willy," Banana Jack said, nudging him, "I think that kid over there is trying to get your attention."

"Where?"

Jack pointed with his chin to a young Indian kid sitting all alone at a nearby table, and when Willy looked over, the kid's pockmarked face brightened. He was tall and lean, with his hair in a ponytail, a hank of which had escaped from the rubberband which held it and hung over one eye. His skin was brown from the sun, striking against the prison whites, and he had a broken nose which was not properly set. Nonetheless, he had a goofy white grin, his teeth perfect, and Willy could feel his own face form itself in the dour moue that was his prison substitute for a smile.

Willy pointed at himself and the kid nodded. Willy gestured him over. The kid got up with his tray, tripped in his eagerness, and skittered nimbly across the floor with the tray in his hand, bent over and holding onto its corner as if the tray had a mind of its own and he was merely trying to keep up. The utensils on the tray almost slid off, but the kid spun around with the tray tilted, keeping them in place by centrifugal force, and completed a pirouette by sitting down, everything neatly in place, in the empty spot across from Willy.

A less hardened crowd would have applauded at such a display. As it was, the men who witnessed it in the green and white din of the mess hall looked at the kid as if he had puked upon himself. Somebody snorted in laughter. The kid smiled winningly at Willy.

"Am I supposed to know you or something?" Willy asked, his face immobile.

"Well, not really. Maybe. Ever hear the name Faith-in-full Goodforks?"

"Nope," Willy said immediately, although he had the vague suspicion that he *had* heard the name before. It was one of those names one might remember.

"That is one fucked up name, kid," Banana Jack said. "I hope it's not yours."

The kid shrugged, bobbing his head, and grinned again. "Bob Two Bears is my mom's bother," he said to Willy, and started eating from his tray.

Bob Two Bears had recently been to the prison for visitor's day and never said a thing about this relative.

"I just saw Bob not too long ago, and he didn't mention you," Willy said.

"Well, I only got arrested just last month," the kid said, "at least this most recent time, and I don't even know if he knows about that yet. He's also the kind of guy who wouldn't mention it.'"

"How 'bout that," Willy said.

"Yeah, I don't think he approves of me all that much, either. He's talked about you, though. You don't see ol' Uncle Bob speak that well of people very often. He does about you, though."

"You don't say," Willy said. "What landed you here, kid?"

"And what's with that fucking name?" Ricardo Espinosa contributed.

The kid grinned and spread his hands. "Sixteen point buck, fellas," said Faith-in-full Goodforks.

So, for the first time- and certainly not the last- the story of Faith-in-Full Goodforks and the Sixteen Point Buck was told in that prison. At least the initial part of the story, that is. The kid was charming and voluble, a natural storyteller, and all of the men present paid attention to his story in spite of themselves.

The kid's tale was just getting fairly interesting when Willy noticed the already-loud decibels of the messhall increasing, and looked over to see that a crowd of prison-white backs had formed around a fracas in the middle of the messhall. Willy sighed and took a bite of dry white turkey, and someone stuck their head and shoulder out of the melee and shouted, "McGregor! It's Squinty!"

141

Willy thought that he might have muttered something to the men at the table around him, something about backup, but before he knew it he had stalked over to the ring of backs and found Pfister holding Squinty the Yegg by the collar with one fist and pounding him bloody in the face with the other while Pfelcher turned and faced Willy, laughing, and said, "McGregor!"

And Pfelcher went for Willy with his shank.

Willy would have been acutely disappointed to know that, at that very moment, Mae and the boys were getting ready for dinner at Emilio and Solveig's and that the boys behavior, especially Chief's, had been getting increasingly unruly.

They were only gradeschoolers, and Mae, already in a tumult of dark emotions about Willy's imprisonment, was torn apart by how her sons responded to the situation. The first few weeks he was gone, she was a bit surprised at how normally they had behaved. It was still summer, and they banged out of the front screen door of the bungalow just as they always would, and came home breathlessly for lunch, just as they always would. Mae was running the bar by herself, but with the practiced assistance of the other employees, she didn't find it too difficult, and made sure she came home at lunch to fix the boys something to eat. At first the boys were so unemotional that she thought there might be something wrong with them; there seemed to be no response. Gordon was a bit withdrawn, but Chief was his old self, at turns daydreamy and rowdy. The boys shot out the door after dinner, although Gordon did it a little more slowly that usual, as if thinking he should rely upon habit. When they came in after if got dark out, after playing up on the bluffs or down by the river or in the park, kickball or army or softball, they settled down in the living room, reading or listening to the radio or playing a board game. It was not unusual for the three of them to be alone at home in the evenings- Willy was often down at the bar- and for many nights, things had the semblance of normality. They went about their days, and Willy's absence, for some time, wasn't mentioned at all. Mae intended to say something about it, but when the words rose in her throat, she swallowed, thinking it better to leave the fragile silence alone while she could.

She took the boys down to the bar one night when Runty had to go home early to look after his own son, Shorty, and she was unable to find Bob Two Bears. It was the first time the boys had been there since Willy had been sent up, and at first they behaved normally, until, apparently, they realized that nobody else was. The regulars, who usually treated the boys with rough good humor, suddenly seemed at a loss for words, awkward and hesitant, smiling at the boys, beaming at them, really. Steve and George and Barnacle Brad, all the others, sat with drinks in front of them, or, in some cases, raised halfway to their mouths, a tableau of well-meaning witlessness.

Gordon glowered at them all for a moment, then burst out with, "Quit looking at me!" and ran through the bar and up the back stairs to Mollie's old room. This broke the tableau, and Barnacle Brad, as was his custom, went to pick up little Chief under the arms to set him on the bar, but Chief broke free, saying "Leggo a me!" and ran up the back stairs in pursuit of his older brother.

Mae was talking to Runty, who was putting on his hat to leave, but when she saw this, she gave him the look that parents share and followed the boys upstairs.

Gordon was in the small bedroom, looking out the window to the cobbled alley, and Chief was curled up on the bed facing the wall, sobbing.

Mae sat by Chief on the bed and put her hand on his shoulder, but he shrugged it off violently and said, "Leave me *alone!* I want my *Daddy!*"

Mae sniffed once and closed her eyes, swallowing hard, willing herself not to cry. When she looked up, Gordon had turned from the window to face her. His face was red and tears rolled down his cheeks. "You see what that's like down there?" he said, pointing down the stairs. "It's like that *all the time!* I hate it! I *hate* him!"

"You hate who?" Mae said, her fine white hands reaching out to him, her eyes wide.

"I hate Dad!"

Chief sat bolt upright, his face red and contorted and wet with tears and snot. "You shut up!"

"Why'd he have to do it! I hate him!"

Chief launched off the bed and drove his head into Gordon's stomach, sending them both banging back into the chiffarobe. They scrabbled for a moment before Mae was able to pull them apart.

"You shut up!" Chief yelled. "You take it back!" He kept trying to get at his brother, but Gordon stepped back and faced Mae.

"Why'd he *do* it?" Gordon demanded, his chin trembling.

Mae opened her mouth to speak, but, being conflicted herself, had no immediate words.

"He did it to protect us," she said finally. "He did it to protect *you*. That man was a very bad man. He killed his own daughter, honey, he killed Mollie, and you loved Mollie. Your father did what he thought he had to. He did the right thing."

"Then why'd he have to go to jail?"

The thoughts swirled in Mae's mind, all of which she had thought before. Because the Sheriff, although he was our friend, was in over his head. Because Willy's attorney wasn't up to the task. Because the prosecutor had a reputation to build and was friends with the judge. And the judge hated Willy. How do you explain that to a boy?

"Because sometimes in the world, the wrong thing happens," she said, moving over so that she could encircle the boys in her arms. "Sometimes bad things happen to good people, and sometimes the other way around. Sometimes bad things just happen, they *do*, and we have to be able to deal with them. One of the things we have to do in life is to make sure the right things happen. It's our responsibility. And your daddy was trying to make sure the right thing happened."

Gordon thought about this in the warmth of his mother's embrace. Chief just buried his face into her and seemed to be smelling her in long, almost sleepy, breaths.

Gordon looked up at her and said, "So Dad shouldn't be in jail?"

And all of Mae's feelings of accusation and resentment toward Willy seemed to wash away downstream, leaving her only with loneliness and love. She swallowed hard and said, "No, sweetie, your dad shouldn't be in jail. He should be here with us."

They held each other for awhile. Eventually, they all went downstairs to the bar, where Bob Two Bears was just walking in the door. With her arms around the boys' shoulders, Mae briefly talked to him before they went out the door, and as they did, Barnacle Brad raised his beer glass, and the others around him followed suit.

"Need a knife to fight, Hank?" Willy said, crouching with his hands out, watching Pfelcher's center. "What a fucking chickenshit."

Pfelcher swiped once and backswiped, and Willy barely moved. Pfelcher swiped again, and Willy darted, grabbing Pfelcher's wrist with his left hand and punching his metacarpal bones with his right. Pfelcher grunted as the knife was knocked from his hand and skidded away, and Willy kicked him in the balls. Pfelcher went down, but not as hard as he should have; Willy knew he'd missed the man's balls with a full impact, kicking slightly behind them instead. Willy twisted Pfelcher's wrist down and to the side to expose his face and kneed him in the chin, but Pfelcher managed to reach out with his right and grab Willy's belt buckle, spinning him around. The ring of men cheered, but no one interceded. Willy kneed Pfelcher in the face again, and felt himself struck sharp and hard in the back. He released Pfelcher, kicking him hard in the cheekbone, and turned around to see that Pfister held the shank, now bloody, and seemed oblivious to the fact that Squinty the Yegg had him by the ankle and was gnawing his calf. Pfister took his turn swiping at Willy, grinning, and Willy just saw Pfelcher's leg lash out to sweep his own and jumped over it when he felt himself punched sideways in the abdomen and looked down to see the shank sticking out of a slice in his shirt on the lower left side. There was no blood for an instant, then it spilled forth, soaking his white shirt and dribbling over his thighs and spattering the floor.

Willy slid the knife out of his side, muttering, "You fucking *ass*hole!" but Pfelcher kicked out again, this time felling him, just as a messhall tray whickered out of the crowd and hit Pfister square in the nose, audibly breaking it. This was followed by a deep-lunged, shocking howl, and the lean figure of Faith-in-Full Goodforks, as if launched from a circus cannon, thudded into Pfister's chest, pounding him back into the crowd. Then men in the messhall rushed together with the sound of two football teams impacting at the line of scrimmage, and Willy looked up to see Banana Jack, his gold dental work glinting in a surprisingly vicious grin, as he used a mess tray as a straightedge and chopped one of the Nazi cronies at the base of the skull. Ricardo Espinosa dove in, and Willy was amused to hear the voice of Ozymandias Root screaming profane threats, although the hideous dwarf was too short to see.

Inspired by this unexpected turn of events, Willy started to sit up. The encouraging shouts had changed into a general roar and he heard the whistles of the converging guards, but he met eyes with Ben Cherry, who was moving to kneel next to him, and he nodded and smiled at Cherry's grave expression. He found it hard to breathe, though, and, seeing how much blood had soaked his whites and spread across the watermelon-green floor, and how much was spurting out still, he came to the conclusion that it might just be a better idea to lie back down and take a nap until the fight was over. He looked at Ben, but saw that he was leveling his gaze at Pfister and Pfelcher as the guards tore into the crowd and pulled men apart.

After that night in the bar, there had been peace in the home for awhile, and Mae had felt a sense of the three of them pulling together. She suspected though, that, kids being kids, they would be soon to forget whatever epiphany they might have momentarily enjoyed, and would be back to acting on impulse unless constantly herded as if surrounded by border collies. Or wolfhounds.

The boys began to get into a different kind of trouble than was usual for their admittedly rambunctious personalities. Gordon, according to the school principal, had become surly and distrustful of teachers and the principal himself, although his grades remained good, and, as far as Mae could tell, he seemed to be studying harder than ever, in a rather dark and distant way. Chief seemed generally happy and rowdy, but had become hair-triggered and indiscriminate about conflict, seeming to find an almost savage joy in one instance in being beaten up rather soundly by a couple of older- and much larger- boys whom, in the past, he would not have antagonized. In spite of a cut lip and a black eye, he proudly brandished his scabbed knuckles. "I'm small now," he said. "Heck, I'm just a little kid. Wait'll I get big like Dad!"

Mae lay in bed at night and tried to sleep, thinking about the boys. When she found herself running in circles on that topic, she worried about Willy for awhile. Her anger had dissipated and now she missed him so badly and worried about him so much that she found it difficult to eat. She thought of him pacing and trapped like an animal in the zoo, imagined him grasping the bars and staring out, muttering her name, and although she thought the image was a bit melodramatic, it brought her to tears. Sometimes in the night she would roll over to find his warmth and encounter only his absence, and then she would cry and cry, silently there in the dark.

In the mornings, though, it was easier to pretend in the clean sunlight of the kitchen that Willy was only away fishing or hunting with Emilio, that he would be back any time. The three who were left went about their routines, Gordon diligently up and washed first, then Mae, as she drank coffee, going through the habitual escalation necessary to get Chief out of bed. Finally they sat at the kitchen table, the boys eating while Mae read the paper, drank more coffee, and waited on them, their conversation sparse and customary.

When Mae asked them what they wanted to be for Halloween, Gordon said that he wanted to be a cop, while Chief said he wanted to be a prisoner in a striped suit, like in the movies. When Mae asked them if they'd come up with this as a plan together, they looked at each other blankly and said, "No." She acceded to their requests for costumes and sewed them herself, and noticed, on that glum and rainy Halloween, that at no time did they play out the roles that their costumes indicated for them, instead they went from door to door rather dolefully, coming home soaked from the rain, and cooperatively splitting their proceeds, unselfishly trading for things the other preferred.

Emilio came by often and took the boys out on the water as the trees changed color and lost their leaves. He was as kind and avuncular as ever, hunkering down and explaining things to them on a level that was eye-to-eye with the boys. Back from the river, they brought home fish, mallards, and a goose or two, and the boys were always cheerful and thankful, but missing a sort of light that they had when they did the same thing with their father. Emilio offered to have the boys stay overnight from time to time, just to give Mae a little time off, but Mae found that, after an hour or so of silence, she missed them so that it was far better to have them around.

When visiting her parents, her mother was always sweet and helpful, while her father- often in the process of becoming slowly drunk- was no longer bold enough to demonstrate his opinion of Mae's jailbird husband, at least not in any overt way, but would snort derisively or make oblique cuts any time the opportunity presented itself. If questioned about his opinions and asked to expand on them, he would hold up his hands and close his eyes and mutter something to the effect that it was far beyond *him* to question a great man like William McGregor. Mae found this at least as annoying as her father's old blowhard demeanor, and made an effort to limit her exposure to him. Her father never went anywhere, though, just stayed at the hotel, usually in some level of intoxication, as the business slowly faded and he rattled around muttering darkly, like a ghost. When Mrs. Parker came over in the afternoons and they drank tea and talked for hours, Mae realized that she had never loved her mother so much, that her mother was the source of her strength and inspiration. Certainly nothing beneficial came from her father.

On Thanksgiving Day, Mae had baked an apple and cranberry pie and made a cranberry sorbet- in keeping with the unstated but unavoidable gourmet nature of the Thanksgiving tradition among their circle of friends- and had some fine plum wine as well. The boys, when told to get ready to go, were quiet, in Gordon's case, and downright sullen in Chief's; he dragged his feet on the carpet in a pantomime of reluctance so convincing that he was able to give his older brother a shock, after which their bedroom door slammed shut and a muffled but thumping altercation ensued. It went on for awhile and then was silent- suspiciously silent- and Mae went to their door and opened it quickly, only to find Gordon tying Chief's little tie while Chief pursed his lips and glared at his brother. Their hair was messed- Chief's more so- and Chief had a red mark on his left cheekbone. They were both breathing heavily and seemed not to notice when Mae came in. Gordon finished tying the tie, and said, "There. Way better than a clip-on." Chief continued to glare at him.

"You boys okay?" Mae asked calmly.

"Yeah," they said simultaneously, eyeing each other.

"No problems?"

Gordon said, "Nope."

Chief said, "I don't want to go."

Gordon made a move as if to punch him, and Mae barked, "*Quit!*" They both froze.

"Why don't you want to go?" Mae asked Chief.

"'Cause the girls are always trying to make me play house and shi- stuff, and they're just... I dunno, I don't want to!"

"You leaker!" Gordon said, and at his tone, Mae slipped between them as Gordon shouted, "You'd lie around all day and let them put makeup on you!"

146

They started for each other and Mae said "Stop! Now!"

There was a moment of silence, and Mae opened her mouth to speak when Gordon pointed at his younger brother and said, "We're going. We're going to do this every year so that when Dad gets home, it'll be like he never left! He can just come back, see, and it'll be like he never left!"

"It's not the same! Dad's not here and I don't want to go!"

Mae said, "Look. Look at me! You're both right, okay? We are going, and we're going to give your father something to look forward to. But it is not the same- it's *not*- and it might never be. You have to realize that. You're going to be getting out of *high school* when Dad comes home and *we can't change that!* He would be *so hurt* if we let our lives fall apart because he's not here. Think about that! He'd blame himself for us not living our lives and being happy, and he'd be sad because we represent him here where we live! So let's hold our heads *up*, okay? *Up*, Chief! Your Dad is a strong man, and we have to be strong like him. He would tell you that strength is a choice, so what are we going to do?"

"Be strong!" Gordon said, his eyes alight. He reached out and nudged his younger brother's shoulder with his knuckles. Chief raised his eyes and looked at his mother, and then at Gordon. Gordon prompted him with a bob of his head, and Chief said, "Yeah. Be strong. Okay. Be strong." His smile was at first tentative but seemed to gain conviction, and Mae put her arms around them.

She felt quiet and peaceful as she drove down the grey street in a whirl of brown leaves, headed for Emilio and Solveig's. With great will, she convinced herself to be calm, to move deliberately, to maintain the silent belief that everything would turn out all right. She had no idea what had just happened to her husband, and it is merciful that she could not see him where he lay, pale and drained, in a pool of his own blood on the green prison messhall floor, surrounded by a flurry of the legs of prisoners and guards.

In the white light, Willy listened to the story that was told, and he was sure it wasn't the first time he had heard it. This comforted him. There was something lively yet reassuring in the voice that made even the most mundane tales entertaining. He was glad to listen to the story again. It was warm and pleasant in the sunlight.

"I get my name, Goodforks, or my family does, from a place where we used to fish on the Ashipunakwa river. It was really good fishing. Still is. Been there a lot of times. There're like these forks in the river there by some rapids where the fishing was always good, and my people, that is to say my family and forebears and whatnot, used to have a village there among a big stand of old oaks on a hill overlooking the forks. Had burial mounds there and everything, people had been there for a long time. Finally got kicked off the land when my grandpa was a young guy and we've been on the res ever since. It was our land, though. It was just real convenient that the folks who took it had a different way of surveying property and whatnot...oh, I don't want to talk about it. We'll have it all back one day after the white folks get done fucking it all up, and in a hundred years, it'll be good as new. Maybe fifty.

"Now, Faith-in-Full I got because my mom, see, she went through a Christian period where she felt pretty beholden to the people who had taught her how to read and write, the same people that tried to get her to forget about who she was and act like a white person. Some people had translated their names to white a long time back, some were holdouts. Anyway, she had me not long after she got out of this one-room schoolhouse run by these Christian folks, and, as I said, she felt pretty beholden to them for all they had done. I guess some of 'em were pretty good people. Not all of 'em though. One of 'em, the one who hated Indians the worst, but sort of tried to cover it up with helpfulness, tried to fuck my mom, no kidding. According to my mom, anyway. She was awful pretty when she was younger. She'd be the first to tell you.

"This didn't sit well with one of the other teachers, who was sort of an old maid type, if you know what I mean, and maybe kind of liked Mom a little herself- that's what Mom thinks- and they got rid of the one guy. The old maid type made sure that my mom thought it was all the doing of the lord, and made my mom promise that she would raise her children, when she had 'em, to be people of *faith in full.* Hence the name, I always say. My mom was carrying me before she got out of that school and my dad got killed in a hunting accident, so they say, and she was left on her own to name me while still in a Christian mood. Hence the name.

"I got in here through a series of events. I imagine the most egregious of 'em was when I was hunting one day and bagged myself one of your short-horned, dappled deer. That's a holstein cow, to those of you ignoramuses who don't know what I'm talking about. It just happened to be on the land of the farmer who had taken over the site of the old village at the Goodforks, and I was in the process loading my kill into the back of my pickup with a winch and some boards for a ramp when all of a sudden I hear someone chambering a shotgun and turned around to see the farmer himself, who didn't look to be too happy about the situation. Didn't seem to sit well with him at all. I told him I was a cityboy from Greysport and acted all proud of the deer I'd bagged, but he wasn't having any of that one and kept his gun trained on me until the sheriff showed up. I got off pretty easy that time, but it became part of my record, naturally.

"Boy, they sure do keep peckin' at ya, though. Guess they figured they'd been lenient enough with me by the time I got my sixteen point buck. Now, I see your question. What, was I hunting out of season? Well, no, not exactly, it's just that it was around midnight and I was driving down a backroad outside of the res with a quart of beer and my rifle, and I come around a bend, and there standing in some brush about three feet off the road is this *huge* sixteen point buck. Rack like this! So, the buck is staring at me and I'm shining him with a spotlight from my pickup and didn't dare get out in case the buck ran away, so happenstance forced me to *plug* it from where I sat in my pickup. Gotta put meat on the table, you know. So I get out and I'm getting ready to gut him right there in the headlights of my truck, when I hear some tires on gravel, and goddam it, there's the *exact* same sheriff who took me in for the damn cow. He'd been catching a nap on the two-rut driveway leading up to some city folks' cabin among a stand of pines- he wouldn't admit it, of course- and I drove right past him in the dark. He gets out of the squad and walks over- big fat guy- and says, 'Goodforks, old buddy, maybe you should consider becoming a vegetarian.' Insult to injury, that was. Got my truck confiscated to cover the fine, got the suspended sentence from the cow *plus* what I got for poaching and being a repeat offender, and I didn't even get to eat the damn buck. How 'bout them apples."

There was some chuckling in the hospital ward. Willy sighed cozily in his morphine doze. It was like when his father, a fine storyteller in his own right, told him tales about Scotland when he was a boy, snug in bed by his window overlooking the moonlit sea.

Faith-in-Full Goodforks continued to hold forth, apparently to the amusement of the others in the ward. "I gotta admit, that's just plain old inept. And here I am, in Oakwood for a couple of days on a two year sentence, I get involved in what amounts to a riot, and get a goddam compound fracture to my leg. German American Bund my ass. Fuckin' Nazis. People aren't gonna be in favor of *them* in a year or so, mark my words. Adolph Hitler, Man of the Year 1938. What the fuck. And you're here for what?"

Willy couldn't make out the reply from the other prisoner and didn't care, but Goodforks continued, "No, not your sentence, what're you in the hospital ward for? Nephritis! Isn't that where you like to fuck dead people? Oh. Sorry. I'm kidding. I know what nephritis is. Damn liver thing. And you got the what? Jeez, well that's rough. Ain't nobody in here but us chickens. What're you layin' over there for? Got all these empty beds, might as well move you closer so we can hear each other better. Oh, yeah. That Ver Voort fella moved the wards around for *him*. Guess he knows you fellas aren't the *Bund* or something." Goodforks laughed at length. Willy breathed deeply, pleasantly.

"You know," Goodforks continued, "this man here is the end of those assholes. You wouldn't believe what I heard from my Uncle Bob. This man is a bona fide war hero. Kicked a *pile* of Hun ass in France. That's a white man's war, not mine. We lost this shit so far." He laughed for awhile, infectiously, and said, "No really. Killed something like a *platoon* of German fellas, rifle, grenade, damn, he chopped their fucking heads off with a *shovel*. Never even talk about it. Got a damn drawer full of medals at home, packed away. He's a war hero, and after that... no, he's old enough to have been over there, see that grey hair there? Gotta say, he's uncommonly strong. Look at him, all carved up with a knife, guts just about hanging out, and he looks like he's taking a nap. Big man.

"He was a kid when he went, lied about his age. After that, he ran booze on the river, married some royal woman, I mean *descended* from royalty, she played piano and fancy music and conducted a orchestra. She still plays piano. His wife-*his*- might be the most beautiful woman on earth. On the outside, yeah, but mostly on the inside, on the inside, know what I mean? No, fuck you. Your mom's okay, but tell her to get my shoes back to me; I left them under the bed. I love those shoes. What an ass! Ho!"

There was a bit of a roar, and Willy faded out, and back in. "My uncle works there, that's how I know him. We're copacetic, friends from *way* back."

There was a bit of silence, of murmuring, and Goodforks said, "He is the one *just* man here. He put a guy down who was gonna do some bad shit to his whole family, done so to others-laid him *low*- and now he's in here, and doing the same. All right, zip the lip on who did what to who, but we know it was those-" a moment of silence- "assholes who got the whole thing together. You oldtimers ought to be surprised that that Yegg fella got out of here with only a line of stitches and two missing teeth. It's a good thing for those cake-eaters that me and Hard Willy are in here, because I'll tell ya, time is limited for *those* boys."

Willy struggled for a moment, opened one eye. The broken-nosed, smiling Indian kid was in a cot, plastered leg in traction, a few feet away. "Hey! Mr. McGregor!" he said. "Holy shit! He's awake!"

Willy tried to talk once, and produced a rasping sound. He cleared his throat, tried again. "Kid," he croaked, "don't you ever shut the fuck up?"

The kid looked over Willy's shoulder and smiled. "Here comes your shot," he said. Soon Willy felt fine again, up where it was white and warm.

Willy had been in the hospital ward for a week and three days, trapped next to the loquacious Faith-in-Full Goodforks, when he heard in the evening of December the Seventh that Pearl Harbor had been attacked by the Japanese and that America, finally, was at war. He thought that the war was inevitable, and didn't worry about it that much; whatever his feelings about it, there was nothing he could do about it. He thought that he'd wasted his youth and, for a time, his sanity, on a war not as righteous as the one at hand, but, again, there was nothing he could do about it. He worried more about having to explain to Mae- to whom he had promised to keep his head down and his ass out of trouble- the healing incisions to his abdomen, back and front. He didn't mind thinking about the punctured lung or the internal damage, put together by the hospital surgeon, unless he thought about her reaction to it, Mae out there where she could do nothing to care for her man.

On Tuesday the Ninth, Pfister and Pfelcher were found bludgeoned to death in a hallway not far from the woodshop, their brains virtually beaten out of their ears, their arms and legs, perhaps gratuitously, snapped backwards at the joints. The Warden came to see Willy in the hospital ward.

"There is an investigation, of course," Ver Voort said in a low tone, puffing his pipe, his legs crossed at the knee, sitting in a chair with his back to the other men in the ward, "but nobody seems to have seen anything. Funny about that. We might never know what happened. Ironically, I was working on transferring our Nazi friends to another facility, but my efforts were being held up by the usual red tape. In a way, this is a fortunate outcome. I see those two as instigators of the worst sort, who didn't belong in a medium security facility in the first place. In light of recent events, I don't think many tears will be shed for members of the German American Bund. Whoever took justice in their own hands, however," Ver Voort raised his voice so the others in the ward could hear, "will be dealt with in a manner consistent with the harshest interpretation of the law."

Willy nodded blankly, and the Warden watched him for a moment, then winked. "We'll need you back at the library as soon as you're able, Willy." He got up and left the ward, nodding at the other men.

Word got around that Willy, before losing consciousness on the floor of the messhall, had said, "Don't tell my wife." Ben Cherry was not the type of man to gossip, so Willy figured that someone nearby during the melee had heard him say such a thing. He had no doubt that he actually had.

150

Perhaps his first clear thought upon emerging from his morphine doze was, "Shit! What am I going to tell Mae?" He was immediately terrified that she would come for visitation and find that he was in the hospital, which would destroy all his efforts to make her believe that his time deprived of freedom was, at the worst, boring. He was relieved to hear that visitation privileges had been suspended during the investigation of the causes of the riot, the suspension being extended after the bludgeoning deaths of the Pfister and Pfelcher. What made it all perfect- although he disliked himself for thinking so- was that Mae would have been unable to come for several weeks anyway, due to the fact that her mother had slipped and broken her wrist while shoveling the sidewalks of the hotel as her husband slept off a morning drunk in one of the guest rooms, a ploy he used so often that Mrs Palmer had given up looking for the old bastard and taken to doing everything by herself. Mae, of course, had to be available to help her mother, as well as run the bar and take care of the boys. Willy received a letter from Mae, eloquent and brave, describing the situation (along with a few paragraphs of vitriol regarding her father), and, although he felt for her and disliked her father more than ever, he was hugely relieved.

Faith-in-Full Goodforks had been moved from his section of the ward and back into the general population, and, with the departure of the others his area, Willy found himself alone in a way that had been impossible since the beginning of his sentence. At first it was a huge relief, giving him time to think and read, but before a surprisingly short period of time had passed, he found himself getting lonely. He even found himself missing Goodforks.

Confined to the hospital bed, and even forced, ignominiously, to use the bedpan, he could feel his strength deserting him. He couldn't work out to keep strong, he couldn't jump rope, he couldn't even walk to the toilet, having to leave the stainless steel bedpan for the trustee who pretended not to notice or care about what he was doing. Willy ignored the trustee when he came in, or lay feigning sleep. He was terrified that the man would say something invasive like, "Hmmm, less blood in your stools today," or "Holy Moly, lookit the size of that one!"

The doctor came and checked on him occasionally, raising his eyebrows and nodding over the charts, but the male nurses were around more often, unobtrusive and matter-or-fact. As much as he loved to read, and was brought as many books as he wanted by Banana Jack- who could never stay long enough for a decent conversation- he could only read so much. After that, he simply lay in bed and thought, or slept whenever the whim took him. Soon he knew he was sleeping and thinking too much, the thinking the kind that just went in circles, accomplishing nothing.

He began to have nightmares. They began at night, but, the more he slept, the more they slipped into the daylight hours. One night, alone in the darkened ward, the black shadows of the walls and floors streaked with the glow of security lights coming in through the uncovered windows, from the walls and guard towers of the prison, making the area look like an Expressionist theater set, he thought he saw a shadow darker than the others down the hall that lead away from the beds and into the bowels of the building. It was just a patch in the dark hallway, and he wasn't sure whether or not it moved. He squinted at it, trying not to breathe, feeling weak and helpless and unable to move, naked. He watched the patch, not sure it was there at all, until it started to move. He was sure it was moving. It seemed to shuffle, to hunch, obliquely approaching through the shadows to where he lay. He soon could hear the shadow shuffling, even muttering. He felt around fruitlessly for any kind of weapon, his eyes wide. The shadow came closer, slowly closer, until it was a hulking silhouette, hovering over the bed, breathing stertorously. The prison searchlight moved along the building outside, coming through the window and illuminating the wall over beds some forty feet behind the figure, and suddenly, in the chiaroscuro halflight, he could see the figure's blue face, wet with black blood, teeth missing, one eye a piglike glint, the other a slick black socket, the figure huge over the bed, holding a carving knife. "I like your wife and kids," Bud Sletto said, laughing with a gurgle of blood.

Willy woke up with a yell which echoed through the ward. The ward itself looked quite similar to the one in the nightmare. "Holy fucking shit," Willy said aloud, his heart like a belabored speedbag in his chest. He forced himself to stay awake as long as he could, but only lasted fifteen minutes.

Sometimes during the day, he would be so exhausted by his nightmare life during the dark hours that he would fade off into dream during the brightest part of the day. During one such dream, he was sitting in the visitation yard waiting for Mae and the boys. They were late, and as time drew on, he worried more and more about where they were. He was soon choked with a claustrophobic dread; something had happened to them and he didn't know what and there was nothing he could do about it. He looked around the yard and they were nowhere. Suddenly there was a rush of dark water at his feet, over the toes of his boots and around his ankles. The water rose in a black flood, filled with huge chunks of ice. He was underwater, thrust along in the current, and had to fight himself to the surface, jostling against the ice, clutching at it. The water then began to recede and he found himself sitting on the drenched, overgrown grass of a graveyard whose old, weathered stones stuck at odd, jumbled angles out of the grass among slabs of ice which were themselves like tombstones. Leaning against one of the old stones, as if deposited there by the receding water, was Mollie, dressed in her plaid skirt and red sweater. She was drenched, and her crimson bra was visible under the open sweater. She was very pale, dark circles around her eyes, her lips cool lavender, but she was quite beautiful. Her eyes seemed to follow Willy's to the crimson bra, and she looked back up at him and moaned, "Who will find me pretty now?"

Willy was about to answer, but she began to smile, her teeth dark, and the smile widened, becoming impossibly wide, showing thirty teeth, sixty teeth, and she opened her mouth wide, her throat black, her uvula ululating purple as she began to wail like a banshee, her dark tongue, long and pointed, lashing over her many teeth.

Willy woke with a shout. The ward was still in the sunlight around him, and off at a table in the corner the trustee on duty looked up from his comic book and regarded Willy for a moment before returning to his reading.

Willy sometimes saw in his dreams things that he had long pushed down into some dungeon of his memory, things he had not thought about or visualized since his days of drinking and debauchery immediately after the war. He dreamt about the time when he had been the only living being in a section of trench, just a boy, with a mortar bombardment going on around him so fiercely that he shat himself. Disgusted, he unbuckled his woolen pants and dropped them to his knees, using his bayonet to cut away the underpants at the sides and casting them into the filthy water of the trench, his only witnesses being the dead men and parts of dead men all around him, one corpse seeming to stare right at him mirthlessly, eyes pale beneath the truncated brow, the top of its head missing. "What're *you* looking at," Willy had said to the corpse, stabbing his bayonet into the wall of the trench and angrily buckling his pants.

Perhaps the worst dreams were when Mae and the boys were in the trench with him, either all together or in some combination. He was surrounded by weapons, but they were all jammed or somehow useless- out of ammunition, their barrels bent- and they all cowered on a landscape that was riven and churned, black and grey and brown and blood, explosions around them, clods of mud and parts of limbs raining down among the blackwater craters and barbwire, the hammering of machine gun fire and insectile whir of bullets incessant overhead. In one version of this hell, he was in a trench with the boys, and Chief began to yell, "Mom! Where's Mom!" Willy looked around in terror, but the color of his wife's hair was nowhere to be seen in the malignant landscape. He gathered his courage- that age-old feeling- and leapt up out of the trench, sprinting low and looking around and diving into a crater, Mae nowhere in sight, and he realized that he had left the boys behind and they were under bombardment, and, whether he moved or not, he was dead.

When he was deemed fit, he was allowed to go back into the general population, back to his cell and the library. He could not remember feeling weaker in his life, and walked slightly hunched with his forearm covering the new scar on his abdomen under the prison whites. He half-expected someone to jump out at him from around any corner to pummel his wounds open, thinking at the same time that he was virtually unable to defend himself. His fear worked itself into a scowl on his face, but those who did not welcome him back or greet him with rough good cheer seemed to stay far away from him, as though he was protected by a shadow of himself far larger and darker than the pale and wispy one to which he felt he had, in reality, diminished.

There had been no resolution to the beating deaths of Pfister and Pfelcher. As was often the case in such situations- although they were rare at Oakwood- unless the perpetrator were caught red-handed, there were no confessions forthcoming, and the inmates met any inquiries with predictable silence. As idealistic as Warden Ver Voort was, Willy thought it unlikely that he would give the investigation his most zealous effort, considering the nature of the men who were killed and the current political climate of the country. On a personal level, he was relieved.

Many of the prisoners believed that there was a hero or heroes walking around unheralded in their midst; such talk would have revolved around Willy if he hadn't had a perfect alibi. As to Banana Jack, he seemed to be the only one to sense both Willy's weakness and his psychological unease, and was kind and encouraging. "Although I don't think anyone here will interfere with you for the rest of your time, it is apparent that your days in convalescence have left you somewhat drained, and it would be best if you were back to top form as soon as possible." His avuncular warmth touched Willy, and the memory of the leathery old gent leaping into the fight choked Willy up and left him muttering and clearing his throat whenever he tried to express his thanks.

He slowly and painfully began to get back into shape. Sit-ups were excruciating at first on his left side, and he was quietly shocked at how much strength he had lost in his upper body and legs. On a logical level, he supposed he agreed with Jack on his status among the population, but on a more fundamental level he felt desperate to regain his strength, ultimately trusting no one but himself to look after his wellbeing. If he had been consistent in his training before, he now became pathological. His punctured lung seemed to have healed completely, although his wind had become short from his inactivity.

Although it was only 1942 and prisoners' rights were not protected as much as they are today, Warden Ver Voort could only enforce a lockdown and revocation of prisoner privileges for so long without crossing a line, the line of his own ethics coming before that of the law. His investigation into the particulars of the two deaths had proven fruitless, which surprised the warden; he'd thought someone would talk to curry favor or get a reduction in their sentence, but it sometimes seemed to him that a dark form of patriotism had silently taken hold of the inmates. Even the intervention of the State Department of Justice had yielded no results. Weekend visitation was allowed again, other privileges returned. No one was even sent to Contemplation; Ver Voort wouldn't have known who to send, and it was a relief to his conscience, the more so when he watched what was going on in Europe and Asia.

Willy had been worried about the revocation of lockdown, knowing that Mae and the boys would be up at their first opportunity, the three of them making the long drive through the woods and the hills to the prison. He had written to Emilio, confiding in him about his wounds and their cause, about his time in the hospital, asking him to come along on the first visit to run interference. It would just be Emilio, Mae, and the boys; Solveig had come once, leaving the girls with her sister, and had broken into uncontrollable tears at the sight of Willy in prison, eventually having to be escorted abruptly out of the facility by Emilio. Willy knew that he wouldn't see her again until he was free.

So the first people Willy saw at visitation in a couple of months were his wife, his boys, and his best friend. He was terrified that his Mae would sense something wrong, and wanted to do anything he could to prevent her from worrying about what she couldn't change. It was a cold January day and visitation was held in its customary hall, and when they came through the doorway, Emilio made an obvious try to get ahead of the rest to check him out but the boys tore around him and ran to embrace their father. Willy found himself hunching over to protect his side from the impact and forced himself to relax, putting his arms around the boys at first then crushing them to him. After awhile he stood up and shook Emilio's hand. Emilio searched his eyes intensely, wordlessly asking about Willy's wellbeing. Willy winked once, released Emilio's hand, and stood looking at his wife.

Her beauty, her beloved face, the face he loved to watch while she slept and while she laughed, the face that now swelled his heart, was a thin patina of unconcern. "You've lost weight," she said, her eyes narrow. "You're pale. Are you all right?"

"Just...yes," he said and took her in his arms, the smell of her and the feel of her like the scent of rain on the wind, a taste of something nourishing and distant, and he thought that and thought it was corny but so fucking what. He crushed her to him, his eyes clenched shut, rocking her in his arms as she held on tightly. After a long time he sat down and talked to them.

He listened to the news from town, not really hearing it, but soaking up their presences. The boys had grown but not changed, talking over each other to wedge in their small stories. Emilio told him a few jokes. Most of the time Willy looked at Mae, whose face blended between love, longing, and suspicion. Before too long at all, it was time for them to leave. He told them all that he was fine, that his worst problem was boredom. He whispered in his wife's ear that he loved her, stopping himself before going further. He shook his friend's hand and gave him a deep look of thanks. Soon they were gone, and he let his smile collapse and he sighed, the warmth deserting him and leaving him with nothing but the old black feeling.

There had been a small welcome back for him when he had returned from the hospital, and the same group of men seemed to be loitering around his cell when he returned from visitation.

"What's going on?" he said, looking around at Banana Jack, Faith-in-Full Goodforks, Ricardo Espinosa, Squinty the Yegg, and a few others, all of whom were grinning at each other.

Faith-in-Full said, "We've been working on a little surprise for you, Mr. McGregor."

Willy looked at him, and at the others, all of whom seemed a bit flushed and jocular.

Banana Jack beckoned him into his own cell, saying, "Sometimes only the elixir of the gods can lighten the burden carried by a heavy heart." And with that, he produced from underneath his bunk a quart jar of clear liquid, less than full, its tin lid loosely attached. Jack unscrewed the lid and handed the jar to Willy.

Willy knew what it was immediately, but bent over to sniff it out of a connoisseur's reflex. "Holy shit!" he said, jerking his head back from the paint thinner fumes of the moonshine.

The men all laughed, and Banana Jack gave a graceful, palm-up gesture for Willy to take a swig. Willy took a large gulp, knowing that the amount that oxidized in his mouth would be the same if he took a small one. The moonshine was milder than he'd thought it would be, even smooth, like a very potent but good vodka. He stood with the jar in his hand, staring off into space as the thread of the liquid slid down his throat and warmed his stomach.

"Not bad," he said, and took another jolt, the men watching and laughing.

"Might even be a restorative for ulcers," Squinty the Yegg said, holding out his hand for the jar. "Who knew."

It turned out that, while Willy was in the hospital, Faith-in-Full Goodforks had gotten a job in the boiler room, befriending there a crazy little redneck by the name of Eddie Zwolanek, usually known as "Swollen-neck" Zwolanek, due to the fact that he was a muscular little bastard with so little body fat and such a spittle-flingingly emphatic nature that in his calmest moments he looked like his veins and muscles were about to burst right out of his skin. Swollen-neck, according to Goodforks, had such explosive energy that he did, among other exercises, an average of fifteen hundred sit-ups a day, just to blow off steam, which contracted his stomach into an array of hardballs, forcing him to walk hunched over, his fists bunched in front of him like lumps of granite. He had had time in Contemplation, not to mention time added to his sentence of Aggravated Battery, for several fights while behind bars ("Done gone from fights *in* bars to fights *behind* 'em!" he was heard to cackle) the last of which involved him coldcocking a six-four, three-hundred-twenty pound, acutely surly black man in the latrine, then dragging the man up to a toilet and beating his head on the porcelain until the toilet broke, all the time laughing like a hyena, standing over the senseless bulk of the downed prisoner as water from the broken toilet washed his bright blood over the green tiles and down the drain. It was fortunate for Eddie Zwolanek that witnesses agreed that his victim had started the fight.

It further turned out that Swollen-neck Zwolanek had a know-how of moonshine making, something he shared in common with the ever-resourceful Faith-in-Full Goodforks. He had sat on this knowledge for some time, attention span not being his long suit, but the appearance of Faith-in-Full Goodforks and his capable attitude had catalyzed the two into taking what they needed from the ample hardware and tools of the boiler room's shop and making a still. Faith-in-Full promoted several bushels of potatoes from the kitchen for the mash, along with some yeast, and they were soon in business. It took all of Faith-in-Full's wily persuasion to keep Eddie from getting drunk during the daytime, but once a habit of discipline was established, they were both sparing and moderate. With the help of a few guards who liked their product, they were able to distribute it, using the ubiquitous crew of janitor inmates as their drivers. The mopsmen simply submerged quart jars in their large, murky buckets of water and swabbed their way right past the cells of the customers, who simply rinsed the bottles off, unafraid of any germs that might come in contact with the liquid held within in any case. It was Faith-in-Full's idea to impose a caveat on the deliveries: any inmate who allowed himself to be noticeably drunk, especially during the day, would be considered a threat to the operation and be cut off for good. It wasn't so much that he expected the men to monitor and discipline themselves, but that those who enjoyed the new service and were in possession of their faculties would monitor (and adjust) the men of a more self-indulgent nature. Willy found it implied among those in the loop that he was somehow behind all of it, and this knowledge imbued the participants with a certain respect.

This aggravated Willy when he found out about it; he'd had nothing to do with the whole operation, but Faith-in-Full had, with artful implication, exaggerated to others the nature of his relationship with "Hard Willy" until Willy was more than even an uncle, but a father figure, almost a patron saint. Whenever Willy picked up a hint of any of this, he winced in exasperation. He remembered that it had been his vain notion that he would invisibly slide through his time in prison. The idea that, through no effort of his own, he had somehow again become linked with illicit trade in alcohol was just plain funny.

So it was that, a year into his sentence, the simple and monotonous habits of his life in prison were established. He slept and had nightmares, he ate, he worked out and coached some boxing (including trying to discipline the gyrations of the propeller-like Eddie Zwolanek), he did his bit in the library, he played cards and chess and Monopoly and anything else he could get his hands on. He allowed himself nightly warming draughts from his stash of potato vodka and occasionally got discreetly hammered after lights out when he had nothing much to do the next day. He very privately beat off with a will late at night, lost in reveries of his naked wife. Every instant when he was not distracted, he was numb with the pain of want and longing, those poisons crouching there indelibly dark in every cell of his body.

On the outside, back on the river, Mae held onto the other half of their sentence. She ran the bar and took care of the boys and the house. She played the piano at home at night, with the windows open spring through fall, and the neighbors were not wrong in imagining that there was a wistful or somber tone to the tunes she played. A few times a month, though, she would have a few drinks at the bar and unwind into forgetfulness by playing raucously, alone or with other musicians, often surrounded by the likes of Emilio and Solveig, Doc Ambrose and his wife, Steve and George and Barnacle Brad. She loved to lose herself at times like these, but when she woke up in the morning and felt beside her for her husband, finding that part of the bed cold and neat, the world crashed in on her again.

The boys grew quickly and went through school, Gordon somewhat more studious, but Chief still getting good grades in his haphazard but intelligent way. They had fun with sports but were not obsessive about it, working out with each other more and more in the basement with their father's weights and boxing equipment, asking Emilio for occasional pointers. Their rowdiness had not diminished, but had taken new forms: if any of the large, cornfed bullies at the school were to pick on a kid who didn't deserve it (as will happen anytime, anywhere, among us primates), Gordon would be the one to somberly stand up and do something about it. If Chief were there, he would be the one to advocate action, whereas Gordon would want a calm resolution, if possible.

Emilio was better than an uncle to them, taking them camping, hunting, and fishing, trying to answer any of their questions on any subject as accurately and clearly as he could, the way he knew Willy would do it. He showed them the fundamentals of woodworking and carving, and was surprised to find that Gordon, in spite of his somewhat more serious nature, was naturally more attracted to the creativity of carving- and had a real gift for it- while Chief seemed to find reassurance in the logic and science of carpentry. He loved his own girls beyond reason, but they mostly seemed disinterested in his work, and the boys' eager minds delighted him.

Solveig got plump and lovely, keeping a giant garden in the fertile soil by the river, and was a kind and doting mother to the girls. The girls themselves were a marvel, bright and lively and each beautiful in their own way, exhibiting what

Emilio- ever the amateur scientist- thought of as an advantageous phenotypic outcome to their mixed Nordic and Latin genotype. He noticed something of a change in the girls' interactions with boys in general and Willy and Mae's boys in particular, and he watched this unfold with covert interest.

Among their group, they got together for cocktails, picnics and dinners, talking about their town, the world and the war. One of Runty Schommer's boys was among the first to enlist and was in the fighting at Guadalcanal. Larry Cornwall's son Dennis survived being trapped in the ice storm those many years ago only to die in the jungle on the Bataan Death March, beheaded by a Japanese sword, although none but surviving witnesses ever knew the details of his death. Jeff the newskid was now reporting the war from London, and was there during the Blitz.

Mae waited for her husband and watched the world, sad for any of the boys who were lost in the war, but secretly relieved that her own were too young to enlist, viciously eager, as they were, to join the conflict, and frustrated by their age.

And for Willy, the painful sameness of his time ground on in prison. He, too, watched the war with impotent interest. Occasionally, a distraction would arise, as when Banana Jack introduced him to the music of Duke Ellington, and they listened to scratchy records on the library's equipment while they sipped Faith-in-Full's vodka, doing both over and over again.

Willy got into the habit of attempting to empty himself of emotion when his loneliness became too great. He would sit in his cell and stare at a point on the wall, breathing deeply and imagining himself as an amphora, filled with a dark and bitter liquid composed of his loneliness, his fear, his want, his anger. Then he imagined that the base of this vessel was filled suddenly with tiny holes, and through these holes the poisons within him drained to the floor, there to flow away, leaving him filled only with light and air. He began to get better at it as he practiced, finding himself after such sessions emptied of everything except, he supposed, peace. Or perhaps patience. He thought he might be on to something, but was embarrassed to bring it up with anyone, even Jack, who he thought might look at him as if he were insane. He kept this process to himself, and practiced it when his longing for Mae and the boys and his friends and the wind and sky and river and the waves of the ocean itself seemed too strong for him to bear.

There were prison conflicts and dramas, but Willy finally found himself at a point where he was left alone as he had always wanted to be. He occasionally had a game of chess with Warden Ver Voort, who seemed mortified about what had happened to Willy at the hands of the prison's representatives of the German American Bund, having almost jokingly predicted that one of them might pull a shank.

Willy ignored the whole thing when Eddie Zwolanek clobbered the shit out of Ozymandias Root for being as unstoppably obnoxious as he always was. Faith-in-Full continued to steadily run the vodka operation while Eddie was in Contemplation again, but Eddie's contribution as anything other than an enforcer was pretty much a thing of the past. The operation had other trainees who would be able to take over no matter what happened, the new men having been judiciously picked by Faith-in-Full, who had a surprisingly canny understanding of human nature and was a good judge of character, however much he could come off as a superfluous blowhard.

Willy was in the midst of a rare conversation with Ben Cherry when Ozymandias Root was called for release. His sentence was up and there was nothing anyone could do about it. Willy's conversations with Ben Cherry had always been brief, but less so after Willy's knifing and hospitalization. Willy thought that the quiet, solitary man was perhaps on the verge of warming up to actual social interaction. Willy banteringly suggested to Cherry that he come by for a drink- he knew that Cherry had quietly observed the furtive goings-on on the cell block- and he was sure that Cherry had almost smiled before he declined. There was something he sensed about Ben Cherry, though, not only his sadness, but an unbendable and heroic goodness, that made Willy refuse to give up. He was about to leave where he stood in front of Ben Cherry's cell and walk back across to his own when two guards came onto the tier, shouting the name of Ozymandias Root.

"Whatch y'all want, motherfuckers? I'm trying to get my goddam beauty sleep!" the hideous little man- his bruises from Eddie Zwolanek still healing- shouted back from his cell.

"Time for you to take a powder, Root," one of the guards said, approaching his cell. "The State decided you're too fucking ugly for us to keep you here any longer. It's depressing to the other prisoners."

Ozymandias Root had known his release was coming, of course, and had decided to just lie back and bait the guards, and everyone else, a little bit. "I'm gettin' outta here? *Me?* Why, this is a most wonderful miracle! I must truly be a chosen one of God! Hallelujah, motherfuckers! Halle-fucking-lujah!" He was ready to go, though, and grabbed his few things, while the other men lining the tiers watched, sickened or numb with envy.

Ozymandias Root walked down the tier, the two guards behind him. "A most *won*derful miracle, yes*sir!* God must understand the *needs* of all the *wimmens* out there that need the *root* of ol' Ozymandias! Praise God and send me the motherfuckin' pussay!"

"Shut the fuck up, Root," one of the guards said.

"*Yes*, sir. *Sorry*, sir. Guess they'd be somethin' y'all could *do* about it if'n I was to pull a shank or some shit, but I am *gone! Gone*, motherfuckers! Gonna get me some big ol' nappy motherfuckin' *pussayyyyy,* all you all jailbird motherfuckers! Gonna get me some tight lil blonde pussay, too, while I'm thinkin' about it. An' some *young* pussay, real young, know what I mean? And some *Mexican* pussay, while I'm on the motherfuckin' subject! Hey, Espinosa, I'll stop by and say hey to yo ol' lady, how 'bout that!"

Friends of Espinosa held him back when he immediately lurched forward, screaming, "I will fucking *kill* you, Root! Come here, *puto!* You're fucking *dead!*"

One of the guards warned Root to shut up again, but he just cackled and licked his sausage-like lips with his huge, demon tongue. Then he noticed he was almost abreast of Willy and Ben Cherry. In an effort to avoid Willy's steady, stony gaze, Root's eyes shifted involuntarily to Cherry's, whose gaze was even more daunting. Cherry quickly moved his shoulder just a fraction of an inch, causing Root to flinch. The guards saw this and laughed, and Ozymandias Root, chagrined, made it almost out of the cellblock in silence before shouting out, one last time, "So long, motherfuckers!"

Not even two months later, in a ghetto in Greysport, he was caught in the act of attempting to rape a twelve-year-old Puerto Rican girl but was stopped by her brother, a member of a gang. The police, who didn't squander much effort on an investigation, never found out the identity of the perpetrator, but it was obvious that Root had been tortured imaginatively and at length before suffocating on his own severed cock. When they received this news, Banana Jack said dourly, "There is no justice that humankind does not exert upon itself. All else in life is adaptation and survival." Willy nodded, he and Jack looking in each other's eyes, understanding.

Squinty the Yegg was released not long after that, but acted to everyone as if they had it better off inside than having to go and live with his wife. "You give her a good schtupping," Willy advised him, just to see if he would laugh.

Squinty did, which was unusual, and said, "Oh, there will be a great schtupping, all right. And a gnashing of teeth and a tearing of hair, if I have anything to say about it." He shook hands with Willy and, leaning close, said quietly, "She's a good goil and I love her very much. You can't really say that in a place like this."

Willy nodded and watched the little man leave.

By the time the war had turned in Europe, it was Faith-in-Full Goodfork's date for release. It seemed a longshot, but the vodka concern was running smoothly, and those who might have been inclined to rat it out were too convinced of the probability of retribution to follow their inclinations, so popular was the operation. A few men had been caught out getting drunk, but swore that they had made the hooch themselves, as is not uncommon in many prisons.

They had a little party for Goodforks on the night before his release, hosted in and around Banana Jack's cell. Vodka was passed, and Goodforks was grinning gleamingly from ear to ear, rubbing the hook in his broken nose with a forefinger in joy and embarrassment. He gave an orotund and lengthy speech, which had the men in attendance alternately laughing and threatening him to shut him up. Ricardo Espinosa asked him what he was going to do when he got out, and Goodforks said, "Go hunting. What do you think?"

Everyone laughed at that, and when it died down, Banana Jack said, "Don't you come back here, son. It can become a habit for some people."

"Don' t worry, sir," Faith-in-Full said, ever polite to his elders. "I've got other plans."

When things broke up just before lights out, Faith-in-Full came by Willy's cell.

"I just wanted to thank you for everything you've done for me while I was here," he said, obviously suppressing emotion.

"Kid, I didn't *do any*thing," Willy said.

Neither said anything for a moment. "You were my friend," Goodforks said, dropping his gaze.

Willy put his hand on the boy's shoulder and said, "Look, if you hit a rough patch, you go and see Bob Two Bears and say I told him to give you a job. We've got a room upstairs from the bar for strays."

160

"Yessir."

"And Banana Jack is right. Don't you end up back in here."

"No sir," Faith-in-Full Goodforks said.

He was gone the next day. Willy felt happy for the boy, but it made him sick to think that, in the possibilities of the world, Faith-in-Full Goodforks could go fishing with his boys and eat at the same table with his wife before he could himself. It turned out that Goodforks' distilling guild had gotten more skilled in its abilities, and the boy had seen to it that Willy was the first to receive a quart of cask-aged sour mash whiskey. Not very aged, not very good, but under the circumstances, quite a treat. When the inmate with the mop made the delivery, Willy laughed out loud on and off for ten minutes.

Then it was Banana Jack's turn for release, just about the time Adolph Hitler took a pistol to his head down in his bunker. The dapper gent played a few last games of cards with Willy in the library while they sipped from the stash of sour mash, and Willy was wordlessly surprised to find that he loved the old conman. They got quite drunk together, and Willy woke up with the worst hangover he'd had since he'd been free. He still managed to get near the fences next to where freed men made their egress, and after he waited for a bit in the sunshine, Banana Jack appeared in his civilian dress: a black and banana yellow checked vest, yellow shirt, tie, slacks, and even shoes, accessorized with a black derby with a yellow band and a black walking stick with a gold lion's head knob. Jack saw him and bowed formally, then straightened and smiled, doffing his derby, his gold dental work glinting in the sun.

"You give those ladies hell, there, Jack!" Willy called, keeping his voice strong.

"Oh, I intend to, my friend, I intend to," Jack said, waving his cane, "and you get on home to that lovely wife!" With that, he turned and strode past the guards and through the gate, walking lively as a twenty-year-old, and was gone.

So Willy became a longtimer and new prisoners came to fill the cells of the departed. He kept his head down and concentrated on going forward through time. He did some monosyllabic coaching of Eddie Zwolanek in boxing, and it was apparent that some web of magic Faith-in-Full Goodforks had woven on the kid had worked; he appeared to revere Willy where he feared no one else, being only laughingly compliant with the guards. Potential antagonists grudgingly gave wide berth, and the perceived strength of their physical alliance was reinforced by the quiet solidity of the booze operation.

Willy, with his close-cropped hair showing more grey almost monthly, he thought, had to admit to himself that it didn't hurt to have a rabid young supplicant at his beck and call. He associated with few other people and was reluctant to make more ties. With an unsettled feeling, he found himself able to read and think, jotting down poems, and, occasionally, try to meditate on emptiness. Sometimes he was successful, but sometimes it was like suffering from sleep apnea; it seemed as if, at the moment of true loss of self, he jerked himself awake again and into his own familiar misery. And there crouched that black poison.

He marked the days through the wheeling of the years by noting the birthdays of Mae and the boys, of Emilio and Solveig and the girls, of Doc and Edith Homburg, the anniversary of buying the bar, of buying the house. The anniversary of their wedding. He wrote poems about the days that moved him and hid the poems away. Sometimes friends came for visiting day, sometimes the boys came with Mae. Sometimes they didn't, and Mae seemed anxious and guilty, and Willy soothed her and told her that they were teenagers, pulling away into their own lives. Maybe, at times, they were disgusted with their father, and when this thought appeared to distress Mae, he said that he was sure they would grow out of it.

His wife was the one who always came, who was always there. She was beautiful to him in a way that was changeless, and every time she sat across from him, the loneliness and the loss were gone for that very short time. Sometimes he thought that she was withholding things from him, things about the boys, things about their life on the outside, but if she were, perhaps it was better that way, and the lurking thing could wait. After all, he hadn't shown her his scars.

On Monday, January 10th, 1949, Willy was called to Warden Ver Voort's office. Ver Voort had changed little since Willy had first met him nearly seven and a half years ago, and Willy was a bit surprised to realize that the man's idealism had not in the least diminished in that time. He seemed, in fact, to believe that his notions of clemency and compassion were more worthwhile that ever.

"Even after everything you've seen," Willy said, sitting before Ver Voort's desk.

"More so," Ver Voort said, looking at his bookshelf distractedly, seeming a little surprised himself. Willy smiled.

"At any rate," Ver Voort said, seeming to come back to himself, "the reason I asked you here today is to give you formal notification of your pending release. You're to be freed at eight o'clock on the morning of Saturday, March Fifth, 1949. There are papers to fill out, other red tape, but that's the long and the short of it. I must confess that I'll miss having a man like you around. Care for a drink?"

"Sure," Willy said, watching as the warden went to the sideboard and poured from a cut glass bottle into two glasses. He handed the whiskey to Willy, who held up a glass and took a sip.

It was Faith-in-Full's cask-aged whiskey. Willy knew it unmistakably and immediately, and was aware that Ver Voort knew. Their eyes met, and the warden said, "That Goodforks was another one I've missed."

Willy snorted quietly and raised his glass, and they both drained their drinks.

On the night before his release, there was a small, customary get-together with some of the men around Willy's cell. Eddie Zwolanek attempted to give a Faith-in-Full style speech, appeared to immediately forget anything he had planned to say, although he stuttered over it for a bit, and finally held up a quart jar and said, "Let's, uh, drink some a this."

The other men held up their drinks as well. They looked back and forth at each other, seeming to think that someone would say something pithy. Finally Willy got it over with by saying, "Down the hatch!" and tipping his drink.

Willy claimed to be tired and alluded to what would happen when he would be alone with his wife for the first time in seven and a half years, and the men chuckled and paid their respects and gradually drifted away. Willy finally sat alone in his cell, the idea of being free the next day surreal to him.

He was lost in such thought when he realized that someone was standing outside his cell. He almost started, but saw that it was, to his surprise, Ben Cherry.

"Ben," Willy said, trying to act as if such a thing happened every day. "Come on in and have a seat."

To his surprise, Cherry came in and sat at Willy's small desk.

"How about a drink?"

Cherry nodded and Willy poured from the quart jar into the tin cup he had by the small sink. Cherry sipped it, his face expressionless, and sat forward with his elbows on his knees, his muscles bunching under his white shirt. He sat like that for some minutes, and Willy took a drink or two from the jar.

Willy was about to say something when Ben said in a deep and quiet voice, "You have been lonely for your family."

"Yes," Willy said. "Yes I have."

Ben nodded and took another drink. Another minute passed. "I have been lonely for mine," Ben said at length.

Willy nodded, looking Ben in the eyes, letting his own hard face fall away.

"You'll go home and see yours tomorrow," Ben said, finishing the cup and holding it out for more with a faint smile. Willy filled it up to the top, watching him.

"I'll never see mine again," he said, and drank. Lights began to turn out along the tier, and guards shouted the time until lights out. Ben, dark in the white prison uniform, sat back in the small chair, which creaked under his solid weight.

Willy cleared his throat and said, "Yeah, Ben. Yeah, I know, and I'm so sorry."

Ben said, "My wife made me promise to survive when I came here, to stay alive and never give up my hope." He shook his head, staring off into space. "Hope. There's a thing." He took a drink and was silent again.

Willy waited for him to talk.

"I came here an innocent man," Ben said, finally. "I think I am a good man. At least, I hold out that hope. I saw that you were a good man."

He stood up very tall. He handed Willy back the tin cup. "You go on home to that beautiful wife an them two boys. You look after them."

Willy stood up slowly and held out his hand. Ben Cherry took his hand, his grasp very strong, but restrained.

"I don't talk to nobody around here," Ben said.

"I know," Willy said.

Ben held their handshake and said, staring Willy in the eye, "I done for them two Nazi boys. I put them boys down hard."

Willy opened his mouth to speak and Ben tightened his grip for a moment, shaking his head.

"You go on home and look after your wife and them boys. They look like strong boys. Like their daddy. You look after them, now."

"Okay," Willy said.

"Promise me."

Willy cleared his throat and said gruffly, "I promise."

Ben seemed to look down into Willy with that hawk's gaze for a few moments. He released his grip. "All right. All right," he said, and turned and walked silently out of Willy's cell.

The next day was balmy for a morning in early March. Willy, dressed in the workshirt, jeans, and boots he had last worn years ago, walked out through the gates. He looked back through the fence and saw Ben Cherry, who inclined his head somberly, turned and walked away.

Outside the gates in the parking lot, Mae stood next to the car. He wanted to run to her but he walked- feeling lightheaded, feeling like his legs would buckle- and he reached her at last after timeless time crunching on the gravel and held her- right *to* him- for what seemed like an hour. He held her like he wanted to squeeze her into him, put her inside where she would never be away again. At length they separated, gasping, laughing, then nuzzling each other, smelling each other. They held each other, eyes closed, breathing in, breathing out.

She got his jacket out of the backseat and they got into the car, Mae driving while Willy watched out the back window as the prison dwindled down the road and was soon obscured by the trees.

Mae drove down the miles of gravel road through the tall trees, speeding fast enough that Willy's guts shifted inside him as she tore up and down over the hills. He sat with his back against the door and his left leg up on the wide seat, watching her, her pale skin, her light blue eyes, her copper hair, as the sunlight and shadows of the pines moved across her face. He had nothing to say and didn't care, just watched that beloved face with its calm eyes fixed out on the road. He could reach out and touch that face anytime he wanted to, and it was no dream, no fantasy. He did so, then sat and watched her some more.

Finally she smiled and glanced at him. "You're making me nervous," she said.

"Sorry," he said, still watching her. He reached out and stroked her face.

The road opened up on the left as they passed a large frozen lake, and when they approached a small parklike area under some pines, Willy said, "Pull over."

She did, and he got out of the car, slammed the door, and came around to her side. She seemed hesitant, looking up at him and squinting against the morning sun. He opened the car door and held out his hand, taking her small, fair hand in his large gnarled one. He took her by the lapels of her checked wool jacket and pushed her slowly but forcefully against the car. Her face relaxed and she turned it toward the warm sun, her lips pink and soft, and he bent to kiss her.

He had thought, in prison, that when this moment finally came, he would be too nervous, or unable to perform. He forgot all about that now, her softness, her scent, her form something now almost alien to him, something that made him dizzy with want.

As they worked at loosening each others' clothes, inexpert now from lack of practice, he feared for a moment that she would see the scars under his t-shirt, and, following an initial impulse, unbuckled her jeans and bent her over the trunk of the car, grasping her soft pale hips in his hands and pounding artlessly into her until they both came. Then he turned her around and opened her flannel shirt and, kneeling in front of her, sucked her tender pink nipples and played with her clitoris until she came again.

He then stood up, buttoned his shirt and buckled his jeans while she watched, then he bent and pulled up her jeans and closed her shirt and put her clothing more or less back in place. She looked at him drowsily and said, "I haven't felt like this in years."

Their arms around each other, they walked over and looked out at the melting ice of the lake. They said nothing, just held onto each other in the warm sun. At last they walked back to the car, and, seeing how drowsy and relaxed Mae was, as if she were limp with several forms of relief, he helped her into the large front seat and got in behind the wheel and drove away. Her head was soon on his thigh and she was asleep, and he reached in the back and retrieved a blanket and put it over her. He drove along with the window open to the crisp air, smelling the pines, amazed by the fact that he was here with his wife, free to drive, free to go home. It was hours before he realized that he was driving on an expired license.

He saw the river for the first time in all those years from a bluff, and the sight of it caused him to breathe slowly and deeply, the scent of snow seeming to be the very scent of freedom itself, and the space of the river the beginning of all the possibility in the world. When they drove down from the bluffs and out onto the highway next to the river, he resisted, for a moment, the urge to howl out the window, and then succumbed and did it anyway. They drove through Black Marsh and down the last big stretch (this part seeming to take hours) along the river to the island bridge, and then rumbled over it and onto the island. It was strange how little was different; except for subtle changes resulting from the war, tattered war bond posters and the like, the place was so much the same that Willy could almost believe that he had never been in prison at all. He stared around, fascinated, seeing the details of things he had long since taken for granted and forgotten. The boathouse, the park where they were married, the town square and the brick buildings and their shops, the cobbled alleys, everything was the same. The little town was never much to look at and maybe slightly seedy, especially under the growing cloud cover of the March afternoon, stretches of melting snow here and there, but it looked snug, settled as it was at the base of the crescent of bluffs, and warm light came from the windows.

It was no surprise when they drove past the bar and stretched across the front was a banner saying, "WELCOME HOME, WILLY!" He saw this and looked at his wife, who shrugged, smiling sunnily.

"And so there's going to be a party," he said.

"Yeah," she said.

"Tonight?"

"Yep. I might be the boss, but I was powerless to resist."

Willy sighed, a little put out, but decided he really didn't mind. It occurred to him that many whom he had befriended in prison would do well to simply slip unnoticed back into society, and that the best of them- Ben Cherry- would not get out at all.

They pulled into the driveway of the bungalow and Willy had the same sensation of remembrance, the same weird feeling. He was sure the boys were inside, or at least he tried to convince himself of that. If he came in the front door and one or both of them weren't there, it would be a sign to him, justified or not, of how their love for him- and loyalty *to* him- had drifted. They got out of the car, Willy gathering his duffelbag of books and other small items, and walked through the slush and up the steps where the dead cat had sat so long ago, through the screen door ruptured in one of the boys' fights, and into the living room, Mae's piano near the front door. There was the couch where Mollie had slept, there the carpet where the boys listened to the radio. The room was empty.

Willy stood in the living room and smelled the familiar smells, so rich and filled with stories and comfort after the antiseptic odor of the prison. He dropped the duffelbag on the rug and looked at Mae. He noticed her age and felt indebted to it, and for a moment the stone face of the prison came right back upon him. Then he heard what could only be the sound of thumping on the heavybag in the basement.

"Boys?" Mae called out. "Boys! Guess who's here?"

The thumping on the bag ceased, there was a moment of silence, and then a surprisingly heavy tread of two sets of feet coming up the stairs. Up into the kitchen and standing in its archway to the living room stood his boys side by side. *Filling* the archway.

They stood shiny with sweat in gym shorts and sodden athletic t-shirts, wearing gloves to work out on the heavybag. Gordon, at eighteen, was almost shockingly muscular for his age- something which couldn't be seen in the loose clothing he had worn during the last visitations- and Chief wasn't far behind. Gordon had an almost stony look on his face, although a hint of eagerness, something wide-eyed, showed through. Chief stood for a moment in the archway with a frozen look of wonder, then burst out of his pose and crossed the space to his father, running and embracing him.

"Dad! Dad!" he cried, giving his father a bearhug which completely threw Willy aback. Willy raised his arms and put them around his son, allowing his discipline to break and to fall to the floor, and Gordon was embracing him, too, and he encircled his boys' heads with his arms and held them to his cheeks, saying, "My boys, my boys, my boys."

He looked for Mae and saw that she was watching them, the knuckle of her forefinger held to her lips, crying and laughing.

They sat together at the kitchen table for awhile, Mae making them all chicken salad sandwiches, the boys talking- with increasing comfort and enthusiasm- about their recent activities. Gordon was a senior in high school and graduating in three months, planning to go to college in Black Marsh or even Greysport after working for Emilio for the summer. Willy was both proud and slightly hurt when Gordon told him that he wanted to pay for college for himself, having saved money from working in the bar and carefully conserving it and the money from other jobs for years. Gordon was less controlled in his behavior, but cheerful and offhand about going to college, thinking that he would join his brother when he graduated.

Willy began to feel warm and sleepy, but sat at the table and talked to the boys. Mae saw his state, though, and soon told him that he should take a nap. When he stood up, he felt almost woozy, more relaxed than he could remember feeling. He told the boys that they'd have plenty of time to talk, and followed Mae down the hall to their bedroom.

The afternoon light glowed on the sheers over the windows, and Willy found himself momentarily transfixed by Mae's feminine things carefully arrayed in front of her makeup mirror. She stood in front of him and unbuttoned his shirt, and he nearly flinched when he thought of the scars underneath his t-shirt. She made him sit in his wing-backed reading chair and helped him off with his boots, then had him lie on the bed and covered him with a quilt. The room had a clean smell, like laundry dried on the line, and he could detect the subtle scent of the sachet from Mae's dresser drawers, something he would never have paid attention to before. She sat next to him on the bed, smiling tenderly down at him, stroking his hair off his forehead. Her face was kind and lovely, an almost unnoticeable trace of fine grey in her hair, and light in her eyes. He meant to close his eyes only for a moment, but was soon fast asleep.

He woke up when it was dark, and he could hear Mae and the boys talking in the kitchen. He came out in his stocking feet, and the way they were all quiet as soon as they saw him alerted him that he had been the topic of their conversation.

"I'm okay now," he said. "We're all here. We're all okay."

Willy grumbled about it, but knew he had to succumb to the party down at the bar. It made him uncomfortable, made him want to go up on the bluffs by himself or out on the river, but he knew that it was something he would eventually have to face and braced himself for it. He dressed in a comfortable old workshirt and jeans, recently taken out of the closet after his years away and washed by Mae. The jeans were a bit loose on him, and he pulled his old belt to a notch which bore no crease from use. The boys had shined his workboots, and the leather smelled good and was perfectly broken in. He had a cup of coffee at the kitchen table as the boys got ready, and when Mae ushered them in, he slapped his hands on his knees and stood up, saying, "Welp! I guess!"

Mae made a slight wifely protest about him driving without having gotten his license back, but he pointed out that there was no sheriff's office here anymore, and there would be no reason for anyone to pull him over even if there were. Besides, he was enjoying the novelty of driving, even for such a short distance.

There was no point in pretending that the party was going to be a surprise, what with the banner stretched across the front of the building, but when he pulled up in front and found that the turnout was so good that there were no parking spaces, he felt the same social discomfort settle over him again. Stopping in front of the bar, he said, "Look, you guys just go in. I'll park around back in the alley."

The boys, still apparently conditioned to do pretty much as he said, opened the door and slid out of the back seat, but Mae said, "Oh, don't you think we should all go in together?"

"It's...I'll be right in, just go ahead."

"Don't be nervous."

Willy just sighed, and she kissed him on the cheek and got out to join the boys on the sidewalk.

He drove around the block and came back up the alley, parking the car by the wooden fire escape to one of the apartments over a shop down the street from the bar. He shut the door and walked up the dark alley to the rear door of the bar, hoping to slip in unobtrusively.

Silhouetted by the light over the bar's backdoor was the figure of a slim man smoking a cigarette, leaning against the wall, one heel up on the bricks. As Willy approached, the man's features became clear. It was Faith-in-Full Goodforks. Willy almost laughed in surprise.

Goodforks took a final drag on the cigarette and flicked it at the brick wall across the alley, the orange sparks falling to the cobbles, and looked up as Willy emerged from the shadows. Goodforks jumped.

"Shit! Boss! You scared the hell out of me!"

"What's this 'boss' shit? What're are you doing here?" Willy was surprised at how glad he was to see the kid, but felt the old stony impassivity on his face.

"Your wife hired me! Gonna be a surprise! My uncle- Bob Two Bears-grumbled about it, but when I told your missus how close we were in prison, she thought it might be a good idea. Guess I fucked that one up."

"We were close in prison, huh?"

"Well, yeah! I've been telling people about how you straightened things out in there, how you were almost the boss of that place, too."

"What? I really wish you hadn't done that."

"Oh, come on," Goodforks said, smiling. "You deserve some credit. Your boys sure liked the stories."

"Goddammit! What're you telling them stuff like that for?"

"Too late," Goodforks grinned and started for the back door.

"Hey, come here, I'm not done talking to you!"

Goodforks turned around, a sudden look of trepidation on his face.

"I'm serious," Willy said. "I don't want to be known for this kind of shit."

"Well, what *do* you want to be known for?" Goodforks asked with a tone of frank curiosity.

Willy thought about his stacks of hidden poetry for a moment and said only, "I don't know. Just something better. If I'm made out to be some kind of hero, we're in bad shape."

Goodforks shrugged and said simply, "Well, you're a hero to me."

Embarrassed, Willy dropped his eyes and said, "You're not getting what I'm talking about."

"Don't worry, I told the stories right."

"You have a tendency to embellish."

Goodforks laughed. "Sure. I told 'em *right*."

"Jesus, did you tell my wife about me getting shanked?"

"Oh, no, no. I'm not an idiot, you know."

"Sometimes I wonder," Willy said

Goodforks clapped him on the upper arm and said, "Not to worry, Mr. McGregor, I did you right."

Willy sighed and shook his head. "Just try to keep a lid on it."

"You've got a lot of people waiting for you in there. Want to go?"

"I guess," Willy said.

Goodforks opened the back door and held it for Willy, gesturing him inside with a smile. Willy walked into the bar for the first time in years, through the very door he had walked in with Emilio when he had first seen his wife playing the piano in the light of the front window. Again, the sensation was heady and unreal.

The bar was crowded, and everyone in it had their backs to him, facing instead the front door, where Mae and the boys stood, also looking at the front door. The door opened and everyone in the bar cheered, and Barnacle Brad walked in,

169

clasping his hands and shaking them over his head like a boxing champ. A few people booed while others laughed, and Brad made his way into the bar.

Emilio and Solveig were there with their three daughters, all of whom had grown up to be surprisingly attractive and buxom. The middle one, Katita, stood next to Chief hugging his arm and looking at him adoringly. Willy shook his head.

Doc and Harriet Ambrose were there, and the veterinarian Homburg and his wife of two years. Steve and George Hansen were present with their wives, Runty Schommer and his boys, and Larry Cornwall- looking somewhat wistful as he watched the Schommer clan- stood nearby. The bar was crowded with other regulars, but there were many people Willy couldn't place, all of whom seemed nonetheless enthusiastic about the goings-on.

In the few moments it took for Willy to take this in, he had the uncanny feeling of being at his own funeral- albeit a festive one- watching old friends and acquaintances conversing among themselves. For an instant, he wondered what his own funeral would be like.

It was fascinating how much was exactly the same and how much had changed. The interactions between people he had long known were precisely the same, yet there were the strange additions of more grey hair, more wrinkles, larger bellies. To see his sons standing strapping and confident, no longer the kids who chased each other around the bar and wreaked havoc at home, to see Chief comfortably beside Katita, all of it was deeply surreal. This was the bar where he had fallen in love with his wife, the bar where he had shoved the barrel of his gun in Bud Sletto's mouth, the place where he would come for breakfast after duck hunting with Emilio, the place where he had worked so long- untold hours, weeks, years- but it still seemed strange to him.

He stood silently, taking all this in, when Bob Two Bears, working the bar, nonchalantly poured a large whiskey and brought it over to where Willy stood.

" 'Bout time you showed up," Bob said impassively, handing Willy the whiskey. They nodded casually at each other, both acting as if they'd done the same thing the night before. Willy just had time to down the half of the fine whiskey before Faith-in-Full Goodforks said, "*Here* he is, folks!"

Willy downed the rest of the booze quickly before the crowd of people reversed their polarity, realized the situation, and crushed toward him- a few people bleating "Surprise!" (being more surprised themselves) and Willy held out the glass to Bob Two Bears, who smoothly took it and refilled it. The bar was quickly elbow-to-elbow with people trying to buy Willy and each other drinks, and Gordon and Chief came around behind the bar and started servicing customers with unthinking ease. People slapped Willy on the back and pumped his hand, and Willy looked over at the crowd and found his wife beaming at him before she turned and sat down at the piano to play Roll Out the Barrel, the lyrics of which Willy always found to be annoyingly nonsensical and convenient. Mae, aware of this, smiled mischievously at him. Soon almost everyone was singing along, though, and Willy found himself trying to carry on five conversations at once with those in his immediate vicinity.

Members of the ad-hoc band were in attendance, and soon had struck up the music, playing with Mae. Faith-in-Full Goodforks and a few others moved the tables out of the dining area and people began to dance. In a moment that seemed as if the people around him diminished in size and the sound of the music grew distant, Willy saw his wife playing piano just as he had first seen her, in that very place, and he muttered an excuse to those around him and found himself walking through the crowd to where she played. She looked flushed and lively, laughing at something the fiddler had said, and as he walked over to her, people retreated out of his way and all the lines of his life lead to her as if she were at the point where they converged. She looked at him, her eyes bright, decades older than the girl he had first loved, lovely and kind, her face made for him, and he held out his hand and she took it, slowly rising to dance. A circle formed on the cleared floor, and the fiddler, accompanied by his friends, played something slow and sweet, lilting and sad, and Willy held his wife close and they danced.

It was a familiar feeling, but one he had almost forgotten. He held her in his arms with his right hand in the small of her back, holding her firmly and close, his large left hand engulfing her small, fair right hand as he spun her softly around, the people and the bar a blurry impression behind her. He was dimly aware of people applauding, of a glimpse of Harriet Ambrose and Solveig Benitez standing side by side with tears in their eyes, his wife's own eyes gleamed up at him and he felt more warm than he had in years.

The song drew to a close and they embraced, and when Willy dipped his wife and kissed her long and well, the crowd cheered. The fiddler then struck up a jig and the circle collapsed, the floor filled with dancers. Behind the bar his sons watched, Gordon with veiled amusement, and Chief with an unambiguous grin.

As people bought Willy drinks and he bought them back, the noise in the bar increased and things slid into full party mode. Emilio stood by his side with a drink in his hand for the first time since before the most recent war, his friend's hair suprisingly grey, smile lines in his brown face, but still the same Emilio. He talked to Solveig and the girls, to almost everyone in turn, and found himself laughing out loud. He was home and he was free.

It was well into the evening when he stood at the end of the bar drinking a ceramic beer stein of coffee to counteract the surprising shine he had put on, when he heard the sound of loud motorcycle mufflers outside, audible even over the din of the bar. Willy watched a bit blearily as the front door opened and a gang of six or seven surly-looking young men came in, wearing black boots, blue jeans, and leather jackets. The gang formed a loose vee behind the shortish but strongly built man who had first come through the door who wore his black hair heavily pomaded into a gleaming pompadour.

Goodforks, who was behind Willy dropping empty bottles down the chute into the basement, said, "Hey, Uncle Bob!" and tipped his head to the gang of young men.

"Yeah, I know," Bob Two Bears said.

"What," Willy said, "who're these guys supposed to be?"

"Just some greasers from Black Marsh," Bob said.

"Assholes," Said Faith-in-Full over his shoulder.

"Might've heard about this thing here tonight," Bob said.

171

Willy watched them for a moment as they moved through the crowd back to the pool table, and looked over at his boys behind the bar, both of whom had stopped what they were doing and stood next to each other, shoulder to shoulder, eyeing the greasers. Willy sighed.

He was soon distracted again by conversations, catching up with all the small things that had happened on the island and up and down the river, still checking on how things were going in the bar, back to his mode of owner in spite of how much he'd had to drink. He wasn't paying attention at all when he heard a glass break and a shout, the unmistakable sounds of struggle, and a fight broke out involving the greasers and locals- a knot of leather, flannel, and workshirts- and while Willy was still somewhat groggily assessing the situation, Gordon threw down his bar rag and strode around the bar, beginning to grab shoulders in the melee and throw people apart. Bob Two Bears swore and grabbed the baseball bat from its corner and came around the other side of the bar behind Willy, Faith-in-Full at his back. Willy looked over at Chief, who was talking to his mother on the other side of the bar. Chief looked over at him and gave him a happy look, and Willy gave him a palms-down sign to take it easy

The situation appeared to be in hand, with Gordon seemingly brokering a peace. When Gordon turned his head to talk to some of the locals, he was slugged in the temple by the greaser with the black hair. That was all Chief needed; and he put one foot on the rack of rail bottles and another on top of the bar and sprang eight feet onto the head and shoulders of the black haired greaser, bowling over the man and several of his companions before Gordon even had a chance to respond.

That was all it took for things to break loose, and the greasers picked themselves up and counter-attacked. Gordon and Chief were punching and kicking, showing greater accuracy than most of the greasers. The black haired one did a left-right combination on Faith-in-Full while Bob looked for clearance to swing his bat. Steve and George Hansen, both quite grey, had tripped a greaser and were kicking him in the corner while Katita poured a drink on his head and Barnacle Brad, jeering, irrelevantly waved his penis at the preoccupied man. One greaser brought out a chain with which to flail his opponents, but Bob Two Bears got a clear shot and swung his bat down on the man's arm, breaking it. When the greaser clutched his arm and glared petulantly at Bob, Bob nodded and gave him a look as if to say, "Yeah, hurts, doesn't it."

Emilio, coming back from the john, was suddenly at Willy's shoulder. They looked at each other and started pulling people out of the way to get to the fray. When a bottle arced out of the crowd and bounced off the oak of the backbar, narrowly missing its mirror (last replaced by Ole) before landing safely in the tub of bar ice, Willy lost patience and roared, "*That's it, goddam it! Knock it the fuck off!*"

His bellow was the loudest sound he had made in nearly a decade, as if he were cracking off the patina of silence he had accreted in prison, the dust he had willed to settle on himself, disguising him in silence. His fists were clenched, his forearms knotted and corded, his neck and face veined and red. People jumped and flinched and froze in mid-action, slowly turning their heads to look at the source of the sound. Somewhere a bottle rolled of a table and smashed on the floor. Then it was silent.

Willy was breathing heavily, his pulse hammering, his eyes wide. Everyone was looking at him. He held his hands out slowly, palms down, calming, and said, "Just...knock it the fuck off. I mean...I just got *home*, okay?"

Chief released the leather collar of the greaser he had been about to hammer with his fist and let his arm drop to his side. Gordon let the black haired greaser out of a headlock and straightened himself up. Willy looked at Mae, who, standing back by the piano, frowned and shrugged. Willy turned and walked toward the back of the bar, hearing as he went Faith-in-Full Goodforks say, "Don't you fucking morons know who that *is*?"

People began to talk again as he walked up the back stairs, and he heard Bob Two Bears kicking the greasers out to the jeers of the others present – "Satisfy your curiosity, dumbshits?" "Nobody fucks with this island, you greased assholes!" "Guess you got what you were looking for!"- and his wife piping up and offering beer on the house as he closed the door to Mollie's old room and sat down on the small, cozy bed. He sat there for awhile, feeling pretty drunk and fingering the fabric of the bed's quilt. He felt bleak.

There was a tap on the door and Emilio stuck his head in. "You okay, buddy?"

Willy nodded, and Emilio came in, holding a bottle of whiskey and two glasses. Willy shook his head and laughed.

"Mae wanted me to check on you," Emilio said. He set the glasses on the dresser and poured them half full, handing one to Willy and sitting next to him on the bed. Emilio held up his glass and said, smiling ruefully, "Welcome home."

Willy snorted laughter through his nose and they clinked glasses. He held his glass up as if to toast, and said, "Oh, shit, what *have* I done."

They downed the whiskey.

Unsurprisingly, Willy woke up to an evil hangover. He realized he was in his own bed and at home, the light of a cool, cloudy Sunday morning coming in through the windows, and, in spite of his condition, he stretched in comfort, feeling somehow purged. He was about to turn over and go back to sleep when he realized simultaneously that he was naked in bed, and that Mae was sitting in a chair in the shadows beside the window, watching him. He remembered his scars and was instantly awake, rolling over onto one elbow and clutching the sheets to his chest.

"Why didn't you tell me?" she asked, tears in her eyes.

He couldn't think of a thing to say and just lay watching her, his eyes wide, not knowing what she would do next.

"It was in your first year, wasn't it?" she asked.

"Yeah."

She nodded, wiping her eyes with a handkerchief.

"How did you know?"

She tilted her head to one side and gave him a bored look, then sniffed and wiped her nose. Willy flopped back in bed and groaned.

After awhile, he said, "I didn't want you to worry."

She sniffed again and said, "I know."

She stood up from the chair and padded over to the his side of the bed. She was wearing jeans and one of his old sweaters and looked as if she hadn't had much sleep. Sitting down on the edge of the bed, she said, "Did it hurt?"

He held his hand up to the side of her face and brushed away some of her disheveled hair. "I guess I was more surprised than anything. After that I was on morphine for awhile."

"Was your life in danger?"

He bit the bullet and lied flat out. "Nah. Looks worse than it is."

She pulled down the bedding and held her fingers to her lips, then reached out and touched the long scar on his stomach. "It may be white now, but it looks pretty bad."

"Ah, I'm tough."

"That you are," she said, reaching lower, past the scar.

He found that, his secret out, he had nothing to be nervous about, and was surprised at the rapidity of his erection. So, apparently, was Mae, whose eyes widened. He was also suprised at how wet she was when she hurriedly stripped off her clothes, and with virtually no foreplay, he was on top of her, she holding her cheek to his bicep and looking into his eyes as he slid into her. Even now, she was hot and tight, his favorite face looking up at him and he down into her eyes as, in minutes, they both came.

They lay there for awhile, gasping and cuddling in the grey light. Before long, she got up out of bed, put on a robe, and brought him back a large glass of water from the kitchen. He drank it down and laid back in bed, and was soon asleep.

When he awoke, the sex and the water seemed to have cleansed his hangover, and he shat, shaved, and showered (the trio of things which will make any man feel better), got dressed and walked out into the kitchen feeling much younger than a man at the end of his forties. He found a note from Mae saying that she had gone to the store, and walked outside to find the boys beside the garage, under the hood of an old 1938 Chrysler for which they had scrimped, scrounged and scavenged. They both seemed almost startled to see him; they'd become engrossed in their task and the sight of their long-distant father sauntering out into the back yard was understandably strange to them. Willy attempted to lessen the strangeness of the situation with contact. He reached out and took both of their muscular necks in his hands and kneaded them, gently shaking the boys back and forth. Gordon was a little grudging at first, ducking his head, but was soon grinning almost as openly as Chief. Willy couldn't help but beaming, which was an odd but wonderful sensation.

Chief was more adept at mechanical and engineering tasks, which came as a surprise to Willy, who thought that Gordon's more artistic nature would have been better suited to Chief's dreaminess, while Chief's skills seemed more appropriate to those of a young man of Gordon's more serious and hardheaded demeanor. Chief turned over the engine to impress his father with its smooth hum while Gordon looked on, half smiling and watching his brother, who seemed a bit impressed with himself.

"Good job," Willy said, and Chief gave him a smug thumbs-up.

"He's got a knack," Gordon said.

Willy stood around with the boys for awhile, talking about nothing in particular, just getting used to their size and their voices, their familiar faces more angular now, and stuck suddenly at eye level on their surprisingly solid bodies. He imagined that, to them, he hadn't changed much, although he was now on eye level with *them*. This was doubtless a peculiar sensation to them, not to mention the fact that he was back in their lives at all after having become, perhaps, almost mythic with distance. Willy stalled for a bit, not really knowing how to broach his subject, but after the three of them had stared uncomfortably at the engine of the Chrysler long enough, he just dove in.

"Look, boys," he said, "I wanted to tell you that I'm proud of how you handled yourselves in that little, you know, set-to last night-"

Chief looked at Gordon with an I-told-you-so look, but Gordon was watching Willy.

"-and I'm glad that you know how to handle yourselves, and can look after your mother. I'm grateful for that. I'm going to have to sit down and think of a way to tell you how proud I am of you, because words seem a bit inadequate.

"I know that a lot of things have been said about me around here, some good, some bad. The truth is somewhere in the middle. I'm sorry for any trouble you've had, and I'm also sorry if you felt you had to live up to some kind of exaggerated reputation. It's just...I'm just your *dad*, okay? I'm not a villain and I'm not a he- I'm not anything else.

"My point is that I don't want you boys to ever- *ever*- try to live up to some kind of horseshit...*image* that *I* might have, okay? I- I mean, look at you! You're young, you're smart, you're strong! You've both got such *gifts*! I want you to make the most of those gifts and not waste your time on any...." He trailed off, shaking his head.

"Okay, Dad," Chief said.

After a moment, Gordon said, "Yeah, well, I'll try."

"Well, good. Your best is all you can do."

They stood around for a bit more, and after a few moments of uncomfortable silence, Chief began pointing out things about the engine. Soon some of the awkwardness was gone, but certainly not all of it. When it occurred to Willy that, being teenage boys, they might have other plans, he told them that he had something he'd had to do for a long time and would be back in a little while. He got the keys to his old pickup truck which was parked in the garage, assiduously tended to by the boys, and, after expressing his approval of their work, started the engine- turning down the corners of his mouth and raising his eyebrows to show his pleasure at the sound of the engine- and went down the drive and out onto the cobbled street.

He drove down through town toward the river and north out of town, toward the bridge that crossed the river, but turned off before it. From there, he went up the familiar hill road past the Coeur de la Riviere cemetery and up into the crescent of bluffs, up to Maiden Bluff where he had gone with Mae when they were younger, and where he had gone with the boys when they were children. He parked the truck and got out as the clouds parted and the sun came out, suddenly warming him. He walked along the path to the north, out onto the limestone bluffs themselves where they towered over the river, looking out to where the constant flow came down broad from the north, around the islands in its midst, down inexorably to the sea. The wind buffeted him, and he walked faster and faster, soon at a trot, looking down at the river as he ran, birds flying beneath him, the clouds moving off to the east and the sun in its dome of sky.

Willy ran along the top of the bluff, far over the breadth of the river, among the naked trees of early spring, almost hot in the sunshine of the unusually warm day. He ran until his chest was heaving in the cool, fresh air, ran until he collapsed to his knees at the edge of the bluff where a shelf of limestone thrust up out of dead leaves and pine needles, and over the edge he could see, far away, a coal barge as it made its way north. He inhaled and exhaled heavily through his mouth until he had nearly caught his breath. Leaning forward on one fist, he reached out with the other hand and took some of the mulch of leaves and needles into it, resisting the urge to take it and rub it on his face and into his hair. He held it up to his nose and inhaled deeply, and, still out of breath, gasped out. He did this again and again until his breathing had calmed, then took up the needles and leaves with both hands and rubbed them in his hair, streaked his face with his fingers like warpaint. He howled in the wind, shortly, more of a bark, did it again, and sat back on the bluff with his legs stretched out in front of him, his head tipped back, staring at the motion of the towering clouds moving off in the crystal hemisphere of sky. He sprawled back, splaying his limbs like an asterisk, and laughed.

Free, he thought. I am free.

Willy readjusted quickly to his life back on the river, although he was often floated on rushes of surreality. Waking up in the dark and thinking for a moment that he was in his cell, but discovering he was sleeping next to his wife, her face in sleep as innocent as a child's. Braving the cold wind on the early spring water with Emilio, their conversation soon over the initial novelty and back to its usual bantering rhythms, his friend the same but different: smile lines around his eyes, his hair more grey, his manner even more relaxed. Walking into the hardware store where he had killed Bud Sletto, his mind on his list of errands, and suddenly remembering where he was with a hot, dizzying rush; reassembling himself and taking his items to the clerk, a kid of about nineteen who had perhaps heard stories of what had happened in this place, but was not at the moment putting two and two together.

Seeing the boys every day, so large and deep-voiced, so much like him; this both fascinated him and filled him with surges of love and dread. That was also the trouble: each in their own way, they were so much like him.

It was nearing Gordon's graduation from high school by the time he *did* summon the courage, and he knew that he had to do it or Gordon would be gone and he would have missed his chance. He considered getting a good buzz on before doing it, but thought that that would remove all doubt, at least in his own mind, that he was a coward, so he steeled himself to take them out on the river and deliver his sermon in the unparalleled cathedral of nature.

The old cruiser now had more than years on it, no longer even close to the cutting edge of such boats, but it had been dry-docked and carefully maintained by Emilio and the boys while he had been "away". All the mahogany surfaces were meticulously varnished, the brightwork pristine, and to have it out on the water brought him back so far, and so lucidly, that seeing it made him remember things he hadn't thought of in years. He had a tiny blast of panic standing on the boat, remembering the last time he had been there- the sheriffs waiting at the dock- but he, Mae and the boys roared off onto the water one Saturday in late May, ostensibly to go up to Black Marsh for Chinese food, for which the boys, Chief in particular, had a liking.

Mae sat sunning herself on the bow of the boat as they cruised north, and the boys sat with him in the cockpit, squinting in the sun's bright light, the wind ruffling their hair. They were already tanned this early in the year, and seemed to have reached a level of adjustment to their father's return. They were dressed, as he was, in shorts, sweaters, and deck shoes, and seemed contentedly silent and still for the moment, something unusual for boys of their energy. In a moment of inspiration, Willy overcame his hesitancy and dove into the conversation he had been rehearsing in his mind.

"You know, boys," he started, "the night that I got back and that fight broke out, it was good to see that you could take care of yourselves. The world is an unpredictable place, and I think it's a basic function to be able to protect yourself and the people you love."

Gordon and Chief appeared to realize that there was a speech coming, but didn't yawn or roll their eyes; rather they appeared to give him their attention, something Willy put down to Mae's constant loyalty and respect.

"I have to add, though, that fighting is nothing to be known for. It's something that's a means to an end at best, that we only do it to preserve the better things and to make possible nobler achievements. I don't think there's much nobility in fighting itself, but it's sometimes a necessary response to a chaotic and unjust world. I wish it were unnecessary altogether, but that's just...not realistic."

He adjusted the course of the boat slightly, watching a barge headed downstream as they passed it, thinking about his words. "When I was younger than you, I lied about my age and went and fought in the First World War. They called it The War to End All Wars, if you can believe that. Not long before that, people had said that everything that *could* be invented *had* been invented, another stupid thing. I think it's a safe bet that the world will continue to get more complicated and dangerous, with no real end in sight. And now we have the bomb and NATO and the Soviets and the People's Republic of China- all things unheard of when I was born- and the world is not more safe but less so. Plato said, 'Only the dead have seen the end of war,' and I think he was right."

"That's why I think about going into the service sometimes," Gordon said.

"Me too," Chief echoed.

Willy felt his heart drop. "No, boys, I...no." He shook his head. "I don't think you're listening. Don't base your manhood on that. Your life has to be about more than that. It's about who you love, and what you can contribute to...you know... *people*. It's not about being rich or famous, or being a hero, it's about building something more, doing something positive."

"You got to have *your* adventures," Gordon said.

Willy considered how to respond, saying finally, "If I didn't have you boys and your mother, I'd have very little to show for how I've lived. I want you both to do better than that. There's nothing wrong with running a bar, I guess, but I want more from you. I want you to use your strengths and do something positive."

"A lot of people around here think you're a hero," Chief said defensively.

"Well, I wish I were known for something else. I wish I were known for something better. And look: my life has been the way it is because I didn't listen to *my* dad, and I expect you guys to be smarter than that. I don't want mistakes I've made to be for nothing, I want you boys to learn from me and not have to go through the same kind of thing. There's no reason that you have to learn from your own suffering, and although you will make mistakes, remorse is something you should have as little as possible to do with. I want you to listen to me. Gordon, you're a good artist. Go to college and study and you could make a living bringing something beautiful into the world, and you could find a great deal of satisfaction doing it. And Chief, you've always been handy in the sciences, you need to go to college and see what it is you can do for the benefit of us all. That's what we should be about, our intellect, not our brutality. See?"

The boys had their eyes on him, watching him. "Just think about it," Willy said. "I don't want you making the mistakes I've made. We should all be working for the beauty of the future, not wrestling with the ugliness of the past."

They *seemed* to be thinking about it. It was a day that would stand out in the future for its rarity. At the time, though, in the mild sunlight, the sky immense overhead with clouds moving in from the west, Willy had a cautious but happy sense of the return of the golden span, even though he knew it wouldn't last.

June came in pleasant, with occasional gentle rains, the high waters of early spring having flowed down their ancient course and out to the waters of the world. Graduation day came for Gordon and for the Benitez's daughter Marita (out of a graduation class of around sixty), and after a tedious ceremony in the high school's airless gymnasium, the sky having threatened rain early on, Emilio and Solveig had the dependable party at their house by the river. The trees were leafed out with fresh green, and boats moved by, up and down the currents of the river. The regulars attended, along with many others, crowds of high school students laughing and unsullied by time. Runty Schommer was there with his ever-expanding clan, Faith-in-Full Goodforks (who had become close to the boys), Bob Two Bears, Steve and George and Barnacle Brad and their wives.

Doc and Harriet Ambrose were there, of course, having watched the boys grow from their birth, having seen them through everything. Doc was quite old now and semi-retired, a young new doctor taking on more of his practice, and Ambrose walked slowly, relying a great deal on a cane, his wife attending him indulgently, although she was only slightly younger.

Doc and Willy stood together drinking hard cider, watching the horseplay of the teenagers and criticizing Emilio's ministrations at the grill, where he was frantically keeping up with demand, flipping burgers and hotdogs, barbecued chicken and bratwurst as Solveig brought out to the long tables more potato salad, three-bean salad, macaroni salad, vast bowls of the dependable and reassuring things.

"You're gonna burn that piece of chicken, there, Emilio," Ambrose said, pointing with his cane.

"I know what I'm doing, *viejo*," Emilio said. "I don't see *you* cook much."

Willy and Ambrose glanced at each other, amused. They watched where Gordon and Chief stood together, Gordon talking to two adorable girls in swing skirts, Chief touching his forehead to Katita's as they whispered, smiling, to each other.

"I'll tell ya," Willy said, shaking his head.

"Been a long ride," Ambrose said.

"Maybe for you," Willy said deadpan.

"I'm seeing more grey in your hair, there, young fella."

Willy snorted.

After a moment, Ambrose said, "I'm getting pretty old for this shit. The only reason I've held out this long is that I want to see what happens."

Willy nodded.

"Curiosity's a good motivator," Ambrose said. "Got me where I am today. Always wanted to see what would happen next."

"What does happen next?"

"We get old. We die. There aren't any happy endings, really, only temporary victories. I just want to die before my wife."

Willy exhaled through his nose, took a drink of cider.

"But really,"Ambrose continued, "I got to train that kid I've got over at the practice. Make sure he doesn't leave a speculum up someone's twat. And I want to see what direction your boys head in. I've taken a liking to them these last eighteen years."

"They do that to you. Then what?"

"I'd like to see the west coast for awhile. Maybe Mexico. Winter around here is hard on the joints. Never did get to travel much; seems like every time I went away for a day, people around here didn't know whether to shit or go blind. Also, I'd like to see if I can make it to a hundred."

Willy glanced at his watch and made a doubtful scowl.

Ambrose laughed. "Those boys of yours have turned out well."

Willy pursed his lips and nodded, flicking his eyebrows up.

Ambrose took a sip from his cider and touched his knuckles to Willy's arm, saying gently, "You did what you had to, son. Our lives are neither neat nor predictable."

Willy shook his head and stared at his cider. He tried to speak and it came out as a croak, then he cleared his throat and said, "Coulda done better."

"Son, when I met you, I thought you'd either end up governor or a suicide. You've done pretty well, all things considered."

Perhaps Emilio was listening, for he said with perfect timing, "Hey, Willy, fill up my cider, okay? I got my hands full."

Willy made a production of it, going to get another jug, and was able to get away from the uncomfortable conversation. By the time he came back, Barnacle Brad had drifted over and the subject had changed to something lewd.

179

As the sun fell into the west over the bluffs, and the high cirrus clouds coursed through gold and orange, ruby and lavender, a fire was built in the fire pit. A blind eye was turned to some drinking on the part of the recent graduates, but those who wanted to party hard- an inevitable rite- gradually drifted off into the deepening night to meet around their own fires at their secret hideouts up in the bluffs and in woods along the river.

Taking a break from constant conversation, Willy strolled down the river to the spur of land which jutted out into the water off the south end of the island. He wondered about the damage he had done to the boys, about how Gordon seemed to view the things Willy told him not quite with skepticism, let alone suspicion, but without the simple, open trust that Chief showed him. Gordon seemed to weigh what Willy said, judging it on its merits and not simply believing it because it had come from Willy's lips. Would Gordon have been this way had Willy not gone to prison? Wasn't he that way with his own father, and hadn't he been so headstrong and cocky that he had disregarded his father's wise advice, an action which had him out to this unforeseeable life on the river? What would have happened to him if he had listened? Would he have been happier? Would he have done more good?

Willy looked back through the trees to the clearing in front of Emilio's house. His eyes had adjusted to the darkness so that he could clearly see everyone who stood within the nimbus of the fire, the complicated rush of conversations over the scratchy sound of the radio on the front porch. Mae talked to Katita and Harriet Ambrose, and the yellow light from the fire made her hair glow and her smile flash. He could tell by their motions that Gordon and Chief were to leave with their attendant girls and go off to their own party, and he was so proud of the boys and the way they carried themselves that it was almost a weight upon him. For all the hardship, how could his life have been a life at all without them? Faith-in-Full Goodforks said something in a circle of men that made them all laugh hard, the sound so familiar. He watched as Emilio- his great friend, in some sense the author of his life- struggled to keep from spitting out the cider in his mouth, the other faces in the circle bright with laughter. He looked out at the river and watched for a few moments as a barge, strung with lights, made its way off into the darkness and headed downstream. He watched it for a few minutes, standing very still, and with a sigh turned at last and walked back up to the fire.

Gordon and Chief both worked at the bar and with Emilio as needed when school was out, Gordon adamant that he had saved enough money and would not need any assistance from his parents to attend college. He had been accepted at the branch of the state university at Black Marsh with no difficulty, but it was when Willy and Mae took the boys to Greysport, away from the river and on the other side of the state on the lake, that things took a turn.

It had taken those months after his return for Willy to settle completely back into his life, and the rushes of surreality eventually faded, but never went away completely. Ever since he had been in the war as a kid he had known not to take things for granted, but being away from everything he had loved the most, having that taken from him, had thrown the preciousness of what was good in life into sharp relief.

He had gotten up before dawn one day, having slept soundly and awakened with an unshakeable restlessness, and had showered and dressed while Mae and the boys were still deep asleep. He had coffee and left the house, strolling the cobbled streets before the town awoke. It had gotten cool overnight, and the humidity had condensed into a slowly moving fog. The solitude was delicious, the scent of the damp air pungent with life, and Willy walked along, sometimes in the middle of the street, with his hands in his pockets, looking at the houses and then the storefronts, their windows dark. The bar, too, was dark, and all seemed to be in order. The river itself moved relentlessly under a bank of fog, and an old pickup truck labored stertorously north by the park along the river road, its headlights on, its racket diminishing in the mist and leaving the town again in silence. He walked down to the park, the place where he had been married, and walked to the bank of the river. He stood there for a moment, thinking about nothing in particular, and wandered off on the gravel edge of the road.

He found himself walking up the bluff to the Coeur de la Riviere Cemetery at the base of the bluffs, the surrounding oaks black and dark green at the forefront of the woods, dripping with moisture. He walked by the graves of those he had known, the gravestones pebbled with dew. He found himself standing in front of the grave of Mollie Sletto. She had been so young, her life so short and brutal. Willy looked out over the river, the fog thinning now, and saw a boat moving down it, its running lights still visible although the sun was almost over the distant trees to the east. The wind freshened with the dawn.

He thought of all the things Mollie hadn't seen, all the things of beauty in the world, and thought of the things she had, the things to which no child should be subjected. His own boys had not had enough beauty in their lives, although Mae had done so well. He thought, though, that for all their solidity and size they were still boys, and perhaps he had a chance to continue to expose them to things which would bring them enlightenment and breadth of vision. He looked back at Mollie's stone and put his hand on its cool, wet surface, standing there for a moment before turning away and walking slowly home.

It was then that it occurred to him to go to Greysport with Mae and the boys. He went into the bedroom when he got home and sat on the edge of the bed as Mae awoke and stretched, yawning comfortably. He brought her a cup of coffee and told her his idea and she agreed enthusiastically.

They considered taking the train, but decided that they would have more freedom if they took the car, and that the boys would have fun sharing the driving. Since it was not a problem to take off work, they set aside the last week in June to make the trip.

The day of the trip, they loaded up the car with luggage, books, sandwiches, and soft drinks and set out, driving across the bridge and up the river road to where it connected with the county road that threaded up into the bluffs and the hills behind them. They drove though the town of Mt. Pleasant, and Willy explained to the boys the influenza epidemic which had nearly wiped the town out, and how many of Runty Schommer's family, by far the biggest name in the tiny town, had bitten the dust. West of Mt. Pleasant, they came into a long area of rolling hills quilted with apple orchards, and when the highway crested a hilltop, they could see such orchards, interspersed with woods and bluffs, reaching to the horizon.

This was in the days when the Interstate system was still just an idea, and they zigzagged across the landscape, going through little towns at intersections, passing tractors that chugged slowly at the side of the road. They drove through the state capital, where the boys had been on a field trip when Willy had been in prison. They could have made a day of that alone, but that was not their objective, and they drove east, where the land flattened out from glaciation, instigating another talk from Willy, who found himself talking like a tour guide to Mae and the boys. It made him smile to think that his father had done exactly the same thing but in his Scots accent. Willy realized how much he had remembered of what his father had told him, although most of it didn't sink in at the time. He made a conscious effort to be informative rather than pedantic.

It was well into the afternoon when they approached Greysport. The towns got bigger and more closely packed until they were nearly continuous. The highway became a street, packed with traffic, trucks and taxis. They waited for nearly twenty minutes at a train crossing by a switching yard, and Willy, having nearly forgotten about ever dealing with such conditions, hung his hands on the steering wheel and stared glumly out the window, nearly hypnotized by the ringing of the warning bell at the train crossing. Mae and the boys, though, found it all rather interesting, commenting on the traffic and the people they saw in cars and walking by on the sidewalks.

When the train passed, they entered a large industrial zone, with huge factories and weedy lots crisscrossed by train tracks. The boys pointed with disgusted mirth at smokestacks pouring multicolored vomit into the sky, commenting on the various colors.

"Look, green!" Chief said.

"More of an olive," said Gordon.

"Orange!"

"Burnt umber," Gordon laughed, elbowing his brother.

"Mister arteest."

Industrial stenches changed from block to block. One moment there was the odor of molten pitch, the next one of fermenting grain, the next one of acetone. They drove through a long stretch where stockyards and slaughterhouses stood shoulder to shoulder with tallow rendering plants, and the boys crowed with revulsion, telling each other to stop farting. Mae delicately held a finger under her nose. Willy ignored it all and threaded his way through traffic.

They went through a series of underpasses and took a right onto a walled freeway, and when the freeway rose to surrounding ground level and the walls dropped away, they were able to get their first unobstructed view of the skyline of Greysport. Willy turned off the freeway and onto a sidestreet surrounded by parking lots and squat buildings, pulling over to the curb to give them a chance for it to sink in.

There was an onshore breeze from the lake, bringing in a fine mist, but the sun was in the west behind Willy and his family, and tall skyscrapers stood out of the mist, their granite, marble, and steel turned pale gold by the sunlight, billowing grey cumulous clouds lit with gold over the lake behind them. Sunlight reflected in the banks of hundreds of windows, and distant gulls wheeled in the air overhead. The timing was perfect; the city looked huge, simultaneously tough and glamorous, a city of industry like something off of a poster.

"Wow!" Chief said.

Willy looked at them in the rearview mirror, and they were both grinning like raccoons, moving their heads back and forth. He glanced at Mae, taking her hand, and she smiled at him.

They checked into the Gander Hotel, a vast granite edifice built at the end of the last century with a gigantic marble lobby complete with ruby red carpeting, enormous gilded frescoes, marble pillars and a fifty foot ceiling. Chief started to crane his neck, but Gordon nudged him and told him not to act like a hick. Willy was afraid he'd become a bit rustic himself, and tried to recall an earlier version of his personality in which was more accustomed to such things. Mae, a child of comparative privilege, stood calmly at the mahogany front desk as Willy signed them in; a comfortably refined bearing was nothing for her to summon.

Once in the room, the boys demonstrated that they were too old to bounce on the beds, but not to old to flop luxuriously down, taking up a queen-sized bed apiece. They dressed for dinner, and Willy stood in front of the mirror for a few moments with his tie around his neck, trying to remember how to tie it. Mae wore a dress of deep red that even made the boys comment, and made Willy wish that he had sprung for two rooms. They had steak and lobster and wine in the hotel restaurant- Willy and Mae a passing a sly glance agreeing to go all the way- and after dinner they strolled the streets of the downtown area, looking at the lighted marquees and in the large windows of the stores.

In the morning, they showered, got dressed, and went out for breakfast at a restaurant overlooking City Park and its trees and statues and large fountain. They stuck to their plan to go to museums which were spaced among the lawns and trees and sculptures of the park, neoclassical structures cool and elegant in the clean light by the lake. They went first to the Hall of Science, where Chief could hardly contain himself; Mae commented that if he'd been just a little younger, he would have sprinted off and they'd have to spend an hour finding him.

There was an exhibit on the manufacturing of steel, one on quantum electrodynamics (which only Chief seemed to find interesting, not to mention comprehensible), and one on the harnessing of the atom, with illuminated displays explaining theory, and a large model city with a futuristic power plant, fantastic buildings and electric cars, all pristine and perfect.

At the Aquila Planetarium, their favorite exhibit was the one entitled Our Future in Space, which featured huge murals of silver rockets standing alertly on the white and grey surface of the Moon, the sky black overhead and aswarm with stars, and on the orange surface of Mars, with brown mountains on the short horizon and a deep blue noon sky overhead, the rockets in the murals surrounded by equipment and rovers with tank treads and crowds of future explorers wearing multicolored space suits with fishbowl helmets. There were models of space stations and demonstrations of the theoretical drives necessary to carry humankind to the nearest stars. Willy kept whistling and shaking his head.

"I'll tell ya," he said. "What a world."

They took a break for lunch, buying footlong hotdogs with the works and sitting under a large elm down by the lake, watching sailboats slipping by in the fresh, cool breeze. The boys sprawled out on the grass, Mae sat with her legs curled under her while she pokily finished her hot dog, and Willy leaned back on his elbow and watched the boats as they all discussed the exhibits.

When they had rested long enough, they made their way across the grass and up the broad steps, flanked with huge stone lions, to the Greysport Institute of Art, which had, along with one of the country's best art museums, an art school of prestigious reputation. There was an exhibit of Impressionism which had Mae so spellbound that, after trying to get her to come along, they left her transfixed in front of a Monet before moving on to a gallery of Romantic Era pieces.

It was in this gallery that Gordon, of course the most avid art lover in the family, stopped dead in his tracks. On a wall in front of him was a painting by Caspar David Friedrich entitled *Abtei im Eichwald*, or Abbey in the Oakwoods. He stood there, his lips slightly parted and his head tilted to one side as he squinted at the small painting. In it was the depiction of the ruins of a cathedral standing almost in silhouette against a misty dark background, a grim late November forest, perhaps, under the dome of a lowering sky with a ghostly new moon. Around the ruined cathedral stood eight ancient and gnarled oaks stripped of their leaves, and before it stretched an undulant dark field, overgrown and studded with tilted crosses, obelisks, and tombstones. Clustered in front of the cathedral were several vague, dark shapes, cowled monks perhaps, or spectres of the waiting dead.

"Wow!" Chief said, but Gordon ignored him.

Gordon stood there for a long time. He walked up to the painting, then back. He stood close to it but off to the side, inspecting the details and brushstrokes. He stood back again, putting his weight on one foot, and, after awhile, the other.

Mae eventually caught up, and the rest of them walked around the gallery twice while waiting for Gordon. Chief moved to rouse him, but Willy silently tapped him on the forearm and shook his head.

A long time later, when the three of them were resting their feet, sitting on a marble bench in front of a towering Roman sculpture of a discus thrower, Gordon shuffled into the gallery, walking toward them but not seeming to watch where he was going.

Mae smiled a curious smile and put her pale hand on his arm. "Ready to go, honey?"

Gordon breathed in, breathed out. "Yeah. Yeah, okay. I want to come back, though."

"You *can*."

"Yeah. Okay."

So the next day after breakfast, when Willy, Mae, and Chief were all set to go to the city's Great Pier, which had had casinos back in the days of Prohibition but now had a Ferriswheel and other amusements, Gordon announced flatly that he would be going back to the Institute of Art and would catch up with them later. For an instant, Willy considered objecting, but saw something in Gordon's eyes which made him hesitate.

Mae looked at Willy, who shrugged.

"There's just so much to see," Gordon explained. "You can't just cram it in. It's...disrespectful."

"Sure, sure," Willy said. "We'll just see you back here."

Chief wanted to go with Gordon, who said that Chief would be too ansty and would distract him. Chief seemed a little put out, but had apparently gotten over it before they were in the lobby of the hotel. They had a fine day on the Great Pier in the sun and the wind, having Italian beef sandwiches from a stand for lunch and strolling along the city's famous Lake Drive in the afternoon, looking in windows and going into stores they found interesting.

When they got back to their room late in the afternoon, a bit tired from all the walking, Gordon was still not back from the museum. Willy stretched out on their bed with a book and Chief did the same, while Mae took a bath in the huge tub.

Willy started out of a doze when the door to the hotel room opened and Gordon came in.

"Thought you'd gotten shanghaied," Chief said.

Gordon had in his hands a rolled up poster which he spread out on one of the beds to show them. It was a print of the Caspar David Friedrich painting he had admired in the museum. Willy looked up at him, and Gordon flicked his eyebrows upward, smiling. Willy saw that he had set down on the desk by the door a folder of some kind, and he asked what it was.

"Application stuff for the Institute of Art," Gordon said, flicking his eyebrows up again and grinning. "I think it'll be tough to get in, but that's what I want to do."

Mae came out of the bathroom brushing her hair, and Chief blurted out to her what Gordon had just said. A smile spread across her face, and she hugged him. She looked over Gordon's shoulder at Willy, who imagined for a moment a look in her happiness which suggested that it was about time someone in the family did something with their talent. He knew, though, that it was only his disgust with himself overlaid on her beloved face.

Willy said, "Well, son, if you're going to do it, you have to go all the way. You have to be in or out."

"Okay, Dad."

"It'll be tough, but you know how to survive."

"All *right*, Dad."

The boys went out to explore after that, and Willy lay on the bed staring at the ceiling, a book forgotten on his chest. Mae seemed to sense his mind, and came to sit on the bed next to him,   putting her hand on his thigh.

"He's going to be fine," she said.

Willy sighed.

"We raised him to have faith in himself," Mae said.

"You did. I've been conspicuously absent."

"Oh, now, come on."

"And I don't provide much of an example. The best thing I ever did with my little poetry obsession was to get you to marry me."

"That was enough. I love you for who you are."

"Sometimes I feel like I tricked you," he said.

"If you did, I'm glad it worked."

They drove back to the river after another day in Greysport, all a little wistful and thoughtful as they reversed the trip. After they were out of the city, though, Chief seemed to have forgotten this mood and reverted to his essential cheerfulness, so much so that Willy pulled over and let him drive. He babbled humorously with his hands on the wheel, not noticing that Mae had fallen asleep, and that Willy and Gordon were gazing silently out the windows of the car, each lost in his own thoughts.

That summer was one which Willy tried hard to hold onto. He knew what would happen, that Gordon would go away to college and Chief would follow him, and that they would then go forward into their lives, returning only for visits, or longer if they hit a rough patch. It was obvious to him that this was so, but it was surprising how much he saw around him evidence that others had little grasp of how fine moments were fleeting and ugly times were inevitable. They treated the precious in a cavalier manner, but seemed surprised when a loved one got sick, or a friend died.

He made a point of telling the boys that they could always come back and have a job at the bar, but made it clear that this was not the most desired outcome.

"Look at Goodforks, there," he said over burgers at the bar one rainy afternoon. "Told that guy he'd always have a place here if he needed it, and before I'd even gotten back from my little vacation, here he was, entrenched."

"Heard it, boss," Faith-in-Full said on his way down the basement stairs for a case of beer.

"And he could have been a Nobel Laureate!" Willy called down the stairs after him.

"Heard that, too!" came the reply.

"He could have?" Chief asked.

Willy and Gordon laughed.

He took the boys boating and fishing as much as possible, and they camped on islands and sandbars. They all got along so well that Willy was almost suspicious. Runty Schommer was always, at any given time, having a feud with at least one of his many children, and was the perfect example of a man who took everything he had for granted. He was a good friend and reliable worker, and Willy had of course known him for years, but Willy saw his method of being a father as questionable. He felt, however- and for obvious reasons- unfit to criticize.

Although there was some red tape about Gordon's belated application to the Greysport Institute of Art, Willy, Mae, and Gordon put their heads together and, with a phone and letter campaign, overcame any obstacles they encountered. He was accepted, and was beside himself with restlessness to leave. Willy didn't want to depress the boy or make him feel guilty about relishing this last summer of his childhood, but he encouraged him, as gently as possible, to pay attention to the time, to notice its details.

Willy was proud of his son. At one of their obligatory dinners at Mae's parents' slowly deteriorating hotel, Palmer had blearily made a derisive comment about Gordon's aspirations, and Mae had stared at him with a dull distaste while her mother said, "Shut up now, dear, and eat your pie."

"And don't worry, Grampa," Gordon said. "If it doesn't work out, I can always run a hotel or something. Better yet, I could take over Dad's bar, if I wanted to occupy a more important position in life." Willy ducked his head to cover a snort of laughter, and Mae smiled.

Summer drew to a close, too quickly for Willy, although it was smartingly obvious that it could never have been quickly enough to suit Gordon. They had an atypically peaceful afternoon one stormy Sunday, the boys forced by the weather to slow down for once. Willy sat in his chair and the boys alternated between the couch and the floor, all of them reading, while Mae went between attending to a pot of stew on the stove and playing the piano. The door was open to the porch, as were the windows on the leeward side of the house, the sound of the rain and the occasional rumbles of thunder blending with Mae's playing of Chopin. For Willy it was a perfect moment, a fragile thing balanced gently between the past and the future. He mostly only pretended to read while he watched his wife and sons, begging the moment to stay, please stay, just please keep it like this. Don't move. No moment can last, though— no pain, no pleasure— and Chief finally broke the spell by asking if the stew was ready. As they were eating the aromatic stew with fresh bread, the rain and clouds blew over and the sun lit up the front porch, turning the drops of water on the screens into tiny prisms. The boys cleaned up the dishes and left to pursue other activities. Willy didn't realize that he was staring off with a furrowed brow until Mae bent over and kissed it. He looked up at her and attempted to put on a pleasant face. She placed her hand on his neck, looked at him sweetly and knowingly, and kissed him on the forehead again.

They had a party for Gordon, of course, at the bar the night before he left for Greysport, attended by all the usual suspects. Gordon was flocked by girls and surrounded by lifelong friends; he was pursuing one of the most interesting paths of all of them, so it seemed, and many of his friends had jobs lined up or were going into some branch of the service. Willy had been watching the events in China, and wondered what kind of trouble those poor kids might be getting themselves into.

They drove up to Black Marsh to see Gordon off at the train. They ate at the Chinese place but Gordon was excited and distracted and barely ate, a rarity. Mae got his pork egg foo young wrapped up to go for Gordon to eat later, and they were finished eating so soon that they had time to kill and went down to a park by the river where a large bridge crossed into the next state. They watched the river traffic and listened as cars and trucks went over the bridge, not saying much, Gordon fidgeting and gnawing at a bit of skin by his thumbnail.

After awhile, Willy slapped his knees and stood up, saying, "Well. We should go."

The train pulled into the station as they arrived, and after all their waiting, they found their goodbyes to be hurried. Gordon hugged his mother hard- she groaned when he squeezed her, her eyes shut tight. He let her go and she put her hands on his shoulders and looked at him keenly, the sunlight bright in her eyes, and said, "You'll make us proud. I know you will."

"Okay, Mom," he said, gazing back at her for a moment before dropping his eyes.

Chief apparently could think of nothing original to say and reverted to a common expression among their group of friends, "Don't do anything I wouldn't do, and if you do, name it after me."

"Sure. I've always liked the name Dumbass." They, too, embraced, slapping each other on the back, and Willy felt a lump in his throat.

Gordon then turned to Willy, and hesitated for just an instant, seemingly about to extend his hand, and Willy again felt the pang- almost sickening- of the years he had lost. The moment seemed to stretch, both of them wavering, and Willy made a minute gesture, spreading his hands a tiny bit. Gordon did the same, and the tension broke and they put their arms around each other. Willy was surprised at Gordon's strength, proud of it.

"'Bye, Dad," he said tightly.

"Okay, now," Willy said. "Okay, now."

They released each other, and Chief picked up Gordon's duffelbag and his knapsack of books. Willy wanted to say something good, something memorable, parting his lips a few times to do so, but there was nothing there.

"Do you have your ticket?" Mae asked.

"Mom, for the fifth time, yes." He shouldered his knapsack and hoisted his duffelbag, going up the steps and into the train car.

"We're proud of you!" Mae called, and Gordon waved over his shoulder, although already seeming to be looking around the train car as he walked into its shadows. The train began to move almost at once, and they stood by the tracks, waiting for him to appear in the window and wave. He didn't, though, and the train gained speed and was soon well away from the station.

"Well," Willy said.

"He'll be fine," Mae said, squinting after the receding train.

"Sure."

"I told him to call when he got settled."

"When can we go visit him?" Chief asked. "It's boring around here."

"I'm sure you'll be somewhere more exciting soon enough," Mae said.

Willy lagged behind a little, watching the remaining members of his family as they walked back to the car.

It was only in the first week of September that Chief created a little trouble for himself, staying out too late on a Saturday night with Katita in the '38 Chrysler. Gordon had relinquished his half of it upon leaving for Greysport on the condition that he could drive it as much as he wanted when he was back, and Willy was not surprised that it took Chief so little time to get in trouble with it.

They went over to Emilio and Solveig's to "talk about it", wanting to bear down on the kids before they got into any serious trouble. There was no yelling, although Mae and Solveig looked a bit tense, and Emilio looked acutely uncomfortable. He and Willy exchanged a glance which conveyed this, and when the kids had been unambivalently admonished and grounded for awhile, exchanging their own doleful glances, they all walked to the door somberly, leaving with muted goodbyes.

Willy was at the bar two hours later, and Emilio came in, blowing through pursed lips and shaking his head. Willy snorted and set them both up with beers and shots. They clinked the shot glasses and drank the whiskey, sipping their beers and talking about their kids' behavior, each arguing that the gender of their own child was more problematic, Emilio (justifiably, Willy thought) worrying about his girls because of the type of boys that he and Willy had been, and Willy making the point that boys were more destructive and had a tendency to do stupid things like getting in car wrecks or going off and getting killed in wars.

"Never thought I'd see the day when we were in a fix like this," Willy said.

"Is not without its irony," Emilio said.

"That wasn't lost on me, Emilio."

They ruefully agreed that it was too late for them to do anything about the predicament of parenthood that they were in; all they could do was ride it out. Willy poured another pair of shots, glad to be with his old friend.

Things slid into a new pattern, accommodating Gordon's absence, and Willy caught Mae once or twice looking at his empty bed. She smiled at him, wrinkles gathering at the corners of her eyes, and he hugged her.

Willy had seen the last several autumns only through bars and over walls, and to be out in October again- perhaps his favorite month, was a wonder. The colors changed from the dusty greens of late summer, slowly smoldering into the yellow, orange, and red that made the landscape magical, reflected, along with the deep blue sky, off the surface of the relentless river. A touring troupe of actors put on a performance of *A Midsummer Night's Dream* in the park , and although their performance was only average, the gemlike colors of their fanciful costumes seemed designed to be seen in the golden haze of an autumn afternoon. Willy sat watching the performance holding Mae's hand, and saw that, a few rows ahead and down the aisle, Chief appeared to be doing the same with Katita.

In the cool evenings when he was not at the bar, Willy sat on the front porch in a wool jacket, having a glass of whiskey with a cigar while Mae played the piano- often something serene and a little sad, a nocturne by Chopin, perhaps- while Chief did his homework at the kitchen table, quiet, comparatively still for a change, and absolutely absorbed. Willy occasionally had the rushes of surreality again, disbelieving his life in this kind place; it jarred against the grinding days in prison. He occasionally wondered about the men he had known there, mostly Ben Cherry and Banana Jack. He thought less about what had brought him to prison in the first place, but put that down in the dungeon of his mind with his memories of the war of his youth, down there in the dark. He emerged again and listened to his wife play the piano, then got up and wandered inside, passing his wife and touching her gently on the head, and going into the kitchen to see how Chief was progressing with his homework.

They had their usual Halloween party (although ,of course, it was not usual for Willy), but on a Saturday night, as Halloween that year fell on a Monday. Chief and Katita, inspired by the play they had seen, came as Romeo and Juliet. This took a bit of either courage or obliviousness on Chief's part; his group of friends ribbed him mercilessly, but he waved them off vaguely and danced a slow number with Katita, the two of them clinging together, their eyes locked. When his friends continued their taunts after the dance, Chief, still gazing at Katita, suggested blandly that they could engage in a circle-jerk if they wanted to, but would have to leave the bar to do so; he, himself, would be busy. Willy overheard this and snorted.

Thanksgiving rolled around and Gordon came home from Greysport, sporting a black sweater and the beginnings of a beard. He seemed to have become a bit opinionated- Willy and Mae exchanged glances across the dinner table as he held forth- but it could have been worse; Willy remembered himself at certain times in his life with a fatalistic sigh. Chief watched his brother and nodded in admiration, glancing occasionally at his mother and father. Willy kept his face just on the pleasant side of neutral, and could tell that Mae was doing the same.

They had the expected festivities, although it had been the first time for Willy in so many years that he thought he could perceive the differences in those present more acutely than anyone else; he had not been there for their gradual change. Emilio was now salt-and-pepper grey and had distinct lines around his eyes when he smiled. Solveig had gotten plump and matronly, and Willy could see her as a grandmother, especially when he observed how attractive and womanly their daughters had become. Doc Ambrose was smaller and more bent, his tweed suit baggy on him, his skin pale, soft, and translucent. His wife doted on him, and Willy detected that their love had gotten sweeter, that they were aware that their time together was slowly slipping away.

There was the obligatory visit to Mae's parents, as long as the family was all together, and it was apparent that Mae's father was losing both his hearing and his mental acuity. Mrs. Palmer looked after her husband with what Willy thought was admirable patience and tolerance, especially considering his frequent querulous outbursts. His diminishing capacity did nothing to slow his drinking, however, and the boys were only restrained from outright amusement by cautionary glances from their mother. Willy thought it was fortunate, in a way, that their grandfather had always kept them at arms length, otherwise his decline would have been a thing of greater sadness.

The hotel guests consisted now mostly of blue-collar workers, steamfitters and the like who were there for the construction of the new powerplant up the river near Black Marsh. They were the type of clientele that Palmer would, at one point, never have wanted, but Mrs. Palmer welcomed them and seemed glad for the business. They were mostly gone for the Thanksgiving weekend, but some of them came into the bar, and Willy gathered that Mrs. Palmer was looked upon as a motherly figure, while Palmer himself was dismissed with not always mild contempt.

The next time Gordon came back was for Christmas. His beard had come in more, and this time he was not so talkative and full of himself. Willy had the sense that something had gone wrong in Greysport; Gordon's grades were good, so Willy and Mae surmised that there were some kind of relationship problems. Gordon said that everything was fine, though, and they didn't press the issue.

New Year's Eve came, and Willy splurged and bought a few cases of champagne. Mae and Solveig indulged unstintingly in the treat, and got goofily drunk, a rarity. Willy was forced to abandon a rather somber speech he had thought up regarding the death of the old and troubled decade and the beginning of a fresh new one when Mae reeled up, a glass of champagne in one hand and a bottle of it in the other, and put an arm up around his neck.

"I love you, honey," she said, "but sometimes ya gotta just loosen up." She pulled his head closer, spilling champagne on his shirt, and kissed him wetly on the lips. Those present hooted at this, and Willy grinned, his speech forgotten. When the clock struck twelve and the new Year was rung in, Willy had his own bottle of champagne in his hand and sang *Auld Lang Syne* as loudly and atonally as anyone else. Later in the night, he looked around at all his friends, loving them, loving his home.

Gordon came home from school in the end of May and attended Chief's graduation from high school and the subsequent parties. It surprised Willy that Chief intended to go to the state school in Black Marsh, rather than following Gordon to Greysport. Mae pointed out that Katita's going to Black Marsh to pursue a career in teaching probably had everything to do with it, and that love had apparently superceded his doggish loyalty to his older brother.

The boys worked for the summer, coming home tired at night but ready to go out soon after a brief bit of rest. They often worked out with Willy in the basement, lifting weights and pounding on the heavy bag, and Willy had to restrain himself from making repetitive comments about their size and strength. Both of them could hit like a mule kick.

Whereas Chief did almost nothing that didn't involve Katita in the evenings, Gordon spent a fair amount of time alone. Willy and Mae were out for a drive one evening, off the island and driving north along the river, when they passed the gravel lot of a fishing spot next to the river. The boys' car was parked there, some yards away from the pickup truck of some fishermen. Gordon leaned against the hood of the car, his hands in the front pocket of his jeans, squinting out over the river. Willy wouldn't have described the look on his face as happy.

Mae put her hand on Willy's forearm. "Oh," she said, "I wonder what's the matter with Gordon."

Willy slowed the car and watched his son, who didn't notice them.

"Let's go see if he wants to come with us," Mae said. "He looks like he needs some cheering up."

They were slowly driving past the gravel lot, and Willy had to look over his shoulder to watch the young man.

"No," he said eventually. "No, let's just...let him think."

Mae was concerned and wanted to question Gordon when they got home, but Willy made a palms-down motion. Patience.

On a hot Saturday in August, Willy was doing inventory at the bar with Bob Two Bears and Faith-in-Full Goodforks when a Cadillac convertible of a deep, candy-apple red with cream sidewall tires pulled up past of the open front door and parked. The vehicle was unusually glamorous for the area, and their conversation paused as the watched the car come to a stop. Only the trunk was visible, and Goodforks, in frank curiosity, went and looked out the front window. His white grin split his face.

"Holy shit!" he said, and went quickly to the front of the bar as Banana Jack, with a large, round, black woman on his arm, appeared at the door.

Banana Jack was dressed according to trademark, with primary-yellow pants, shirt, and tie, with a black and yellow checked vest -all beautifully tailored- and a black hat with a yellow headband. The woman on his arm was rather beautiful, in her mid-forties with a large smile and warm skin like polished cherrywood. She wore a dark red silk dress and a matching hat with artificial cherries on it, and a ruby brooch on her breast. Willy laughed and shook his head.

"Good afternoon, gentlemen," Banana Jack said. "And greetings to you as well, Mr. Goodforks."

Willy came around the bar and pumped Jack's hand, slapping him on the shoulder repeatedly. Goodforks was nearly jumping in excitement, and, in all of this, introductions were made. Even Bob Two Bears, eyes narrowed watchfully, could not help by smile; people with this kind of style were rare in MacDougal.

The woman with Banana Jack was Ruby Rose Redmont, a blues singer from Greysport. The story came out that they had met, fallen in love, and pooled their resources to buy a nightclub down the river in New Orleans, and that Jack had insisted on stopping for a visit before making their way south.

"Give this man a constructive outlet for his talents," Ruby said to Willy as she sat at the bar, discreetly pressing her large breasts up against Jack, who obviously loved it. Willy kept smiling and snorting laughter as he fixed Jack an Old Fashioned and poured a glass of wine for Ruby. Jack caught his eye and waggled his eyebrows lecherously.

"I had to make up for lost time after my incarceration," he said after a few drinks. "I had a surfeit of energy."

"Ooooh, I know *that's* right," Ruby said, looking Jack up and down rather smokily. Jack beamed. The afternoon got late and the drinks flowed. Willy called Mae, and while they waited for her to come down, the regulars came in and put a face to all the stories they'd heard from Goodforks, who had listened attentively while Jack gave him an avuncular lecture about securing his future and making a life for himself.

"I've got some plans," Goodforks said, nodding. "I've got some plans."

Mae came down at sunset, immediately hitting it off with Ruby, and after a few more drinks it took little persuasion to get Ruby to sing while Mae played piano. Most of the bar's ad hoc band showed up as well, and on a muggy night, the joint was soon jumping. Ruby handed Mae sheet music for some tunes she didn't know well, including a favorite of both of theirs, "At Last" by Mack Gordon and Harry Warren, as Ruby introduced it. She did indeed have a terrific voice, and those who were not dancing- the dancers including Chief and Katita- were watching with rapt attention. Willy was busy behind the bar, but took moments to pause and watch his wife as she played, her eyes narrowed, her head weaving. He wanted nothing more than to dance with her.

During a break, he and Mae, Banana Jack and Ruby, Chief and Katita sat at a table and talked. Willy was at first a little nervous about either or both of the boys meeting Jack, seeing as he was a friend from prison and he didn't want to do anything that could possibly glamorize that grim experience. Then he thought that the damage had already been done through the tale-spinning Goodforks, not to mention that he was slightly ashamed of himself for even thinking that he should do anything less than welcome his friend completely and without hesitation. When he saw how Chief leaned close to listen to what Jack had to say, though, and that Jack spoke to his son kindly and warmly, he just sat back and watched.

At the end of the night, Willy offered to put them up at the house; Gordon was off "being moody" somewhere, according to Chief, and was probably not coming home that night, and Chief was glad to sleep on the couch if they wanted his and Gordon's beds. Jack and Ruby demurred, though, and insisted on staying upstairs in the spare room which Mollie had used. Willy was almost glad for this, as if their presence might overlay memories of sadness with something new.

Willy came down in the morning, a little sluggish from the late night, and found that they had already gone, leaving a note behind on the made-up bed. Emilio came in for coffee shortly after that, back from being out of town, and was disappointed for missing out on everything.

"Oh, we'll see them again," Willy said. He never did, though. They corresponded with some regularity over the years (in part out of a fruitless campaign to get Ben Cherry out of prison, another story altogether) but Willy was never to see his friend again. Their business was to do well and would actually become somewhat famous, especially among music aficionados, for decades.

Toward the end of August, Willy was relishing the last days before Gordon went back to Greysport and Chief left home for the first time. He couldn't seem to make the days last long enough, getting up very early and staying up late, spending as much time as he could with his boys as they slowly faded into the men they would become. They still slept like teenagers, late on weekend days if possible, and he and Mae quietly opened their doors to watch them as they slept, no longer children but young men with stubble and occasional bad breath. Willy could see the sadness in Mae's eyes, the yearning, but when she spoke about it, it was always with a tone of pride. She never once said anything critical about all the years he had been in prison, all the years he had missed. She was not the type of woman to stab him with recriminations in the first place, and she obviously knew how much he tormented himself, because the only things she ever said about his absence were calming and conciliatory. She tried to make him feel better, and many times it actually worked.

They were trying not to count the days before the boys left. Chief was almost jumpily excited, and had rushed conversations on the phone with Katita about their preparations to go to Black Marsh. They had dorm rooms in buildings next to each other, and spent considerable time on the front porch looking at what classes they intended to take, looking at the map of the campus and figuring out the most logical times to schedule their classes and in which buildings.

Gordon didn't seem much excited at all, and Willy didn't think it was because he had already become such an old hand at going to college in Greysport. Willy couldn't figure out what was on his mind; the recent reticence, the solitude, the moodiness. At one of the last dinners they had together, his curiosity was relieved.

"You haven't said much about going back to Greysport," Willy said to him. Gordon shrugged.

"Well, are you looking forward to it?"

"Sure am."

"Got your schedule all worked out?"

"Sort of."

"What do you mean, 'sort of'?"

Gordon set down his fork and stared at his father. "I'm going to Greysport. To enlist. I'm going to go to Korea."

The only sound was Mae drawing in her breath, then the ticking of the wall clock.

Willy stared back. "You're what?" he said.

"I'm going to enlist. I'm going to go to Korea."

"You goddam well are *not*," Willy said quietly.

Mae was white, staring at her son. Chief's eyes flicked between his father and brother.

"You can't tell me what to do, Dad," Gordon said. "I'm old enough to make my own decisions."

Willy's heart was thudding so hard that he was sure it was moving the front of his shirt. He forced himself to breath slowly and deeply. "We've talked about this. This is not for you."

"It's my time, Dad," Gordon said calmly. "I have to do it."

"You do not have to do it. This is not what makes you a man. We've talked about this."

"It's what I have to do. And we have not talked about it. We haven't talked about what happened to you in the World War One. You always talk around it."

Willy looked at Mae and saw terror in her eyes. "I don't talk about it because...it's nothing I ever want to even think about."

"Maybe it's time you *should* talk about it, Dad," Gordon said with what Willy thought might be slight contempt.

"Gordon, honey," Mae said, "you have to go to college. You have your future-"

"Mom, it's okay," Gordon said, laying his hand on hers. "I'll be able to save my money and pay for college on the G.I Bill. I'll go when I come back."

Willy nearly said, What makes you think you *will* come back? The look on Mae's face stopped him.

"Your mom is right," Willy said.

"I'm going, Dad. You can try to talk me out of it, though. You can tell me about what happened to you. Tell me the real thing. All I've ever heard is stories from other people. Tell me what really happened."

Mae was looking at him with naked trust. He sighed.

"Okay, son," he said. "But your mom doesn't need to hear any of this. Not again." He got the keys to the truck.

"I have to...." he said to Mae, jerking his thumb over his shoulder.

Mae gave him a solemn nod.

"I'm going, too," Chief said.

With all three of them in the cab of the truck, they drove in silence to a spot on the river road between town and Emilio's Point. Willy parked the truck and they got out, walking down to a place in a grove of trees next to the river.

Willy sat down against an old oak, resting his head back against its gnarled bark. The boys sat down cross-legged in front of him, and it took a moment for him to realize that it was something they had done together since the boys were small. The memory of them being those small, brown boys was tenuous, though, overwhelmed with the vision of the young men who sat in front of him, calves crossed, elbows on their knees, muscular and intent.

Willy said without preamble, "There are doors you can go through that are one way doors, and once you're through them there's no coming back. I want you to listen to me. We don't have to keep making the same mistakes over and over. We don't always have to learn the hard way. So listen. And *hear* me."

He searched their eyes for their attention.

"There are some things that are impossible to completely imagine. I think that's one of the great failings of our species. We can hand down factual information, but we can't hand down experience, can't hand down the wisdom won at great price from experience, and for this reason we make the same mistakes over and over again."

The boys didn't fidget or even move. They watched him and waited.

"When I came home from the war, what I had seen, what I had been through, convinced me that there would never be another war. There was no way that such a thing could be forgotten, I thought. Such ghastly deeds would surely be branded on the human consciousness, and our world would change."

He sighed and shook his head. "Our species is apparently neither that noble nor that intelligent. The war that I was in was seemingly only a warm-up for what was to come. When the death camps were discovered at the end of the Second World War, I just...we...no one could believe at first that such places could exist. No one could think that humanity could be that depraved. And I had thought that we would learn. We don't learn. We just grow new crops of fools."

"You're talking around it again, Dad." Gordon said. "What *happened* to you?"

"I was getting to it," Willy said a little sharply, instantly regretting it. "I know that you can't fully imagine what I tell you. If you could, going to enlist would not even be a consideration for you. I could tell you and that would be enough.

"Can you just *try* to imagine, though, what a graveyard looks like after it's been shelled, with coffins blown out of the ground and lying shattered open by craters, the bones and decomposing bodies of the dead scattered on the... fresh-turned steaming dirt? Can you imagine what that smells like? I couldn't have imagined it before I saw it, and after I did, I fought for years to keep the images of it out of my head. I have known men who came back unable to feel any happiness or pleasure again; seeing such things had ruined the world for them, and anything good seemed like a deception. I was one of them for awhile- do you see?- but meeting your mother and having you boys brought me back to the land of the living. You are in the land of the living now, and you have to *realize* it. You cannot take this for granted! You must listen to me! What you have right here is what is good, and you have to preserve it. It will go away soon enough. Tragedy will come, death will come, and boys your age are in such a rush to meet these inevitable things."

He paused for a moment before saying, "There were times when I was on body detail and had to pick up parts of men and try to reassemble them. I picked up, with *these hands*, the head of a man I knew. He still had a cigarette in his lips. There were times when there was little point in picking up the remains at all; there were just shreds and bits. Do you want to be looking at the woman you love someday and have something like that flash into your head?

"Some men lost their minds, of course. Some adapted to the situation in ways that might later have driven them mad. On that same body detail, I came over a knoll to where bodies and parts of bodies were being laid on the grass, and two men had taken various mismatched parts- arms, legs, torsos, heads- and put them together on the grass in a way that resembled a whole body, like Frankenstein's monster. They were falling on the ground laughing about it."

The boys were silent for a moment, then Chief said, "What did you do?"

"I remember having to be held back," Willy said. He looked over their heads and remembered the time when he, too, had laughed like that. A German soldier he and members of his squad had thought was dead, lying as he was among dozens of other bodies, had sat up and begun to point his pistol at Willy. Willy's friend, standing off to the side, had gotten off a shot first, though, aiming his rifle and shooting from a distance of no more than six feet. The round pierced the man's helmet and exploded his head, splattering Willy with it, including an eyeball which landed in the crook of his arm in a fold of his jacket. As Willy stared at this, his friend said, "Watch it, he's got his eye on you." They were helpless with laughter for almost half an hour. It shamed Willy to think of it, a memory he had mostly sealed away for so long, and it disgusted him that part of him still found it funny.

"Something decent in you dies when you are part of such horrible things, when you...*do* such horrible things. I've shot men, I've stabbed them to death. I beat a man to death with a shovel. You don't want that, you don't want to be like that. *This does not make you a man.*"

"There is no coming back from it. It's because of that, because something inside of me was poisoned, that I killed Bud Sletto. Because I was poisoned. What normal person could do something like that? I don't want you boys to become poisoned. You have to do better than that or it's all...just in vain."

"But most people think you're a hero for what you've done," Gordon said.

Willy shook his head and sighed again. "No, son. No. You have to be known for something better than that."

They sat for awhile and looked out over the river. "On top of all of that- because of it- I lost so much time from your lives. That's...difficult. Only my love for you and your mother makes everything tolerable. I love you boys very much."

Gordon was watching him with what might have been cautious sympathy, and Chief with open adoration. "We love you, too, Dad," they chorused.

Willy hoped he'd made some kind of impression on Gordon, but the young man said next to nothing before he got on the train back to Greysport.

He said, quite earnestly, that Willy had given him a lot to think about, and that he was still enrolled in the next semester and that was the way it stood for the time being; he hadn't made any final decisions. They hoped for the best. Gordon hugged Mae, but the way he shook hands with Willy seemed a bit cool, yet somehow searching. After a moment's hesitation, they embraced.

Chief was enrolled for his own first semester, and their house was in chaos as he prepared. Willy had similar reports from Emilio, with the additional- and not completely helpful- factor that Solveig kept bursting into tears as she helped Katita get ready to leave home. The preparation and the details kept Mae busy, and she was hard-headed and practical, working down sets of long-prepared lists. Left to his own devices, Chief might have simply stuffed a knapsack with a few t-shirts and sweatshirts, a pair of jeans, an odd number of socks, and a half dozen books, then gone out to the road and hitchhiked- or even hopped a train- up to Black Marsh. Mae kept him in line, though, and it was apparent that he was grateful.

They took him up to Black Marsh on the Saturday before classes began, loading his carefully planned cargo of belongings in the trunk of the car and half of the back seat. Mae checked off her final list one more time, and soon they were crossing the bridge and headed north on the river road.

"You can always come home on weekends," Mae said.

Chief was glum about the fact that they hadn't let him take his and Gordon's car, but Willy insisted that, in his first semester of college, he should be as undistracted as possible. Willy had foreseen problems with Chief and Katita, more or less unsupervised, having access to a car. "Show me some good grades at semester break and we'll talk about it," Willy said. "In the meantime, use some of the cash I gave you to take the train home. And don't just go and blow all of it."

"I've got money saved up," Chief said.

"Okay, well, stick to a budget."

It was practical discussions like these that kept Willy and Mae from thinking about their youngest son leaving home. Chief, himself, was oblivious to any emotions his parents might be feeling, squinting out the window of the car and chomping away rapidly at a wad of gum.

They drove through the campus, looking at the old stone buildings and the walks between them crossing the broad grass lawns shaded by large oaks and maples. Chief's dorm overlooked the river, a three-story brick building with young men going in and out, a few tossing a football desultorily not far from the front entrance. Willy and Mae were aware that Katita's dorm was only a short distance away.

They helped carry Chief's boxes and duffelbag up to his room, after getting directions from an officious-looking resident assistant behind the front desk. The room was on the third floor, small but sunny, with windows looking out through the trees and over the river. One bed was piled with boxes of books, mostly science fiction, and an open suitcase, apparently abandoned in the midst of being unpacked. Willy and Chief looked at this, then each other, and shrugged. On the other side of the room was a neatly made narrow bed and stark walls, and the three of them set their things on and around it.

"Let's help you get settled in," Mae said.

"It's okay, Mom," Chief said. "I've got it."

"You sure?" Willy said.

"Yeah," he said.

Mae flashed Willy an overly bright smile and said, "Well, then!"

"Yep," Willy said.

Mae and Chief hugged, and stood slightly apart. Chief took his mother by the shoulders and kissed her on the cheek, saying something reassuring to her, kissing her on the cheek again with a smacking "Mwah!" Willy watched them and thought of how much they had been through together, feeling slightly outside of their bond for a moment. Then Chief turned to him and held out his hand. When Willy went to shake, Chief snatched his hand back and ran it through his hair, saying, "Suh-*moooooth*."

When Willy jerked his head back a fraction in surprise, Chief said, laughing, "Dad, it's a *joke!*" and wrapped him in a bearhug. Willy hugged him back, holding his son's head to his and clenching his eyes shut, but eventually getting himself to laugh.

At that moment, a slim, pale blonde boy, his translucent skin lightly freckled, came into the room and cautiously introduced himself as Patrick Pinkwater.

"Dan McGregor," Willy watched his son say. "Everyone calls me Chief. These are my parents."

Pinkwater shook hands formally. "I guess I'm your roomie," he said.

"Guess I'm yours," Chief said, shaking his hand. "You like sci-fi, I see."

"Oh, yeah," Patrick Pinkwater said.

"*Worlds Beyond?*" Chief said.

"Yeah! *Galaxy?*"

Chief spread his hands and tilted his head to one side. "Read Asimov's *Foundation?*"

"Hell, yeah!" Pinkwater said, but drew up short and looked at Willy and Mae with his eyes wide.

"Don't worry," Chief said, "We all run a bar. You can't shock them. We're copacetic."

"A bar?"

"Yeah," Chief said, looking at the books.

Pinkwater drew his narrow shoulders together, looked around furtively, and giggled, saying, "Wow."

Willy saw that Chief had noticed this, but remained pokerfaced. "What's this one?" Chief asked, pulling a paperback with a lurid cover out of the box. Pinkwater tilted his head to look at the book.

"I've got better than that in there," he said.

They started to look at the books in Pinkwater's boxes, and Mae said, "I guess we'll be going."

"Oh! Yeah!" Chief said. "Sorry to be so-"

Willy gave a palms down and shook his head. "Just give us a call when everything's rolling."

"And bring your new friend down for the weekend some time," Mae said. "He can come to the bar." They eased out into the hall.

"Your mom's pretty," they heard Pinkwater say. "And I bet nobody crosses your dad."

"Yeah," Chief said. "Didja see *The Day the Earth Stood Still?*"

"'*Klaatu berata nikto!*'" The boys were laughing as Willy and Mae went down the hall, occasionally jostled by other young men.

They walked out to the car and drove off.

"Well, we got *that* over with," Mae said. "Jesus!" She was sitting with her head turned, looking out the window. Willy put his hand on her thigh.

They were driving south along the river and halfway home when they saw Emilio and Solveig driving in the opposite direction with Katita. They waved, and the other three waved back, Katita beaming, Solveig sobbing and wet with tears but faking a smile, and Emilio looking tired and disgusted, covertly giving Willy the finger as they passed. Willy and Mae laughed on and off for the next several miles.

They came home to a house so quiet that they both noticed the sound of the living room curtains moving in the breeze from the open windows. They walked into the middle of the living room and looked around, then faced each other. Mae flicked her eyebrows up and pursed her lips in a smile. Willy did the same.

"Finally got rid of the little fuckers," he said.

"Yep," she said, laughing, and they embraced.

Their sex life spiked for a bit, and they did it almost everywhere in the house that would have been too risky with the boys coming in and out at unpredictable moments. They did it in the kitchen, the living room, on the boys' beds, even on the front porch late at night. Mae drew the line at any such activity in the basement, which she considered to be too "icky". Otherwise, things got exciting.

Willy and Mae vacillated on the new silence in the bungalow, not always experiencing the same emotions at the same time. Willy might be sitting in the kitchen with a cup of coffee and the newspaper, paying attention to neither but staring at a random point, thinking about how much time he had lost with the boys, thinking about the ringing silence of the place. Mae would breeze in the front door with groceries, chattering, seeming oblivious to Willy's mood until she had changed it. Willy might then catch an instant of a look on her face, a flash of concern, and he would realize that she had known his mind ahead of time and set about cheering him up.

He tried to do the same with her, when he saw her staring out through the front door to the yard and the sidewalk, as if waiting for them to run around from behind the house or up the sidewalk from town. Once or twice he found her pointlessly straightening their rooms, tugging at the corner of a bedspread, minutely adjusting a chair in front of a desk, taking a book off one of their shelves and looking at it. He would clear his throat or make other noise so as not to startle her, then come into the room and put his arms around her.

"The good thing about you having them so early," he told her once, "is that I've still got a young, sexy wife." This changed her mood immediately, and they were soon making love in the sunny bedroom, not having to worry about the noise they made.

Doc Ambrose understood the absence of children, he and Harriet having raised a few themselves. He was now quite old, his skin soft, supple and hairless. He had attained a patience, a quiet dignity, which surpassed even his previous levels. He commiserated with Willy and Emilio at the bar one day over a game of chess. "You get used to your kids being gone," he said, check-mating Emilio. "It affords a lot of freedom."

"I've still got some at home," Emilio said, setting up the pieces again. "It's not over yet."

"Make use of your time," Ambrose said, nudging his pieces into perfect order. "It is inestimable and fleeting."

Willy didn't mention his growing worry about Gordon enlisting. He just watched the game and kept his thoughts to himself.

Sometimes it was almost disconcertingly quiet around the home after the novelty of the boys' departure wore off. When he and Mae ate breakfast in the morning, the clank of their silverware on their plates seemed to reverberate in the kitchen. He realized how accustomed he had been to the bantering of the boys voices; even when Gordon was in Greysport, Chief had chattered nonstop. Willy took to turning on the radio and listening to the news to fill in the silence.

In the evenings, Mae still played the piano, and it was more comforting than ever. Willy could tell that she was trying to cheer him and herself up by the uptempo tunes she played; she seemed to avoid anything that had even a hint of sadness or melancholy to it. Chopin was out. She put on a brave front, though, and Willy made silent gestures of kindness, bringing her bouquets of flowers and other little presents.

One afternoon he caught Mae with her guard down when he came home from the bar and found her in the bedroom, going through a box of old pictures spread out on the bed. He'd intentionally made plenty of noise coming in, but this did not stop her from what she was doing. Among the pictures in front of her were snapshots taken at the county fair, or the carnival in town, of the boys on the boat, of all of them together with Emilio and Solveig and their children, of the boys standing looking acutely bored in front of Mae's parents and the hotel. There was even the photo of them and the boys taken at the bar when the photographer had set his hair ablaze with the flash of his old-fashioned camera. The memory of this almost made Willy laugh, but the look on Mae's face restrained him.

She reached out and gently touched- almost caressed- a photo of the boys by the river. Chief was perhaps four years old, his bare feet muddy, and Gordon was holding a stick as though he were pretending it was a rifle. They both squinted in the sunlight, smiling at the camera.

"My babies," Mae whispered. Willy said nothing, simply sitting on the bed beside her and taking her in his arms.

They received several post cards and phone calls from Chief before they heard anything at all from Gordon. Willy was often nauseous with worry, and he could tell by the frozen look on Mae's face, as if she were trying to keep from furrowing her brow, that she felt the same.

Faith-in-Full Goodforks took a leave of absence to go up north, and Mae took the opportunity to fill in at the bar. She worked longer hours than she had since Willy had gotten out of prison, and Willy saw that she did at least as good a job of running the place as he did. He began to get angry at Gordon for not writing to them, and the only number they had for him had been disconnected over the summer. This made him furious.

Mae checked the mail on a Saturday and came into the kitchen where Willy was reading the paper and listening to the news. The front page article was about the "police action" in Korea, as was the current topic on the radio. She said nothing, but laid down next to his right hand an envelope. Under Gordon's name, the return address was a military base in the south.

"Goddam it," Willy said. He folded the paper and set it down. He stared out the kitchen window, then picked up his coffee cup and sipped from it without moving his eyes.

"Why don't you open it," he said.

Mae paused, but said, "All right." She used a knife from one of the two place settings to do it.

She read aloud, "Mom, I love you. Don't worry, I'll be okay. Dad, I had to do this. I heard what you said, but this is my time. I'll be in touch when I can. Love, Gordon."

She handed it to Willy, and he read it for himself. "Goddam it," he said again. His anger picked up momentum and he swore vilely on and off for almost fifteen minutes. Then he went down into the basement and hammered at the heavy bag for at least a half hour more. When it was quiet, and Mae smelled cigar smoke, she knew that he was drinking potato vodka and scowling at nothing, down among his tools and weights, cans of nails and screws and nuts and bolts, his trunk of old poetry, his stash of old coins. When he finally came up the stairs and stood in front of where she sat on the couch.

"It's my fault," he said.

She started to say something, but he held up his hand. "It's my fault," he repeated. "You know it is." He walked out the front door before she could say anything else.

Chief came home that weekend, getting a ride with Emilio and Solveig, who had gone to pick up Katita. There was no room in the front of Emilio's pickup for the four of them, and, as Chief had invited his roommate Patrick Pinkwater home for the weekend, he would have had to sit in the bed of the pickup in any event. When Willy heard this he smiled, knowing Emilio's other reason for keeping Chief in the back.

Pinkwater was from a suburb of Greysport and had never really seen the river, let alone ridden in a pickup truck, and the fun and beauty of the ride- the autumn bluffs on one side and the river on the other, the blasting wind, having to shout to be heard- had him running off at the mouth when Emilio dropped the two boys off in front of bungalow.

Chief and his friend were so ebullient that Mae and Willy agreed, in a mutual glance, that they would leave off mention of Gordon's enlistment until later in the weekend. They offered to have a cookout in the backyard for the boys, but it was obvious that Patrick was wild about the notion of going to the bar. For Chief, the idea of being in the bar was not novel, of course, but he pitched it to his father on behalf of his friend, after having tried to talk him into seeing some of the area's natural beauty, even with the enticement of a few sixpacks of beer.

"He just wants to see himself as experienced," Chief explained.

"Okay," Willy said. "But keep a lid on it."

Amazingly, he held himself back on a lecture on the subject that all young people wanted to see themselves, and to be seen, as experienced, and that that was why Chief's brother was now going to Korea. He repressed the urge to shake his head like a bloody dog when he thought of it. Then, wherever he was, the thought of his son going there made him throw back his head and clench his eyes in pain.

Chief and Patrick, though, had a good time. On a Saturday night, young Pinkwater got to drink beer and play pool. He got to do shots- when Willy wasn't looking- with Barnacle Brad and the Hansen brothers, the former lighting the end of his increasingly white beard on fire, to the amusement and disgust of the boys and other patrons, while the Hansen brothers generously tipped a dour Bob Two Bears to give the boys shots of whiskey. Chief did well, tossing down shots and beers in cool way which impressed, to the point of consternation, the onlookers who had known him when he was young.

Not so, though, for young Pinkwater, who got slurringly hammered. He began to give a speech about the honor he felt to be in the bar of a hero (Chief held his hands up in an attempt to prevent this), and all the regulars tried to shush him when, at the other end of the bar, Willy seemed to hear it, his eyes clicking over to them while he talked to a patron. When Mae sat down to play the piano, though, the young man appeared to lose notice of everything else, swooningly fixed on his friend's beautiful mother. Mae played away, and, over the course of a half hour, the ad hoc band set up around her and began to play along.

The pallid and inebriated Pinkwater reached his peak when he said, "I love these fuckers!" He tipped back his mug of beer and sloppily misaimed, two rivulets running from the corners of his mouth to soak his shirt. Chief, safely drunk himself, howled, and Barnacle Brad and the Hansens laughed at the whole thing.

Pinkwater seemed to take the laughter as positive attention, pouring himself more beer from the pitcher and slopping his mug around, his lips wet, saying, "Hey! That shit! Fuckin'..."

This was immediately followed by a convulsion of his stomach and a hunching of his shoulders, his mouth working. He bolted out the door. The Hansen brothers and Barnacle Brad roared at this.

"Pop goes he weasel!" Brad howled. Chief joined them briefly in their laugher, but quickly went out the door to look after his friend, who was spewing between two parked cars.

The next day, young Pinkwater was saved from a savage hangover only by the fact that Chief had taken him home, supporting the reeling and vomit-breathed but still jolly boy all the way, and making him stay awake until he had consumed at least a gallon of cold water, giving him aspirin at the end of the process, The boy was still a little bleary, but not nearly as bad as he would have been if left to his own unsophisticated devices.

When Willy found the two boys sitting at the kitchen table in the morning- this time Chief was getting Pinkwater to drink orange juice- he came and sat down, bringing the letter from Gordon with him.

"So," he said, "are you fellas feeling a little more *experienced* this morning?"

The two young men looked at each other and shrugged.

"Sure, Mr. McGregor" Pinkwater said.

"I guess so," Chief said, a bit warily.

"You want to know a good way *not* to get experience?"

The boys shrugged again.

Willy flipped the letter on the table. Chief spread it out and read it. His eyes widened, and he looked up at his father.

"Did you know anything about this?" Willy asked.

"No sir, I sure didn't." Willy could see his surprise and knew that he was telling the truth. Willy watched him for a moment nonetheless.

"Patrick," Willy said at length, "I've talked to my boys time and time again about what's important in life. About when to fight and when not to fight. About when it's right and when it's not, and when your capacity for it as a young man is simply being used. Have your folks ever talked to you about anything like this?"

Pinkwater looked at Dan, who was watching him but remained expressionless. "Uh, no sir," he said. "I guess not."

"No?"

"No sir," Pinkwater said. "They don't really talk to me about much at all, come to think of it."

Willy exhaled through pursed lips, got up and poured himself a cup of coffee. He sat back down at the kitchen table, leaned back in the chair, and stretched his legs out next to the table.

"Allow me to explain," he said. Willy felt that Gordon, if present, would have gotten up and left, or at least rolled his eyes, but Chief- to his credit- leaned forward and prepared to listen again.

"I thought I'd gotten through to Gordon," Willy said, summing up, "or at least I'd hoped I had. I guess he was going to do what he was going to do all along, though. There's no talking sense to some people. I know. I've been one of those people. I'd like to think it's different with you two, though. Imagine how it'd be if we could hand down wisdom, and people wouldn't have to constantly learn old lessons the hard way. Imagine what a world that'd be."

Willy gave the boys a ride back to Black Marsh, Pinkwater in the front, and Chief and Katita sitting in the back, managing to do nothing that Willy could see in his rearview mirror. Willy treated them all to lunch at Fung's Golden Dragon, their favorite Chinese restaurant, before he left, first reminding Chief to keep his nose to the grindstone.

His drive back consisted of little but worry about Gordon. When he got home, he saw that Mae was in the same state. They didn't conceal their feelings from each other, but there ultimately wasn't much to say on the subject. They wouldn't receive another letter from Gordon until he was done with his basic training, and the military jargon the young man used brought home the reality of the situation to Willy unsparingly. Meanwhile, Chief called from school and dropped a hint to Mae that he was considering marrying Katita.

"What next," was all Willy had to say.

While the two of them were worrying about the boys, life pulled one of its surprises when Mae's father, in his seventies and quite drunk by ten-thirty in the morning, fell down the entire flight of wooden stairs from the second floor of the hotel. Amazingly, he'd broken nothing- not even the glass which had held his gin- and when Mae's mother ran over to where he sprawled in the sunlight on the oriental rug at the base of the stairs, he simply got up, dusted himself off blearily, told his wife to unhand him, and staggered over to a couch in the sitting room before the large front windows of the hotel.

"Are you sure you're all right?" Mrs. Palmer asked him.

"Of course I am, dammit!" he yelped. "Now leave me alone."

He stretched out on the couch and almost instantly passed out. Mrs. Palmer shook her head in disgust and walked into the kitchen, caring little if a guest came in and saw him. He looked harmless enough.

She came out awhile later when a new guest rang the bell at the front desk. She had hoped to beat her husband there, but could see over the guest's shoulder that Palmer was still on the couch, and was thankful for it. She smilingly gave the guest his key, told him where to find the room upstairs, and waited until he had gone up with his suitcase. Then she came around the counter and walked into the sitting room.

"Get up!" she said, standing over him. "Get up! Go to bed and sleep it off!"

Palmer didn't move. She repeated herself. Then she realized that not even his chest was moving. She reached out, took his wrist, and felt for his pulse. After several moments, she dropped the wrist, saying, "Huh!"

She sat down in a chair next to the couch.

She was still sitting there half an hour later when the recently arrived guest came back down the stairs, ready to go about his business. He began talking to her in a cheerful manner, walking across the floor, when he took in the scene and stopped in his tracks.

"Is...he okay?" he asked.

Mrs. Palmer looked up at him, sighed, and smiled a tired smile.

"Drunk?" the guest asked conspiratorially.

"Nope," Mrs. Palmer said, still smiling. "Dead."

Doc Ambrose's young partner determined the cause of death to be a subdural hematoma. When he'd gotten up from his spill, Palmer had already been bleeding inside his skull. When he'd staggered over to the couch and passed out, the increasing pressure of the bleeding in his skull guaranteed that he would never get up again.

When Mrs. Palmer notified Mae, driving over to tell her, Mae sat down at the kitchen table. Her reaction was the same as her mother's.

"Huh!" she said.

When Willy came home- she didn't want to bother him with a call at the bar- she told him, seeming distant and a little puzzled. Willy's dislike for the man was no secret, of course, and he wasn't a liar. He just kept his mouth shut and sat down on the couch next to her, holding her hand.

The funeral was sparsely attended. Chief came down from school with Katita, inevitably, by his side. Emilio and Solveig and the rest of their clan were there out of solidarity, along with a few other of their other friends. Palmer, himself, had had no friends of his own to attend, although Mae later joked that she was surprised that a bill collector didn't show up. Mrs. Palmer was dry-eyed and matter-of-fact about the whole thing, and surprised the hell out of everyone by saying that she'd buy drinks at the bar afterwards. Willy and Mae looked at each other with expressions of amazement.

"Oh, it's about time," Edith Palmer said. "Jesus!"

"Okay," Willy said, "but you're not buying. It's on me."

"We'll see about that, young man."

The atmosphere was less than doleful. Mrs. Palmer asked for champagne, and when it was poured for those clustered around, she raised her glass in a toast. "Here's to me selling that damn hotel!"

Mae did a puzzled double-take between her mother and Willy, and laughed out loud. She clinked glasses with her mother, still with a look of amusement and disbelief.

Her mother talked easily with Barnacle Brad and the Hansen brothers, and it was a side of her that no one could remember seeing. It didn't deter Mae, though, and she soon sat down at the piano and began to play The Beer Barrel Polka, which Willy couldn't remember her playing since the Halloween at least ten years before when she'd dressed as Marie Antoinette and he as a pirate.

The whole thing got rather raucous, unsurprisingly. Willy felt one of those perfect moments when he looked around the bar, saw most of his friends smiling and talking and laughing, saw his wife standing close to her mother, also laughing and drinking. The sight of his mother-in-law like that was such a pleasing visual non sequitur that he shook his head in marvel at it. At one point, Mae and Edith each had drinks in their hands and their arms around each others' shoulders, and seeing his wife so happy next to her mother made it one of the best moments in his life. They laughed together at something Barnacle Brad said, and then, almost immediately, there was an instant of shared sadness. Their eyes teared and they touched their foreheads together- something Willy had never seen them do- but then they pulled their heads apart, brushed their tears away in a remarkably similar gesture, and clinked their glasses together again, suddenly laughing.

The ad hoc band trickled in and people, without being asked, moved away from the space by the front windows and the piano so that they could set up. Willy sent them pitchers of beer, and they began to play. The man with the tin whistle was first- always the most perspicacious, his notes piercing the din of the crowd, getting their attention- and the others soon joined in.

They played a few jigs and a reel, standard fare which everyone loved, as much as they had the one-time-only appearance by Ruby Rose Redmont. Mae stayed away from the piano for most of the tunes, sitting down to play only occasionally, and on request.

When the band played a slow and sad tune, Bob Two Bears, to the amazement of those still capable of it, came around the bar and held out his large hand to Mrs. Palmer, who sat in a chair weaving her head to the music. She replied by clapping her attention to the large man, holding up an index finger while finishing her drink, and getting up to dance.

Everyone else cleared away or sat down. The two danced slowly, Mrs. Palmer with her head to the chest of Bob Two Bears, whose own eyes were closed. Mae and Willy exchanged a glance so subtle that those who saw it would be unable to decipher it: peace, it said. Happiness. Resolution.

The dance ended, and Bob Two Bears held Mrs. Palmer's fingertips and bowed. She curtsied back, although a little creakily, and sat back down at her place. Those around her congratulated her, and she was given another drink.

When Willy judged things had gone on long enough- and he was confirmed by a thumbs-up from his wife- he acted like he was taking his mother-in-law into the back of the bar, inviting her with some seriousness. When he got her moving, he took her out through the darkened restaurant section into the alley, where he had parked their car.

"I'll just take you home," he said. "It's been a pretty long day for you."

"I always liked you," she said a bit blurrily. "Might have gone a bit far protecting my daughter and grandkids, but it's nothing *that* old son of a bitch would've done. Ever. You've got my vote, kid."

He smiled that she called him "kid", and opened the passenger door for her. "Your daughter's worth it, ma'am," he said.

"Worth time in prison?" she asked, looking him keenly in the eye as she got into the car.

"Oh, yeah," he said, and shut the door.

When he got back to the bar, things were so loud that only a few people had noticed him missing, and most of those wanted something from him. He poured a mug of coffee for himself, and many drinks for others.

Mae's essential cheerfulness deflected much of the intended commiseration of those leaving the bar at closing time. She accepted drinks or took rain checks, which accounted for her being only moderately tipsy when the bar was empty. Chief, Katita, and the employees had already left.

Willy wiped down the bar as a matter of habit while Mae sat watching him, her cheek in the palm of her hand.

"You okay?" he asked.

"Peachy," she said.

Willy shut down the lights and walked her out into the alley. It was so beautiful out, they decided to leave the car where it was. She took his arm and leaned her head to his shoulder as they walked.

"One thing I'll say for my father," Mae said, "he made me appreciate the man I've got."

Willy scowled, made a fist, and bunched his large biceps. Mae felt it, narrowed her eyes, and said, "Ooooh!"

They walked home and turned on the lights in the silent living room.

The next day, Mae drove up to the hotel, parked the car, strode into the lobby and into the large front room of the hotel. Her heels alternately clacked on the hardwood and clumped on the oriental rugs. She walked into the large front room with its tall windows overlooking the river. There sat the grand piano Frederick Ferrier had once played, the one from which she had been banned by her father.

It had been decades in coming. Mae walked over to the piano, pushed out its bench seat with a loud, vibrating screech, and sat down. She tested the keys, found them adequate, and began to play a polonaise, warming to it and soon pounding the keys vigorously. Her mother heard the sound and came into the room, stopping for a moment as a smile spread across her face, then sitting on the couch where her husband had died. She nodded her head in time with the music. Mae looked at her and smiled, playing in the sunlight.

She was quiet but smiling that night as they read in the living room, and Willy knew that she would be all right. For the time being, at any rate. It was getting undeniably crisp in the mornings and the trees went to their customary explosion of color, a phenomenon forever reinvigorated for Willy after his deprivation in prison. Willy and Mae got Emilio and Solveig and the girls on Willy's old cabin cruiser and motored up to Black Marsh. They had called Chief and Katita to warn them that they were coming, not wanting to interrupt anything embarrassing. They took their time on the trip, stopping for lunch at a little restaurant by one of the locks upriver, then cruising up to where Chief could see them from his dorm window.

Chief and Katita ran out across the autumn lawn of maples and oaks hand-in-hand, chattering and laughing and looking witlessly youthful. Willy and Emilio exchanged a dour glance: these kids had no idea that was in store for them.

Solveig, now quite round and large-butted, said, "Ohhhhh, they're so *cute!*"

Mae sighed, holding one hand over her eyes against the sun and waving with the other to the kids. "Yeah," she said. "Yeah, they are."

Willy pulled up next to one of the small docks of the college boat club when he saw the kids. Emilio stood on the starboard side of the boat, his knees slightly bent to accommodate the bobbing, extending a hand as the kids jumped aboard. Willy pulled away and out into the river.

"Have you heard anything from Gordon?" was the first thing out of Chief's mouth.

"No," Willy and Mae said simultaneously.

Chief's face was unreadable, but he settled into the cockpit sitting very close to Katita, who joked with her sisters.

"You?" Willy asked. Chief didn't answer, smiling and watching Katita and the girls.

"Chief," Willy said.

"Huh?" Chief said, turning to his father with a smile on his face.

"Have you heard anything?"

"Nope," Chief said, making eye contact for a moment before turning back to the girls. Willy couldn't tell whether or not Chief was trying to deceive him.

They had a picnic out on the river, dropping anchor downstream from an island. The kids gathered on the bow of the boat, laughing and shushing each other, while the adults stayed in the cockpit, pretending not to listen to the kids and to have a good time.

Chief and Katita made no mention of anything regarding marriage, although the adults were already prepared with a line of reasoning in case they did. They had to finish college first, they were too young, there was plenty of time; it had all been discussed beforehand and the parents had a unified front. The fact that it never came into use puzzled them, but, as Emilio later pointed out, it was better to be overprepared than underprepared for just about anything.

They dropped the kids off later in the afternoon and cruised back down the river, tying up at Emilio's dock before dark. Emilio and Solveig invited them in, but they claimed to be tired and left, driving home in silence. The house, once again, seemed more silent than ever when they got in the door.

In November, they finally received a rather terse note from Gordon saying that he had finished basic training and gone into advanced. He said that he had gotten surprisingly accustomed to being continually screamed at and to lousy food. Although the tone of the note was wry, even cynical, nowhere in it did he say that he might have done the wrong thing. All in all, it was so emotionally neutral and devoid of content that it answered almost no questions, merely alleviating their worry for the moment. Gordon said that he would not be coming home for the holidays, and signed it with love to both of them.

Willy went duck hunting with Emilio when it began to get cold out and the leaves were being blown off the trees by the grey north wind; there was great reassurance in that old ritual. They drank coffee from a thermos in the boat, sitting and not saying much. Willy had always been able to talk to his old friend about everything, but one of his current subjects of worry was that Chief was going to get Katita pregnant, and it was a topic he couldn't begin to guess how to broach. He was virtually positive that his son and his friend's daughter were having sex, but he also knew what a protective and doting father Emilio was. His daughters were still his babies, and Willy thought he was obdurately unwilling to see his eldest as a sexual being. Willy had talked to both of the boys about their responsibilities regarding sex and methods of contraception, but he knew that it was a far easier thing to talk to them than for Emilio to even imagine doing with his daughters. Willy visualized Emilio clapping his hands over his ears and simply walking away if the subject ever came up between Solveig and the girls, but knew that, in reality, Solveig would have thought that it was quite improper to ever discuss such things at all. In the end, he had to trust what the boys would do with the knowledge that they had taken away from his and Mae's unusually candid approach to such topics, and let his best friend dwell in the false security of his rare blind spot. He kept his mouth shut and watched Emilio scanning the sky with a peaceful and patient look on his face.

He and Mae talked about their sense of the wheeling of the years, that they simultaneously wanted to squeeze all that they could out of each day- the older they got, the more they recognized their preciousness- but at the same time, they wanted to get through the next few years quickly without mishap befalling their sons. The things that were beyond their control they responded to with a relaxed attitude, riding the inevitable waves of circumstance, but there would always be those worries about things closer to their heart that they would be unable to put away.

Mae was beautiful in her early forties, and Willy, who became more obstinate about his working out than ever, was tougher and in better shape than most men twenty years younger than he. Willy never questioned the worth of his continued training and honing of his skills; he pounded on the heavy bag and lifted his weights in the basement as a matter of ritual, feeling slightly nauseous and ill-at-ease if he missed doing it for more than a few days. Most of the time he didn't think about his years in prison or what had put him there, he simply found pleasure in the routine and the rhythms of his life and tried to pay acute attention to the simple moments of happiness it provided.

There was another opulent Thanksgiving, the cast of characters changing somewhat but the essential nature of it the same. They missed Gordon, but had known for years that such absences would be inevitable, having talked- even when the boys were quite young- about the likelihood of their moving away one day, even far away. They joked about what a relief it was too have them out of the house, and this alleviated some of the loneliness.

"I always saw our mission as parents," Mae said, "as successfully working ourselves out of a job."

"So far, so good," Willy said.

They went up to Black Marsh to get Chief for the holiday break. The dormitory room Chief shared with the Pinkwater kid had become a shrine to science fiction, with movie posters adorning the walls, and shelves that Chief had installed bulging with paperbacks, no apparent concern having been given to order. Both the boys were, in fact, sprawled on their respective bunks, reading science fiction novels and eating potato chips when Willy and Mae arrived.

"Hard at work?" Willy said as they came in the door.

"Hardly workin'," Chief laughed, putting down his book and standing to embrace his parents. Pinkwater also rose, shaking hands rather formally, which struck Willy as odd. He put it down to the boy being shamefaced about getting riotously drunk on his visit, and let it go at that.

When Chief was ready to go, Mae and Willy wished Pinkwater happy holidays.

Pinkwater shrugged. "My folks aren't like you," he said. "I'm anticipating acrimonious arguments. I wouldn't go home if they weren't paying my tuition."

Willy was slightly taken aback, "Well, uh, try to have a good time anyway, Patrick."

"Yessir."

"And you come down to visit us any time you get the chance," Mae said.

"Yes ma'am," Pinkwater said, smiling and- if Willy wasn't mistaken- even blushing a little.

"He was dreading going home, but not finals," Chief said on the way out to the car. "His folks are always going at it."

"Maybe, but I bet his parents were both always around when he was a kid," Willy said, and immediately wondered where it came from.

"He thinks you guys are great," Chief said. "He thinks you're the most interesting people he's ever met. He thinks you're a hero, Dad."

Willy felt his old disgust, but kept his mouth shut.

Christmas went well, the highlight of it being that they went up to the hotel and actually had a good time. Mae helped her mother put on a large spread, and they made a party of it. It was the only time Willy could remember seeing the front hall of the place crowded with happy, laughing people, and it was made precious by the fact that it seemed almost certain that Edith Palmer would successfully sell the place before the next Christmas rolled around.

After the party, he dropped off Mae and Chief at the house. Finding himself in a pensive mood, he walked down the street as it began to snow. As happened from time to time, he found himself wandering closer and closer to the cemetery. He walked up the hill towards it, and soon found himself standing in the snow in front of Mollie's gravestone, as he had so many times before.

He thought about the Christmas she had spent at their house, and how it seemed, with just a little care, she might end up with something that resembled a happy life. He stood with his hands in his jacket pockets and stared abstractedly at the stone. He thought of the boys buying Mollie the red bra and he laughed softly. He thought about how precarious it all was, and that knowledge of this precariousness enabled one to live life more fully, recognizing the slippery moments of beauty and of goodness. It seemed, though, that most people would walk or drive by this very cemetery every day and pay no more attention to it than they did to a brick wall or a stand of trees, so engrossed were they in small concerns, thinking about the things they wanted to buy or an argument they had had at work or what color they wanted to paint the living room. Palmer, his father-in-law, had been such a person, and there was his tombstone some yards away, soon to be ignored and forgotten, and it would be rare that anyone would stand in front of that stone and wonder who he had been.

It was in January that they got their next letter from Gordon. Willy had been hoping that he would have gotten a posting in Germany or Japan, somewhere out of harm's immediate way, but no, Gordon had pushed to be sent to Korea and hadn't encountered much resistance. In the letter, he wrote: "Crossing 5500 miles of Pacific Ocean to Japan was one of the most- no, *the* most- hellish experiences of my life. I was one of about five thousand other guys on the troop transport, some of whom had never even been on a boat before. You know me, I don't really get motion sick, but with a few thousand other guys puking their guts out all around you, sometimes biology just takes over. When I get back and go back to school, I'm going to do a sculpture in bronze called The Pukers, involving six guys bent over the railing of a boat, all blowing chow from their heels up. It'll be my little homage to the military. Maybe we could have the town commission it and put it up down in River Park, right by where you guys got married. I can see it in my head. It's noble, hilarious, disgusting and sad, all at the same time. That strikes me as fitting."

Willy thought about his own first passage of the Atlantic and shook his head.

Gordon talked about Japan for a bit- his writing neat and tiny to fit on the flimsy airmail page- about how the people were industrious and polite, although he could feel an undercurrent of both awe and hatred directed at the American troops. "I'll be shipped to the front eventually," he wrote. "No matter what happens, it can't be as bad as our little cruise across the Pacific."

It was after this that Willy allowed Chief to have his and Gordon's old car. With resignation, he knew that there was little he could do to influence the boy's actions, and if Chief and Katita were going to get into some kind of serious trouble, they were perfectly capable of doing it without the car. Chief's grades had been excellent, and he seemed to be on track with his difficult chemistry and engineering courses. Emilio drove his truck while Willy took the '38 Chrysler up to Black Marsh. It had recently snowed, but the river highway was clear and black, steaming in the sunlight of the unusually warm day.

He met Chief in the entrance to his dorm, and the boy was almost dancing with excitement. Willy didn't say anything, just raising his eyebrows and inclining his head while staring Chief in the eye. He held out the keys and jingled them, and when Chief made the grab, Willy snapped them back into his fist.

"Do I have to give any lectures?" he asked, pinning Chief with his gaze.

"No! Jesus!" Chief said, holding out his palm.

Willy narrowed his eyes skeptically, and very slowly placed the keys in his son's hand. Emilio watched, smiling.

"Thanks, Dad!" Chief said, bolting down the stairs while throwing on his jacket.

They had thought to take the kids to lunch, but realized that might have been unrealistic under the circumstances.

Willy finally succumbed to the television craze and got a deal on four General Electric TV sets from an appliance dealer he had known in Black Marsh since Prohibition. Emilio chipped in for one of them, and he got one as a present for the ancient Dr. Homburg, so he could watch baseball games at home.

"I tell ya," Homburg said, shaking his head in marvel after Willy and Emilio trundled it into his living room from Emilio's truck and set it up. "This is what I'm always talking about, Willy. I'm motivated to stay alive just to see what happens next."

The other two TVs went in the living room of the bungalow and at the bar, where Emilio attached it on a frame just below the ceiling so everyone seated at the bar could watch it, a novel concept at the time. Someone had to get up on a barstool to change the channel, but, since there were only three channels, the issue didn't come up much.

At first it was an unsettling sight to see men sitting around the bar, their drinks in front of them, watching the television together, the bar otherwise silent for long stretches of time. Willy noticed that the regulars drank more at night when the TV was turned off and the jukebox or a band was playing, and was fairly certain that people drank the most and the fastest when they were listening to sad songs. He had no idea why this was, but refused to exploit it. When the novelty of the television began to wear off that summer, he found it pleasant to come into the shady, cool bar on a summer afternoon and watch a baseball game with old friends as they nursed their pilsner glasses of beer.

Chief and Katita took the car home from school on weekends, although with less frequency as they made new friends and were gradually distracted from their ties with home. Chief brought Patrick Pinkwater home once or twice, and, although they were welcome in the bar, they stayed away from indulging as much as they first had.

They got letters from Gordon every three or four weeks, and he downplayed being near the conflict. He wrote, instead, about the men in his unit, and his plans when he got home. He thanked his mother for the food she sent, cookies and candy and sausages, and made joking comments about how good it was going to be to have a beer and to get out on the river when he got home. Although Willy said nothing, he knew that Gordon was sanitizing the letters for the benefit of his mother.

He was proven right when, one morning in April, he received an airmail letter addressed to him alone at the bar. Gordon knew that, although his mother frequently worked at the bar, she always got there later than Willy, and that Willy was always the one to get the mail.

Willy took a deep breath and opened the letter. The handwriting , as always, was tiny block letters crammed efficiently onto the flimsy airmail paper.

Dear Dad, it read, *I'm sending this to the bar for obvious reasons. Actually, I got the idea from you, when you got sliced up in prison and kept it under your hat for the rest of your time. Of course this puts you in a position where you can't say anything to Mom, but that, obviously, is something you are capable of doing.*

Willy wondered if Gordon were taking a shot at him, but read on.

I'm going to come right out and give you the chance to say 'I told you so'. I'm willing to admit that this was not such a hot idea. I'm off the MLR (Main Line of Resistance) right now after my first stint on the line. I almost had to come back early anyway. I cut my right thumb pretty bad on a the lid of a can of beans, and my whole hand got so infected that the red, infected part went up over my wrist, while leaving the tip of my little finger unaffected, for some damn reason. My hand was swollen like a rubber glove full of blood, and the knuckles were dents. Almost no one goes off the line unless they're wounded, but it was to the point where I couldn't bend my trigger finger and was worried about gangrene. My buddies wanted me to report it, but I didn't want to because I'd be letting them down. Then we were relieved anyway.

You would be familiar with this situation, except for some new developments in the decades since you did it. I live in a bunker with some of my buddies, dug into the reverse side of a hill close to the line. The bunker has sandbag walls and a timber roof with ponchos over the door. It was really damn cold there for awhile, but I think things were a lot better than they were last year, when guys supposedly were losing toes and feet to frostbite if they didn't just freeze to death out on an ambush. When it's like that out, anyone who gets hit and killed will be laid out and wrapped up, frozen solid in no time flat. Good thing we did a lot of outdoor stuff in the winter when I was a kid. Some of the guys had never experienced anything close to it, couldn't even imagine it. I know one guy who had never even seen snow before, and came here. How about that!

I got a doc to look at my hand and now it's almost better, although it's taking a long time to write this. The swelling is down, but dead skin is peeling off where it shrank. I can bend my fingers pretty well. When we got back off the line, I hadn't had a shower in four weeks. I hope they burned our clothes. After a hot shower, even with the delousing, I never felt cleaner in my life.

You were right about many things, I see that now. Maybe as a species we lack the imagination to really understand what this is like without seeing it. You were right that perhaps our greatest failing as a species is that we can not hand down wisdom. If everyone on the planet could see in their minds what you and your buddies saw (and your enemies, who were almost as much like you as your buddies), there would never have been another war. But we are a pretty stupid species, aren't we, and keep making the same mistakes over and over again.

I thought I was a pretty tough guy. I thought I could take it. Maybe I can take it, but I'll tell you, I'm not so tough. When you've seen a buddy torn up by artillery or mortar fire (and you know what I mean: torn up), you've seen someone missing their legs or an arm or with their head shot off, the theoretical notion of something like that happening can never, ever match the reality. It is images like that which, if we could beam them into the head of millions of other people like something from one of Chief's science fiction books, none of this shit would ever happen again. Guess we're still pretty much just primates, though, huh?

I am just a primate. I have to admit that something in me enjoyed killing someone who threatened me and my buddies. I've shot North Koreans and CCF guys (usually called gooks and chinks, respectively) and got a guy with a grenade one night as they tried a raid up our forward slope. I saw his body in the snow in the morning and the middle two-thirds of him was just blown away, leaving shreds hanging off bones like a turkey at Emilio's after everyone's been at it. His face was still perfectly intact, just staring off to the side, not even a look of surprise. I saw a B-26 napalm a hilltop on The Other Side, and I cheered as it went up. It looked like a volcano. I've never seen anything like it. Then I started to cool down and felt sick and ashamed of myself.

Even worse was seeing what happens to civilians. And I like the Koreans. They are cheerful and resourceful, all while living in the most fucked up situation imaginable. And then they're taken out in hundreds, thousands, and shot. The fighting, of course, has just gone back and forth over the same ground. One time we were advancing after the enemy as they pulled back, and outside a town I saw a lady lying in a ditch beside a field, shot dead. She looked nice. Her three little kids were sitting by her crying and pulling at her clothes. They were too young to know what had happened. I went to help them but was ordered- ordered- to get back on the road and keep going. Then, inside the village, we came on a place where there were long trenches dug in the square. The trenches were piled with the bodies of the people of the village. Piled with them. They'd machine-gunned them all when they retreated. We were up on the line not long after that, and that vision made it a lot easier to kill. At least in the heat of the moment.

It's stuff like that that is branded into my brain, as if you could screw off the top of my skull and still see the smoking mark in my gray matter. It will never go away.

Now I know why you did what you did. Now I know why you came to live on the river in our stupid little town. You wanted some peace, and some of the time you got it.My hand hurts like shit. My buddy Karl got a bottle of vodka somewhere. He wants to come visit when we get out of this. I love you, Dad. I understand. I'll write again pretty soon. - Gordon

PS: Don't tell Mom about this, obviously. And do not let Chief come here! He's a good kid, and he really loves Katita. Do not let him come!

"Yes," Willy said, gently setting down the letter. "Yes."

Willy kept his mouth shut about the letter. He was so used to speaking candidly with Mae on any topic that it proved, in these circumstances, to be a distinct disadvantage. On the verge of saying aloud something he was thinking about

Gordon- the comment seemingly right there behind his teeth- he somehow always managed to bite it back in time. He felt terribly guilty about it, until one weekend when Chief was home, the boy startled him with a revelation.

Willy was sitting in the kitchen drinking coffee and reading the paper. Chief came in and turned down the radio, then sat at the table.

"I've been getting letters from Gordon, too," he said.

Willy set down his mug and the paper. "What?"

"I've been getting letters from Gordon," Chief said. "He tells me all the bad stuff that he could never tell Mom. He also said he was writing to you. Pretty much the same stuff, although, knowing him, he's trying to scare me."

Willy sat still for a moment. "Are you scared?"

"Why should I be? I'm not over there. In my own life, the only thing I have to worry about is finals in a month."

Willy watched his eyes. "Gordon's okay," he said. "He'll be okay."

"Did he write about his hand?" Chief asked.

"Yeah," Willy laughed. "I wonder if Doc Ambrose has got a lifetime list of all the injuries and stuff you guys have had. You scared the living shit out of me with the polio."

"We can survive anything."

"I suspect you're right."

They were quiet for a moment, then Chief said, "You probably shouldn't mention this to Mom."

Willy smiled thinly. "I am aware of that."

"You shouldn't feel bad about it, either," Chief said. "It's all in a good cause."

This time, Willy forced his face to remain blank. "Okay. I won't."

"It wouldn't do Mom any good just to worry needlessly about this kind of thing."

"Nope. It sure wouldn't."

"Well," Chief said, getting up. "I'm going over to Katita's. I have to help her on some math homework."

Willy nodded, then said, "Uh, Chief?"

"Yeah?" he said, stopping in the doorway to the living room.

"You're not going to give your mom anything more to worry about, are you?"

Chief gave him an exaggeratedly puzzled look. "Like what?"

"*I've* given your mom plenty to worry about," Willy said, "and now Gordon's doing it. We really don't need any further contributions. Let's just hope Gordon gets home safe as soon as possible, and let's just make sure your mom is happy."

Chief gave him a look saying that this was obvious, then turned to go.

"Chief!"

"*Yeah*, Dad."

"I'm serious. Don't go doing anything crazy. You're doing the right thing, right now. You have a great life ahead of you."

"I *know*, Dad," Chief said. "It's *all* under control."

He turned and left.

For a few weeks in May, the lilacs were in bloom, white, lavender, and purple up and down the street. Willy's favorite was a deep purple one right beside their front porch, and he sat out there, listening as Mae played the piano and the cool evening breeze carried the scent of their blooms to him. Lilacs always made him slightly sad, beautiful almost to the point of magic, their scent heady, and gone so soon.

Inspired by the ephemerality of things the next day, he packed a picnic basket with cold chicken and grapes, fresh bread and white wine, and took Mae by the hand and put her in the car. Without saying where they were going, he drove up into the hills near Mt. Pleasant where the apple orchards were in bloom.

From a high point, they could see for miles over the rolling hills covered with orchards and their white and pink blossoms. The sky overhead was huge, a deep blue with towering cumulous clouds swelling brilliant white in the sun.

Willy parked at the side of the road and got the picnic basket out of the back of the pickup, taking Mae by the hand and going back into the orchard. The grass was fresh and green and they were surrounded by a maze of blossoms, enveloped by their scent and the sweet breath of clover.

He spread out a floral quilt and set up the picnic punctiliously, as Mae stood with the knuckle of her forefinger to her lips, laughing, touched. He saw the love in her eyes and it made his heart swell, that sensation he had felt thousands of times and yet remained undiminished.

They ate the food and drank the wine, talking, never running out of words after all the years, but content to sit in silence if it suited them. They lay for awhile, Willy with his back against an apple tree, Mae with her head and hand on his chest, her knee over his. It was a Sunday, and Willy, knowing the owner of the orchard (one of the network of Runty Schommer's relatives), knew he would not be around. With a look of mischief that made Mae laugh, he began to unbutton her blouse. Soon they were naked on the quilt, kissing, the breeze loosing occasional petals from the apple blossoms, which fell and touched their skin. They made love, and, knowing there was no one near, they did it loudly.

Afterward they laughed about it, panting and touching each other lazily. Willy looked at his wife in the uncompromising brightness of the sunlight. Her breasts were not those of a twenty-year-old, the fine, white skin of her belly had faded stretch marks, and there were tiny crowsfeet around her eyes. These were things she did not like about herself, but which suffused him with tenderness. She was curvy, smooth, and lovely. The very sight of her seemed to make his body warm and relaxed, as it always had; her simple physical presence always capable of purging care or tension or anger. He looked down at himself, at his large chest and arms, his stomach, certainly no longer flat, laced with its faded white scars, his chest hair turning grey.

"We have had an unusual life, I think," he said, and pulled her closer to him. When they had met, when they had been married, if anyone had told him that that was just the beginning of his love for his wife, that his love for her would increase with each year, ever into some unguessed territory, he would have called them a liar. He could not have known. He told her this.

She kissed his chest several times. The wind blew, and a shower of blossoms covered them. Thinking about this, he felt a sudden pang of sadness, a sharp sense of the passing of time. He looked at his wife's beloved face and sighed, then sprang up suddenly and began to run naked and hooting through the trees, leaping in the air and slapping his ass. Mae watched him, laughing. He kept it up until she was doubled over and helpless.

Chief and Katita finished their semester and came home. The families celebrated the completion of their first year of college, but Chief seemed a bit distant. Mae noticed and whispered it to Willy, both of them watching as their son seemed to be going through the motions of the party. They talked about it later in bed, each of them offering up theories for the other's opinion, but they struck on nothing which seemed quite accurate.

Willy checked the mail at the bar first thing every day, but found no letters from Gordon. One came addressed to both of them, but it was the way he always wrote if his mother was going to be one of the readers, descriptions of the country and his unit, derision of his superior officers, whom, he said, consisted of almost everyone. "Both of you taught me to believe that I'm pretty special," he wrote, "but life in the military soon disabuses a guy of such notions. I'm a hell of a shot with a rifle, but other than that I am just a replaceable unit, that much is clear."

The rest of this letter was a description (a vague and euphemistic one, Willy saw) of the diversions he and his buddies got into when off the line. They bartered with the British troops, exchanging fruit juice and peanut butter for British beer rations. "Once I got over my amazement that they would make such a trade," Gordon wrote, "I did it as much as I could." He also described developing a taste for the local beverages, including So-ju, a hard liquor, and Chung-ju, a strained rice wine. "They take some getting used to, but you'd like them, Dad. You could sell them as a novelty drink at the bar. And don't worry, Mom. I'm not becoming an alcoholic. I'm just a soldier, which, I suppose, is bad enough."

Willy and Mae just looked at each other and sighed.

Willy hired Katita to waitress at the bar for the summer, covering for another girl's leave of absence. Faith-in-full Goodforks had gone missing, so Willy was glad to have her cheerful help along with his old stalwarts, Bob Two Bears and Runty Schommer. There was some symmetry in the fact that Chief was working for Emilio on a carpentry project which would take all summer.

With these rhythms just established, Willy was puzzled when Emilio came into the bar on a Monday, saying, "You'd better come with me."

"What is it?" Willy asked.

"I...it...just come on," Emilio said. Willy looked at Bob Two Bears, who waved him away irritatedly.

"What is it?" Willy asked.

"We have to go to your house."

"You'd fucking well better tell me what's going on."

"Easier to show you. Get in the truck."

They pulled up in front of the bungalow. In the driveway was Mae's car-normal enough- but also Chief's car, tools in the backseat, and Solveig's wagon behind it. Emilio gave him a nervous look as they went up the walk to the house.

"Your son quit his job," Emilio said.

"What!" He didn't have time to think about it, though, as they walked across the porch and into the living room.

When Willy saw the tableau which awaited him there, it was as though his brain stopped for a moment, and there was a blank hum in his head instead of its usual function. Chief was there, and Mae, looking rather pale and apprehensive. Solveig sat on the couch in tears, a soggy handkerchief wadded in her plump hand (nothing too strange in that), but Katita sat next to her, and it was obvious that she had, too, been crying. The strangest thing of all, a complete visual non sequitur, was that Patrick Pinkwater was there, a duffelbag at his feet.

Willy stood squinting at this, his eyes flicking back and forth.

"It's going to be *okay*, everyone. Jesus!" Chief was saying, and Willy's brain seemed to kick into gear again.

It's not Gordon, he realized. Why would the Pinkwater kid be here. It's-

"You two idiots enlisted," Willy said.

Chief laughed witlessly. Pinkwater looked at the carpet.

"Goddam it! You two fucking idiots *enlisted*!"

The smile dropped from Chief's face. "Dad, come on! It's going to be okay!"

Willy went and sat in his reading chair, which, he realized later, had been left conspicuously empty. He took a breath. "Daniel McGregor-" he started.

"Dad! It's okay! I've got it all figured out!"

"Daniel McGregor!"

"Dad, think about it! There are peace talks going on, okay? It'll all be over by the time we get there! We get training and the G.I. Bill!"

With an effort, Willy controlled himself. "I can *not* believe my ears," Willy grated. "Tell me you are not doing this."

Chief's placatory attitude vanished, and he said, "It's done. We signed up."

"Did you have anything to do with this, Patrick?" Willy asked, but when he looked at Chief, at his size and his attitude, then looked at the skinny Patrick Pinkwater and the way the kid could barely look him in the eye, he knew the truth. Pinkwater started to stammer something, but Willy waved it off.

"My dad said he was proud of me," Pinkwater persisted.

Willy took a very deep breath, staring at the kid, but let it out and said, "That's fine, son."

He looked around the room. Mae stood there straight, but her face was pale and set. Solveig sat damply on the couch, Katita beside her, her own face (cool blue eyes in a café au lait complexion) a teary mixture of fear and pride. Emilio patted his wife absently on the shoulder, but was gazing at Willy with a look of understanding. Patrick had unconsciously moved behind Chief, who had held his arms crossed over his chest in a protective posture, but then dropped them to his sides. He was no longer joking, he was no longer soothing. He looked at Willy levelly.

"There's everything you did, and there's Gordon, Dad," he said. "I couldn't be the one not to go."

And that was the way it happened. Chief and Patrick Pinkwater were gone almost at once for basic training. Willy tried to talk them into finishing college first so they could go in as officers-gambling that the war would be over before they did- to no avail.

Chief and Katita had announced that, when Chief got back, they were going to get married as soon as they finished school. Katita would finish first and get a teaching job, and Chief would go through on the G.I. Bill, saving them a lot of money. Gordon would be home by then, and he would finish school in Greysport, then maybe they could all live somewhere near the river and be together.

"See, Mom? Dad?" Chief said. "It's not so bad. It's not bad at all! Gordon will eventually find someone nice, and you guys'll have a bunch of grandkids!"

Mae smiled artificially, while Willy tried to look like it sounded reasonable to him. He knew immediately that his attempt at the pleasant side of neutrality had failed rather pathetically.

Just before he left, Chief said, "Dad, you know me and Gordon. We can survive anything."

Willy got him in a bearhug. They were about to let each other go, but Willy crunched him in his arms again.

"Dad!" Chief said, his voice tight. "Need to breathe. Can't show up dead for my next physical."

Willy let him go and watched as Chief tenderly held his mother for a long time. They murmured things to each other, Mae looking up into his eyes, and Willy stood there feeling sick.

The next thing they knew, he was gone.

Beginning in June of that year, there was cruel and intense fighting along the MLR in Korea. Willy could barely read the news, although there was much less coverage of the conflict than there had been in the Second World War. The populace was seemingly weary of such things, intent on shifting their focus to Prosperity. Mae read as much about it as she could, also watching anything she could find on the television, and Willy shook his head at her calm. He consoled himself by thinking that Chief was still in basic training, peace talks were on, and Gordon was tough and had probably already seen the worst of it. As the summer got hot, though, it was blissful to walk down the shady street and enter the bar to watch a double-header in the cool shadows.

Dr. Ambrose, in spite of having the TV at home, tottered down to the bar to join him.

"She wants to watch those soap operas," he confided. "I like it here."

Ambrose had been such a pillar of stability in Willy's life for so long that he found it hard to imagine his life without the old man. His kindness and support seemed inexhaustible, even though he seemed to become more and more transparent, like a watercolor dropped in the river, eventually to disappear altogether, which of course he would.

Willy, naturally, had told him all about the goings-on with Chief, and Ambrose had nodded wearily. "It's an old saying, but it bears repeating," Ambrose said, taking a delicate sip from his glass of beer, his voice competing with the sound of the baseball game on TV, "'It's what you learn after you know it all that really counts.'"

The letters they received from Chief were terse but upbeat, the young man lacking Gordon's artistic abilities. It was his acumen in the sciences, however, that got him into training to become a medic when he got out of basic. Pinkwater, no slouch himself, was going into the same training, and the two had somehow worked it so they could stick together.

"Things are great!" Chief wrote. "Going to be a medic! Look good on my resume!" Willy, on a hunch, scanned the letter, and found that it did, in fact, have more exclamation points than periods.

"That kid," he said.

It was in that very cruel and intense fighting along the MLR- pounding the earth around the 38th Parallel again and again, back and forth over the same riven ground- that Gordon lost his right earlobe. He was the rear man on a stretcher, carrying a wounded buddy off the line, when he tripped on a rock a lurched forward just as a round from a rifle, originally intended for his whole head, merely clipped off the little nubbin of flesh instead.

"Ow! Fuck!" Gordon yelped. He couldn't let go of the stretcher, though, and just kept trotting, in spite of the blood spattering his shoulder and chest.

His buddy on the stretcher laughed in spite of his leg wound. "Think you lost part of your ear, there, McGregor."

The man on holding the front end of the stretcher craned his neck around and said, "Yep."

"Tough shit," Gordon shouted. "Least I can still run, you gimp-ass motherfucker, so let's get the fuck outta here!"

When his ear was cleaned and bandaged, he went to check on his friend, whose leg was neatly bandaged and who was enjoying the benefit of morphine. He pointed to his leg, smiled, and said, "I get to go home with this one."

Gordon fingered the bandage over his ear and said, "It's back to the line for me."

"On your way, why don't you go fuck yourself," his doped-up friend said amiably.

Gordon smiled wearily and flipped him off. "I already did by signing up for *this* shit."

Not long after this, Gordon received a letter from Mae, telling him straightforwardly that Chief had enlisted and would be going to Korea. "If you get a chance," Mae wrote, "look after your little brother."

Gordon felt nauseous with fear and anger, but read on." This is not your father's fault. He tried to talk Chief out of it just as he tried with you. Please come home safely and soon, sweetheart. *This is not your father's fault.*"

"Of course it is," Gordon muttered, but smoothed the letter and put it in his pocket.

It was fall by the time Chief had finished medic training and was ready to make the same trip Gordon had across the Pacific. Gordon, meanwhile, served in various capacities but was due to go back to the line, lacking the points necessary to go home. By the time Chief got to Korea, Gordon had already been deployed, and it seemed that they would never be able to get together.

When winter came on Chief was assigned (still, through steadfast ingenuity, with his friend Patrick Pinkwater) to the MLR and saw for the first time what his father and brother had described to him. He, too, had that one-way realization, that recognition of reality which could never be retracted. As a medic, he saw the things that others on the line were too busy to see, and saw it in great concentration. He was silent and serious when they had a moment to breathe, but Pinkwater, in private, sobbed quietly and at length.

Gordon was back on the line, up in the hills, accumulating points. On Thanksgiving Day, he was huddled in a bunker, sharing a bottle of whiskey with his buddies after a meal of pork and beans and a dessert of canned peaches. He told his buddies about his Thanksgivings at home, an unconscious but understandable echo of his father in prison. At first his friends were enthralled, almost drooling over the descriptions, but they finally begged him to shut up.

A week later, he was walking along the foot path on the ridgeline from his bunker to the command post. Along with the occasional artillery and mortar barrages from the North, the landscape had been hit with a heavy snowstorm. The day was brilliantly clear, though, and as he walked along the footpath on the reverse side of the ridgeline, he wore only his woolen shirt and pants over his long woolen underwear. Occasionally, through gaps between the granite, he could look across the snowy valley to the enemy ridgeline, but could see no fortifications or movement of any kind, only the deep snow and outcroppings of rock jagged against the sky.

He was on his way down the crude stairs chipped into the ice and snow when he hit a patch of ice which had gotten slick in the sun. His left foot slipped while his right had traction, and he felt his right knee twist and heard something pop and crunch and with a shout he slid down the slope. He tried to arrest his fall, but went off the edge of a small cliff where the stairs formed a T with a footpath. He fell ten feet and hit with his right thigh on a granite outcrop, shattering the bone. He tumbled into the deep, powdery snow, sliding and sliding, and finally came to rest. He lay there in the snow, breathing heavily, melting powder on his face, staring at the sky, his eyes wide with the unbelievable pain. Groaning, laughing angrily at how bad the pain was, muttering to himself about it, he got up on his elbows and looked at his leg. A large lump stuck out inside his pantleg, as if he had a baseball in his woolen longjohns beneath the bottom of his cargo pocket, and blood was soaking through from underneath, a compound fracture.

"*SHIT*!" he bellowed. "*Mother*fucking fucking cocksucking *fuck*! Fuckin'... *MEDIC*!"

He thought that it was ironic that his little brother was a medic somewhere in the world, someone he could trust, and then he lost consciousness.

So Gordon never got to see Chief in Korea. In the hospital in Japan the young American surgeon who had done his best to repair the leg told him that, although he might walk with a limp for the rest of his life, his time in Korea was over.

"That's gotta be good news, huh?" the surgeon prompted when Gordon didn't say anything.

"Kind of," Gordon said. "My stupid little brother is still over here."

"Oh," the surgeon said, suddenly at a loss for words.

Gordon went home while Chief was up by the MLR. Chief wrote sporadically to Mae and Willy, usually telling them that everything was fine. They got the impression that he wrote to Katita considerably more, although that was to be expected. Katita and Mae got closer than they had ever been, Katita using the boys' car to come home for the weekend, sometimes working at the bar for a little extra cash. "After studying, what else am I going to do on the weekends?" she said.

It was in April of that year when things were getting muddy on the line in Korea, just months before the end of the war, that Chief and Patrick Pinkwater and some other buddies had gone to the rear to a little village, getting some food and doing a good deal of drinking, some of the boys looking for whores. Peace talks continued, but so did the hostilities, back and forth, back and forth.

Chief was more adventurous about the local cuisine than most of his buddies, and had developed a taste for kimchi ("Fermented vegetables, cabbage, and chili peppers!" he wrote home) and especially pulgoki ("Kind of a Korean barbecue- it's great!"). Chief ate everything as spicy as possible, most of his friends laughing and shaking their heads in disbelief. He tied a bandanna around his head to absorb the sweat, beaming happily. When his friends laughed harder, he laughed as well, chewing his food and flipping them off with both hands. They had returned to their barracks near the front pretty well lubricated.

Somewhere during the course of the day, they had picked up some food poisoning. By nightfall, many of the boys had been vomiting off in the muddy fields in the dark, but some began to have more serious symptoms.

"It's that fucking gook food," one of then said, just back from the latrine.

"No it isn't," Chief said. "Jenkins is foaming at the ass, and he didn't eat any."

"It's the gook food!" the young man persisted.

"You idiot," Chief said.

"Hoo, boy," Pinkwater said. "I'm not feeling too good. Not too good at all, in fact."

Chief looked at him and laughed. "Me neither," he said. "I'm still going to eat kimchi and pulgoki every chance I get."

"Uh oh!" Pinkwater gasped, and staggered through the tentflaps, fumbling with his trousers.

"Jesus, McGregor," one of the peaked young men said, "are your guts made of lead pipe or something?"

Chief had been hiding the fact that his guts had been gurgling ominously. He winced. "Guess not," he said, getting up and going outside. Jenkins, the soldier who eschewed the all but military issue food, followed him.

Patrick was coming out of the latrine- luxurious for the fact that it had walls around it and an actual wooden seat- as Chief and Jenkins approached.

"Keep it all warm for me, Pat?" Chief asked.

"Steamin'," Pinkwater said. "They don't call me Pinkwater for nothin'!"

"Hurry the fuck up, Chief," Jenkins said.

"Oh, this won't take long at all. This is going to be one high-speed, explosive shit. I'm gonna shit so hard my fucking *lungs* will be in there. Besides: fuck off. There's another latrine right over there." He closed the flimsy door.

"I won't make it," Jenkins said. "I'm clamping it shut as hard as I can."

"Tough shit, I beat you to it." Chief groaned as the sound liquid on liquid came from the latrine.

"Hurry the fuck *up*, Chief!"

Patrick, his guts still rumbling, was laughing at this exchange and halfway back to the tent when the barrage came from the north. Incoming shells exploded among the barracks, detonations huge, numbing, as mushrooms of yellow, orange, and red flame curled up, blackening, into the night. There were several strikes in the area of the main command post. Men were running everywhere, shouting. Small arms fire started up.

Pinkwater turned in circles for a moment, and was facing the latrine when it was hit. The explosion killed Jenkins- instantly and unambiguously- and blew the walls of the latrine to firewood.

"Fuck!" Pinkwater screamed, running across the dark ground. He tripped and fell, as if in a nightmare, but got to his feet and continued running.

He found Chief lying in the debris of the latrine, covered with splinters and fragments of boards, as well as cold shit and piss. Chief was riddled with wounds. Patrick wetly evacuated his bowels.

"You just shat yourself, buddy," Chief pointed out.

"Oh," Patrick said in the din of the barrage. "Uh-"

"You'd better take your belt and tie a tourniquet around my leg, there. Right about mid-thigh."

"Yeah! Yeah! I'll do that!" Patrick began frantically undoing his belt.

"This is pretty funny, when you think about it," Chief said, and he died there in dark with the base in flames and men screaming around him.

Patrick Pinkwater would eventually return and tell Willy a stylized version of these events. At first he had tried to talk to Mae, but burst into tears at every attempt, Mae finally ending up consoling him. When he calmed down, she sent him down to the bar, following him a few blocks behind, watching him hesitate and pace up and down, ducking his head and peeking through the very window which was the same one since Bud Sletto's failed firebombing.

Mae watched from the shade under a blossomless lilac bush, her arms crossed over her chest. "Go in, kid. Go on in," she said. Pinkwater went in.

Pinkwater sobbed at the bar when he told his story to Willy. The old timers stood by the boy as he wept, putting their hands on the young man's shoulders, most of them weeping themselves, men who posed as ungentle.

That wouldn't be for more than a year, though. Before that, on a Saturday morning, Willy and Mae would receive a simple, stark telegram.

They were both at home when it arrived. Mae put her hand to her throat and sat down on the couch. Willy took the telegram from the quiet deliveryman and closed the door behind him. He read it and said, "Well, honey, Chief is gone."

Thus ended their Golden Span.

The news of Chief's death crashed through the town like a wave. Willy called Bob Two Bears at the bar to tell him he wouldn't be coming in, and, although he could barely speak the words, he had to say something eventually.

"Chief was killed," he said, simply relaying the information. His mind was numb; he couldn't fully embrace the reality of it, and so merely said the words.

Willy could hear the television on in the background. Finally, Bob muttered something and the line went dead.

Mae called her mother and was equally terse and unemotional. Mae hung up the phone, saying, "She's coming over."

Willy next steeled himself to call Emilio, knowing that this news would be terribly hard on Katita. He looked out the kitchen window at the cool April day, some flowers coming up, the trees beginning to bud. He took a deep breath and made the call. He was dreading that Katita, home for the weekend, would answer the phone, and sure enough, she did.

Willy swallowed hard. "Could I speak to your dad, honey?"

"Sure!" she chirped. He heard what sounded like Katita holding the phone to her chest and calling for her father, a muffled sound which expanded like the sound of a breaking wave when she handed over the phone, saying "It's Mr. McGregor."

"Hey, Willy, what's up?" Emilio said.

Just hearing his old friend's voice made tears spring to Willy's eyes. His words caught in his throat, but he coughed and said, "Chief was killed."

"*Ay Dios mio*," Emilio whispered. He swore softly in a vicious spate of Spanish, then was silent for a moment. Finally, he said, "I am so sorry, my brother."

"Yeah."

"No one will ever learn."

"No," Willy said.

Willy imagined his friend nodding sadly on the other end of the line. He could see his face clearly in his mind. He thought about what Emilio would have to tell his daughter.

"We'll be right over, my brother," Emilio said.

Willy considered telling him not to come, but his mind seemed limp, so he said, "Okay," and was about to hang up but added, "and take care of Katita."

He hung up the phone. Then he threw up in the sink. He regained himself, though, looking out the kitchen window at the back yard as he ran the faucet and cleaned out the sink. He turned with the intent of finding his wife but found her, instead, coming through the archway to the kitchen. A strand of red hair fell over her eye. She was pale, and looked somewhere to the left of him. When he walked toward her, her eyes did not shift, but she held out her arms and they embraced.

Mae's mother was the first to arrive, bringing with her supplies from the hotel. Within an hour, the living room and the kitchen were filled with people, who then spilled over onto the porch and into the front yard. Mae and her mother made sandwiches and coffee in the kitchen. Katita sat with her own mother and her sisters on the living room couch. After an hour of crying, she could do nothing more but cling to her mother and moan, her pale eyes reddened, tears threading her cheeks. Solveig, having summoned some form of hidden serenity, held her, shushing her and kissing the top of her head as her sisters wept beside her.

Bob Two Bears and Runty Schommer had closed the bar, leaving a note on the front door, and had brought cases of beer in the back of Bob's pickup truck. They now sat next to each other on the front porch, each dangling a bottle of beer from one hand, sipping occasionally. Runty had his arm around the large shoulders of his friend, who sobbed openly, tears running down his brown cheeks, stopping to drink from his beer and say, "What the *fuck*," and drinking from it again.

Willy tried to help Mae and her mother (who politely declined all offers of assistance), bringing out plates of sandwiches, and finally getting Barnacle Brad, who kept sniffling and shaking his head, to set up some folding tables on the front lawn, covering them with the linen tablecloths Mae had saved from their wedding so long ago. The tables were soon covered with pies and casseroles brought by newcomers, and Willy roused Bob and Runty to go back to the bar for more cases of beer and a keg.

Friends and neighbors, almost all of them genuinely stricken, kept giving Willy their condolences, touching his arms and his shoulders. Willy imagined Chief describing this as a primate pack behavior, and felt disjointed for a moment, the words of those around him fading to a buzz. He found himself staring at someone's shoes as a voice in his head said, over and over: Oh no, oh no, oh no, oh no. There was a roaring in his ears, and he realized that someone was gripping his elbow with some pressure and saying his name sharply. He raised his head and found himself looking at Doc Ambrose and Emilio.

"You'd better come with me, son," Ambrose said. Willy allowed himself to be led down the driveway to the back yard. Ambrose sat him on the back steps and said, "Now stay there. Breathe deeply and keep your head between your knees. You were about to pass out."

Willy obediently sat on the steps and did as Ambrose told him while the doctor sent Emilio into the house for a glass of water. Emilio brought it back and handed it to Willy, his face set and grim. Willy guzzled the water, handing the glass back to his friend.

"Oh, my boy, my boy," Ambrose said, putting his hand on Willy's shoulder. Emilio did the same.

"Is my wife okay?" Willy asked.

"For now," Ambrose said. "She's busy. It won't last. You'll have to pull yourself together in a bit. She's going to need you."

"For the rest of her life, *mi hermano*," Emilio said softly.

"Okay," Willy said. "Sure."

Then there was nothing to say, and the three men sat quietly on the steps.

After a long time, Willy sighed, slapped his knees, and stood up. "I have to look after Mae," he said, and went up the steps and into the house.

Mae and her mother ran the show from the kitchen, and Willy was kept busy doing errands for them and talking to those in and around the house. For Mae, the work was her anodyne, and seeing her work with her mother, a few quiet words between them, gave Willy a tiny bit of peace.

After nearly passing out on the front lawn, Willy was back in control of himself, and having the same repeated conversations with people he had long known seemed to have a numbing effect. People expressed their condolences, Willy nodded and thanked them quietly, and responded to a lifetime of habit by offering them something to drink. Habit was good.

As often happens at such gatherings, it was not all sadness. People who hadn't seen each other for awhile caught up, talking about banal things. There were even bits of laughter, more after some drinking had been done and people forgot to be embarrassed. Willy stood by nodding or overheard as people shared stories about Chief, funny stories, touching stories, as Chief began the process of changing from being a living person to being a memory, a character in a story.

As the sun went down and it gradually got chilly out, people began to drift away. Soon only Emilio, Bob Two Bears and Runty Schommer were left outside, helping to clean up. Katita was curled up on the couch, asleep with her head in her mother's lap, her sisters dozing together under a blanket on the living room rug. Solveig stroked Katita's hair absently, her eyes blank.

When the house was tidy, Mae's mother hugged her and quietly left, Bob and Runty behind her. Emilio woke his daughters on the floor and then gently shook Katita, who opened her eyes, blinking for a moment before her brow furrowed and she closed her eyes again with a soft moan, covering her face with her hands. She allowed herself to be led out to the car by her father and mother.

When they were gone, the house was very quiet. Mae sighed deeply. Her face looked like she had never smiled in her life.

"I'm exhausted," she said. "I'm going to bed."

As she walked by Willy, he stopped her with his hands on her shoulders, pulling her to him. He encircled her with his arms and held her to his chest. She put her arms around him, seemingly as a reflex, but there seemed to be no strength or will in it. Finally she extricated herself and gave him an automatic peck on the cheek.

"Are you coming?" she asked.

"I'll be along in a bit," he said.

She went into the bedroom and closed the door.

Willy stood there blankly for several moments before wandering into the kitchen and getting a bottle of whiskey and a glass out of the cupboard. He turned the radio on low, and sat at the bare kitchen table, distracted by the sound of the radio but not listening to it, the thought of the silence itself too painful. He drank from the glass of whiskey, adam's apple bobbing three times, set it down and poured again.

As often happened, whatever was on the radio was not enough for him to pay attention to for any length of time, but did distract him enough to go off on tangents of his own thoughts without getting bogged down in the monotonous recording of self-recrimination which played again and again in his mind when it was too quiet. Soon, he had gotten out the pad of paper and a pencil from under the phone book in the corner drawer of the kitchen, and was writing things down in little bursts, holding the glass of whiskey and staring at nothing when his right hand was not in motion.

Hours later, the bottle empty, he got up from the kitchen table and turned off the radio and the lights. He checked the front door, weaving a little as he walked, and bumped into the doorjamb on his way into the bedroom, where Mae was curled up in bed under the quilt, motionless in the temporary peace of her sleep.

Willy awoke with a sickening hangover and remembered that his son was dead. Mae's side of the bed was empty. He got up and shuffled into the bathroom in his boxer shorts and took a piss, then brushed his teeth and held a cold washcloth to his eyes.

Mae was not in the living room or the kitchen. He poured himself a cup of coffee and sat at the kitchen table, trying to remember his train of thought the night before when things had begun to get blurry.

As he sat there, Mae came in from the back yard and sat down in the chair opposite him.

Without preamble, she said in a mystified tone, "I don't know what I could have done any differently. I don't- I tried to tell them what I could, what I knew-"

Willy shook his head vehemently, his hand on her forearm. "No, honey, no, no. Sweetheart, it was my fault."

"It was not your fault!"

"Yes! My example! The things I did! I-"

"You did what you had to! Are you talking about Bud Sletto? *Fuck* Bud Sletto! I wish you could do it again! You shouldn't have gone to prison, you shouldn't-"

"No, it's not that," Willy said. "I should have...dispelled their illusions."

"You tried to."

"I-" He thought about what Gordon had written about beaming knowledge into a person's head. "I didn't succeed. I failed. I failed our boys."

"No," she said, grabbing his wrist and gripping it until he looked her in the eye. "Willy. No."

He hung his head and stared at his cup of coffee.

They sat like that, silently, for some time.

"We are not going to bury him in that cemetery," Mae said finally. "Not in that... place."

"Okay," Willy said, looking up sharply. "Yes, you're right."

"We're going to scatter his ashes on the river. He loved the river."

"Yes," Willy said.

"And when I go, you're going to scatter my ashes there, too."

Willy said nothing, held himself together. Mae did; she was dry-eyed.

"All of us should have our ashes scattered on the river," she said.

"Yes, Mae."

The next day, they got a telegram from Gordon. "I'll be coming home soon," it read. "Don't do anything until I get there."

And so they began to wait for their sons to come home. Gordon would come when he had finished his rehabilitation and was released from service. Chief's body and personal effects were shipped to Japan, not far from where Gordon was in the hospital, and then placed in a refrigerated container with the bodies of many other young men shipped home under the auspices of Operation Glory, the new effort of the US Army's Mortuary Affairs division to repatriate the dead. Willy, with complete recognition that his boy was gone, could not stop himself from visualizing his sweet face, as if sleeping, pallid and quiescent, lying among strangers in the dark.

Willy and Mae tried to go about their daily routine as they waited. They ate in silence, but were kind to each other. Willy walked down to the bar in the morning, Mae usually came down some time later. The mood in the bar was grim and somehow apologetic for the first week or two, but the pall gradually dissipated, and things slowly settled into a new normal. The ad hoc band played one night, and Willy realized later that no one had mentioned Chief for the entire evening.

For both of them, though, their private pain did not diminish, and never would. Willy mowed the lawn before it needed it with the old push mower after taking too much time oiling it and carefully sharpening its blades. He soon ran out of things to repair at the bar. Mae did the laundry and cooked, but was so typically quick and efficient that she was soon helping Willy with whatever work they could dream up at the bar. They went to the hotel now and then for dinner, and although Edith was at ease, seemingly herself at last, the place was cool, echoing and empty.

They indulged in the chores they could think of, doing the seasonal upkeep on the old boat, scraping and painting the south side of the house next to the driveway together, always working efficiently and quietly, saying little.

Mae did not play the piano, and Willy wouldn't suggest it.

One Sunday morning in the cool bedroom, they held each other and began to kiss. Soon they were making love. In the midst of it, though, Mae sobbed once, hard, and Willy looked down into her eyes, which were lensed with tears, overflowing and rolling down her temples and into her hair. His breath caught in his throat and he moved off her with a hand frozen in the air as if to touch her, the need stilled by fear, as though she were too fragile to touch. She sniffed once, got up from the bed and went into the bathroom and closed the door. Fifteen minutes later, she came out and began getting dressed.

"Sorry," she said, watching her hands as she buttoned her linen blouse.

"Yes," Willy said, nodding rapidly, his eyes wide. "It's okay. It's all right."

Gordon and Chief both came home in May.

There were no bands for those who returned from Korea, no official greetings. They met Gordon when he got off the train in Black Marsh. The passengers who got off before him dispersed in their own directions, and Gordon got off last, dressed in uniform, going down the steps one at a time using a cane and holding the handrail, one leg obviously stiff.

He dropped his duffelbag and embraced his mother, favoring his leg but putting both arms around her, the cane in one hand. He held on to her for a long time before letting her go. Willy was sure that Gordon was merely going to extend his hand to him, but again, after a moment's hesitation, his son embraced him. When they stood apart, Willy noticed the puckered purple scar at the bottom of his right ear where the earlobe had been shot away. He didn't mention it.

Willy shouldered the duffelbag as they walked back to the pickup, Gordon arm in arm with Mae, limping and using the cane. It crushed Willy to recognize the look in his son's eyes, the look that left Gordon old and sad and grave, as if his gaze were fixed not on the good in the future but the evil in the past, the look he knew might be irrevocable.

They spoke little, suddenly a quiet trio instead of a pair. Willy placed the duffelbag in the bed of the pickup and they got in, Mae sitting in the middle.

When they got home, they stood in the living room for a few moments, wordless, before Willy cleared his throat and took Chief's duffelbag to his old room. When he came back, Gordon sat on the aging couch, the couch Mollie had slept on, his mother beside him. He absently stroked the fabric of the couch, and although his face was stern, his lower eyelids held thick crescents of tears. They finally fell, almost simultaneously, rolling in thin, shiny streaks down his face and dripping off his chin onto his uniform, leaving two small dark dots.

"Fuck it," he choked, the corners of his mouth turned down. "Fuck everything."

Gordon found that his old clothes were too big for him, but said he didn't like them much anyway. In the cool days of spring, all he wore was a frayed pair of shorts and a t-shirt with an old black sweater over it, deck shoes with no socks. He began to grow back the beard he had sported in his days in Greysport, although now it did not seem like an affectation.

He read constantly, books that Willy knew he had read before, along with a great deal of Chief's science fiction, seemingly mowing through the dead boy's shelf. He sat on the porch and read until it got too chilly, then went to his old room, his room from childhood, and was still reading when Willy went to bed. Even when he came home late from the bar, Willy saw the crack of light from under his door.

Mae told him that she had come home from shopping one day and found him sitting in Chief's room on the bed, his elbows on his knees, face blank, eyes wide. She went to put away the groceries, expecting him to come in and help. When she got done and went to check on him, Chief's room was empty and his own door was closed.

Katita came to see him, driving their old '38 Chrysler. Willy was in the kitchen when Gordon answered the door, going out onto the porch to talk to her. He couldn't make out everything they said, but saw Gordon put his hands on Katita's shoulders and lean down to touch the crown of his forehead to hers. He could hear enough to discern, at one point, that Katita was trying to give him back the keys to the car, but Gordon repeated firmly that he wanted her to have it, and it was obvious from his posture, his head now raised and his shoulders squared, that he was remaining adamant. He could see from their body language that she finally gave in, but also saw her gesture over her shoulder with the car keys in her hand. He then opened the screen door and said that he was going for a drive with Katita. Willy lifted his chin at his son in acknowledgement, and they were gone.

Other than occasional drives with Katita, Gordon refused to see anyone. If old friends came to the door, he had Mae or Willy send them away. Willy was certain that, when he was home alone, he didn't go to the door at all, simply waiting on his bed with a book until they stopped knocking.

He never came down to the bar and only went out late at night, sometimes for long walks, although Willy had no idea where they took him. Concerned about his weight loss and apparently declining health, Willy tried to encourage him to work out in the basement, to lift some weights and hit the heavy bag. When Gordon refused, his face unreadable, Willy went down to the basement himself and made noise with those activities, hoping that Gordon would be drawn down the stairs, but he always finished his workout alone.

In one sense, Willy was almost grateful for his son's withdrawal, in that it gave Mae something to think about other than the arrival of Chief's coffin. She even called Doc Ambrose, who, of course, knew everything about Gordon that there was to know. The old man talked with Gordon on the couch while Willy and Mae discretely tended to some weeding in the front yard.

When Ambrose came out of the house at last, they both gave him anxious looks, ill-concealed on Willy's part.

Ambrose, leaning on his cane said, "He's sad."

Willy snorted. "No shit."

Mae put her hand on Willy's arm and Ambrose continued.

"I told him it was normal," Ambrose said. "It is. And if he believes it's normal, he stands a better chance to forgive himself for feeling this way. Like a lot of young men in his position, he thinks, from what I could glean, that he should just 'soldier on'. He finds himself unable to do this, thinks he's weak for this inability, and hates himself for the weakness."

Willy closed his eyes and sighed, as Mae said, "He's just a boy."

Ambrose looked at her levelly and said, "He'll always be *your* boy, but he'll never be a child again."

Doc Ambrose tottered off down the street, and Mae went inside to make Gordon some lunch. The day was beautiful, and Willy realized that he hadn't even noticed that the lilacs by the front porch were in bloom. He remembered the weekend day a year before when he and Mae had been up in the apple orchard, back when they still made love. He spent the next few hours puttering in the garage and the basement, leaving Mae and Gordon alone together in the house.

He thought about what Ambrose had said as he puttered, and finally went into the house, washing his hands at the kitchen sink. He went to Gordon's room, knocked and entered, finding his son stretched on the bed, one forearm under his head, holding a paperback in the other hand. He pulled the wooden chair from the small desk where his son once did his homework, sitting on it backwards with his arms resting on its back.

He watched his son for a bit and said, "You know I know how you feel."

Gordon, groaning softly, put his thumb in the book to hold his place and rested the book on his chest.

"You know I know," Willy said when Gordon met his eyes.

"I suppose you do."

"So, let's talk."

Gordon didn't say anything.

"You leave it in there, building up pressure like live steam, and it's just going to boil your brain." He said this in a mildly jocular tone, but Gordon drifted his gaze to the ceiling.

"You want to say something," Willy said. "Just say it."

"You're the one who wants to say something," Gordon said.

"Like what?"

Gordon snorted and glanced at his father disgustedly, then let his eyes slip back to the ceiling.

"Really, Gordon, like what?"

"Dad, come on!"

"*You* come on."

"You want to say 'I told you so'! Just say it! Get it off your chest! Jesus!"

Willy was silent for a moment, then said, "I wasn't thinking anything like that, Gordon, I assure you."

"Bullshit."

"Son, I just want you to know that you're not alone. I want you to know that I have felt this way, the way you're feeling. When I came back from the war...." he sought the words and petered out, thinking about what to say to his son.

"We've both seen how ugly our species can be, and it's so bad, we're sure that others who haven't seen it can't understand it. We've both seen how ugly we *ourselves* can be. After witnessing such things, many people feel that there's no hope, or redemption, or... joy."

He got up from the chair and went to look out the bedroom window at the back yard.

"You see normal people walking around happily with no knowledge of this, and you wonder if they're insane or if you are."

He realized he had Gordon's attention, but continued to look out the window, as if he were afraid to spook a wild and suspicious animal.

"They're not insane, and you're not insane. You *do* know more about the nature of human reality, though, on a deep level that most of them can never understand. I have found that this can be an advantage, although it took me a long time to figure it out.

"When I came back from the war, I was adrift. I can tell you this now. I felt little happiness, but didn't feel quite bad enough to kill myself. I just didn't care one way or the other. There were guys I knew who did it- killed themselves- but I always thought that they had made things much worse for the people who loved them than things were for themselves. They had survived the war, so had their families, and then they threw away the gift that was the rest of their lives. They left their families to wonder what *they* had done wrong. They squandered whatever gifts they had been born with.

"My own parents died when I was overseas, and I didn't really have anyone left alive who would mourn *my* passing, let alone bear the weight of it, which is usually the case with suicides. I wrote to Emilio and a few other people, but there was no real reason to stay alive. I just... diverted myself."

Willy pretended to look at an angle out the window, as if examining the neighbor's spring garden, but was able to see with his peripheral vision that Gordon appeared to be listening.

"I had some adventures. That kept me going. Curiosity about what would happen next; the kept me going, too. Old Doc Ambrose said the same thing not too long ago, and he's something like two hundred and seventeen years old."

Willy wasn't sure, but he thought a wisp of a smile might have come and gone on his son's face.

"You have to find something you love, I think. You have to...I started writing poetry after the war, did you ever know that?"

Gordon sighed and said, "Yeah."

"You did?"

"Yeah. Mom told me. Me and...Chief. She said that's how she fell in love with you."

"She did, huh?" Willy tried not to go too fast, tried to let Gordon ease into the spaces of silence.

"Yeah," Gordon said finally, "she told us stuff like that when you were in prison. It explained all the times I saw you up late at night in the kitchen, scribbling away at the table."

"I guess I never noticed." Willy couldn't believe they were having this conversation.

"I'd be going to the bathroom or getting a drink of water. I could stand in the dark in the living room for a long time," Gordon said. He even laughed, shortly, quietly. "You never even knew I was there, and you usually know everything that's going on in the house."

It might be all right, Willy thought.

"How about that," he said.

"Yep. You'd sit there like this." Gordon sat up to imitate him, scowling and holding his left thumbnail to his lip while miming scribbling from left to right across a page.

"I look like that?"

Gordon nodded, not quite smiling, but his look mild.

"That's how you look when you draw," Willy said.

They both snorted through their noses.

"You should go back to that," Willy said. "Go back to school. You're very good. It's something to love."

"What about your poetry?" Gordon asked.

"Oh, I still do it."

"I know."

Willy looked at him; his face was unreadable.

"Maybe you should publish your life's work," Gordon said.

"You guys have been my life's work," Willy said.

Gordon watched him for a few seconds, his eyes lidded. "Nice job," he said.

No! Willy thought, but before he could say anything else, Gordon said. "I'm really tired, Dad. I think I'll take a nap. Would you mind?"

Willy didn't know how to pick up the sudden pieces. "Okay," he said, and got up and walked to the door, closing it behind him, allowing himself to get kicked out of his son's bedroom.

A few days later, Chief came home on the train, in a coffin on a cargo car. Willy had received notification of when it would arrive, and had set it up so that his longtime acquaintance Sam Feeney of Feeney Funeral Home was there to receive it.

He had wanted to slip out and be there when Chief's body arrived, hoping to avoid subjecting Mae to any unnecessary sadness, but she had known that he was concealing something and had gotten it out of him.

"What were you thinking?" she asked him. "We can't avoid the sadness of this. And if we can't avoid it, we have to push our faces into it. We have to *drain* it."

"Just trying to protect you," Willy said.

"I know," she said, and kissed him dryly on the cheek.

Mae told Gordon, and half an hour before the train was due to arrive early on a Thursday morning, he was dressed in jeans and a black jacket, waiting on the porch. They filed out to the car and drove up the river road to the familiar train station in Black Marsh. They didn't say a word from the time they left the house until they stood together on the cobbled brick platform beside the station. Gordon still looked strong, although pale and drawn, his beard and the score of his scar in sharp contrast to his pallor. His face would have been expressionless had it not been for his slightly furrowed brow. Mae, too, was pale, clad in her dark, cool-weather coat, and wore her version of the same expression, her red hair tied up simply in a black ribbon.

Willy talked to Sam Feeney for a moment, then came back and stood with Mae and Gordon as Feeney got a clipboard out of his plain hearse and stood with his assistant a discrete distance away.

The train pulled in punctually, and they waited as the passengers got off and spread away in their various directions. Feeney approached the conductor and spoke quietly to him and boarded the car while his assistant readied the collapsible cart he pulled from the rear of the hearse. With practiced ease, the men moved the plain military coffin from the train onto the cart. Feeney signed some papers and handed them back to the conductor, and he and his assistant began slowly rolling the coffin to the hearse.

Gordon stood with one hand on his mother's shoulder, and Willy stood behind them, placing his hand on top of Gordon's. They watched, listening to the idling of the train's engine down the track, to the sound of the cart's rubber wheels thumping over the cobbles of the platform, to the sound of Feeney's voice as he said softly to his assistant, "Easy, there. Watch the... yeah. Okay."

Just as they were about to slide the coffin into the back of the hearse, Mae started forward. Willy and Gordon stood frozen for a moment as she went over and stopped beside the coffin. Feeney and the other man hesitated. Mae reached slowly out and put her pale hand on the lid of the coffin. She stood there, motionless, the morning breeze lifting her hair. The train engine idled, the scent of diesel in the air.

Gordon went and stood next to his mother, putting his hand beside hers. A man passing by to board the train slowed his walk to stare, and Willy gave him a look that made him drop his eyes, muttering apologetically, and hurry around the front of the hearse. Willy stepped forward and put his hand the coffin, softly at first, then heavily, suddenly leaning his weight on it, enough to shift it a little on the cart.

"Willy?" Feeney said, and Willy controlled himself.

Mae didn't appear to notice. Her lips pursed, her brow furrowed, she stared at the lid of the coffin. After a long time, she tapped the lid twice with her fingertips and nodded. The three of them- she, Willy, and Gordon- stepped back to allow the men to slide the coffin into the hearse.

They stood and watched as the hearse drove away in the cool light of the May morning.

When they finally stood alone on the station platform, the train pulling away into the distance, Mae said that she wanted to see Chief's dormitory. Willy and Gordon shared a look and quietly agreed, and they all got back in the car. They drove through the campus, where students busily walked to and fro, books under their arms.

"Finals," Gordon said, and laughed.

They pulled up to the small parking lot next to the dorm and got out. The oaks and maples on the lawn were leafing out, apple and crabapple trees in bloom here and there. Kids were everywhere, on the steps of the dorm, on the lawn, down by the river, studying, playing catch, making out. As the remaining McGregors walked slowly across the grass and down to the pier on the river, it seemed to Willy that the young ones around them were moving in fast motion. A kid going long to catch a football missed running into them by a foot, calling, "Sorry!" but none of them changed their pace or even acknowledged his presence.

They came to the pier, the sound of their heels thumping, the lapping of small waves familiar. A young man lay on his back, holding a copy of Homer in the air above his eyes, and a couple sat at the end of the pier with their arms around each other, looking out over the water.

Willy and Gordon stood still behind Mae as she watched all of this, her hands in the pockets of her jacket, her ponytail and its black ribbon riffled by the cool breeze. At length, she turned around and exhaled through her delicate nose.

"Let's get something to eat," she said.

"Where do you want to go?" Willy asked.

"Where else?" she said.

At the Chinese restaurant, they were surrounded by students, many talking brightly, some studying. When the doors with small round windows to the kitchen thumped back and forth with the passage of waiters, Willy heard the shouting in Cantonese and the clatter of plates and utensils, the hissing of steam in the white kitchen. He wondered what the was dialect of the men who had killed his son, the men who had been just as terrified, the men who had families and children, mothers, fathers, brothers-

Mae nudged him and he came back.

They waited for their customary booth by the front window to be wiped off my a smiling young Chinese woman, thanking her quietly and sitting down. Students around them talked and laughed. A girl with a volume of Keats, wearing a perfectly frayed black turtleneck, sipped tea. A couple of round and redfaced railmen halfheartedly studied the menu while eyeing the female students, nudging each other and smirking. Willy sighed.

Their order was taken by a young Chinese man in a white jacket who spoke English with a bit of a Greysport accent. Gordon stared at him, more with wonder than malice.

The young waiter seemed bored with such attention, and said to Gordon, "Uh, hey, man, do I know you?"

Gordon stared at him silently. The waiter stared back, raising his eyebrows and spreading his hands.

"What, never seen a Chinese guy before?"

Gordon's eyes widened slightly, but he said nothing.

The waiter finally sighed and said, "Well, I can tell you're one *crazy* cat, dig? While you decide what you want, I'll just get the orders from the beautiful lady and Mr. Knuckles here."

Gordon got more erect in his seat.

"Don't...fucking..." he muttered, but stopped when Willy put a hand on his wrist.

"I'll come back when you're ready to order," the young man said, narrowing his eyes at Gordon and moving away.

"Gordon?" Willy said, his hand tight on his son's wrist. Gordon's eyes fixed on Willy with such a dark and recognizable look that Willy took his hand away.

Mae, oblivious, put down her menu and said, "Let's just order."

When Gordon calmed down, he ordered Chief's old favorite. The food came, and Willy offered to share some of his and sample some of theirs, the old family tradition, but he was ignored as the other two picked away at their plates. The people around them chattered and laughed and lived.

The ashes were ready in a week, and Willy and Mae went to pick them up.

Again, Willy had wanted to go alone, but Mae wouldn't allow it. They pulled up in front of Feeney's, a grey stone building with black trim and black wrought iron gates and fixtures, iron work from nearby Mt. Pleasant done by a relative of Runty Schommer's. Willy was about to mention this irrelevant fact to Mae, but realized that his mind was wandering as a means of protecting itself. He shook his head minutely and tried to focus.

They pulled open the heavy oak door by its iron handle and went inside. The carpet in the front hallway was deep red, the walls dark oak, the light fixtures and door handles bronze. The place was silent but for the ticking of a large grandfather clock at the end of the hall opposite the entrance. Willy wondered if it was meant as a reminder that those who entered upright would one day enter horizontally.

"I always thought this place was a little posh for this town," Mae whispered. In spite of the wry comment, her face was serious.

"Old money from the Irish mob in Greysport," Willy said. "They had to launder it at a discrete distance."

They padded down the hallway and stopped, listening to the resolute ticking of the clock. Sam Feeney came silently out of a dark side door.

"Hello, Mae, Willy," he said, shaking their hands. Willy had always liked him; he was not unctuous or fawning; rather he was straight and matter-of-fact, working in a business of absolute necessity so grim and routinely tragic- a business that would break many people- and yet was kept at a distance by most people in the community, if not treated with what amounted to mild scorn or even revulsion by those who would one day need him. He knew everything about the sadness of life that most people never see, and yet he bore it quietly and with mild humor. He had an unsurprising fondness for whiskey, but always maintained an even keel, and on the infrequent occasions he came to the bar (always finding himself soon surrounded by empty barstools), he drank his fill and talked to Willy calmly, his demeanor never changing even if he'd had several glasses of whiskey neat. Willy had given up chiding his regulars for their superstitious avoidance of the man.

Feeney ushered them into an office off the hall, also well-appointed with stained glass windows and a heavy desk. As Willy expected, Feeney offered them a drink. Mae shook her head, but Willy nodded and Feeney poured them both a healthy Jameson's. He handed Willy one of the glasses and sat behind the desk. In the center of the gleaming wood of the desk's surface sat what appeared to be an eight by ten inch box wrapped in white silk.

"Allow me again to say how sorry I am," Feeney said. "Chief- Daniel- was such a good boy. He would have been a fine man." He looked at them both levelly and did not embellish. Willy took a sip from his drink, but Feeney paid no attention to his own.

Willy and Mae quietly thanked him.

"You said you didn't want an urn," Feeney said.

"We're scattering his ashes," Mae said.

"Yes," he said. "Here they are." He picked up the silk-wrapped box and came around the desk, extending it in both hands to Mae.

"It's so heavy," Mae said. Willy watched for tears, but none came. She handed the box to Willy.

"So small," Willy said.

"Again," Sam Feeney said, "I'm very sorry."

When they closed to doors to the place behind them, they walked to the car squinting in the sunlight. Once home, Mae put the box on the center of Chief's bed. The door to Gordon's room was still closed.

They left a note for Gordon and went down to the bar for the Saturday night crowd. When they got back, they found Gordon asleep on Chief's bed, a science fiction book in one hand, the other hand resting on the box.

They scattered Chief's ashes on the river a week later.

Only those closest to the family came, a small, quiet gathering at the same pier which Willy and Mae had left from their wedding, the pier to which Willy and his family returned to the waiting sheriffs the night of the final confrontation with Bud Sletto. These recollections were completely absent from Willy's mind as he saw the faces of those assembled. He looked at his old boat tied up at the pier. It was almost a living thing to him; it had brought him all the way up the river, to his life, to his resurrection, to his fate.

Katita stood with Gordon, who had shaven and was neatly dressed in khakis and a white oxford shirt. She was quietly talking to him, watching his eyes, which were focused on the water beside the pier. Emilio stood with Solveig, who had her plump hand in the crook of his arm. The other two girls stood near them, their eyes large and gleaming. Solveig was wearing a pink suit and hat, although Emilio was dressed somberly and wearing a tie.

Doc Ambrose, who had brought the boys into the world ("Our usher into this global theater of the weird," Chief had once joked), was there with his wife Harriet. They leaned on each other, and it was quite clear that they were very much in love. Near Mae stood her mother, looking almost stern as she reached out and smoothed her daughter's hair. Mae had a look on her face similar to Gordon's, and to the one she wore when she laid her hand on the coffin; her brow was lightly furrowed, her lips slightly pursed. She looked out at the water.

She seemed to sense that Willy was watching her, and shifted her eyes to meet his. She nodded once.

"Well, everyone," Willy said, "we should get going."

They boarded the boat one by one. Gordon and Emilio helped Doc and Harriet Ambrose aboard, then Emilio got on with his wife. Willy helped the girls over, leaving Gordon on the pier to untie the bow and stern lines. He started the engine and nodded to Gordon, who cast off and got on, his leg still stiff.

It was a windy and brilliant day, and the clouds moved swiftly overhead. Willy squinted against the sunlight and pushed the throttle forward, accelerating the boat over the waves. People had settled themselves in the seats and looked out over the water. Doc Ambrose was talking over the sound of the engine to his wife and Mrs. Palmer, but the rest were quiet. Emilio sat with his hand reassuringly on his wife's lap, and Solveig held her hat to her head. Willy went up the river for a quarter of an hour, heading for an island where the boys had always liked to fish. Gordon leaned out over the gunwale and watched keenly as the island drew close. When they neared the island's south side Gordon went to the bow and dropped anchor, which didn't have far to go in the translucent brownish water before it struck a sandy bank. The anchor bit into the bank and the bowline went taut.

Mae sat in the cockpit with the silk-covered box in her lap, her hands resting on top of it. Her mother had her arm gently resting across her shoulders, but Mae seemed unaware of this. She looked out over the water, lost in thought, then seemed to come to a conclusion and back to herself.

She sighed and patted the box. "Willy?" she said.

Willy stood up, loosely compensating for the boat's rocking, and came to her, taking the box from her hands and slipping it out of its white silk cover. Inside was a cherrywood box, polished and neatly crafted. Katita, watching intently, sniffed once and began to cry. Her mother moved to comfort her. She began to shudder with sobs and a bubble of mucus popped from her nose. Her mother gently wiped it away.

Willy and Mae stood together in the stern of the boat and faced the others. Gordon got up and joined them. Willy held the box on his upturned hands, Mae and Gordon each placed a hand atop it.

"This is our boy, Daniel James McGregor. He was bright and young and strong, and adventurous. We all...we loved him so."

Katita was sobbing, and Solveig grimly patted her shoulder. The girls were weeping quietly, clinging to each other. Emilio was pale and looked like he had aged fifteen years. Doc Ambrose sat with his wife, too unstable to stand with the rocking of the boat, and Willy saw thin tears running down his softly lined cheeks.

Willy continued. "Chief now knows the mystery that awaits us all. If anything exists after this, he has been enlightened by it. If he can watch us, he's watching us now."

"Chief!" Katita wailed. She was sobbing so hard she drooled, and her mother and father supported her to keep her from falling to the deck.

"If there is nothing after this," Willy continued, "then our boy is far away from sorrow, and far away from pain. He can never be hurt again, but is immortal in our hearts."

He looked at each of those present in turn, ending with Mae and Gordon.

"Does anyone have anything they want to say?"

There was silence.

"That was good, Dad," Gordon said as Willy slipped the cherrywood box out of its silk cover.

"The poem," Mae said.

"Oh," Willy said, holding the box out for Mae and Gordon to hold. He took from his jacket pocket a piece of paper, written on in broad-nibbed pen so that the letters looked like calligraphy.

"Could you-" he said to Mae and Gordon, indicating that they get ready. They nodded, and went to the stern, leaning out over the water. Katita keened while everyone else watched silently.

Gordon and Mae opened the box. Inside was a sealed paper packet, large enough to hold a couple of books. Mae set the box on the deck while Gordon tore open the corner of the packet. Together, they held the packet over the side and poured the gritty grey contents into the water. The ashes formed a cloud in the current and began to dissipate.

Willy read the poem:

Waves will run under endless sun
Long after deed of man is done

Take our boy and set him free
Softly, softly to the sea

Gordon limped back into the cabin and brought forth a wreath of apple, crabapple, and lilac blossoms. He cast it on the water where the ashes were borne downstream, and, caught in the current, it floated away.

They all watched for awhile. Soon there was no trace of the ashes, and the wreath had been borne away on the strong and unending current of the river.

Willy had left a sign on the door of the bar saying, "Closed for Private Function", although this was necessary only for people coming in from out of town; all the regulars would know the reason. Prime rib was roasting, and Willy and Mae had made the preparations in advance for mashed potatoes and fresh asparagus, bread from the bakery and a good red wine.

They'd moved the other tables and chairs in the dining and dancing area aside, leaving a few tables together in the center of the room, covered with tablecloths and set with silverware and candles. While Mae and Solveig did the final preparations in the kitchen, Willy opened wine and made sure everyone had a glass. Fresh bread and butter were passed around.

When Mae and Solveig brought in the vegetables, Gordon, to everyone's surprise, began to giggle. It was looking at Solveig that apparently set it off, and although Gordon tried to stifle his laughter, this only made things worse.

Everyone knew what it was about. When they had tied the boat up at the pier and gotten off, Solveig had been comforting the still-sobbing Katita when a gust of the strong wind had snatched her improbable pink hat, momentarily unprotected, from her head and lofted it out over the river, where it finally plimped into the drink to float away.

Solveig, her arms still around Katita, had watched the hat wistfully and said, "Ding dong dammit!"

Emilio had promptly told her that they would get a new one, and the other men had ignored it while the women had made tisking sounds. No mirth was expressed until Gordon started to giggle, apparently set off by Solveig's wind-stricken hair as she set down the mashed potatoes.

Gordon took a sip of wine and attempted not to laugh, but noseburped and started to laugh harder. He tried not to look at Solveig, but when he glanced at her for a moment, he snorted again and laughed out loud. The girls looked at him and began to smile. Willy looked at his son and was flooded with such relief that he began to laugh, too.

Gordon laughed harder, apparently provoked by the look on Solveig's face, which was a placid version of a glare. He slapped the table and Ambrose and his wife began to laugh.

"I'm sorry, Mrs. Benitez," Gordon choked, "but the hat! It's just the hat!"

Eduardo began to laugh and imitated his wife: "Ding dong dammit!"

"Some cracker down south is going to fish it out and wear it to church," Doc Ambrose said, and now everyone was laughing.

Except for Mae. Willy could tell that she was trying to smile, but he also knew that the look in her eyes was one of sadness and love for all of them there, that mirth was beyond her. She turned and went into the kitchen.

Willy offered Gordon a job at the bar, just to give him something to do while he sorted himself out. Since Gordon had taken care of the place with his mother and brother while Willy was in prison, he was certainly capable of running the show himself.

"You've got enough people, Dad," Gordon said, stretched out on the couch and not moving his eyes from the book in his hand. "I appreciate it, but I know you don't need me."

"Okay. I just thought I'd offer."

"Thanks anyway."

Willy watched him for a moment and said, "I'm sure you're thinking about going back to school."

"Yeah."

"You've got the G.I. Bill and everything."

"Yeah."

"And you've got a lot of talent, son. You don't want to waste that. You need to think about how you're going to contribute-"

"Dad! Okay!"

Willy gave up and left the room.

Things went on like this for another month, as it began to turn into a muggy summer. Willy became accustomed to being crushed with grief- he winced most mornings when he awoke and remembered- but other emotions began to compete. Mae functioned well, but emotionlessly, seeming blank, with neither highs nor lows. She helped her mother with the sale of the hotel to a hopeful young couple, she completed all the tasks she had ever done, while Willy did his. When he tried to draw her out of her blankness, she would kiss him coolly on the forehead or cheek and drift quietly away.

Gordon gave moments of promise, having conversations with his mother and sometimes with Willy, and was occasionally pleasant. His basic mood, though, was one of gloom; it would have been mere sullenness if exhibited by a young man his age who had not been through as much.

One day Willy came home at lunch and was pleased to hear the sound of the heavybag in the basement being pounded. He walked quietly through the living room and stood at the top of the basement stairs, listening. He realized that Gordon was muttering as he slammed the bag, growling, "*Fuck* you! *Fuck* you! You *fuck*, you *fuck*, you *fuck*! You *motherfucker*!"

Willy blew air silently through his lips and left the house without a sound.

So he waited for what was left of his family to come back to him, simply ticking off his life's to-do list in the meantime. He began to get annoyed with Gordon's lassitude and felt ashamed at his own reaction, as he did regarding his feelings about the apparent death of his and Mae's sex life. These things embarrassed him and made him feel petty, and he tried to keep as busy as possible in order to ignore them.

With the money from the sale of the hotel, Mae's mother stored the possessions she didn't auction and went to visit her sister, whom she had not seen for years, in New England. They'd had a final dinner at the hotel before the closing, and Willy still found it surprising at how unemotional his wife was, as was her mother. When they parted, it was casual, as if they would see each other again in a week, but Edith Palmer had made it clear that she had no immediate plans to return, and she was well into her seventies. They seemed to have tapped into wells of hidden strength or numbness, Willy couldn't decide which. It was something he would once have discussed with Mae, but a slow fog seemed to have drifted between them, silently building in density until they could no longer see each other at all. Not knowing what to do, he left it alone.

Whenever he had done every conceivable thing that needed doing around the house and the bar, when he had worked out and watched a baseball game with Doc Ambrose and Barnacle Brad, the Hansen boys, Bob Two Bears and Runty Schommer, when he had tried yet again to initiate intimacy with Mae and again been airily rebuffed, he went up to the bluffs or out on the river. It was in those places that he could not avoid his thoughts.

How much was he responsible for his son's death? If he was only minimally responsible, what was it that had coaxed Chief toward it? Was it Chief's brightness and his strength, his adventurousness, that ended his life, when a more torpid boy would still have been among them? What was the human compulsion which made the young yearn for their own tales of hardship, what caused them to think that they needed to survive trial in order to feel worthy? What was it in some young people that made them want to see things they would later wish they had not seen, endure that which they would wish they had not endured?

And they became another link in the ancient chain that faded back into time, and their wisdom and their warnings would go unheeded by a new wave of the young who would find it impossible to resist the drive to become hardened by fresh tragedy.

He talked to Emilio about it, out on the river.

"It is the kind of human tendency that can be used," Emilio said. "They will call it glory, they will call it duty, and they know it will lead to the death of children."

"It's amazing our species survives," Willy said.

"So far," Emilio replied.

It was a muggy Saturday in August when the bar was busy with regulars taking refuge from the heat. It was cool and dark, the brightest light being that of the sunlight coming through the dusty front windows onto the unused piano. The dining area was empty, but almost every seat at the bar and surrounding tables was taken, pilsner glasses golden in the diffuse light. The Hansen brothers were watching cartoons on television before the baseball game, Steve laughing the

240

hardest, holding a beer in one hand and a cigarette in the tobacco-stained fingers of the other. Willy did a crossword puzzle while Bob Two Bears took his time waiting on the patrons, always seeming to move unhurriedly, but never allowing anyone to be left unattended.

When the game was about to begin, the door opened, and, as often happens in small town bars, everyone turned to see who was coming in. To Willy's surprise, it was Gordon. Although he was greeted cheerfully, he seemed a little hesitant, even glum, but allowed himself to be seated at the bar, and accepted the first of many offers of a beer.

Willy set down his crossword puzzle and stood in front of Gordon.

"Well, hi, son," he said.

"Just thought I'd come in and watch the game," Gordon said. There was a general hubbub about the game, everyone chiming in, and the noise in the bar increased by several decibels. In the din, someone insisted on doing a shot with Gordon, pressing him when he demurred. He finally relented, but when he was toasted as a "young hero", he winced slightly before he did the shot. The men on either side of him slapped him on the back as he sipped from his beer. Willy gave him a look that told him to take it easy, and Gordon nodded solemnly.

The game began, and from the first inning it was clear that it would not be boring. Willy wasn't very interested in it, but he had begun to associate the drone of the announcer's voice and the occasional roar of the audience on the television and around the bar with a lazy summer afternoon, and the feeling was not unpleasant. He was able to watch his son's face when his eyes, like those of the men around him, were fixed on the television, and Willy smiled when Gordon swore at an error or hooted at a good hit or surprising catch. The novelty of his presence seemed to be getting him a lot of free drinks, and Willy wanted to caution him again, Gordon not being much of a drinker, but he looked relaxed, distracted, maybe even a bit happy for once, and Willy didn't want to spoil it.

When the game was over, the men in the bar were cheerfully buzzed, and even Gordon smiled cautiously. Willy drank a cup of coffee and began to set up the dining area for the evening, and when he was done with this, he noticed that Gordon had left.

"Where'd my son go?" He asked the men on either side of the empty barstool.

They shrugged. "Just muttered something and left," one of them said.

Willy told himself not to be worried.

It was getting late, dinner rush long over. He and Runty and the part-time waitresses were cleaning up when Gordon came back. Although Gordon's expression was impassive, Willy could tell from his slow eyes and his subtle weave that he was very drunk, although he might not have drawn any attention from a stranger. Before Willy could intervene, Gordon had sat among the bar crowd and Bob had poured him a gin.

Every time I turn my back on those boys, Willy thought.

Gordon may have been thinking along similar lines. As Willy walked over, Gordon was shaking his head and sliding money across the bar at Bob, who seemed to want to give him the drink for free, and when Gordon saw his father in the mirror of the backbar, he said, "Bob, were you here that time, that one time?

241

My brother and I were kids, okay? It was here, I mean *right here-*" he slapped the bar twice- "okay? And I was chasing Chief, and he jumped up on the bar and was running down it- on top of the bar *right here-* and he turned to see if I was chasing him and tripped and broke his fucking arm."

Gordon laughed and Bob Two Bears smiled patiently.

"It's probably time to switch to coffee, son," Willy said. "That or go home and go to bed. Drink a lot of water first, though."

Gordon turned to him, weaving slightly. "You were out of the room," he said, pointing at Willy. "I remember. Ol' Doc Ambrose- holy fuck, was he *always* old? Like, physician to Henry the Eighth or something. 'Your wife has a headache, your highness? I've got something that'll fix it!'"

He laughed. "Ol' Doc Ambrose probly got sick of patching us up. But Chief broke his arm, anyway. You were out of the room. The end." He took another gulp of gin.

Willy and Bob exchanged a glance, and Bob brought Gordon a cup of coffee and a large glass of water. Gordon didn't seem to notice.

"Go on home after this, Gordon," Willy said gently. "I'll give you a ride if you want."

Gordon just stared at himself in the mirror. Willy watched him for a few moments, then went back to his work.

Ten minutes later, he was making sure everything was neat in the kitchen when Bob came in and motioned with his head, Come with me.

They went out into the bar, and Willy saw that Gordon was sitting at the bar quietly weeping. Somehow he had gotten a shot of whiskey- probably from the often well-meaning but equally witless Barnacle Brad- and he held it in his hand.

Willy put his arm around his shoulders and said, "It's okay, son. Let's just go home."

Gordon hung his head and shook it, and tears tumbled down his cheeks.

"Come on," Willy said. "You don't need any more, okay?"

Gordon seemed to relax against Willy for an instant, then tensed and hunched over his shot. "Leave me the fuck alone," he said.

"Let's go. I've got the keys. We should go."

"Why?" Gordon said, suddenly belligerent.

Willy spread his hands. "Because it's the right thing to do, okay?"

"The right fucking...." Gordon snorted in disgust and did the shot. "Is it what *Chief* would do? Huh, Dad? *Huh*? Is that what *Chief* would do? He was always kissing your ass, he was always your biggest fucking acolyte!"

"Okay-" Willy started.

"That stupid fuck!" Gordon said, raising the empty shotglass to his lips, staring at it for a second, and slamming it down on the bar. "That fucking stupid *fuck*! And *you*, goddam it," he shouted at Willy, coming at him, "he went because of you! It's your fucking fault! All this grandiose bullshit! Fucking tough guy! Who did you save? Did you save Chief? Did you save Mollie?"

Bob had come around the bar and tried to get in front of Gordon, his hands up placatingly, and Gordon shoved him into Barnacle Brad, who spilled his beer. Both Bob and Brad began to protest when Willy had had enough.

"That's *it*, goddam it!" Willy barked. "Gordon, knock it off!"

Gordon came forward and swung at Willy, but, drunk as he was, he was slow. Willy dodged and used Gordon's momentum against him, spinning him around and getting him in a full nelson. Gordon struggled, and was still strong in spite of his months of inactivity, but when he tried to drive the crown of his head back into Willy's face, Willy swept his legs and they both landed on the barroom floor.

Willy tightened the full nelson and shouted, "Goddam it, Gordon, that's enough! Enough!"

Gordon began to struggle, but Willy tightened the hold again and growled softly, "No, son! No!"

After a few moments, Gordon relaxed and began to weep. Willy eased the hold and shushed his son. They lay on the floor, side by side in a semicircle of old friends slowly relaxing from frozen poses of intent.

Willy slowly got up as Gordon rolled on his side and pulled his knees towards his chest , the injured leg bending less, and covered his eyes with his elbow.

Willy watched him, his heart breaking but his face feeling like stone. "Come on, son." he said, "Let's go upstairs."

Gordon went limp and rolled on his back. He took his elbow away from his eyes and laid there for a moment, his eyes closed but his face peaceful. He sniffed once, hard, then opened his eyes and held out a hand for assistance. Bob grabbed his wrist and helped him up.

He stood, and Willy nodded toward the back stairway. They went up without words to Mollie's old room, stark but clean, with the trapunto quilt and the window overlooking the dark alley.

Gordon's face was contorted now, tightened like a fist, but seeming to flicker through bad emotions.

"Dad-" he started.

"It's all right, son," Willy said. "You just rest."

"Okay, just for a bit," he said, and fell onto the bed, rolling on his side and facing the wall. Willy opened the window and to let in the damp river air, and got a sheet from the chiffarobe and spread it over him. He went downstairs and brought up a pitcher of ice water and a glass, then left the room, turning out the light, and closing the door behind him.

He checked on him later, just before he locked up. Gordon was in the same position as when Willy had left him. He snored softly, and when Willy came around the bed and stood by the window to look, he saw that his brow was slightly furrowed in his sleep.

Willy awoke at nine the next morning. Mae, as was usual these days, was still asleep, her face peaceful. Willy quietly left the room, softly closing the door behind him.

He started some coffee and was going to shave and shower, then go down and check on Gordon, who he thought would be just about ready to wake up to a bad hangover. He looked in his room out of habit, though, and to his surprise found a note on a yellow legal pad squarely centered on the bed.

I HAD TO LEAVE, was all it said.

Willy looked around. Most of Gordon's things were gone, except for his dress uniform, which hung in the closet. Willy sat slowly down on the bed. He looked at his watch and wondered when Mae would get up.

It would be years before he would see Gordon again.

Willy found out the same day where Gordon had gone. He called Emilio and talked first to Katita, who said that she had taken him to the train station in Black Marsh. He was going to Greysport.

"I thought you knew," she said.

"Nope," he said.

She seemed at a loss for a moment, then said. "I hope I didn't do anything wrong."

"Oh, no, sweetie. Gordon just...has to figure some things out. He'll be in touch."

"He said he'd write," Katita said, sounding a little worried.

"He will. It'll be okay."

He told Mae about it and she didn't respond, just sitting at the kitchen table with a cup of tea in front of her, looking at the window over the sink. After awhile, she sighed.

Time passed. Just as when the boys were overseas, Willy and Mae checked the mailbox (if they didn't personally intercept the mailman) every day, and Willy went through the mail at the bar as soon as it came, hoping that Gordon might send him something as he had before. When Katita came home from school for a weekend, she said that she had received postcards from him with small prints of artwork from the Greysport Museum. She didn't have to look to know they were from Gordon; the subjects were usually gloomy. The writing was so vague as to be without content.

Willy came into the bar on a Tuesday in early October, sorting through the mail, expecting to be disappointed, and of course he was. He had seen that Bob was behind the bar, putting the cash drawer in the register, but had not noticed that the man sitting across the bar from him was Faith-in-Full Goodforks.

Willy hung his head, the hand holding the mail dropping to his side. "Oh, shit," he said, laughing and shaking his head. Goodforks grinned his white grin and spread his hands, nodding his head.

Willy threw the mail on the bar and embraced him, slapping him on the back. Strangely, he found himself choked up to see the kid. Holding him by the shoulders at arms length, he noticed that Faith was no longer a kid; he had faint lines around his eyes and tiny creases in his lean cheeks, and even a few grey hairs in his ponytail. Willy shoved his shoulders playfully and said, "What the fuck."

"He was wondering if he could pick up some hours," Bob said, pursing his lips and shaking his head.

"Perfect timing," Willy said.

He explained that Runty Schommer had had to take over not only the load of their last kids in school, his wife having understandably gone on strike after years of endless toil raising their huge gaggle of children, but thrown into the mix was the care of their two preschool grandchildren, Dwight and Don, staying with them while their parents effected a move to Greysport, where their father Shorty was seeking work in a steel mill. Runty's wife claimed to be suffering from "nervous exhaustion", but Willy knew from Mae and Solveig that she just sat on the couch drinking tea, eating coconut macaroons and watching soap operas (something Willy thought justifiable) while Runty, a fine short-order cook, got the last of their kids off to school and looked after the toddlers. The idea of having Goodforks back at the bar was a relief to Willy, and never a problem; workers came and went, and Willy often gave people hours when he didn't need the help, even secretly contributing money to the tip jar at the end of the night if things seemed to be spread too thin.

"You can stay upstairs in the spare bedroom, if you want," Willy said.

"That'd be great," Faith said. "Won't it, Uncle Bob?"

"Nope."

"You don't like me all that much, do you, Uncle Bob?"

"No, not all that much, actually," Bob said, unnecessarily wiping down the bar with a clean rag.

Faith grinned at Willy and leaned over the bar to poke at Bob with his fingertips. Bob remained stony for a moment, and his face crumpled into a smirk and he leaned over to shove back.

This made Willy feel happier than he had in a long time, happier than seemed reasonable. He whistled when he went down into the basement to check the inventory.

Things soon got back into the groove of having Goodforks around, and, as always, there seemed to be a positive energy from his presence. He joked with people and always had a story to tell, and Bob Two Bears was his dour straight man. He always seemed to have a big idea, a grand scheme for the future, and it was so often lampooned that he took to ridiculing himself, imitating Spencer Tracy in *Northwest Passage*, standing with his legs spread apart, his fists on his hips, affecting a visionary squint and saying, "I don't know if it's ever been done before, but that doesn't mean that it *can't* be."

His current scheme involved entrepreneurial activity on Indian land which was prohibited elsewhere.

"I'm thinking about it," he said. "I've got to do some research. But Indian land is Federal land, right, and that allows a certain legal latitude that wouldn't be available elsewhere. See where I'm going?"

"No," Steve Hansen said, sitting at the bar with a handrolled cigarette in one hand and a beer in the other.

"Well, gambling for example. There might come a time when gambling could be legal on Indian lands in this state where local regulations would prohibit it in occupied territory. Think of the money in that. And the profits would all go to the tribe."

Bob Two Bears watched his nephew for a moment and slowly began to smile. "Time to take something back from the white man," he said.

Goodforks grinned and nodded slowly. "Yeah," he said.

Before he could think to keep his mouth shut, Hansen said, "Jesus, what'd the white man ever do to you?"

Willy said nothing, just watching. Bob and Faith slowly looked at each other, Faith's mouth dropping open in amused disbelief.

"What? I mean, *what*?"

Bob turned to bore into him with unbelieving eyes, and Faith said, "Are you fucking kidding me?"

"No, I-" Hansen sputtered.

"How about our *country*, okay? Our culture, most of our population? Any of that ring a bell?"

Hansen appeared to realize his *faux pas*, but was too pigheaded to back down and admit he was wrong."Well, look at all the benefits we-"Ohhhhh, fuck *you*!" Faith said. People rarely saw Faith angry, and watched with amused anticipation, Hansen always having been known as a bit of a bonehead. Willy just sat and watched.

Before it could go any further, Bob Two Bears started chuckling. Just a little at first, then louder and louder, from deep in his chest. Soon he was fighting doubling over with laughter, thudding the surface of the bar with his large brown hand. The looks on the faces of the others around the bar were those of reflexive sympathetic laughter and fear.

Bob gasped, tried to speak, pounded out a few more barks of bass laughter, before managing, "Steve, you have always been one of the most ignorant motherfuckers I have ever known. Read a fucking book, you incredible dumbass."

He started laughing again, deep, hard, and very loud. Then Faith was laughing, and when they looked at each other, they laughed even harder. It was so infectious that soon everyone was laughing but Willy and poor Steve Hansen, to whom Willy gave a conciliatory beer and a look that said, in this case, that was as far as his support could go for an incredible dumbass.

For the next hour, whenever Bob and Faith looked at each other, they began to chuckle again.

"If we ever do get gambling going on the reservation, Steve," Faith said, "you just come on up. Your money will always be welcome."

Bob snorted again and lumbered down the old stairs to the basement, his laughter echoing up from below.

Willy was used to waiting. Waiting to get home from a war, waiting for his life to mean something, for Mae to love him, waiting to walk out of prison, waiting for the boys to come home, waiting for Mae to love him again, waiting for one boy to come home. So he waited.

He worked and worked, although he had more than enough people to take care of everything. He put new gutters on the house, raked the yard, mowed the lawn for the last time of the year. He did projects at home and at the bar until he ran out of things to do, then tried to dream up more.

He occasionally bounced rowdies and drunks from the bar, suddenly feeling, when trouble arose, that *here* was something useful for him to do. He waved off any offers of assistance and took care of it himself. The moment of conflict, the shot of adrenaline, made him feel alive and twenty years younger.

He refinished the hull of the old boat with Emilio on weekend afternoons, their ritual of many years. All Emilio's girls were now out of the house, and his old friend was glad for something to do. They hunted for deer and goose and duck together, although the large, festive dinners they once had seemed to be a thing of the past. Thanksgiving was at Emilio's again, the girls home from college, two with friends, but the warmth had a small cool spot in it. Mae sat at the table, emotionless, and it seemed as if she were surrounded by empty chairs.

Christmas was small, and they gave little gifts to each other. They had company, but again, they seemed to be walking through the hours rather than living them. When they took the Christmas decorations down after the holidays, Mae picked up the wrapped shirt and sweater and books they had gotten for Gordon and put them on a shelf in the hall closet.

And so another year went, turning like a wheel with twelve spokes, seeming to slowly accelerate. Willy slid into his mid-fifties, working out and trying to push back time, but nothing could stop its slow gain.

Mae got too thin. She was sweet and kind, in a faded sort of way, and they lived together quietly, but her love had gone cool and dry.

That winter, there was a large blizzard in mid-January. Willy walked to the bar, just for the fun of it, and shovelled off the sidewalk himself, delighting in the huge falling snowflakes. The regulars were hardy Northerners, and it was a point of pride that they wouldn't let something so insignificant as a blizzard keep them coming to the bar. Bob Two Bears cooked up a vat of chili and they made hot rum drinks, and in the late afternoon the atmosphere was warm and golden, while snow, lit by red and blue neon, fell outside the windows against the early lavender twilight.

Willy thought that old Doc Ambrose would drive down with his customary great care in inclement weather- one of many rituals which he claimed kept him alive- and after he didn't show up for a few days, Willy got concerned and called his house. His wife Harriet answered, and Willy learned that Ambrose had gotten pneumonia.

"Well, he's a tough old geezer," Willy said, thinking, Oh no, this is it. He told Harriet he'd like to stop by the next day if she had no objections, and Harriet seemed relieved.

"Sure, Willy," she said. "He could use the company. He's an ornery old bastard when he's under the weather. He could grumble at *you* for awhile."

Willy hung up wondering how they did it, how they kept up their banter when they knew that each day was one subtracted from the finite amount they had together, and that their stack of days was getting short indeed, now perhaps perilously short.

He called Mae and told her the news, and heard more of a spark in her voice than he had in a long time.

"Oh, my!" she said. "Well, we have to go over there."

"Maybe you could fix some of your venison stew," Willy said. "Doc always likes that."

"I'll start right now," she said, and hung up.

Mae seemed partially brought back to life and purpose. She was more animated when Willy came in the front door, holding the lid of the slow cooker in one hand while she seriously regarded the contents.

"Harriet told me he doesn't have much of an appetite," she said, "but you never know, this might do the trick."

They went over to the Ambrose's house late the next morning, a Saturday. It was brick colonial up the hill from the river, one of the last houses before the encircling crescent of bluffs, which stood tall and snowy, thick with dark oaks. A neighborhood kid was just finishing shovelling the walk; Willy and Mae knew him as the son of somebody, squinting at each other trying to remember whom. It was sunny and cold, a beautiful day, and Willy looked at the dark windows of the house with trepidation. The young doctor who had eventually taken over all of Ambrose's practice, Bill Harrington, was in the house, his car parked on the snowy street.

Willy held the slow cooker, keeping the storm door open with his shoulder as Mae clacked the brass knocker. Harriet Ambrose opened the door and showed them in, sounding cheerful as she brought them into the kitchen, thanking them for the stew. Willy saw that, although she smiled and made small talk, when she thought no one was looking, there was a dark look of terror in her eyes. Mae stayed with her in the kitchen to talk for a bit while Willy went up the stairs to the large master bedroom.

His eyes had adjusted to the inside of the house, and the bedroom was bright and cheerful, sunlight coming in through the lace curtains. With Harrington leaning over him, a figure in black, Ambrose lay in the large bed under white quilts, coughing weakly into a wad of tissue. From the doorway, Willy saw how he looked and sighed once, deeply, before putting a sarcastic look on his face.

"Don't try to tell me my job," Harrington was saying. "Do as I say and you might just live to torment your wife for much longer than she's willing to stand it."

"She was never willing to stand it," Ambrose wheezed.

"Then out of mercy towards her, I shouldn't have given you the penicillin." Harrington followed Ambrose's gaze and turned around to see Willy. They greeted each other, and Harrington turned back to Ambrose and said, "Try to eat something. Stay in bed. You know the drill. I'll be back later."

On the way out, Harrington gave Willy a disposable mask to wear, leaving several more on the dresser next to the door.

"Bacterial pneumonia is spread by airborne droplets," he said. "Can't be too careful." He shook hands with Willy on his way out, and Willy thought that the look on his face when he turned away from Doc Ambrose would most accurately be described as somber.

"So," Willy said when they were alone, "I brought the paper to read to you, and Mae brought you some venison stew."

"Oh, shit. That was unnecessary," Ambrose said, "but thanks."

Willy put on the mask, drew up a chair, and started reading to Ambrose from the paper. He read him the funnies, Ambrose wanting to hear *Peanuts* first. When Willy read it to him, showing him the cartoon, Ambrose had a coughing fit.

"I like those kids," he wheezed, once he regained his breath.

Willy then read from *Pogo*, this installment featuring the character Simple J. Malarkey, a thinly disguised Joseph McCarthy, and Ambrose began coughing again.

Willy contemplated reading to him from the front page article on the McCarthy hearings, and another story on a Gallup poll indicating McCarthy's fifty percent approval rating, but thought that either might induce a seizure of coughing that would finish the old man off. He stretched out the banal reading of the paper- which was most of it- for as long as he could, spending a lot of time improvising on the classified ads.

"Outboard motor for sale here," he said. "Probably a piece of shit. Job opening as a plumber's helper. Is that a plunger, or do they actually use a person for that? You should look into it. You need a new career, something to keep you busy."

"I've been up to my elbows in enough plumbing in my day, but thanks," Ambrose said raspily. "That reminds me: you should have your colon checked."

"I'll have it looked into," Willy said, causing some rasping.

Willy read on for awhile, trying to be amusing, and when he looked over the paper at one point, he noticed that Ambrose was resting limply on the white pillows, his skin translucent in the sunlight, gazing at Willy fondly.

"How come you never published any of that poetry of yours?" Ambrose said clearly.

Willy watched the old man. A clock ticked on the oak dresser in the corner.

"It's not- I'm not ready," Willy said.

"Bullshit," Ambrose said. "You've been ready for years."

"Other things got in the way."

"Well, that happens. But look at you. Big strong guy, you look tough enough to eat ball bearings. And if you don't have something to write about, nobody does."

"I'm working on it."

"Don't be afraid to show what's inside. It's the best part of you."

"Okay."

"Make it a distillation of everything you've learned the hard way. Maybe a perceptive soul could glean something from it."

"Okay, okay. Jesus."

"I mean it. It's not like a critic is going to do any worse to you than you've been through already."

"I suppose not," Willy sighed.

"All right, then," Ambrose said, and began coughing once more into the tissue.

Willy was relieved to hear Mae and Harriet coming up the stairs. They came into the room, Mae carrying a breakfast tray with stew, a glass of milk, and bread on it. She spoke reassuringly (going a little too far, Willy thought), just as she would with the boys when they were sick, and felt Ambrose's head after gently setting the tray over his lap. Ambrose wriggled pleasantly under her touch. She leaned over to adjust the tray, her breasts close to Ambrose's face, and Ambrose gave Willy a subtly lecherous look. Willy snorted.

"What's funny?" Mae asked over her shoulder.

"Nothing," Willy said, staring at Doc as the old man leered.

They all sat around the bed in the sunny room while Ambrose had a few spoonfuls of stew, moaning approvingly, but he almost immediately began to look drowsy, and they quietly took their leave.

They came back the next day. Willy didn't want to miss time with the old man, and Mae seemed rejuvenated with purpose. It was snowing again, and grey. The bedroom was darker today, and had a closer smell. Willy thought it would benefit from an open window, but one look at Doc Ambrose shut down that idea.

They both did without masks this time. Mae sat by the bed and made smalltalk for a bit, then went downstairs with Harriet to make tea. Alone again with Ambrose, Willy saw that he looked worse than the day before. He thought about glossing over his bleak thoughts, about saying something that swept the real situation under the rug, but the old man had always been straight with him, and he appreciated that.

He cleared his throat and said, "So, what's the prognosis, Doc?"

Ambrose regarded him over his reading glasses." Well, I'm old, so that's not good. This kills a lot of people my age. I've got the whole thing: the coughing, the chest pain, difficulty breathing, greenish sputum, you name it."

He paused to catch his breath, and Willy waited. "*Streptococcus pneumoniae*. Complications can include respiratory and circulatory failure, sepsis affecting the liver, kidney and heart. Patient can develop bacterial abscess." Doc shrugged.

Willy exhaled through his nose. "Why don't you go to the hospital?"

"I'm trying to avoid it. I hate that fucking place. My wife and that Harrington kid might make me, though."

They sat in silence for awhile, then Doc said, "I'm sorry about your boy, Willy. So sorry."

Willy sat, looking at Doc's knees under the quilts. "I know."

"I brought him into the world, and I wish I'd never seen the day that..." he trailed off, shaking his head.

Willy sat forward in his chair, elbows on his knees.

Doc sniffed, and Willy was pierced to see tears in the old man's eyes.

"This life. It's just...so sad. So sad." Tears slipped down his translucent cheeks. "I love my wife so much. It's not enough. I know more about what happens at the end than most people, I know what to expect, always have, no surprises. And it's just not enough. Not enough time."

Willy leaned forward and put his hand on Doc's wrist. Doc patted Willy's hand.

"I love you, boy," he said.

"I love you, too, Da-" Willy cut himself off. He hung his head, tightening his grip on Doc's wrist. They sat like that for a long time.

We humans are tribal animals. We have evolved that way, and over the ages it has protected us, it has ensured the survival of our species.

So ancient is this tendency that it is the very fundament of not only our society, but the function of our brains. We seek inclusion, we seek friendship, we seek love.

Rarely do we stand back to contemplate our need for these things, for friendship, for love, for this simple inclusion. It is difficult for us to stand outside it, to see that it is the medium in which we live, the source of our light and warmth. Only when it is stripped from us do we recognize what it is to us, and there we lay gasping, like a fish pulled from the river.

The price of this inclusion, this primate closeness and mutual reliance, is the pain of parting, either for a little while or forever. The price of love, ultimately, is sadness, and if we recognize that, we will make the most of love while it lasts. We know that, ultimately, we all must part, and we shy away from the contemplation of the time and the place of this parting, of how it will look, of the shape it will take. Such contemplation is valuable, though; it makes us look with revived perception upon the faces of those we love, it allows their voices and their laughter to swell our hearts.

Doc Ambrose did not die that winter, but it was close. As old as he was, he would not die for some time. Although his body had become frail, his will was keen and strong; he was better in a few weeks, much better in another month. When the first big thaw came in March, he tottered down the wet sidewalks from his house by the bluff and had a single beer, waving off the salutations of the regulars.

So Doc Ambrose, to everyone's relief, was not the next one to die. The next one was predictably unexpected.

The forces of geology exert themselves upon the bluffs along the river, just as they have for millions of years, and will continue to do long after humans are gone. Water erosion, expanding and contracting ice, the growth of roots, all work cracks and fissures into the ancient stone.

One huge block high on a bluff above the river road had been worked upon by these forces for millennia, and succumbed after the ice of a final winter and the long rains of that April. A witness at the top of the bluff would have heard, under the steady hissing of the rain, a deep, heavy sound- CRUNK- so low in the human range of hearing that it would almost be felt as a vibration in the bone marrow. They would then see a crack appear in the soil and leaf matter under the long grass that had found purchase there, and the crack would widen, slowly at first, then faster, gaping black with the rain falling into it before the stone toppled majestically away, spinning dreamily in the air, smashing through the tops of huge trees, the splintering sound an accompaniment to thunder as it closed the gap to the river road two hundred feet below.

Steve Hansen had been driving down the river road from Black Marsh, a trip he had made so many thousands of times in his life that it had become far beyond boring. He was not a person susceptible to the beauty of nature, and lacked the ability to find something new to marvel at every time he took the drive. To alleviate his tedium, he pulled his rusty 1942 Ford pickup under an oak tree by a boat launch and rolled a joint of his special Bluff Blend reefer, left over from last year's growing season. He smoked the joint and listened to the radio, annoyed by the lightning.

When he was pleasantly high, his rheumy pink eyes at half mast, he pulled back out onto the road and headed south. The wipers swiped rhythmically but ineffectually across the windshield, their effect soporific.

"Whew! Sure is stoned out," Hansen said.

He realized he was being tailgated when a car behind him flashed its brights in his rearview mirror. With his left hand, he motioned for them to pass, and when they didn't do so, he pulled off onto the shoulder and motioned again. The car pulled up beside him and the passenger rolled down his window.

"You're doing half the speed limit, you old fuck!" the man shouted over the rain.

Hansen smiled, tonguing the hole left by his missing upper incisor, and gave the man the finger. The man flipped him off in return, and the car sped off in a roostertail of rain.

"Must be from outta town," Steve mumbled, and puttered down the road.

His fate was at the intersection of his horizontal path down the river road and the vertical path of the huge stone block toppling down from above. Among the sound of thunder, there was a crack of branches overhead half a second before impact.

There is no word for the sound of the impact, which caused the gravel and stones in a hundred foot radius of it to jump in an expanding wave on the shoulders of the road. The sound was a sub-deep *FUMP*, so low and profound that, some distance away, slickered fishermen on the river looked at each other, then up at the sky, before shrugging and casting again.

Hansen's pickup was smashed almost completely flat. On the front end, the headlights and the bumper were intact, but the radiator was crushed and steaming; on the rear, the bumper and the license plate remained, shattered taillights still recognizable. Both ends curled up around the edges of the block, out of the giant rectangular hole it had stomped into the blacktop. The plates were helpful to law enforcement, as it was the only way that Hansen was initially identified before his mangled and sodden driver's license could be finessed from the wreckage.

Traffic on the river road had to be diverted while the Sheriff's department and road crews cleaned up the obstruction, the latter using jackhammers to split up the block of stone before it could be moved with heavy equipment. The crushed scrap metal of the truck, with the paste of Steve Hansen inside, was dragged by a winch up onto the flatbed of a tow truck, covered with tarps, and taken back to the garage at the Sheriff's department up in Black Marsh.

When news of the event spread- quickly, of course- it was rare that anyone's reaction was of sadness or loss. The most common response was, "No! What?" or "Bullshit! Hansen?" or "Yeah, sure." Incredulity was standard, and mirth common.

"It's a shame," a railman was heard to say.

"How so?" was a bargeman's response.

"It was the hand of the Almighty striking down a sinner," said one pious and disapproving bonehead.

"If that standard were applied with any rigor, we wouldn't have any bluffs around here at all," said the bonehead's more realistic friend. "Besides, he sold you your weed."

Willy, Bob Two Bears and Faith in Full Goodforks heard the news at the bar. The regulars were there in the rainy afternoon, Hansen's usual stool empty.

Bob and Faith looked at each other, seemed about to laugh, then got thoughtful and serious. A few people around the bar did laugh.

"Hey, come on," Bob said.

"What?" someone said. "You were arguing with him all the time."

"I do that with *you*," Bob said.

The person snorted and said,"Yeah, but he was the most worthless-"

"He was our friend," Faith said.

Not unlike Hansen himself, the obtuse regular didn't know when to shut up. "Yeah, but why?"

There was a moment of silence and Willy said, "Proximity. Most of the time that's all it takes."

People seemed to think about this for a bit.

"He was still a dumbass," Barnacle Brad observed, shaking his head disgustedly. "Owes me five bucks, too."

Steve's brother George, with whom he was stuck on the island in the big freeze more than twenty years ago, seemed to be, more than anything else, puzzled by Steve's death. No one, of course, said anything derogatory about Steve in his presence. Willy realized how old George looked, his hair now completely white, the lines in his face suddenly pronounced as he furrowed his brow.

"Huh," he kept saying, shaking his head. "Huh."

"Well," a regular said by way of consolation, "Your brother grew some great reefer."

"Yeah!" others chorused, looking for something positive to say.

"He was probably stoned when he was driving," George said, picking up his beer and watching its rising bubbles. "If he hadn't been stoned, he would've been driving a little faster. The boulder would've fallen behind him."

Someone snorted, and the man next to him gave him the elbow.

"Well," George said. "Huh."

After the funeral Willy walked down the street with Doc Ambrose on a sunny afternoon. They were both lost in thought. After Chief's death there had been, and still was, an enormous chasm. Hansen's death was a pothole. He said this to Ambrose.

"I was thinking along similar lines," Ambrose said, stopping to lean on his cane.

"You know, I've seen a lot of shit in my life," Willy said. "I thought I was burned out when I was twenty and now I'm in my fifties. But Steve was a good guy, and I...I don't know. I'll miss him. You've been around a long time, you've seen so much, had so many people die on you. Does it ever get any easier?"

Ambrose leaned on his cane and squinted, sucking his teeth. At length, he cocked his head to one side and said, "No. If anything, it gets harder."

Willy snorted, nodding ruefully.

"That doesn't mean that Hansen wasn't a jackass," Ambrose said

"No, of course not," Willy said, holding out his elbow for Ambrose to take before continuing down the sidewalk.

Emilio's take on it was characteristic. They were out fishing, feeling strongly alive in the bright sunshine, and Emilio leaned over the gunnel of the jonboat, splashed his hand in the river, sending droplets twinkling in the sunlight.

"Like these droplets of water, espinning in the sunlight, so are our individual lives. We come from eternity, have a moment of individuality, and to eternity we return. Our lives are but a brief respite from oblivion. We should have the sense to love it while we can."

Willy, smiling, watched his friend for a few moments. "That was pretty deep," he said.

Emilio closed his eyes and nodded serenely. "I am a very wise man."

Anniversaries were bad with Mae. There was the anniversary of learning of Chief's death, a day which passed grimly. Mae said nothing out loud and Willy didn't dare to, but the day went by gloomily, heavy clouds pressing down from overhead. The days of Chief's birthday and the scattering of his ashes were both in May, a month of apple and lilac blossoms, but no matter how sunny and beautiful the day was, how fragrant and kind, a funereal darkness seemed to seep up beneath the surface of things.

To make matters worse, even Katita stopped receiving communication from Gordon; he could have been anywhere. Mae continued on in her cool way, not seeming terribly disturbed by Gordon's absence.

"He'll be in touch," she said. "When he settles, he'll be in touch. Nothing can happen to him. It's statistically impossible."

Mae said this to Katita when she stopped by to visit, but Katita was young and restless and had obviously become obsessed with the remaining brother. At the end of the semester, she came home and announced that she would be leaving for Greysport.

"That's where he is," she said. "I know it."

Emilio and Solveig wanted her to finish school, convinced that Gordon would eventually return, telling her that it would be impractical to just point off in an almost random direction with no plans, and without completing what she had started.

"I have to find Gordon," she told them. "I can't stand the thought of him roaming around out there all alone."

She told Willy that she wouldn't be working at the bar that summer and kissed Mae goodbye, and with the little savings she had, she loaded up Gordon and Dan's old car and headed for Greysport.

In June of that year, they finally received a postcard from Gordon. It was from Martha's Vineyard.

"Came here to see where Dad's dad and mom lived," Gordon wrote. "Trying to figure out how things fit together, and where I am in it. Don't worry about me. I'm fine. I'll stop and see Grandma Palmer. Love, Gordon."

Mae set the letter on the kitchen table. She sighed deeply, and slowly began to smile. Resting one hand on the postcard, she held out the other and put it on top of Willy's. She smiled more broadly.

"You were right," Willy said.

Mae, almost grinning, nodded emphatically.

While running errands, Willy stopped and talked to Emilio and Solveig at their house to sound them out on this development, hoping that they would get Katita to see that she would be wasting her time in Greysport and should get back in school.

"She shouldn't be waiting for him," Willy said. "Who knows when, or if, he'll be back."

Emilio and Solveig sat on the couch of their living room, saying nothing. Solveig looked at Emilio and took his hand, dropping her eyes.

"I don't think she's coming back soon herself," Emilio said, and Solveig looked like she was about to cry.

"Why not?" Willy asked.

"We had an argument before she left. I said that-" he paused, seemed to gather his thoughts, and proceeded delicately, "I said that sometimes young men die in ways that are just wasteful, even criminal, and..." he shook his head.

Solveig cleared her throat and raised her head. "Katita thinks Chief died a hero," she said.

"Oh," Willy said.

There was an awkward silence. Willy picked at a spot of dried paint in the knee of his jeans. Eventually Solveig excused herself and went out to the kitchen. The two men walked out onto the porch.

"She thinks my boy died a hero," Willy said, looking out over the river. An image of scattering Chief's ashes in those waters flashed into his mind and he pushed it away. When he looked at Emilio, his friend's face was grim. Emilio put his hand on Willy's shoulder.

Before Willy got back into his truck, he could hear the two of them shouting at each other in their kitchen.

He hated to witness discord between his old friends, sighing as he clumped slowly up the steps and onto the front porch of the bungalow. When he walked into the house, he was astonished to find Mae in the kitchen with the radio on, something she hadn't done in almost a year and a half. He was further amazed to see that she was cooking something other than simple fare, was actually making one of his favorites, beef bourguignon.

"What the hell," he said, stopping dead in the archway to the kitchen.

In front of the stove, Mae had her apron on and was stirring the steaming pot with a wooden spoon. "I just thought..." she shrugged, smiling.

Willy took two strides to her and put his arms around her waist, pulling her to him. He was almost afraid to take the chance, but was in the midst of it and went ahead, kissing her. She opened her mouth and responded, kissing him back. They kissed for some time, Mae's arms around his neck, the spoon hanging from her hand. It was like the first time they had ever done it, there on the rainy street many years ago, the feeling just the same. Willy felt dizzy and broke away with a wet smack. "Wow," he said.

"Yeah," Mae said, smiling, her cheeks pink. "I have to turn this down and let it simmer for awhile, so..." she inclined her head in the direction of the bedroom.

"Yes!" Willy said. "Oh, please, please, *please* yes! Let's go, let's go, let's go!"

They went at it like kids, and when they both came, it was explosive. Willy lay in bed, stunned. What the fuck just happened? he thought. He entwined his fingers with Mae's, gazing at her. She looked young.

"Good to see you, honey," he said, and she snuggled close to him. They lazed for a long time. When they got up, he was ravenous. They ate the beef bourguignon with fresh bread and home made plum wine, there in their humble kitchen, and Willy had to concentrate to remember the last day that was so good.

He ambled down to the bar later, feeling blissful. When two youngsters, emboldened by beer, squared off and got ready to brawl, Willy just sauntered around the bar, grabbed each of them by the back of the neck and squeezed until they dropped their arms and stood grimacing.

"Now, is this any way to act?" Willy asked them jovially. "Of course not. Just be nice, and don't ruin a beautiful evening."

He made them shake hands and apologize, and that was the last trouble he had at the bar for a long time. He walked home late at night, smelling of smoke, and took a hot shower before getting into bed, just as he always did. He wasn't sure if the splendid afternoon was a fluke, but when he got into bed, Mae rolled over and cuddled up to him. His nose stung and his eyes filled with tears. He kissed Mae on the forehead and held her for a long time before falling asleep.

It was later that month that Patrick Pinkwater came back to tell Willy as much as he could about how Chief died. Willy knew that the young man avoided saying anything too gruesome to Mae before she had sent him down to the bar, but he wanted to hear it, wanted to force himself to listen to it. He wondered what Katita would say if she knew the whole truth.

Willy and Emilio took Patrick out on the boat and cruised up the river. They dropped anchor at the bottom of an island and dropped in some lines, but Patrick's mind was obviously elsewhere. The two of them tried to make him feel that he was not alone, to let him know that they had felt as he had, and that there was hope for a happy life in the future. He seemed grateful, but they weren't sure that he got the message. Willy wished again that he could beam what he had learned through his own hardship into the mind of another, but knew that he had done what he could and that the rest was up to the desolate young man who sat before him. Patrick got a little buzzed on beer as they fished, and Willy was afraid he might get morose. To his surprise, though, Patrick appeared to lighten a bit, and was soon telling jokes and taking an interest in the fishing. Once he was living right there in the sunny day, among men who understood him, he seemed- momentarily at least- capable of happiness and peace. When they got back to the pier, Patrick thanked them sincerely.

As he drove away, Willy felt a welcome bit of optimism.

That summer, the sleazy carnival showed up again. Its appearances were always sporadic, and Willy put that down to the overall shadiness of the operation. After the lunch rush, Willy and Bob Two Bears, a reflection of themselves a decade and a half earlier, stood in front of the bar and watched as the carnival was set up.

"That's the same piece of shit Ferriswheel they've had forever," Bob pointed out.

"Same everything else, too. Same Neanderthal trailer, same tilt-a-whirl," Willy said.

"It was probably dangerous fifteen years ago."

Willy was touched when Bob offered to take over running the bar for the weekend, suggesting that Willy use the opportunity to get Mae out on the boat, as they had once done frequently.

Willy looked Bob in the eye. He had known him so long that he was sure he could read his friend's impassive face, and was further sure that Bob's intent was also to get him away from memories of the day which had deflected his life in an unanticipated and unwelcome direction.

"You serious?" he asked, squinting up at his friend.

Bob shrugged slightly. "Yeah. Go on."

"*Okay*. Don't burn the fucker down."

"Wouldn't do it without you."

He tapped Bob on the forearm with his knuckles and double-timed home, trotting down the sidewalk. When he got to the driveway, he had a cramp in his side, and thought about how easy it had been to jog such a distance when he was twenty years younger and forty pounds lighter. Old man, he thought. He shook it off and burst into the house. Going from room to room, he called his wife's name.

He finally found her in the back yard, tending the garden. She smiled up at him, holding her gloved hand up to shade her eyes. He told her the plan.

"Okay, let's go," she said.

Willy almost laughed with relief.

They cruised up the river well past Black Marsh, up and up and up. Bluffs and islands flowed by and the years dropped away. They pointed out to each other sights they'd seen long ago, laughing. A cloud seemed to pass in front of the sun when memory involved the boys, but Mae appeared to make a conscious effort to overcome it, and this helped Willy to do the same.

They stayed again at the little hotel in Omicron Falls, fortunate enough to find room eleven free. After they had made love, they told each other that it was the same as the first time they had done it in that room. Willy knew that it wasn't, and knew that Mae felt the same way. For all the honesty between them, the difference made by the weight of years was something they did not discuss, something they glossed over. The first time they had made love in the room had been an occasion of vigor and hopefulness, both resurrected in Willy by Mae, a testament to his resilience, he now saw. It had been the beginning of their Golden Span. They had thought that they knew everything. Now, though, more than two decades had flowed down the river, washing any remaining innocence along with it. What they were left with was a tenderness born of the recognition of their finite days. Willy thought that this might have been even better than their witless youthful vigor and (a grim part of him almost laughed to think it) of their completely unfounded hopefulness.

After leaving Omicron Falls, they dropped anchor downstream from a small island thick with pine trees half an hour before sundown. For the sake of simplicity, they heated up some soup, which they ate in the cockpit with ham sandwiches and cold beer. They sat close together, feeling the breeze, saying small things. A loon called in the distance.

Willy thought about what he was going to say for awhile, then just decided to blurt it out. He stood up and faced Mae.

"Let's just sell everything," he said, intent, looking into her eyes and putting his hands on her shoulders. "Let's sell the house, sell the bar, sell the car and the truck. Okay? Let's get out of here. Let's go down the river and sell the boat. We'll get rid of it in New Orleans, check up on old Jack and Ruby. You liked them. We'll take a boat to Scotland and Ireland, see where our ancestors came from, then cross the channel and go to France, okay? We'll-"

Mae laid her hand on his forearm, smiling a little and shaking her head.

"I love the way you think," she said. "I always have. But we have to wait here for Gordon. We have to wait and see."

"See what? We have no reason to believe that he'll come back. Ever. If he does, he's sure to look in on Emilio and Solveig, and we'll leave word with them."

She smiled, almost laughing, shaking her head. He loved her eternal patience with him.

"No, honey," she said finally. "No."

He dropped his hands to his sides.

"Okay, we'll wait," he said at length. "We'll wait."

But at night, when she was asleep and he had lain there long enough, he went up on deck and looked at the depth of stars. Mae had faith in Gordon, had been through more with him than Willy had. Willy loved him painfully but saw and understood his bitter confusion. He had no reason to believe that his son would return. Willy hadn't when he was young.

And the river flowed down to the sea, out into the world. He saw himself flowing with it, out, out, out.

Free.

They stayed, though, and they continued with their lives. Over the next few years, he brought up the idea of dissolving their life in MacDougal and slipping away, down the river until the island town was a dot behind them and then nothing. Mae wouldn't bite, though, convinced that Gordon would come back.

"It's not a matter of whether or not he loves *me*," she would say. "I know he loves me, and he knows I will love him forever. I know he loves *you*, too. He is ashamed of himself, though, and looks up to you, even if other emotions sometimes get in the way of that. He wants to do something that will make you proud of him before he comes back."

Willy thought that it was he himself who should be ashamed, he who had to prove his worth, and it was this idea that convinced him that his wife was right. Mae saw them being grandparents, having Gordon and his wife and children over for the holidays. She would teach the little girls grandmother things, give them piano lessons (although she no longer played herself, which Willy elected not to mention), bake with them, grow things in the garden. Willy, she said, would show the boys how to fish and box and hunt, teach them his love of literature and poetry, show them the majesty of nature, and how to always be gallant and loving, just like their grandfather. She thought they might name the first boy Daniel, after Chief's given name.

Willy knew that she was right, but he still was wistful when he thought of other places, and would find himself lost in reveries when out on the river or up on the bluffs, watching barges and other boats as they moved downstream. He felt his fifties slipping by him.

He found the most contentment in the fact that his wife had returned. She would never be the woman she was before Chief died, but neither was she the ghost that had drifted through their home for so long. The sadness which lay as silently as dust around them also made things more precious. Broken forever was the illusion that their time was limitless; Mae now understood what Willy had meant when, long ago, he had talked about the Golden Span.

She never pestered him about publishing any of his poetry. "You'll be ready when you're ready," she would say. "That's about *your* fulfillment. Having *you* is about mine."

He hated to see that she no longer played the piano, though. He tried to entice her into it, and even made a point of having the pianos at home and at the bar tuned, setting it up so she was in each place while the work was being done. She acted, in both cases, as if the man doing the work were not there at all, and went out to dig in the garden while he was inside the bungalow. She didn't mention it, and he let it go. He occasionally stood looking at the piano at home, remembering her giving the boys piano lessons, seeing them small beside her on the piano bench, swinging their feet as they plunked dutifully away. He knew exactly what she was thinking. Give it time, he thought.

Solveig gave everyone a scare by having a heart attack. It was a mild one, but she was in the hospital in Black Marsh for quite some time, and Emilio was up there constantly. On one occasion when Willy and Mae visited, Marita and Gabriela were there with a new husband and a fiancée, respectively. Solveig seemed flattered by all the attention, but although Emilio made a show of being cheerful and positive, Willy could see his worry. Solveig had gone past the point where she could be politely referred to as plump, and it seemed improbable that she would change her habits. He also noted that no one mentioned Katita's absence.

Faith-in-full Goodforks announced that he would be leaving again.

"Gotta expand my horizons, boss," he said one morning as they prepared for the lunch rush. "I've piled up a bit of money."

"I was wondering when you'd decide to do it," Willy said.

They had a going away party for him. It got raucous fairly quickly, the flames fanned by Faith buying everyone drinks, which called for rounds of reciprocation. Mae sat at the center of the bar with the same half glass of wine in front of her for most of the night, and when anyone asked her to play the piano, she demurred.

Faith gave a long speech which started out as a toast. He stood on a chair above the crowd and spoke, the people around smiling in anticipation with raised glasses. When they realized that the toast was becoming a speech, the glasses wavered and were lowered, and the smiles faded to smirks Willy would later be unable to remember what the speech was even about, but recalled that people laughed and booed. At length, Faith thanked them all for everything, ever, and the crowd cheered and drank.

They had him over for lunch the next day, catching him before he left town. "I'm going to explore the possibility of gambling on reservations in the state," he said a little grandly, although he seemed to catch this and put his fists on his hips like Spencer Tracy again in a bit of self-mockery.

"I knew you'd never cool your heels here for long," Willy said. He struggled with a moment of restraint and hugged the young man.

Faith put his arms around Mae, then held her shoulders and stood back, saying, "Remember: life is beautiful."

She smiled. "Take care of yourself," she said.

Then he was gone, and life adjusted its constant flow to his absence, as if he'd been plucked from the water.

They finally received word from Gordon. It was more terse than his letters during the war ("He only wants to report something positive," Mae noted), but he said that after some wandering, he had found a job logging in the North Woods.

"What the hell," Willy said, puzzled.

The letter went on to say that he liked working outdoors, and was unable to see himself back in school at that time. He planned to save up money and go back to the Greysport Institute of Art on the GI Bill, he wrote, "So I can concentrate on my studies."

"He's going to get off track," Willy said.

"He'll figure things out," Mae said. "Trust me. You did *your* wandering."

She was reading the letter at the kitchen table, and Willy, standing behind her, looked at the back of her head, opened his mouth to say, Yeah, a family trait, and see where it got me. He clamped his mouth shut, though, and put his arm around her, reading the letter with her.

It appeared Gordon had a love interest, but he was vague about it, as always. Mae said that they'd know it was something serious if he ever mentioned the girl's name. "Maybe I can come home for the holidays," Gordon wrote. "We'll see how it goes."

He signed it simply with his name in bold capital letters.

Gordon never appeared to have the time to come to visit; he'd become so involved with his life in the North Woods that he claimed to have difficulty getting away. He made the occasional long distance phone call- seen as something of an event- but the conversations were always far more banal than Willy wanted them to be.

During one such call at Christmas, Mae talked to him on the wall phone in the kitchen the way mothers will as long as telephones exist. Willy waited a few feet away, occasionally holding out his hand for the receiver, raising his eyebrows. Mae held up an index finger and kept talking.

"Just so long as you're warm enough. Dress for the weather," she said, ignoring Willy when he rolled his eyes. "Be sure to eat enough. It takes a lot of energy to stay warm. Are you seeing anybody? But it's not serious? Okay. Your father wants to talk to you. Say goodbye before you hang up."

Willy got the phone. "Hey, son," he said.

"Hey, Dad."

Willy felt words bulging in his throat, thought of all the things he wanted to say and then imagined how they might offend or alienate Gordon, and edited most of them. He felt his cheeks get hot when he found that they were discussing the weather. Then they were talking about Sputnik and its implications, then *On the Beach* by Nevil Shute, then a French writer Gordon liked named Robbe-Grillet.

"So, are you going to go back to school?" Willy asked in as light a tone as he could manage without sounding completely false.

The pause told Willy he should have kept his mouth shut. "Yeah, Dad," Gordon finally said. "Just...I have some stuff I have to do first."

"That's fine, son, that's fine. Just remember you have a lot of talent."

260

"Yeah. I'll remember, Dad. Could you put Mom back on for a sec?"

Mae and Gordon were then off on a discussion of Gould's *Goldberg Variations*, which Gordon had sent Mae for Christmas. Willy puttered in the kitchen, pouring himself a glass of water and looking stonily out the window while fuming to himself that he had said anything which might alienate his son. He was simultaneously angry with Gordon for isolating himself in the woods when, with his talent and cultural curiosity, he could be having a much more interesting life if he could just pry himself loose and get back to Greysport. He wanted to hug him; he wanted to shake him by the shoulders, turn him around, and give him a boot to the ass. Then he wanted to hug him again.

In the end, though, he took the phone back from Mae once more.

"So when are you going to come down for a visit?" he said.

"Soon, Dad, soon."

"Okay. Well, here's your mother. M'bye."

Mae talked for another few minutes. She hung up, and came and stood by Willy, smiling a little and flicking up her eyebrows. Willy sighed.

It wasn't until February of 1958 that they saw Gordon again.

Chief had been dead for nearly five years, and they had adjusted to the fact of it as much as they were going to. Mae talked about giving piano lessons to children from the neighborhood but never seemed to get around to it. For all that she had been through, she looked younger than her fifty years, and Willy still found himself gazing at her at times, smiling faintly, until she realized it and did something to break his small trance.

Barnacle Brad had developed diabetes, but still stopped at the bar every afternoon for drinks. Doc Ambrose would sit next to him, nursing his one beer and making disparaging comments about Brad's intelligence.

"Drinking when you have your condition is ridiculous," Ambrose would say, shaking his head.

"Yep," Brad would reply, holding up his beer. "Down the hatch."

There was always a new crop of kids to come into the bar, and some of Chief and Gordon's classmates had long since become regulars. Willy hired local kids to work as waitstaff during the dinner hours. They came and went, and he relied especially on Bob Two Bears as his mainstay, Runty Schommer having reduced his hours to very part time, and seemingly only to keep his connection with the town hall aspect of the bar's environment. He brought in his two youngest grandsons from time to time, and it drew out the true colors of some of the regulars, who usually posed as tough guys. Barnacle Brad himself was particularly susceptible, squatting down and talking to the kids, something of an evolution from when he had made faces at them and spoken a form of idiotese when they were smaller, anything to make them laugh. To make up for the ribbing he received, though, he dubbed the kids Stumpy and Nubby, as an extension of the family tradition started with Runty and carried on by his son Shorty, the boys' father. Unfortunately for young Dwight and Don, the names stuck.

There was a snowstorm that February, and when it passed, the landscape was dazzling under the deep blue sky, the frozen and snowcovered river looking like Siberian tundra. Willy was shovelling the walk in front of the house when Mae called from the door of the porch and gestured him inside. He thumped his boots against the porch steps, knocking off the snow, and walked up onto the porch.

"Gordon's coming!" Mae said, beaming.

"What!"

"Yeah! He's up in Black Marsh at the Chinese place."

"What!"

"Yeah! And it sound like he's got someone with him. A girl!"

"A girl?"

Mae held her palms up and nodded vigorously.

Willy felt his whiskers, thinking. "Well, what the hell," he said. "When's he going to be here?"

"Within an hour! I've got to, got to, *do* things! Make something to eat!"

"Calm down, he just ate," Willy said. "Well, what the hell."

Mae settled for making coffee and whipping up a quick batch of cookies. Willy waited, not knowing what it was all about and refusing to do much until he did. He was watching out the window of the front door when Gordon pulled into the driveway.

"He's here!" he called to Mae in the kitchen.

Gordon was driving an older station wagon which was obviously packed for a move. Next to him in the front seat was a blonde woman in a dark coat. Willy and Mae went out onto the front porch, their breath smoking in the cold. Gordon and the blonde woman thumped their car doors closed. The woman was pretty, smiling sunnily. "Hi!" she called, waving.

"Get inside," Gordon said, coming up the walk. "It's cold out."

Gordon had a dark beard and was wearing a knit cap and heavy jacket. The young woman, pretty enough to be a model, was wearing an expensive-looking coat and ear muffs. Gordon hugged Mae hard enough to make her grunt, then turned and pumped Willy's hand.

"This is Ingrid Carlson," Gordon said, helping the girl off with her coat.

"*McGregor*," the girl said, nudging Gordon and holding up a manicured left hand to show the wedding ring on her finger.

"McGregor!" Gordon said. "I'm still not used to it."

Willy huffed in surprise.

Mae's mouth dropped open and she hugged the girl. She stood back, her hands on Ingrid's shoulders.

"And you're pregnant!"

When the girl saw Mae's approval, she smiled, shyly at first, then beaming.

"Yeah, we're just full of surprises," Gordon said, grinning.

"We're going to be grandparents!" Mae almost shrieked at Willy.

"Well, what the hell," Willy said, and hugged his son.

"Why didn't you tell us you were getting married?" Mae asked.

Gordon looked significantly at Ingrid's midsection and said, "It was something we had to take care of without further ado," he said.

They'd met while Gordon was working at a lumber mill up north. Ingrid's father was the owner of the mill and a lumber yard, one of the wealthiest men in the area, and, although it wasn't mentioned, Willy could see that Ingrid was coddled, especially by the standards of the rather spartan living of the woods. He also guessed that the relationship developed without the father's approval, which would have made it more attractive to Ingrid.

"Gordon was different from the local boys," Ingrid said later. "He reads a lot, been lots of places, been in Korea. There aren't many guys like him where I come from. Nobody as talented."

Aside from apparently spoiling his daughter, Ingrid's father was a gruff and disapproving man. He had gotten to know Gordon and liked him as a worker and especially as a veteran (something Gordon wouldn't even talk about), but was dismissive about Gordon's artistic aspirations. Gordon was a stranger, and Ingrid's father saw her marrying someone of her own social stature (Willy and Mae exchanged weary smiles, remembering their youth), and much of their romance had been on the sly. When Ingrid had gotten pregnant, Gordon had already planned to go back to Greysport and take her with him. She wanted to avoid the predictable explosion from her father, preferring to leave a vague note and call him from Greysport after the baby was born, but Gordon refused to sneak away with the man's daughter.

The confrontation had come, and had nearly resulted in a brawl. Ingrid's father had backed down, though, the first time Ingrid had ever seen it (she hung on Gordon's arm during this part of the story), and they had left. The wedding had taken place at a small chapel in the woods, in a clearing surrounded by pines. They had pictures of it.

"So I'm going to get back in school," Gordon said. "The baby's going to be born in Greysport."

"Why don't you have the baby here?" Mae asked, obviously a bit hurt.

"We'll be fine, Mom," Gordon said. "I've wasted enough time."

"What are you going to do for money?" Willy asked.

"I've saved up a bundle, and can go to school on the GI Bill. A buddy from the service has me lined up with a job at the port. We'll be fine. And living in Greysport will be great for the kid."

"I hope it wasn't *that* bad growing up around here," Mae said.

"Mom, no. It was great. I just want something different."

After dinner, Gordon wanted to go down to the bar to show off his wife to his old friends. It was encouraging; he never seemed to take earlier relationships seriously, and it appeared that he was dedicated to the idea of making a life with Ingrid. That the pregnancy was an accident didn't seem to deter him, which was a good thing, considering their limited and undesirable options.

They spent the night, and as there was no large bed other than Willy and Mae's, Ingrid slept in Gordon's old room, and Gordon in Chief's.

In the morning, they had breakfast in the sunny kitchen together, the room smelling of bacon and fresh coffee. As good as it was to see Gordon (now a burly man, most of his boyishness gone), Willy still had some misgivings about Ingrid. She appeared to move Gordon to do things for her with small displays of petulance, although Gordon, obviously transformed by the idea of being a father, seemed to either not mind or not notice. He doted on his wife, and it was apparent that she expected it. Willy said nothing, but he could tell that Mae had seen the same thing.

They tried to persuade the young couple to stay, but it was obvious that they were anxious to get under way, to get started with their new lives. Mae wanted them to stay for a week ("It's been so long since we've seen you!"), but, typically, stopped short of doing anything that might make Gordon feel too guilty.

It was getting cloudy as the young couple got ready to go. Mae fixed them a thermos of coffee and some sandwiches for the road, and Willy, for lack of anything productive to do, checked the tire pressure on the station wagon. He then tried to hand Gordon a roll of bills, which Gordon brushed off.

"Dad, come on," Gordon said, blocking Willy's forearm, but smiling a little.

It was just beginning to snow as they got into the car and backed out of the driveway. Willy and Mae walked down the end of the driveway and stood amidst the mounds of shoveled snow, waving as the youngsters drove away. They watched until the car was far down the road by the river, and it turned towards the bridge and drove out of sight.

When early spring came, Gordon's job at the port started in earnest. They had found an apartment on the south side of the port, in the unimaginatively named

Portview, a neighborhood populated by German, Irish, and Italian immigrants and their descendants. In letters and phone conversations, Gordon said that he loved the neighborhood, which had a profusion of restaurants and bars, and was close enough to the port that he could walk to work if he had to.

He'd gotten a job as a longshoreman. Things were slow in the winter when the locks in the east were closed and the conditions on the lakes were too dangerous for shipping. In April through December, though, things would be busy, and it was Gordon's job to work offloading the steel which would eventually go to the many huge factories that took up sprawling areas around the south side of Greysport.

Mae spoke on the phone with Ingrid far more than Willy, with whom the young woman was pleasant but not talkative. Ingrid's own mother had died when she was young, and it was obvious that there was a ready niche for Mae to fill. The pregnancy seemed to be going well, but Mae seemed less than impressed with Ingrid's mothering instincts.

"She'll learn," Mae said. "I guess."

Although Gordon never complained, at least not much, it was obvious that his wife's psychological state during pregnancy was sometimes difficult for him.

"She gets a little...unpredictable," Gordon said cautiously during one phone conversation.

"If it gets too rough, just put your head between your shoulders and make for the door," Willy said. "Shit, the night you were born, Emilio and I got kicked out of the house and were out on the river in a snowstorm."

"Heard about that one," Gordon said, and Willy could hear him smiling.

They made plans to drive to Greysport when the baby was born, and aside from that, there wasn't much they could do.

Gordon sent one letter which made Willy and Mae think that he was a bit overwhelmed with the concept of fatherhood, but which was, at the same time, a hopeful sign about his psychological well being.

The letter was all about the sculpture section at the Greysport Institute of Art, and he went on at length. Although the museum was, since the first time he had been there, a holy place for him, he seemed to have exploded into a fascination with sculpture. The museum had a famously extensive collection, and he slid off into a series of digressions, writing in detail about the pieces from India, China, Angkor, about his fascination with Greek and Roman sculpture and their relationship with the geniuses of the Renaissance ("How did Michelangelo make so unyielding a medium look as soft and supple as living flesh?" Gordon wrote), about marble, bronze, limestone, granite, porphyry. He went on and on.

"What the hell is porphyry?" Willy asked.

"Got me," Mae said, and they read on.

It sounded as if he went to the museum, on the other side of the harbor, on a few of his days off, and that Ingrid rarely accompanied him. He didn't say anything too specific, but always seemed to refer to himself in the singular.

They looked at each other, narrowing their eyes, thinking about it.

"Hmmmm," Willy said.

They deduced that he might be experiencing a bit of panic about fatherhood, and that Ingrid might occasionally be making it hot for him at home.

265

"That's okay," Mae said after thinking about it. "It gives them a little time apart, and it feeds his fire."

All in all, though, things seemed to be going well for the young couple, and even Mae didn't worry too much.

Ingrid was due in mid-May, right around the time of Chief's birthday. As the month began, the blossoms everywhere again for their short time, Willy and Mae got ready to depart for Greysport to be present for the birth of their grandson. Mae went over lists of what to bring, and was overprepared, as far as Willy was concerned, but he dealt with it as patiently as possible.

Mae showed no sign of discomfort regarding becoming a grandmother, and Willy admired that. Some woman could not be faced with the notion, tripping over their own vanity, but Mae was beside herself with happiness. She had always been so very composed, but now the mention of the coming baby brought her almost to tears.

"My baby is having a baby," she would say with a faraway look, and Willy put his arm around her shoulder and kissed her head.

The child was born that May in Greysport, in a good, boisterous immigrant neighborhood at Greysport Memorial Hospital. The baby came before Willy and Mae could get there; they were on the road when he was born, taking the series of county roads and highways that led them across the state.

They were held up even more by the frustrating Thursday afternoon traffic, something they were unaccustomed to with their life on the river. Mae lightened the tone by reminding Willy of the time they had faced a similar snarl when bringing the boys to the city to see the museums. He noticed that she did it without sounding sad about Chief; she was merely recalling a happy memory. Willy sighed and hung on the steering wheel, forcing a smile.

When they got to the hospital, it took them awhile to find the room in the labyrinthine old building, a structure which had been added onto at least once a decade for the past eighty years and was proportionately confusing. They arrived at last after asking at a final nurses' station, and paused outside the door for a moment before going in.

"Okay," Willy said. "You ready?"

"Of course I'm ready. What are you stalling for?"

"I just want to make sure you don't faint or something."

Mae gave him a sour look and shook her head as if to clear it. "Let's go, tough guy," she said.

Ingrid lay in the hospital bed, looking out the window at the view of the harbor and the lake. Her face was pinched and pale, a little plain without makeup, her hair in a ponytail. She seemed to be ignoring Gordon, who stood in a corner by the window in his work clothes. The baby, wrapped in a white blanket, was in his arms. He smiled as he talked to it in a low voice, rocking it gently. When he saw his parents, his face lit up with the purest happiness that Willy had seen there since before he had gone to prison.

The decibel level in the room increased as greetings were exchanged. Mae hugged Ingrid (who summoned a wan smile), and went to hover over the baby.

Willy, not knowing what to do, engaged in inane small talk with Ingrid while his wife made high-pitched sounds over her grandson.

"The delivery was okay?" he said, his grin feeling witless.

"I guess so," Ingrid said. "I was knocked out on ether."

"Yeah, I suppose, huh?"

"And we got a kid out of it, to boot," she said, flopping her hand in the direction of Gordon and the baby.

"That's fine, that's fine. What the hell." He knew he sounded like an idiot, but was unable to stop himself.

He went over to look at the infant, standing next to Mae, who had her head tilted to one side, speaking soothing nonsense down at the baby. Its little pink face was peaceful, eyes closed, tiny lips working. It moved a little hand out of the soft blanket, and when Willy held out his gnarly index finger and touched the hand, the baby grasped his finger. Willy exhaled sharply through his nose, feeling as if his heart had heated and expanded in his chest. When he looked at Gordon, he saw that his son's eyes were filled with tears. Gordon grinned, and the movement of his cheeks sent the tears rolling down.

Willy cleared his throat and said, "Oh, he's a fine boy, Gordon. Just fine."

"Thanks, Dad," Gordon rasped, and started to laugh, lifting the baby up to his shoulder with scabbed and callused hands. "Thanks."

"What are you going to name him?" Willy asked.

Gordon, holding the baby in his arms, gave Willy a puzzled look.

"Dan," he said. "What else?"

When Ingrid was asleep and the baby in the nursery, Willy took Mae and Gordon for beers and burgers at a bar down by the port. It was the same kind of bar as the one they owned, the difference being that the clients were rail and port men rather than rail and barge men, sailors and steel mill workers rather than river rats, and not a single farmer in sight. Both bars had power plant workers, who could have been interchangeable. Willy was sure that he recognized a rail man as a customer from years ago, but lost sight of him and turned his attention to the conversation.

Gordon seemed to be as stunned about the birth of his son as Willy had been when Gordon himself was born. Watching Gordon was, in a way, like looking back through the years and seeing himself in the same state. Gordon seemed at once overjoyed and overwhelmed, and when Willy asked about his plans, his son seemed to shake off a creeping reverie and try to concentrate on the conversation.

"We've got it all figured out, Dad," Gordon said. "Don't worry."

He was too blissful to be put out when Willy offered financial help. He started to talk about their plans for the child, where the boy would go to school, how often they'd be able to come back for a visit.

"I don't want him to be any stranger to life on the river," he said, "but this is something different. This'll be good here."

"When he gets a little older, he could come and stay with us in the summer," Willy said. "Give you kids a break."

"Sure. I'll keep it in mind."

Mae offered to stay with them until Ingrid got back on her feet, but Gordon seemed hesitant. "Our place is kind of small. It's nice and everything, but I don't know. Thanks, though."

They stayed long enough to see the new family home from the hospital. Their apartment was indeed pleasant, a sunny place on the third floor of a brick building, up on a hill with a view of the port. Much of what they looked down on was an industrial area, but the lake glinted in the sunlight not far away, stretching to the distant horizon, and the neighborhood was busy with bars and small restaurants, delis, bakeries, butcher shops and the like.

Willy and Mae wouldn't talk about it until they were on the drive home, but Ingrid didn't seem overly interested in taking care of the baby. She fed it and held it, but only in a noticeably lackluster manner. She kept Gordon on the jump, and he seemed eager to help in any way he could, was even fussy in a manner that Willy found atypical but amusing. When he thought about how protective Gordon had been towards Chief- in between their brotherly brawls, that is- it began to add up.

Gordon would need to return to work before long, though, and Ingrid would have to be able to function alone. Willy was sure she could do it, in spite of her lack enthusiasm. He kept his mouth shut, and so did Mae, who offered to stay a few more times before giving up. She gave Willy a look that summed up her feelings.

It was harder to leave than ever. They covered their emotions by being brisk and businesslike about it, and soon were on their way. In an hour, they were out in the country, and Willy felt as if he were decompressing.

"I don't know about Ingrid with the baby," Mae said at one point. "Sometimes young mothers get depressed after giving birth. She might not be up to the task."

"Oh, it's all instinct," Willy said. "She'll be fine."

Mae was clearly unconvinced.

The kids finally came out to the river that Thanksgiving. Mae had offered to stay with them yet again, but hadn't pushed too hard, sensing Ingrid's mood, not to mention Gordon's desire to keep things as peaceful as possible in his young family. Willy got the sense that they had enough arguments on their own that they didn't need the insertion of in-laws to provide another topic.

There were times in the intervening months that Willy got frustrated, got antsy again, and could see no practical purpose for their remaining where they were.

"Let's just go," he'd urge Mae. "Let's just sell everything and go."

"Willy. No."

"Big world out there, sweetie. We have plenty of money. There's a lot to see."

"He's going to need us. I know it," Mae said, and Willy knew that look.

"He's going to need us," she said on one occasion, "and I'm going to be here. You might not. You haven't been before."

This was as close as Mae had ever come to a rebuke for the years he was in prison, the years he was gone from the boys' lives.

"So go on," Mae said, throwing out her hand as if scattering seeds to the wind. "Go. Do what *you* want, Willy. Go on down the river. I'm staying. He'll need us. I know it."

Willy watched her, his lips pursed. "All right, all right," he said finally. "Jesus."

That Thanksgiving, though, Willy knew that his wife was right. She had always had the ability to see clearly in his blind spots. The young family came and stayed for the weekend, and they had a dinner at Emilio and Solveig's like the ones years ago. All who had been to those legendary dinners knew they were experiencing something magical and transitory, and those who were new to the experience couldn't help but get caught up in the feeling. Even Ingrid was pleasant, and seemed to like showing off the baby, especially to Marita, who was now pregnant herself, and Solveig, obviously champing at the bit to be a grandmother. The women present (along with a smiling Doc Ambrose) clustered around the baby, while the men drank and talked in the living room.

At one point after dinner, Willy and Emilio stood in the brisk dark on Emilio's front porch, smoking cigars and drinking scotch, the golden glow from the windows bathing their shoulders. Emilio was pensive about Katita not showing up- yet again- and Gordon had no information about her, even seeming reluctant to discuss such matters in front of his wife.

Willy knew the state of Emilio's mind. One daughter was missing, Solveig's health was not the best, and yet a new generation was on its way. Willy watched his friend, whose eyes rested on the dark river, but whose attention was elsewhere. He could practically see the thoughts in Emilio's head.

"We're both almost sixty," Willy said. "Think of that. Sixty."

Emilio exhaled through his nose, shaking his head.

"We are just rocketing through this life," Willy said.

Emilio pulled on his cigar and blew the smoke out, watching it drift on the breeze.

"If we can accept the sadnesses and imperfections," Emilio said at length, "the rest is beautiful. The fact that it is slipping away so fast makes the beauty sting."

Willy nodded.

"Let us hold on, my friend," Emilio said. "Let us hold on."

Willy clapped his hand on Emilio's shoulder and watched the darkness with him.

In April, almost a year before little Dan's first birthday, Willy surprised Mae with a little picnic up on Maiden Bluff, over the river where he had run when first freed from prison, always a favorite place of theirs- of his when he was alone- a place of escape. After they'd eaten, they lay under a large old oak tree nearing the end of its life, some of its limbs already naked of bark, exposing the silvery dead wood. Willy had his head on her stomach, reading a book, and Mae stroked his hair.

"This tree reminds me of that poem of yours" Mae said, looking up into the branches. "You know the one."

"Yeah," Willy said, following her gaze. "It's old."

"Standing here like a sentinel, all these years."

"Hundreds of years. Think of all it's looked out upon."

That gave Willy an idea.

He bought a hundred oak saplings, just before little Dan's first birthday. He planted them in the boy's honor, in places where they had a good chance to grow and thrive, places where they might stand witness to the life of the river for hundreds of years, just like the old oak on Maiden Bluff. That, in fact, was his favorite place that he did the planting, the new saplings there to take the place of the old oak.

There was something holy in the planting of a tree, something which had such promise, such purity. It was an act devoid of selfishness or ego, cleansed by its anonymity and hope for the future. He would only tell Mae and his grandson about what he did, Mae because she would want to know what he was up to, and little Dan because it might inspire him to do something similar. He hummed to himself as he dug holes in the soil, again and again, up on the bluff in the breeze of spring days, the timeless river far below.

Letters and phone calls from Gordon were not as frequent as they would have liked. Over the next few years, they saw each other no more than two or three times a year. Gordon, Ingrid, and the baby would come up for Thanksgiving or Christmas, but rarely both, and Willy and Mae drove to Greysport around the time of Danny's birthday.

When they did get together, it was apparent that Gordon's was not the happiest of marriages. Ingrid had been warm towards them the first time they met, and afterwards seemed to be struggling to be on her best behavior. It was obvious that she resented any motherly advice Mae had to give, however obvious it was that she needed it. She bordered on neglectful, and appeared to be annoyed by demands that other parents would find to be a source of joy. Gordon seemed to fill the gap, looking harried, and Willy and Mae wondered what Ingrid did when Gordon was at work.

Ingrid seemed especially cool to Willy, who cared only because she was married to his son and was the mother of his grandson. Willy imagined that her attitude could be a reaction to what she thought about his past; he had run into it before. He thought again about how absurd it was that he had been seen as a hero for things he had done in the war, but as a murderer for his actions defending his family from someone like Bud Sletto. There was little he could do about it, though, so he retreated to a default position of being as pleasant, helpful, and close-mouthed as possible.

As his sixtieth birthday grew near, Willy's state of mind changed continuously. On the one hand, he was amazed that he was alive at all and that he had enjoyed as much happiness as he had, and all the sadness- Chief's death, Molly's murder, the deaths of friends, his time in prison- seemed like a bearable weight, given all the good that had come in its midst.

Then there were times where he was tired, beyond tired, crushed and worn. People depended on him, though; he knew there was only a thin layer of ice between Mae and her vast gulf of grief, he knew that people depended on his steadfastness, needed his constancy. So he pushed himself to his feet at times like this, put one foot in front of the other, mechanically going through the motions of his day.

At an age where most of his contemporaries had long since stopped such activity, he worked out diligently in his sanctuary in the basement. He lifted the weights the boys had once lifted, he pounded the old heavy bag. His strength and speed were slowly sliding away from him, but he pushed back against this. His strength would be needed. *He* would be needed.

"Do not go gentle into that good night, old man," he would mutter to himself as he thumped down the stairs one more time.

There was always some young idiot who would start trouble in the bar; it was a workingman's bar, after all, where people came to blow off steam, where rowdiness was the norm and decorum ridiculed. In spite of Willy's age, his reputation seemed to screen most of this behavior, but every once in a while something slipped through. He had to straighten out the ex-boyfriend of one of his wait staff, a boy who had a problem with taking no for an answer. He finally made it clear to the young man that his presence was not wanted in or around the bar, or anywhere in the girl's life.

"I'm not going to involve the sheriff's department in this," he told the kid as he held him up against the brick wall of the alley. "You're just going to get the message and leave her alone."

"Maybe I should call the cops on *you*," the kid said.

Willy bunched the kid's jacket in his fists and pulled him close enough that he was breathing in his face. Then he slammed him back into the wall, bouncing his head off the brick.

"Just get out of here, kid," he said. "Don't come back."

271

For a week or two, he thought the kid might do something stupid, following the girl or doing damage to the bar, but nothing happened and he eventually forgot about it. When he did think about it, he saw how similar it was to events earlier in his life, saw how little had changed. He knew better than to suggest to Mae, yet again, that they leave.

He was tired. Part of him wanted Gordon to come back and take over the business, although he didn't bring the subject up with him. He wanted to go away, take Mae and go somewhere that no one knew him, where he wasn't bound by his history and could simply settle into being an old man. He would be needed, though. He would be needed. Mae would always be right about that.

He managed to sneak past his sixtieth birthday without much ado. He begged Mae to simply keep it quiet, and got her to ask Emilio and Solveig to do the same. Gordon seemed to have let it slide, but remembered the next year and brought his wife and son, now four years old, out to the river.

The boy was the very image of Gordon and Chief when they were that age, although he might actually have been more rambunctious. At a get-together at the bungalow, the boy charged around with a safety pin holding a bath towel around his neck, pretending he was a superhero. He ran into furniture and the legs of adults with abandon, imitating the sounds of explosions rather than giving any apologies. He kept Gordon running, too, which Willy and Emilio found amusing, in the way of grandparents getting a bit of revenge on kids who once drove them to distraction.

"Shoe's on the other fucking foot now," Willy muttered to Emilio.

"I never get tired of watching the girls change diapers," Emilio said, laughing. "I almost forgot how disgusting it can be."

The next day, when they put Dan down for a nap, he was, predictably, less than willing. He finally complied after much cajoling and calming down, and Gordon softly closed the door to his old bedroom behind him. Ingrid had gone to lie down in Chief's old room, Mae had found an excuse to run errands. Willy and Gordon sat out on the front porch having coffee and sandwiches.

It was the first time they had been alone together in years. They talked about banalities for awhile, Gordon telling Willy that he couldn't afford to take off work and go to school right now, but that he'd get around to it. Willy kept his advice to himself and followed Mae's suggestion that he be a good listener.

"I put in a lot of hours at this time of year," Gordon said.

"Gotta be tough," Willy said.

"It's worth it when I come home and see that kid." Gordon smiled, shaking his head.

"He's a little character."

"Yeah. Handful. And I know he's only four, but he's got a knack for art. Way beyond his age."

"Chip off the old block."

"He could be way better than I'll ever be. Something about him, I'll tell ya. And I'm not just speaking as a proud father here."

"You're entitled."

"I give him lessons," Gordon said. "He takes right to it. It's gratifying. You were always teaching us stuff. Now I get it."

Willy almost said, It's great when a kid *wants* to listen, but stopped himself.

As if Gordon were reading his mind, he said. "There are a lot of other things I wished I'd listened to when I'd had the chance."

Willy considered his words and said, "Mark Twain said something like, 'It's funny how, the older I became, the smarter my dad became.' I went through the same thing with my dad. Don't feel bad about it."

"I do feel bad about it," Gordon said, leaning forward with his elbows on his knees, a line down his forehead.

"Well-" Willy began.

Gordon cut him off. "Look, Dad. I have to say something. I've been thinking about this for years and...just didn't have the balls to say it." He stopped, scowling at the floor.

When he didn't speak for some moments, only opening his mouth as if to start, Willy said. "Gordon. Gordon! Look at me."

Gordon slowly looked up.

"It's okay," Willy said. "It's okay, son. You're safe. Here. With me."

Gordon swallowed hard, rubbing his eyes with the heels of his hands, then running his fingers back through his hair. He looked at Willy.

Willy nodded, trying to look kind.

Gordon took a deep breath. "Look," he said, avoiding Willy's eye, "when I got back from...Korea, I was pretty angry. I said some stupid shit. I blamed you for things and I shouldn't have. I was angry at myself, and you got in the way. You know?"

"Son, it's all right-"

"No, let me finish, Dad. This is really hard to say and it's been in my head for fucking years. Jesus. Years."

He drank some coffee and said, "Now that I have a kid, I see it. That little kid in there, my son, he liberated me.

"I blamed you for shit that now makes perfect sense to me. You killed that Bud Sletto. He was going to do something bad to us and there was no one you could rely on to do anything about it. No one but yourself. Shouldn't have been that way, but it was. And you protected us, you saved us, and then you went to *prison* for it. Prison! And I *blamed* you for that!

"Then I *had* to go Korea in spite of everything you said. *Had* to go. And when I was there, I didn't want to let my buddies down. You know how it is. I didn't want to let them down, couldn't stand the idea of it."

"Well, that's okay, son," Willy said. "Once you were there, you could do no less."

"Yeah, but Dad! In the end, I let my own brother down. My brother! Fuck!"

Gordon slumped forward on his elbows, shaking his head. With no clear idea what he should do, Willy started to get up from his chair.

At that moment, little Dan came out onto the front porch.

"Dad!" he piped. "Grampa! Come see what I did!"

Willy and Gordon looked at each other. This took too long for Dan, though, and he grabbed Gordon's wrist and pulled against it, his little body at nearly a forty-five degree angle in his effort. "Come *on!*"

The look of suspicion on Gordon's face was replaced with a slow grin. "What is it?" he asked, getting up.

"Just come *on!*" Dan grunted, tugging on his father's arm. Willy and Gordon smiled at each other and followed the boy through the living room.

He took them back to Gordon's old bedroom, where the shade was pulled down for the boy's nap. When their eyes adjusted to the gloom, they widened.

"See?" Dan said, holding out his arm like a showman.

He had taken crayons and done a rather elaborate drawing on the wallpaper. It was apparent that he had drawn as far as he could reach while standing on the bed, then had moved to the floor beside it and continued his theme, which involved knights and dragons, the former attacking the dragons, torn to shreds on the ground, or in the process of being eaten, the latter either doing the eating or flying menacingly overhead.

"Dan! Jesus!" Gordon cried.

Willy, over his astonishment, began to laugh.

"Dan, Danny, you can't do that, buddy! Oh, man!" He looked over at Willy and said, "Wow, sorry, Dad!"

Willy laughed harder and harder.

Dan looked up, delighted, and pointed at the wall by the door, where another drawing was on the wall. This one showed a knight standing on top of an obviously dead dragon, a bloody sword held triumphantly overhead.

"That one's me!" Dan said.

"Oh, man!" Gordon said, laughing, his hands on his head. "I get you art supplies! Use those! And you were supposed to be taking a nap!"

"Naps are for babies," Dan said contemptuously.

Willy laughed and laughed. When he managed to get control of himself, he noticed how good the drawings were, as if drawn by someone much older than the little boy. "Those are amazingly good," he said. "I mean, have you had this boy tested?"

"Yeah, we've talked about it. God, this wallpaper has been here as long as I can remember."

"What's this?"

Willy turned, and there was Ingrid, blearily looking around Willy's shoulder and into the room. Willy immediately smelled vodka on her breath.

"Danny! God damn it!" she barked. "What the hell did you do?"

"It's okay," Willy said. "We were going to redecorate in here anyway."

Gordon gave him a glance that told Willy he knew he was lying, and said, "It's okay, honey. We were just talking about it."

"He should get a spanking," she said, and the boy looked up at his father.

"Oh, no," Gordon said, patting the boy's head. "That's not necessary. Just a little excess creative zeal."

"Creative *zeal*," Ingrid scoffed. "Okay, then. You take care of it. I need some more sleep."

274

Willy rubbed the bridge of his nose with his forefinger and walked over to pull up the shade.

"I'll repaper in here, Dad," Gordon said.

"Boy, I don't know," Willy said. "That might be like throwing away something Mozart wrote when he was a kid. You weren't kidding."

On the last afternoon of Gordon and Ingrid's stay, Willy sat on the porch with Dan on his lap. Dan was playing a game he had learned from his father, which his father, in turn, had learned from Willy. The game was called the Claw, and involved the child holding up a hand with its fingers hooked in order to elicit a surprised and terrified reaction from the adult.

Since Willy was an old hand at the game, he played it well, and the boy was delighted.

"Look around! Look around!" the boy piped, and Willy, according to the rules and tradition, was expected to search the ceiling and the walls, innocent of the fate that awaited him.

"Lah di dah," Willy said, "Sure is nice to sit here with my grandson, enjoying the-"

It was then that young Dan would hold up the Claw, and Willy would make cartoonish squawks and shrieks of terror.

"Yah! Gak! It's the Claw! The Claw!"

This apparently struck Dan as funny enough when his father did it, but having the gnarled Willy doing it- and arguably better- drove the boy wild with laughter. It was such an infectious sound that Gordon looked out from the living room, he and Willy glancing at each other, smiling, unable to kept the mirth off their faces, finally laughing out loud.

"Do it again! Look around, look around!" It could, apparently, go on forever. Willy eventually got tired and convinced the boy to show him his new toys out in the back yard.

After they'd had dinner and talked around the table for awhile, they watched Dan play with Tonka construction toys in the sandbox Willy had made for him. Little Dan was oblivious to their presence, talking to his dump truck and bulldozer in different voices, making the sounds for them as he moved sand around. Mae smiled, her sweet face creased with tiny wrinkles. The boy was happy, Gordon seemed at peace.

After awhile, when Gordon was in the house fixing more drinks, Dan came up from the sandbox and, without hesitation, sat in Willy's lap. Gordon brought the drinks out to the picnic table, setting Willy's in front of him. Dan got wriggly, then seemed to remember something, and, putting on a ferocious face, once again held up The Claw.

Willy laughed and played the game, but it was near bedtime and he wanted to avoid getting the boy too active. During a period when the boy had settled down somewhat, he matter-of-factly stuck his tiny middle finger in his nose and ate the booger it produced.

"Oh, hey, little buddy," Willy said, "don't do that, that's disgusting."

Dan made The Claw again, squinching up his face, and when Willy did his best to feign terror, the boy grabbed him by his upper cheek, jamming the boogery finger in his eye.

"Shi-!" Willy cut himself off, squinting his smarting eye, and said, "Well, it must be time for someone to put his jammies on and go to bed."

Gordon and his little family left the next day. Willy's eye was infected for a week.

The fall of 1963 started well but deteriorated toward the end. Mae got word that her mother was sick in October, and waited to hear about the severity of her illness before deciding to go and see her. She'd been feeling guilty about not visiting her mother for the years she had been living back east, and with this development, she became grave and preoccupied.

At the same time, Harriet Ambrose became ill as well. She was taken to the hospital in Black Marsh in a converted Edsel Amblewagon, which, Willy noted, was the same model that Sam Feeney of the funeral home used, only the ambulance was done up in the comparatively more cheerful colors of sterile white and ruby red. Some of the ruby red parts were flashing as the ambulance drove away.

Willy realized the strange tangent of his thoughts and came back to himself. Doc Ambrose stood next to him, watching his wife get driven away.

"We'll take you up there," Willy said, just as Mae pulled up with her sedan, as quick and efficient as a getaway driver.

"Hop in," she said, completing the illusion. Nobody joked about the fact that Doc Ambrose was far past his hopping days. They crossed the bridge and drove up the river road in silence. They had all been through too much together to succumb to bullshit.

Harriet apparently stabilized, but Mae's mother didn't. Two days after they had driven Doc Ambrose to the hospital, Willy saw her off at the station in Black Marsh. Willy said that he'd follow if necessary, but Mae shook her head.

"She's old. She wants it this way. She'd be mortified if she thought anyone would make a spectacle out of it."

"And she doesn't want to be buried back here," Willy said, trying to sound helpful.

Mae gave him a look.

"Well," Willy said in a placatory tone, "we don't know what's going to happen."

"What's wrong with you today?" Mae said.

"Okay, okay. Fuck me for asking."

"No time. Train's about to leave."

He stood on the platform and waited for the train to pull out. When it did, he watched the windows for her face. She saw him, and he looked around once, then did strongman poses and his impression of a gorilla for her as the train gained speed and rolled away.

He could see that she tried not to smile at first, then did and began to laugh. She was laughing and waving as the view of her window went from perpendicular to acute. Soon the train rolled through the rusting trees and out of sight.

Doc Ambrose brought Harriet home a few weeks later. The traditional Halloween was held at the Eyrie, but Willy let Bob Two Bears handle it. He found himself getting slowly drunk, and turned out the lights in the bungalow and thumped down the stairs to the basement, listening to the radio and the sound of kids ringing the doorbell. Mae is gone, he thought, so what the fuck. He put his bottle of whiskey on the workbench, pushing aside some disorganized tools to give it space, and thumped halfheartedly at the heavybag.

"The Great Fucking Willy McGregor," he said, taking faster pops. Soon he was pounding on the bag.

"Fuck! Fuck! Fuck!"

When he realized he was doing the same thing Gordon had been doing years ago, he stopped. He felt sick. He went back up the stairs and into the darkened house. In the kitchen, he poured a large glass of cold water from the tap, then stood in the arch between the kitchen and the living room. He stood where the boys had when he had come home from prison, the two of them strong and invulnerable. He stood where he had watched Molly sleeping on the couch. He stood where he had watched Doc Ambrose go back into the bedroom to deliver Gordon. He stood....

The house was dark. Jack-o-lanterns still glowed at the neighbor's houses. He teetered in the living room.

"What have I done?" he said to the silence.

Mae called every night. It was not to give him an update on her mother's condition- it was obvious that she was near death- but she was lonely for him.

"There's nothing you can do here," she said. "You should stay and see if Doc needs any help."

"You're sure."

"Yes! It's better this way. It's all right. We've had a lot of time to talk. She knows it's her time, and she seems to feel a lot of peace. She said good things about you."

"That must mean she got the check I sent."

Mae laughed. "It's okay," she said. "It's all right. It's very sad, but it's all right."

Their phone conversations usually went like that. It reassured him, but he still didn't like the feel of the empty house, the silent bedroom, the sound of the radio in the kitchen when he had his coffee.

He did as he was told, though, and checked on Doc and Harriet. Harriet seemed cheerful when he came up to visit, Willy apparently one of the few people she would allow to see her in such a state. It was also apparent that Doc coddled her; there were books and newspapers around the bed, teacups that needed to be taken down to the kitchen. Willy insisted on helping with this, and was washing dishes at the sink when Doc tottered in behind him. Willy turned off the faucet and dried his hands.

"Why don't you sit down for a minute, Willy," Doc said.

Willy pulled out a chair and sat down across from Doc at the kitchen table.

"She has ovarian cancer," Doc said without preamble, as usual. "It's inoperable. There's nothing we can do about it."

Willy exhaled hard. He stared at the table for a moment, then dared to raise his eyes and look at the old man. Doc smiled.

"It's all right," he said.

"But...it'll get painful," Willy said.

"We have plenty of morphine. There's no need for anyone to be in any pain."

"What will happen?"

"Well, she already has metastases, of course. They're growing. As they grow, they'll create blockages in the internal organs. Fluids will begin to accumulate."

Willy shook his head, searching for words.

"You needn't be so distressed, son," Doc said. "This is what happens. You're far too old and have been through far too much to think anything different."

"It's still not enough, though, is it?"

"It's never enough," Doc said. "That's what makes it so beautiful, I suppose. Besides, if people didn't die, it'd get pretty fucking crowded."

"It's too crowded now."

Doc held out his hand, palm up. "My point exactly."

"Are you going to take Harriet back to the hospital?"

"She hates that place as much as I do. She's not going to die there. Neither am I, for that matter."

Willy nodded. "Let me know what I can do."

"You'll know what to do, son," Doc said, patting his hand.

On the Friday a week before Thanksgiving, Willy was out running errands for the bar when it occurred to him to stop by Ambrose's to check in on them. He had heard from Gordon that he would be unable to make it this year.

"Why can't you come?" Willy had asked.

"I'd really like to, Dad," Gordon said. "It's just too complicated right now."

"We'd sure like to see the boy."

"I know, Dad, I know. Maybe for Christmas."

Willy knew without doubt that Ingrid was behind it, but didn't want to fan the flames by saying anything negative.

"Well, okay, son," he said. "Let me know if anything changes and you can make it."

"Sure, Dad."

Willy was thinking about this when he parked in the Ambrose's driveway. It had snowed recently, but was warm enough out that the accumulation on the driveway and sidewalks had melted, although there was still a layer on the grass and the branches of the trees. The garage door of the house was closed, and Willy had the impression that Doc had not stirred from the house that day.

Willy opened the storm door and rang the doorbell, waited, rang it again. The wind gusted, rustling the dead oak leaves in a nearby tree. He waited, then rang the bell again. Finally, he used the brass knocker.

"It's me, Doc," he called. "It's Willy."

He stood with his hands in his pockets, staring absently at the shrub next to the front door. He was about to use the knocker again when his chest was washed with a surge of misgiving. He tried the doorknob. The door was unlocked, and he stuck his head in.

"Doc? Harriet? It's me, Willy!"

Part of him knew what he would find, but he went into the house, calling their names. He tried to make his voice sound cheerful as he slowly went up the stairs. The house was chilly.

"Better answer! I don't want to catch you in the middle of anything!"

The door to the bedroom was ajar, the room behind it filled with the grey light of the overcast day outside. Willy reached out and pushed the door open.

"Ohhhh," he said. "Damn."

Doc and Harriet Ambrose, happily married for sixty years, lay together in bed holding hands. Harriet's hair was brushed, and she'd put on some lipstick. Doc lay beside her, his hair neatly combed. Their faces were calm, and, if anything, might almost have been smiling. An empty vial of morphine and a syringe were on the nightstand.

"Ohhhh," Willy said again. He sat down in the chair by the bed, the chair in which he had sat when reading to Doc during his brush with pneumonia.

There's no need for anyone to be in pain, Doc had said. You'll know what to do.

He sat in the chair for an hour. The only sound was the ticking of the clock and occasional gusts of wind against the panes of the window. Willy almost expected them to open their eyes, to yawn and stretch. Their hands were clasped together. Their chests neither rose nor fell.

He finally got up and walked over to the bed. He leaned over one side and kissed Harriet on the forehead, then went to the other side, standing over Doc. He touched the old man's fine white hair, stroked it, then bent over and kissed his forehead as well.

He walked silently out the door and down the stairs. He stared at the wall phone for a moment before picking it up and dialing.

Willy was at the house for hours, trying to stay out of the way of Bill Harrington, the "young doctor", then the coroner from Black Marsh, then Sam Feeney, who, as always, was calm and capable. When Doc and Harriet had been taken away, he locked up the house and drove down to the bar in a daze.

279

He expected the place to be buzzing at this hour on a Friday afternoon, but it was silent, the regulars leaning on the bar, silently watching the television.

"What's going on?" Willy said.

"Some fuckers shot President Kennedy," Bob Two Bears said.

Willy was forced to conclude that Thanksgiving that year was just about as bad as the one where he had been shanked in prison. It was a toss-up.

In the days after that evil Friday, everything in the town seemed to move more slowly, more quietly. Playing children, oblivious to the atmosphere, were shushed. Once or twice Willy saw people crying on the street, and he didn't know if it was for Doc or for the gallant young president. It seemed like the world had shifted away from an older paradigm and that a new one, subtle and oppressive, held sway.

Emilio and Solveig's Thanksgiving, needless to say, was less than cheerful. To make matters worse, Katita came home from Greysport for a rare visit, and the already small and morose affair degenerated into an argument between Katita and Emilio (who had had a bit more than usual to drink), which soon became a shouting match involving the whole Benitez family, which in turn started the babies crying. Willy tactfully extricated himself. Emilio shot him a look which conveyed fear, envy, and desertion, making Willy smile for the first time in days. He went to the bar, where Bob was looking after a few somber patrons there to escape similar scenes in their own homes.

"Thanks again for being here, Bob," Willy said.

"It's always good to spend time with people who enjoy Thanksgiving as much as I do," Bob said.

As Bob had a rule against drinking with people on the other side of the bar, Willy came around and sat with him, pouring them both large whiskeys and a couple of pints. They drank together, and took turns waiting on the quiet customers.

More people came in as the night went on, and the ad hoc band (long since officially referred to as the Ad Hoc Band, so named by Willy) drifted in and began to play. The bar gradually went from gloomy to loud and cheerful. Willy found himself letting go of worry and sadness, and soon was laughing and joking. Bob was smiling as well, occasionally loosing his booming laugh, although he would still only drink with Willy and accept nothing but tips from the patrons. Willy soon decided that he would be performing a public service by keeping the bar open after its legal time. He made sure to caution patrons to keep it quiet on the streets; he didn't want to disturb neighbors, who might wake the skeleton crew of the Sheriff's department to drive all the way out to the island on a noise complaint. The night became hilarious and blurry, and Willy found himself guiltily liberated by Mae's absence.

He woke up blearily in the morning, his bladder splitting full, and only remembered that Bob had slept there when the door to Gordon's old room was practically rattled by a thunderous fart from within.

"The Trumpets of Dawn!" Willy said to the door. "Breakfast, Bob?"

"Fuck you," Bob grumbled. "You are a bad, bad white man."

At the Ambrose's funeral, some people cried, of course. The worst ones were the couple's own children, two daughters and a son, all of whom bemoaned that fact that they hadn't spent time with their parents. Willy said some words over the two caskets, thrust again into being in charge when he had only the vaguest idea why that would be so. He felt again as if he were standing in while the real Man in Charge- although who that might be, he had no idea- would finally show up. The only person he felt he could talk to about such sentiments lay before him in a casket.

Willy didn't feel all that sad about it; after all, he would prefer to live to be so old with Mae, and to make his exit with her, so that neither of them would have to be alone. He felt wistful, and knew that he would miss the old man, but that when everything was added up, this was the best outcome that could be expected.

The story in the community was simply that they had been found peacefully dead together; Willy managed to work it so that no mention was made of the details. Sam Feeney had said that it was one of the few beautiful death scenes he had ever witnessed. Some in the community said that it was a miracle, others derided this notion but admitted that it was fitting.

The Ambrose children were a captious trio, Willy was surprised to discover. Not only did they fight among themselves, they were obviously put out by the fact that Willy (to his surprise) had been named executor of the estate. Doc had also left him an embarrassing sum of money, although nothing compared to the bequeathment he left to the library.

"He left us almost nothing," one daughter whined to Willy. "Why is that?"

"Yes, why?" the other daughter said. "Why would he make *you* the executor? Why would he leave you money?"

"That old man owed us!" said the son, who was nearly Willy's age.

"I really can't say," was all Willy allowed, a thin membrane of tact barely keeping him from loosing a font of castigation, if not violence. He knew, in fact, that the greatest regret Ambrose had had in his life was his perceived spoiling of the children; they had lived a comparatively lavish life in Greysport until the children were off, when he and Harriet had sought a simpler and possibly more redemptive life out on the river. It was the fact that his children always seemed to think they were owed something, after being given the kind of upbringing which was better than a fair person would have any reason to expect, that had caused Doc consternation. Willy could see the old man shaking his head, slowly releasing a breath through his nose.

"I really can't say," Willy repeated. The adult Ambrose children left after the burial of their parents in the old cemetery, seeming, in fact, eager to do so. Willy never saw them again.

Mae's mother died in her sleep not long afterwards. Willy had been waiting for the call, of course, but was yet again surprised by his wife's composure.

"It okay," Mae said. "In fact, it was beautiful. When she went, she had been free of That Old Bastard"- Willy heard the habitual capitals in her speech- "for a long time, and she died her own woman. I was never more proud of her."

She forbade Willy from travelling all the way out for the tiny funeral, citing her mother's wishes.

"I'll be back before you know it," she said. Willy missed her to a distracting extent, and the occasional feeling of liberation when he was at the bar late at night did little to compensate for it.

When Mae returned, there were only a few weeks left until Christmas. He picked her up at the train in the flurries of a dark afternoon, and he accidentally bumped people out of the way as he shouldered through the slow-moving crowd dispersing from the passenger car. He excused himself perfunctorily and grabbed his beaming wife by the lapels and pulled her close to kiss her.

They drove home in the dark, swarms of snowflakes in the headlights, Mae sitting on the bench seat next to him, holding hands.

"This is where Steve Hansen got killed by the boulder," Willy pointed out.

"Oh, yeah," Mae said, raising her head to look out the window.

They talked about recent final conversations. Mae's mother had said to her that most people only really began to understand the preciousness of their lives when they had squandered half of them, that it was a tragedy that we couldn't pass down this knowledge, instead leaving it to be learned over and over again. Willy told her what Doc had said about attaining a certain age where death was sometimes sad, sometimes not, but usually not a surprise, a matter of not If, but of How and When.

It might seem odd to some that it was not a depressing conversation, but rather a clarifying one. They knew, at this point, that their time together was finite, a thing to be completely savored. When they talked about the growing number of people they knew in the town's cemetery, it made them feel nothing if not fortunate.

"We just don't need any more surprises," Mae said.

"Oh, we're gonna hold on, young miss," Willy said. "We're gonna hold on."

The next unsurprising thing to happen was the end of old Barnacle Brad. How it happened, though, was unanticipated, as it often is.

Doc Ambrose had been customarily correct about Brad's combination of drinking and diabetes, but Brad's thought was that his condition was advanced enough that it didn't make much difference if he drank or not. It was fun, and it eased the increasing pain in his feet. "Nature's analgesic," he was given to say, holding up a glowing glass of beer or whiskey in the slanting sunlight through the windows of the bar.

It was after he had had a few toes amputated due to decreasing circulation that he began taking morphine as well. It was an activity few knew about, almost unnoticeable in conjunction (not quite to the point of synergy) with the steady consumption of alcohol.

When he had finally had both feet amputated, he began to get fed up. Partially recovered, he rolled himself down to the bar in the wheel chair, where it angered him to be seated at eye-level to the elbows of others, next to his usual stool, which stood as empty as Steve Hansen's had for some time after his melding with the boulder.

"Fuck!" Brad shouted. "This is intolerable! You guys pick me up and put me up on that stool, will ya?" A bargeman and a railman each took an arm and, grunting, lifted him into place.

"Thanks. That's more fucking like it," Brad said. "Bob, give these guys a couple of shots."

Bob Two Bears gave him a deadpan look for several moments, then slowly went to comply.

That set a precedent, and Brad would sit at the bar, dangling his stumps, his wheelchair empty behind him, until it was time to go home or until his wife Patty came to roll him out.

Use of the morphine made Brad constipated, though, and on one occasion he had struggled too hard to "cap one off", as he said, and passed out, falling sideways off the toilet seat and onto the floor. He had suffered the humiliation of being found by Patty, who not only had to get him up off the floor, but had to clean him up first, seeing as he had been halfway to success in his initial mission when he had lost consciousness.

This presented Brad with a dilemma: he had to give up morphine or give up shitting. It seemed to him that the latter was only slightly more necessary than the former, so the decision was difficult. Brad was a pragmatist at heart, though, and bit the bullet and got himself off the use of the narcotic, assisted by the dawn-to-darkness consumption of Greysport Lager. After a week, he was able to unburden himself at regular intervals once more, and often explosively, due the cleansing and cathartic nature of his favorite beer.

The pain in his abbreviated extremities was much worse without the morphine, even though he didn't talk about often. He said so to Willy when they were alone in the bar one afternoon, Willy having lifted him up by the armpits and placed him on his stool.

"I don't know how much more of this bullshit I can take," he told Willy. "I'm not sure it's worth it."

"Beats the alternative," Willy said.

"Yeah, maybe," Brad said, downing his sixth lager, one third of the way through his usual quota.

Barnacle Brad apparently came to the conclusion that it was, in fact, not worth it on a fine day in June. Patty had taken him fishing on a shady little pier under a willow tree on the banks of the river, setting him up with a cooler of beer, a tackle box, and a rod and reel. It was one of the few things they did together, living under the same roof mostly out of habit.

Patty later said that Brad had cast his line, leaned back in his wheelchair, and said, "This was a good idea. You've always been a real sweetheart. I have no idea how you've put up with my sorry ass all this time."

"I did it for the glamour, obviously," Patty had replied.

She went so far as to drink two beers with him, a rarity, her vice being quilting. Before long, she had gotten up, saying, "I have to take a pee."

Always fastidious, she had to find the proper place back behind some bushes where no one had a chance of seeing her, not that there was anyone around. When she was ready to drop her pants, she realized that she had forgotten to get toilet paper, and returned to the car to get some tissue from the glove compartment. At this point, she was nearly hopping with the need to pee. She pulled her pants down to her ankles, squatted, and let go, sighing among the green leaves and shifting yellow dots of sunlight.

She went back to the car and called out to Brad, asking if he wanted a sandwich. He didn't reply, and she couldn't see to the end of the pier, which was down a slope and behind a curtain of thickly leafed willow branches. She took some sandwiches from the car and walked down the slope and out onto the pier. When she parted the curtain of light-green leaves, she found that the pier was empty.

Patty ran to the end of the pier, jumping from foot to foot and fluttering her hands in her overload of anxiety. She looked up and down the river, calling out his name, but there was no Barnacle Brad to be seen. It was only when she had screamed herself hoarse, and was hanging her head disconsolately and staring at the water at the end of the pier that she saw, in the yellow diagonal beams of light in the shallows, Brad's wheelchair.

Brad himself was found two weeks later. A body submerged for that length of time in the summer can often be difficult to identify, but the fact that the body found by two fishermen in a downstream backwater marsh sported a long grey beard and truncated legs was a "dead giveaway", as the local joke immediately went.

The press didn't cover the fact that, when he was found face-up a foot below the surface, Brad's long beard had yellowed in the turbid river water and was twisted with weeds, and that fish or turtles had seen to his eyes and lips, and that he was grinning whitely, Brad always having had good teeth.

The kids visited in the summer of 1964, not long after Barnacle Brad's departure. Gordon was saddened by the death, having known Brad his entire life, but had to shake his head and repress a smile at the appropriately Bradlike end.

"He loved the river and he loved to drink," Gordon said. "And he went by drinking the river."

"What a loser," Ingrid said, and Willy could see Gordon keeping his mouth shut and forcing himself to breathe slowly and deeply.

Little Dan was now six, and his rambunctiousness seemed to have more focus. Willy and Gordon went down to Emilio's house with the boy for a visit, and he could hardly be restrained to sit still for a few minutes while Solveig tried to spoil him. After the heart attack scare, she had gotten serious about her health and cut out all sweets and bakery items. As a result, she was more slim than she had been since her teen years, but had only apples and oranges in the house to offer the boy. Matters were made worse by the fact that there was mention made of showing him how to shoot a .22 up at the base of the bluff in the pines behind Eduardo's house, at which point Dan almost had to be physically restrained.

"Be polite," Gordon said. "Danny. Be polite. Mrs. Benitez has a nice apple for you, so take it and say thank you."

The boy hung his head exhaustedly and he intoned, "Thank you Mrs. Benitez." He took a bite of the Granny Smith.

"You're welcome, young man," Solveig said, beaming- almost leering- at him in a way that apparently made him uncomfortable.

He took a bite from the apple and set it on the coffee table, craning his neck to look out the window at the warm summer day.

"Can we shoot the gun now?"

Before acceding to his itch, Gordon got Dan to draw a sketch of Solveig, which made the kid groan and throw his head back to stare at the ceiling in disbelief. With the bait of shooting the rifle, though, he complied. Given some paper and a ballpoint pen, Willy watched him struggle to concentrate for a moment, then click into acute focus, something almost like a trance. It was interesting and even a little weird, a thing Willy would see many more times but always find fascinating.

The kid was motivated, though, and did a sketch far beyond his years in the skill it showed. He was obviously in a rush, but glanced at Solveig then flickered the pen over the paper, glanced and flickered, glanced and flickered. Finally, as if he were being timed on it, he slapped down the pen and said, "Done!"

Emilio, sitting on the other side of the coffee table, slid the paper over, turned it around, picked it up so that he and Solveig could look at it.

"*Dios mio*," Emilio said, looking from the paper to the boy.

"Holy shit," Solveig said, too stunned to be aware of her words. She looked at the boy almost as if she were a bit frightened by him, but it was also clear that she was flattered.

Willy came around and looked at the drawing in Emilio's hands. It was extraordinary. It was also done in such a favorable way, with such kindness to Solveig, that it might have been done with the intention of currying favor. So he could go and shoot the gun. Willy wondered what the boy might have done if he'd wanted to be cruel.

"Can we go now?" Dan said.

Later in his life, Dan McGregor would remember that day (although he would have to be reminded about the part where he drew Solveig's likeness) and see himself as unusually fortunate for having learned how to shoot from three veterans and hunters. He would always be an excellent shot, and, as far as he would ever tell stories about himself, that would be one of his favorite days in his childhood.

The three men and the boy took their .22 caliber rifles and walked up the shady slope through the pines, the needles a scented padding under their feet. There was a large clearing at the base of the towering bluff, oak trees atop it roaring in the summer wind overhead. Setting steel beercans on boulders and outcrops, Gordon showed the boy how to be safe with the gun, then how to load with it.

"Never, ever, point a gun at something unless you intend to shoot it," Gordon said, making sure he had been understood. Willy and Emilio exchanged a glance of veterans: never point it at *someone* unless you intend to shoot.

Gordon then got down on the pine needles and demonstrated shooting from a prone position, telling the boy its advantages. Dan's concentration was absolute, but his hands kept jerking to hold the gun.

Finally, Gordon let him shoot. They weren't lying far from the target cans, but the boy missed.

"Dang it!" he said.

"That's fine, don't worry," Gordon said. "Stay calm, it makes you a much better shot."

Gordon showed him how to breathe, how to squeeze the trigger. Dan made the second shot, the gun popping and the small round plinking the can off the rock.

There was a chorus of approval from the men, and Dan looked over his shoulder, his face the picture of delight.

They moved farther back from the targets until Dan started to miss a bit more. Willy and Eduardo then demonstrated their skill from a variety of positions farther and farther from the targets. Dan was gape-mouthed in awe, but still wanted to shoot more. When it was time to leave, and they all picked up the torn cans and shell casings, Dan made it quite clear that he would have kept shooting as long as the ammunition held out, whether it got dark or not.

They took the opportunity to go fishing as long as the kids were visiting. Ingrid stayed at the bungalow with a headache. Willy looked at Mae when he heard this; Mae closed her eyes and shook her head. It seemed to be a relief to Gordon, and to Mae, who had spent the afternoon of the target practice with Ingrid. No one said anything, but it was obvious that a pall had seemingly lifted with her staying behind. Willy was sure that didn't bode well for their marriage, but the times he got to spend with Gordon and Danny were so few that he didn't really care at the moment.

It was apparent that Gordon and his son didn't fish much in Greysport, although he had taken the boy smelt fishing with some friends from the port one night that spring.

"I got to stay up all night!" Dan said.

Gordon shook his head minutely and muttered to Willy, "He made it to about ten-thirty."

They took the aging boat to an old favorite fishing spot at the bottom of an island and dropped anchor in the shade. When Gordon was bending over Danny, showing him how to bait the hook, Willy looked at Mae and saw that she was simply glowing. Being in the boat with all her three generations of men, she was in a state of bliss. Chief had been dead for over ten years and the grief would always press down on her like additional gravity, but this, this moment, she was light, she was buoyant, she was young again. She looked from the younger ones to Willy, smiling, and put her hand on her heart. Willy went and sat next to her, putting his arm around her, kissing her white-streaked red hair.

As always, it was difficult when Gordon and Dan left, the only thing lessening the sting of it being the departure of Ingrid. They didn't know what to think, couldn't see a way for the young couple to straighten things out. If they hadn't had Dan together, the solution would have been simple. The fact that they boy did exist was obviously the best thing in Gordon's life (although not, apparently, in Ingrid's), and the trade-off, the bitter compromise, was that he had to try to make a life with her.

This was never clearly stated by Gordon, although Willy and Mae, being of the same opinion, barely needed to talk about it. The relationship seemed incapable of being fixed, so when would it get to the point where they admitted that staying together was not for the good of the child? Furthermore, if they got divorced, Ingrid would get custody of Dan, such a prospect being the legal standard of the time. They only saw her infrequently, but it seemed unlikely that she was a better mother in her day-to-day life than she was when out for a visit, when, it seemed reasonable to believe, she was on what was as close as she could come to her best behavior.

Being parents, they worried about it. Being parents of an adult child, there was little they could do. Willy found himself, during the course of his usual activities, daydreaming about Ingrid succumbing to a brief but severe illness, and Gordon bringing the boy out to the river to live for good. It was a tasteless fantasy, and he tried to shake it off, but somewhere later in the day or the week it would reappear.

The cheesy carnival that had come to town for so long was not going to make it that year. The spottily maintained, and- as Bob Two Bears had pointed out- dangerous rides lived up to their potential when, in a town down river, the Octopus ride had been at full spin when some rusted bolts disguised with a coat of fresh green paint had finally given way and sent a car and its occupants on a screaming trajectory up over the ticket booth for the ride and into a nearby cotton candy stand, killing four. Another death had taken place simultaneously when a bystander, gasping at the surprising turn of events, had aspirated a good chunk of a footlong hotdog. The man had fallen to the ground, choking, and might have been saved had it not been for the chaos surrounding the crumpled Octopus car and the shattered remains of the confection stand. One observant good samaritan recognized his plight, though, and knelt down to help him, finally realizing the cause and compressing the man's chest, the expelling trapped air behind the section of dog sending it out with a pop to bounce off the samaritans's face. The samaritan looked around for affirmation of this deed (not realizing that he had not saved the man at all, merely loosing the dog with his trapped final breath) but was crestfallen to find that all attention was focused on the four victims of the confluence of the Octopus ride and cotton candy stand, who lay in gauzy shrouds of multi-colored cotton candy, as if mummified by a festive giant spider.

Other sordid news for the summer came from teenaged Stumpy and Nubby Schommer, who now bussed tables for Willy during the dinner rush. They had an uncle who halfheartedly ran a blacksmith shop up in the bluffs in the town of Mt. Pleasant, mostly using it to launder money for his marijuana-growing operation (this last fact had come not from Stumpy and Nubby, but long ago from Steve Hansen, an old cohort of the boys' uncle, who had come in with the man from time to time, goggle-eyed and smirking from weed). The story was that a neighbor of the uncle, a man known for his junk-strewn, weedy mess of a yard surrounding his tilting, paintless house outside of the intersection which constituted Mt. Pleasant, a man who kept to himself but was noted for his bachelorly peculiarity when in public, had been caught red-handed boning another neighbor's calf. The owner of the calf and his son had been stunned into immobility by this discovery, and the odd bachelor, apparently, had kept boning diligently away, after a curt and businesslike nod to the two. The father and son, laughing disgustedly, had jumped into the pen to pull their neighbor off. A scuffle had ensued, during which the peculiar neighbor had tried to run but had become tangled in the pants around his ankles and fallen in the slurry of mud and shit. The aggrieved calf took this as an opportunity to kick him soundly in the head, after which he was limp enough to be extracted by the two owners. They tossed him, pants-down and dungcovered, in the grass beside their gravel driveway, keeping an eye on him until the Sheriff's deputies could arrive.

When the deputies, grimacing with mirthful revulsion, tossed the man in the back of one of the squadcars, he began to protest his treatment at, apparently, everyone's hands, starting with the parents who had left him the farm, and ending with the owners of the calf and the deputies. He, himself, was blameless and misunderstood.

"Just look in her eyes! Look in them and you'll understand! Those eyes are wells of understanding! Those eyes are love!"

When the calf mooed- perfect timing- the man had called, "I love you, too, my little coquette!" He saw one of the deputies looking at the calf with a puzzlement which the man must have mistaken for desire, for he started to scream, "Don't look at her! She's mine!"

As he was driven away, he called from his slumped and handcuffed position from the backseat, "I love you honey! I forgive you for that little kick you gave me! You was just scared!"

The deputy got him to lie down, telling him that it would be all right. After they'd been on the river road for fifteen minutes, the man staring listlessly out the window, he did as suggested. When they got to the station in Black Marsh, the deputy went to rouse him from the back of the squad, but found that he was dead. Smiling like a man in love, but dead.

Every now and then, they got a call from Gordon when things were in crisis. There were the normal calls, once a week or so, when they described the rhythms of their lives, and then there were the calls when Gordon, a man of the world, nonetheless gave his father the respect of asking for his opinion. He did a good job at covering his desperation, but Willy could see that he needed to be a calming and logical voice in Gordon's realm of chaos.

During one such call, which Willy had at first thought was one of the normal ones due to the length at which Gordon and Mae had calmly conversed, he had been given the phone and was talking to his son when Gordon had interrupted and said, "So, Dad, I guess you never had any problems with Mom going nuts before, right?"

The conversational change was so abrupt that Willy snorted with laughter. "Well, no, not exactly," Willy said. "You know your mother. She's got a pretty even keel."

"Yeah."

"That doesn't mean that, in my wilder and less responsible days, I didn't run into that kind of thing from time to time. With other, shall I say, lesser women." Willy restrained himself with manners and didn't ask directly what it was that Ingrid was up to this time.

"Yeah, I suppose," Gordon said abstractedly, as though he were listening for something on his end.

"I've told you before, when it gets bad, put your head between your shoulders and make for the door."

"That is great advice, Dad, but sometimes I don't want to leave Dan alone, you know?"

Willy paused for thought, finally saying, "Son, that's not so good."

"Tell me about it."

It was then that Willy could hear an increase in volume from Gordon's end, the slamming of doors and Ingrid screaming viciously, "What kind of *man* wants to be an *artist*, a *sculptor*. Jesus, what a loser! Real men run lumber mills!"

"Uh, Gordon?" Willy said.

"Hang on a sec," Gordon said, and Willy heard him putting his hand over the receiver, but could still hear, "Will you control yourself? You're scaring Dan!"

She continued to rant, and Gordon added, "You're probably scaring the neighbors! Shut up!"

"Fuck you! Fuck the neighbors! I want my Daddy!"

Willy heard Ingrid's noise lessen and visualized Gordon going into the pantry off the kitchen.

"Dad?"

"Yeah. Good times, huh?"

"Shit."

"She wants her *Daddy*?"

"Uh, apparently."

Willy kept his mouth shut.

Then it seemed like the pantry door was yanked open and Ingrid was yelling, "And if you get laid off, we're not going out to that *fucking* river with your *fucking* ghost of a mother and your *fucking murdering jailbird dad*! I want my *Daddy*!" Willy was sure that the percussion he heard was Ingrid stomping her feet.

"Dad, I'll ...call you back." Gordon said coolly.

"That sounds good, son," Willy said, staring wide-eyed at the receiver after he heard the click.

Ingrid's father, a stern bastard, refused to come down to Greysport to rescue her, and she had little ability to take care of herself enough to just pick up and leave, which, Gordon confessed in one conversation, he had encouraged her to do. He was terrified that she would take the boy, though, and she knew it. Not wanting Dan for herself, she appeared to see it as completely sensible to use him as a tool against her husband. And so it went.

The stalemate was broken when Ingrid's father had a stroke. He had alienated her siblings enough that none of them would take care of him, and absence had made Ingrid's heart grow so fond of him (in utter disregard to the facts of her childhood), that she saw it as the solution to all their problems if they would move back to the North Woods. To make matters worse for Gordon, he had eventually been laid off for the winter and Ingrid had made frivolous expenditures with their careful savings. The last nail in the coffin was pounded securely home when Ingrid, in one of her manipulative sweet phases, told Gordon that her father wanted him to be manager of the lumberyard.

"I thought he couldn't talk," Gordon said.

"Well, he...let it be known," she said, attempting to be charming.

"How?" Gordon persisted.

"He wrote it with a crayon," she admitted.

In this rare window of clement relations, Ingrid further told Gordon that her father wanted him to run the lumber yard and eventually the mill because he respected him, Gordon being one of the very few people to stand up to him, and the only one to get him to back down. This might have been flattery on Ingrid's part, but it did make a certain amount of sense. She was at her most honest when she was at her most cruel, though, when all manipulation was set aside; in at least one argument, she had quoted her father as saying that Gordon would be a hell of a man if he "got kicked hard enough in the ass to get the *art bullshit* knocked out of his head ." (The end of that particular argument entailed Gordon taking Dan by the hand and taking the bus to the art museum.)

All this was in the works, and Willy knew what was happening when Gordon reverted to form and went silent for a month. When they tried to call and found that the number was disconnected, they knew exactly what had happened.

They got a letter from Gordon eventually, a sure sign that he was chagrined and wanting information to go only one way. It wasn't that Mae or Willy would chastise him or say anything negative, but he was sensitive enough that, in the wrong kind of pause or inflection, he could hear their carefully avoided censure, and that would be enough to put him in a funk. Mae was more perceptive about these kinds of things than Willy, habitually, and when she pointed it out clearly to him, it made sense.

"Let's just write him a letter back," Mae said. "We'll be encouraging."

"What's so bad about managing a lumber yard, anyway?" Willy said, looking for a positive point of view. "The old geezer's had a stroke, so at least he'll shut the fuck up. I wish Gordon'd move here with the kid and take over the bar but...." he spread his hands.

"Maybe they can just see it through, sell the place, and then move down here. It might be that we look pretty good in comparison to Ingrid's relatives at that point."

"Stranger things have happened," Willy said.

A letter from Gordon- in response to their carefully positive letter- said the same thing, but only as a misty possibility. Then he changed the subject: "I can keep my hand in with sculpting," he wrote, "although not in as august a manner as I had hoped. Woodcarving has been interesting, and, seeing as I work at a lumber yard, I have it on good authority that I should be able to find materials. It's a new medium for me, but fairly self-explanatory and entertaining."

"I worry about Dan, though. I don't want to be the kind of dad who lives through his kids (thanks for suppressing that desire, Mom and Dad), but he really is so talented, and was thriving on his regular exposure to art in Greysport. For his sake, I'd rather we returned to the city."

"Things will work out though. We might see this through and come down to your neck of the woods for awhile-" Mae gave Willy a told-you-so look "-you never know. Ingrid's dad isn't going to last forever, or even for very long, not to sound heartless or anything."

He signed off wishing them good health and giving his love.

"It'll work out," Mae said.

Willy flickered his eyebrows noncommittally.

Running the lumber yard hadn't proven much of a challenge for Gordon; in fact he seemed to have a knack for it, although it would obviously get more hectic in the summer. Ingrid had two brothers whom the father had alienated, and an aunt (her father's sister) who was at loose ends and had become the father's caretaker, pushing him around in his wheelchair, spooning baby food into his mouth, even changing his diapers, all, Ingrid assured Gordon, in the hopes that he had written her into his will. The aunt, unlike Ingrid, was a good cook, though, and kept things together, even doting on Dan a little bit.

This freed Gordon up to run the lumber yard, even leaving him enough time to doodle away in his office at ideas for sculptures. In his later years, some of Dan's happiest memories of those times would involve being in the paneled office with his father, both of them lost in their own art projects when it was snowy outside and business was slow. He would also remember their walks in the winter woods near the large old log home where they lived, the target practice among the towering trees, and coming home to the kitchen for soup and sandwiches, where they laughed together and tried to ignore the old man grunting in the corner in his wheelchair, a bib under his chin spattered with a slop of something pureed.

Gordon took immediately to woodcarving on the dark, snowy days. He'd gotten a taste of it as a boy under Emilio's supervision, and was now working away in one of the yard's woodshops, relearning how to use the carving knives, chisels, gouges, veiners, the attributes of oak, mahogany, tupelo, basswood, chestnut, walnut. He always wrote his longest letters when enthusiastic about a subject, seemingly oblivious to the interest level of the letter's recipient, but it amused Willy and Mae the way he rambled in print. Even in his thirties, he exhibited the same tendencies that he had as a child; they had merely become more nuanced and fine-tuned.

He wrote about little Dan and how he was fitting in at the new grade school, the friends he was making, his grades, how he got off the schoolbus and ran through the snow into the shop or the log home, wherever he thought he might find his father. Gordon rarely even mentioned Ingrid in the letters, something Willy and Mae found worrisome.

Along with one of the letters, Gordon sent a package containing a bas relief in applewood of a young family picking apples, appropriately enough. There was surprising detail to the work, which showed what appeared to be a strongly built father, a slender mother, and two sturdy boys in an idealized orchard. Mae had Willy mount it on the wall in the living room.

As if to remove all ambiguity about his subject matter, Gordon next sent a large box containing a sculpture in wood. As soon as they opened the box and freed the piece from its wrapping paper, they knew the photographs Gordon had used for reference, ones taken by Emilio, who had gotten the family to stand together by the river. The boys had still been in their teens, and Willy had been standing behind the three of them, one arm around Mae, one over Gordon's shoulder, Chief standing in front of them with Mae and Gordon each resting a hand on Chief's shoulders. Chief had been grinning, his head tilted slightly back, as if he were laughing or enjoying the feel of the sun on his face. Gordon had executed it perfectly.

"Well, I'll be," Willy said.

"That kid," Mae said.

Mae cleared away some things from the top of the piano and set the sculpture there. They stood back and admired it.

When they called Gordon to thank him, they could tell from the tone of his voice that all was not well. He told them that they'd be unable to make it down for Christmas, but would be sure to come next year.

"Who knows if we'll even be living here by then," he said to Willy.

"It's a pretty good gig you've got there," Willy said.

"It's nothing I ever saw myself doing," Gordon said.

"It often isn't."

"I've got to get back in school."

"Do what makes you happy, son," Willy said, sticking with his policy of blanket encouragement.

Dan got on the phone and chattered at both of them, telling them nonlinear stories about his friends, the woods, the wildlife, a jumble of things. If he was aware his parents were having difficulties, was inured to it.

Doc Ambrose had once said that it's not the If, but the How and the When. Even with that message taken deeply to heart, there will always be surprises, no matter how much someone as sweet and kind hearted as Mae would have loved to live out her years in peace, no matter how much someone like Willy, always looking in the wrong direction for calamity, would have loved to join her.

He was looking in the wrong direction on a Saturday afternoon in January. He and Emilio were performing their winter ritual of the careful maintenance of the old boat, which was approaching its fortieth year and had attained the status of a collector's item. They did the usual meticulous maintenance, sometimes talking, sometimes working in silence or listening to the radio, two grey-haired men who had said everything to each other.

Willy thought, as he often did, about bringing the boat to this place years ago, a lost young man, spiritually gutted, seeking a friend he hardly knew, seeking something, somewhere, without even knowing he was doing so. In this boat, he had drifted up against the powerful flow of the river and washed up upon this shore. Upon this shore, this random shore, his life had accumulated.

They were getting towards the end of the day, talking about what to do for dinner. They often took The Girls, as they habitually called their wives, out for dinner on Saturday nights, and Willy could tell that Emilio was leaning towards a prime rib dinner, although he was, as usual, too accommodating towards the wishes of others to forcefully state his own. It was an old routine.

"So, just say it," Willy told him, smiling down from the top of a ladder where he was doing some sanding. "If you want to have prime rib, just say you want prime rib,"

"No, really, it's not important. We'll see what the girls want to do."

Willy tried not to smile and continued needling. "Emilio. Just say it. Loud. I want. Some fucking. Prime rib."

"It doesn't *matter*," Emilio said, with enough of a snip to his voice that Willy knew he had succeeded. Willy looked at his friend, and saw that he had stopped what he was doing and frozen in place. He followed he eyes to where Mae stood in the door of the boat shed. In her dark coat, the snowy afternoon light behind her, Mae was very pale, her face blank, her eyes wide.

Immediately, Willy knew that it was either Gordon or Dan.

The news of Gordon's death was so thunderous that, when the facts of it were made clear, it was like the ringing in their ears after the blast. To those on the scene, though, it was apparent what had happened.

Gordon had gotten up on a Saturday morning with a vision in his head and had gone out to execute it. When Willy was in the woodshop at the lumberyard some time later, he would see the sketches and the photographs that Gordon was working from. His idea had been to carve, from a giant dead oak in the woods a few hundred feet from the log cabin, a sculpture in wood, a kind of icon, a pagan god in a the clearing. It was to be something magical, something Druidic. Willy would see exactly what was in his son's mind, how the thing would look in the towering dark woods in summer, how it would appear ancient and arcane.

Armed with a chainsaw and a ladder and the vision in his head, Gordon had walked through the fresh snow in the pink dawn to make the broad strokes in the dead tree, blasting the peaceful silence with the grind and whine of the chainsaw. The tool had slipped its chain, though (a broken linkage), and the chain had lashed out, a steel bullwhip, striking him in the left side of his neck.

The deputy who wrote the report, an experienced Northwoods hunter adept at reconstructing a scene from tracks, would say that it was obvious that Gordon had tried to hold his hand over the wound, had panicked for a moment before making for the cabin. The wound was too deep, though, and he had fallen to his knees and then to his side to bleed to death in the snow.

This much was plain to the deputy, but he and others on the way to the bloody clearing had disturbed and hidden other tracks, tracks that might have been those of a running boy at first, tracks that had touched their toes in the outermost spray of blood on snow, then reversed their direction and before shuffling back to the cabin. It was the blood and the body that got the attention, and the small prints in the fresh powder would be wiped from memory, lost from mind.

Mae was beyond speech, beyond grief. She was hardly even there. She cooked for the inevitable people who showed up at the house, she nodded and did not respond with more than single words. Willy had a vision (had he seen it before?) that she might just lose all color and dissipate from the world.

Willy made plans. Of course it was this way; he had learned the reality of the world as a boy at war. In his conversations on the phone with Ingrid, it was ringingly clear that she was incapable of dealing with the situation. She could barely put together a coherent sentence.

"I'll take care of it," Willy told her.

"What a loser thing to do!" Ingrid screamed into the phone. "What about me? What am I supposed to do?"

"I'll take care of it," Willy repeated.

The notion of burying Gordon up there in the woods glinted in Willy's mind for less than a second. He called the eternally prepared Sam Feeney, who was, as ever, calm and methodical.

"I'll drive up and get Gordon," Feeney said. "I assume we'll be cremating him."

"Yes," Willy said. "Thanks, Sam."

It was obvious that their lives were over, and that they were merely waiting for them to physically end. Willy settled into the familiar patience that he had known so many decades before, in the time before the Golden Span, the time when he had seen the world clearly, unveiled by illusion.

Sam Feeney called from a phone at the lumber yard.

"I've spoken to the county coroner. Gordon's there, and I'm on my way to pick him up."

"All right," Willy said. "Bring him home."

"Count on me," Sam said. "I have to make you aware of something, though."

"Yes?"

"I...stopped by where Gordon was living, a log cabin in the woods. It was just a courtesy call to his wife, to let her know that everything was taken care of, to see if there was anything else I could do."

"Okay?"

"Willy, the situation there is not good. Ingrid is, well.... She has every reason to be distraught, of course, but she's fallen apart. She's not taking care of things. There's supposed to be someone around, Ingrid's aunt, maybe? I don't know where she is, but there's an old man in a wheelchair in the kitchen, the place is a mess, and your grandson was outside in the snow."

"I'm on my way," Willy said.

"I put him inside, fixed him some soup in the kitchen, set him up with a pile of sandwiches."

"Okay, good."

"His mother was passed out on the couch. There was a vodka bottle and, you know. It was obvious. I have to tell you, Willy, if it wasn't your family, I would have called someone. I would have had to. And it's not like I could take the little kid along with me to the coroner, or the drive home."

"No, you did the right thing. Thanks, Sam. I won't forget this. You bring my son home. I'm on my way."

Willy found Mae sitting on the couch in the living room. She sat there, no books, no radio, no television. She sat there. The dusty piano stood five feet away. He sat next to her and told her the situation. He didn't ask if she wanted to come. As strong as she had always been, she was obviously at the end, and didn't need to see what he knew he would find.

"I'll take care of this," he told her. "You've been strong when I've been weak. I'll take care of this."

"Bring home our boys, Willy," she said. "You go get them and bring them home."

Willy sped north. The woods grew denser and darker, more pines standing in the snow, closing in on the road. He thought he might see Sam Feeney driving in the other direction, but didn't, unless he went by while Willy was lost in thought, or took another route.

It wasn't hard to find the lumber yard, its trucks and equipment cold and snowcovered in the twilight, the windows dark in all the buildings. He found the log cabin next door, through a small stand of trees. The only light was the flickering of the television in the living room. Willy knocked on the door, not expecting an answer, and let himself in.

Sam Feeney was right; the place was a shambles. He could see in the dim light through the kitchen windows that the place was a mess. Expecting to find an old man in a wheelchair, he found instead a note placed atop the cluttered kitchen table caught Willy's eye. "Ingrid," it read. "I have your father with me. G."

Willy walked out of the kitchen and into the living room. What appeared to be Ingrid was curled up on the couch facing away from the room. A nearly empty bottle of vodka sat next to a glass on the coffee table, and an empty one lay beneath it. Ingrid's form was motionless in the flicker of the television. He moved toward her, reaching out his hand, when she breathed deeply, sighing.

Willy turned to where Dan sat four feet from the television, a bag of potato chips in his lap.

"Hey, Dan," he said. Dan didn't reply.

"Hey, buddy," Willy said, his throat tight, "it's me. Grampa."

Willy didn't expect the boy to ask him to do The Claw, but his lack of response was disturbing. The boy finally looked away from the television.

"Hi, Grampa," he said.

"Whatcha doing, Dan?"

"Watching TV."

"What's on?"

"*My Favorite Martian.*"

"Never watched it. Is it any good?"

"Yeah."

"We can watch it together next week," Willy said. "Look, let's go get something to eat, okay?"

Dan shrugged.

"I'll leave a note for your mom," Willy said.

"She's sleeping," Dan said, his eyes on the TV.

"Yeah. That's okay."

He found the boy's room and gathered some articles of clothing, sniffing them first, and a few other odds and ends. Back in the living room, Dan was in the same position.

Willy gathered the boy up, put him in a jacket, gloves, and a knit cap.

"Gotta keep warm!" he said. "Gotta be prepared, right?"

He got the boy a hamburger at a diner next to a clean little motel, then checked into a room.

"You're going to come stay with us for awhile, okay?" Willy said. "It's too late tonight, though, and I'm pretty tired. We'll get a good night's sleep and leave in the morning after we talk to your mom. Okay?"

"Okay," Dan said. The boy was so quiet.

Willy had the boy put on his pajamas and brush his teeth, folding back the crisp white sheets and the clean trapunto quilt. Dan came out of the bathroom, looking scrubbed, but with circles under his eyes, which looked strange in his perfect young skin.

"Hop into bed there, buddy," Willy said. "Want me to tell you a story?"

"No, thank you."

"All right, then. I tell pretty good stories, though."

"No, thanks."

By the time Willy came out of the bathroom after washing his face and brushing his teeth, the boy was deeply asleep. He turned back his own bed, then turned out the lights and opened the blinds, looking out the window at the few cars in the lot of the motel, the color of the neon light on the snow. Where the light faded out, the highway began, grey compressed snow against a jagged black wall of pines. He knew he would be unable to sleep at all without a drink, and produced a bottle of whiskey from his duffel bag, unwrapping the paper from one of the motel glasses. As he stared out the window, it began to snow lightly. Occasionally a car or truck crunched by.

Little Dan was sound asleep an hour later when Willy first made a sound other than the clinking of glass.

"My boys, my boys," he whispered. "My beautiful boys."

He awoke early with too little sleep and a mild hangover.

His grandson was still sound asleep. His face was serene, his mouth slightly open, and at that moment he did not seem as strange as he had the day before. He was just a boy in peaceful slumber.

Not having the heart to wake Dan, Willy showered and dressed in minutes, locking the hotel door behind him. A man in a plaid winter coat, leaving a room a few doors down, nodded cheerfully to Willy in the early light and crunched over the packed snow to a semi with a flatbed full of lumber. He started the diesel engine as Willy got in his car and drove away.

No one was at the lumber yard yet, and Willy poked around. He found the shop with Gordon's drawings, gathering the drawings up, rolling them into a tube, and putting a rubber band around them. He went out and followed the tracks that led away from the yard and through the woods, back to the clearing where Gordon was going to work on his project.

He knew of Gordon's love for Caspar David Friedrich, and he knew his son's mind when he walked into the clearing. He could see the work his son had done on the old oak, and knew from the drawings what Gordon had been doing. Indeed, in the early light, the morning sky pink and orange behind the clearing's circle of dark trees, the rough, unfinished icon at the center, there was something powerful and primeval about the place.

Although it had snowed, it was plain that many people had been in the clearing within the last few days. It had not snowed enough to cover the blood, or the extent of it. His son's blood. It was pink under the white dusting. Willy felt dizzy, a roaring in his ears. He turned and left the clearing, forcing himself to breathe deeply and walk right, forcing himself not to stagger.

In the house, Ingrid was vomiting in the kitchen sink, holding her hair back with a sweaty, trembling hand.

"I let myself in," Willy said, standing in the doorway.

She glanced up at him, then turned on the tap and washed her face.

"Dan's with me," Willy said. "You seem like you could use a break."

She turned, straightened up, and was about to say something when she heaved, held up an index finger, and turned to vomit in the sink once more. Her body was so consumed by it that her stomach contracted visibly, and she stood on her toes with the effort.

"Oh, God," she said. "Oh my fucking God."

"Can I help?" Willy asked, only because it seemed like the right thing to do.

She leaned on the sink and looked over at him. There was vomit in some of the blonde hair she had been unable to hold back.

"Yes, you can help," she said. "If you wouldn't mind."

Willy was a little surprised at her mild tone.

"Anything," he said. "You name it."

She held up a finger again, went partway up the wave of a retch, but slid back before going over. She rinsed out her mouth and breathed deeply.

"You can help," she said.

"Yes. How?"

"You can help by taking that little *freak* of a kid, your *loser* son's little *freak*, and getting him the fuck *out* of here!"

Willy felt himself pull back slightly in shock.

"He's with me," Willy said. "He's safe."

"Fine!" she screamed. "Take him!"

Willy turned and made for the door.

"Your son ruined my fucking life!" she screamed after him. "And you ruined his! Fucking murderer!"

As he closed the door behind him, stepping out into the clean cold, he could hear Ingrid ranting as he walked away.

"Daddy!" she screamed inside the log cabin. "Where are you, Daddy?"

The boy was still sound asleep when Willy got back to the motel. He sat and watched him for awhile, then roused him reluctantly.

"Can't we stay?" Dan said. "I like it here."

"We have to get going, buddy," Willy said. "Your gramma's waiting for us."

"Okay," Dan said.

He turned in the room key at the motel desk and got breakfast for them at the diner. When the boy was in the car, he called Mae from a payphone and told her that they were coming home.

"Be back soon," Mae said softly.

"We're on our way."

Willy and the boy didn't talk much on the long drive back. Willy wanted to speak to him about Gordon's death, but it still seemed too tender, too early. He'd wait until he got the boy his feet under him, got used to feeling safe. He knew that Dan understood on some level, though. The boy was not his rambunctious self, only sitting and watching out the window, his brow slightly furrowed, the image of his father. They came at last out of the woods, down the bluffs, the frozen white river suddenly broad beside them. Willy let him fiddle with the radio until he found some Beatles, whom Willy knew from the Schommer boys insisting on having it on the jukebox. Willy wasn't sure if he liked them or not, but he wasn't going to tell Dan he couldn't listen to it.

"Maybe, after you get settled, we could go over to Mr. Benitez's house and shoot the .22."

"Yeah," Dan said, watching the snowy river roll by, squinting his blue eyes against the sunlight."And we'll go fishing this summer. Get out on the boat. It'll be great."

The boy didn't say anything.

When they parked in the driveway and came in the front door, Willy dropped their bags and placed Gordon's rolled up drawings on top of the piano. He could smell that Mae had made beef stew while she waited.

"Look what I found," Willy called, trying to sound cheerful.

Mae came in from the kitchen and stopped in the doorway, her eyes bright on the boy. She moved quickly to him, knelt in front of him and held him close. She took off his knit cap and kissed his static-feathered hair a dozen times. He hesitated for a moment, as if taken aback, then threw his arms around her and nuzzled into her neck.

Later that evening, when the boy was in bed, they sat together in the kitchen.

"I knew we were waiting for something," Mae said. "Not this, but something. I knew we'd be needed. Remember how you wanted to go away? Wanted to leave? We might be happier somewhere else?"

Willy didn't say anything.

"Well, this is why we're here. That little boy sleeping in Gordon's room- I guess it's his room, now- that little boy is why we're here. Our *happiness*"- she said the word almost with contempt- "has nothing to do with it."

Willy nodded.

"My mother lived through worse than this," Mae said. "She had three brothers and her sister out east, and the three brothers died. My mother lived through far worse than this. We can do it."

"Yes," Willy said.

"We've *been* happy," Mae concluded.

Willy had nothing to add after that.

They knew what to do this time, when they picked up Gordon's ashes at Sam Feeney's. They brought them home in the cherrywood box and set them on the piano, there to rest until the ice had broken and was gone from the river.

The wake was something that they saw as an obligation to others who had loved Gordon, although neither of them wanted to do it. All the people in their lives who had known Gordon came to the bar. The entire Benitez family was there;

even Katita was back from Greysport. Her mother had gotten lean and Katita had gotten plump, her mother was sad but composed while Katita was just in tatters. She bubbled inarticulately on Willy's shoulder, wiping her nose and eyes with a soggy handkerchief.

Bob Two Bears appeared to have vowed not to drink, perhaps not wanting to cry in public after this particular death. With the assistance of young and gangly Stumpy and Nubby Schommer, he kept things moving smoothly in the bar. The two young brothers seemed puzzled by the turn of events. When someone like Brad died, it seemed normal. He was old. Gordon's death was something that happened to a young man whom they admired, and the fact that it had happened in such a manner was something which, Willy could tell, was virgin territory for them. They seemed relieved to have Bob tell them what to do.

Mae wouldn't play the piano, and nobody asked. When someone from the Ad Hoc Band got up and sang *Danny Boy* beautifully (something Willy would have stopped had he known it was coming), she got up and left the room.

Willy looked around the bar for faces that were gone forever, now replaced by those who seemed only recently to have been children. When the roaring in his ears came, he went down into the basement to sit, and did it by himself, Doc Ambrose being gone and unable to help him.

They did not hide away from reality. They took Dan to Bluffside to enroll him in second grade, walking together up the steps of the appropriately situated three story brick building housing kindergarten through high school students.

"This is our grandson, Dan," Mae said to the principal. "He's going to live with us, and this is his new school."

Principal Baumeister, a tall, soft, well-dressed man with carefully tended hair, was a bit overly solicitous of Dan, knowing, as one might expect, the family's entire history.

"You'll be just fine here, Danny, just fine," he said, leaning over the boy condescendingly.

"My name's Dan," the boy said, recoiling slightly, perhaps from the man's cologne.

"We hear you're quite the little artist," Baumeister said.

Dan turned around to look up at Willy and Mae.

"He's got talent," Willy said.

"That's *terrrrrific!*" Baumeister said, and Willy almost laughed.

When they left Dan to be introduced to his new class, Willy looked back to find the boy giving him a rather dark look.

Spring came slowly, in fits and starts, and they quietly established a new routine. Mae shopped again for food that boys would like, finding that many things had changed. She bought him breakfast cereals that he asked for, Quisp and Quake, although, she said to Willy, she thought of them as breakfast sugars, and tried to get him to eat something more nutritious.

Willy read him stories at night after they watched something together on television, their favorite programs being *My Favorite Martian, The Addams Family* (which actually made Dan laugh hard) and *The Alfred Hitchcock Hour,* which was a treat for the boy, being on after his bedtime . They made sure that there was quiet time spent reading in the living room together, where Dan could be found surrounded by books ranging from *The King's Stilts* and *Bartholmew and the Oobleck* to books on paleontology, astronomy, the Dutch Masters, Goya and Michelangelo, all of which he appeared to find equally fascinating.

Mae had to restrain herself from spoiling him, and admitted as much to Willy. The deep horror of the loss of both their boys was somewhat mitigated by Dan's presence.

He never spoke about his father or mother. He got dressed in the morning, ate his breakfast quietly while Willy read the newspaper and listened to the radio. Then he was off to school, sometimes walking down the sidewalk lost in thought while other children ran and shouted around him.

They managed to keep from Dan the conflict they had with his mother, waiting until he was out wandering around alone. Ingrid hadn't called to talk to the boy once since Willy had seen her. Finally, Mae had called Ingrid to ask if she could ship them, at her and Willy's expense, any of Gordon's clothing, artwork, books-anything, really- that little Dan might want to have one day.

It took Mae several attempts to even get Ingrid on the phone. When she finally did, she was unsurprised to find that Ingrid was drunk. She mimed this to Willy, who sat listening at the kitchen table.

"If you could just box up anything you can part with and send it to us, we'd be glad to pay for it."

"Part with it?" Ingrid said. "I could part with all of it. I threw the shit out."

Willy could hear Ingrid's side of the conversation from where he sat. He grimaced in anticipation, ready to get up.

"You did...*what*?" Mae said, her face suddenly turning pink.

"You heard me. I threw the shit out!"

Willy was frantically writing WE DON'T HAVE LEGAL CUSTODY on a piece of scrap paper to show to Mae when she barked into the phone, "You little bitch, I'm gonna come up there and rip your *scalp* off-" Willy showed her the paper and she shoved it away, so angry she was spitting- "I'll kick you in the cunt so hard your fucking *teeth* fall out! I'll reach up your whore cunt and rip out your fucking uterus so you can *gum* it, you fucking-"

She was holding the phone in her fist, shouting into the mouthpiece when Willy was horrified to hear a shrieked, "Let's see you try it, gramma!" before the loud click from the other end of the line.

Willy cautiously took the receiver from Mae's hand and hung up the phone.

"Come on, sit down," he said. Mae had gone pale with rage, eyes wide, her breathing shallow, almost gasps.

"Oh, that little...I'm gonna...." She didn't seem aware of her surroundings, but allowed Willy to sit her at the table and bring her a cup of tea.

When Dan came home an hour later, Mae had a bowl of tomato soup, a glass of milk, and a coldcut sandwich waiting for him.

"How was school, sweetie?" she asked. Any trace of what had happened was pushed down.

"Okay," the boy said, busy eating. Mae busied herself in the kitchen, kissing Dan on the head almost every time she walked by.

300

They had never changed the wallpaper in the room Dan had embellished a few years before, when he was supposed to have been taking a nap. They allowed him to put up new drawings, though, and Willy was interested to see that some of them appeared to be in emulation of his own father's sketches of the idol in the clearing, which they had also put up on the wall of his room. Willy found it interesting, though, that while one of Gordon's sketches in particular was done in pastel and seemed to show what he intended the idol in the clearing to look like during a lush and leafy summer, Dan's renditions were rather stark and wintry, even threatening. One, in particular, showed the trees as a spiky black wall, the sky red overhead, and the old oak luminous in the center.

"Why did you decide to do it like that, buddy?"

Dan, already at work on another drawing, just shrugged.

The boy seemed to like watching Willy lift weights and thump the heavy bag in the basement, and sat four steps up from the bottom of the basement stairs, watching the old man go at it. Willy found this to be helpfully motivating; he was at a point where it took a great deal of will to get down there and do it, even though it was his firm conviction that working out pushed back the hands of time. Dan watched, and Willy gave him pointers.

"Don't forget, though," he'd caution the boy, "you never want your whole life to center on being a tough guy. Good skills to have, but we should aspire to something better. Right?"

"Right," the kid said without conviction, but Willy thought the message might sink in with brute repetition.

May came. The boat had been in the water for a few weeks, and they had been out a few times already. When it was cool and brisk, early in the morning, Dan seemed to like it most, wanted to be up in the bow as they shot across the reflective water, the bow sending up thousands of droplets like tiny prisms in the light.

With the boat in the water, though, and the ice long gone from the river, it would only be a matter of time before they would have to scatter Gordon's ashes. It was something they never mentioned, and, of course, the ashes would keep in the cherrywood box. There had been little hesitation with Chief's ashes, though, so there should be little with Gordon's. It was just something they couldn't bear to talk about, and along with it went the unspoken notion that it was too early for the boy to be part of such a thing. This was nonsense; if they had buried Gordon, he would long since have been in the ground, and there would now be layers of days between then and the present. It would be the final letting go, though. It would do no harm to wait another week. And another.

It was a matter of some concern that Dan didn't seem interested in making friends. They could see that he was thought of as strange by other kids in the neighborhood, but the contempt went both ways.

"Other kids are boring," he confessed under questioning.

Willy could see why this might be so. Dan's imagination- dark for anyone, let alone a kid going into third grade- was considerable, and he apparently thought that doing something like playing baseball, with its narrow and simplistic rules, was nowhere near as entertaining as what he could come up with in his own mind.

301

His one acquaintance who could almost be termed a friend was Bobby Dolan, a fat (there's no other way to say it) little kid from the neighborhood who was scared of bees, worms, moths, caterpillars, you name it, and seemed to have trouble keeping his large glasses on his small nose. Willy had actually witnessed it when Dan and Bobby had been inspecting some dogshit by the curb, and when Bobby had bent over heavily for a closer look, his glasses had slid right off his nose and plopped into the dogshit.

"Not *again!*" he'd squeaked before running blindly home, eventually getting his mother to retrieve the besmirched eyewear. Willy watched from the living room, shaking his head, and saw that Dan, too, was shaking his head, his eyes narrowed, as he watched Bobby Dolan flee.

The Dolan kid had his uses, though. In whatever games and scenarios Dan could dream up, Bobby was always a willing second banana. Playing army, or better yet, medieval knight, or even better, Mars Explorer, or any of the other scenes Dan could dream up, Bobby allowed himself to be borne along in the wave of Dan's imagination. Even that had limited appeal, though, and Dan still spent a lot of time alone. Willy suspected that the Dolan kid had a threshold, however unusually high, for being bossed around.

They had gone up to Black Marsh to see *Mary Poppins* at a second-run theater, and while Willy had found his mind wandering during the movie, Dan had come home fascinated with the idea of sidewalk art. It was raining when they got back from the movie, but as soon as the sun had burned the sidewalk dry the next day, he took his colored chalk and went out in front of the house, on his knees for hours. Willy would poke his head around the house to check on him, and Mae would get up from the garden, go into the house, and bring him out a glass of lemonade. He hardly seemed to notice.

He hardly seemed to notice, either, when he was accosted during his work by a couple of sixth graders, both children of someone Willy knew but couldn't keep straight, kids who would live here all their lives and become customers at the bar before Willy could think twice about it. Willy was again in the living room, watching Dan as he was lost in his own head, when the boys came up and saw an opportunity which could not be passed up.

"Oooooh, look at the sidewalk artist," the first kid said.

"What a faggy thing to do," the second kid said. "Faggy faggot. What a fag."

Not to be outdone, the first kid came closer to Dan and kneed him in the back. "You're fuckin' up my sidewalk, fag."

"It's not your sidewalk," Dan said, obviously annoyed at being disturbed. Willy watched.

"Is too, kid," the first one said, kneeing Dan in the back again. "I can even piss on it if I want. See?" He looked over his shoulders, stood slightly sideways and pulled out his pale nubbin, pissing on Dan's artwork. Dan ignored the nubbin, watching the kid's eyes with a bored expression.

"See?" the first kid said again.

"Yeah," Dan said.

"So don't be such a faggy faggy faggot," the second kid said. The first kid kneed Dan again for good measure.

They walked down the street, pleased with themselves. Dan gathered up his supplies and made for the house.

Willy went into the kitchen and pretended to be busy making coffee. Dan came in and put his supplies on the kitchen table.

"How's it going, buddy?" Willy said.

"People are idiots," Dan said.

"Can be," Willy agreed. "Anything I can help you with?"

"No," Dan said.

"Wanna help me work out?"

"Okay."

It rained later in the afternoon, long and hard. Bob was taking care of the bar, Mae was in Black Marsh with Solveig, and Willy and Dan were left to their own devices reading a novel and a comic book, respectively, on the front porch. Every now and then, Willy, over the top of his book, saw Dan look thoughtfully out at the sidewalk.

The next day was sunny and dry. Willy went out and looked, finding the sidewalk to be washed by the rain to a blur of pastel colors. After Mae made breakfast, Dan was out the door, creating a new world on the fresh concrete. They watched him from inside, smiling.

It had rained a great deal in the past few weeks farther north and in states to the west, and with the unusual saturation of the soil in those regions the previous fall, not to mention a snowy winter, the conditions combined to set the stage for a flood. It was in the papers and on the television at the bar, and everyone braced for the coming event, thousands of times more destructive than any avalanche, almost unimaginable to those who have not seen it with their own eyes.

Willy had gone to the extent of taking the boat out of the water, with Emilio's dependable help. People sandbagged where necessary, although the town of MacDougal was situated fortunately, most of it being just far enough above even the worst flood levels.

To make matters worse, or more exciting as Dan appeared to see it, thunderstorms rolled over from the west as the river got higher and higher. The boy was having a sandwich at the bar as the oldtimers watched the television and shook their heads. Outside the open front door of the bar, the rain came down and the thunder boomed. Dan was so distracted that he could hardly concentrate on eating his sandwich, his attention being torn between the storm outside and the television footage of partially submerged towns upstream.

The waters rose overnight until a good deal of the town's river park was under a foot or two of the milky-coffee river water. Large trees and other flotsam moved by on the current which roiled and boiled and spun the trees majestically around. Emilio called the bar to tell Willy that the battery of his truck was dead and to ask if Willy could take him into town to replace it. Dan was as delighted as he could get when Willy asked him if he wanted to go along.

Dan was craning his neck to see past Willy as they drove along the river road to Emilio's, pointing out things being borne downstream. The water was ominously high, almost at the level of the river road itself, and the tires of the truck splashed through muddy runoff. Dan was too taken by the spectacle to notice Willy's concern.

"What's that!" Dan said, his pointing finger in front of Willy's face.

"Appears to be an old water heater," Willy said.

"Lookit that! Is that a dead cow?"

"Where?"

"There!"

"Oh," Willy said. "Yeah. Yeah, it is. Some creatures downriver are going to enjoy snacking on that."

"What's that? There!"

"I have to drive, buddy."

At Emilio's enclave, the dock was submerged. His house was snug up among the pines, though, and he seemed unconcerned, taking his time walking out to the truck in a rain poncho.

"Third time that battery died," he said by way of greeting. "Time to get a new one. Hi, Dan."

"Hi, Mr. Benitez,"

"Did you know," Emilio said to the boy as he got in, "that water weighs about eight and a half pounds a gallon?"

"No," Dan said, his shy affection for Emilio obvious.

"It's true. And how many gallons do you think are going by out in that river right now?"

Dan thought about it. "Wwwowwwwwww! Gazillions!"

"Yes. You are witnessing something magnificent and terrifying."

Dan was in an awed silence for awhile after that, sitting between the men on the truck's bench seat, gazing out the window.

They picked up the battery and went back to Emilio's, all of them marveling at the level of the water. After pulling into Emilio's shed, Willy got a stool for Dan to sit on and watch while Emilio changed the battery.

"Can we shoot the .22?" Dan asked.

"It's raining out, buddy," Willy said. The boy seemed disappointed, but was never one to beg.

"Can we watch the river when we're done?"

"Sure."

It was because of Dan's interest that they found themselves just far enough away from the lake park to see the old boat house meet its end. The three of them sat in the cab of the truck, the men drinking coffee and commenting on the fact that the pier was submerged and possibly gone and that a good section of the bank of the park had eroded away. As they watched, the side of the old boathouse next to the river suddenly moved, a jolt. The earth and grass underneath it slumped into the water and disappeared, the dirt seeming to dissolve, the grass swirling momentarily on the water's turbulent surface before it was sucked under as well. This left half of the old boathouse hanging in space over the powerful water, almost seeming to tremble. The three of them held their breath.

"There she goes," Willy said as the clapboard siding splintered, beams and floorboards squealed and cracked, windows shattered, and half of the old boathouse leaned out, splashing into the water to be washed downstream spinning slowly. They could see the old woodstove topple in heavily, sending out a fan of water.

Dan was delighted. The old men sighed and shook their heads, exchanging a glance.

"That was cool," Dan said.

"*Sic transit gloria mundi*," Willy said, and Emilio laughed.

"We can build a better one," Emilio said. "Remember the time with the ice storm? The night Dan's dad was born?"

Willy cut him off with a glance- Let's not discuss Gordon- shaking his head a little. Emilio's weary look said that the subject could not be avoided forever. The boy, fascinated by the carnage, seemed not to have noticed.

It was things like that which made Willy wonder if he and Mae were taking the right approach with the boy when it came to dealing with Gordon's death. Dan knew, of course, that his father had died, having said as much when they had taken a collective deep breath and broached the subject. They rarely mentioned his mother, having nothing good to say and not wanting to lie, but the boy didn't seem to want to talk about her either. Willy adopted Mae's approach, which was to show him as much love and consistency as they could. They were prepared, after raising Gordon and Chief, to be consistent in discipline as well, but the boy was so quiet and introspective that it was hardly an issue. He did his chores without complaint, seemed buoyed by his grandfather's attention, cuddled into his grandmother's doting, and lived his little life.

They knew, also, that he had saved them from the real depths of their grief, that his life and his presence abated the true horror of their own lives, that all of it would have been for nothing, a pointless dead end, without him.

Willy understood his wife's wisdom over all those years, understood her insistence that they stay put and wait, her conviction that they would be needed. He loved her more deeply and sweetly than ever before, and this seemed to grow by the day.

There were times, though, that she gave him concern. Once, in the middle of the night, Willy started awake, sure that Mae had just said something.

"What?" he said, struggling to wake up.

"I don't think I can bear it," Mae said.

He sniffed and rubbed his eyes with his fingertips. "What?"

"I can't bear it," she said.

"Can't bear what?"

She was quiet for a moment. "Nothing," she said finally. "Go back to sleep."

He fought his grogginess, wanting to talk to her, but she got up and went to the bathroom. He surrendered and fell back asleep.

He asked her about it the next day.

"It was nothing," she said. "Just a bad dream."

He watched her. She seemed as good as could be expected. He kissed her on her forehead and went down to the bar.

There were times when Willy unlocked the front door to the bar in the morning and wanted to scream. He knew the conversations that would take place, having listened to them hundreds of times. He knew any regulars' position on any given subject. Arguments broke out over the war in Viet Nam, but those, too, were foreseeable. The best conversations he had were with Bob Two Bears, usually late when the bar was closed. They both mentioned, as unsentimentally as possible, that it wouldn't be a bad thing if Faith-in-Full Goodforks were to return, always having been unpredictable and entertaining. He had started a bingo parlor up north on the reservation near the place he was born, though, and was parlaying it into a larger gambling enterprise. He would not be returning, although he wrote from time to time to tell them of his life. He was married now with two teenage children and had settled into a relatively happy existence, his wild years behind him.

The Schommer boys were amusing, and Willy liked it when they worked their part time hours. They had both gotten tall, such an anomaly in the family that there was speculation that they might have had a different father than their siblings. Their bickering and brinksmanship were usually amusing, although harrowing. Both had talked about enlisting, and every time they made such pronouncements, Willy watched them motionlessly, groaning inside.

Mae was entertained and distracted by the approach of Halloween, the first time she had been excited by the holiday in years. Willy had been reading *The Hobbit* at night to Dan- for the second time- and the boy had to be a hobbit for trick-or-treating. Mae dove in, reading the descriptions of hobbit dress from the book and making Dan a costume with red tights, a gold tunic, and a green cap, all with a convincingly medieval look. She topped it off with pointy latex ears and large latex feet which fit over the boy's shoes like rubbers, obtaining these hard-to-find items at a novelty store in Black Marsh while shopping with Solveig. Dan was delighted with the overall effect, and would remember it for the rest of his life.

The night of Halloween, Dan went out trick-or-treating with his friend Bobby, whose lassitudinous former beatnik parents had apparently, at the last moment, decided to dress their round kid as a black cube, having him wear black pants and turtleneck underneath a spraypainted black cardboard box with holes for his head and arms. The kid looked disconsolate, as if his lame costume exposed some horrible shortcoming in his parents, which it obviously had. He had a hard time angling his arm around to finger his glasses back onto his nose, finally figuring out that he could retract one arm, turtle-like, into the cardboard exoskeleton to reach up through the head-hole to accomplish the task. He was egged in the head later in the evening by a passing car of teenagers and had run home crying, leaving Dan to go door to door for another hour by himself, or going up with a crowd of other children, acting like he was one of their number.

The holidays were more subdued than those in the past, but as pleasant as could be expected. Willy and Mae pushed down their sorrow for their sons and filled it in with doting on Dan, although they showed as much restraint as they could muster and pulled back from spoiling the boy outright. He got everything he had asked for that Christmas, though, perhaps in part because he was so quiet and understated in his requests. In return, he gave them a drawing apiece.

They were surprised when, in February, a large box came with the return address of the cabin up north. Inside were some of Gordon's books on art, a black baseball cap, a short-sleeved shirt of his with black and white checks like a finish-line flag, and the framed print of Friedrich's *Abtei im Eichwald*, the very one he had gotten during the family trip to Greysport so long ago.

They were surprised that Ingrid hadn't actually thrown out all of Gordon's things. There was no note of explanation in the box, no letter that a mother might be expected to send her young son.

"I wonder what that little bitch is up to," Mae said as they hung the print in the living room.

Unless she was taking care of Dan, Mae usually seemed vague and absent. Willy accepted it as the new norm. With the boy, she was always cheerful and loving, and he seemed to grow in that warmth, trusting it. After that, though, she appeared to have nothing left. Willy didn't complain; in fact, he understood. If she used all her remaining capacity to nurture on that deserving boy, he thought the effort was well placed. He saw it as his role to love and support them both.

Mae removed any of Willy's doubt about her emotional state when, on a school day, she announced to Willy that she wanted to take a little drive in her car. This was unusual, and Willy immediately agreed to go.

He was surprised when she drove them up to the old hotel her parents had owned, vacant now for many years. They pulled up into the driveway, parked and got out. The day was dreary, melting snow on the ground, the river below showing broad amoebic patches of soggy grey ice. The old hotel was in an ongoing state of dilapidation, paint peeling, a broken window here and there, along with evidence that teenagers came here to party. He remembered what it had been like when he had first come to this place, when he was a lost young man.

Mae sighed, a thoughtful, perhaps skeptical, look on her face.

"I just wanted to see it," Mae said. "I've been avoiding it for so long, and I just wanted to see what it made me think."

Willy waited for his wife to say something else, and when she didn't, he prompted her. "What *does* it make you think?"

She took a deep breath and let it out slowly. "Sometimes, especially late at night when you're snoring away, I just wonder what the point of it all is. I wonder what this has all been about. I miss the boys so badly; I miss my mom. I miss Doc and Harriet Ambrose. I even miss my dad sometimes, that old son of a bitch."

Willy smiled and put his arm around her.

"I miss them so much that I find myself wondering what justifies the misery. Is there any point to it, or is it all just a painful road leading to a dead end."

Willy covered up his essential agreement with her thinking by saying, "Cheerful subject."

"Yeah," she said.

"So is there a point?"

"Yes."

A moment. "And?"

She narrowed her eyes. "That boy is the point. That poor, good boy. We might not know what this all means ourselves, but if we care for him and help him grow, he might find out. It's like you planting trees."

"Yes."

"There's that," Mae said, "and each other. We give each other meaning. For all our hardship, Willy, I have loved you long, and I will cling to you in the gathering darkness."

The poetry of this statement arrested him. He took his wife's small face in his hands and tipped it up to him. Her eyes were still their lucid blue, her face still soft and fair, if tinily lined. He kissed her gently, and she reached up and held his forearms. They stood in the slush holding each other, her head against his chest under his chin, his arms around her, one hand on her hair. Their breath steamed in the damp chill, and their attention was on neither the trees nor the river nor the abandoned hotel behind them.

They put off scattering Gordon's ashes by unconscious agreement. They had put them on a high shelf among books he had loved as a boy, and that was good for the time being. Dan seemed content in his life, and neither Willy nor Mae wanted to do anything that might disturb that.

Dan still played with Bobby Dolan most consistently, although he had vague friendships with other kids in the neighborhood which drifted in and out of allegiance, as happens with children. Dan would always prefer games which involved imagination, and the scenarios he dreamed up were popular with other kids, especially as they dealt so often with death. Kids apparently found Dan's capacity for the morbid fascinating, which fed his desire to accumulate more knowledge on such subjects; it was his area of authority. Willy found him out by the garage one day, explaining to a small crowd of kids the function of a hangman's knot, and the concept of the Drop. Two kids a few years older than Dan were listening as intently as if Dan were an expert lecturer on the subject.

"So, the bigger the guy," Dan explained, "the shorter the drop. You want to snap the neck without strangling the guy, but you also don't want to tear his head off."

Some of the kids were wide-eyed, and the older ones nodded, fascinated.

"A real good hangman will be able to tell a guy's weight by shaking his hand," Dan summed up. "Others will weigh him to figure out how long the Drop should be."

When Willy later asked him where he had come by this knowledge, the boy said, "Books," but didn't expand on this statement. Willy perused the shelves in the house for books the boy might find interesting, and found some with placemarks of little strips of newspaper. One marked the Rembrandt painting of an autopsy, which Willy recalled him studying before. Willy had put it down as the boy's precocious interest in the Dutch masters in general, but was beginning to revise his opinion.

The capacity for other kids to pay attention to such things was limited, though, and sooner or later they drifted away. Dan never tired of it. Willy was concerned when he found Dan in the sandbox in the backyard, playing with blocks and plastic soldiers. The blocks had been formed into a large rectangle, forming walls. Inside the walls were the green American soldiers. Atop the walls themselves were grey Nazis. Willy didn't get it until he asked.

"Whatcha doing, son?"

"Playing prison camp," Dan said, not looking up.

"Oh," Willy said, "That's interesting."

Willy went into the garage to putter while he took a moment to think about this, and when he came out, he suggested that they go fishing. Dan was delighted, and soon his mind seemed to be in another place.

Whatever of Dan's tendencies Mae saw, she apparently ignored. The most she would say was, "That kid's got quite the imagination." Willy didn't mention the hangings and firing squad executions of GI Joes, or how many times he might overhear the boy mention death while playing with other kids. Things would never be perfect, and their grandson was just a little odd.

An old widow living alone in a bungalow up the street went into the hospital briefly and died, and her house was sold by her children. It was bought by a woman in her forties who had moved from Greysport after a divorce, Mae soon found out.

"She was an art teacher," Mae said. "She took the money from the divorce and came out here to open up an art studio. She does watercolor, among other things."

"Sounds like you've got a new friend," Willy said.

"I've been thinking about doing watercolors again myself."

"There you go."

"And maybe we could have Dan take some lessons. He's a little beyond what they can teach at his school."

"Sure. Keep him out of trouble."

Julia Hannah quickly became a friend of the family. Blonde and a little sun-frazzled, she soon had an opulent garden bursting forth in her back yard. She did plein air painting with Mae, and was taken aback by examples of Dan's work, surprised at the boy's age when they first met.

"Well, you're only, what, eight?"

"Yep," Dan said.

"I have a couple of nephews about your age. How'd you like it if they came out for a visit?"

Dan glanced at Mae, whose smiling expression invited him to be polite.

"Sure," he said.

Julia's presence was a balm to Mae, a draft of something fresh and new. She didn't want to hurt Solveig's feelings, but Julia seemed to understand this, and tried adroitly to involve her in their activities. Willy was flabbergasted when, walking home from the bar one afternoon, he thought he heard the sound of a piano coming from the direction of the bungalow. As he came up the walk, the sound was unmistakable, punctuated by shrieks of laughter.

He came in the door to find Mae at the piano, Julia doubled over with laughter on the couch, and Solveig in the middle of the living room, apparently in the midst of pantomiming having an enormous penis and making thrusting motions with her hips to Mae's burlesque accompaniment. The makings for white russians were on the coffee table, and all three women had drinks either in their hands or nearby. When Willy came in and stood in the doorway, they were all silent for a moment, their mouths open. Then they all looked at each other and howled with laughter. Mae leaned forward, plunking her forearms on the piano keys, barely able to breathe, she was laughing so hard.

"I hope I'm not interrupting anything," Willy said.

"Nope, nope," Solveig said, mimicking a man's voice and pretending to hitch up her trousers and give her balls a scratch. "Just between us fellas."

The women laughed even harder. Willy made a polite face and went down the basement stairs, where he stood for a moment, smiling as he listened.

"Ah could walk a lot easier if Ah didn't have these damn huge balls," Solveig continued, to the sound of more laughter and icecubes clinking in glasses. Willy left discreetly, never really knowing what it was about, but happy to hear his wife laugh so hard.

Willy hated to fire employees, but the matter came up when he caught Stumpy and Nubby Schommer smoking dope in the basement of the bar. He loved having them around, and the fact that they were the grandsons of Runty, his durable worker and friend from the early days of the business, made it more difficult. Their presence had changed the bar; their wheedling insistence of having current music on the jukebox- the Beatles, the Rolling Stones, other freaks and oddities, in Willy's opinion- had changed the nature of the bar at night, after the remaining old regulars had left at the end of happy hour. There were the nights when the Ad Hoc Band played, Prime Rib Saturday night seemed to be a permanent favorite, but the composition of the bar had changed. Willy had never gotten around to thanking the Schommer boys for that.

There were things about their employment which bothered him, though, however much affection he had for them. Still in their teens, they had developed an affection for Harley Davidson motorcycles, which they rode roaring up the brick alley to the bar on their way to work. The sound of it made Willy wince, and he couldn't help but think about the bikers who had enlivened his homecoming from prison. Friends often showed up at the back door of the bar when the boys were working, and Willy had told the boys, with increasing emphasis, that when they were at work they needed to be working, and could save socializing for afterwards

When he parked next to their bikes in the back alley and came down the stairs to the basement, he smelled the unmistakable scent of weed. Marijuana was a substance which he didn't enjoy personally, although he had nothing against it. He was of the belief that the public relations movement against it since his youth was the work of William Randolph Hearst, who wanted newspapers to be printed on paper made of wood, in which he had large financial interests, and not the durable and multipurpose hemp. Smoking dope had always made Willy feel uneasy; he had never felt the pleasant, humorous lassitude that long time smokers like Steve Hansen and Barnacle Brad had seemed to experience.

Nonetheless, it was a personal pursuit, and he didn't want anyone doing it on the job. Sniffing the unique odor, he crept down the sturdy old stairs into the basement. The lights were on, but the main part of the old, stone-walled room was empty. He moved back along the stairs, past the tall shelves of stock, the empty kegs. In the last row of shelves he found Stumpy and Nubby. They were sitting on crates, illuminated by a bare lightbulb overhead. They were sucking smoke out a mysterious contraption, a long, clear plastic tube with four inches of water in the base which bubbled when the smoke was drawn through it. Nubby was holding the tube, and Stumpy was holding a lighter over a small metal bowl with smoldering orange contents.

"What the hell is that thing?" Willy said.

Stumpy jerked and put the lighter in his pocket. Nubby, just finishing the bubbling pull of smoke into his lungs, held the smoke there and said in a constricted voice, "It's a bong."

"Bong, huh? Let me see it."

Nubby handed it over. "Interesting," Willy said, looking at it and handing it back. "You can take it with you when you leave. You're fired."

"What!"

"We were just-"

Willy held up a hand. "Nope! When you're on the clock, you're getting paid to work for me, not to get hopped up on reefer. I've talked to you about being here when you're here."

"But Mister McGregor-"

"Sorry, boys. Your family and mine go way back, but it's a matter of respect. You're showing disrespect by your behavior. Won't have it."

"But-"

"Pick up your checks on Friday from Bob."

They realized their appeals were fruitless and shuffled glumly towards the stairs. Stumpy, in possession of the bong, poured out its rank water in the basement sink, after a look asking for permission from Willy. He politely ran water in the sink to rinse it out, then stuffed the bong in a backpack and went up the stairs.

"No hard feelings, boys," Willy said as they shuffled out the back door. He watched as their motorcycles rumbled down the alley.

Bob Two Bears was surprised at the turn of events. "Huh," he said. "I thought those guys'd be working here for a long time, even if it was on weekends while they were in college."

"Guess not," Willy said.

"Well, they needed a kick in the ass."

"That was my point."

The departure of the Schommer brothers created more work for Willy and Bob, not to mention the other employees. Willy put up a help wanted sign in the window.

A few days later, the boys came back and stood humbly outside the back door, waiting while Bob interceded on their behalf. Willy came and eyed them skeptically.

"So, you want your jobs back," he said at last.

"Yessir," they said in unison.

"I don't know, you guys."

"This is the coolest job around, Mr. McGregor-"

"We'll even cut our hair if you want-"

"We won't fuck up anymore-"

Willy regarded them for a moment. "Okay," he said. "But I'm watching you. No more smoking reefer, no more fucking around. You're getting paid to work. Got it?"

"Yessir!"

"All right. And why would I give a shit about your hair? You *have* seen some of the river rats who come in here, right? Sometimes I don't know what you kids are thinking."

He let them in and Bob gave them a list of things to do, all of which Willy had suggested they put off until the boys came back. When they were hard at work, he took the help wanted sign out of the front window.

The living flowed into the empty spaces left by the dead, as they always will, and moved through their lives in the new configuration. Within a year of Dan coming to stay with them, they existed in a comforting routine, and three years later, it was a little difficult to remember having lived otherwise.

Dan seemed particularly adaptable. Although consistently darkminded, he was somewhat cheerful about it, and was never more delighted than when the subject was morbid. He was fascinated with the Coeur de la Riviere cemetery, a place which terrified most of his contemporaries (when they gave it any thought at all), and Mae had shown him how to do charcoal rubbings on newsprint applied to the faces of old headstones. She tried to keep it light, treating it as a history lesson, and on any little trip up and down the river road, they stopped to investigate old cemeteries up in the bluffs. Dan compiled a collection of such rubbings, piecing together family histories from the stones, tales of infant death, men killed in wars, women pulled from the stream abruptly by illness, leaving nothing but carved dates as witness to the brevity of their forgotten spans.

Willy had his questions about this, but their lives, although somehow in shadow, were as happy as could be expected, and he would do nothing to jeopardize the happiness, knowing that such a state was permanently tenuous.

It didn't surprise him when Stumpy Schommer (whom he always called by his given name, Dwight) enlisted in the service, but it saddened him. After all the lectures he had given the brothers on the subject of war, of how young men's desire for tales of glory were used by the old and the cynical, of how the young men were the ones who paid the price, all of these lectures had fallen on ears just as deaf as those of Gordon and Chief.

"This is a bullshit war," he told the tall, lean Stumpy Schommer as they sat at the bar. "You're risking your ass for bullshit."

Stumpy shrugged it off. "I didn't want to go to college right away, and if I enlist before I get drafted, I've got an advantage."

"Some advantage."

"Sure, I'll probably go to Germany. Drink a shitload of beer," he grinned. "No offense, sir, but you enlisted."

"Yeah, and I lied to do it. I was even dumber than you are."

Stumpy seemed hurt, and Willy put his hand on the young man's forearm. "Look," he said, "don't do this. Get in college in Black Marsh. I'll help you with the money."

"Thanks, Mr. McGregor, but jeez, nothing will happen to me."

"Something eventually happens to everybody, kid. No need to push it."

"Well, it's too late anyhow. I already enlisted."

"Ah, Dwight. Shit. Don't you remember what happened to my boy Chief? Didn't you listen to any of the stories I told you about myself?"

"Sure. You guys are heroes. Sometimes the world needs heroes."

Willy sighed explosively, went around the bar and poured a stiff drink.

They had a party for Stumpy before he left for basic, even though Willy was strongly considering ignoring his departure.

"It's the least we can do," Mae said, finally persuading him.

"I guess," Willy said.

Getting custody of Dan was harder than they had expected. Ingrid's father had finally died, they were able to find out, and, before his stroke, had left the business to her and Gordon. She wanted nothing to do with it, and sold it to her two brothers. The aunt- whom Willy knew only by the initial G which she had left on the note he had found in the kitchen when retrieving Dan- was never mentioned, although Willy and Mae suspected she had been given short shrift, loyalty, apparently, not being the strong suit of the Carlson family. They found their official adoption of Dan at an impasse.

And the silt of days accumulated on him, a growing weight. In his late sixties, it often hurt just to get up out of bed in the morning, his knees and back sore. He was motivated often only by obligation. When he worked out in the basement, it was with a sour recognition of his diminishing strength, but he knew that if he stopped altogether, he would fall apart. Someone had to remain sharp. His strength seemed to improve when Dan came down the stairs to watch and work out a little himself, although he was still too young to reap much benefit.

Emilio was getting creaky as well, but was as tough as beef jerky after a life of labor. His hair was almost completely white, his brown skin furrowed, deep smile lines around his eyes. Every once in a while Willy would see his old friend and, for an instant, fail to recognize him, which caused him to go and look in a mirror, sometimes having the same reaction to what he saw there. When they talked about their wives, it was clear that Solveig was healthier that she had been twenty years before, and Mae was lean and calm, although she seemed, at times, to be experiencing shortness of breath. All four of them lived for their grandchildren, who gave them life as if turning cranks in the backs of rusty, forgotten machines which were slowly winding down.

Willy and Dan both became avid fans of the space program. To Willy, born right after the turn of the century, the whole thing was completely amazing. To Dan, it was a part of the background saturation in which he was raised, but nonetheless seized the interest of the part of him which loved to play Mars explorer. Willy could practically see the gears turning in his head; *I could be there, I could be on Mars.*

The art lessons with Julia Hannah hadn't worked out as hoped. As well-intentioned and obviously skilled as she was- her neat, well-appointed house unobtrusively fixed with her own work- she seemed to lack the ability to get a boy like Dan to sit still and do anything that he wasn't immediately interested in doing.

"He's just like my nephew Charlie," she once said. "Talented kid, unable to sit still. They're sure to get along."

It had also proven impossible to get Dan to sit still for piano lessons, no matter which angle Mae tried to work. It was likely that her softness toward the boy was what got him off the hook, something that never would have worked with Gordon or Chief.

"I'll teach him when he settles down a little," she said, and Willy knew that she believed it just about as much as he did.

Willy thought that there was something about the kid that was the substrate of stubborn. It didn't come down to a battle of wills; if he was disinterested in an activity, he was disinterested. Nothing could change it. If someone pursued *getting* him interested, he seemed to just check out, and no amount of haranguing, cajoling, pleading, or even threatening appeared sufficient to get his attention. He was obedient about his chores, having been taught their necessity, but after that, given the slightest opportunity, he would zip out the door, letting it slam behind him with the exact same sound as it had when his father and uncle had been boys. Mae and Willy would look at each other, sad, resigned, mirthful.

Julia Hannah's nephews Charlie and Jim came to stay for part of the summer after Dan finished fifth grade. There were two older siblings at home, a brother and sister apparently old enough to take care of themselves. Julia had told Mae that, yes, the father- her brother- was fobbing them off on her, but she saw their visit as a means to open their eyes to the world outside of Greysport.

Charlie and Jim Gates were one year older than Dan and one

year younger, respectively. They were lean and tan, handsome lads with blue eyes and white-blonde hair that hinted at beaches and vacations in tropical places. They seemed disinterested in being on MacDougal Island, disinterested at having their eyes opened any more than they already were, and disinterested in meeting Dan.

When Dan first saw them, he was walking up the sidewalk with Bobby Dolan. They were lounging on the front steps of Julia Hannah's bungalow, wearing cut-off jeans and sneakers, both reading Marvel comic books. Dan couldn't tell if the two boys in the neighbor's yard had seen them at all, but they were new kids, and as such, seemed as out of place as two figures cut from a picture in a magazine and stuck to the front of a familiar painting. Dan didn't like the sensation.

He stopped on the sidewalk in front of his own yard and eyed them. Charlie, the older one, glanced up from his comic book, locked eyes with Dan for a moment, and sighed, dropping his eyes back to the Fantastic Four.

Bobby Dolan took note of Dan stopping, followed his eyes, and said, "Look, new kids." He waddled across the lawn to where the brothers sat and said, "Hey, you guys."

Charlie Gates looked up slowly. "Who the fuck are you?"

"I'm Bobby," the boy said amiably. "Just one of the neighborhood friends."

The brothers exchanged an unreadable look. "Well, *Bobby*," Charlie said, "we're trying to read here, so why don't you take your fat ass and go be friendly somewhere else."

Dan turned and went up the walk and onto the front porch. He watched through the screen as Bobby recovered from his shock, dropped his head, and wandered away from Mrs. Hannah's front yard. Apparently he was so astonished at his treatment that he forgot he was with Dan and went home, too shocked even to be in tears.

Dan went to a window where he could watch the new boys. They continued reading their comic books just as they had been before, as if used to thwarting intrusions. Dan would later remember not liking them all that much.

Mae and Julia were friends, though, and, knowing nothing of this beginning, tried to force the boys to get acquainted. Julia brought her nephews over, and Mae called Dan out to the back yard. The women introduced the boys- Jim actually made the effort to shake Dan's hand- and chatted while Dan and Charlie regarded each other. After awhile, seemingly sure that the boys would be fast friends, the women went into the house for iced tea.

"This place is a shithole," Charlie said as soon as the women were out of earshot.

Dan had never considered this possibility.

"Fucking sucks, man," Jim said.

"If it's so bad, what are you guys doing here?" Dan said.

"Wasn't our fucking idea," Jim said.

"Our dad's boning his new girlfriend in Switzerland," Charlie said. "If it's anything to you."

Dan shrugged as if he knew people who boned their new girlfriends in Switzerland all the time, and that it *wasn't* anything to him.

"You live with your grandparents?" Jim said. "What a fucking drag."

Dan shrugged again, trying to think if he had ever before been so relentlessly offended.

"You don't have any brothers or sisters or anything?"

Dan shook his head.

"Where's your mom?" Charlie said.

"Where's yours?" Dan replied.

"Who knows. She took off. Probably realized what a pompous, useless asshole our dad is."

"She was pretty worthless anyway," Jim added.

That comment had Dan feeling a brief, wavering sympathy, when Charlie said, "So, what, your dad cut his head off with a chainsaw or something? What the fuck. Must've been one stupid hick."

Dan gasped. "Don't talk about my dad," he managed.

"Oooh, hit a nerve. Sorry."

"Just don't do it."

"Okay, okay," Charlie said.

A moment or two passed, and Charlie said, "But did he?"

Dan pounded his right fist into Charlie's mouth so hard that the taller boy landed on his back on the driveway. Jim seemed too stunned to react. Dan was stunned himself, seeing the amazing effects of hitting the heavy bag in the basement. He managed it, though, and stood in a boxer's stance.

"Told you not to say anything about my dad," he said.

Charlie's mouth was bleeding, his lip split. Jim stared at him wide-eyed, his mouth open, as if expecting something terrible to happen. Charlie smiled, his teeth slicked with blood. He spat a red gobbet on the driveway.

"You can hit, kid. You a boxer or something?"

Dan stood there.

Charlie held out his hand and said, "Help me up."

"Think I'm stupid? Get up yourself."

Charlie did. They eyed each other. At that moment Willy pulled into the driveway and parked. Seeing the boys, he walked up.

"Hey there, fellas," he said. "You guys must be Julia's nephews."

They introduced themselves with polished politeness.

"What happened to your mouth, son?" Willy said to Charlie.

Charlie looked at Dan. "We were just messing around, sir."

Willy looked at Dan and back to Charlie and Jim. "Well, okay. Don't mess around too hard, though. Hate to have to take you to the hospital."

Oddly enough, the boys' little set-to seemed to establish the parameters of respect, and Dan began a wary friendship with Charlie and Jim Gates. They were both much more bright and imaginative than Bobby Dolan (whom Dan began to avoid), but this tended to take a risky bent. They were immediately drawn across the bridge to the railroad tracks along the river, where they waited for trains to

316

pass, putting pennies on the track then searching for the flattened coins when the roaring cars had passed.

"We should hop a train," Charlie said.

"Yeah, we could run away," Jim said. "See what Dad thinks about that."

"Kid got killed doing that last year," Dan said.

"No shit?"

"Yeah, about a mile that way." Dan didn't mention that he had gone up the tracks alone, pulled to investigate, to see what had happened. He had found the place, the splattered tissue frozen to the inside of the tracks under a low November sky.

"Wouldn't happen to us," Charlie said. "We're too cool for that. Ever watch *The Train*, with Burt Lancaster?"

"No."

"Yeah, no shit," Jim said. "You got, like, one and a half TV stations here. Fucking sucks."

"Let's go find that kid's guts!" Charlie said.

"Yeah!" said Jim.

"What, are you stupid?" Dan said, suddenly angry. "They're not there anymore."

Jim watched his brother as if anticipating trouble (perhaps no one talked to Charlie like that), but Charlie's look was guarded.

"He's got a point," Charlie said after a moment. "Crows probly ate 'em and shit. Rain washed 'em off."

"Too bad we couldn't be here when some kid *did* get run over," Jim said, by way of leaving things on a positive note.

The river itself was also magnetic, not only the acres of marsh, in which they played Vietnam or Guadalcanal, but the vast, sedulous power of it, where a kid could throw something in and see it pulled away to who knows where.

"Mexico!" Jim said.

"Brazil," Dan said.

"Kamchatka," Charlie said, nodding at the coolness of his idea.

Dan had no problem keeping them interested in Jungles of Venus, an experiment in imagination he approached with caution. There was real danger as well as the imagined, at least for the unwary.

"We have to be careful around here," Dan told them at one point. "A kid drowned right near here last year."

"They ever find his body?" Charlie asked.

"Yeah."

"Too bad. We could look for it. See if we could find his skull."

When he told them that he had shot guns, they went berserk. They began to badger him ceaselessly about getting to do it, but the thought of the two of them together with a gun made Dan's hair stand on end.

Willy put a stop to it by saying that the boys had to have permission from their father, holding up a hand when they started to interrupt.

"Nope! And I have to hear it first hand, okay? A lot of people don't like guns, and I have to admit that I can see their point."

317

"Excuse me for asking, sir, I don't mean to be rude," Charlie said, "but why do you have them, then?"

"I don't like them or dislike them, son. Any more than I do...hammers. They're just necessary."

Charlie and Jim nodded, cheerfully reasonable. As soon as they were in the alley behind the garage and had made sure they couldn't be heard, they were fuming.

"Where does your grampa keep his guns?" Charlie spat.

"No way," Dan said.

"We could wait until he goes to the bar and sneak them out." Jim suggested.

"Are you nuts? I said no way."

He walked down the alley and they were at him from both sides, cajoling him in stereo. Wracking his brain for a way to change the subject, he hatched an idea.

"If you guys shut up, I'll show you something cool," he said.

That actually worked. They immediately shut up, looking at each other.

"How cool?"

"Just come with me," Dan said.

It took almost twenty minutes to walk to the old hotel. Dan had to keep reminding them to be patient, that it was a surprise. They walked up the driveway through the trees, the dense leaves hissing and shifting overhead in the growing breeze.

"Really," Charlie said, "what is it?"

"Keep your pants on. We're almost there."

The trees opened up, roaring in the wind around them, and they walked out onto what was once the lawn in front of the old hotel. It was now overgrown, the grass long and rippling in the wind. The view of the river was stupendous, rolling off in the distance, islands and a barge on its expanse.

The old hotel stood off to the side. Slowly becoming swallowed by the untrimmed trees, its peeling paint and dark windows looked ominous sheltered in the shade from the sunny day. Charlie and Jim didn't even glance at the wonderful view.

"Holy fucking shit!" Charlie shouted. "Are you kidding me!"

"Why didn't you tell us!" Jim yelled, slapping Dan on the arm and following Charlie at a run into the open door of the abandoned hotel. They ran whooping into the reverberant front hall. Dan walked in behind them.

The inside of the building had been stripped of anything overtly valuable, leaving worn floorboards, stained and peeling wallpaper, rusty beercans and broken liquor bottles. Charlie sprinted up the stairs and called down from the landing, "We can be the kings of this place! This is nuts!"

"Who owns it?" Jim asked.

"My gramma's parents used to. They're dead."

"Oh, man, this is great!" Charlie shouted. "This can be our clubhouse!" He whooped again and ran off down the upstairs hall, running from room to room, his shouts echoing down. Jim ran up the stairs to join him.

Dan couldn't help but be infected by their enthusiasm. It hadn't occurred to him to take them to the old hotel; the place had always struck him as terribly sad, a fact it would never occur to him to admit. Charlie and Jim's reaction swept away that somber perception like dark fog before a crisp wind, and he began to see the potential.

Jim was about to throw a bottle through the glass of an upstairs window when Dan stopped him.

"Knock it off," he said.

"Why?" Charlie and Jim asked simultaneously.

"Just...don't, okay?" he said slowly, holding his palms down in and looking in their eyes. "We should look out for this place, not fuck it up. Then we can stay here."

Charlie and Jim looked at each other. "Okay," they said. Jim tossed the bottle in a corner, where it shattered.

Dan stared at him.

Jim grimaced and put a finger to his lips. "Shhh! Sorry!" he said.

They walked out into the littered hallway and Dan made an attempt to change the subject.

"There used to be all kinds of people who stayed here," he explained. "River boat captains, guys like that."

"Probably loaded with ghosts," Jim said hopefully. Charlie jumped at him suddenly- "Woo!"- making him start.

"Knock it off, asshole," Jim said.

Dan, getting into the mood of it, said, "No, he's right; this place is probably crawling with ghosts! I'm pretty sure my great-grandfather died here, for starters."

"How'd he die?" Jim asked.

"Suicide, I think," Dan improvised, his creativity in gear. "I think he was this evil guy or something. That's what I hear from my grandmother."

"Man," Charlie said, "your family is so fucked up."

Dan looked at him slowly and Charlie said, "Not that ours isn't."

They explored and made up stories about the kind of ghosts that might inhabit the place until it was time to go home for dinner. As soon as they could bolt down their food, they met on the sidewalk in front of their houses. Charlie had a knapsack of items pilfered from his aunt, which he revealed when out of sight of the house: candles, two cans of baked beans, some hot dogs.

"We have to have supplies to make it our base camp," he said.

Walking back down the road to the old hotel, the boys did their best to appear nonchalant. Charlie and Jim's natural boisterousness was overlaid with their secondary demeanor (the difficult one to maintain), pleasant innocence. As soon as they came to the road up to the hotel they looked around to see that they were not observed, then tore up the incline into the trees.

The sun had already gone behind the bluffs to the west, leaving the sky light blue and the trees dark. Dan found that time of evening mysterious and beautiful, and was reminded of the painting *Empire of Lights* by Rene Magritte, which he had stared at in one of his grandmother's books. He was about to venture explaining it when he realized that he was lost in thought and the other boys had already run into the house.

Within minutes, the boys had put their innate skills for pyromania to work and had a fire going in the large old fireplace in the front hall, candles placed on either side of it on its raised stone hearth. Even though they had just eaten dinner, they sharpened green sticks from outside and roasted hot dogs, just for the novelty of it.

"We should save the cans of beans for later," Charlie said.

"We can build a stockpile," Jim said. "We could get a five-finger discount on stuff in town, pile it up."

"Yeah," Charlie said, "that way, if the Russians drop the Big One, we can come here and hide out while civilization falls around us."

"What," Dan said, "you think we wouldn't get any fallout here?"

"Well, yeah. But we'll escape the chaos that follows." He grinned at the idea, nodding his head gleefully.

It got darker outside as they talked about postapocalyptic scenarios, allowing their imaginations to take off. Charlie and Jim's imaginations were nearly as feverish as Dan's, and Dan found this to be constantly refreshing. He'd never seen anything like it among the local kids, and as the fire and candlelight began to outshine the fading glow outside, the shadows around them growing deeper and wavering in almost-recognizable shapes, their talk got spookier and they lost track of time. One minute, they were discussing turning the place into their stronghold, about saving Aunt Julia and Gramma and Grampa McGregor from the fallout, and then from radioactive zombies.

"Your Grampa would let us shoot his guns then, I bet," Charlie said. "We're young and we have good eyesight."

"Yeah, I bet he would," Dan said, doubting it but not wanting to dispel the illusion.

When they realized how dark it was and how late it had gotten, they hurriedly prepared to leave, hiding the cans of beans and blowing out the candles. This left only the orange light of the coals in the fireplace. They looked at each other silently, their faces strange in the dim glow. When they summoned their courage, they burst from the door of the hotel and into the dark ringing with crickets, sprinting down the dark gravel road with visions of slavering zombies emerging on all sides from the unreadable dark.

They burst onto the road and into the comparative light of the broad night-time sky over the river, but were all a little shaky until they walked into the warm glow of the town, all three acting nonchalant in the light.

In spite of his apparent fear of the Gates brothers, Bobby Dolan, perhaps motivated by boredom and loneliness, came moping around to see if Dan was free. Dan wasn't, having planned to go with Charlie and Jim to the old hotel, but the morose look on Bobby's face gave Dan a twist of guilt. He let Bobby hang around while he finished mowing the lawn, then enlisted his aid to take some boxes of junk that Willy had set aside out to the curb. Dan was hanging around with Bobby on the front steps of the bungalow, in a spell of speechless summer listlessness, when Charlie and Jim showed up.

Dan was embarrassed, and thought that Charlie, at least, would say something cruel to Bobby. To his credit, Charlie remained silent, although his treatment of Bobby was cool. When Bobby was distracted by scratching a design in the dust at his feet with a stick, Charlie and Jim both gave Dan looks: what's *he* doing here? Dan shrugged and spread his hands.

It went without saying that Bobby wasn't cool enough to include in the zombie-fighting brotherhood of the ghost hotel, which left them with the dilemma of what to do with the time before he wandered away. Bobby himself suggested going to the hobby shop in town to look at models, and again, the brothers showed admirable restraint in not ridiculing him. Charlie snorted, and Jim rolled his eyes and sighed, but that was as far as it went.

The problem was to construct an activity that was not too boring, yet not too destructive. In a blaze of inspiration, Dan came up with what he thought was a brilliant compromise.

The game of Hotfoot was something he had devised while similarly bored but with no one around. It involved taking the red plastic gas can from the garage into the back yard, pouring a bit of gas onto the bottom of his sneaker, and setting it alight with a match. The object was to let the gasoline burn off, stamping it out on the lawn before the bottom of the sneaker melted. Dan explained it to the other boys, two thirds of whom were enthusiastic.

Dan smiled, trotting into the garage to get the gas can. When he came back, the other boys were in the middle of the back yard. Charlie was grinning, Jim looking around for possible witnesses, although it was a weekday, the surrounding houses empty. Bobby hung his head.

Dan ignored Bobby and got a book of matches from his pocket, separating it from his pocket knife and a few folded dollars.

"Here's how you do it," Dan said. He held up one foot, turning up the sole of his sneaker, and poured a half-ounce of gasoline on it, then quickly set down the can and lit the gas with a match. The gas alight, his jumped around one foot.

"Hot foot! Hot foot!" Charlie and Jim chanted, laughing. Bobby stood by wide-eyed, his hands flittering uselessly at his sides. Finally, Dan stomped out the flame and spread his hands.

"Lemme try it!" Charlie said. He was less accurate with his pour than Dan, and slopped more gas onto the bottom of his foot, but lit it successfully with his stolen lighter.

"Hot foot, hot foot!" Dan and Jim chanted, laughing hard.

"You guys are nuts!" Bobby piped, edging back a few feet across the yard.

Trying to outdo each other, the boys got more generous in slopping on the gas. Bobby could not be persuaded, no matter what the inducement, to do more than hover nervously by the fence. The boys soon came to the conclusion that the best thing they could do would be to light three shoes at once, one per boy, The Triumvirate of Fire, as Charlie put it.

This was more difficult to execute, as all three boys had to have access to the gas and to flame in quick succession. They formed a triangle and put the gas can in the middle, Dan going first. The gas on the bottom of one shoe, he stood on one leg with his matches ready, as Charlie took the gas can and applied some to his own foot.

"Hurry up!" Dan said. "My gas is going to evaporate!"

"Go ahead and light up!" Charlie said.

"Gimme the gas!" Jim said, taking the can and slopping too much on his foot in his haste.

They all lit the bottom of their feet at more or less the same time. They had intended to stand with their ignited feet triumphantly aloft before stomping the flames out, but things went awry when Jim lit his foot, where the carelessly applied gas had soaked into the fabric of his shoe. Seeing that his shoe was ablaze, he tore it off his foot and threw it, suddenly realizing that the sock underneath was lit as well. Dan's foot was aflame, but the sight of Jim dancing around on one foot with a burning sock was so funny that he lost his balance and stomped his foot to the grass. This ignited some unlit gasoline on the ground, which sputtered a foot or two across the lawn and lit the spilled fuel on the side of the plastic gas can.

All of the boys but Dan scattered. Running across the lawn put out Jim's sock, and he and Charlie nimbly vaulted the fence at the back of the yard. They later agreed that they had never seen a fat kid move so fast; Bobby literally dove over the fence into the next yard and rolled to his feet with surprising agility. The only reason he didn't lose his glasses was that his mother had made him wear them with a strap. He didn't stop running until he was home, where he hid in the basement with an old television set, trying to act nonchalant. He was so nervous at dinner, so petrified at the thought of getting in trouble, that his mother believed him to be sick and sent him to bed.

When the side of the gas can lit, the oily red and black flames seeming to creep slowly up the metal fill tube to the opening, Dan's only thought was a flash of how pissed Willy would be if he blew up the can in the back yard. Dan hesitated only as long as the span of time between his blazing foot causing the ignition and the flames reaching the side of the gas can. He took two steps, snatched up the can by its handle, and ran across the yard to the unused sandbox his grandfather had built for him when his was little. Setting the can in the sandbox, he scooped up handfuls of sand and threw them on the can, putting out the flames. The fire out, an explosion averted, he sat back in the sand and started to laugh.

Charlie and Jim had stopped in the alley and watched what Dan had done. Now they walked slowly back into the yard.

"Holy. Fucking. Shit." Jim shook his head in disbelief.

"You have balls, McGregor," Charlie said. "I'll give you that."

Any flame damage to the back yard was fairly easily concealed with a rake and a hose, although the gas can had to be replaced, as the side of it was scorched black. Fortunately, it was new, and when they bought a replacement at the hardware store, it looked exactly the same. The burned can they concealed and took to the hotel, to be part of their stockpiled provisions.

"You never know when you're going to need some gasoline," Charlie said.

"The events of today prove that much," Jim added, and they all laughed.

The moon landing interrupted their plans to make the old hotel into a stronghold. Everything involved in the mission took far longer than any boy should be expected to tolerate, but it would have been unthinkable to miss anything.

"When I first came to this town as a young man," Willy told the boys as they sat at the bar over ginger ales, their eyes on the black and white screen over the bar, "they still delivered milk by a horse-drawn cart. Can you believe that?"

"No sir," Charlie and Jim said automatically, but Dan thought about it. His grandfather had told him that Neil Armstrong was about his father's age, and had also been in Korea. This grabbed Dan's interest. What might his father have done if the accident hadn't happened? Wasn't he the kind of capable hero that Neil Armstrong was? Might Armstrong and his father have been friends? This line of thought had him staring at a point above the television, the voice of the newscaster a drone from outside his mind.

When the moon landing finally took place, Charlie and Jim were at home with their aunt, and Dan sat the bar with Nubby Schommer. The young man, always friendly and amusing to Dan, had gotten his hair cut short, although his eyes still had their dreamy look, which often turned pinkly glassy if he were in the bar after work. The moon landing appeared to have redirected his mental focus from its usual point of obsession: his brother Stumpy being in Viet Nam.

"Those dudes are gonna be on the moon, man," he said. "Actually *on* the moon. Far fucking out."

Willy sat next to Dan when the landing took place. It was a Wednesday afternoon, but the bar was packed, the focus of dozens of pairs of eyes converging on the gritty image on the television, everyone silent. When the words came, "Houston, Tranquility base here. The Eagle has landed," everyone roared. Willy and Dan hugged, patting each other on the back.

"Helluva world, boy," Willy said. "Helluva world."

In the hours before the actual moonwalk- there could be no longer wait for a boy- Dan went out to look at the moon. It was at the half-moon phase, and would set at 2210 hours; Dan had checked. There were men there, men like his father. It was a place. Mars was a place. His mind drifted off.

He was staring at the moon when Charlie and Dan walked up.

"Hey, spacecase," Charlie said. "Aunt Julia said we could watch at the bar for awhile, see them walk on the moon."

"Why the hell don't they just get out and do it?" Jim said. "I mean, what the fuck? What are they sitting around for? What are they doing, watching themselves on TV? Beating off? Jesus!"

There was only so much waiting they could stand, and were playing pinball when Mae rounded them up to watch Neil Armstrong set foot on another celestial body. His static-hissed transmission came through, and the bar again exploded. Charlie and Jim thrust their fists in the air and ran around the pool table hooting. Dan looked at his grandmother and grandfather embracing, oblivious to the noise of the bar, their eyes locked. He saw there a look that he would only later fully recognize, one of love, of longing, of sadness, of the recognition of slipping time. As a boy, though, he only saw that the adults in his life, those who loved and protected him, were deeply in love with each other. It filled his heart so warmly that he felt on the edge of tears.

Rather than do that, though, he thrust his fists in the air and joined Charlie and Jim, hooting as they chased each other around the bar, out into the street, under the dark August sky where the moon had already set behind the trees and bluffs to the west.

The routine of the boys had been to meet outside, after breakfast, lunch, or dinner. To be indoors was too confining, especially with the river, the marshes, the woods, the bluffs, and finally (and best of all) the old hotel to attract them, as the presences of adults propelled them out the door. It was only on one of the last full days of their stay- the Friday after the moon landing- that Dan took Charlie and Jim into his room for more than a few seconds. The fact that it was pouring rain outside helped them stay in one place.

Dan made little of his artistic talent, but he couldn't avoid having to say something when they finally spent time in his room.

"Man, who did these drawings?" Jim asked, looking around.

"I did," Dan said.

"Coooool."

"They're like some way older kid did them," Charlie said.

"Or, like, a grownup. They *are* cool."

"I made these for you guys," Dan said, holding out two drawings. "Going-away present."

The drawings were of Charlie and Jim holding Thompson submachine guns and blasting away at a circle of ghastly, clutching zombies. The rendering of the brothers was accurate, the attention to the splatter of blood and tissue painstaking.

"Oh, man!" Jim said.

Charlie stared at his for awhile, fascinated. He finally looked up, nodding and smiling. "Fucking excellent, man," he said. "You're a genius."

On the Saturday night before Charlie and Jim were to catch the train back to Greysport, the boys persuaded the adults to let them pitch a tent and camp out on the bluffs on the north side of the island. Mae and Julia were hesitant, due to the boys' ages, but the boys leaned on Willy, who they suspected would encourage them if left to his own devices. The women relented, and set about trying to pack too much food.

"All we need is beans and hotdogs, really, Gramma," Dan said.

"How about some cans of chili instead?" Mae said, kissing Dan on the forehead.

"Even better."

Willy questioned them about the contents of their packs, making sure they had mess kits, matches, sleeping bags. The weather forecast was for clear skies, so they packed light, leaving a puptent behind.

"It got pretty soggy yesterday," Willy said to Dan. "You can still find dry kindling and make a fire, right?"

"Yep."

"Okay. And no falling off the bluff to your doom, right?"

"Right."

"In fact, no doom of any kind."

"Okay," Dan said.

They stopped at the bar on the way to the bluffs; Nubby had said he wanted to give Dan a surprise. At the back door of the bar, the boys waited as Nubby went inside and got a paper bag from his backpack. He handed it to Dan, his face expressionless.

Dan opened it up and looked inside, to find dozens of squat red cylinders equipped with green fuses. "M-80s!" he said in a croak, stopping himself before he shouted.

Charlie and Jim shouldered in to look.

"Holy shit!"

"Excellent!"

"Thanks, Nubby," Dan said, holding out his hand to shake.

Nubby seemed touched and amused by this adult gesture. "You're a cool dude, Dan. Enjoy. But don't let these two maniacs swallow them when lit or any crazy shit like that."

"I'll keep an eye on 'em."

The gift of a bag of M-80s was utterly irresistible to the boys, who tried to remain calm and stuck to the plan of at least walking out of town with their backpacks before blowing any off, although a few trash cans and mailboxes along the way presented nearly irresistible targets. They went up past the cemetery to where the hill road led up the bluff. There they stashed their packs in some heavy underbrush, and, instead of going up to the top, went down a path to a marshy area at the base of the bluff. Once there, they broke out the M-80s.

Charlie made sure that he was the first to try them out. Holding the explosive in his right hand, he cocked his arm backwards in a pitching position, and said over his shoulder to Dan, "Light me."

Dan struck a match and held it to the fuse, which lit and hissed sparks. Dan waited a second- Jim's eyes were wide- and tossed the M-80. It hit the water next to some cattails and exploded in a geyser of water, black marsh mud, and shreds of reed.

"Ho, baby!"

"Yeah!"

"Gimme one!"

"No, me!"

"He gave them to me," Dan said, holding the bag up next to his shoulder. "Everyone gets an equal amount."

When they had all had a few turns, they moved through the marsh blowing things up in increasingly imaginative ways, the most gratifying being those which sent up water, mud, or debris. The sound of the detonations themselves were always amusing.

"These'd be great with pumpkins," Jim pointed out. "Blow the shit out of 'em."

When they realized that they had gone through a considerable amount of their stash, they had to force themselves to desist.

"Just one more," Charlie said, pointing to a dead carp by the water. He took a final M-80 and stuck in the mouth of the carp, leaving enough fuse sticking out that he could light it. He did so, and ran back to where the other boys waited among some reeds. At first they thought the fuse had gone out, Charlie making a move to investigate, when it exploded, blowing chunks of the carp corpse into the air and plopping into the reeds and water, leaving the tattered back third of the fish next to the smoking hole in the bank.

"Ohohohoho, man!"

"Did you see that?"

"Just one more."

"No way," Dan said, rolling up the top of the paper bag with finality. "We've got to save some, and we already went through, like, half. You don't know what else we might need them for."

They walked through the marsh grass to the base of the bluff and up the path to the top, the marsh and the river getting farther and farther below them. Once at the top, Dan showed them a clearing under some oak trees where they could make a fire and have room for their sleeping bags.

Dan started a blaze with little difficulty, and soon they were cooking some chili, listening to the wind in the trees and watching boats on the river as the light slowly faded. Charlie fished out some cans of pop from his pack and handed them around.

Once the chili was eaten and the pop consumed, boredom soon began to set in. In the glow of the fire, the undersides of the leaves illuminated against the darkening sky, the boys seemed to have run out of conversation. Dan was perfectly content to sit there and look out at the night, or read a book by the firelight, but this obviously wouldn't sit with Charlie.

"Let's go over to the hotel," he said. "It's a perfect night for it."

"Ah, man," Dan said. "I'm all comfortable."

Jim was up for it. "Let's go! It'll be cool! We can play hide-and-seek in the dark rooms or something."

"Hide and seek?" Charlie said, regarding his brother disgustedly. "What a dork."

"Fuck you," Jim said, and went for him. In the wrestling match which ensued, Dan crouched like a referee between the boys and the fire or the edge of the bluff. When Charlie pinned Jim- as almost always happened- the boys lay there, laughing and panting.

"Fucker," Jim gasped.

"So," Charlie said when he caught his breath. "Let's go to the hotel."

"Fine," Dan said, imagining them being tired enough to sleep, rather than roll off the bluff or set themselves ablaze, when they got back.

"Bring the M-80s," Charlie said, stuffing them in Dan's pack and handing it to him.

"What for?" Dan said.

"Better to have them and not need them than need them and not have them. That's what your grandfather always says, right?"

Dan shrugged and brought them.

They walked slowly down the path in the dark, Dan leading the way. The cemetery was dark and sufficiently spooky, but they had to avoid the lights of the town so as not to be seen by adults, it being late enough that their presence might arouse suspicion. A car sat in the parking lot by the new boathouse, and they had to duck below the river bank to avoid being caught in its headlights. All of it got them in the right mood.

"We're spies," Dan said. "We're going to blow up a Nazi installation."

"Check!" Charlie said.

"Fucking Nazis," said Jim.

Clouds covered the moon and the road was dark, the river to their left and the bluffs hulking to their right. The overgrown road up to the hotel might have escaped their notice if they hadn't known where it was, but they darted into its shadows as a car drove south from the town. They hung back in the shadows until the car whooshed by.

Nearing the top of the bluff and the hotel, they could faintly hear music playing. As they got closer, the music got louder. They slipped into the dark clearing and could see that a couple of muscle cars- a GTO and a Malibu SS were parked in front of the hotel- and that lantern light came from inside.

"Fucking seniors," Dan said. It made him angry that anyone would be here.

"Their music sucks, too," Jim said. "Fucking hate that country shit."

Howling and the sound of breaking bottles came from inside the hotel. Voices blended with the din from the portable radio, and although the words were mostly unintelligible, it was obvious the people inside the hotel were drunk.

"Let's get closer," Charlie said. "It's light in there and dark out here. The can't see us."

Crouching down, they crept through the grass, getting close enough that they could see into the big windows of the hall at the front of the hotel. Inside, they could see a Coleman lantern on the mantelpiece of the fireplace- the boys' candles standing unnoticed nearby- along with assorted bottles of booze. Open cases of beer stood ready, and the young men, local would-be hoodlums, standing with their backs to the windows also held beers, and cigarettes, in their hands. Dan recognized most of them, and knew that Nubby was acquainted with them but not their friend, as they were the type who might have wanted to beat Nubby up for being a hippie were it not for the fact that none of them could have taken him in a fair fight. There were at least six of the young men standing in a semicircle around the fireplace, chanting at someone who could not be seen, exhorting them. It didn't make sense; Dan wanted to see more.

One of the young men turned around to get another beer from an open case. He was laughing as he did so, saying, quite audibly through a missing window pane, "Yeah! Pull that train, Donna!"

As he bent for the beer, the boys caught a glimpse through the gap in the young men. There they could see, just for a moment, that a chubby young woman was bent over with her hands on the hearth of the fireplace. She had her skirt hiked up over her hips and her panties down around her knees. She grunted as one of the young hoods thrust into her from behind.

"That the best you can do?" she said over her shoulder in a surprisingly gravelly voice.

The young man reaching into the case retrieved his beer and stood back up, laughing.

Jim snorted laughter. Charlie grabbed Dan's forearm and mouthed What the fuck?

Dan was frozen, torn by fascination at witnessing a glimpse of sex, and by the anger he felt at this place being desecrated. He motioned with his hands for the other boys to crouch in the shadows beneath the window.

"I'm going to throw some M-80s in there," he whispered.

"No, no, no, no," Charlie hissed back. "Let's watch!"

"I'm doing it."

One of the hoods inside said, "I'm gonna fuck her in the ass."

"What, are you a fag?" said the hood of the train-pulling comment.

"No, I just like ass," Ass Fucker said. "If I was a fag, I'd fuck *you*, and not have to wait."

"Homo," Train Puller said.

"You're the homo," Ass Fucker said, drinking his beer.

Jim slowly sank to the ground trying to stifle his laughter. "Shut up!" Charlie croaked, punching his brother in the arm. "Let's just watch a bit," he said to Dan.

"Gimme your lighter," Dan said, fishing through his pack for some M-80s.

"Okay, okay! After we watch for a bit!"

Jim, his laughter tentatively in check, stood up, a look of bliss on his face; he could not believe his luck.

Things came to their conclusion with the hood who had been boning Donna apparently finished his task.

"Who's next?" Donna said in a perfunctory tone.

"Me," said Ass Fucker.

"Here we go," Donna said. "Something I can feel."

Jim held his hand over his mouth to stifle laughter, but some escaped in a snort. The boys tensed and crouched, ready to run. Train Puller straightened a bit, half-turned toward the windows. Dan held the other boys' forearms.

"Ah!" Donna's raspy voice was suddenly louder. "That's more like it! Unh!"

The hoods inside cheered, and Train Puller turned back to watch over the shoulders of those in front of him.

"Gimme the fucking lighter," Dan said.

"Oh, please!" Jim wheezed at Dan.

"Fork it over," Dan said.

"Okay," Charlie said, "but you owe us."

As cheering came from inside the hotel, Dan took four of the M-80s from his pack and twisted the ends of their fuses together, then slipped the pack back on.

"They're going to expect us to run down the drive," he said, "so take off over there"-pointing in the direction opposite the drive to the darkness under the trees across the overgrown lawn- "and duck down. Stay down until they leave."

He held out his hand for the lighter, which Charlie surrendered with a look of disgust and resignation. Dan motioned with his head the direction in which they were supposed to run, raising his eyebrows to make sure he was understood. The other boys nodded grudgingly.

Dan slipped around to the big front doors of the hotel, finding the left one ajar. Looking inside, he could see things from a different angle, see that Ass Fucker was going at it with abandon and Donna was bracing herself with her hands against the stone of the fireplace, grunting. He watched for a moment, surrounded by anger, fascination, and mirth, then clicked open the lighter and flicked it, putting the flame to the fuses of the M-80s. When they lit, he tossed them underhand into the large room and took off, sprinting back around the front of the hotel.

The M-80s went off as he drew next to Charlie and Jim. The four detonations were shockingly loud in the reverberant hall. Screams and shouts followed. Donna shrieked continuously, and one of the hoods- Ass Fucker, it sounded like- screamed, "She shat on me! She shat on me!"

They had to yank Jim away from the window, breaking his spell, but not before Train Puller turned toward them. His head jerked forward and his eyes went wide. "Kids!" he shouted.

"What!"

"Two of 'em, maybe three. Two blond ones, anyway!"

"Where!"

"Out front!"

"She fucking shat on me, man!" Ass Fucker continued hysterically.

"Let's get the little fuckers!"

Dan led the way, zigging towards the driveway- in case Charlie and Jim's hair was visible- and zagging back through the long grass and into the trees. They flattened themselves in the undergrowth and watched as best they could, keeping perfectly still, their hearts hammering.

The hoods piled out the front door of the hotel. Two got behind the wheels of the muscle cars and started them up, revving their engines.

"Come on!"

Donna and Assfucker were the last to come out.

"You shat on me, goddammit!" Assfucker was saying as he buckled himself up.

"Well, I guess that's what they mean when they say something scared the shit out of you," Donna sneered. "Wash it off later and quit whining. And I drink free for a couple of weeks now, dumbass."

"Shat on me. Damn!"

"Let's go!" the driver said, blasting his horn.

In their histrionic anger, not to mention the sudden need to demonstrate their automotive virility, the drivers of both cars revved their engines and patched out, as much as they could on the overgrown lawn, throwing grass and soil and gravel into the air. The GTO ran into the right rear quarter panel of the Malibu, and everything came to a halt.

The boys watched as best they could from the cover of the trees and long grass. Jim was laughing so hard, and trying to smother it, that Charlie, snorting enough that he shot some snot on his upper lip, punched him in the back of the head. Dan put a hand on Charlie's and Jim's shoulders in an attempt to calm them both down, but was giggling silently himself.

The drivers of the cars screamed at each other, the sound of the engines covering most of their mutual threats. The boys watched the drivers pushing each other in the headlights. Charlie pointed to Assfucker taking the opportunity to wash his dick with a beer, while Donna, in her customary skirt-up-panties-down position, squatted in the long grass.

After some further shouting, everyone piled in, and the drivers of the two muscle cars peeled off, as much as possible, down the tree-clustered old road.

The boys waited until they could hear crickets. Then they started laughing out loud.

"Somebody actually shat on somebody," Jim said, gasping for breath. "I can't wait to tell people at home about this."

"What the fuck," Charlie said. "That was sosososososo great. Fuck! Nobody will believe this shit, man! Not where *we* live. Nobody!"

Dan's laughter trailed off and he said, "Hey. They left all their shit. Think of that?"

Charlie and Jim looked at each other, their eyes widening.

"Man, you're fucking smart," Jim said. "But we can't do it. They'll be right back."

"Not that soon," Charlie said. "They're looking for us, but not here."

The lantern was still lit on the mantelpiece, and Dan grabbed it, holding it out. He marshaled the boys to take the bottles of liquor and put them in the empty spaces of the cases of beer, then showed them out the back, along past the old kitchen, and up into the dark woods leading up to the bluff, carrying a case, as he had been shown by Bob Two Bears, on his shoulder.

"Come on!" he said. "Those fuckers'll be back!"

They put the cases of beer and the bottles of booze in a space amongst the rocks at the base of the bluff. They covered their treasure with leaves and vines, anything available. Charlie looked at the stash and said, "We can save this stuff. Most of it. But let's take some back with us. Let's get drunk."

"How much should we take?" Jim said, looking down in the direction of the drive.

"I don't know," Charlie said, looking at Dan.

"Guys at my grampa's bar drink a lot," he said, "but I think they're pretty good at it. Takes practice. I think if we take, like, four apiece, that oughta do it."

"Let's take some whiskey!" Charlie said.

"You ever taste whiskey?" Dan said. "It's like fucking gasoline. Besides, it's really strong. You'll fall off the bluff. To your doom."

"Come on," Charlie said. "We're going to do it eventually anyway. Bring a bottle of the whiskey, and if we don't like it, we'll chuck it off the bluff."

"And we'll probably need more beers," Jim said. "I've seen our dad's grad students drink, and they do more than four."

Being around his grandfather's bar so much, Dan had seen enough drunk people that the idea of getting drunk himself held little mystery to him. The Gates brothers' yearning for it fueled his own, though. He not only relented, but became enthusiastic.

"Okay," he said. "Whiskey's like gasoline, but you chase it with beer. I see guys do it all the time."

"I may not have mentioned this recently," Charlie said, "but you have the coolest life in the world."

They stuffed the pack with beer and a bottle of whiskey. Dan shouldered it. They stopped long enough, Charlie and Jim anxiously outside, for Dan to slip into the doors of the old building and put the lantern exactly back where he'd found it. Charlie laughed at that, backhanding his brother's arm.

At the bottom of the gravel drive, they stood next to the undergrowth, waiting for a car to pass. They were just ready to go across the road to the safety of the river bank when they saw two cars heading down from town.

"It's those dudes!" Charlie yelped.

"And Donna!" Jim added.

With the slipperiness of boys, they darted into the brush, just as the cars turned in and headed up the drive, spitting gravel, country music blaring on the radio. The sound faded as the cars drove up the bluff.

"Shit!" Dan said. "Ditch!"

They ran across the road and down the short slope to the river bank. Keeping themselves concealed, ducking whenever a car passed, they made their way back to the bluff, going past the pitch-black cemetery and up the path to their campsite. The pack was heavy, but Dan said nothing. These were the best friends he'd ever had. He soon had the fire blazing again, and the boys opened their first beers together with the opener on his pocket knife.

"Ya gotta clink 'em together," Dan said. "Like this. Cheers!"

"Cheers!" the other boys said.

They tried to act mature and sophisticated, then tried to act drunk.

"I don't think I'm actually, really drunk," Dan said.

"Let's have some more beers, then," Charlie said.

Before long, they summoned up the nerve to drink some whiskey. Charlie was first, then Dan, then Jim. Charlie gulped it, bubbles going up into the bottle. He handed the bottle immediately to Dan, then drank from his beer.

"My theory is," Charlie gasped, "that if you don't let the whiskey oxidize in your mouth, you won't taste it so much."

This made sense to Dan and Jim, who followed suit.

Before long, the boys were actually, really drunk, laughing around the fire.

"I think I was pretending I was drunk before," Jim said. "Now I really am. You think that Donna would let me do it with her if I gave her a bunch of beer and whiskey?" Charlie and Dan roared.

"You might have to do it in her butt," Dan laughed, and took a drink from his beer.

"Something I can *feel*," Charlie grated in a low voice, and they fell over each other, howling like young wolves around the campfire.

Charlie and Jim were gone not long after that night. It was a good thing, too, because a short time later, at the end of August, Dan came into the bar for a hamburger and a ginger ale and found Donna, Trainpuller, and two other hoods sitting in a booth. He almost tripped when he saw them, but was able to summon the presence of mind to appear casual. He thought that he might be recognized at any moment, but began to relax when nothing happened, feeling happy about the fact that his hair was dark rather than a nearly white blonde.

Bob Two Bears had his hamburger on the grill, giving him a ginger ale with a maraschino cherry and an orange slice in it, a little extra thing he always did for Dan.

"Hey, do me a favor, buddy," Bob said to him, "take this burger and fries over to those guys in the booth. The one with the chunky chick smoking a cigarette." He meant Trainpuller and Donna, of course. The hair on Dan's neck stood up.

"Okay," Dan said, taking the plastic baskets of food over to the booth, trying to breathe slowly and keep a neutral look on his face. "Who's got the burger and fries?"

"I got the burger," Trainpuller said, not even giving Dan a second glance.

"The fries are for me," Donna said, taking a long drag from her cigarette before crushing it out in an ashtray. The raspy sound of her voice almost made Dan laugh out loud. "Aren't you a good little worker," she said, and Dan snorted.

"What's so funny, kid?" Trainpuller said, smiling a little.

"A joke I heard," Dan improvised.

"What's the joke?"

"It's...I don't know."

"No, go ahead. We're listening."

The only thing he could think of was one of his grandfather's favorite jokes, one he even remembered his dad laughing about. "Two guys are walking down the street," Dan said, "and they come upon a dog licking his, you know, his dick. The first guy says, 'I wish I could do that.' Second guy says, 'You'd better pet him first.'"

The hoods at the table were silent for a few seconds, then burst into laughter. Donna laughed so hard she started to choke, and the hood next to her had to slap her on the back.

"Better pet him first," one of the hoods repeated. "Shit."

"Give the kid a tip," Donna said, gasping for breath.

Dan walked away with a dollar in his pocket. He couldn't wait to write to Charlie and Jim about it.

To Willy, a good deal of Dan's life was opaque. Most of the summer, he was out the door as soon as he could eat breakfast, just like Gordon and Chief. He came home or to the bar most days for lunch- unless he had packed something and was off in the woods and marshes- and came home for dinner as late as he could push it. Now that it was October and he was back in school, his days remained cloaked in the same opacity, although a good amount of his activities took place at school. Willy wished he could sit up among the trees on the bluff behind the school and watch through the windows with binoculars, or stand unobserved on the steel bridge that crossed from the upper floor of the school to the leaf-littered sidewalk that led along the base of the bluff. He could imagine what Dan did there during the day, but had no detailed knowledge. He imagined the boy alternating between paying attention when interested, and gazing off into space with his brow slightly furrowed, daydreaming the way he often did at home or when they were out on the river.

He mentioned these thoughts to Mae. "I think he's fine," Mae said. "He comes home and seems happy to be with us. Gordon and Chief used to squirm a bit if I

332

hugged and kissed them, but he sort of melts into it. I think he needs it more. If he feels loved and protected, we're doing our job."

The conversational way Mae spoke of their departed sons spilled a sad peace into Willy's chest. He knew that she had healed as much as she could, and that the boy lit her up when he came near.

Emilio had his thoughts on the matter. "I think about that all the time," he said. "I always did, wondered about what happened to them during their day. When I could watch them asleep at night, I knew, and I was quiet in here-" he tapped his chest- "but at other times, who knows? Think of how old Katita is, and I still worry about her every day."

"When was the last time you talked to her?"

"April," Emilio said, and Willy could see the weariness of worry in the wrinkles around his eyes.

Mae insisted they talk to Dan's teacher, Mrs. Chilton, and the principal, Mr. Baumeister. Willy sighed and rolled his eyes at this; Baumeister's foppishness struck Willy as somewhat annoying, out of context as it was in a small river town, but it was more Willy's suspicion that Baumeister was a dilettante in education and a blowhard to boot. He went to the meeting anyway, not wanting to fall short in his grandfatherly duties.

"We put a great deal of emphasis on education here at Bluffside," Baumeister said from behind the protection of his grandiose desk.

That's good, you're running a school, Willy thought, and caught the subtle look from Mae which conveyed the fact that she knew what he was thinking.

"Dan gets good grades," Willy said, "we'd just like to know how he is in class, what he's like. He's had a bit of a tough time, and we'd like to know if there's anything we should be concerned about."

"Well, he never gets sent to my office!" Baumeister said with a hearty laugh. Willy showed his teeth in as polite a way as he could manage, but was apparently unconvincing, and the mirth left Baumeister's face.

"Really, though," the principal said, "his day-to-day behavior is not precisely my bailiwick. You'd have to ask Mrs. Chilton."

Bailiwick, thought Willy. Not his bailiwick. Willy wondered what his old prison warden, Dexter Ver Voort, was up to after a quarter century, and if he'd be ready for a new job. He was sure the high schoolers would agree that the positions were similar, and there was no question that Ver Voort would be good at it.

Mrs. Chilton, unlike the principal, had an aura of competence and calm. "Dan's an unusual young man," she said, thinking about it. "At first I thought he was going to be a problem, always doodling in a notebook and appearing not to pay attention. When I made him put the notebook in his desk and keep his focus on me, it wasn't long his eyes would seem to glaze over and, although they were pointed at the front of the room, they weren't looking at me."

"He does that a lot," Willy said. "He's sort of looking back into his own head, with his eyes pointed outwards."

Mrs. Chilton laughed. "Yes, exactly."

"He gets that from his father, and from Willy," Mae said. "His father was an artist, and Willy's a poet."

"A poet!" Baumeister said. "Well!"

Willy made a self-deprecating grimace and waggled his hand, giving Mae a dirty look.

"Well, you are," she said.

"So," Willy said, changing the subject, "you found that if you let him scribble away, he's actually paying better attention."

"That's it! And to call what he does 'doodles' is a little dismissive. He's by far the best I've ever seen for a boy his age. Better than any I've seen in high school, for that matter! We really don't know what to do with him in that regard."

"Quite the little wunderkind!" Baumeister said. "We have plans in place to improve our art program here at Bluffside." The carefully neutral look on Mrs. Chilton's face told Willy that this was bullshit.

Mae said, "We have him taking lessons from a friend of ours, Julia Hannah, when we can get him to go. She's not quite sure what to do with him either."

They talked a bit longer. When Mae's concerns had been allayed, they left as soon as was polite.

"I'd love to read some of your work!" Baumeister said to Willy with a comradely pat on the back.

"Thanks. That's something to think about," Willy said, and left it at that.

As much as Mae doted on Dan, the boy was Willy's little buddy. In the years since his father's death, Dan had adapted to life on the river, and made little mention of the days before, either living in Greysport or the time up north. The latter, in fact, he never mentioned at all, although a reference to Greysport occasionally came out in connection to another subject.

They took the old boat upriver one day, and were having a little picnic on the bow- ham and cheese sandwiches, apples, and a quart of milk- when Willy noticed the familiar pensive look come across the boy's face. He sometimes got a short deflection when he asked the question, but occasionally the boy would open up, and Willy would get a glimpse into his mind.

"What are you thinking about?" Willy asked tirelessly.

Dan munched his sandwich for a bit, swallowed, and took a drink of milk from a tin cup.

"My dad," he said, his eyes distant. "He used to take me down to the lake a lot."

The boy took another bite of his sandwich. Willy waited to see if he continued, but Dan just watched a flock of Canada geese flying north up the river.

"So, what about the lake?" Willy persisted.

"Oh." Dan said, turning his blue eyes on Willy. "Well. It's really beautiful. It's huge, you know. My dad said it was an inland sea."

Willy kept himself from grinning. "I am aware of that."

"And it's beautiful," Dan said. "This is beautiful, but that's another kind of beautiful. It's kind of...."

Willy waited for a moment and said, "Majestic?"

Dan looked at him.

"Grand," Willy said, holding his hands out and tilting his head back towards the sky. "August. Lofty. Noble. Above the usual."

Dan thought about it.

"Yeah," he said. "Majestic."

"Well," Willy said. "You can move back there. Here's what you do. You get through high school, and we'll get you into college back in Greysport. And *finish* college, too. Your dad didn't. I didn't. But *you* finish. Then you can live by the lake. You can sit on the beach and paint the waves coming in, paint storms over the huge water. How about that?"

"Could I paint shipwrecks? There are hundreds of shipwrecks out there."

"You bet. You'd probably paint the best shipwrecks ever."

Dan took another bite of his sandwich. After a few moments, he said, "Will you come and live with me?"

Willy's throat tightened. He coughed. "Sure," he said, tapping the boy's arm with his knuckles.

Mae wanted to help the boy with his costume for Halloween, but he said he already had a plan. She pestered him about it, but he seemed to have his mind made up. On a sunny Saturday afternoon when Dan was obviously at loose ends, they drove up the bluffs into the hills around Mt. Pleasant in search of pumpkins. The land was brilliant with orange, yellow, and red, with the darker gem tones of huge oaks blended in, dried cornstalks the color of brass in the fields, all under a deep blue sky.

Dan sat on the bench seat of the pickup between Willy and Mae.

"Majestic," he said, smiling.

"Yep," Willy said, tousling his hair. "Majestic."

They found a stand selling pumpkins, honey, apples, and cider. It stood brilliant in the angled rays of yellow sunlight coming through the changing trees; the apples gleamed, the jars of honey and jugs of cider were illuminated, looking like huge samples of polished amber. Willy found Dan staring at them, and touched the boy on the shoulder, snapping him out of his trance.

They got some of everything, putting the purchases in crates in the back of the pickup. Willy let the boy ride in the back on the way home, ostensibly so he could keep the crates from sliding around too much. At one point he had a start when he glanced in the rearview mirror and saw that the bed of the truck was empty. When he turned around to look over his shoulder, he found the boy lying sprawled like an asterisk in the back, bracing the crates with his feet and squinting up at the sky with a look of rapture on his face. Willy tapped Mae, who turned around and smiled at the sight of him.

A storm came in that afternoon, and it got gloomy outside. They spent the time in the kitchen listening to the radio, Willy and Dan carving pumpkins while Mae made pumpkin pie and prepared a Canada goose for dinner. With his typical aplomb, Dan (who had come up with the idea of using old jigsaw blades as tools) carved jack-o-lanterns which were actually rather disturbing. Willy thought his attempts were almost embarrassingly simple by comparison, and he laughed out loud about it.

"I'm not kidding, son," Willy said, "you've got talent."

Dan smiled and waggled his eyebrows.

The feeling of levity inspired Willy. He remembered making Gordon and Chief laugh when they were kids, and decided to try the ancient joke on Dan.

335

"Pull my finger," he said, holding out a gnarled, pumpkin-slick digit. Dan pulled it, and Willy farted at length.

Dan pealed laughter, and Mae said sharply, "Willy! Not in the house! Jesus! You men!"

Dan settled down after awhile, but giggled intermittently while carving a pumpkin in the bright kitchen, thunder rolling overhead.

On Halloween, they lit the jack-o-lanterns on the porch and got ready for the neighborhood kids. They had no idea what Dan's costume would be; he'd been mysterious about it. As it got dark out, he locked himself in the bathroom and got ready. Willy and Mae sat in the living room watching television, taking turns answering the door for younger kids out early.

The heard the bathroom door open in the hallway, the light from the fixture over the sink spilling out. They heard the click of the switch, and the light went out, leaving the hallway dark.

"Ready?" came Dan's voice from the darkened hall.

"Ready!" they said simultaneously.

Dan leapt into the arch of the doorway. Dressed in black jeans and t-shirt, he wore a black fright wig and had green skin.

Green. Skin.

His mouth was filled with large red fangs, from which dripped what appeared to be blood. He had on green latex monster feet over his sneakers, completing the costume.

"Omigod!" Mae said in a gasp.

"Holy shit," Willy said, shaking his head and laughing.

"Like it?" Dan said, his speech altered by the fangs.

"It's horrible," Willy said. "I love it."

"What did you do to your skin?" Mae asked.

"Food coloring."

"Oh, my. How about that blood?"

"Also food coloring." He took out a small vial of it and dripped some drops in his mouth. He grinned and rivulets or red ran down his neck.

"Don't get any on the carpet," Mae said. "In fact, you'd better go out through the kitchen."

He set off into the dark to meet a group of friends, just as the doorbell rang again. They held out the bowl of treats for the last of the young children who would come that night, complimenting them on their costumes.

Sitting on the couch, they watched the television, holding hands. Mae put her head on Willy's shoulder. Soon she was asleep.

He let her doze like that for awhile, leaning forward to gaze on her face, the fine lines, the soft lips, the sweetness there. Thinking she would be more comfortable in bed, he gently roused her and took her into the bedroom, helping her off with her clothes and tucking her in.

Unable to sleep, he wandered down to the bar, unobtrusively looking in the window to see how the annual party was going. Bob was behind the bar, dressed so accurately as Sitting Bull that Willy almost did a doubletake.

He ambled off, occasionally seeing the forms of older children darting from the shadows, sometimes touched by the glow of a streetlamp through thinning red and orange leaves. Laughter came from random, invisible spots in the dark. At one point he heard the thump of eggs on siding, at another the sound of pumpkins tossed into the street.

Eventually, he found himself down by the river, which was almost entirely covered by the slow congealing of a heavy fog. After some time, he turned around and walked back home. Dan was asleep on the couch, the frightwig and fangs gone. It was obvious that the boy had tried to get the green dye off his skin, with little success. Willy roused him and took him into the bathroom, where they got most of the dye off- with the exception of a dozen green-tinted blackheads- with the cold cream Mae had left there for that purpose.

The wheel turned, a year passed. It was a soggy day in mid-November when they saw Ingrid again.

For awhile, weather had gotten cold and windy, and the trees had lost most of their leaves. It had then gotten unusually warm and rained for two days, and the air smelled of sodden leaves and coming rain. Willy and Dan were raking up the soggy mats of decaying leaves in the back yard while Mae made lunch; Dan was promised that he could take off after he had helped with this chore and eaten. They worked mostly in silence, and Willy only occasionally had to remind him not to daydream. The only sounds were the tines of the rakes on the lawn, the croaking of crows, and occasional honking and wingbeats of northbound geese.

Mae came to the back door, and Willy thought she was there to call them for lunch until he looked at her face and saw the fear and anger there. He turned and looked at the boy, who was facing the rear of the yard, raking back in the corner around the old sandbox. Willy narrowed his eyes and spread his hands. Mae nodded to the front yard.

As they walked down the driveway, Mae said quietly, "Ingrid's in the front yard. With some guy."

"What?"

"I happened to look out the window," Mae said, white with anger. "She went to Julia's by mistake. Didn't even remember the right house."

"It's okay. We'll take care of it."

They walked to the steps of the front porch, and there in the middle of the freshly raked front yard stood Ingrid. She was thin but puffy-faced, with circles under her eyes, and her clothing was more humble than she once would have tolerated. Next to her stood a large man with a buzz cut, wearing khaki work clothes and a quilted black nylon jacket. His arms were crossed and he looked displeased.

"Oh, here they are!" Ingrid said to the man. "We finally found you!"

"Ingrid," Willy said, nodding once.

"What do you want?" Mae said.

"Well, I thought it would be nice to have a little reunion with my son and his grandparents-"

"A reunion?" Mae spat. "You dissolve when Gordon dies- I can understand that- but you just fade out of that poor boy's life, you don't even call for all this time, and you want a re*union*?"

Ingrid's smile faltered, and the big man beside her drew himself up. "He's my son, after all-"

"You gave him up. You left him here. He's happy now, at least as happy as he can be, and you're going to leave him alone."

"Told you this would happen," the big man said.

"Shut up, Mike," Ingrid said. "Look, Mae. He's my son."

"Not any more he's not. You gave up that right."

"Not legally," Ingrid said.

"You little bitch," Mae said.

Shit, Willy thought. He and Mike sized each other up.

Ingrid's gaze shifted. She leaned forward and put her palms on her knees. "Well, there's Danny!" she said sweetly. "There's my young man! It's your mom!"

Willy and Mae turned around.

Dan stood there with a rake in his hand, his eyes narrowed.

"Come give your mommy a hug, Danny."

Dan looked at Willy, at Mae, and then at Ingrid. He didn't move.

"Come on, Danny," Ingrid pleaded. "Come and give mommy a hug. And shake hands with Mike, here. He's going to be your new dad."

Dan's eyes went wide. He threw down the rake and ran down the driveway, across the back yard, and jumped over the fence.

"You're coming with us eventually, kid!" Mike called after him. Dan was gone.

"Great!" Ingrid said, throwing up her hands. "That's just great."

"You get out of here," Mae said. "Get out of here and don't come back."

"Fuck you, Mae," Ingrid said. "He's my kid and he's coming with me."

"Better leave," Willy yelled to Mike, who gave him a look which said he knew Willy, knew all about him, and he wasn't done with him.

"We'll be back with the sheriff!" Ingrid called over her shoulder.

"I'll kill you!" Mae screamed. "And my husband is going to kill your fat fucking boyfriend!"

"Back with the sheriff!" Ingrid called in a singsong before getting into the car.

Mae screamed as they drove away.

In the end, there was nothing they could do. Willy talked to a friend at the Sheriff's Department (the same man who had dealt with the calf-boning incident), who told him that, although they could fight it in court, Ingrid was the surviving parent and had legal custody of the boy.

"There's nothing you can do at the moment," the deputy to Willy. "You have to hand him over. Talk to a lawyer, I guess."

"We have."

"Well, I don't know what to tell you. He's got to go. Things could get bad for you legally if he doesn't. Sorry, but there's nothing else I can do."

It was grim and silent in the bungalow as they readied Dan's things. They packed a suitcase for him, and put a few books and his essential art supplies in a box, promising to mail the rest later, once he sent them an address.

"I don't want to go," he had whispered when they had sat him at the kitchen table and told him. "Please don't make me go." He was trying not to cry, being almost twelve years old, but his chin quivered and he kept his eyes on the table.

"You have to, Dan," Willy said. "There's nothing we can do about it."

"For now," Mae said. "For now. Okay? Now look at me. Look at me, Dan." She tipped his chin up gently with her fingers and he looked her in the eye. "You belong here. We're going to fight for you. Understand? You just be patient and we'll start working on it, okay? Okay, Dan?"

"Okay," he said finally, and dropped his eyes again.

She hugged him for a long time, pausing only to kiss him repeatedly on his cheeks. Willy laid his hand on the boy's head and watched.

When they walked him out of the house, a Sheriff's deputy was parked behind Ingrid and Mike's car. Mike sat behind the wheel, facing away, but Ingrid stood by the open passenger side door. She smiled primly at Dan.

"No," Dan whispered.

The deputy walked over to Ingrid and talked to her, then turned and said, "Okay, folks, we should probably move this along." Willy noted the young man's look of embarrassment.

Mae smiled at Dan and kissed him on the forehead. "I hardly have to bend down to do that anymore. You're getting so big."

"No. Please," Dan said.

"You have to, son," Willy said. "We'll be working on it." He took the suitcase and the box and walked over to the car.

"Mike!" Ingrid said. "Open the trunk, Mike."

Mike slowly got out of the car and walked back to the trunk, unlocking and opening it. He glowered at Willy.

Mae hugged the boy while the deputy glanced at his watch. Willy patted him on the shoulder and said, "We'll talk to you soon, son."

Dan stood staring at the car. He took a deep breath, blew it out between his lips, and walked across the lawn. He stopped as though he were about to turn around, then simply got in the back seat of the car and shut the door. Mike started the car and drove away. Mae waved, but Dan sat staring straight ahead. Soon the car was out of sight.

The deputy apologized to both of them.

"Sometimes I hate this job," he said.

"There's nothing you could do," Mae said, and turned to walk back to the house.

"Well, that's that," Mae said once they were inside.

"We'll fight it," Willy told her. "Just like you said."

"I don't think I'll ever see him again." She sobbed once, sharply, but stiffened, shaking her head minutely. "I'm going to make some tea," she said.

Not knowing what to do with himself, Willy wandered out into the back yard and picked up his rake. He stared at the leaf pile Dan had been working on for a moment, then continued the task, although he only seemed to see what he was doing in his peripheral vision.

Their lawyer told them that it would be difficult to get custody of Dan if the mother was opposed to it, although if they could get her to sign the proper papers for termination of parental rights, it was not impossible.

"We don't even know where she is," Willy said. "How can we start any proceedings if we don't know where she is?"

The lawyer pursed his lips and nodded. "We'll get everything ready that we can. Then we'll have to wait for them to surface."

"What a fucking mess," Willy said.

"Hang in there," the attorney said. "We'll get him back."

Yeah, Willy thought, hang in there. He supposed he could always hang himself in the basement; that'd be hanging in there. Too ugly, though; Mae would be the one to find him, and he couldn't have that; he wanted her years to be as happy as he could make them. Nor could he depart if there was anything he could do to save the boy. If there was the least chance he could do anything to help that poor kid, set him on the right track, he was obligated to do it. If the rest of his own life didn't matter to him, he knew it mattered to the boy, and to Mae.

Bob, who missed the boy a great deal himself, seemed to understand. They sat at the bar on a slow afternoon when the lunch rush was over, Willy pretending to watch the television.

Bob eyed Willy for a while and said, "Obligation."

"Huh?" Willy said.

"Obligation. Sometimes that's the only thing that keeps a man going."

Willy snorted and shook his head. "Got that shit right."

That night Willy avoided going home. At first he felt cowardly about it, knowing that he couldn't bear, just this one time, seeing the look on Mae's face, or seeing the boys' bedrooms once again empty. He was disgusted with himself until he'd had a few drinks and shot a game or two of pool and a few of darts. It got later and more raucous. He bought shots for the regulars and laughed at a few jokes. Bob stuck to his rule of not drinking with customers, but Willy found himself feeling so expansive that he insisted Bob sit on the other side while Willy poured him drinks. At one point he realized that Bob was sticking around out of friendship to Willy.

"You are one tough old bastard," Bob said at one point, after many drinks. "The shit you've been through. You could live through fucking anything."

"I have no proof that I am not immortal," Willy said, and they both laughed.

Emilio, too, understood. They went out in the jonboat to get in a final day of goose hunting before things iced over, cruising up to a spot near where they had found the dead men frozen in their boats nearly forty years before. The sky and the water were grey, the dead blond marshgrass on the nearby island changing color beneath the shadows of the rolling clouds, the brown and black trees moving in the chill breeze.

Willy thought that it was somber but beautiful, a good place to have a final moment. If he were here alone, he could just roll over the side of the boat into the freezing water, dive down deep, exhale, and take in a great breath of the river water, just like Barnacle Brad. With any luck, his body would never be found, would dissipate in the flow, be borne down to the waters of the world. Softly, softly to the sea. What freedom, what relief.

"I sometimes think," Emilio said, making Willy jump, "that all my most beautiful days are behind me, the days of my greatest vigor, my greatest strength. My daughters are gone, I'm sore all over, my wife won't fuck me anymore. Not that I want to. She's so skinny now that her flesh hangs in an unpleasant manner. Like flaps."

Willy laughed in spite of himself, snapping his careful sorrow.

"And I think to myself," Emilio said, "what is the point?"

Willy flicked his eyebrows up, nodding.

"Then I think that the point is this day, all the days like it. Death is my hole card. Whatever it is, if it's just nothing, like before you were born, we'll find out eventually. No rush. So even though I'm old, and sometimes it hurts to walk, and sometimes my back is fucking killing me, at least I have days like this. I can go home, hug my wife- it's a secret, I really do love her- and I can sit by the fire with a glass of whiskey. I can read a book. I can do a project up in my shop, although slowly, and I can walk in the trees. I can see my grandchildren.

"You'll see Dan again. He'll be living with you. I know this. But now you've got this day. And you've got Mae."

Willy gave him a sour look and shook his head. "You exasperate the living shit out of me, you know that?"

Willy opened his thermos and poured coffee for both of them. When a vee of geese flew north overhead, the joints of their wings squeaking, the two grey haired men hardly noticed.

Willy thought about what Emilio had said, as usual. He woke up before Mae the next morning, went out to the kitchen and put on some coffee, listening to the public radio station. When he checked on her and noticed she had begun to stir, he began making bacon and eggs and toast. In the bedroom, he opened up the blinds to the cool light of the late fall morning and said to his wife as she moved to get out of bed, "Ah! Nope! Stay in bed."

"Why? I smell bacon."

"Stay there!" He left the room and brought breakfast in on a tray.

"Well, aren't you sweet!" Mae said, attempting a smile.

"If you think so, yeah."

Willy watched her while she ate. She was dainty, as always, and he loved the way she did things with her small, pale hands. She dipped the toast in the egg yolk, taking a small bite of it. The way she did it made his muscles relax in warmth.

He didn't say it much; it took courage to do so. He mustered the necessary gumption, though, saying it straight out, flatly, "God damn, I love you Mae."

He was about to tell her why he loved her: because she had saved him, because she had picked him up out of nowhere and set him down, making his roots grow, giving him a place, a reason. He wanted to tell her that the loss of the boys had broken his heart and would have ground the life out of him were it not for her, that she was his meaning, she was his light.

As he opened his mouth, though- just barely parting his lips- Mae said, "Could I have some jam? On another piece of toast?"

Feeling reprieved, he sprang up and went to get her another piece of toast. He brought it back to her with the jar of jam, knowing that she would pile it on so thick that he could never have done it right himself.

"Do you want to know where we're going, Danny?" Ingrid said as they drove.

Dan didn't answer.

"I said," his mother repeated, turning around to face him from the front seat, "Do you want to know where we're going?"

Dan glared at her and stared back out the window.

"Answer me, sweetie," she said.

"Better answer her, kid," Mike said, looking in the rearview mirror.

Dan stared at him, too, and said quietly, "Okay, where?"

"We're going back to Portview, in Greysport!"she said. "How about that! Huh?"

Dan put his head back on the seat and sighed.

"And we got an apartment back in the same building we used to live in before we went up north, which is where I think everything, you know, went wrong. It's not the *exact* same apartment, but one just like it on a higher floor. What do you think of that?"

Dan remained silent.

"Do you remember how happy we were back in those days, Danny?"

"No," he said. "And it's Dan."

"Hey!" Mike said. "No smartmouth!"

"It *is* Dan!"

"What did I just say?"

Dan sighed loudly and kept quiet, his heart hammering.

"Don't mind Mike, honey," Ingrid said, "he's just grumpy. Just a big old grumpy junkyard dog." She patted his cheek and he grumbled, but Dan got the impression that he liked being referred to in such a manner.

"Oh, it'll be wonderful," Ingrid went on, looking out the windshield. "Back in the old neighborhood with all the shops, just a bus ride to down town. We can go to the beach in the summer. We can start over, better, and just pretend that unhappy things never happened."

Dan crawled back into his own mind and directed his eyes out the window.

He had forgotten his mother's tendency to perceive any silence as uncomfortable- although she was right about this particular one- and fill it with babble. When she ran out of something linear or relevant to say, she just improvised, often with anything that crossed her mind or vision. "Look at that farmhouse there. Spooky. I wonder what those people *do* in there? What are their lives like? Lonely. It's lonely out here. I bet they wished they lived in Greysport. It was lonely where I grew up. I had a dog. Daddy killed it."

When this went on long enough, Mike snapped on the radio, tuning it to an AM talk station, on which the current subject was the war in Viet Nam. Dan could watch Mike becoming more and more angry.

"Cocksuckers," Mike erupted at one point. "Oughta drop the A-bomb on all those cocksucking gooks and get the fucker over with. Fucking slopes. That'd show their yellow asses."

"Language, honey," Ingrid said. Dan could see his neck getting red.

"Hey, if the kid hasn't heard talk like that yet, he's probably a faggot. You a faggot, kid?"

Dan acted like he didn't hear.

"I asked if you're a faggot." Mike said, the tone of his voice tipping over into menace.

"No," Dan said, wondering what Mike might have happened if he had answered in the affirmative.

"You sure? You're into all that artsy-fartsy stuff, right? Seems pretty faggy to me."

Dan was surprised by the realization that Mike was trying to make a connection with him.

"I'm not a faggot," he said.

"Listen to that, a whole sentence! Shit! Do you like gooks, Danny?"

Dan didn't dare say that his name had only one syllable, playing it safe instead. "I don't know any."

"Gooks or faggots?"

Dan blinked and took a breath "Do you mind if I take a nap?"

"No, honey," Ingrid said. "Go ahead. You just stretch right out on the seat back there."

He did so, covering his eyes with his arm. Pretending to be asleep, he listened.

"They oughta nuke the niggers on the South Side, too," Mike said.

"You're so bad," Ingrid said, chuckling.

They seemed to loosen up when they thought Dan was asleep. He heard the sound of the movement of fabric, and Ingrid said, "Mmmm, yeah, I love it when you touch me like that."

Dan heard a rustle of cloth and the sound of a zipper being opened.

"Go ahead," Mike said.

Some time later, they started talking about money. It was the first time he heard mention of Ingrid's father in the same sentence as the term "trust fund", and that Dan was linked to it in some way. He didn't know what that was, but it seemed to be about money. They were talking about that in the front seat when he fell asleep.

When they woke him up for lunch, he didn't know where he was, or who he was with. The recognition of it came over him, and he felt sick.

"Time for some lunch," Mike said. "Get up! And we're still an hour away from the fucking Interstate. Fuck!"

They went into a tavern in a town which was no more than an intersection in a cornfield standing among some hills, with a church on one corner and bars on all the others. Mike ordered a beer, an old fashioned for Ingrid, and a coke for Dan. Dan wanted the kind of drink that his grandfather or Bob made for him, a ginger ale with a maraschino cherry and a wedge of orange, and the image of it depressed him. He thought Willy might come through the door at any minute. How could he not?

While waiting for their hamburgers and fries, Ingrid put down two drinks, and Mike two beers. They both smoked as if it were a chore they'd gotten behind on. Ingrid gave Dan some money to play pinball, and on the way over to the machines, he stopped and looked out the window. He wouldn't have been surprised if he'd seen Willy's pickup driving up, but nothing was moving, only a thin grey dog trotting along on business of its own.

By the time they had finished eating, Ingrid was fairly drunk. She insisted on staying a bit longer, claiming to find the bar "charming", and becoming involved in a conversation with some of the locals. Mike seemed indifferent, as long as Ingrid bought him beer. She also gave Dan a pocketful of change to keep himself busy with pinball.

Dan played the pinball, but the machines were set up in such a way that he could keep an eye on Ingrid and Mike at the bar. Mike didn't seem interested in conversing with the locals, but Ingrid talked to them energetically, making sweeping gestures with her hands, occasionally leaning on them or putting her arms around them as if they were old friends. The locals seemed to enjoy her unusual presence, especially when she bought them drinks.

When they all seemed occupied, Dan slipped away from the jukebox and went to the payphone in the dark foyer to the bar. He put in the change from his pocket and dialed the phone number of his grandparents.

Mike reached over Dan's shoulder and pushed down the silver lever of the payphone.

"Nunna that," he said, his solid, smoky, thick presence surrounding Dan as he reached over and took the returned coins from the slot. "Come on."

Mike took him by the collar and lifted him up so that his toes just touched the linoleum, scrabbling.

"Look what I found," he said to Ingrid, setting him down.

"Well, *here's* my little boy," Ingrid said. "Here's my little genius! Show these people what you can do! Come on!" She held out a pencil and a pad of paper.

Dan looked at all the faces. They were round and red and yellow and orange in the light of the bar. Bits of black, blond hair. The surreality of it roared at him, and the faces seemed to expand.

"Come on, Danny," Ingrid said, a bit impatiently.

"Fuck you!" Dan shouted, and ran.

His grandfather would be out there if he ran fast enough. His grandfather was old but strong as old wood, big as a fridge, and tough and tough and tough. His grandfather towered over these fuckers.

Then Mike tripped him with a pool cue, and he skreeped across the linoleum by the back door.

Mike waggled the cue.

"I told you nunna that shit, you little fuck," he said.

He picked Dan up by the collar again, seemingly without effort. This time Dan's feet didn't touch the floor. The sweater his grandmother had knit for him was ripping when he was set next to Ingrid.

"Hi, Danny!" she said, weavingly drunk. She turned to the locals and said, "What were we talking about? My round!"

Dan sat waiting for rescue. The bartender gave him a Coke. No one said anything about what had happened, and Dan realized he was alone.

Mike leaned forward and muttered in his ear, "Even when you think I'm not watching you, I am. Got that, you little fuck?"

Dan nodded in a way that he hoped was convincing.

The landscape was familiar when they drove in to Greysport that night. The freeway took them over a rise, where the city center stood like an improbable organization of fairy-lights to the north, slightly hazed by the mist of the river. The tall buildings stood up out of the mist.

To the south, where the shoreline angled away, amber lights of increasing density led to the glow and underlit smoke of the foundries and steel mills. The port lay directly to the east. A foghorn sounded. Soon they were in the neighborhood of Portview, old brick apartments rising dark from the street, misty smears of light from bar signs and the occasional streetlight.

"You're home, kid," Mike said. "You grab your shit and I'll grab your mother."

It was the same building he had lived in so long ago. Dan looked around, puzzled. Did I live here? he thought. Is that where me and my...dad caught the bus?

"Snap out of it." Mike said, "I'm getting your mom up in bed. She looks like she's gonna puke. She pukes, you clean it up. That's your new function, recruit."

The apartment was the same as the one where he had lived with his dad, but the walls were painted differently and had an overpoweringly strange smell. Mike tossed Ingrid on the bed in the largest bedroom, the springs squeaking.

Dan thought about the old pickup truck Willy drove. He and Uncle Emilio kept it in pretty good shape, but suppose it broke down. That's what had happened. It broke down.

Mike showed Dan his room. It was small and narrow, but clean, with blue walls and a small bed covered with a grey wool blanket. The walls were bare, and there was a small window out into an airwell.

"Wasn't my idea, kid," Mike said.

Ingrid let him take off a week of school before enrolling him. Then it became two.

"We'll give you time to get readjusted to being back home," she said by way of explanation.

They didn't appear to care much what he did, so he stayed out as much as possible. He quickly understood that the environment in the apartment was entirely unpredictable. He might be reading peacefully in his bedroom, enjoying a few fragile moments of sanctuary, when he would get rousted out to do some chores or perform a meaningless task for his mother which she could easily have done for herself. Mike turned out to be less of a problem than he had first seemed, often giving him a few dollars and shooing him out of the house. It was Ingrid who was much more the wild card; he never knew what combination of emotions or reactions might come from her. It could be different every time, like pulling the arm of a slot machine.

There were, however, two basic forms of Ingrid's behavior: effusive drunk or mean drunk. There was arguably a third: wincing hangover with bitter cantankerousness, but this was usually redirected into one of the first two after a few morning eye-openers. Dan eventually concluded that the effusive drunk had to do with the pills she sometimes took with her vodka, valium, most frequently. When in this state, she would call him from his room and out to the kitchen table, where she almost invariably had a screwdriver and a cigarette going, although on festive occasions she might have a tequila sunrise.

"You can do anything you want to," she said on one occasion, draping her wrist on his shoulder. "You have a talent that's just...*uncanny!*" She made a sweeping motion with her arm and dropped cigarette ash on the floor. "You can do anything you want to, Danny. You just have to believe in it. *Believe* in it with all your heart."

"Okay," Dan said, trying not to recoil too obviously from her breath.

"Your father had talent. But he was lost to us."

Dan said nothing.

"Fix me another drink, okay, sweetie?" she said. "That's one good thing about your living with those people out on the river. You'll make a good bartender. Always have something to fall back on."

He knew when the mean drunk was coming by the changing expression on his mother's face. The corners of her mouth pulled down, her eyelids went to halfmast, her head wove, and it was obvious she had trouble focusing. She looked like a version of the tragedy mask, one with a drink and a cigarette usually in front of it.

"Your father was a loser," she said one day when well into the latter state, "your grandfather was a loser- a loser and a *murderer*, by the way- but your father probably was too, in Korea- and you're a loser. All these dreeeeeamy McGregor assholes- do you know your grandfather wrote poetry? Hah! They all look so tough on the outside but are made of *shit* on the inside. Like a fucking shit Twinky."

He developed the habit of nodding reasonably and heading for the door, often using the excuse of having to take out the garbage, one of his assigned tasks. It usually seemed pointless to try to communicate with her, but on one occasion he said, "Why am I even here? What am I doing here? You don't want me around. I want to go home."

Her response was terse. "Your grandfather- the good one, *my* dad, not the convict- wanted me to take care of you. And he set up something called a trust fund to help me. Okay? I take care of you and the trust fund takes care of us."

"Is that why Mike doesn't have to work?"

"Mike has a back injury. He used to work on the docks like your fucking father. Now I just want him to be a dad to you."

"He's not my dad," Dan said slowly. He looked into the living room where the television was on and Mike was asleep on the couch.

"You'd be lucky to have a dad like Mike," Ingrid said, the corners of her mouth turning down. She was suddenly on the verge of tears.

"I'm going out," he said, going to the front hall and putting on a coat and knit cap.

Willy would find him, because Willy was a weathered god. Dan drew pictures like this.

The neighborhood had a different scent depending on the direction of the wind. From one direction came the warm, malty smell of the breweries, from another the tang of molten pitch, from yet another the rich smell of a chocolate factory. When the breeze came in off the lake, it was crisp and invigorating. Sometimes it was foggy and still, and the shrouded neighborhood smelled of rotting leaves and wet pavement, foghorns both near and distant tolling arhythmically as if conversing through the gulf of gloom. There was an Italian bakery nearby, and if he slipped out of the house before dawn on the motionless, foggy mornings, the wholesome scent of the bakery permeated the neighborhood.

Dan often walked down by the port, down the hill the way his father had gone to work, although he didn't realize he was walking in his father's footsteps. The port was desolate in the winter months; he remembered being fascinated by the activity in the summer, but the misty loneliness of it- the occasional semi driving by, the cries of gulls- made him think of post-apocalyptic movies he had seen, and the thought was beautiful. He turned up the collar of his coat, and pulled his hat down over his ears and walked on, unconsciously mimicking his father.

It was an unusually warm November, and although there were occasional flurries, fog was the more frequent state. After he had slipped out of the house on the night of a forgotten Thanksgiving ("I kept meaning to cook something," Ingrid had slurred), he walked the long distance to some abandoned warehouses by the mouth of the harbor. The brick buildings, mostly devoid of glass in their arched windows, were on the upcurved part of the C of the harbor. Standing inside the damp ruin the first time, Dan was mesmerized as the east wind drove curling waves into the harbor, the city dark and cloudridden in the mist, a light here and there. Greysport might have looked the same way after a staggering plague. It gave him a great sense of peace, the sound of the waves rolling by sussurant and soothing, their slowly pulsing booms on the breakwater rocks an excitement, the tolling of the foghorns a call home to those lost in countless frigid shipwrecks. It made him shudder as much with delight as with the cold.

When Dan walked home, though, it was always with increasing dread. Mike was irritable, but consistent; that was one thing he could depend on. If he came home and the apartment was empty, he knew that they were out at a happy hour, and that he could make himself a can of soup, or take something from the refrigerator if anything was fresh.

As terrified as he was of Mike finding him making a call- and the thought of a call to Willy and Mae was enough to make his hands shake in front of the phone- he was able, while the two were out, to call Charlie and Jim. He didn't have their phone number, but looked in the phone book for the most likely Gates listing, and was right on the first try. Gates, Henry Bosworth. They'd said he thought highly of himself. Who else would include his middle name?

A woman with a sweet Latin accent answered the phone, and, after a muffled rumbling, Charlie answered. Dan announced himself.

There was a missed beat, and Charlie said, "Hey, motherfucker!"

Dan heard the shocked utterance of the woman in the background. Charlie said, "Fucking cool it, it's my friend. What's happenin', man?"

Dan, not used this urban form of salutation, said, "Uh, well, not much."

"You sound like you're nearby."

"Yeah, I'm down in Portview."

"What!"

348

"Yeah," Dan said, and gave Charlie a version of events which he hoped sounded nonchalant.

"Man, that sucks," Charlie said. "Your grandparents are cool. Well, you have to come here! You can hop on a few buses and be here in an hour."

Dan thought about how Ingrid and Mike would respond to him doing such a thing, sensing also, in an unconscious way, that it would be made worse by Ingrid's resentment towards the privilege of the Gates family. She wouldn't mind them being wealthy if she were herself. There was also the question of busfare. "That might not be a good idea right now," he said.

"Jesus, come on," Charlie said. "Don't be such a pussy."

"I'll get around to it."

"Come *on*!"

"Cool it, cheesedick," Dan said, smiling.

They left it that Dan would visit during the holidays, although Dan knew he'd have to run away to do it. Charlie gave him his address and directions, even looking up the number to the Greysport Transit Authority so Dan could call and find out which buses he should take. Dan said that he'd do his best.

Ingrid eventually enrolled him in school. She moaned and huffed angrily through the entire procedure, but eventually got it done, dealing with the indifferent personnel of the crowded and noisy school as if she resented them for not showing her enough respect. Dan remembered his grandparents enrolling him in the comparatively serene Bluffside school in MacDougal, and the thought made him intensely homesick. He even missed the smarmy principal Baumeister.

"Okay!" Ingrid said when they were done. "You're officially a student at Portview High!" She leaned forward and pecked him dryly on the forehead before leaving. He squinted at her sour breath.

Dan stood there alone in the tiled hall in front of the school office. The class bell rang like a burglar alarm, and he jumped. The halls were immediately packed with yelling kids. Completely overwhelmed, he put on a face as impassive as his grandfather's and found his way to his first class.

While he waited for rescue, he settled into a makeshift routine. When the last class bell rang, he tried to avoid eye contact and made for the door. This usually worked, but twice he was accosted by older kids who needed to test him. The first one he gave a left to the solar plexus, as his grandfather had taught him, and a right to the cheekbone as he was going down. The right had been meant for the kid's jaw, but he had dropped so fast that Dan didn't have the chance to hit him there. The second kid he simply kicked in the balls, then stood in the stance his grandfather had taught him. After that, he felt safe in carrying art supplies to school.

As far as that subject was concerned, he now found himself with another art teacher who didn't know what to do with him. Mr. Kinder was a barely restrained hippie, slim and furry with a delicate goatee and John Lennon glasses. Dan could usually smell dope on his breath, if not his clothes. He knew this, naturally, due to his tutelage under the Schommer brothers, not to mention half of the other patrons of the bar.

"Man," Kinder said, looking at Dan's halfhearted work for class, "this shit is far out. *Stuff* is far out. *Stuff*. 'Scuse my language. Your expertise took me the fuck aback. I mean hell. *Hell* aback. Heck, even. Fuck, kid, you know what I mean. Shit, I just said fuck. Man. Whew."

Dan smiled, but ducked his head to hide it.

"Look," Kinder said quietly, as the class around him erupted in cacophony and chaos, "just do some good shit that we can enter in a contest, and we don't have to pay attention to any rules. And do well in your other classes. We're headed for a revolution, but you still have to stay invisible to the Man, dig? Just good thinking."

Dan didn't stay invisible to the Man. The fact that he cut class as often as possible contributed to his poor grades, other than the A in art and an A-minus in science. He knew that any truancy notices would pile up in the mailbox until he took them out himself, and that if Ingrid were called, she'd hang up or not answer at all. Dan simply walked out of the classes which took effort and strolled down to the port.

He kept in his pack- along with a his art supplies, a few science books, and his copy of *The Two Towers*- a knife, a few boxes of wooden matches, and a spoon lifted from the school cafeteria. In the ruins of the warehouse, he stacked white driftwood which had washed up on the huge blocks of the nearby breakwater. Twilight came early and the snow began to pile up, flakes fluttering through the dark arches, but in his corner of the old warehouse, he had a good fire and a few stolen cans of pork and beans warming next to it, rather like being in the old hotel up on the bluff. He felt comfortable staying there until he knew that Ingrid and Mike would be prostrate and snoring in the sizzling blue light of the television.

A few times he fell asleep next to the fire, waking only groggily to toss on more driftwood, then to curl back into a fetal position with his hands in his armpits, feeling half as close to safe as he would out on the river, but half was close enough.

When he went home at dawn, Ingrid and Mike were so solidly out that he tested how much noise he could make before they would stir. Finally he summoned the gumption to make a few chicken pot pies, slamming the door to the oven when he was done. Mike remained unconscious, snoring wetly. His mother stirred, half-opened her eyes, and flopped back down on the couch, farting at length, also wetly. Trying not to breathe, he took the pot pies on a plate into his blue bedroom with the grey blanket, there to finally fall asleep in real warmth, if not in actual peace.

Christmas, too, was nearly forgotten, although Mike had gone to the effort of bringing home a small tree. Perhaps it was a branch sawed off a pine in someone's yard and affixed, with a single nail, to an X of lath; Dan didn't know. After this valiant gesture of holiday spirit- a cause for raucous drinks- the sad tree lost its novelty and slumped purposelessly in a corner. No one ever got around to decorating it, but Ingrid claimed that it was festive.

She had also neglected to go to the store to buy anything for Christmas dinner, although the supply of vodka and orange juice was well-stocked. She even got tequila and grenadine to make tequila sunrises.

Mike was heartily game about the lack of dinner. "Fuck it!" he said cheerfully, raising his drink. "We'll go out for chink food, like kikes! On me!"

"Let's exchange gifts first," Ingrid said.

She gave the boy a ten-pack of knee-high tube socks, and a used copy of Hans Christian Andersen fairy tales in a large format, designed for children. Dan would find the illustrations puerile, but the stories amusingly dark. He had a chance to read it while Ingrid and Mike made more drinks and lost their focus on the proceedings.

When their attention returned, Mike gave him a football, which had obviously been well used, a gift which, for a moment, puzzled Dan, before triggering his well-concealed contempt.

"Gee," he said, keeping his face blank. "Thanks."

Dan had acquired the habit of hiding out a few afternoons a week at school, in Mr. Kinder's loft artroom high above the rest of the school and coveted for its northern light. It was here he had finished his presents for Mike and Ingrid. Mike's was an acrylic, in the Frazetta fashion, of Mike standing on top of a rock, stormclouds behind him, a blazing automatic rifle in each hand. His shirt was ripped open, clothes in revealing tatters. Improbably muscled, he had two buxom, black-clad women, apparently vampires, clinging to his massive bronze thighs.

"Holy shit," Mike said. "You did this?"

Dan shrugged, feeling a tiny twinge of affection for Mike, while watching his mother readying to tear the butcher paper off her obvious package. Dan went to pour himself a drink of orange juice before she used it all for screwdrivers, and waited for her response.

"Oh, Danny," Ingrid said, fingering a corner of the paper, "you can do anything you *want* to. You can be *anything*. You just have to set your mind to it, give all your heart."

He managed not to make a face at this common refrain.

"Think I could make it as an artist?" he asked cautiously.

Her smile faltered. "Well...if that's what you *want*, dear. Yes," she said, suddenly affecting saintly vision pointed at the wall behind his head. "Oh, yes."

"I can do anything I want if I set my mind to it?"

"Yes, Danny," she said. "Yes, you can."

"Great. I always wanted to levitate."

His mother, in spite of herself, scoffed.

"What, Mom? Can't I levitate? Like, if I want it with all my heart and soul and try really hard?"

"Danny, it's..."

"Maybe if I concentrated hard enough, I could have a giant, veiny head like those guys on *Star Trek*, the Talosians. That'd be cool. Maybe if I started right now. Do you think? I'm concentrating. I'm trying really hard. See anything?"

"Now you're just being sarcastic. And mean!"

"Okay, sorry. How about if I could shoot laser beams from my eyes? That'd be excellent. Could I do that, if I tried really hard?"

"Hey!" Mike barked, swizzling icecubes.

"I'm not even talking to you anymore," Ingrid said "Get me a drink."

351

"Aren't you going to open my present?" Dan said.

She sighed, finished her current drink in a gulp, and gave him a look that said he was being naughty and she was disappointed but tolerantly amused. She took the wrapped package in her hands.

"Oh, what could it be?" she said, tearing off the butchers paper.

The painting was beautifully executed. Over a scorched-earth landscape, under a dark sky, buildings burning in the distance, Dan levitated. A crimson robe flowed around him. It was recognizably him (his accuracy always astonishing to others) but for the giant, bulging cranium: grey, hairless, and covered with finger-thick veins. Twin ruby beams needled from his eyes, striking his mother, who was running away in the foreground of the painting, screaming, her hair bursting into flame.

Ingrid's face flushed with pink.

"Thanks for always helping me *believe* in myself, Mom," Dan said earnestly. "Merry Christmas."

That was the first time Mike hit him, and the first time he ran away. That first time was only a backhand, but it sent Dan stumbling backwards, knocking over a chair on his way to the floor. He got up a little dazed, but somehow relieved that the tension had broken.

"You fucking asshole!" Dan said- almost laughing- and Mike came at him again.

"What did you say to me?" Mike said, lunged.

Dan quickly evaded him, getting the kitchen table between them. "I *said-*" he feinted left and right to taunt Mike into making a move- "you're a fucking *asshole*! Are you deaf, too?"

"C'mere, goddammit!"

Dan kept him going until he was winded and panting. Already fairly drunk, he was soon almost staggering. Ingrid shouted at them to stop, but Dan would dance just out of Mike's grasp, and Mike would make another lunge. Mike finally caught his feet in the overturned chair and tumbled heavily to the floor, where he lay wheezing and glaring, his red eyes enraged and boarlike.

Dan smiled and gave Mike the finger, then went for the door, where his pack and jacket sat for just such an occasion. His mother threatened and implored, but he put on his things. Mike made a weak attempt to get to his feet, but slumped back, his eyes drilling into Dan.

"See ya later, kid," Mike huffed.

"Yeah," Dan said cheerfully. "Merry fucking Christmas."

Ingrid got up to stop him, now wearing the tragedy mask, but he shook her hand off his shoulder and went down the stairs two at a time.

It was snowing again, and as he headed down to the port, he knew it would be too cold to hide out in the warehouse. It was still only late afternoon, but darkly overcast, the port deserted and beautiful for it.

Without really thinking about it, he found himself at a bus stop in front of a storage warehouse. The service was limited on a holiday, but he only had to stand hunched against the cold for twenty minutes before a bus came by. He got aboard, nodding at the driver and dropping his change in the receptacle. The bus roared away and headed uptown through the snow.

The only other passenger was an old woman in a ratty, pea-green jacket and a hand-knit pink tam. The lighting of the bus made her skin look yellow with purple blotches. In spite of her unpleasant appearance, Dan had a small hope that she would make eye contact with him, that they would talk. She stared stolidly out the window, though, seemingly watching the yellow headlights of the traffic as it flowed in the slush and the growing dark.

Dan got off the bus downtown. The snow was coming down heavily now, illuminated by the festive department store windows and the streetlights, although the large buildings overhead were dark grey and black against the city's reflected golden glow on the clouds, all of it largely lost in the swirls of snow. The thought of Andersen's little match girl popped momentarily into his mind, along with a vision of himself freezing to death tragically in an alley. He shook his head in amusement and disgust at himself. He paced indecisively for a moment, then took his time looking in shop windows, not admitting to himself that he was searching for a payphone.

Finally confessing his mission, he went into a bar called the Swinging Door. Willy might have called the place "swanky"; it had red stained-glass windows with a blue and white crest in the middle, and the door was heavy, polished oak, as was much of the interior. Dan came through the door and entered in a swarm of heavy snowflakes.

In spite of the surroundings, the patrons seemed underjoyed to be there, although Dan found the smokiness, warmth and jukebox Christmas music to be immediately comforting. The bartender was pouring a scotch rocks (something Willy would have considered vile if the scotch was good) for one of the hunched and silent patrons, and looked at Dan as if kids came into his bar every day. He told Dan where the payphone was, around the corner and back in a dark room with dimly lit dartboards and a few tables.

Dan hesitated for a moment, then told himself that there was only one way forward. He dialed Charlie's number.

The woman with the Latin accent answered again- didn't she ever go home?- and got Charlie on the line. He picked up another extension, and there was music and laughter in the background.

"Dan?" Charlie said. "What the fuck, man! What are you doing?"

"I'm downtown," Dan said.

"What the hell are you doing there?"

Dan made some filler syllables while he thought of what to say, but before he had to ask for anything, Charlie said, "Well, that's bullshit, man. My brother Hugh is here. We'll come and pick you up."

"Yeah?" Dan said as unemotionally as possible. "Great." With a bit of skeptical relief, he gave Charlie his location.

When Dan hung up the phone in the booth, he turned around and almost jumped when he found one of the bar's patrons standing just behind him. The man was bald and tall, wearing a beige canvas coat. His form was backlit, his face hard to read, but his eyes reflected the light of the payphone booth.

353

"Done with the phone, kid?" he said.

"Yeah," Dan said. "It's all yours."

"Maybe I should call my mother," the man said. Dan went to walk around him.

The man put his hand on Dan's shoulder, not in a harsh way, but in one that was soft and kneading.

"You lonely or something kid?"

"No."

"You like beer?"

"It's okay," Dan said.

"Well, I could get you some beer," the man said. "We could go back to my place and have a party."

"No, thanks," Dan said. "Some friends are picking me up."

"You sure?" The man's hand kneaded Dan's shoulder through his jacket. It dawned on him what the man wanted, and things Willy had told him about some men and how they felt about young boys, his grandfather never wanting to shelter him from the world. Dan remembered the wristlock Willy had shown him, but didn't want to use it. It might seem rude.

"Yeah, I'm sure," Dan said.

"Come on, kid," the man said. "It'll be fun. You'll like it."

"I'm getting picked up," he said. "Some friends are going to be here. They're badasses, by the way." He slipped the man's palpating grip and made for the door, thinking about putting the wristlock on him and thumbing him in the eye.

Dan stood in the doorway to the bar, refusing to act cold- making himself relax against shivering- when the Gates entourage showed up in a black Saab. The street was slick with the deepening snow, and the car almost went sideways into the curb, the engine revving then quieting to a lull. The back door opened, and there was Charlie in a black mohair overcoat and white dress shirt, looking surprisingly posh. Jim was similarly dressed, crowding into the middle seat to see Dan.

"Hey, motherfucker!" Charlie shouted. Jim was laughing, and punched Dan on the arm when he got into the car.

"Let's go, I'm getting sober! And I want to smoke some pot!" came a woman's throaty voice from the front passenger seat.

"Jesus!" the driver said, "did you forget the bottle of scotch you put under your seat?"

"Oh, yeah," the woman said, bending over to search. Groping for the bottle she inadvertently pushed it under the seat toward Dan, who retrieved it and handed it to her.

"Here you go, miss," Dan said.

"Thank you!" she said. "Miss. What a gentleman. You should learn, Charlie. Jim, pay attention."

The driver, tall and lean, dressed in black, reached his hand over the seat in spite of the awkward angle, offering it to Dan. "Hi, I'm Hugh. The older brother."

"Half-brother," Charlie said.

"You just say that because you don't like fags," Hugh said.

"I don't mind fags," Charlie said. "I just don't like *you*."

They both laughed.

The young woman with the scotch screwed off the cap of the bottle and took a swig. Dressed entirely in black, with hair Dan thought to be dyed black, cut with bangs touching her eyelashes, nape-length and otherwise straight, sides curling up around her pale cheeks. No one on the river looked the way she did, and she was beautiful.

"Hi, nature boy," she said, putting a cigarette in her mouth. "We've heard a lot about you. I'm Gigi. Hugh the Fag's sister, half-sister to Thing One and Thing Two back there."

Dan wasn't sure what to make of any of it and just kept silent. Hugh drove, slipping occasionally in the snow, while Gigi smoked, drank scotch (the liquid splinking in the bottle when she tipped it to her lips), and criticized Hugh's near-perfect driving.

"*Please.* I'm driving," Hugh said, laughing, when she tried to make him drink from the bottle. "I'll party when we get home."

"Come on," Gigi said. "It's Christmas."

"Don't be a little bitch."

"I won't if you won't."

If Gigi was drunk, Dan thought, she didn't seem like it. Just talkative. Smoking and drinking, she laid out the family dynamic: Hugh was ten years older than Charlie, Gigi eight. Her name was actually Guinevere, which became, at her insistence, Ginger for awhile. Her initials and the way she signed notes led to the name Gigi. They were the kids from the first marriage of their father, Henry (as they all called him), although they all seemed to hold him in roughly the same bemused contempt.

"He teaches at University of Greysport," Charlie said.

"Ethics, oddly enough," Gigi said, and they all laughed, even Jim, although he seemed almost as mystified by the joke as Dan.

They drove north from downtown in the deepening snow. Traffic was light, and Dan split his attention between the barrage of questions from Charlie and Jim and the ornate displays in the store windows. Soon they were on Lake Drive, with bright highrises on the left and the vastness of the dark lake on the right.

Dan was startled when Hugh began to sing in a polished, professional baritone.

"It's the most wonderful time
"Of the year
"While Santa's ho-ho-ing
"The elves are all blowing
"Each other with cheer!
"It's the most wonderful time
"Of the year!"

Everyone in the car laughed but Dan, who was too taken aback, although he still smiled tentatively. The others all sang the chorus, and Charlie soloed with,

"Your breath is so scrotumy
"Don't say hello to me
"Don't stand so near!
"It's the most wonderful time
"Of the year!"

Dan caught on that it was a game in which the purpose was to improvise lyrics, and desperately tried to think of something to contribute, while Gigi took her turn.

"I gotta get outta me

"Whiskey lobotomy

"Settle for beer!

"It's the most wonderful time

"Of the year!'

"Good one!" Hugh said.

"Wait, wait!" Jim said. "My turn:

"Don't think it's heinous

"I'm scratching my anus

"Got tapeworms I fear!

"It's the most wonderful time

"Of the year!"

"Dan?" Gigi asked, turning around

Dan, laughing, spread his hands and shook his head.

"You'll get the hang of it," Hugh said.

"He doesn't have to," Gigi said. "He's too cute."

"He's an artist," Charlie said. "Fucking genius."

Dan gasped in mortification, giving Charlie a look of betrayal (Mae would have seen Willy clearly in this response), but Charlie turned down the corners of his mouth and shrugged. It was true.

"Genius!" Hugh said. "Well! That means a lot, coming from *that* malignant little bastard."

They drove up a hill, away from the dark lake, and into a neighborhood of old trees and stately houses, some of which had gatehouses finer than the best homes on MacDougal Island. All stood far back from the street behind broad yards deep in snow, and all had subtle but magnificent displays of Christmas lights.

They turned into the long driveway of one such place. Dan would think of it only as a mansion. Past the wrought iron and stone gate ("We are entering the Gates of Gates", Hugh intoned), up a drive lined with small, pale lights, past the three car garage and what appeared to be a large gardener's building- in which Dan would happily have lived- both built of stone with black trim and doors to match the mansion itself.

In each of the tall, rectangular windows of the mansion was a single electric candle, over twenty in all. Neatly trimmed, snow-covered bushes flanked the broad stone steps that led to the huge black front door, which was adorned with a simple wreath wound with gold ribbon, placed symmetrically around a large gold knocker. Gold lamps lit the door and the steps in a pool of light flurried with snow. Dan tried not to look astonished.

"You live here?" Dan asked.

"This is the place," Charlie said.

"We tell kids it's got ghosts," Jim added.

"It looks impressive at first," Hugh said, "but don't let it get to you. It's just our house."

"Yeah," Gigi said, "we're as fucked up as anyone else."

356

"Maybe more," Hugh said, and, after some thought, added, "No. More. Definitely more."

Hugh let them out and parked the car in the garage while the rest went up the steps. Jim opened the big black door and swung it inward. The Gates siblings stomped their feet, dusted off their coats, chattering among themselves and hanging their coats in a cloakroom off the entry vestibule. This entryway went through glass-paned double doors of heavy polished oak, into a large hall.

Dan was hardly aware as Gigi took his grubby coat, but walked into the hall in his soggy sneakers. He stood in the hall and looked up, feeling his eyebrows slide up his forehead.

The floor of the hall was polished stone, with a large oriental rug in the center. A broad sweeping staircase with a wrought iron railing went up to the second floor to a balcony looking down on the hall. In front of this was a Christmas tree at least twenty feet in height, so broad at the base that all three boys could have crawled in and hidden behind it. The tree was densely populated with fanciful ornaments, gold, silver, the colors of gems. Minute multicolored lights- not the kind of big, hot bulbs his grandfather and grandmother had- gleamed from the pine branches like a tiny civilization of elves. By many of these lights were delicate butterflies made of pastel-colored feathers.

Jim nudged him, breaking his trance. "See the star on top?"

Dan did. It was the size of a serving tray, beautifully crafted. For all Dan knew, it might have been made of real gold.

"I get to put that up there," Jim said. "I'm the youngest."

"What a dork," Charlie said. "That's a big deal when you're, like, six."

Dan thought *he* wouldn't mind putting the star up there, but kept this to himself. He imagined falling into the tree, through its dark branches and magical lights, there to be arrested in his descent by a fairy like Tinkerbell, taken back to her village in the boughs to be raised in their midst, leaving only to ride into battle on the back of a ruby dragonfly.

"Come on," Charlie said. "We'll show you around."

"Shouldn't I meet your dad?"

"He's in his study," Charlie said. "You can meet him later."

"Yeah," Jim said, "We'll take you up to our rooms."

The place was so huge that Dan immediately wanted to explore, but Charlie and Jim seemed bored by the idea.

"The attic must be big," Dan said as they walked down a long hallway, their footsteps made silent by thick carpet.

"There's a couple of them," Jim said.

"A *couple* of them?"

"All kinds of crazy shit up there," Charlie said. "Our great-grandfather used to live here, then our grandfather, then us. Shit accumulates."

"Let's go check it out," Dan suggested.

"Ah, later," Charlie said. "Maybe you want to change into some dry clothes. My stuff'll fit you."

When he saw Charlie and Jim's rooms, he had gotten accustomed enough to his surroundings not to show his amazement. A large oak door opened into a huge common room, the boys' bedrooms through two more doors to the right and left. The high ceiling was raftered, and large windows looked out on the nighttime darkness of the lake. The room itself was filled with distractions: books, globes, a telescope by one window, a slotcar set on the floor, a microscope, two desks, a drafting table, hockey sticks, baseball bats. Posters on the wall were of rock bands or psychedelia, along with maps of the Moon and Mars. He was flattered to see that the artwork he had done for them was in a place of some prominence.

Dan said, "Shit, you could put a boxing ring in here."

The brothers looked at each other, amazed.

"Yyyyyeah!" they cried simultaneously.

Dan took them up on their offer of a shower, and when he came out, he found clean clothes laid out on a couch in the common room.

"Here's some hiking boots you can have," Jim said. "They were a present, but they're too big."

"I couldn't take those," Dan said.

"I've got more," Jim said. "And I'd get more if I didn't."

"Here's a spare jacket you could have," Charlie said. "See? Down. It's really warm."

"I can't," Dan said, embarrassed.

"You're our guest, man," Charlie said. "We'd be offended if you didn't take some stuff. Your Christmas already sucks. We've got tons of everything. Just please take it."

"Share and share alike," Jim said, slapping Dan on the shoulder.

"Okay," Dan said. "Thanks. I owe you."

"We owe *you*," Charlie said. "You're, like, our guide in the wilds of the river. You've got a reputation around here already. You've got to meet some kids tomorrow. Everybody thinks you're the Wild Boy."

"How long can you stay?" Jim asked.

"I guess that's up to me." He knew what he was going to face when he went home, and was willing to put it off for as long as possible. In the meantime, he intended to find distractions to keep his thoughts off the humming bass note of worry and anxiety in the back of his mind, one instrument in the band of unfaced music.

He was anxious to explore the house, although it was obvious the brothers were less than interested. They were focused, instead, on a game of foosball, apparently a thing of ongoing rivalry.

"Let's check out the attics," Dan suggested.

"In a minute," Charlie said, clacking the ball into the goal and thrusting his fists in the air. "Hah!"

"Game's not over, dickhead," Jim said, and they started again.

Charlie was in a good mood after beating Jim, who took the loss with practiced good humor and an equally familiar vow of revenge.

"Okay," Charlie said, "Let's show him around."

"Attics or basements?" Jim asked.

"Basements?" Dan said. "Plural?"

"Yeah," Jim said. "The place is built on a bluff, so there's, like, sub-basements and shit. There's gardens and terraces that go down to the beach."

"Wow," Dan said.

"It's all right," Charlie said. "Where you live is cooler. It's all just a bunch of boring fuckers around here."

"You've got gangs and shit where you live," Jim said.

They started on the top floor, each room a wonder to Dan. The first floor of his grandparents' house could have fit inside the master bedroom, which looked rather uninhabited and too perfect, like a display. Hugh and Gigi had apartments downtown, but came and went, staying in their old rooms for the holidays, or whenever else it suited them. Hugh's room was neat and tasteful, Gigi's strewn with clothes, books, and magazines, many of them dealing with the topic of sex.

It went on and on. The kitchen was huge and immaculate, the dining room had a table which could seat fourteen. A vast living room had a grand piano and was lined with books and artwork in gold frames, had windows which overlooked the terraces and the lake, and had, Dan was puzzled to discover, another Christmas tree in it, not as large as the one in the front hall, but huge nonetheless, although it seemed somewhat in scale under the beamed eighteen-foot ceilings. Dan looked out the window into the dark, where he could make out a snowed-over pool and stone poolhouse. There was a library with leather chairs and thousands more books, and next to it, off a carpeted hall, was what Charlie said was a study. The door was closed, but Dan could hear what was apparently one side of a conversation behind it.

"That's where Henry, I mean, our *dad* hangs out," Charlie said.

"Do you want me to introduce myself?" Dan asked.

"Nah," Jim said. "He's on the phone."

"I don't want to be rude," Dan said.

Charlie snorted. "He doesn't give a fuck. He doesn't know what's going on around here most of the time, anyway."

"He's *distracted*," Jim said, making air-quotes.

They went down a servant's stairway leading to a paneled hallway with dark red carpeting. Dan heard the clack of poolballs, and they went through a door to find Hugh shooting pool at a large table. Dan realized how small, stained and cigarette-burned the one in his grandfather's bar was. Gigi came around from behind the large wet bar with a drink and plopped down on the leather couch.

"You finding everything okay, sweetie?' she asked Dan.

"I'd get lost in this place," Dan said.

"You get used to it," Hugh said, taking a shot and sinking the ball. "Make yourself at home."

"We're still showing him around," Jim said.

Other rooms contained a sauna, a gym, an office, and what Dan considered to be mystifyingly superfluous guest bedrooms with French doors opening to a terrace with a classic sculpture of Bacchus standing dimly visible in the snow.

"Holy shit, you guys," Dan said. The brothers ignored him.

Another basement held a wine cellar with thousands of bottles, all under stone arches which seemed almost medieval.

"We can walk around in here, but Henry would get seriously pissed if we broke or took anything," Charlie said. "He's an oenophile."

"A what?"

"Guy who likes wine," Jim informed him.

"Not to be confused with pedophile," Charlie said, "although the two aren't mutually exclusive."

Another, smaller set of stairs led down to a long, dark stone tunnel.

"Where does that go?"

"To the beach. I think they ran booze in through here back in the gangster days. And people could split if there was a raid and escape to the beach."

"Wow," Dan said. "Let's go down it."

The brothers looked at each other. "Sure, why not," Charlie said.

Jim clacked on a heavy old lightswitch. The tunnel was like a long bunker, the lights protected by wire cages. They went down to the end, where a large door on great hinges was protected by deadbolts and a heavy crossbar. All were covered with cobwebs.

"We don't come down here much," Charlie said, a little apologetically.

"Are you nuts?" Dan said. "I'd be down here every day. Let's open it!"

The other boys seemed hesitant, but Dan went forward and lifted off the crossbar with some effort.

"Shit," Jim said. "I didn't think you could lift that."

Dan opened the deadbolts with consecutive thumps, then grasped the wrought-iron door handle. It wouldn't budge.

"Gimme a hand, you guys," he said.

The handle was large enough for three pairs of hands, and they all pulled, grunting, Dan with his hiking boot against the doorjamb. The door finally gave with a creak, opening halfway with a rush of snow and cold air. A hundred feet away, waves boomed in the darkness. The boys laughed in delight.

"And you guys don't come down here much," Dan said, smiling and shaking his head. "What the fuck."

"Guess you should visit more often," Charlie said.

They ran out into the snow and onto the broad beach. Waves rolled in, their sound crisp and rhythmic in the night. The half moon was visible through occasional gaps in the clouds, the falling snowflakes set aglow in its light. To the south, the glow of Greysport lit the gigantic clouds from underneath. Behind the boys, the terraces led up to the mansion towering above them, its windows warm in the darkness.

Dan breathed the cold air, smiling, tilting his face up to the falling snow, all worry forgotten.

A snowball hit him in the back of the neck. He turned around to see Charlie laughing.

"You dick!" he shouted, packing some snow and pitching it back, hitting Charlie in the chest. Not wanting to omit Jim, he packed another snowball and hit him as well, then ran off towards the waves. The boys chased him, laughing and shouting, their breath steaming in the snow and the moonlight, their laughter thin, light, against the boom and hush of the waves.

Back in from the beach, red-cheeked and panting, they made their way up to the kitchen through the hallways and flights of stairs. Hugh and Gigi were gone, and the boys set upon the refrigerator. The choices were overwhelming, and Dan found himself standing holding the door to the appliance open, lost in thought. It made him think about how spartan and practical his grandparents were, and the thought of his mother's fridge, usually empty, the freezer containing pot pies, pizzas, and orange juice concentrate, was something he pushed down and away from him.

They stayed up late watching movies on TV. Once in bed, Dan pulled the covers up to his shoulders in the cavernous dark room. The sheets smelled as if they'd been dried on the line, but it was too cold out for that, and it was hard to imagine that the Gates laundry was treated in such a manner. The room was warm and peaceful in spite of its size, and he felt truly safe for the first time since leaving MacDougal Island. It occurred to him that his grandparents might never pick him up, that perhaps they didn't want him and never had. In light of that, he wondered if it might be possible that he could live here, if there was any way the Gates family would accept him and bring it about. It seemed possible. Anyone with this much had to have the ability to make things happen.

If a thought about Mike and Ingrid came up, he quickly forced it from his mind, replacing it instead with images of running on the beach or exploring the house's attics. He could live here; maybe he could live in the attic. His thoughts slowly lost their shape and blurred into dreams.

He woke up in the late morning, remembering where he was and wondering, for an instant, if his mother had the police searching for him. The thought of the trouble he was in and the inevitability of returning to Portview poured heavily over him. He lay in the clean bed thinking about it, breathing deeply through his nose, almost panting. He finally got up and wandered off to the bathroom.

When he got back to the bed to look for his clothes, he realized that they were gone, except for the new hiking boots and down coat he had left around a chair. On a chest behind the head of his bed, he found two wrapped presents with little tags with his name on them. Opening one- "from Gigi"- he found a black cashmere sweater. In the other, from Hugh, was a copy of *Slaughterhouse Five* by Kurt Vonnegut. Underneath both were clean, folded jeans, socks, underwear and t-shirts, all in his size.

"We're washing your other clothes," a note said. "These are yours to keep, sweetie-pie. G.G."

After he had showered and dressed- he kept unconsciously stroking the arms of the cashmere sweater, fascinated by the texture- Charlie and Jim were still asleep. He occupied himself by looking out at the lake, the view stupendous in the daylight, with the sky clear and blue, the water deep blue at the distant horizon, the color of jade near the shore. Looking at things through the telescope, he watched the occasional solitary person far down on the beach. When Jim straggled out of his bedroom an hour later, he hardly noticed Dan reading the Vonnegut on the daybed by the window, shuffling by him to the bathroom, scratching his tufted blonde hair with one hand and his buttocks with the other. Charlie came out of his room awhile later in much the same way, muttered something, saw that the bathroom was occupied, and shuffled, almost sleepwalking, to one down the hall.

Dan wished for an instant that he was one of these brothers, that they were a trio, that his hair was the color of theirs and that he had the right to be here.

Terribly hungry, but not wanting to say anything, he seemed to wait forever for the boys to get showered and dressed. Finally, they went down to the kitchen, where he was introduced to one of their housekeeping staff, Elpidia, a trim Latina who had been beautiful, but was growing into a lined and tired look. Her accent reminded him of Mr. Benitez with a sudden pang, and when he spoke a few words of Spanish, the lines seemed to leave her face and she smiled brightly.

"*Ay, que bueno!*" she said. "*Y guapo tambien!*" she tousled his hair and demanded to know what they wanted for breakfast. Chorizo and eggs was a favorite, apparently, which pleased Dan immensely; he'd had it so often at the Benitez household that it gave him another sharp pinch of homesickness. When it was ready, he attacked it with a will.

They were informed that the Dr. Gates was gone, as were Hugh and Gigi. It was apparent that this was normal, and that the boys had the run of the huge place with little or no supervision. Charlie and Jim seemed puzzled when Dan offered to help clean up after breakfast, but Charlie said, "Suit yourself," and the two brothers wandered off. Dan stayed in the kitchen talking to Elpidia after they were finished. In spite of his being enthralled by the lavishness of the lives of the Gates family, not to mention the excitement of possibilities around him, it was the first time he had really felt comfortable in the huge house. Of course he felt safe, but comfort was another thing.

"Well, they are a smart bonch," Elpidia said, bringing Dan a glass of milk. "You might not be able to tell that with Charlie and Jim," -she pronounced it *Jeem*, of course- "but they are like the Dr. Gates. And like Gigi and Hugh. All very intelligent. The boys cover it up by being little *malditos, me entiendes?*"

"*Si*," Dan said.

"I think you are the same way," she said, patting his hand.

No, I'm not, Dan thought. I'm just a *maldito*. Otherwise someone would want me.

"Don't you be intimidated by them," Elpidia said. "You are just as good as they are."

Being in the kitchen with Elpidia felt somehow like being with his grandmother when she was cooking; it was calm and peaceful, seeming to make his heart warm, to beat more slowly. He stayed as long as he could, until he thought he was being a rude guest. He then excused himself politely, not wanting to go.

"Ay, those two *pendejos* don't care what you do," flicking her hand as if brushing away a mosquito. "They're probably just watching TV or pulling their *pingas*. But you go ahead. Come back if you want something. And remember: you are just as good as they are. Better."

Dan wondered for a flickering moment what it was she saw about him that called for such reassurance and encouragement; was he so obviously tainted? About the boys, he thought she was probably right; they almost certainly were watching TV or pulling their *pingas*. Only wanting to find them in the midst of the first activity, he tried to imagine where they might be engaged in it. He checked all around the vast first floor. The living room, the giant library, dazzling now with

362

light reflected off the snow outside, were empty; wastefully so, Dan thought. The view of the vast blue lake hypnotized him for a moment; he tilted his head to one side and thought about painting it, about what color it was, then shook his head and continued.

He dared to look in Dr. Gates's office. Large and oak paneled, it had an enormous desk with a leather chair which resembled a throne. The room was lined with books with incomprehensible titles; diplomas and awards adorned the walls, oil paintings with sailing scenes. Dan wondered how he would measure up in Dr. Gates's eyes, and, without forming the thought into words, knew that he would have to make a good impression if he were ever to live here.

Dan found the boys in the pool room with the large television on loud, but ignored. They played pool for awhile, and Dan's skills, attained in his grandfather's bar, came in handy against the brothers, who had obviously sharpened their own skills against each other (and under Hugh's tutelage) during hours in this room. In spite of the magnificence of the table, which was half again as large as what he was used to, and had no dents, scratches, or cigarette burns, Dan soon got anxious to do something novel in these tempting surroundings.

Eventually, he persuaded Charlie and Jim to explore one of the attics, an idea which obviously bored them, but to which they acquiesced. It took some considerable tramping to get from the pool room up to the attics, up flights of stairs and through doorways, finally up a length of uncarpeted wooden steps to a large door. They opened it and came into a huge room, lit from either end by small windows, the hard winter light from outside making the looming shapes around them dark and shadowed by comparison. Dan could immediately make out a stuffed bison head and large old steamer trunks, and then, off by one of the windows, a glint caught his eye. He approached it, and saw that it was a suit of armor.

"Armor?" Dan gasped. "You have a suit of *armor*? *Jee*-ziz, that's the coolest thing I've ever seen! What the hell is it doing up here?"

"It's old," Jim said.

"No shit it's old, genius," Charlie said. "It's fucking *armor*. Who uses armor?"

"Old guys, asshole," Jim said defensively.

Dan didn't know where to start exploring. He opened up a steamer trunk and was examining its contents: old dresses with high collars, mothballs, boxes of costume jewelry. He had gotten engrossed with a box of yellowed sepia photographs of men and women in old clothing standing front of huge ships in a port when Jim cried, "Holy shit! Check this out!"

"What?" Charlie said, going over to look.

A large cardboard box held a few dozen Barbie dolls, along with numerous Kens and Skippers, plastic horses, dogs, a jeep, a convertible, even a panda and a zebra.

"So what?" Dan said. "You've got a suit of armor up here and you get excited about Barbie dolls?"

Charlie and Jim looked at each other, grins spreading across their faces.

"The pellet guns!" they cried simultaneously.

When properly motivated, the Gates boys acted quickly. Before Dan could think of what was wrong with what they were about to do- this could make a terrible impression on Dr. Gates!- they were in their coats, had gotten two pellet guns from their room, and were dragging the box down the flights of stairs, going past the kitchen and out the door to the back terraces.

Elpidia opened a kitchen window and barked, "Hey! What are you *culicagados* doing?"

"Nothing!" Jim called.

"Getting some fresh air!" Charlie called. "It's good for us!"

Dan gave her a nervous look and a little wave. She shook her head wearily and closed the window.

They went past the poolhouse and down the snowy steps to a lower terrace where they could not be seen from the house. There the brothers began to set up.

"Astronaut Barbie must be the first to die," Charlie intoned. "Set her up against the wall."

Dan felt torn. "So, aren't these, like, Gigi's or something? Won't she get pissed off?" He liked Gigi and didn't want to hurt her feelings.

"She likes dick and weed, in that order," Charlie said, pumping up his pellet gun. "And booze, naturally. She won't even know these are gone."

"Ready?" Jim asked, sighting down the barrel of his pellet gun.

"For your transgressions against the state," Charlie said, aiming, "your life is forfeit."

Dan remembered his trepidation at the thought of the brothers handling his grandfather's guns, and thought that his feelings were justified. They fired: tap-tap. Astronaut Barbie jerked against the stone wall and pitched forward into the snow.

"Die, capitalist pigdog," Jim said. Dan smiled, then snorted with laughter in spite of himself.

"Here," Charlie said, handing Dan the pellet gun. "your turn."

Jim stood the doll back up and moved out of the way. Dan sighed, walked several paces back while pumping the gun, aimed, and fired.

"Oooh hoo hoo, head shot!" Charlie crowed.

Dan narrowed his eyes in thought. "Let's put a Ken over there. He looks like a smug asshole." Dan's background feeling of guilt slipped away when he imagined lining Mike and his mother up against a wall, visualizing them both cowering as he took aim. He shot again and again.

Over the next hour, they came up with more and more inventive scenarios as they decimated the large box's population of dolls. They laughed hardest when setting up Barbie, Ken and Skipper in different sexual positions and blowing them apart.

"Talk about your coitus interruptus," Charlie said.

"In flagrante delictooooo," Jim said.

"Fuck me?" Dan said, aiming. "Fuck *me*? Fuck *you*!"

Charlie and Jim laughed, delighted with his vicious tone.

When they had shot everything they could, Charlie stomped on some of the pieces.

"Just to be thorough," he said.

They stood around in the afterglow of the carnage, smiling at each other.

"Guess we should clean it up," Dan said.

"Nah," Charlie said. "It's gonna snow again. Nobody'll see it 'til spring."

"What then?"

"Gardener'll clean it up," Jim said.

"He won't say anything," Charlie said.

"We rip off bottles of booze for him," Jim added. "He's our buddy."

Satisfied and a little tired, they walked back to the kitchen. Elpidia made them soup and sandwiches for lunch, scowling at them throughout, apparently aware that they had been up to no good, but not sure what, exactly, that no good might have been.

As long as he could keep himself distracted, Dan was fine. He got the impression that he made Charlie and Jim do more around their own home than they otherwise would have done. He induced them to work out in the gym, which led to wrestling matches. Although Charlie was a year older than Dan, and now taller, Dan was solidly built and had benefitted from his grandfather's set-up-which Dan was now forced to admit was rather primitive- in the basement of the bungalow. Their matches were competitive to the point of being brutal. It was obvious that Charlie did not like to lose, but he had somewhere learned good sportsmanship and was analytical about it. Jim was the youngest and therefore lowest on the totem pole, but he had such heart, such a willingness to go at it again, that it made Dan and Charlie smile at each other.

"One day I'll be able to beat both you fuckers," Jim said, panting, lower lip bleeding, after one tough bout with his brother. "At the same time."

They took a sauna at Dan's insistence, the brothers amazed that he had never had one before. "Shit," Dan said, "this is great. I don't know why you guys don't do this every day."

The brothers seemed happy to please him, and it was only when Dan met some of the kids from the neighborhood the next day that this seemed to make any sense at all.

A trio of them came over, ushered in the front door by Elpidia. All three of the boys treated her as if she weren't there, and she regarded them with flinty eyes, her lips pursed. Dan saw this, and immediately knew what to think of the kids.

All of them looked soft, and, to Dan's eye, overdressed. There was blonde kid named Scotty, who slouched into the library where Dan, Charlie, and Jim were playing Risk. He was followed by a chubby, dark-haired boy named Ian, and a small red-haired boy with protuberant eyes named Joel, all introduced by Charlie as they came in. Dan's eyes met Elpidia's for a moment before she slowly rolled her gaze away, as if to say, No comment.

"Elpidia's got a great ass," Scotty said after she'd left the room. "I'll bet she was a great fuck when she was younger."

"What would you know about a great fuck?" Charlie said.

"Oh, I know," Scotty said. "I know."

"Too bad we can't own slaves," Ian said. "We'd make her fuck all of us."

"Yeah, *fuck* us," Joel giggled.

"Cool it, assholes," Jim said.

Scotty ignored this. "So, what's your deal, uh, Dan, is it?"

"What do you mean, what's my deal?" Dan said.

"Where do you live? Where do you go to school?"

"Right now, in Portview."

"Portview! What a shithole! You in a gang or something?"

"He's in *our* gang, *Scotty*," Charlie said. "Quit being such a dick."

"Hey, I'm just asking a friendly question. Jesus. You mind if I ask you a friendly question or two, Dan?"

"Guess not."

"So, you used to live way out on the river, right? D'ja know any Indians or anything?"

Dan thought about Bob Two Bears, always kind and friendly to him, and wondered what Bob would make of this boy.

"Yeah, I know some Indians," Dan said. "Why?"

"Just wondering, just wondering. Did you learn anything cool from the Indians? Like how to eat dogs? Skin 'em and shit? I just want to know if I should bring Patches in tonight. I don't want you eating my dog if you get hungry."

Ian and Joel laughed at this.

"My dad's CEO of a food distribution company," Scotty said. "What does your dad do?"

Dan blinked once at this question. "He's dead," he said, feeling his pulse speed up and his face get hot.

"Dead?" Joel said. "Bullshit!"

"Oh, now I remember!" Scotty said. "These guys told me all about it! Your dad's dead, and you used to live with your grandfather, who's a murderer, right? Wow. *Cool.*"

Charlie and Jim both got in front of Dan before he could cross the room to the kid. In his mind, Dan clearly saw himself pounding the kid in the face until the blood flew, and he only had to get *that far* to make it happen. Charlie and Jim struggled to hold Dan in place.

"Drama!" Ian cried delightedly.

"Scotty," Charlie said over his shoulder, "you better shut up, or we're going to let him go."

"And you don't want that," Jim said. "You just got your braces off."

"Hey, sorry," Scotty said. "Really. I was just giving the kid a little shit. See if he could take it. No offense, Dan, okay?"

Dan watched him, breathing deeply. Charlie and Jim slowly released their hold.

"Man, you've been through a lot," Joel said. "I didn't know people actually lived lives like that."

"Not around here, they don't," Ian said.

"That's why he's cooler than you fuckers'll ever be," Jim said.

When things settled down, they all sprawled on the floor to play Risk. With the violent fantasies Dan was having about Scotty, he could barely concentrate on the game, and finally made some intentional bad moves to be out of it. He got up and crossed the library to sit with a book on Michelangelo by the windows overlooking the lake, but had a hard time even looking at the pictures in the book. Instead, he watched Scotty, holding the book in front of him so that it masked most of his face.

The game came down to Jim and Scotty, and when Jim had the smug boy cornered in Kamchatka, ready to finish him off, Scotty fell forward from a kneeling position and thumped his head into the board, scattering the pieces.

"You asshole!" Jim cried. "Just can't fucking lose, can you, Scotty!"

"Hey, it was an accident!" Scotty said innocently.

"Dan," Charlie called, "Scotty's ready for his beating now!"

Dan lowered the book and watched Scotty, who saw him and looked away.

"Well, that was fun," the boy said, standing up. "I guess we'll be off. Come on, guys."

Joel and Ian got up and walked out after Scotty. Dan set down the book, ready to follow Scotty outside if he made a parting comment, but the boy left the room without looking back.

Charlie saw them out the front door and came back to the library.

"Those guys are your friends?" Dan asked him.

"Well, more like neighbors, really."

"They go to our school," Jim said, bobbing his head apologetically.

"Now you can see why I hang around with Bunghole, here," Charlie said, punching his brother in the shoulder. "Bunch of jagoffs in this neighborhood."

"Punch me again and see what happens, asshole," Jim said, shoving his brother. A wrestling match ensued, which Elpidia broke up, screaming at the boys to take it down to the gym.

Dan was beginning to wonder if Dr. Gates lived in the huge house at all. He'd been at the Gates home for days and not seen him once, and when the boys had shown him their father's bedroom, it hadn't looked as if anyone actually lived there.

"He's probably boning one of his grad students," Charlie said. Dan still didn't fully understand what a grad student was, but he got the general idea.

The house was large enough that he imagined it was possible to live in it without running into another person for some time, but he thought it strange that they didn't seem to eat together. Out on the river, dinner together with his grandparents had been reassuringly punctual, a realization he had now that those dinners were a thing of the past. The other end of the spectrum was life with his mother, which was too chaotic to provide any routine whatsoever. It seemed that Charlie and Jim's routine was to eat dinner with Elpidia before she took the bus back to the South Side, and Dan supposed that was good enough.

They were in the pool room shooting a game of eightball when Elpidia called on the intercom to tell them that their father was home and they'd be eating dinner at six. Dan immediately felt nervous about this, and Charlie read it on his face.

"Jesus, don't worry about it, man," he said. "Our dad's a doofus."

They were on their way to the formal dining room when Dr. Gates came out of the door to his study.

"Oh! Boys!" he said.

"Hey, Dad," they said.

Dan didn't know what he was expecting, but he'd had the idea that Gates would somehow be more imposing. The man before him was shortish, with a bit of a belly, wearing a corduroy jacket and reading glasses perched on the lower third of his nose. He was not impressive in the least.

"And this must be Dan! Young Huck! The Wild Boy of the River! A pleasure to meet you!"

"Likewise, Mr. Gates," Dan said, holding out his hand.

"*Doctor* Gates, actually," he said, shaking Dan's hand.

"Sorry, sir."

"Sir! Hear that boys? Gigi said you had good manners, Dan. You're welcome in our home. Stay as long as you like."

A glow of hope welled in Dan's chest. Maybe it *was* possible. Maybe he'd never have to go back to his mother's apartment. He knew he had to make an impression.

"This is a terrific house you have here, sir," he ventured.

"Ah, this old place. You get used to it. I'm sure these two take it for granted."

"This neighborhood sucks," Charlie said.

"It's boring around here," Jim said.

"See, Dan? How sharper than the serpent's tooth, how sharper than the serpent's tooth."

Dan had no idea what the man was talking about, but nodded amiably anyway.

The four of them sat at the end of the long table in the dining room. Dan wondered why they didn't eat in the kitchen, which would have been more practical, not to mention easier for Elpidia.

Dinner was not what Dan expected, either. Although the food was excellent, as he had come to expect, Gates didn't interact much with the boys; rather he ate his meal, drank wine, and talked *at* them. After asking Dan a few polite questions about his life, he stared off into space and gave a discourse on the life of Samuel Clemens, the state of the country in his time, and the geological history of the river. This, somehow, became a talk about the Aztecs and the Mayans and the relative merits and shortcomings of their civilizations.

Charlie made eye contact with Dan at one point, and interrupted to say, "Our father is a gigantic suppository of knowledge."

"I think you meant to say 'repository', Charlie," Gates said.

"No I didn't."

Gates gave Charlie a droll look, but continued his lecture. At length. Dan wandered so far off in his own thoughts that he lost the thread of the subject matter.

"Not that European civilization at the time left nothing to be desired, of course, Dan," Gates said at one point, and Dan jumped at the sound of his own name, dropping his knife with a clank on his plate.

"Are you all right, son?" Dr. Gates said, his eyes on Dan over his reading glasses, his sudden focus unnerving.

"Just slipped," Dan said.

"Oh. Well. More roast?"

"Yes, sir."

Dr. Gates finished his first bottle of wine, and got up to open himself another. Dan looked at Charlie, who was rolling his eyes elaborately, and Jim, who sat at the table with his mouth and eyes wide open, as if he'd been lobotomized. Dan laughed.

"Sesquipedalian motherfucker," Charlie said to the other boys as Gates returned to the table.

"What was that, son?" Gates said as he sat down.

"I said, 'sesquipedalian motherfucker'."

"Okay, Charlie," Dr. Gates said mildly, "watch your language."

"Sorry," Charlie said. "I guess I meant to say 'pleonastic motherfucker'."

"That's enough, now."

"*Wordy* motherfucker? *Verbose* motherfucker? What exactly do you want me to say?"

"Say goodbye. You can leave the table."

"I was leaving anyway," Charlie said. He tossed his napkin on the table and walked out. Jim did the same, looking at Dr. Gates and shaking his head.

Dan suddenly felt small in the huge room, sitting motionlessly for some time. "Thanks for dinner, sir," he said finally.

"Oh. Yes." Gates said, as if just realizing that Dan was still there. "Of course. Go ahead and join the boys."

Leaving the room, Dan glanced back. Dr. Gates was now the one who seemed small in the room, as if diminished by the absence of even an unwilling audience.

If Dan felt a bit sorry and embarrassed for Dr. Gates at the hands of Charlie and Jim, it was nothing compared to what would happen when Hugh and Gigi joined in.

Gates was hosting a party on New Year's Eve, with colleagues and students invited. Hugh and Gigi had returned home for it, finding the boys in the poolroom.

"Can't miss Dad's parties," Gigi said, walking in and hugging Dan, giving him a kiss on the head. "They're hilarious."

"I have an idea of how to make it better," Hugh said.

Gigi eyed him with a slow smile. "Uh oh," she said.

"Yeah. Uh oh."

Charlie and Jim had explained that, while the relationship shared by Dr. Gates and Hugh seemed warm enough, there were shifting undercurrents to it which eluded the uninformed glance.

Dr. Gates, whose full name was Henry Bosworth Gates V, had had a son with his first wife and given that son the succession of his name, Henry Bosworth Gates VI. This child had died at less than a year old, and the parents were heartbroken. They tried again, though, and Hugh was born, followed shortly thereafter by Guinevere. Dr. Gates's first wife had then died when Hugh and Gigi were still in gradeschool, and Charlie and Jim were born to his second wife, who had died of an overdose of sedatives. None of the children appeared to fault him for "boning grad students", so dismal had his luck been with mates.

"In a way," Gigi had said, "at least we still all have each other, however fucked up that might be."

369

Dan didn't think it was fucked up at all; he thought it was the best thing in the world.

The missing eldest brother was referred to as Six, and was often invoked at such times.

"Of course," Hugh said, "things wouldn't be fucked up at all if *Six* were still here."

"Of course not," Gigi said.

"Yea, Six!" Jim cheered.

"Good ol' Six, you dead-ass motherfucker," Charlie said.

Some of those dark and shifting undercurrents involved Henry Gates's feelings toward his eldest son. It seemed that, as much as Gates denied it and tried to cover it up, he resented Hugh for being gay.

"They were too filled with superstitious dread to name me after Dad, to continue the linkage," Hugh said, "which wouldn't have made a bit of difference anyway, since I'm not going to have kids. If I did, and named the kid Henry Bosworth Gates VI, who, in turn, could have spawned a Henry Bosworth Gates VII, well, then I'd really be somebody."

"You are somebody," Gigi said. "You just prefer dick."

"You prefer dick, and nobody makes a big deal out of *that*."

"Touché," Gigi said.

"Dad might hate me for being a faggot," Hugh said, "but it kept me out of Viet Nam."

"All because you were willing to demonstrate that you prefer dick. Think of that."

The five of them were summoned for dinner in the large dining room while caterers busied themselves with party preparations throughout the first floor of the house. All the Gates siblings seemed perfectly relaxed in the formal surroundings, although it still made Dan nervous. He made eye contact with Elpidia as she got ready to leave for the evening, and she winked reassuringly.

Dr. Gates took off almost immediately, first talking about the advent of the microprocessor, then about the statues on Easter Island and the collapse of the civilization which created them.

"They failed to live within their means, the people of Easter Island," Gates said. "A lesson to us all."

Hugh and Gigi attempted to be polite throughout this, muttering to each other and the boys to pass dishes or making a quiet comment which went unnoticed by Dr. Gates.

Gates began talking about Odysseus, then about the mythical creatures in such stories. When he went on at some point about the Cyclops, it got Dan's attention. In an attempt to make conversation, Dan asked, "Was there a country that the Cyclopses came from?"

Charlie said, "Actually, the plural of Cyclops is *Cyclopes*."

"Ah!" Dr. Gates said, "You've done your reading, Charlie! Good eye!"

Groans followed at the unintentional pun (while Gates looked momentarily puzzled), and Hugh said over them, "Yes, he's a fine pupil!"

Barks of laughter punctuated the groans when Gigi said, "Okay, let's put a lid on it."

"Iris *just* going to say that!" Jim laughed.

"Ah, a little aqueous humor," Charlie put in.

Dan realized that attention had subtly moved to him. The pause became uncomfortable.

"I've got nothing," Dan said, but just as Hugh began to cover for him, he said, "I guess I deserve a thousand lashes."

The Gates clan cheered. Feeling his face redden, Dan leaned forward to inspect his plate.

"He's got his foot in the door," Hugh laughed.

"Got his toe in the water!" Gigi put in.

Dr. Gates, caught up in the mood, laughed and laughed, holding up his drink in salute.

"That was an arch comment," Charlie said, looking over at his father.

"Don't be a heel," Jim crowed. "Dan got off a good one."

Again the attention turned to Dan.

"I guess I might have nailed it," Dan allowed. There was a pause. "You know, toe nail."

Dr. Gates ultimately had to be thumped on the back to relieve his choking. Dan felt as if he had walked through a door into a warm and protected place, as if he'd been given a set of golden keys.

Dan had never seen caterers before, and wondered why they had to be hired when there were perfectly able-bodied people lounging around the house, waiting for things to begin. It seemed to take forever, but soon cars began to pull into the large driveway as the boys watched from an upstairs window.

"When Dad has parties, we can get away with almost anything," Charlie said. "And I mean more than usual. Anything gets broken, it's one of the guests who did it."

"Booze can go missing," Jim said, shrugging and spreading his hands. "Things can happen."

"Shit could explode and nobody would notice," Charlie said.

Soon the mansion was filled with a throng of people, with susurrant waves of conversation and the clinking of glasses creating a din which the boys had to talk over when slipping, ignored, through the crowd. A jazz quintet was gathered around the grand piano in the living room, but the efforts of the musicians, unless one stood right nearby, were generally washed into the flood of sound.

It was the first time Dan ever saw a woman wearing a sari, or a man a turban. The only Asians he had ever seen had been at the Chinese restaurant in Black Marsh, Fung's Golden Dragon, but there were a variety of them here tonight. It was fascinating. He forgot his background suspicion and fear, and wanted to move through the crowd and listen to all of them, to ask them questions. They encountered a towering, twig-thin man with an unusual, fluid accent and skin the color of an eightball who looked as if he didn't belong in grey slacks and a black turtleneck; Dan envisioned him in loose, garden-colored robes and perhaps a fez. The man took the time to talk to the boys, asking them genuinely interested questions about themselves, baffling them with magic tricks done with a deck of cards, and telling them that they should experience the wonders of the Mother Continent, before he was summoned away by new arrivals. Charlie and Jim greeted people they knew, but were generally treated as if they were invisible. They had to pull Dan away by the elbow from time to time.

At one point, they were on their way down the hall to the kitchen when they saw Hugh and Dr. Gates having intense words near Gates's office. Hugh was facing them, and glanced at them over his father's shoulder as they slipped by, his face atypically stony as his father leaned in, almost hissing at him, and poked him twice in the chest. The boys couldn't hear the words exchanged over the general noise.

"They're at it again," Charlie said. "Come on."

Dan looked back. A guest saw Dr. Gates down the hall and called to him with loud cheer. Gates cut off the conversation- or diatribe- put on a delighted face, and hurried down the hall to shake hands with the guest. Hugh watched him go, a look of tired contempt on his face. When he saw that Dan was watching him, he smiled and waggled his eyebrows.

"Hugh said he's got a surprise for Dad later," Jim said.

"What is it?"

"I don't know. That's why they call it a surprise."

The kitchen was another form of chaos, and going through the door an abrupt transition. Catering staff dressed in white shirts, black pants, vests and bowties moved efficiently around with trays. A large black man in a white uniform and chef's hat calmly directed the staff, and when he saw the boys, said "Charlaaay! Jimbo! Other kid!"

"Hey, Greg," Charlie said. "Just grabbing some beers."

"Well, you live here," the chef said, "you know where they are. There's lots more out on the breezeway. Veronica! If you drop those hors d'oeuvres, I will wait until you're pregnant and beat your fetus! I will reach in there and punch that little fucker in the face, so help me!"

"Thanks, Greg," Jim said.

"Later, fellas. And go easy, you're kinda young."

With a case of beer from the breezeway, they went down to the poolroom.

"This can be our base camp," Charlie said. "From here we can fan out."

"I'm surprised Gigi isn't down here making out with some guy," Jim observed.

"She hasn't found one who would piss Dad off enough yet," Charlie said.

They opened their beers and clinked them together, acting debonair. Charlie racked the pool balls and Jim grabbed a cue.

"What the fuck?" Dan said. "We can hang out down here any time!"

"Be cool," Charlie said. "Wait 'til it gets drunker and louder. Then I'll show you the type of shit we can really get away with."

"We run this place," Jim said.

"Besides," Charlie said, "I've got something you might be interested in." He went around the bar and stooped down. After moving some things around, he stood up, producing a joint.

"Know what this is?"

Dan gave him an irritated look. "Remember that guy that gave us the M-80s? Went to Viet Nam? Him and his brother were always stoned."

"Have you been?"

"Well, no."

"Always a first time."

"We stole it from Hugh," Jim said. "He'd kill us if he knew. Says he wants us to do well in school."

"Yeah, and that's bullshit. It's natural. All the negative talk about it is just propaganda. They used to say it would drive you crazy, and you know *that's* bullshit."

"We should probably go down in the tunnel and smoke it," Dan said. "He could come in any minute."

"Good idea."

They took several beers and went down the stairs past the wine cellar to the old tunnel. It was cold, and they could see their breath by the light of the caged bulbs on the stone wall. Charlie produced his lighter.

"Here goes," he said. He lit the joint, inhaled, and held it out.

Dan took it, holding it between thumb and forefinger. He wondered what his grandfather would think about him smoking pot; the old man had a relaxed attitude about such things, but probably shared Hugh's viewpoint. On the other hand, his grandparents had watched him be driven away and hadn't done a thing to stop it, or to find him. He put the joint up to his lips and inhaled. When he started to cough a little, Charlie said, "Hold it in! Don't waste it, it's good shit."

Dan nose-burped a couple of times and handed the joint to Jim. They passed it around between them, taking sips of their beers between hits, until it was down to the roach. Dan didn't feel any immediate effect, but Charlie and Jim, who had presumably smoked a bit more, looked different. Charlie looked less focused than usual, with one eyelid lower than the other. Jim's eyes were slightly puffy and he blinked a lot, looking around him as if mildly surprised. Dan felt no symptoms other than a kind of thick warmth which permeated his head and body, in spite of the chill in the tunnel.

"Feel anything?" Charlie asked.

"Nope," Dan said, staring at the wall. "Did you ever look at the texture of these stones? I mean, seriously. Check it out."

Jim snickered. "Yeah. Check it out."

"It's all porous. Looks like the surface of the moon."

Charlie snorted. Jim started laughing, and soon Dan was laughing, too. Charlie threw his empty beer bottle, smashing it against the heavy door, and said, "Let's go upstairs!"

They had intended to go up and infiltrate the party, but got distracted by a game of pool and a few more beers, then got distracted, in turn, by the New Year's Eve coverage on the television.

"It's New Year's on the east coast," Charlie said. "It's not, here. That's really weird, if you think about it."

Jim wandered off and opened the French doors, walking out into the snow. This suddenly looked interesting, and Dan and Charlie followed him out. It had begun to snow again, and they found themselves standing around the statue of Bacchus.

Jim looked up at the sky. "Sure is stoned out," he said.

This struck Dan and Charlie as hilarious. They were still laughing as they walked back into the pool room, just as Gigi came in. She was wearing a simple black dress and heels, with black earrings and bracelets, dramatic against her pale skin. Dan stopped in his tracks, immediately fascinated by her dark red lipstick, by the shape of her lips. He found himself slowly licking his own lips, imagining the feel and taste of her mouth, and felt the tingling of an erection. He quickly turned away and pretended to be captivated by the television.

"What are you guys up to?" Gigi said.

"Just about to come up to the party," Charlie said.

"Good timing. Hugh's about to do his thing."

As they made their way up the stairs, Gigi said to Dan, "Do you like that sweater?"

"I love it. Thanks."

"You look really cute in it," she said, running her finger down his spine. "I love the feel of it."

Dan felt a hot pulse go from his head down to his groin. He fought the urge to flee down the carpeted hall to the party, or to lock himself in a secluded bathroom and masturbate furiously.

"I think it's all set up," Gigi said to them over the growing din of the party. "Hugh's by the piano, and Dad should be there, too."

The party was drunker and louder, as Charlie had predicted. The huge living room was packed with people, and the boys and Gigi came in through the kitchen hallway to avoid the crowd packed to near immobility around the front entrance to the room. Dan saw Dr. Gates not far from the grand piano and the jazz quintet. He was surrounded by a circle of young people who Dan assumed to be his students, the boys carefully scruffy, all sporting some form of facial hair, the girls young and attractive, mostly with long hair parted in the middle. One especially comely girl stood close to Gates on his left side, and, when Charlie nudged him, Dan saw that Gates was covertly fondling and probing the girl's round ass with his left hand while sipping from a wine glass in his right, all the time talking. The girl laughed at something Gates said, subtly grinding her ass into Gates's hand. Dan tried to show no reaction, but the way Charlie smirked and slowly nodded his head- see?- it was difficult.

Hugh stood less then ten feet away, talking to some urbanely dressed people with champagne glasses. Gigi came and stood next to him, deftly grabbing a champagne flute for herself from a waiter's passing tray, exchanging an almost invisible look of communication with Hugh, who, in turn, gave a blankly innocent glance to a sophisticate in a grey jacket and white turtleneck by his side.

The man cleared his throat, and said, "So, Hugh, how are your studies going?"

"Oh, perfectly well, thank you," Hugh said.

A nearby woman in fine attire asked, "And what is it that you're studying, Hugh?"

374

"Voice, in the music department at the University."

"He's getting his Master's," the man in the grey jacket said. "Very talented. I have no doubt we'll be seeing him at the opera."

"Oh, how wonderful!" the woman said.

"David, you're embarrassing me," Hugh said.

"Don't be ridiculous!" the woman said. "Or modest! You can't be modest if you're going to perform on stage, now can you?"

Hugh bobbed his head modestly.

"Please, favor us with a song," the woman said.

"Oh, I couldn't."

"Now, I won't take no for an answer," she said, putting her hand on his forearm. "Please!"

Hugh and Gigi traded a delicate look. "Well, if you insist," he said.

The quintet stopped playing, and Hugh spoke to the pianist, who played a refrain from Sinatra's "A Very Good Year" with enough emphasis to get the attention of most of the crowd.

"This is for my father," Hugh said, "your host, Dr. Henry Bosworth Gates V."

There was a sprinkle of applause. Gates closed his eyes and nodded in appreciation. The girl next to him bounced excitedly and pushed a breast into his arm.

The pianist played the opening chords, and Hugh came in with a clear and resonant baritone.

"When I was seventeen
"I was amazingly gay
"From sunsdown to sunsup
"I buttered my buns up
"And buggered away
"There's not much more I can say
"I was amaaaazingly gay"

Some people looked bewildered, some smiled, some laughed out loud. Hugh continued, belting it out with passion, as if it were the most poignant song he knew:

"When I was twenty-five
"I was fantastically queer
"With all the fisting and felching
"And cumbucket belching
"I should have steered clear
"Oh, but I never came near
"I was fantaaaastically queer."

Most of the crowd was laughing and applauding, although some looked offended. Across the room, Dan saw the tall black man with the cards throwing his head back and laughing. Dr. Gates had a polite smile frozen on his face, as if a photo had been taken of him halfway through being delightfully surprised. The young woman next to him giggled into her little fist, and the students were struggling not to laugh. Gigi had her head on Charlie's shoulder, helpless with laughter.

The song went on, its revised lyrics increasingly raunchy. Hugh finished strongly, with bravado. The crowd applauded and cheered, even those who had at first seemed offended. Hugh gave a neat stage bow with great gravity. The pianist and the rest of the quintet were smiling and laughing. They started right in to playing something up tempo.

Dr. Gates ignored those around him, watching his son with the same frigidly pleasant look on his face. Hugh winked soberly at his father and left the room through the back. Gigi and the boys followed.

In hall outside the kitchen, the siblings collapsed on each other with laughter.

"Omigod," Gigi said. "Omigod. Dad is going to be *so* pissed."

Hugh shrugged, smiling. "He never hesitated to tell me that I embarrassed him. It feels good to take an active part."

"I hope it was worth it," Charlie said. "You could get cut off for this one."

"It was worth it," Hugh said. "It was worth it."

They counted down to New Year's in the pool room, cheering at midnight. Hugh opened a bottle of champagne, warning the boys not to drink too much. Gigi danced with Hugh, and then with Dan, who went stiffly through the motions, trying to remember what his grandmother had taught him in the living room of the bungalow.

When Hugh and Gigi left to go to a party downtown, Charlie said, "Okay, now I'll show you what we can do around here. Get your jackets."

They went outside and around the house to the front, going between the house and a fence that separated the property from a wooded ravine which led down to the lake. In front of the house, the long drive was packed with cars, as was the street in front of the gate, with a few people coming and going.

The boys, apparently unnoticed, followed Charlie to the gardener's building in the front yard. Inside, Charlie turned on the light and looked around, gathering some empty quart bottles, a funnel, a large gas can, and some rags.

"I was thinking about this for awhile," he said. "I got the idea from our little game of hotfoot that we played in the summer. That, and a book by Abbie Hoffmann."

Charlie used the funnel to pour gasoline into the quart bottles.

"Ho, man," Jim said, laughing and shaking his head. Dan cracked the door and looked out to see if anyone was coming.

"Don't worry," Charlie said. "Who's going to come out to the gardener's shed at midnight on New Year's?"

Dan watched, in a mixture of fear and delight, as Charlie tightly stuffed the necks of the bottles with rags.

"Gentlemen," Charlie said, "I give you…the Molotov cocktail."

Charlie put the bottles in a crate and stood up. "Let's go."

They headed for the back of the building, Charlie carrying the crate. Thirty feet away, an elegant couple headed away from the house toward the cars in the street.

"Have a good time?" Charlie called.

"Yes!" the couple replied.

"Great! Happy New Year!"

The couple waved cheerfully and continued on their way. Dan laughed and shook his head.

They went back along the fence through the snow, down the stairs of the terraces to where they had decimated the Barbies. The statue of Bacchus appeared to be the only witness.

"Hokay!" Charlie said in a businesslike manner, setting down the crate. "One of you guys is gonna light the rag here, and what I'm gonna do is aim for those boulders down there. Simple!"

Dan looked up at the windows of the house, all warmly lit, the muffled sound of the party drifting down towards them in the darkness. The house was high enough on the bluff that, from where they stood, no people could be seen, only the tall windows and the ceilings of the rooms inside. No one was outside on any of the balconies.

Charlie handed his lighter to Jim, then took a bottle from the crate and cocked the bottle over his shoulder. "Just like with the M-80s," he said. "Light me."

Dan stood back. Jim clicked open the Zippo and held the flame to the end of the rag. It caught, and Jim shouted, "Well, throw it!"

"Wait a sec," Charlie said, holding the bottle until the rag was halfway ablaze. Then he tossed it, the fluttering flame arcing out into the darkness. It dropped to the rocks and exploded in a mushroom of fire.

The boys cheered. Jim shouldered over to the crate for his turn, selecting a bottle. Dan looked up at the house, saw no one, and watched as the brothers repeated the procedure, another blossom of flame billowing in the darkness. When crowds failed to pour out of the French doors of the house to pursue the young anarchists, Dan took his turn. He was breathing hard when he tossed the bottle, and when it exploded, he leapt in the air with glee. The boys jumped around, laughing and slapping each other on the back, their breath steaming in the cold.

With the last Molotov expended, they wandered back to the house. Just before they went through the doors by the pool room, it began to snow in large flakes.

"See?" Charlie said cheerfully. "This will cover the evidence. We are beloved of the gods."

The pool room was not exciting enough, so they made a final foray of the adult party, which had gotten even louder. They saw Henry Gates going into his study with the student of the fondled ass.

"He's out of the picture for awhile," Charlie said.

The party itself had gotten raucous. Some adults were reelingly drunk, some redfaced with laughter. Greg, the chef, was standing by the piano drinking with the jazz musicians, all of them laughing and openly passing a joint. A woman in an evening gown sat on an antique chair between two potted plants, alternately sobbing and sipping from a martini. Charlie and Jim laughed at her. She cried harder. In a side room off the main hall, they flicked the lightswitch and found the black man of the card tricks standing behind the woman in fine attire from the piano, who was bent over a sofa, clutching its cushions, her face twisted and her skirts around her waist. The man pumped into her from behind, not deterred by the sudden light.

"Ah, boys!" he said. "Would you be so kine as to turn off the lights when you leave?"

"Sure thing!" Charlie said obligingly, flicking the switch.

"Thank you!" the man called from the darkness. The boys leaned on each other laughing in the hall.

Not satisfied with the evening so far, they got the pellet guns and stole across the street in the dark, dodging behind bushes to avoid passing cars. A few blocks away, they came to another stately home in the neighborhood, buffered from the street by a huge, snowy yard.

"Scotty's house," Jim said. Dan didn't need to hear another thing.

Careful to leave no footprints in the snow, they went halfway up the driveway. Checking to make sure there were no witnesses, they pumped up the guns and took turns shooting at the house, popping tiny holes in its large windows. When they thought they had done enough, they slipped back into the shadows and made their way home.

"Scotty always was a dick," Charlie said.

When Dan woke up, it was Sunday afternoon. Charlie and Jim had yet not stirred, although they had gone to bed before him. He had stayed up watching the sky turn purple over the huge water, almost nauseous with the thought that his flight from the reality of his life was almost over. When he finally got out of bed, he went and retched over the toilet, producing nothing but a strand of drool.

Charlie and Jim were in the large room when he came back. They laughed at first.

"Heard ya ralphing," Charlie said.

"Maybe it's a hangover," Jim said.

"We didn't drink enough to get a hangover," Dan said.

"How do you know?" Jim asked.

"He grew up in a bar, dumbass," Charlie said.

"Oh, yeah."

"You look like shit, though, man," Charlie said. "You okay?"

They looked genuinely concerned. Dan realized that these two boys were the closest people to him, the only ones he could trust. They seemed to envy his life, oddly enough, yet he thought that if they knew the reality of it, this would stop. Perhaps they would even stop liking him, in which case he would be completely alone. He looked back and forth at their faces. Then, overcoming his shame and embarrassment, he took a deep breath and told them about his life. Once he had started, it kept coming. Almost fifteen minutes had passed before he had finished. It felt surprisingly good to reveal it, to throw the secret pieces of himself in the air and let them fall where they would.

The looks on their faces told him that he had been right to trust them.

"Man," Jim said. "That's the most I ever heard you talk at once."

Dan and Jim both looked at Charlie, who sat staring at the floor, his brow furrowed.

"Okay. I'm thinking." Charlie said at last. "This is messed up. No one should have to live like that."

"They do all the time," Dan said. "There are kids at my school who have it way worse than me."

"Doesn't make it right."

"Guess not."

Charlie sat, eyes narrowed in thought.

"And you haven't heard anything from your grampa or gramma?"

Dan shook his head. "They didn't want me anyway. They don't care where I am."

"How do you know?" Jim asked.

"They never called. Not once. I thought they were going to come and get me, but they didn't even call."

"Maybe they don't know where you are," Charlie said.

"Nah, they...." He stopped. Maybe they *didn't* know where to find him. No, they knew. "They don't care."

"You should at least call them," Jim said.

Dan didn't say anything.

"We have to do something about this right now," Charlie said. "School starts again tomorrow."

Dan held his tongue, not wanting to ask, not wanting to bring up what had been on his mind since coming here.

"He should just live with us," Jim said to Charlie. Dan could have hugged him.

"Yeah. Let's go talk to Dad."

Rather than search the house for Dr. Gates, they first looked out the front windows. The garage door was open, Gates's car gone.

"We'll have to wait," Charlie said.

They went to the kitchen, and while Charlie and Jim attacked the leftovers from the party, Dan sat with a glass of orange juice, looking out the window to the terraces and the lake. It was snowing again. He felt that he would cry if he only knew how.

Gates finally came home, and the boys caught him as he was going into his office. Charlie framed his question as a request for his father's advice, something that apparently came as a surprise to Dr. Gates. Charlie described the situation clearly, sitting on the arm of the couch in the office. Dan sat in a chair, feeling as if he were in front of a judge.

Gates sat behind his desk, leaning back in his chair, fingers steepled, glasses at the end of his nose.

"I'm sorry things are like this for you at home, Dan," he said finally. "I'm sure you wish you were back out on the river, at times."

Dan moved his shoulders indifferently.

"Well," Charlie said. "We were thinking that maybe he could live here."

"Oh, Charlie..." Gates said, sighing and slowly shaking his head. Dan's nausea returned.

"Why not? We've got tons of everything, plenty of room. He could go to our school."

"It's not as simple as that."

"How much more simple could it get?"

"Yeah!" Jim said.

"His mother has legal custody of him," Gates said. "We can't interfere with that."

"You're always telling us to do the right thing!" Charlie shouted. "Doesn't that mean anything?"

"Yes, of course it does."

"Then *do* something!"

Dan had never seen Charlie so angry.

"Charlie," Gates said slowly, "you see the world in black and white, but usually it exists in shades of grey."

"This is about as *black* and fucking *white* as it gets! This is your chance to actually *do* something!"

"Charlie...."

"Fuck it," Charlie said, his animation suddenly lost. "Fuck this."

He stalked out of the office, Jim following.

Dan got up slowly, resigned, but hoping Gates would change his mind.

"Dan," Gates said. "I'm sorry, son. Things will look up. You'll see."

Dan nodded and walked out.

Charlie was so angry at his father that he vowed not to talk to him for a month. Dan realized that he had to embrace the inevitable, "march himself up to it", as his grandfather might have said. It had gotten difficult to imagine what his father might have suggested.

Back in the boys' rooms, Dan slowly gathered his things together. He put clothes in his pack, the book Hugh had given him, along with the sweater from Gigi. He would rather have worn it, but thought it might raise too many questions, once he returned...home.

Charlie called Hugh to ask him to give Dan a ride. "We can at least see that you don't have to take the bus."

They waited for Hugh to arrive, all of them somber. Charlie and Jim did homework they had ignored for the entire holiday, while Dan did a few drawings of Gigi as a present, hiding in the process of the artwork, his long hair hanging in his face as he bent over the paper. When he was done, he took the drawings down the hall, leaving them on the pillow of her bed.

Hugh came into the room just as the boys had turned on the television. He stood in the doorway, tall and lean in his black overcoat, looking apologetic. Dan stood up and put on the down coat the boys had given him. Charlie looked as if he were masking his emotions with impassivity. Jim lowered his eyes and dropped his head.

"Well," Dan said, "see ya. Thanks for everything." He put his pack on his shoulder and walked out into the hall.

When he got down to the foyer, he heard the thumping of the boys' feet running in pursuit. He turned around to see them coming down the staircase from the balcony, past the unlit Christmas tree.

"We'll work on the old man," Jim said, punching Dan lightly on the arm.

"Yeah," Charlie said. "Don't forget, we run this place."

Dan attempted to smile. Again, he felt that he would cry if he knew how, and the thwarted desire made his face feel thick and numb. Instead, he turned and walked through the foyer, out the large front door.

Hugh drove him downtown from White Birch Pointe, reversing the trip they had taken on the evening of Christmas. They didn't talk much. Hugh asked a few polite questions, but Dan was so quiet and preoccupied that he soon gave up, only asking for directions as they crossed the bridge over the river and into Portview. The snow at the sides of the street was grey and dirty in the diminishing light, the brick apartments, corner stores and bars cheerlessly flanked by naked black trees. The tightly parked cars were mostly beaten and rusted older models, Hugh's Saab the finest car on the street.

"That's it," Dan said, pointing at the apartment building. "718 Pier. Don't stop in front, just drive by." Hugh did so, Dan looking up out the window, trying to deduce something from the lights on in the apartment.

He asked Hugh to pull over in front of an Italian deli. Before Dan got out, Hugh said, "Dan, you give us a call if you need anything, okay? It won't be like this forever."

"What won't?"

"Your life."

Dan looked at him skeptically for a moment.

"Thanks," he said.

He got out of the car, waving limply as Hugh drove away. He looked around for awhile for a piece of pipe or something to conceal under his coat, finally settling for chunk of brick. Still feeling numb, he sighed and walked up the steps to the apartment.

The holidays passed grimly. For the sake of simplicity, they agreed not to give each other Christmas presents, although they both got presents for Dan, which they put in the closet, as if it were routine. They were invited to Emilio and Solveig's, but they begged off, knowing that Katita was in town, a rarity, and that unpleasantness would result. They stayed home instead, and, against their agreement, Willy gave Mae a copy of Beethoven's Seventh. She gave him a blue sweater.

On the first day, Willy wore the sweater while she listened to the album. When she began to listen to it every day, especially the second movement, Willy stopped wearing the sweater and started leaving the house.

At the end of January, a blizzard heaved over the river and the little island, lacing down thick and piling against the windward side of things. Willy knew that he and Bob would be shoveling snow on and off in front of the bar, so he thought he'd get to the driveway and sidewalk of the bungalow first. It seemed rather pointless; the snow kept coming down.

He dressed lightly, knowing it would be hot work once he got going. Mae- still in her pajamas and housecoat, an unusual thing- had been complaining of back pains and nausea, and he thought he'd do the shoveling and let her rest, as much as she had once done the whole job herself.

"I'm going out to shovel!" he called from the door to the porch.

"Okay," she said from the kitchen.

"Drink tea," he said. "Get comfy. When I get back in, I'll start a fire."

"Okay!"

The snow was thick on the bottom and fluffy on top. He tried to get down to the concrete of the walk, thinking that Mae might slip on any ice left behind. Cutting at the deepening snow, he worked back down the driveway, starting to huff and sweat. After an hour, he chunked the shovel in the snowbank and went up the back steps and inside to the kitchen.

"What's for lunch?" he called, taking off his boots and setting them in the stairwell.

In his socks, he went over and looked at the stove, where a pot sat on the unlit burner, a can of chicken noodle soup nearby.

"Mae?" he called.

Willy knew Mae was dead when he saw the teacup on its side on the rug in the living room. One of a set, an heirloom from her mother, it was milky white with a pattern of gold, brown, and orange, a precious thing. Leaving the teacup on the rug was simply something that Mae would never do. The fact that she lay curled on her right side, knees up, ankles crossed, thin left arm behind her, was less shocking to him than the teacup on the floor.

"Oh, no," he said. "No, no, no, no."

He fell next to her, called to her. He took her soft face in his hands and shook her gently, saying her name. He felt her neck, felt her wrist, felt the bones of her narrow chest.

William McGregor came to himself after some time, leaning against the couch, his wife's head in his lap. Easing out from under her, he stood. Bending down, he clutched her to him, lifted her, and took her to the bedroom. Setting her on his side of the bed, he turned down the covers on the other half. He took off her slippers and her housecoat, leaving her in her pink flannel pajamas with little red flowers. Then he picked her up again, moved her to her side of the bed, and pulled the covers up to her chin.

Before getting in bed himself, he closed the door to the bedroom and opened the windows. It was still snowing outside; the pulses of wind at times shook the open windows.

Willy got into bed and pulled up the covers. He leaned over to kiss his wife on the forehead.

"I love you," he said.

The apartment door was ajar, the sound and flickering light of the television coming from within. Dan stood outside for several minutes, stock still, his head cocked to one side as he listened. Hearing no snoring or muttering, he realized that Mike wasn't home, imagining, instead, his mother asleep on the couch in front of the television. He slowly opened the door and crept inside, leaving his pack out of the way, but close to the door. His fingers touched the chunk of brick in his coat pocket.

Ingrid lay on the couch, almost exactly as he had visualized her. He walked into his room and turned on the light. The blue walls, the grey blanket, his few possessions were precisely as he had left them. Thinking for a moment about climbing into bed and just going to sleep, he realized that he might get jerked awake in the middle of the night when Mike came home and wanted to take care of unfinished business.

Instead, he went out to the kitchen, turned on the light, and sat at the kitchen table with the book Hugh had given him. When Mike got home, Dan would be waiting.

He waited until midnight, finishing the book. Worry made him want to sleep, but he was determined to fight the urge. His eyes stung; he closed them for a moment and put his head on his arms.

The sound of the toilet flushing woke him up. He jerked, and looked up to find Ingrid, disheveled and bleary, standing on the other side of the kitchen table.

"Well, look who's here," she said.

"Where's Mike?" Dan said.

"Like you care," she said.

Dan did, but not for reasons she would want to hear. "Where is he?"

"He's in jail, if you really want to know."

Dan almost laughed. "In jail?"

"Yes, and it's your fault. You're ungrateful, you know that? Mike really cares about you."

"He does, huh?"

"Yes. He was very upset after your little…altercation. He had a bit too much to drink for a few days, and got into a fight in a bar down by the port. He also had a few warrants, some kind of misunderstanding. So he's in jail. No thanks to you."

"For how long?"

"Don't know yet. Why, do you want to go visit him?"

"Not really."

"Mike cares about you. And you don't care about him one bit, do you?"

Dan studied her face. Her eyes were pink and watery, with bluish smudges underneath them. Lines were becoming more pronounced on her face, small pouches forming on her jawline. He had the odd urge to get out pencils and paper and draw her face, to capture some of the sadness there, to let this brief moment of pity guide his hand.

"Is there anything to eat?" he asked, just to change the subject.

"Have some pop tarts," she said. "I'm going to bed."

"Fine."

She turned before leaving the room. "I'll tell you something, mister," she said. "I would've called the cops on you this last week if we didn't have enough trouble already."

"Okay," Dan said.

It only occurred to him much later that she never asked where he had been, or showed any concern about his well-being. She didn't remind him that he had school in the morning, or offer to fix him some food or to tuck him in, as his grandmother would have done. He didn't think about it. The fact that he had gotten away with his flight, and that Mike was gone, was all he needed for a solid night's sleep.

Dan woke up in the morning and got ready for school, leaving before Ingrid regained consciousness. The rattling din of the schoolbell, the roar of kids in the halls, told him that he was back to his reality. The thought of the days at Charlie and Jim's only served to make him unhappy, and were already being compartmentalized in his memory as some kind of unattainable dream. He could have been their brother, blonde hair and all.

He avoided fights and did his homework, sometimes staying after school in Mr. Kinder's classroom, sometimes sneaking into the gym to work out; if he got strong enough, he'd never have to fear Mike or anyone like him. When it wasn't too cold out, he went to the old warehouses by the port, often making a fire. For a couple of weeks, he had a routine which seemed almost tolerable. Getting home when it was dark outside, he went into his room to read or draw. Ingrid might fix a frozen pizza, or, if she happened to be in an expansive, vodka-and-valium mood, order out for Chinese food. They hardly spoke, although occasionally they would sit and watch a television program at the same time. If she began with any derisive comments, usually after a few more drinks, Dan simply got up and went to his room. Once there, with Mike gone, he could generally depend on some peace. He thought that it might have been worse.

The month passed like this before Ingrid told him that Mike would be getting out of jail, which slid Dan into a panic. At first, she wouldn't tell him when, exactly, Mike would be getting out, so Dan stayed away as long as he could and came home late. Weekends were a relief; prisoners weren't let out until Monday, and Dan knew he had a reprieve.

The last weekend of January brought a blizzard, crossing into the state from the river and rolling eastwards over the hills and woods and farmland to the city. The snow began to deepen. Dan stood by the front windows of the apartment, watching the street below as people shoveled out their cars, got stuck, revved their engines and spun their tires in futile attempts to get free. He watched an altercation start when two men double-parked a car to jumpstart a snow-covered van with a dead battery. When a rusty Lincoln pulled up behind and couldn't pass, words were exchanged and soon four men were slipping around in the street, attempting to exchange blows. It ended when all the men, panting and exhausted, no one badly hurt, got the van running, then went their separate ways.

Snow continued to pile up that Sunday. With Mike scheduled to be released the next day, Dan curled up in his room, obsessively reading a book to shut out nausea. Ingrid stuck her head in his room at two in the afternoon.

"I'm going out for a bit," she said.

Dan knew this to mean that she was out of vodka and was going to one of the bars down the street, the only thing that could shake her out of the house in such weather. He also knew that she wouldn't be back until much later. Listening to her go down the stairs, he ran to the front of the apartment, watching as she walked gingerly down the packed and trodden snow of the sidewalk until she was out of sight.

He sat for an hour staring at the phone. Charlie and Jim had been right; he should call his grandparents. Perhaps they would simply feel guilty enough to come and get him, however much they didn't want him. It was just a delaying tactic, but if they came and got him, he could escape from Mike and his mother. His hand moved to the phone, but he drew it back. They hadn't called, they had never called. But Mike was coming.

Saliva gathered in his mouth, and the contents of his belly felt slick and volatile. He went back into his bedroom and read for half an hour, when the thought of his mother coming home roused him again, forcing him to walk out and stand in front of the phone.

The wind gusted across the windows of the dining room, the diagonal torrent of heavy snowflakes nearly obscuring the grey bricks of the apartment building next door. He picked up the phone, put his finger in the rotary dial, and ratcheted out the digits of the bungalow.

Almost panting with anxiety, he listened as the phone rang. He let it ring eight times, sixteen, thirty, before slamming the receiver down in the cradle.

"God *damn* it!" Willy and Mae were down at the bar, which was cheerful and warm. They were laughing with Bob Two Bears, with Mr. and Mrs. Benitez. There were burgers on the grill, people were eating the Sunday night special, and some kid was drinking a ginger ale with a slice of orange and a maraschino cherry.

Picking up the phone, he tried again. He let it ring until his biceps cramped, then set the receiver down next to the phone, staring at it as it rang. The bungalow would be dark, the phone ringing in the empty kitchen. Perhaps it could be heard in the quiet of the street, where the snow continued to sift down in silent drifts. Why would anyone leave such a snug and welcoming place?

Off and on for the next several hours he made the call, his fear of calling replaced by frustration. The call was never answered.

When he heard Ingrid stumbling up the stairs, he gave up and went into his room. He tried to read as he listened to her clatter around in the kitchen, cursing when she broke a glass. Pulling the grey blanket up to his shoulder and covering his head with a pillow, he finally went to sleep.

Ingrid was snoring on the couch when Dan got up. Mike was not there, the master bedroom empty. Dan showered, then stealthily ate a bowl of cereal. With his down jacket on, his hiking boots with two pairs of socks, he put on gloves and a watchcap and shouldered his pack. Walking quietly on the outside edges of his feet, he crossed the floor onto the rug in front of the couch. Ingrid lay under a macramé blanket of rust, orange, and green, the colors seeming to intensify the pallor of her skin, the color of plucked chicken, and the purple smudges under her eyes. She snored wetly. Dan could see that her teeth had gotten bad, and could smell her breath from where he stood.

He had a faint memory of loving her as a child. Now, looking down on her, he felt a thin stroke of pity, although it was almost overwhelmed by anger and disgust. How could his father, kind and strong, the memory of his face washing away, how could his father have loved this person? She had been young and beautiful. Had he been susceptible to such distraction? Hadn't he been wise? Now his father's mistake was in Dan's flesh, in his bones, in his teeth and guts and eyes and fingers, ineradicable for the rest of his life.

Ingrid snorted once, sharply, the intensity of it occluding her throat. She coughed a few times, rasping, then farted. Her eyes opened slightly, blindly, and she groped around the coffee table, patting the surface, a pack of cigarettes just out of reach. She put her hand in the bristling ashtray before flopping back on the couch, rubbing her face and smearing it with ashes.

Dan crept out of the apartment and down the stairs.

When he got to the school, it was closed. He had begun to suspect when he saw the emptiness of the streets, and checked the clock inside a store to make sure he wasn't late. Snow was drifted in the basketball courts behind the chainlink fence, and obscured the steps to the big main doors. He shook the door handle just to check, and was looking into the window at the empty hall, his gloved hands cupped around his eyes, when the school bell rang pointlessly, its burglar alarm ring, making him start.

Mike would get out this morning and would take the bus home, Ingrid wouldn't drive in such weather, so he had a few hours. The day was cold and pleasant, though, and when the sun broke through the clouds, he wandered off, choosing any direction that would take him away from the apartment.

In front of a small Mexican food store with a tiny dining counter, he came upon Jorge Lopez, a friendly kid from his science class. Jorge was shoveling the snow in front of the store, which belonged to his parents.

Jorge saw him and laughed. "Snow day today," he said. "Didn't your parents tell you?"

"No."

"You idiot. You got out of bed for nothing."

"I'm an idiot? You're the one who's shoveling snow. I've got the day off."

"Yeah? Well...okay, fuck you."

Dan started to walk away, but Jorge invited him in for some fresh tamales. They sat alone at the small, worn linoleum counter, eating the steaming tamales. The smell was wonderful, and other things were obviously cooking in the kitchen. The sun shone brilliantly through the large windows into the clean little shop. As the boys talked and ate, and with the smell of it, the comfort of it, the wholesome feel like an Edward Hopper painting, Dan thought he could have stayed there forever.

When Dan asked Jorge if he wanted to go downtown, or over by the port, the boy told him that he had to stay around and do chores.

"They won't let me off the hook that easy," he said. "If I get a day off school, man, I'm their slave. You get to do whatever you want. You're lucky."

Dan didn't even respond to this, just thanked Jorge and left.

The dim image of his father persisted in his mind. He thought of the times that they would escape the apartment together and go to the art museum, his father holding his hand as they went up the broad steps. Inside those quietly echoing halls, smelling of marble, were things which transfixed him, which opened his eyes. His father explained histories and techniques, and sometimes they sat on benches in the middle of one hall or another, silently, awash in thought and beauty.

With a walk of a few blocks, he could be on the bus downtown. He stood across the street from the bus stop, and visualized the steps to the Greysport Institute of Art, and the giant stone lions which had fascinated him as a child, the place where he had sat with his father and eaten hotdogs in the summer. The memory, the image of it, weighted him with sadness. He watched as the bus drove by, then walked down the hill to the port.

Snow was drifted against the brick walls of the abandoned warehouses, and deep in the broad grid of lanes which had once hummed with traffic, silent, now, silent, but for the occasional whickering sound of the wind. His cheeks were numb, but the sky was dazzling overhead, a deep blue with painterly cumulous clouds. Warm with the tamales, invigorated by the chill and the solitude, he wandered off among the buildings, inspecting rusty barrels and piles of scrap, picking up a piece of pipe and bashing random things as he walked by.

On a side spur off a main avenue, he went through a rusted gate, the snow around it untrodden, his the only footprints. Finding an old brick guardshack, its door open slightly, snow piling in, he pushed the door open and went inside. The floor was littered with paper and other trash, the windows whitely translucent with grime and dust. A faded calendar was on the wall, along with dated pictures of buxom women and a framed print of a hunting scene. There was a wooden desk and a few chairs, and, to his delight, a small wood-burning stove in the corner. He kicked the snow out of the door and pushed it closed. In minutes, he had a fire going in the little stove.

Here he passed the afternoon, shutting out the feeling of eventuality. Tipping back in a chair, he put his feet on a desk and sat next to the little stove, reading a book. When he became restless, he got up and went out into the cold, exploring the network of abandoned buildings. He regretted not having brought food, and, as it got dark out, it took more and more concentration to ignore his hunger.

Dan had never given Charlie and Jim his number in Portview, and he was too embarrassed to call them. He supposed they might have tried when he was out, or his mother might have answered the phone and simply hung up, as she often did. The notion crossed his mind to take the bus downtown and transferring to their posh neighborhood (where buses were intrusive, the transportation of servants), but this struck him as so pathetic that he dismissed the idea.

In the end, he left the guard shack when the snow outside turned orange with the setting sun. He took the precaution of finding a twelve-inch piece of pipe in a scrap pile, knocking off the rust and snow and dirt, and slipping it into his jacket before he shuffled through the snow and back up the hill to the land of the reluctant living.

On the street outside the apartment, he stood looking up at the number on the building, then up to the windows. They seemed cheerily lit, as if in welcome, and this puzzled him. Taking his pack off one arm, he unzipped his jacket and secured the length of pipe under his armpit, then walked up the stairs.

Every light was on in the apartment. The door was ajar, and he came in and put down his pack just inside. The cheap chandelier over the dining table, which was never used, its unshielded light seeming perfect for interrogation, was on, which deepened Dan's apprehension. At the table, eyes sunken, forehead and cheekbones made stark by the glaring overhead light, sat Mike. Ingrid sat next to him, holding his hand, sickly in that same illumination.

"Well, there he is!" Mike said heartily. "We were just talking about you, Danny!"

Dan stood where he was, holding the pipe in his armpit under the coat.

"Come on in, come on in," Mike said. "Come sit at the table."

As Dan walked carefully to stand across the table from Mike, the man stood up and held out his hand. When Dan ignored it, standing sideways to present a smaller target, Mike smiled gamely and sat down.

Mike cleared his throat nervously and said, "Um, I just wanted to say that I've had a little time to think about things, and, uh, I guess I got a little out of hand there, back around Christmas. Maybe had a bit too much to drink, I don't know. You can be kind of trying, too, Danny, you have to admit. So you had some part in it. Maybe a big part in it."

Dan stood at the table, letting his bangs fall in front of his eyes, watching Mike nonetheless.

"So, anyway," Mike continued, "I thought we'd make a clean start of it, let bygones be bygones, okay? And we're not going to be drinking too much around here, which might possibly be part of the problem. Not much, but part."

Dan looked at his mother, who was trying to appear supportive, but for a moment dropped her eyes to the side and looked bleak.

"So, what do you say?" Mike said. "Pals?"

"Sure," Dan said. "I'm going to my room."

Closing the door behind him, he sat on his bed, thinking. Taking off his coat, he hid the length of pipe under the bed. As hungry as he was, he still didn't leave his room, waiting until morning to have a bowl of cereal and leave the house for school.

Suspicious of this truce, Dan went about the motions of his life. He often stayed in Mr. Kinder's studio after school, so engrossed in projects that he lost track of time and of his sense of worry. Darkness would seep into the view of the port outside the studio's large windows, and Dan would be entranced until Kinder came in to lock up. When the kindly hippie asked Dan if there was anything wrong at home, Dan just put on a pleasant expression and shook his head.

Jorge Lopez became a friend, at least when he wasn't kept busy around his parent's shop after school. Dan thought that he might get a part-time job there (anything to stay away from the apartment), but it was obvious that Jorge's parents thought of their numerous children as a source of free labor, making it unnecessary to consider hiring a scruffy kid from the neighborhood. They were always kind, though, and if Jorge was granted any free time to escape with Dan, it usually ended with the boys back at the store or the Lopez kitchen for a hot meal.

At home, Mike's friendly demeanor and his sobriety seemed strained, but he kept at it, even going so far as to ask Dan about his homework and attempting, once, to sit down with him to work on it. Ingrid looked nervous and shaky, and from time to time, when Dan got up in the morning to get ready for school, she was retching in the bathroom.

The strangest turn of events was Mike's insistence that they go to a Baptist church on Sunday mornings, something entirely foreign to Dan. The first time he witnessed the spectacle of the minister's rant, with its blustering theatricality and references to unknown people with peculiar names, Dan was nearly slackjawed with mystification. The second time they went, the minister's spittle-flecked tirade started him giggling, and, try as he might, he was unable to stop. Ingrid sat next to him, staring off into space, but Mike noticed, leaning forward to glower around Ingrid at Dan. Mastering himself, Dan took a deep breath and held it, but when the minister gestured so violently that his glasses spun off his head and landed ten feet behind the pulpit, Dan snorted laughter, sending a rope of mucus across his lips and chin. Having no tissue or handkerchief (Ingrid merely stared dazedly at him), he covered his face with his hand, excused himself, and walked out from the pews to find a bathroom.

When he looked back into the church, he decided he'd chance Mike's anger (the fact that he was struggling to be positive was in Dan's favor), and slipped out the front door. He only came back once more.

The truce between Dan and Mike lasted until the end of March, when Ingrid had a miscarriage.

Dan came home from school to find his mother gone, and Mike sitting at the table with several empty beer bottles and a bottle of vodka in front of him. His eyes had the boarlike look, and he glared at Dan as he came through the door and put down his pack.

"Your mother's in the hospital," Mike said.

"What?"

"I said she's in the hospital. She had a miscarriage."

"A what?"

"You little dumbfuck. *She lost a baby!*"

The fact that Ingrid had been pregnant at all was news to Dan, and the notion that she would have been healthy enough for such an enterprise seemed farfetched. He found that he wasn't all that concerned.

"How long is she in the hospital for?"

"Like you care!" Mike shouted. "It's the strain of having a kid like you that made her lose it! That might have been my son! *My son!*"

To Dan's surprise, Mike began to weep. Moist and blubbering, he hung his flat-topped head over his thick forearms.

Dan stared at the large man, slumped over the table, his shoulders jerking.

"It might have been a girl," Dan said. He couldn't help himself.

"What did you say?" Mike said, aiming his red eyes across the room.

"Might have been a girl. A girl would've been nice, too."

"Get the fuck out of here!" Mike bellowed.

Dan smiled, picked up his pack, and went down the stairs. Some time later, he was at the abandoned guard shack, heating a can of pork and beans on the little stove, reading by candle light. He slipped back into the apartment when he thought Mike would be solidly out. The door was locked (only Ingrid left it ajar, something which annoyed Mike), and Dan feared the sound of the key in the lock and the initial creak of the opening door might wake Mike up. His snoring was loud, though, and Dan crept into his bedroom.

In the middle of the night, Dan was awakened by a slap in the face. The lights were on in his room, and Mike had him by the shirt, slapping him back and forth.

"What did I do? What did I do?" Dan shouted, trying to get his forearms up to block the blows.

"You little shit!" Mike barked, his eyes bulging and face as red as if he were strangling.

Dan pulled away, hard. His shirt tore and he rolled under the bed, scrabbling for the piece of pipe. Mike tried to reach under the bed for him, and Dan swung with the pipe, but ineffectually, his motion impeded by the narrow space. He rolled out from under the bed away from Mike, and when Mike came around the bed toward him, Dan swung, hitting Mike soundly in the knee with a crack. Mike shouted, clutching his knee and thumping to the floor.

Dan stood over him with the pipe in his hand, ready to bring it down on Mike's head. Mike kicked out, though, sending Dan to the floor, the pipe clattering away from him. Mike got up with a wince, retrieved the pipe. He came and stood over Dan, hefting the pipe. He raised it as if to strike, and when Dan cowered, he laughed. Taking the pipe, he limped out of the room. There was something in the roll of his shoulders that showed his sense of victory.

Dan closed the door, wedging a chair under the doorknob. He realized his nose was bleeding, and mopped at it with his torn shirt. He expected Mike to rant from outside, or to try the door and come back in, but all he could hear was the sound of an old movie on the television.

The next day, his left eye was swollen, with purple areas on both lids. Some of his teachers seemed to notice, but only Mr. Kinder asked about it.

"I got in a fight," Dan said. "It's okay."

When Ingrid got home from the hospital, she seemed a little dazed, but was apparently comfortable with the fact that she didn't have to live in a dry household. If she noticed Dan's bruises, she didn't mention them.

"You might have had a little sister or brother, Dan," she said at one point while making herself a drink. "Wouldn't that have been nice?"

She met Dan's eyes, her own aswim with vodka and tranquilizers. She didn't seem sad, just woozily detached, and Dan realized that her gaze was only generally fixed on his face. Another flicker of pity went through him.

"Yeah," he said.

"Don't ever drink, Dan," she said suddenly. "I don't want you to ever drink."

"Okay," Dan said, edging away.

Mike was generally angry, but apparently struggled to keep it in check, as he did with his drinking. He still went to church on Sundays, although even Ingrid's interest in feeding the façade had faded. Mike seemed so dependably touchy when he got back that Dan knew that was one day of the week when he should avoid being home altogether. Creeping in late at night, both adults usually unconscious in the arrhythmic pulses of pale blue light from the television, Dan went into his room and wedged the chair under the doorknob, stealing out in the early morning after stealthily working out with improvised weights.

With the coming of spring, it was easier for him to stay outside more. Making the long walk to the beach south of the port became customary, the spans of sand empty in the damp grey spring, woefully unappreciated, Dan thought, watching the waves that tumbled in. He collected sea glass and other interesting objects he came across among the beer cans, dead fish, and even a well-decomposed deer, half-covered in the packed sand near the water's edge.

Jorge Lopez was a good companion, when available, and this usually led to a good meal. Dan thought about what his grandfather would have said about him mooching, though, and always offered to help around the little shop in compensation, something Mr. Lopez was happy to encourage, so long as it didn't involve actual pay.

Among the many Lopez children was Adriana, a year younger than Dan, who often worked the counter of the store and rang up items on the cash register with the impressive ease of an adult. She was adorable, if a little chubby, and grabbed Dan one day, taking him into a storeroom to make out. This was a hot and dizzying enterprise for Dan, who soon had the experience of slipping his hand under her bra and feeling her round young breasts, then working his hand into her panties. There was always the fear of getting caught (Mr. Lopez being hotheaded about the sanctity of his daughters), but Jorge understood the situation and became their lookout. A certain amount of smirking and suggestiveness was involved on Jorge's part, but Dan took his collusion as an enormous compliment; Jorge was otherwise violently protective of his sisters.

With May, Dan's birthday came and went, forgotten by his mother and Mike. While Dan was briefly in his room after school, the phone rang, Ingrid answering it. The sound of her side of the conversation was muffled by the closed door, but Dan thought he heard her say, "He's not here. I told you before not to call."

When he came out of his room on the way to the door, he asked his mother who had been on the phone.

"No one," she said. "Salesman."

The fact that his birthday was forgotten meant nothing to Dan; he was actually relieved. Who knew how badly things might have gone awry if the adults in his life went through the motions of a celebration. Instead, he went to the Lopez store and had a burrito, followed by a dessert of flan and a heavy session with Adriana in the basement. When her father came into the store (and she knew the sound of his footsteps), she went up the stairs to distract him while Dan slipped out the basement door, up the concrete stairs, and down the alley, still frustratingly turgid. A cardinal sang in a budding tree which grew tenaciously in the alley, though, and Dan thought, on his way to the abandoned warehouse, that a birthday might have gone worse. Fucking happy bird.

Mike made a valiant last attempt to cut down on his drinking, frequently going to church instead of a bar. Dan would have preferred him to drink, however; although it was a crapshoot how alcohol might change his mood, there was a fair chance he might be jovial. When he came back from church, he was tense and dependably mean, and if Dan provided him an opportunity, Mike would take it to slap or punch him, usually quoting scripture to justify his actions. Ingrid said that Dan would thank Mike one day, that a kid like him needed a strong father figure.

Toward the end of the school year, Mr. Kinder seemed to overcome some tactful reticence when Dan showed up with a swollen eyelid, a little purple in the fold, and a cut lip. Kinder said nothing during class, although Dan knew he was discreetly checking him out while Dan hunched over a drawing, attempting to hide behind his bangs. After school, Dan debated ignoring a spring storm and going to the warehouse, but the rumbling darkness outside the emptying halls convinced him that it would be better in the warm and brightly lit art studio.

Kinder puttered around the room while Dan tried to immerse himself in his drawing, one of a growing series of intricately drawn human mutations. He used a copy of Grey's Anatomy for reference, being one of the only students allowed to take the tome off of Kinder's high shelf of sacred texts. He knew what was coming as Kinder sidled over, although he tried to focus his concentration on the delicately executed drawing of a human skull with three eye sockets.

Kinder came and stood next to him, leaning over to study the drawing. Dan looked up.

Kinder stroked his goatee and said, "I don't have to tell you that's excellent. Weird, of course, in the normal McGregor way- they'll be calling it McGregorian one day, watch- but shit, man, it's fucking excellent."

"Thanks."

"Don't tell anyone about my language, okay? I keep it together during the day, but it kind of comes toppling the fuck out when they day's over, you know?"

"Yeah."

"So I can trust you, right?"

"Sure."

"Well," Kinder hesitated. "You should, like, trust me too, man."

"Okay."

"For example, you could tell me why you keep coming to school kind of, you know, bruised up."

Dan kept drawing.

"You're a pretty tough kid, I can tell from looking at you. And I don't think its other kids who are beating you up."

Dan looked at him, tossing his head to get his bangs out of his eyes.

"Trust me," Kinder said. "You can trust me."

"Why?" Dan said.

"Huh," Kinder said. "Good question. I guess I'd say you can trust me because not everyone is bad. I'm not bad. I'm good, at least I think I am. I'm good, and you're good, no matter what's happened to you. If there's something bad in your life that I can help you fix, I want us to fix it."

Dan watched him.

393

"You're a good person, okay? And I'm not talking about your talent, which is, like, fucking huge. Shit, I said fucking. Fuck."

Dan smiled.

"So, just tell me who hit you. Was it someone at home?"

What the hell, Dan thought. "Yeah, it was my mom's husband."

"You mean, every time you've come in here beat up or something, it's been him?"

"Pretty much, yeah."

Mr. Kinder sighed and shook his head.

"How about your mom," he said. "Doesn't she do anything?"

"Hell, no. She thinks he's right to do it. That and she's either drunk, hung over, or about to *get* drunk."

Mr. Kinder stroked his goatee and squinted, as if trying to cover the compassion in his eyes. "Okay. We're doing something about this shit. This isn't right. Nobody gets to mess with you like that, Dan."

In short order, Dan found himself in the school counselor's office with Mr. Kinder and a young black woman who introduced herself as Miss Robinson of Social Services. Having the three adults looking at him with kindly concern was unnerving. He wanted to crawl back into his anonymity, to hide out at the beach or the warehouse.

After some prefatory questions, he repeated much of what he had said to Mr. Kinder about what went on at his mother's house. Miss Robinson was kind and patient, taking notes on a clipboard.

"Do you have any other relatives nearby?"

"Well, no." Dan said.

"None at all?"

"I used to live with my gramma and grampa."

"And where are they?"

He told her. "It doesn't matter, though. They don't want me, either."

"What makes you think that?" she asked.

"They would've come and gotten me by now."

"Maybe they don't know where to find you."

Dan blinked twice. "What?"

She repeated herself. "Did you ever try to call them?"

He thought of the time in the January blizzard, letting the phone ring and ring. He dropped his eyes.

"Well," Miss Robinson said, "we'll look into it. Would you like to live with them again?"

Dan shrugged. "I told you. They don't want me."

"Let's just look into it, okay?"

The next week, there was a meeting with Miss Robinson and other workers from Social Services. Tipped off, Ingrid cleaned the apartment from top to bottom in an unprecedented flurry of effort. She drank nothing but orange juice for two days, and was still young enough to bounce back reasonably well, although she was shaky and watery-eyed. To prevent any unpredictable behavior, she made Mike stay with friends for a week, muttering a convincing argument to do so which Dan couldn't hear, and made a believable stab at eradicating any negative signs of his presence.

When Miss Robinson showed up for the appointment with two of her co-workers, the place was neat, with soup on the stove and a premixed loaf of bread thawed out and baking aromatically in the oven. Dan thought this might have been going too far, and saw what was perhaps skepticism on Miss Robinson's kind young face.

Ingrid lied glibly throughout the interview, starting right in by saying that her husband was out of town on business. What business? Dan thought. He was enraged and disgusted as he watched his mother, in her barfly charmer mode (amazingly, without a drink in front of her), minimize any of the statements Dan had made as she attempted to twist her image into that of an overwhelmed and misunderstood mother. She didn't hesitate for a moment to throw in the miscarriage in order to highlight the tragedy of her life. About Mike, she lied outright, looking earnestly and unblinkingly in the faces of Miss Robinson and her colleagues.

"I think Danny is just mad at Mike," she said, laughing a little, giving Dan a lovingly chiding look. "Mike can be a bit strict."

"But he's never hit Dan," Miss Robinson persisted.

"Oh, no. No, no, no. They're friends, really. But you know how boys are at this age."

It was unsurprising to Dan that the meeting was inconclusive; he didn't have much hope to be dashed. He saw himself running off and joining the military like his grandfather when he was sixteen (or like his father and uncle when they were not much older), but that wouldn't be for another two years. Even the prospect of going to Viet Nam seemed like an improvement. He would have to keep his head down and persevere until then, he knew, having nowhere else to go.

Summer vacation started poorly when Mike made Dan get his hair cut. At first he didn't tell Dan where they were going, apparently guessing that he would bolt if he had known. When they turned the corner of the block and Dan saw the barber pole, he looked up at Mike for a second, but when he thought to run, Mike clamped his hand around the back of Dan's neck.

"You look like a fucking hippie faggot, kid," Mike said genially, grinding his thumb into the pressure point under Dan's ear. "And that shit just ain't gonna work."

The barber was a man with an iron-grey flattop and blurry Navy tattoos on his forearms. He seemed to not only know Mike, but to sympathize with him. Mike stood leaning against the jamb of the front door, his meaty arms crossed, grinning as the barber put a cloth around Dan's neck and turned on his clippers.

"I do this all the time, kid," the barber said. "Couple a minutes, and nobody'll be confusing you for a girl anymore."

At least the resulting haircut was not a flattop, as Dan had feared. The barber had left some bangs but cut it short on the sides, with high, neat arches over his ears. Dan watched as piles of hair accumulated on his chest and lap. When he turned Dan around to see the results in the mirror, Dan took one look and saw his own eyes widen. As the barber dusted his neck with scented talc, Dan stared at Mike's reflection.

"You'll thank me for it one day, kid," Mike said.

I'll *get* you for it one day, Dan thought.

"Next thing we're gonna do is change your last name to mine," Mike said as they left the barber shop.

Dan lagged behind Mike on the sidewalk and said, "To Krapczak?" he laughed. "No way."

Mike turned and crossed his arms, his eyes narrowing. Dan knew he was not only far enough away to escape Mike, but that Mike's actions were constrained, at least for the time being, by the threat of intervention by Miss Robinson and Social Services. On the toes of his sneakers, Dan danced backwards a few sidewalk squares.

"Krapczak? Crapsack, is what I say."

His words had the desired results; Mike's face turned a dark pink, but his eyes were calculating.

"Danny Krapczak," Mike said. "Has a nice ring to it. It's not a pussy name."

"My name's McGregor, asshole," Dan said, holding up his hands and revealing both middle fingers.

This appeared to push Mike's temper over the levees of his self-restraint, and he lurched forward.

"McGregor, Crapsack!' Dan shouted over his shoulder as he trotted away down the street, ready to sprint. "My friends call me Dan. You may call me *Mister* McGregor."

"See you at home, Danny!" Mike called after him.

Dan McGregor came home late and left early for a week, until he thought Mike might have given up on thoughts of immediate revenge.

With the warm weather and freedom from school, though, Dan spent as little time as possible at 718 Pier, as he had come to think of it. There might be a home for him somewhere, but that wasn't it. Out of simple embarrassment, he didn't call Charlie and Jim, although he wondered if, when his mother answered the phone and murmured before hanging up, the call wasn't from them. Figuring that anyone he needed to talk to could be found in the neighborhood, he ignored the telephone. And, carrying on, he adapted.

A job of a few hours a week cadged at the nearby Italian deli gave him more independence. The pay was tiny, but there was always food so good that he had never experienced anything like it, and, due to the punctiliousness of the owners, the Grazianos, anything which had passed its expiration date was destined, without exception, for the dumpster. Here Dan staked his claim. Antipasti, bread, fruit, and more, all of these things went into his backpack before he headed to the port or to the beach.

The way to the beach itself was treacherous. A swampy landfill had to be crossed, its soil seeded equally with weeds and shredded plastic. This was followed by an expanse of boulders, dropped off by the dumptruck load in order to abate erosion. When these obstacles were crossed, however, one could jump down on the broad sand and trot over to the water. If the wind was right, the waves rolled in, their sound somehow cleansing. Even on the most still days, the water of the inland sea quiet, there was a gigantic, relieving sense of freedom. The sound of gulls overhead would be, for Dan, for the rest of his life, the sound of freedom.

There were few companions in his life. Jorge Lopez occasionally escaped with him to the beach when freed from chores, although Adriana was rarely released, her father's suspicion apparent. A kid from school, Darnell Watts, tall and gangly with an immense afro, often came, supplying the weed. The boys frequently crouched behind the last of the boulders, trying to stay out of the wind to light the one-hit pipe. Once sufficiently high, they wandered out onto the beach.

"Man, I am hungry as a motherfucker," Darnell said on one occasion. "I wonder if anyone around here got some antipasti or shit like that."

"Don't be pushy," Dan said, smiling from his high, "I might have to knock you over to see if that 'fro bounces you back up."

Jorge, who giggled most of the time while baked, giggled.

"If you wasn't such a antipasti-bringing motherfucker, and also built like a fireplug, I might have to take your ass down-"

"The bigger they are..." Dan began.

"Yeah, fuck that shit. Let's eat some motherfuckin' antipasti."

Dan gave him a look.

"Ahright. *Please*, motherfucker."

Dan nodded obligingly and opened his pack.

Jorge snorted with laughter as Dan broke out a lunch of cheese, bread, antipasti, prosciutto, and, as an extra surprise, two wine bottles, only partially filled, but corked.

"Mr. Graziano said they'd go bad," Dan said, smiling. "Turn to vinegar."

Jorge snorted guiltily, looking over both shoulders.

"Daaayyyyamn!" Darnell said. "You all right for a white boy. Ima hafta break out some more weeeed after this."

Dan and Jorge laughed, digging in. They passed around the bottles of wine. The waves were roaring that day, and they were happy.

Such days of companionship were rare, though, and Dan was usually left to shift on his own. He had no idea if Miss Robinson, backed by the apparently illusory assistance of Social Services, had made any inroads into changing his situation. He doubted that she ever would.

Accordingly, he picked up a wool blanket at a thrift store, and some bungee cords to affix it to his pack. Another find was a camouflage poncho, apparently free of holes, which he bought for fifty cents. With that, a used sheath knife and a black baseball cap (together costing less than a buck), he felt free to roam the ruins and the beach. A patch of dunes and sea grass lay two miles south of Portview, and it was there that he often slept, happy and protected in his blanket and poncho, in a rift between the grassy dunes. And the sun broke orange over the grey water, with gulls to wake him in the morning.

This was how he spent his summer, being home as little as possible. Often wearing nothing but a pair of cut-off jeans, his possessions stashed in the rolled poncho and hidden in the dunes, he combed the beach for interesting finds. On two consecutive days, he found a gold ring and a functioning watch, trading them in at a pawn shop after arguing over the price.

Days on the beach, as wonderful as they could be, often made him restless, after he had read and roamed and swum as much as he could. The idea of the Greysport Institute of Art kept surfacing in his mind, and, in spite of the sadness the image brought, he found himself pulled to the place, as much by the desire to see what was inside as by the need to conquer his fear.

On a day in late June, he left the apartment as early as usual and walked to the bus stop. The bus was crowded at that time of morning, and he hung on a bar, stonily avoiding eye contact, as the lurching vehicle made its way into the city.

The bus stopped downtown beside the wide sidewalk in front of the Institute. Dan got out with a dozen other people, who dispersed as he stood there, shifting his pack and looking up the broad steps at the grey pillars and arched windows at the front of the building, all of it looking as if it had been beamed forward in time from ancient Rome. Now the only person on the steps, he walked slowly up in his sneakers, crossing over to one of the lions he had loved as a child. His father had sat there, right there. Reaching out slowly, Dan caressed the flank of the lion.

To his disappointment, he realized that he'd come two and a half hours before the museum would even open. With the time to spare, he explored, wandering the noisy, crowded streets. With foot traffic moving too fast for his distracted pace, he walked down an alley, looking at the back doors, loading docks, and delivery vehicles, inspecting the occasional dumpster. A rat the size of a raccoon trotted nonchalantly along the base of a brick wall, its footlong tail striking Dan as almost contemptuous. He picked up a chunk of loose asphalt to throw at the thing, but when he looked for it, it had disappeared.

Finally, he had eaten up the time until the opening of the museum and returned, this time walking faster than the people around him. Having actually walked up the steps earlier seemed to have dissipated some of the weight that oppressed him, and he walked up to the large bronze doors just as they were being unlocked.

The late June morning had been getting hot, and he only noticed when he walked into the dim interior of the enormous building. As his eyes adjusted to the comparative darkness, he looked around for a legend which would tell him where to start. A brochure with a map gave him an idea; one section had Egyptian and Etruscan, Greek and Roman sculpture, jewelry, vases, mosaics. Another section had Asian art, another African. Contemporary, Medieval and Renaissance, all of them drew him. He almost went first to Arms and Armor, but the huge European Gallery won out by a hair, and for no concrete reason.

In the large, cool rooms, he walked past work after work. Some interested him only marginally, while some immobilized him in front of them. He stood close, then walked back, then up again to see the texture of the brushstrokes in light reflected off the surface of the painting.

Hieronymous Bosch amused him, especially his visions of Hell. Wilfrid Constant Beauquesne *The Death of Sister Claire* was darkly interesting, and Charles Emile Champmartin *Study of the Head of a Corpse* fascinated him, reminding him of the Rembrandt he had studied secretly as a child in front of the bookshelves at his grandparents' house. Arnold Bocklin's *In the Sea* gave him ideas. When he walked around a corner and came upon *The Song of the Lark*, by Jules Adolphe Breton, he stopped dead in his tracks. The poignancy of the image of the young woman standing in the twilit field with a sickle in her hand, the orange sun on the horizon, was somehow full of both sadness and hope. He studied the painting so long that he lost track of time, eventually sitting on a bench in front of it, people walking in and out, sometimes in front of him, as he sat immersed in the painting and in his thoughts.

When he left late in the afternoon, he was exhausted. As tired as he was, though, he decided to stay out until later, not wanting to take his chances in his room at 718 Pier. Stopping by the little Lopez store, he saw Adriana and Jorge behind the counter. Jorge greeted him cheerfully, while Adriana gave him a lambent look. Dan considered sneaking off with Adriana and making out, until Mr. Lopez came in and gave him a cool look, then seemed to hover, puttering around in the kitchen and throughout the shop. Dan bought a couple of ginger ales, though, stretching them out until the kids closed the store under Mr. Lopez's supervision. Lopez gave the kids some further chores to do (as a means to keep them busy, Dan was sure), and Dan had to leave as they locked the door behind him. He loitered around the streets until he was reasonably certain it was safe to go inside 718 Pier.

Thoughts of what he had seen at the museum kept his mind busy the next day as he was set to the task of cleaning out a basement room full of trash at Graziano's deli. Images of art were in his mind just as clearly, and as frequently, as those of the perfect ass of Adriana Lopez. Going up and down the stairs to the dumpster, his mind was crowded.

After an attempt to get Adriana to sneak away was thwarted by Mr. Lopez's forbidding presence, Dan impulsively got on the bus and took it down town. In front of the museum, he walked up the stairs, touching one of the lions before entering the building.

The last foray had taken him through only part of one wing, and the thought of even completing that section at the moment was daunting. Instead, he went through Arms and Armor, which was fascinating, but not overwhelming.

It wasn't until the Saturday before the Fourth of July that he saw one, small painting which jolted him to the core. He might have even walked past it before, lost in thought about another, grander work, shuffling by without even noticing it. It wasn't large, and was placed simply, almost in a corner, with a small plaque to its right. It was the painting his father had so loved, *Abtei im Eichwald* by Caspar David Friedrich. His vision seemed to tunnel down to the painting alone, and he walked toward it slowly. The image of the dark woods, the ruined cathedral, the tombstones and shadowy figures (a resonant memory of childhood), the original work, in *this* place...his hair stood on end. Then his throat tightened, he wanted to weep, but the feeling was too far down, a vein too deep. A confluence of crosscurrents washed through him: the memory of the painting, the memory of his father, the memory of his father *in these halls*...could he turn around at just the right speed and find his father standing behind him?

Turning slowly, he scanned the hall over his shoulder. Thirty feet away an elderly couple stood, their backs to him, studying a large painting on the opposite wall. Aside from that, he was alone in the gallery. No one else was there.

He studied the painting for so long that he lost track of time, that he felt numb. At last, he wandered away, out of the museum and into the warm afternoon sun. Finding himself in the large park behind the building, the lake visible not far away, he sat under a young tree in the shade of the museum.

There was something more about the painting, something heavily familiar from childhood. Try as he might, though, that memory was too deep to see.

The Fourth of July was on a weekday, with a large music festival going on within walking distance of the museum. Dan tried to interest his few friends in going in and sharing his experience, but he could find no takers. Jorge couldn't seem to understand why anyone would be interested in doing such a thing as going to a museum, and Darnell said bluntly that art was for pussies. Dan promptly did a drawing of him as cool private detective John Shaft. Executed with a ball point pen and a piece of typing paper, the drawing put Darnell's head on Shaft's body, complete with wedge sideburns, turtleneck, and gleaming revolver.

"Damn!" Darnell said when given the drawing. "You did this?"

Dan nodded.

"You a freak, man," Darnell said, shaking his head. "You ain't a pussy, but you a freak. I ain't goin' with you to no museum. I'ma hang on to this drawing, though, if you don't mind."

"I drew it for you, dickless," Dan said.

Quiet little Adriana would have gone to the museum with him, if only to be by his side. Mrs. Lopez, who liked Dan considerably more than her suspicious husband, thought it would be a good idea for them to go together.

"It's the Fourth of July," Mr. Lopez said, as if exposing Dan in a lie. "The museum will be closed. You should have gone on Cinco de Mayo. They don't close *anything* for that."

In the end, Mr. Lopez, apparently with great misgiving, relented to his wife and allowed Adriana to go with Dan to the music festival and fireworks, as long as Jorge was there to keep an eye on things. Darnell went along, all the kids getting on the packed bus to go downtown. They jammed into the back of the bus, where Jorge searched out the back window to see if his father was following. Dan and Adriana made out fiercely. Darnell, taller than most of the surrounding people, ignored them, hanging on to the metal bar and swaying with the movement of the bus.

It made Dan a bit wistful to get off the bus in front of the museum and actually walk around it. When they did, though, it was a visual explosion. Thousands of people were in the park, sprawled under trees, walking on the sidewalks, lined up in front of vendors. Streets through and around the park had been blocked off, and evenly spaced bands competed with each other: reggae, mariachi, rock. Dan and Adriana held hands as they walked through the crowds, Jorge and Darnell acting as icebreakers.

Late in the afternoon, they paused in a rare empty space under a tree. Mrs. Lopez had set them up with snacks and Mexican soft drinks, which they had put in

Dan's pack. The soft drinks were warm and the tamales cold, but, with the help of a joint passed around by Darnell as they sat cross-legged on the grass, everything looked and tasted ambrosial. A cop walked by while they were passing the joint, and Dan was sure they'd been seen. Darnell nodded at the cop, a pleasant and innocent look on his face as he hid the joint between his legs, and the cop continued on.

Watching bands to kill time before the fireworks, they wandered through the crowds as it got dark. A temporary fence had been erected around the fireworks launch area, and they got a place as close to the fence as possible, Dan taking the bungee cords from around his blanket and spreading it on the ground.

"You like a old man," Darnell said. "What kind of motherfucker your age brings a damn blanket?"

"I'm thinking ahead, like I was when I brought these," he said, producing a couple of bottles of wine, hidden by a towel, from the bottom of his pack.

Jorge looked around for cops, and Darnell said, "Well, all right."

They drank the wine as it got dark. Dan and Adriana had a few polite sips from the bottles then left them to the boys. Rolling up together under the blanket, they kissed hotly, sloppily, with an abandon impossible anywhere near the watchful Mr. Lopez. Dan got his hand under her shirt, feeling her hard-nippled little breasts. She panted and ground her wet little mouth, as succulent as a sun-warmed apricot, into his. With some difficulty (the procedure seeming strange to perform on another person), he undid the button of her shorts and unzipped her pants. Slipping his hand inside, under her panties, he felt the warm pelt of her fur, then slid down and curved a finger into her slick warmth. She moaned and ground against him.

The opening boom of the fireworks display seemed to thud his chest. Adriana, just as startled, bit his tongue. Dan yelped.

"Sorry!" Adriana said.

Groggy with lust, Dan pulled the blanket from over their heads.

Darnell had his back to them, his afro in silhouette against a burst of color directly overhead.

"They're starting," Jorge said pointlessly, turning around and grinning at them.

The moment was broken. Dan cuddled with Adriana under the blanket. She kept her head on his shoulder and they watched the show, although for a while it was difficult for Dan to concentrate, what with the sweet-scented girl in his arms and the ripping turgidity in his pants.

On a night in August, Dan and Darnell arranged to meet after one in the morning and roam the streets. Dan had stayed up until Ingrid and Mike were snoring on the couch, so it was easy for him; he simply walked out of the apartment. The adults in Darnell's household were more watchful, and, after Dan had given a low signaling whistle outside his window, Darnell made a rather acrobatic escape involving window ledges and a drainpipe.

The main streets were still active, even for a week night. They watched a brawl take place in front of a bar, the scuffling limned in the blue and red light of the beer signs in the windows, the men cursing and thudding into parked cars as cheering patrons piled out to watch. The boys watched from the shadows under an elm tree across the street until one participant gave up, trying to save face by saying that he'd slipped on the pavement. He was helped down the street by a woman with ratted blonde hair who seemed unsure how to help him while holding a beer in one hand and a cigarette in the other.

Dan and Darnell got into two parked cars and stole their stereos, to sell later to older kids. Dan hid them under the useful towel in his backpack, although, in the unlikely event that they were stopped by the overworked police, their strategy was to bolt. Almost no cop was the equal of a teenage boy when it came to a foot chase, they knew.

They parted ways before dawn as the sky went from black to purple and grey over the lake. Exhausted, Dan decided to take his chances sleeping at 718 Pier, although he went to the now-customary precaution of putting the chair under the doorknob in his room.

Before nine, he was awakened by pounding on his door. Groaning when he realized where he was, he covered his head with a pillow. The noise continued- the bony taps from his mother and the meatier sound of Mike's palm on the wood.

"What!" he shouted at the door.

"Come on out here, honey," his mother said. "We want to talk to you."

"What for?"

"Out!" Mike barked. "Now!"

"All right, all right. Give me a minute." Wanting to cover his bases, he dressed and got his pack ready.

His mother and Mike sat at the table, both smoking cigarettes. Mike exhaled voluminously through his nose and shook his head, glowering.

"You need another haircut, Danny," Mike said.

Dan had an idea where the conversation was going to go, and kept his mouth shut for the moment. The look Mike gave him tempted him to bolt immediately for the door.

"We've hardly seen you recently, honey," Ingrid said. "We just wanted to see how you've been. Come sit down and talk to us."

Dan stood where he was.

"Sit down," Mike said.

"I'm fine right here."

"When I tell you to do something, you do it," Mike said, scraping his chair back a few inches. Dan stood still, visualizing his pack in his room and the distance to the door.

"Boys, boys," Ingrid said, "let's all just keep it friendly, all right?"

Dan and Mike stared at each other, and Dan fought the temptation to give Mike the finger. The idea of doing it made him smile a bit. Mike appeared to notice this, and his face got a little more red, his breathing a little more deep.

"Well, we've been talking, sweetie," his mother said. "We've wanted to talk to you about changing your name. We're all a family now, and we should all have the same name, don't you think?"

"No."

"This is your home now, like it or not. You should make the best of it."

Dan stood there. The two of them sat at the table, looking at him. Mike stubbed out his cigarette and lit a new one.

"Well?" his mother said finally.

"Well what?"

"What do you think about changing your name?"

"I'm not doing it."

"Why not?"

"Because my name is Dan McGregor. You can call me whatever you want, but my name is Dan McGregor."

"What's so great about that name, honey?"

"Beats the shit out of Krapczak. Are you kidding me? Are you fucking stupid?" He laughed.

"Goddam it," Mike muttered, scraping the chair back. "I told you. This kid's gotta learn who's boss around here." He stood up and began taking off his belt.

"You shouldn't talk to me or Mike that way, Dan." Ingrid said.

"Fuck that," Dan said. "You pull any of that shit, and I'll call Social Services and ask for Miss Robinson. She'd *love* to hear about this."

"Those liberal pussies aren't going to raise my kid," Mike said, although the concept seemed to slow him down. "My old man used to wail on me, and look how I turned out."

"First of all," Dan said, "I'm not your kid. Second, you turned out to be a piece of shit, and when I get big enough, *I'm* gonna wail on you."

That was enough for Mike, who tore around the table- Ingrid protesting- and thumped across the floor. Dan saw that there was no reason to resist temptation, and gave Mike the finger before darting to grab his pack. Mike was almost upon him, but Dan ducked under his arm and was out the door, taking the stairs down to the street two at a time.

"You'd *better* run!" Mike shouted from the top of the stairs.

"Hey! Original!" Dan shouted back, giving Mike two fingers up the stairwell before freeing himself to the street.

Dan knew that Mike would be looking for him, and that it might be a good time to avoid a shared location for a protracted period. A week, perhaps. There had been some gang activity by the old warehouses, and the last time he had gone to the old guard shack, he saw that it had been taken over by some of the Latin Lords. Deep clouds were piling up in the west, and he knew that there would be thunderstorms later in the day, so the beach was out.

On an impulse, he got on a bus to go downtown. Knowing that the art museum, (or the planetarium or the science museum, for that matter) only provided a day's worth of shelter, he found himself thinking about his vacation from reality at Charlie and Jim's house back in the winter. Before he had thoroughly thought it through, he had transferred buses and was headed north to their neighborhood, White Birch Pointe. In August, the area of fine houses north of downtown was lush with old trees and tended gardens, the drone of mowers and the scent of fresh-clipped grass coming in through the open windows of the bus. The heavy leaves of the trees were brilliant in the morning sun against the grey and black wall of clouds to the west, and Dan thought it looked like a negative of Magritte's *Empire of Lights*. He wondered what would happen when he simply showed up after half a year, not having heard a thing from the brothers, but he decided to take his

403

chances. The need of a place to go had overwhelmed his embarrassment; he felt liberated with resolve.

Getting off the bus at a corner, he walked the long block to the mansion, past others equally grand. He wondered if, in his t-shirt, cut-off jeans, and sprung converse sneakers, he looked a little shabby for the neighborhood, if he might attract attention, although the memory of popping away at the little asshole Scotty's house with the pellet guns made him smile.

Parked just inside the gate was a rusty pickup truck with rakes, spades, hoes, and a push mower in the back. A middle-aged Asian man in clean khakis was putting away a riding lawn mower in the gardener's building next to the driveway, and Dan knew the man was the brothers' ally and paid accomplice. He adjusted the pack on his back, walked up to the gardener's building and introduced himself.

The man thought a moment, then pointed at Dan and said, "Oh, yeah. The artist."

Dan shrugged.

The gardener, Ng, had a friendly face with crowsfeet from smiling in the sun. Dan liked his accent. "They're not here," he said. "They're in Europe."

"In Europe? Shit!"

"Yah, nice, hey? They won't be back for two weeks."

A thought occurred to Dan, and he said innocently, "So, who's watching the house?"

"Nobody. All locked up. Is not like somebody gonna come up here from the south side and break in."

"No, I guess not," Dan said, although he couldn't imagine why it didn't happen frequently, this being the land of plenty.

"Cops come by once in a while," Ng said, "they look at the house, check the door. But they lazy around here."

"Yeah," Dan said. "Hey, you think anybody'd mind if I went around back and took a swim?"

"Hell, no," Ng said, waving his hand. "I just clean it, too. Knock youself out. Storm coming, though. Don't get electrocute."

"Okay," Dan said, shaking hands with him and making for the terraces behind the house. Once concealed by bushes, he watched as Ng locked up the little building and drove away in his pickup.

Following the path he and the brothers had taken on New Year's Eve, he followed the fence along the side of the house and back to the top terrace. Seen now in the summer, the terraces stepping down to the lake were clearly Ng's masterpiece. Flanked by perfectly trimmed hedges and immaculate flower beds of prismatic color, the broad expanses of flagstone bright in the sun, Dan could have seen Louis the Fourteenth, dressed in gold, doing a minuet. Bacchus, liberated from snow, stood not far from the sparkling pool.

Dan smiled a little to himself. "Excellent," he said.

Before diving into the pool (which was hard to resist), he gave in to his pragmatism and trotted down the stone steps of the terraces to the old door once used by rumrunners. He had a moment's anxiety that it wouldn't be open, but had gambled that, since only Charlie and Jim knew that it had been opened at all, it would continue to be forgotten and overlooked by anyone else. He laughed to himself when the door opened into the dank black tunnel.

Trotting back up the steps, he scanned the windows of the house once, carefully, before stripping naked and diving into the pool. He swam several laps, then relaxed with his back against the edge of the shallow end, his arms stretched on the concrete.

The sensation of solitude was delicious. It was silent except for the sound of the pool's water circulating through the filter, and the cry of gulls down by the beach and overhead. There might be some small risk of the obnoxious neighbor kid Scotty showing up with his minions Ian and Joel, but he thought that it was negligible.

The storm front had been moving from the southwest, skirting north of the city in a diagonal line, but finally moved east enough to darken the sky overhead. As Dan got out of the pool, there was a flash and then a boom of thunder. He slipped on his cut-offs and sneakers, pulling his t-shirt on over the beaded water on his skin. Rain began to tap the stone around him as he went down the steps and into the old door.

As he clacked on the light switch in the tunnel, it began to rain hard behind him. He pushed the door shut, and went up the tunnel. Although he knew no one was home, his heart thudded in his chest. Up past the wine cellar, into the carpeted hall outside the poolroom and the gym, he padded down the hall, carefully checking the empty rooms. It was strange to have it so silent, so empty of the voices of the Gates siblings.

It seemed smart to stay downstairs, but his curiosity got the better of him, and he went up into the house. The kitchen was spotlessly empty, except for a note on the counter. "Dear Elpidia," Dan read, "We'll be gone until the 25th, as I said. When you return on the 24th, please order fresh milk, fruit, and other perishables. Hope you had a nice vacation. Doctor Gates."

Dan noted that Gates had spelled out his title. He rolled his eyes and put down the note. The refrigerator was full, the freezer packed, the shelves and the pantry filled with such a backlog of canned goods that he thought he could eat whatever he wanted for a couple of months and not make much of a noticeable dent. The Gates family was oblivious to this plenty, and if any supplies got low, Elpidia would simply order more; it wasn't *her* money.

The entrance hall looked even larger without the Christmas tree. The living room was huge, the rush of rain outside the windows making it seem somehow more empty. He plinked at the grand piano, the sound echoing in the space, then sat down and tried to remember something his grandmother had taught him: *Fur Elise*.

Continuing from room to room, he sat in Gates's chair in his study, putting his sneakers up on the desk. The idea of Gates being offended by this amused him. He carefully searched the large desk, and was delighted to find a stash of pornography in a bottom drawer under some papers. What a horny old goat, Dan thought. Feeling a resentment towards the man, he made sure to rub the mouthpiece of the phone on his butt before leaving the room.

The upstairs was neat, except for Charlie and Jim's rooms, which were a disaster; clothes, shoes, books, comic books were scattered everywhere. It felt mildly like a violation to be in their room without their permission, and he walked out slowly.

The same feeling of misgiving came over him outside of Gigi's room, but was overridden by his curiosity. He had not often (in fact, never, now that he thought about it) had the occasion to rifle through an attractive young woman's things. Opening her closet, he looked over her clothes, lifting the sleeve of a silk blouse and pressing it to his face, inhaling through the fabric.

Gigi's underwear drawer was a marvel, too. Dan had never known that such a variety of silky garments existed, thinking underwear to be strictly practical, there to hold things in place, and to catch the occasional drip or skid. Adriana's bras and panties were made of cotton, one pair, notably, having little monkeys on them. Gigi's garments were of a different order entirely. When he found some red and black silk crotchless panties, he puzzled over them for some time.

"Holy shit," he said when he finally figured them out. He immediately developed a bulging hardon. Putting the panties neatly back in the drawer, he barely restrained himself from running through the house and down the stairs to Henry Gates's study. Grabbing a few of the porn magazines, he went into the study's bathroom and closed the door, unable to overcome the habit of beating off in privacy, whether people were around or not.

A little jumpy the first night, Dan stayed in the poolroom, not wanting to turn on any lights upstairs. The refrigerator behind the bar had enough food, mostly frozen, to keep a gang of boys going for days. His first dinner was a pizza heated up in the little stove beside the refrigerator, and a couple of bottles of beer. He took a sauna, then flopped on the couch and watched a Marx Brothers marathon.

When he woke up the next morning, he had the familiar sensation of not knowing where he was. The midmorning sunlight angled through the French doors, backlighting the empty beer bottles which stood next to the crusted disk of pizza cardboard. Listening carefully, he pulled the blanket from him and crept upstairs barefoot. When he was sure he was alone, he had an orange and a small container of yogurt for breakfast (a treat, considering his usual morning fare), then went down through the doors of the poolroom and swam in the pool.

For the next several days, he got more comfortable in the house. It finally occurred to him that he had moved enough things around that he might lose track of what belonged where, and he made a list of things he had used or handled, and where they belonged. Comfortable in his surroundings, he explored as much as he liked, something in which it had been difficult to interest Charlie and Jim.

When he had exhausted his interest in the attic and the gothic basement and sub-basement, an undertaking of some commitment, he found himself gravitating toward the library. Pulling down interesting books from the giant shelves, he took them to various chairs and couches in the huge room just for a change of scenery. He spent a whole afternoon hypnotized by large art books, then opened a bottle of wine from the cellar, a bottle which looked so suspiciously old and dusty that he didn't think that Gates would miss it. He found that he preferred the taste of Boone's Farm, or the chianti from Graziano's; the contents of the bottle tasted, somehow, as old and dusty as its exterior, with a hint of loamy dirt, but it was open already, and free.

Once fairly buzzed, he thought it might be a good idea to run up and down every hall naked, which he did, with a thumb over the top of the wine bottle to keep it from spilling. The orange rays of the setting sun pulsed on him as he leapt past open doorways.

When it got dark, he swam in the pool, naked in the blue light of a gibbous moon. He got out, put on his cut-offs and sneakers, and wandered down to the beach, where low waves hushed in to the shore. The beach was empty in the high-noon brilliant moonlight, and he had the pleasing sensation of being the last person on earth, living in a land populated only by ghosts, as the works of humans were gradually, sedulously, subsumed by nature.

Dan grew accustomed to morning workouts in the gym, then walking out naked through the French doors, nodding to Bacchus, and diving into the pool. It was a ritual he could have performed forever, and he kept from the surface of his mind the fact that each hour that passed brought him closer to another return to reality. This time, though, he wasn't as sickened by the idea. For the moment, anyway, he enjoyed a relaxed fatalism. Putting even that out of his mind, he floated on his back in the pool, concentrating instead on the shape of the clouds, and just what kind of blue was the color of the sky.

Pulling himself dripping from the pool, he stretched out facedown on the warming concrete to dry in the sun. When the beads of water were almost gone from the hair on his forearms, he got up and walked into the poolroom. He stood in the center of the room, his eyes adjusting to the darkness, when Gigi walked in the door. Seeing him, she shrieked.

"Jesusfuckingchrist!" Dan shouted, covering his genitals and looking around desperately for his cutoffs. Finding them by the French doors, he bent over to pick them up.

Gigi was laughing hard.

"Nice bunwad," she said.

Dan faced away from her, zipping up the cutoffs. He turned around, mortified, only able to glance once at her eyes.

"Sorry," he said. "Sorry, sorry, sorry. What are you doing here?"

She was still laughing. "I didn't go to Europe, *those* guys did. I'm going to France in a few weeks. What are *you* doing here?" she asked. "Looking so tan and mmmmuscly, I must say."

Dan sat on the couch and told her the story. He kept it simple. As he told it, she came and sat next to him, taking his hand. "You poor thing," she said. "Charlie and Jim told me about some of this, you know. They've tried to call you. They said some woman would answer the phone and say you weren't there. Henry made them stay out of it, said it wasn't their business."

She waited as if expecting him to reply, but he remained silent.

"Well, you just stay here," she said. "I have some time off, and we'll have the place to ourselves. We'll have fun. It's a pleasant surprise, actually. Really pleasant. Great, in fact. Let's smoke some dope."

Dan felt a little nervous and tongue-tied being alone with her. Even near the end of summer, she was pale, with an easy refinement and beauty that made Dan feel a little unworthy to be in her association. She went behind the bar and got her stash, then came out to the couch and rolled a joint over the coffee table.

"Charlie and Jim know where my stash is," she said. "I don't care. I replenish it from time to time."

She lit the joint and handed it to Dan. "Hugh doesn't approve of them smoking much dope," she croaked, holding the smoke in. Releasing it, she said, "Ol' Hugh. The mother we never had." She laughed.

When they'd gotten fairly high, Gigi got them a couple of beers from the refrigerator. "What the hell," she said. "Vacation! Cheers!" They clinked the bottles together.

Dan imagined how Jorge and Darnell would react to see him in this situation. They'd *have* to see it, otherwise they wouldn't believe it. The experience would be so far removed from their daily lives (as it nearly was from his own), that they'd be tempted to believe he was lying. He hardly believed it himself when Gigi leaned forward and kissed him.

He jerked back an inch in surprise. "You're just so damn cute," she said, closing the small distance and kissing him again. "And *sweet*."

Realizing he had no reason to resist, and opened his mouth, kissing her back. They put their arms around each other and rolled back onto the couch hard enough to click their teeth together. Gigi laughed and continued kissing him voraciously, sucking his lips and tongue.

Dan was used to Adriana's timidity. He kissed back in a frenzy caused as much by his intense horniness as by an almost panicky desire to simply keep up with Gigi. When she reached down and felt his granitic hardon, he was astonished. She loosed it from his cutoffs and he wondered if someone his age could have a heart attack. He was almost hyperventilating when she took it in her mouth; he was lucky that he had beaten off that morning, the only thing that kept him from exploding instantaneously.

He came back from the brink when she loosed his cock and stood up, taking off her shorts and t-shirt. Curvy and pale, with pink nipples, dark, trimmed pubic hair, and a glimpse of pink labia, she stood before him comfortably, a little smile on her face. It was all so surreal that for a moment he felt dizzy, goggling at her nakedness. She snapped him back to reality.

"Here," she said, "lick me for awhile."

He had little idea what he was doing, but was immediately, ecstatically, face down in Gigi's lap. The slightly briny taste was not what he expected (although he didn't know what he *had* expected), but was also so clean and delicious that he lapped away like a dog at a bowl of water. Enthusiasm alone was not enough, apparently, and Gigi gave him some pointers, seizing his hair and pulling his face away from her crotch.

"Okay, here's what you do," she said, looking him in the eye. "You lick around here first, around the lips. Slowly. Then you gradually move up around the clit, here, and do slow circles. Around it, not right on it. Okay? When my breathing gets faster, and pay attention to it, make the circles smaller, tighter, and faster. In the end, when I'm really going, go right for the clit. Got it?"

He nodded almost angrily, shaking her hand off his head, and went back to it. After awhile she was moaning, saying, "Yeah! Good! A little faster! Tighter circles! Ah!"

When she came, shouting, he stopped only when she pulled his face away and rolled on her side, bringing one leg up over his head and putting her knees together.

"Wow," she said, breathing in pants. "Was that the first time you did that?"

He nodded, smiling.

"Could've fooled me. Come here and fuck me."

This is it, this is it, he thought. She laid back on the couch and spread her legs again. "Don't worry about it," she said, "I'm on the pill."

He hadn't actually been worrying about it at all, had only been thinking about getting *in* there. The mechanics of it threw him off for a second, but he got between her legs, and, leaning on one elbow, put the tip of his hardon up to her cunt.

"Even though I'm wet, you should still go slowly at first," she said. He did this, entering her gradually until he was all the way in.

"Okay, now fuck me," she said. He did.

Having beaten off earlier and downed a few beers, he was able to go for awhile. Gigi moaned and ground into him. When he came, it was stronger than he had ever come before, as if she were sucking the orgasm out of him with a pneumatic mouth between her hips. He spasmed and swore, arching his back and trembling, feeling himself go cross-eyed, his eyelids fluttering. He pulled out, collapsing between her legs, his head between her breasts.

She played with his hair. When he had regained his breath, he looked at her, grinning.

"Oh, you're gonna be *good*," she said.

He laughed out loud.

Gigi gave him the assignment of reading *The Sensuous Man*, which he couldn't put down. She fixed them dinner in the enormous kitchen, and he sat by the window reading the book. She snapped him out of his trance, and they ate dinner on the terrace outside the kitchen with a bottle of wine. After dinner, they drank more wine and smoked a joint, and Dan lit hurricane candles when it began to get dark.

Gigi smoked a cigarette and tossed back her wine, asking Dan questions about his life. Although he was reluctant to say much at first, she was persistent and funny; their intimacy, too, put him more at ease than he almost ever felt. When she began asking him questions about his father's death, though, his immediate impulse was to push such thoughts away.

"He died," he said, a bit more sharply than he had intended. "It was an accident. My grampa came and got me. Okay?"

Gigi clicked her tongue. "Okay," she said, her eyes narrowing in sympathy. Leaning forward, she put her hand on his. "It's okay, Dan."

He realized that he had been staring off over the dark water long enough that he had developed a small headache from furrowing his brow, as if a knot were tied, hard, just behind the skin of his forehead. He felt self-conscious, depressed about his life, but at the same time he was getting attention for his moodiness. Not knowing what else to do, he continued to scowl.

He would always remember what Gigi did next; it was as if she had read his mind and decided to do something about it. She had been stroking his hand, but suddenly slapped it.

"Well, then!" she said, suddenly standing up. "Are you going to be the kind of guy who capitalizes on his gloom and tragedy, or are you going to snap out of it and go skinny-dipping with a hot chick?" She stood up and took off her top, freeing her breasts.

"Come on! I'm waiting!" she said.

When she straddled him, then leaned forward and thrust her breasts in his face, he snorted laughter.

"Time's up," she cried. "What's your decision?"

"Skinny-dipping with the hot chick," he said.

"Good choice!" She pressed closer, holding her breasts from the side and pushing her nipples into his closed eyes. "Up periscope!" she cried.

This caused him to laugh hard, and, on an impulse, he took one of her nipples in his mouth.

"Ooh, you've been reading the book," she said. "The benefits of education."

They didn't make it to the pool immediately. First, Gigi decided, Dan had to experience fucking a woman on a table, with her ankles up beside his ears. Less than grudgingly, Dan complied.

When their time was drawing to a close, with only two days until Elpidia returned (three before the return of Charlie and Jim), Gigi turned Dan on to acid for the first time.

"You've been curious about it, right?" she asked him.

"Hell, yeah," he said. He'd read everything he could on the subject, trying to tease the truth from the fiction. The Schommer brothers had certainly done acid, and had talked about it in glowing terms, saying only that Dan was too young to try it.

"It's the easiest way to another planet," Gigi said. "And at a cost somewhat cheaper than the NASA program."

Gigi prepared everything meticulously. She set hurricane candles around on the terraces as the sun began to go down, made sure that beer and wine was available ("to keep the edge off," she said). Dan opened a beer and waited on the terrace while Gigi went into the house and got the acid.

She came back out with a tiny glass canister with a black lid. Taking off the top, she shook out what appeared to be two tiny, square pieces of amber plastic.

"It's windowpane," she said. "Go like this..." she touched one piece with the tip of her index finger, brought it to her mouth and licked it off.

Dan did the same with the remaining piece, washing it down with a beer. "I don't feel anything."

Gigi laughed. "It's not like smoking weed. It takes awhile, longer than you want it to."

She was right about that. It took forever. Dan drank two more beers while Gigi had a glass of wine, and they watched the huge expanse of water and sky change color.

Soon it got dark enough to light the hurricane candles. They did this together, walking around the terraces until many candles were lit. Gigi was talking about the French and sex.

"They call orgasm *la Petite Mort*," she said. "The Little Death. Isn't that cool?"

"Yeah," Dan said, somewhat distracted by a strange feeling in the back of his throat. A little catch back there, behind his uvula, something that made swallowing feel a bit funny.

"My throat feels weird," he said.

Gigi gave a wicked grin. "You're getting off," she said. "No going back now."

Dan took a swig of his beer. As he did, he felt a tingling at the base of his skull, something which seemed to spread out, rippling down his limbs to the tips of his fingers and toes. He shuddered, the sensation pleasurable.

"Huh," he said. "Weird."

"Let's go down to the beach," Gigi said.

They trotted down the stone steps of the terraces. Dan felt an odd, wiry energy, a sense of his own strength. Gigi skipped ahead of him, and he got distracted by the texture of some of the stones beneath his feet, which seemed to reflect the dying light of the sky and the purple of twilight, a pointillist rendering of the stone in purple and orange, like a refined test for color blindness. He wasn't colorblind at all, though; quite the opposite. He bent over to look at the stone, fascinated.

Gigi called to him from the edge of the sand. "Quit spacing out! Come on!"

Dan stood up straight. Very straight. His eyes felt as if they were as open as they could be, as if they couldn't take in enough information. He took in a deep breath of the fresh lake air, letting it out slowly. This seemed to have a cleansing effect.

"Whew!" he said, and sprinted across the sand to Gigi.

For what seemed like its own age, they ran up and down the beach. It was hard to hear each other talk over the sound of the waves, but when Dan raced by Gigi and slapped her round little ass, her squeal was a sharp point of punctuation in the sussurant rush. She showed him how she could do cartwheels, and he responded by doing handstands and kip-ups. When it got quite dark and they were both crusted in sand, Gigi suggested they go back up by the pool.

Dan was clenching his teeth rhythmically, feeling his jaw muscles bunch. He breathed deeply, his heart pounding. The waves roared down on the beach, and an onshore breeze made the leaves of the hedges along the sides of the yard whisper and hiss, as if unseen creatures murmured to him from the depths of the leaves, almost visible, their speech almost intelligible. Were those faces there in the dark green foliage, watching him? He leaned forward, staring and tilting his head, trying to make something out.

When Gigi called him up from the darkness to the pool, it was as though he had left one gallery of the art museum for another. The pool lights were on, and a rippling blue glow underlit Gigi's face as she stood by the pool. Hurricane candles of different colors were everywhere, and the effect was startling.

Gigi's eyes had a look he now recognized, one of intensity, enlightenment, a glow he thought he could now perceive from across a room. She seemed to note his recognition, to see something similar in his eyes. They began to laugh, and soon were helpless with it. Hanging on each other, they gasped for breath, wiping their eyes.

They sat down at the table and drank beer. The conversation changed wildly, from stars overhead and the possibility of life on other planets to the glaciers that carved out the huge body of water before them to nuclear war and giant plagues. When Dan, unusually talkative, began to talk about how doing art made him see the world differently, Gigi said, "I bet doing acid will make you see the world differently."

Dan gave a low whistle. "No shit." This caused another bout of laughter.

Diving into the pool together was like entering another completely different gallery of experience, a unique realm. The sensation of the water was, at first, a shock; his body rushed with ripples of tingling. He took a deep breath and swam the length of the pool, and it was like flying. The bottom of the pool was seemingly laced with minute patterns of purple and magenta, as if reality were diaphanous, and something more real, a larger truth, lay just behind it. It reminded him of things Mr. Kinder had shown him, like Sierpinski triangles, Heighway dragons, and Julia sets. He burst through the surface of the water and looked up at the Milky Way, noticing that it was vastly deep, three dimensional, something he had never seen before. Perhaps he was part of a tiny eddy of reality, and he was perched, trembling, on the verge of seeing the next level, and his place in everything. He spent a half hour which seemed like a century trying to explain this coherently to Gigi as they moved slowly around the shallow end of the pool. He knew he was having a gigantically important epiphany, and it was crucial that she share it with him. She smiled, stroked his wet bangs from his forehead, apparently amused by his rambling. Finally, she gave in to his relentlessness, and started talking about infinite regression in Hindu traditions.

Dan was mesmerized. "Yes! Yes! Exactly!" he said, taking her pale shoulders and shaking them gently, kneading them. The human contact! The union of souls! We are not alone!

They went inside to get warm and put on dry clothes, and fell into an epoch of playing pool. Here, too, Dan saw patterns, saw the shots mapped out in magenta lines as if he were in geometry class and the teacher was doing diagrams on the overhead projector. It was fascinating. His concentration felt so intense that it was almost as if he could explode the cueball with his vision if he could just find the right way to concentrate on it.

He swilled beer and it seemed to have no effect. They played game after game of pool until they noticed the sky was turning dark purple outside. This ushered in the era of sunrise. They took a bottle of wine down to the beach and watched the metamorphosis. Dan was certain he had never seen anything so beautiful.

The sun was a palm-width above the horizon when they realized they were coming down. Their energy waning, they trudged up the steps to the house.

"Did you like it?" Gigi asked.

"I can't wait to do it again," Dan said.

They were exhausted and fell asleep in Gigi's large bed, far too tired (and in too cerebral a place) for sex. When Dan woke up, it was early afternoon, and Ng was mowing the front lawn.

Before Elpidia returned, Gigi gave Dan a ride home. He insisted on taking the bus, not wanting to impose.

"Impose?" Gigi said, clicking her tongue. "Oh, you are just the cutest thing."

The drive to Portview was mostly silent. Dan wanted to tell Gigi how much he needed to be with her, cooking up desperate plans of how to do it, but couldn't even articulate them. He kept glancing over at her while she drove, opening his mouth to speak from time to time, but never summoning the critical amount of courage.

Dan had Gigi park close to the landfill by the beach. He took her hand, and the look in his eyes must have betrayed him.

"Jesus, don't go falling in love with me or anything. You're too young, and I'm too messed up."

"Well," Dan countered, "I won't be young forever, and I'm messed up, too."

Gigi laughed.

"I'm going to France, anyway," she said. "I might come home for Christmas. Might. I won't be back for sure until June."

A rock formed in Dan's throat. He looked out the window.

"Oh, sweetie," Gigi said. "You have to get out of here just as soon as you can. My dad won't help you. He's all talk, nothing will happen. You're going to have to do it yourself. Call your grandparents."

Dan shook his head.

"Social services, then."

He gave her a disgusted look, and shook his head harder.

They sat in the car together for a long time, looking out at the overcast day. Finally Dan kissed her on the cheek and got out of the car. As he headed for the beach, she rolled down the window and called to him. He waved over his shoulder and continued down to the water. When he heard the car drive away, he turned and watched.

When he went back to 718 Pier, he didn't wait for Ingrid and Mike to be asleep, rather confronting their reaction straight on. He listened outside the door before going in, then went in quietly, keeping his pack ready on his shoulder.

Mike and Ingrid sat on the couch in front of the television.

Ingrid saw him and said, "Well! We almost called the police this time!"

Dan said, "Sure you did. That'd make you look great with Social Services."

Mike was glowering, but said nothing. Ingrid looked him over and said, "You don't look much the worse for wear. There's leftover pizza in the fridge."

She turned her gaze back to the television, and Dan walked into his small room and closed the door. He made sure to put the chair under the doorknob.

The last days of summer evaporated. After the time he spent with Gigi, Adriana and her monkey-print underwear no longer filled the bill, and Dan found himself in the miserable and craven position of trying to avoid her. Although he thought he knew what his father or grandfather would say he should do, he still found himself sneaking through back alleys and going out of his way so as to skirt the tienda. He justified his actions by telling himself he had enough to contend with at the moment.

Between his time at the museum, the beach, and the warehouse ruins (apparently abandoned, however briefly, by the gangs), his hours at Graziano's, he had hardly spent any time at 718 Pier. On the infrequent occasions that he saw his mother, she made sure to point out exactly how much time was left in the summer vacation, seeming to take enjoyment in his discomfort. Mike, if awake, rarely did anything but glare at him from the couch.

Dan weighed his options about going to school at all. He contemplated running away, as he did every day, but the conclusion was always the same: he had nowhere to go, and, when he was eventually caught, he would end up in foster care, which might be worse than his present situation. At least at 718 Pier, he had some control. Better the devil you know than the devil you don't know, his grandfather would've said. The old asshole.

What were they doing, he often wondered. What would happen if he just hitchhiked across the state, back to the river. Would they take him in? Would they turn him over to the foster people? When he let himself think about it at all, the idea of their abandonment stung him.

He explored the ruins with Jorge and Darnell, getting Darnell to stop by the tienda. Dan knew far more about abandoned industrial area, both of the other boys having homes which would not fling them so far afield. Acting as their guide, he showed them through the weedgrown avenues, to the guardshack and out to the warehouse on the harbor where Dan had spent so many hours the previous winter.

"Man, why didn't I ever come out here?" Darnell said, looking out through one of the brick arches, over the misty harbor to the city beyond. "This is beautiful."

Dan showed them how to make a fire from driftwood, and they roasted stolen hotdogs. On their way home in the dark, Darnell split off.

"I think I'll just let you go home by yourself," Dan said to Jorge.

"I hear you," Jorge said. "My dad doesn't want you coming around anyway."

Dan stood across the street in the dark, watching while Jorge went into the well-lit store. Jorge talked to his father, little Adriana watching them both and then looking out into the dark. Dan wandered away, and sat reading a book under a street lamp in a little park until it was time to go home.

School was a shock to the system at first, but at least this year it was a place where he felt at home, for all its faults. The din of students in the halls between class, the contemplative silence of Mr. Kinder's studio when the regular day was over, were things he found, in some way, pleasant. It was only the reality of going back to 718 Pier every night that wore at him, and it was that which he closed out of his mind when he bent over a drawing.

Mr. Kinder provided him with a rudimentary set of oil paints, and some basic instruction. He got Dan books on the subject out of the library, along with volumes with good prints of the works of masters. Dan took to it immediately, although he saw that it would be nowhere near as easy as simple illustration, the complexity of the process being much greater. The smell of the paints, of the linseed oil and turpentine, were soothing to him, the act of blending paint on the canvas almost hypnotic. He couldn't wait to try it on acid, and almost broached the subject with Mr. Kinder. Watching the man putter around, distractedly mumbling to himself, picking up a drawing pencil and looking at it as if suddenly surprised by its appearance, Dan thought it would be safe to procrastinate on bringing up the subject.

The grind began when he went back to Pier Street. Dan had the impression that Mike was struggling through another dry period, and that it had something to do with a visit to the doctor's office; at least that's what he derived from hushed conversations between the two adults. He had no idea what would happen in his life if Mike were to disappear, although it was a subject of daydreams. He'd still be stuck with Ingrid.

"It wants to be an artist," Ingrid had said one morning when she happened to be up early enough to see him before he left for school. Looking at her in the morning light, he was shocked at how haggard she looked (forty wasn't *that* old), but ignored her as he had a bowl of cereal.

"Artists do no good in the world," she said as he read the back of the cereal box. "What good have artists ever done? Your father wanted to be an artist, and look what happened to him. Wash that bowl before you leave for school. It's a stupid idea, wanting to be an artist. It's not manly."

Dan rinsed out the bowl, although he was tempted to simply leave it; Mike was a stickler about such things. He got his pack ready and made for the door.

"Don't I get a kiss?" Ingrid said.

Dan turned and gazed at her, not quite sure he'd heard her correctly. Shaking his head, he opened the door and left.

"I just want a normal family!" she called after him. "God damn it!"

Perhaps it was Ingrid's desire to have that normal family, along with Mike's need to fit in at his church, that led to them forcing Dan into attending a potluck dinner. Dan couldn't see Ingrid fitting in with that kind of crowd at all, even with a moderate social vodka buzz on, nor could he understand why she would want to placate Mike in such a manner in the first place. When he thought about it, her desire to be with Mike at all made no sense. Perhaps she thought he was "manly"; Dan didn't know and would never have bothered to ask. The only thing that did add up was that they seemed to deserve each other, and Dan let it go at that.

On the matter of the potluck, he debated running away again, but it was grim outside, atypically cold for the end of September. Things weren't so desperate that he needed to hide out at the warehouses, and the sort of people who had been frequenting the area recently made such an idea less than attractive. Thinking that it might be better to simply go along with the notion of the potluck, he convinced himself that he should go simply out of morbid curiosity. Mr. Kinder had said that an artist should always throw himself into new situations; you never knew what fresh ideas would come of it.

Before they left for the dinner on a Thursday evening, Dan made sure to heighten his sense of the weird by going down to the basement of the apartment building to smoke some dope before they left. Back among the screened-in storage units, he did one-hits from his small stash, taking a pinch of the diminishing leaf

415

and firing it up in a small pipe. He hid the plastic bag of weed and the pipe behind a loose brick in the basement, knowing that nothing was safe in his room, and that his mother or Mike would not hesitate to tear apart his pack.

Pleasantly high (or "reefereshed", as Charlie would say), he returned to the apartment. Ingrid and Mike looked unnaturally groomed and oddly shiny, and Ingrid had gone to the surprising effort of making a green bean casserole out of canned beans and cream of mushroom soup.

Mike seemed a little nervous, and for an instant, Dan felt sorry for him.

"People hardly believe I have a family," Mike said, "so, you know, be nice." He looked Dan over, and Dan saw his eyes move to Dan's hair, which had grown back. If Mike had been about to say anything, he decided against it.

"Have you been smoking?" Ingrid asked.

"No," Dan said. "You must be smelling yourself."

They went down to the car. Dan thought that, if they were seen by strangers, they might pass for a family. The idea almost made him laugh.

Dan had walked by the church regularly and never given it much thought. He had stolen a stereo from a car parked in the dark lot behind it, and the church itself had provided a good impediment to the eyes of cops in rolling police cars. Mike parked in the lot a few yards away from where Dan and Darnell had boosted the stereo.

The crowded basement of the church was too brightly lit, with linoleum tile floors regimented with folding tables, these covered with hot dishes and pitchers of soft drinks. Dan noticed that there was no liquor anywhere, and slipped a look at his mother to gauge her reaction. She had her best smile frozen on her face, and was keeping up a reasonable façade of normalcy. Mike was being hale and friendly, shaking hands in a brisk and manly way. Dan was introduced around, lifting his chin at people and attempting to keep something resembling a smile on his face. He wondered how many of those around him were utter frauds as well, and scanned their faces. Most of them, he thought. Most of them.

Mike went out of his way to introduce Dan to the minister, a florid, fat man in a three piece suit with a squishy handshake. Dan felt as if the man were trying to mesmerize him, to overwhelm him with the force of his personality as he continued to moistly shake hands, holding Dan's one with both of his.

"I've heard a lot about you, Dan," the man said, staring into Dan's eyes with a cheesy intensity, as if he had read a book somewhere about the power of personality. "Sometimes, when we're troubled, the church is a place where one might find surcease and sanctuary."

Dan pursed his lips and nodded placatingly, but when he tried to remove his hand from the man's damp grip, to break eye contact, the minister refused to let go, instead gripping the hand more tightly and moving his face in front of Dan's eyes to re-establish union.

"Any time you feel troubled, Dan, don't you hesitate one bit to come and talk to me, all right?"

Dan agreed in order to get the man to let go of his grip. "Okay. Yes," he said.

The minister moved on, and before he escaped to find a bathroom and wash his hand, Mike said, "The Reverend is a rare man. He has a power about him."

Ingrid concurred absently and Dan excused himself.

"Don't you go running off," Mike said.

There were other kids his age from school in attendance, and although none of them were among his small circle of friends, none of them looked happy to be there, either. A junior he knew from school looked unnaturally pressed and combed, his long hair slicked into place, wearing a tie the size of a lobster bib. Being older, he would not, under normal circumstances, have deigned to acknowledge Dan's presence, but this situation was unusual. When their eyes met, the kid rolled his eyes, and the two of them shared a smirk.

It dawned on Dan, when he looked around, that the older kid's smirk was for good reason. There, smiling freshly beside her parents, was a girl from school whom he knew to be a slut, whom he had seen stand by laughing while watching a fight between two boys, both of whom she had boned. There was a mailman who was said to have beaten a dog to death, something Darnell had told him about when they saw him viciously kick another dog, which lent credibility to the story. There was a man who Dan had seen making out with another man late at night outside a bar seemingly set aside for such things, yet here he was, mysteriously, with what appeared to be his wife and kids. The list went on and on. And when he looked at Ingrid and Mike, mingling and shaking hands, making benign conversation (strangely free of spicy language), he saw how well they fit in, how it all made sense. He was surprised his mother didn't want to come here more often; she melded perfectly with the others, making bland and pleasant conversation as if she were possessed. It was fascinating.

And yet when it came time to share a prayer before sitting down to dinner, all of the people in attendance fervently reciting the words, he had to struggle to keep from laughing. The young slut, at whom Dan wouldn't have minded throwing a bone himself (the idea nearly making him snort), looked as fresh and unsullied as a drop of dew. He looked around as unobtrusively as he could. They all seemed so sincere.

It must be nice, he thought, to put down any burdens and wrap yourself in an invisible cloak of sanctimony. How did someone maintain that level of self-delusion? He almost envied it, knowing himself to be, as Elpidia would have put it, a *maldito*. And that was that.

He was smiling about the thought of being naked with the slut, doing with her things he had done with Gigi, when he looked over and saw Mike eyeing him expressionlessly. He watched Mike for a moment, meeting his gaze, before looking away. The prayers ended and they sat down.

When they got back to Pier Street, Dan went immediately to his room. Mike had said nothing on the way back, and Ingrid had managed to keep her derisive comments aimed at Dan down to a minimum. The atmosphere was relatively peaceful, but Dan still put the chair under the doorknob before getting into bed to read.

The experience at the church stuck with him, though, and it seemed like a good idea to boost a few more stereos from its parking lot. Who more deserving? he thought. There were people from whom he would not steal, like the old lady who took his deliveries of groceries from Graziano's, an immigrant with a heavy Italian accent. She kept a roll of bills in a coffee can in the cupboard above her sink, which she produced in order to tip him, and she always offered him a piece of fruit or some other treat. Her back door was usually unlocked, and Dan knew it would have been a simple thing to dodge in the door and grab the coffee can. The fact that he didn't had nothing to do with her rumored "connections"; Dan didn't even consider it as a possibility because, to him, she had always been fair, generous, and kind.

"You Italian, keed?" she had asked him on at least three occasions.

"No, ma'am," Dan replied.

"Too bad," she would say, patting his cheek with the palm of her hand hard enough to make Dan wince. Leaving the kitchen (the scent of which invariably made him salivate, even on the unusual days when something was not simmering on the stove), made him wonder how he might get her to adopt him. She seemed so alone in her house.

Nor would he steal from the Tienda Lopez or any of their family, even though Mr. Lopez didn't like him, and was rumored to like him even less now that he no longer pursued Adriana, which Dan found inexplicable.

"My dad's weird," was how Jorge put it, lending no clarification whatsoever.

Dan had made himself scarce enough around the store that Adriana's affection for him waned, and he eventually saw her with another boy, a Latino whom, he felt sure, Mr. Lopez would find only slightly less objectionable. In spite of the fact that Mr. Lopez didn't like him (why would he? Dan thought), Mrs. Lopez had always been sweet and funny. He wouldn't have stolen from them even if he felt comfortable, or was welcome, around the store.

The members of Mike's church were a different matter, though. Darnell was always up for a little adventure, and on a foggy Friday night, the boys brought their tools to the parking lot. Except for a streetlight or two, it was dark, and Dan slimjimmed the door of the minister's car in seconds. Darnell scouted other cars as Dan slipped in and got to work.

He removed the faceplate or the stereo with a screwdriver and got to work taking out screws. Everything he took, he put in his pack. The last screw was hard to get out- was it stripped or something?- and he was working at it, cursing, when he heard Darnell's warning whistle. He popped his head up over the dashboard and there was the fat minister approaching the car only ten feet away.

Dan bolted from the car as the minister was beside the front bumper. He flung the door open, slipping on the wet pavement, and tore off through the lot.

"Hey!" the minister shouted. "Come back here, you little cocksucker! I'll kick your motherfucking ass, you little shit!"

"Catch me, you fat fuck!" Dan yelled back, sprinting after Darnell's fleet form slipping down an alley.

They stopped in the alley beside a dumpster two blocks away, panting and laughing.

"Did he see you, man?" Darnell panted.

"No, I don't think so," Dan said. "It was too dark. Hope we gave the fat asshole a heart attack."

Darnell laughed. Dan took the faceplate of the minister's stereo and tossed it in the dumpster. Bubbling with adrenaline, they waited outside a liquor store until they found an adult who would buy them beer, then took the fire escape to the roof of Darnell's apartment building to drink the beer and look over the smeared lights of the foggy harbor.

Dan was wrong about the minister. He had recognized Dan, even in the dark, and came to 718 Pier early the next morning. He had called first; Dan had heard the phone, but was used to never receiving a call and so had dismissed it.

When Mike woke him up by barking his name and hammering on his door, Dan knew he was caught. He came out into the living room, finding his mother and the minister sitting at the kitchen table, Mike standing beside the minister with his arms crossed, his eyes wide with anger.

"Do you know what this is about, son?" the minister said.

Dan relaxed his face into innocence. "No."

"You sure?"

"No. I mean yeah."

"Yes *sir*," Mike said.

Dan said nothing.

"You don't know anything about a couple of boys breaking into a car last night at the church, trying to steal a stereo?"

Dan spread his hands.

"Oh, Danny," Ingrid said, adding a quaver to her voice, "I'm so disappointed."

Dan almost laughed, but said to the minister, "I don't know what you're talking about."

"I could have come here with the police, you know," the minister said. "I thought it was better to do it this way, to handle it among the members of our church."

"I'm not a member of your church," Dan said. Mike looked like a pit bull on a tight leash.

"Well," the minister said, "we'll see. I think if you come around after school, we can find something for you to do at the church to make restitution."

"Restitution for what? I didn't do anything."

"I saw you, Danny. You were in my car. You ran away with that nigger kid."

"He's *black*, you asshole," Dan said. Then he closed his eyes and hung his head.

"There!" Mike said, jabbing a finger at Dan. He jerked forward, but the minister mildly held up his hand, and Mike stopped.

The minister smiled. "Okay, then. Danny, we know you were there, we know what you did. A real man would *confess* what he did. You think about that, and we'll talk about it next week when you come to see me at the church."

"I'm not coming to see you at any fucking church," Dan said.

Mike gasped. "Oh yes you are," he said, almost panting.

"Oh noooooo I'm not."

The minister smiled benignly and stood up, thanking Ingrid for her hospitality. To Mike he said, "We'll see the boy next week. No need to involve the authorities.

419

As we know, ours is the *real* authority. If you need any guidance, feel free to call me. And, as always, consult the good book."

The minister left the apartment without giving Dan a glance.

Dan stood ready for Mike, but Mike walked around the table on the opposite side, went down the hall to the front room. He pulled aside the curtains and looked down at the street, watching for nearly a minute. Finally, he let the curtains drop and walked slowly down the hall. He stood in front of Dan and sighed. Dan was on his guard.

"We could have been friends," Mike said. He turned to walk away.

"No, we couldn't," Dan said, and Mike punched him in the face.

The pain was bright, a flash, and the sound of the hit actually echoed in his skull. He found himself on the floor, a surprising amount of blood flowing from his nose onto his shirt. Ingrid got between him and Mike, who aimed a kick at him. Dan brought up a knee and elbow to cover himself. Ingrid and Mike were both shouting, Ingrid about Protective Services, Mike about not giving a fuck. Part of Dan wanted to laugh, but he curled into a ball, putting his face almost under the couch. Blood flowed across his cheek and dripped off his face. He could hear it hit the floor, tap tap tap, even with the shouting.

Eventually things quieted down, with Ingrid hushing Mike's rant.

"Goddammit," Mike said at last, and stomped out of the apartment.

When he was gone, Ingrid stood looking at Dan for a moment, then said, "Okay, get up."

Dan did, and Ingrid walked him over to the kitchen table. "Just like my dad and my brothers," she said, sighing. "Let's take a look at you. Jesus. I don't think your nose is broken, but you'll have black eyes. Why do you have to provoke him like that? What's wrong with you?"

She dabbed at his face with a cold washcloth, dipping it in a bowl of water from the tap. Dan glanced down and saw the water in the bowl turn pink.

He decided to relax to her tenderness.

When Dan went to school with two black eyes, things began to happen in short order.

"What, did you get in a fight?" Mr. Kinder asked him. Dan couldn't remember seeing him angry; he was almost shaking, and stroked his goatee rhythmically in his agitation.

Unable to lie him, Dan sighed explosively and rolled his eyes.

"We're going to see about this," Mr. Kinder said.

"What are you going to do," Dan said, "go and kick his ass? He's a veteran or some shit, and he's three times as big as you."

All the time, Dan knew that Mr. Kinder was not the ass-kicking type, and that he meant the thing that Ingrid so feared: Social Services. Living in a foster home might be better than being at 718 Pier. Dan was now willing to take his chances.

In his social science class, Dan sat at his desk, ignoring the lecture and thinking that, if he waited any longer, Ms. Robinson was going to show up at the school and have him called out of class, and that things, at that point, would get out of control. He got up, shouldered his pack, and made for the door.

"Mr. McGregor," the teacher said, "may I help you?"

"Yeah," Dan said. "Fuck yourself."

The class wooed, even louder when Dan flipped the teacher off over his shoulder. It felt great. He didn't know that he'd never see the teacher again. He walked down the empty halls for the last time, hard and fast, pleased with the echoing thumps of his boots.

He avoided going home for awhile. Without giving it much thought, he wandered to the Tienda Lopez after school. He knew it wasn't logical, but went there nonetheless, somehow wanting to be in a place that smelled good. Upon seeing him, Mrs. Lopez threw up her hands, astonished, clapped them together, and came to inspect Dan's face.

"*Es tu padre, no?*" she asked.

"No, ma'am," Dan said, "My dad's dead. He's just some guy who married my mom."

Mr. Lopez walked in from the kitchen, did a double take, and said, "Wat de fock happen!"

Mrs. Lopez rattled at him angrily in Spanish too fast for Dan to understand, but he did catch *pobrecito* and *justicia*. Mr. Lopez looked him over, leaning close, scowling and grumbling, thumbing up both of Dan's eyebrows and looking at the purple lids. Dan was surprised to see compassion in his eyes when he pulled away.

"Dat focking osshole," Dan heard Mr. Lopez say to his wife in the kitchen. When she began an angry diatribe in Spanish, Lopez said, "In English!"

There was a moment of silence before Mrs. Lopez said, "Jes, I thin he iss a osshole."

Although Dan was both touched and amused, he kept the emotions back behind his purpled eyes. When Adriana came in with her new boyfriend, he saw from the light in *her* eyes that she didn't hate him for the cowardly manner of his breaking up, in fact coming over to look at his face with a keen of concern. The boyfriend, a kid Dan knew from school sporting a feeble attempt at a moustache, glowered at Dan in an apparent attempt to appear protective and menacing. Dan ignored this and accepted a fresh glass of pineapple juice from Jorge.

They all had dinner together in the Lopez's noisy, aromatic kitchen, something Dan wouldn't have done when he was dating Adriana. Mr. Lopez glowered occasionally at the boyfriend (who sheepishly avoided his gaze), but was actually friendly towards Dan, although in a rough, terse manner. Dan found the man looking at him occasionally, his expression opaque. At one point, after a moment of hesitation, Mr. Lopez reached out and patted Dan's forearm roughly. Dan looked at him, and the man nodded his head, pursing his lips and blinking both eyes. It'll be okay.

Dan left after dinner. Jorge wanted him to stay, but Dan didn't want to push Mr. Lopez's change of heart; he was, after all, a boy who was fairly recently trying hard to get into the pants of the man's daughter. Instead, made his excuses, lying to Mrs. Lopez to allay her fears. He spent the night at the beach, where he made a fire among the dunes.

It was brisk in the orange morning when he woke to the sound of waves and gulls. He was peaceful, though, and refreshed, and lay in his bedroll, resting his head on one arm while he watched the sun rise over the broad and empty beach. It was too good a day to go to school, and people would be looking for him there.

Instead, he went to Graziano's to get some back pay and a little food. He took alleys and weedy lots on the way there, a longer route, but one intended to avoid Mike, who might be about in the neighborhood. With day-old bread, antipasto, oranges, and a muffaleto sandwich, he returned to the dunes, where he spent the day reading and doing sketches on a notepad.

It occurred to him to take the bus to the museum, but the idea of being around people seemed unpleasant to him. He thought about the time he spent alone at the Gates mansion during the summer, about the peace of his solitude there, and realized that he was almost exactly as happy here among the dunes as he was at the mansion, with all it had to offer. If Gigi were here, he would lack for nothing.

After three days, he went back to 718 Pier.

He was prepared to dodge Mike, whose anger usually abated in a few days anyway. When he found the door ajar, he knew that Mike wasn't home. Ingrid sat in front of the television, drinking a screwdriver and looking even more bleak than usual.

"Well," she said when she saw him, "the lord of the manor."

"Where's Mike?" Dan asked as he went into his room.

"He's out drinking, no thanks to you," she called after him. "You've created a lot of trouble for you and everyone else with your little hijinks. He can't even show his face in church."

Dan thought of several replies, but didn't bother. He closed the door and took off his rank clothes. Putting on a bathrobe, he walked to the bathroom and closed the door.

"I want to talk to you when you're done!" Ingrid said.

He turned on the shower and got in. Soaping himself thoroughly, twice, he tried to think of what to do next. It was obvious that things would only get worse with Mike, and yet the other options could prove worse still. He couldn't simply run away; he had little money and nowhere to go. A run-in with Social Services seemed inevitable. Letting the water run over his head, he made the shower last as long as he could, hiding in the noise of it.

As he returned to his room to dress, Ingrid said, "I told you I wanted to talk to you."

Dan sighed and got dressed. Such a phrase never sounded good.

He came out into the living room and said, "What do you want to talk about?"

"I've been on the phone a lot lately," Ingrid said. "There's going to be some changes in your life."

"In my life? There have been enough changes in my life. Change your own life."

"Don't be flip."

"Flip who? Flip Wilson?"

"Funny," Ingrid said, finishing her drink with a rattle of ice cubes. "Why don't you mix your mom another drink, funny guy."

She looked so pathetic, so prematurely aged, that he had one of his slippery moments of pity for her. He snorted and took her glass. "Sure. Fine," he said. "I'm getting dressed first."

"You'll have to make some more orange juice in the blender," she said.

Dan ran a frozen canister of orange juice concentrate under hot water from the tap, opened it, and let it plop into the blender. He took three canisters of cold water and poured them into the pitcher as well, running the blender on high to make it frothy, the way Ingrid preferred it.

When he turned around, he found Willy standing on the other side of the kitchen table.

"Hello, son," Willy said. "Pack your stuff. We're going home."

Willy had lost a great deal of weight. He no longer had a belly, and his old leather belt holding up his jeans was cinched to the last hole, dark creases left by the buckle as evidence of this contraction. His face, though brown from the sun of the river, was ravaged, neck wattled, watery eyes glowing pink and skyblue from the sockets. His hair, solid white, was dense and tufted, his shoulders still broad, and the rolled sleeves of his work shirt revealed gnarled brown hands and cabled forearms.

"Don't stand there with your mouth open," Ingrid said from the couch, "you look retarded."

Dan ignored this, eyes only on Willy. The old man smiled, but the sadness in his eyes made Dan think of the sound of wind.

"Come on, son," Willy said. "Get a move on. Your mother and I have to talk."

Dan was too stunned to do anything but comply. Almost dizzy, he performed triage of his possessions. The first things he set among what he would take were all of the gifts he had received from the Gates family at Christmas: the down coat, the sweater (carefully folded and hidden away), the books. He left his artwork; he could make more of it. The used football he had received from Mike was in his closet. This he punctured with the knife from his pack and left on the bed in the cell of his room.

Trying to keep his composure, to keep from becoming frantic, he slowed himself down and breathed deeply. The thought that Mike might return at any time threatened to spill into panic, but he kept about his task. At one point he looked out into the dining area. His mother sat at the table with a screwdriver at her hand as she signed a stack of papers. Willy leaned on the table, watching. A thick stack of cash sat next to the screwdriver.

"You'll get more when everything goes smoothly," Willy said. "No one from the trust has to know, and I won't tell them. How many times did I say that on the phone? By signing those papers, you terminate your rights. I'll take care of the rest of it."

Ingrid signed the last paper with a sigh. "So you're sort of buying my kid."

Willy straightened up. "You think this was going well? You think you're cut out to be a mother? You said yourself that it wasn't and you aren't. It was that Robinson lady who called me, you'll remember. Look, I know you're really tired. I know it's been hard. I'll give you this money up front, and more in a year. You'll be covered. All you have to do is sign these papers. And a receipt, for the money.

This way things end up the how they were going to anyway, but that boy isn't in a foster home and you have some money."

"All I wanted was a normal family," she said.

"That was never going to happen," Willy said, his voice quiet.

Ingrid saw Dan watching and said, "Stop eavesdropping."

Willy turned and said, "You almost ready?"

"Yeah."

"Okay, then."

Everything Dan wanted to take fit into his pack and the duffelbag he had brought when he came. Looking around the place, he felt nothing. When he looked at Ingrid, he felt the same. He shouldered his pack and set the duffelbag on the floor, trying to think of something to say.

Ingrid beat him to it. "You go and live with your grandfather for awhile," she said. "It's better that way. That Robinson woman from the services made me see that. I guess I'm not the best parent in the world."

"No shit," Dan said.

"Don't get smart," she said.

"Why the fuck not!" Dan shouted.

"Dan!" Willy said. "That's enough. It doesn't matter."

"It matters! What was this all about?"

"People make mistakes," Willy said. "They're imperfect. Let's go."

Ingrid said, "You could've been more grateful for what we tried to do. You were always just a little shit."

Dan huffed in disbelief, thinking about where to even begin.

"Dan." Willy said. "Let's go. This is pointless."

"Give your mother a kiss before you leave," Ingrid said. Her head was beginning to weave a bit, and her eyes were less than focused.

"You've got to be kidding me," Dan said.

When Dan heard the distinctive stomp of Mike's boots on the stairs, he suspected for an instant that the vision of his grandfather had been an illusion. He picked up his things, wanting to tell his grandfather- so diminished- to go down the fire escape in back, but he hesitated when he saw how Willy set himself, looking at the door.

Mike came in, red in the face from drink, but only loaded enough, Dan could tell from experience, to be belligerent.

Mike's head jerked back when he saw Willy. "What the fuck is all this?" he said.

"Honey," Ingrid said, "I was going to tell you."

Mike's eyes never left Willy's, and Willy stared back.

"What the *fuck is this!*" Mike bellowed. "*Why are you in my house?*"

He came across the floor and grabbed Willy's workshirt and bore him back across the room and against the kitchen counter, slamming him into the toaster oven and scattering some plastic bowls. Dan watched amazed. Ingrid screamed. When Mike raised his fist to hit the old man, Willy reached out, grabbed the pitcher of orange juice from the blender, and swung it into Mike's head. The pitcher shattered, sending glass and orange juice across the linoleum floor. Mike

424

fell to one knee, his hair and shirt soaked first with orange juice, then with spreading threads of blood.

"You old fucking bastard!" he cried, and Dan ran over, raised a boot as far as he could behind him, and kicked Mike in the face.

"Aaaaah!" Mike cried, falling back against the cabinet. Dan kicked him twice more in the face. There was no delight like seeing Mike with a broken nose and mashed lips, his face and hair bloody and soaked with orange juice. He went in for another kick, simmering with glee, when Willy pulled him off.

"That's enough," Willy said.

"I'm gonna sue your ass, old man." Mike said.

"We won't be hearing from the cops or anybody else about this," Willy said. "Might go badly for you, assaulting a kid and an *old man*, as you say. You already have a record."

"So do you," Mike said, blowing a bubble of blood when he spoke. "And you're old. Too old to go into the can."

"Sure, I'm getting old," Willy said, "but if you cause any shit, I'll just pay to have you killed. I don't imagine it'd cost much. Around here, I could probably find plenty of people to do it for free."

"I would," Dan said.

"There you go," Willy said.

Mike slid down until he was resting on one elbow. He looked over to where Ingrid had been sitting. She was gone, Dan saw, and so was the stack of cash.

"Ready?" Willy said.

"Yeah."

"Let me get that duffel bag."

"I can get it."

"I bet," Willy said. "You're looking mighty strong."

Willy ignored Mike and walked out of the apartment. Perhaps his step was light, cheerful, as he went down the stairs. Dan smiled, and looked back at Mike as he picked up his things. Mike was still slumped over on his elbow, and although his eyes were pointed dejectedly at the linoleum, Dan flipped him two middle fingers anyway.

On his way out the door, he heard the toilet flush. Halfway down the stairs, he heard Ingrid say, "Are they gone?"

Then the apartment door slammed. He laughed, and went out onto the street to where Willy was waiting by the truck.

THE YOUNG OAKS

continues ....

With

BOOK TWO

UNUSUAL GIFTS

for availability information
please visit:

www.theyoungoaks.com

Made in the USA
San Bernardino, CA
16 June 2017